GOOD BOY BETTER DRUGS

MANZO

I could call this a memoir but it is a work of fiction. Although the content depicted in this book, including but not limited to events, locales, entities or persons, living or dead, were inspired directly or indirectly by real-life counterparts, I would like to make it very clear that they have been significantly adjusted and recast as a work of almost believable fiction.
Any stories/events with a factual basis have been altered or included for expressive use, and the names of some individuals have been changed to respect their privacy. Any jokes or references made in this book, are meant as harmless fun, so relax.

Cover image by designer:
Greg Munson
www.gregmunson.info

CONTENTS

Chapter One

BROKEN WINGS

The cocaine tasted bitter and my eight-year-old-tongue disappeared.

I looked at the chalky substance inside the aluminum foil as if I had discovered alien dust.

The numbness forced me to repeatedly bite my bottom lip like I did after I left the dentist.

The only other time I ever saw cocaine was when I had watched the movie *Scarface* with my dad when I was five years old. I couldn't understand why all of those *Puerto Ricans* was killing each other for all that flour.

My mother fried chicken with flour—was someone going to blow her away too?

"Manzo just grab the coupons and come the hell on!" my mother yelled from the front door as she and my Aunt Sheila awaited my return. We were on our way to the supermarket.

"Don't make me come back there boy!"

"I'm coming now Mommy!" I hollered back.

Quickly refolding the minuscule wrap of foil, I placed it back on the floor by my father's jeans, ran around the bed to the dresser, and snatched the wad of coupons.

I was the fastest boy my age in the projects already, but that day I had a powdered boost to my Sky Jordan's.

Almost out of the bedroom, I turned around and looked at my father on the bed sleeping, snoring with his mouth wide-open.

I smiled and felt the need to kiss him on his forehead, so I did, and then *Carl Lewis'ed* out of the room.

* * *

The Wagner Houses, or better known as Wagner Projects, were located between Second Avenue and Pleasant Avenue and spanned from 120th Street to 124th Street.

Wagner was a massive housing complex that had twenty-six buildings and was the fruit of Spanish Harlem.

Once the murderers, drug users, backstabbers, and pedophiles were peeled off, there was a core of Puerto Ricans and Blacks who learned to integrate and live together through their common bond of poverty and prayer.

Nothing rivaled the energy and excitement of Wagner in the summer of 1986. Children played on the monkey bars, the center baseball field, and the basketball courts.

Most of their mothers sat on benches eating sunflower seeds, braiding hair, and gossiping. Everyone was in everyone else's business—but had no business.

Black people played Spades, listened to Run-DMC and Luther Vandross blasting from boom boxes, drank Pepsi, and chased pussy.

Life was good.

Puerto Ricans banged dominoes on tables, listened to Tito Puente and Hector Lavoe thundering out of an open-windowed apartment, drank Malta, and chased pussy.

Life was *bueno.*

The young women sashayed through the projects with their Wimbledon tennis skirts and *Fifty-four-eleven* Reebok Classics looking to gain the attention of a young hustler—to buy them more skirts and more Reeboks.

The high-top, soft leather sneakers were called "Fifty-four-eleven's" because each pair cost fifty-four dollars and eleven cents.

To have all the colors was a status symbol, which generally translated to either the girl being a "slut", or her boyfriend had money.

Hustling was the way of life in Harlem, which brought excitement in the neighborhood.

Whether the goal was sneakers, drugs, money, or sex, everyone was grinding and figuring out how to score.

Once someone scored, he or she had to score again. There were no moral victories or participation trophies given. Feeding their addictions was the point.

When there's competition for any *championship*, there will always be people who would do anything for the title.

Greed, jealousy, and envy plagued Wagner Projects.

People who had nothing, prioritized having a little more of nothing—even if it meant betraying, robbing, scheming, or killing their neighbor to attain it.

Often, individuals with the same treacherous agendas spoke freely to one another—unconcerned by who was listening.

"I *want* his woman."

"I *want* her man."

"I *want* their drugs."

"I *want* their money."

"I *need* that life."

Human nature didn't skip the ghetto, but on a bright and sunny afternoon, Wagner Projects looked like the world's largest barbecue.

There were no signs that our hood led New York City in murders and were filleting each other.

People blanketed their fears with faith and street wisdom. If one didn't work, hopefully the other one would.

* * *

My mother, Karen Peña, was an imposing, redbone beauty with high cheekbones, a delicate nose, and fine hair that dropped to her shoulder blades like pieces of black silk.

Her features were uncommon for the non-Puerto Ricans in our neighborhood, and even her own aunts and siblings questioned who her real father was.

Either way, my mother identified as an African American woman, although, a Hispanic man clearly had dipped his coconuts in grandma's chicken grease.

The questionable half-breed was raised in Wagner since her birth in 1955. She watched the projects grow from a puppy to a beast, with an appetite for the young.

Kids, as young as ten years old, were murdered senselessly over arguments, debts, drugs, girls, or simply being at the wrong place at a wicked time.

My mother understood that the beast had to be fed from time to time but refused for any one of her children to be on the menu.

Keeping a close eye on us, we could never play anywhere out of her sight, and the minute she couldn't see us, she would scream our names until we came back to the base.

"Manzo! Javier! Alejandro!" she yelled.

The entire projects echoed with my mother's voice calling the three *Black* brothers with the Spanish names and *good* hair.

Once she had confirmation that we were safe, she would just give us a look that screamed, "Keep your little Black asses where I can see you!"

Mommy, as we called her, was our protector and our guardian angel. While my father was at *work* most of the time, she disciplined us with the strength of both parents.

Mommy demanded respect and obedience. Going AWOL wasn't an option. Either we followed her command, or we got beat. Simple rules.

"Don't talk to strangers."

"Drink your milk."

"Do what I said."

The *Mommy Way* was the only way, and she did an amazing job at keeping drugs and danger from directly affecting our lives.

Yes, we heard gunshots outside at night from our apartment windows.

Yes, we knew people who had been murdered.

Yes, we knew junkies and dope pushers, and violence was all around us.

Although we witnessed the madness a few times, we heard about it far more often than we saw it.

"You know they blew Ms. Taylene's son's head to pieces right?"

"Man, those crazy ass spics told that nigga get off the block or he's dead!"

"*So-and-so* owed that dude money—that's why they slit the motherfucker's throat!"

Each day, someone would give the "ghetto four-one-one" of another tragedy in our community.

I would get on the elevator with my mother to go outside, and before we even had a chance to get off, someone got on the elevator and explained the latest murder—in all its gruesomeness.

"Oh my God!" my mother would respond and hold her mouth. "I used to change his diapers!"

"Yup Karen, shit getting crazy out here," the current anchorwoman always replied as she shook her head.

They always tried whispering, but whispering was never Black people's strong point. I would hear every heart-crumbling word and hold back my little tears, because I also knew the victims.

I knew what death was, and I also knew when death hunted in the projects —at night.

Religiously, Mommy would have her children upstairs right as the sun was going down.

As an eight-year-old boy, I never wanted to go home to our sanctuary, especially because most of the other *mothers* stayed out late with their children. The demons did not scare me. I wanted to have fun.

I didn't care about the night someone started shooting, and Mommy picked up Alejandro and grabbed my hand, before we sprinted to our building.

I didn't care about the night we were outside, and we heard horrifying screams coming from 2375, my Aunt Ree and Aunt Renee's building.

We looked up and witnessed Ms. Mary screaming for help as she was being choked to death with a phone cord by a girl high on crack—the girl was Ms. Mary's own daughter.

Her daughter's boyfriend was in the apartment just watching—police never confirmed the rumor he was eating a bag of popcorn.

Mommy played the odds and taking her children upstairs before death started to deal was her ace in the hole.

Although always disappointed, I had to put on my poker face, get my brothers and fold—the deck was stacked against us. I would have to wait for the sun to rise for another chance to win.

The daytime was our time, but even the devil liked to enjoy the rays every now and again.

The only way to ensure that we never saw any violence and keep us away from the animals was to trap us in the house like animals. My mother wasn't a zookeeper though, nor a prisoner of our reality.

It's not healthy, mentally or physically, to keep children in a cage and not let them out, even if it's just to roam in a larger one.

There's risk in life. There's an even bigger risk in life in the projects.

My mother prayed to keep her children safe and begged God to spare us from further witnessing the cruelty *His* children bestowed on one another.

She prayed a beautiful prayer, but at times...no one seemed to be listening.

* * *

"Mommy after we bring the food upstairs can we come back out, so I can play with my friends?" I asked while I pushed the shopping cart down 123rd Street.

"Girl let me tell you, if I were her, I would've been left that no-good nigga!" Mommy said to Aunty Sheila.

"I hear that Karen! Charlene told me that he was with—"

"Mommy can I PLEASE come back outside?" I interrupted Aunty Sheila.

"Manzo calm the fuck down! Can't you see grown folks are talking?" Mommy yelled.

Looking down, I just continued to push the cart and think about all the fun that my friends were having at the monkey bars.

My lips were no longer numb, but I still licked them with confusion and felt more hyper than usual. I feigned to play.

"Shit Karen, Diana told me that the other day she saw him leaving at 1:00 AM and—"

"Mommy can I play when we—"

SLAP!

Lips numb again.

Shit that hurt!

"What did I tell you?" Mommy asked. "Boy stop being rude. What the hell is wrong with you today?"

"It's OK Karen. He just wants to play," Aunty Sheila answered for me. She always had my back.

Thank you, Aunty.

Pushing along, I just stared straight ahead toward the projects. I watched all my friends across the street laughing and running around as Mommy and Aunty Sheila analyzed my dismissive behavior.

Zoned out, I pictured myself playing Tag with the kids. I paid no attention to Mommy and my aunty describing my actions in the supermarket.

"...and why in the hell was he running all around the supermarket bringing back that bag of flour, knowing damn well we just had fried chicken last night?" Mommy asked Aunty Sheila.

"You know how much Manzo loves fried chicken. Maybe the lil' nigga is hungry Karen...you know he likes to eat, ha-ha!" Aunty Sheila said and laughed uncontrollably.

Run Matthew!

"...that is the problem! He just sleeps and lets the kids do what they want and then I have to deal with the bullshit!" Mommy complained.

"Relax a little bit—Los is getting money all night. Y'all are good parents."

Matthew got tagged! He's slow!

"...raising these kids all day by myself. Shit is no joke Sheila!"

"Manzo tell your mom you're sorry for being rude."

Don't let him tag you Keisha!

"Manzo!" Aunty Sheila repeated.

"Boy, you better listen to your aunt!" Mommy popped me on the back of my head with her hand. "You better snap out of it before I tell your damn father!"

Usually a child would get paranoid with the threat of his father being told of the child's unruliness, but not my brothers and me.

My father was the *good cop*, and he really didn't like confrontation. His way of showing his authority would be by saying, "Do what your mother says, or I won't buy you that toy you wanted."

"Sorry Aunty Sheila," I cluelessly blurted.

"Not me Manzo—say sorry to your mother." Aunty Sheila rubbed the back of my head.

"Oh, sorry Mommy," I smiled, sticking my tongue through my missing bottom tooth.

The tooth fairy's scowl transformed, and she surprisingly returned a smile.

I didn't hear their conversation, but I knew that Aunty Sheila had softened up the old lady for me. My mother had never forgiven me so quickly.

Thank you, Aunty!

"It's OK baby," Mommy said as she rubbed the other side of my head.

"I'm going to take the groceries upstairs and go get your brothers while your aunt stays out here with you, so you can play with your friends."

"Yes!" I shouted. "Thank you, Mommy!"

As we crossed Second Avenue, I watched my peers swinging from the monkey bars, and I couldn't wait to join the action.

The traffic light almost turned green, and I was too excited to notice or hear one word of Aunty Sheila and Mommy's conversation—but I did feel Mommy grip my arm tighter as she hastened her pace.

With Taino Towers at our backs, we reached Wagner's side of the avenue and I could hear with great clarity the sound of kids' laughter.

There were just as many adults outside chuckling and conversing, but nothing could ever suffocate the high pinched crooning of children at play.

A child's laugh was removed of worry and filled with infinite hope.

Drawn to the happy sounds, I watched little Black kids, with arms resembling pieces of chiseled chocolate—swing faster and faster on the steel yellow monkey bars with the silver undertone.

Even at age eight, the kids' muscle structures appeared to develop twice as fast as their Puerto Rican counterparts playing stickball.

Blame it on Kool-Aid or genetics, either way, the browner babies were the bosses of the playground.

The *Boricuas* were forced to play a sport where there was minimum running, so stickball was a natural substitute. They learned early that catching little Leroy was basically impossible.

A few feet from my paradise, I noticed Matthew come from behind a tree and smack Keisha on the back of her purple Cabbage Patch Kid t-shirt.

She had attempted to hide behind the fattest steel post that supported the monkey bars, but every kid in the projects knew that post was the first option for the skinny kids to try to go undetected.

Keisha's four-foot two-inch frame probably weighed fifty pounds.

"Tag, you're it!" Matthew shouted, dashing away. "You ain't never gonna catch me motherfuckers!"

Keisha immediately began to chase Matthew all around the playground as I frowned and mentally rooted for Matthew to get caught. He was my friend, but he always liked to play dirty.

"Try this!" he screamed and ran up the silver bars on the side of the *jungle gym.*

Propelling himself up to the top of the eight-foot monkey bars, he planted his feet on the first of nine bars, stood up, and proceeded to tightrope the bars with confidence and precision.

"Not fair Matthew!" Keisha complained and crossed her arms.

With both arms raised to his side, Matthew laughed and steadily walked back and forth on the monkey bars.

His untied Converse Chuck Taylor's leaned to the side of the steel bars with each step.

"Manzo can you do this?" he asked as he looked at me and stepped simultaneously, never once glancing at his feet.

Of course I could!

The sun shined on the performance and I was eager to join my play brother.

Without hesitation, I released the shopping cart and turned to Mommy who was already shaking her head and smiling at me.

"Bye Mommy I love you!" I spat too quickly for her liking. I looked back up at Matthew, but the Tango was over.

He stood motionless with his head tilted upwards and his back to me. With one strap of his Osh Kosh Bigosh striped overalls dangled off his left shoulder, Matthew had both feet glued to separate bars.

He faced building 2390 and, in a millisecond, my vision was one with the child giant as our innocent eyes watched an endangered species descend rapidly from its nest.

Tenth floor.

Its wings flapped fiercely.

Eighth floor.

Faint sounds of cawing could be heard.

Fifth floor.

A shriek of desperation was released.

Third floor.

It covered its beak.

Second floor.

"That's all the love I get?" Mommy questioned.

First floor.

BOOM!

CRUNCH!

The Black *bird* landed and pounded against the concrete before bouncing a foot in the air and landing again.

Dust engulfed the bird, and its body grilled in a coat of blood.

Neither God nor a spatula could save the barnyard pimp from frying in hell.

Every limb was cracked to pieces and a sharp wishbone protruded its neck like an antenna—but there was no reception.

"Aaaaaahhh!" Mommy howled along with the others who had just witnessed Raymond "Bird" Williams get tossed off a sixteen-story, project rooftop.

"Oh my God!" someone screamed, and the commotion spread.

My first time ever seeing a dead body; I stood in silence and never flinched as I studied the carcass.

Everything went black.

Mommy placed her hand over my eyes and cradled my head as we swiftly began to walk away.

I could no longer see the violence, but I could still hear the pandemonium. I could feel the pain.

"Oh my God—it's Bird!"

"Ah fuck, that's Raymond—nooo!"

"Kids get the hell away from there!"

The more people expressed outrage, concern, and sorrow, the faster we walked.

Never removing her hand from my eyes, Mommy hollered, "Sheila stop looking! Bird's gone—go get the cart!"

Mommy then proceeded to sob while she whispered in my ear and hugged my brain firmly.

"It's gonna be OK honey. I will keep you safe. Nothing will ever happen to you," she said.

Did Raymond's mother tell him that too?

A heinous circumstance was the catalyst to an epiphany and lost innocence. July 25, 1986 was the first day that mattered in my young life.

I realized that I had to get out of Wagner Projects, my mother truly loved me, and I truly loved...cocaine.

Chapter Two

BIG CATCH

The smells of last night's menu, *arroz con pollo* for the Boricuas and fried chicken for the Blacks, clung to most of the kids in Science 101, so I always sat in the front row, closest to the window.

Combine the war between the underarms of the children that couldn't afford the luxury of powdered fresh armpits with the girls who borrowed their grandmother's "Stank Flowers of 1967" perfume, simply learning without vomiting was a daily science project.

The mustard colored walls were bare. There weren't any encouraging words, stickers, or an inspirational poster of a kitten dangling for dear life that read, "Hang in there." There weren't creepy old White guys in lab coats or pictures of Alf either.

There was just a dirty blackboard, a seven-foot fan, and forty moveable metal desks and chairs. Welcome to New York City Public *Schools*.

"If you take the protons and neutrons of this compound and compare it to..." Mr. Glennon spoke and stared at me as if Science 101 were a private lesson between us.

My seventh-grade science teacher, Mr. Glennon—had all the stereotypical elements of a Jewish fella. He had a big nose, nasally voice, glasses, and a Jew-fro with the receding hairline.

I guessed from his thrift store threads that he was cheap as fuck too, but shockingly, Mr. Glennon was not Jewish—he was a few protons and a couple of latkes short of being kosher.

A brilliant man, he knew all the sciences and was cool as hell, although he lacked the chemistry and melanin to have a chemical bond with all thirty-seven of his minority students.

But I was the voluntary muscle in his class, and Mr. Glennon could always count on my participation and straight A's. My mother would have rocked my world if I had gotten a B in her favorite subject.

While other kids sat in the back, passed notes, mentally time traveled back to their beds, or attempted to blast off little rockets under their desks, I was busy learning as I always did.

I was beyond ever letting another student enter my space and disrupt my journey for knowledge.

"In Einstein's Mass-Energy Equivalence, the C in E=MC2—"

"Speed of light!" I blurted out, never raising my hand as usual.

"Correct Manzo…as if anyone else gives a shit," he mumbled underneath his breath.

"Ha, ha, ha," a few kids laughed.

KNOCK.

Oh shit!

Gums swallowed.

Books opened.

Chairs screeched.

Zippers zipped.

Conversations stopped.

Every kid in the class knew the drill when someone knocked on the classroom door. Anyone, from a parent, to Ms. Moore, the principal, to even the police—could've been planning an invasion.

Even the cool kids, who supposedly didn't give a shit, knew that getting caught in class with their dicks out and chewing bubble gum didn't look too good on the ole record.

Harbor was a performing arts school, and each student had five majors to pick: Drama, Instrumental, Dance, Circus Arts, or Chorus.

Being a Drama major, I could recognize acting talent, and my entire science class deserved the lead in the next school play. They were some sneaky little bastards.

As Mr. Glennon shuffled to the classroom door and began to open it, the guys and dolls choked their pens, opened their books, and pretended to do work.

We silently prayed that luck was a lady, and the education gangsters weren't about to attack.

Did I do my homework in all my classes? Yes!
Was I late? No!
Did I ever have a fight, cheat, or skip school? No!
Did I get anyone pregnant? Hell No!
OK, I'm good.

I never had anything to worry about when someone knocked on a classroom door but out of nervous habit, I always asked myself the same set of questions like a paranoid little maniac.

I just could never completely relax, because I've seen too many parents beat their children's asses right in the damn classroom.

I have also witnessed twice as many kids get taken out in handcuffs, and the scenes were not parts of any play.

Mr. G, as we called him, because most teachers felt way-cool to be called by the first letter in their last name, stuck his head out of the ten-inch opening, and the fogged glass made it impossible to get a visual of the abductor.

Mr. G exchanged some muffled dialogue as the students in the classroom, stiff with anxiety and anticipation, looked at each other while they hypothesized which kid would be cooked.

I feel sorry for the asshole in trouble.

"OK, one moment," he said as he pulled his head back into the classroom.

He closed the door just enough to keep our mystery guest a mystery. Emotionless, Mr. G looked at me!

My stomach twerked, and my heart moonwalked to my asshole, but I was not ready to boogie.

Please don't say my name!

"Manzo get your shit and go outside please," Mr. G ordered.

Silence.

This must be a joke!

"What?" I mumbled.

"Manzo, get...your...shit...and...go...outside...please—I have a class to teach."

More confused than scared, I stood up and packed my book bag.

"Hurry up son, let's go!"

I'm moving dickhead!

Only a few feet from being out of the doorway and into purgatory, I shivered as Mr. G continued teaching, but not a soul listened.

The faithless judged amongst themselves as whispers of my damnation resonated.

"I told you that nigga was getting locked up..."

"He gotta be selling crack 'cuz he never wears the same sneakers even twice..."

"He ain't smarter than we is..."

"My best friend's cousin is Manzo's momz best friend, and I heard Manzo's father banged my best friend's cousin...*and* her sister—"

"OK y'all be quiet and let's continue!" Mr. Glennon ordered.

Am I really going jail?

I've never committed a crime in my life, but my classmates' expert commentary on my kingpin status had me believing otherwise.

Opening the door, I had expected to see two fat Irish detectives with Burlington Coat Factory suits waiting to bring me to the slammer—but I didn't see anyone.

Who wants—

A hand tapped my left shoulder, the door closed behind me, and the thirteen-year-old bitch jumped out of me.

Completely scared, I raised my hands to protect my face—until I recognized the executioner.

ANGELA?

"Ha, ha, ha!" Angela laughed.

"What the fuck?" I looked at her with a mixture of lividness and relief.

"Chill out Manzo! Let me find out you really are the scariest boy in Wagner Projects!"

"Shut up, I ain't scared! You just surprised me!"

Angela Cortijo and I have been friends since we started kindergarten together at the East Harlem Block School on 109th Street and Madison Avenue.

High yellow, tall, and slender with a big forehead, she had the same features as Mommy, so any romantic encounters would've never been an option.

With my Cocker Spaniel not barking, I could actually listen to a girl. We never had the desire to bone, but I loved and really appreciated her.

Both half platanos and half collard greens, the two mixed breeds always had each other's back.

"How did you—"

"We don't have time Manzo!" she placed her finger on my lips and explained.

"Nicole is in the staircase right now waiting to talk to you. This is very serious Manzo! Go talk to her and then go back to class.

"Mr. G thinks you're with Ms. Walsh discussing the play really quick—and don't worry, they hate each other's guts, so they won't discuss this.

"But hurry up! You have about ten minutes before the end of the period. OK, I'm gone handsome."

"Uh, damn. Thank you," I said.

Without another word, Angela skipped down the hall, and I didn't get a chance or wanted to question anything she said.

Knowing she always had my best interest at heart, I turned and sprinted toward the staircase to meet Nicole—my girlfriend.

* * *

There were no lounges or conference rooms for teenagers. All personal matters were dealt with in seclusion within the specific timeframes per the schedules of the faculty.

Some issues could wait to be handled during lunch, gym, between classes, or after school.

Other issues were pertinent and needed immediate attention, and for those issues, the staircases provided the security and privacy for America's future.

Bonds were made and broken in a school's staircase, and only the serious shit was discussed, so my mind really had begun to wonder—and with wonder came fear.

What could it be? Does she have another man?

She's a carpet muncher? She's burning?

Nicole sat on the narrow stairs with her head in her lap. A sea of liquorish smoothed her scalp as black waves transcended into a long-braided waterfall with a pink beret dam.

Moist baby hairs on her forehead protested laying down—the perspiration kept them awake.

Even with her face unseen, Nicole had a special beauty, and the freshness of her scent raised eyebrows.

From my vantage point, anyone would have anticipated a lovely young lady of a different variety to resurrect and share the masterpiece that was her face.

She picked her head up from her lap and the tears sparkled off her hazel eyes.

The water on her cheeks glossed her perfections like a newly stained wood deck on a rainy day.

The blue Gap button-up shirt with the red flowers screamed a tale of innocence while her sister's animal print Nine West heels whispered, "fast hoe." I really liked her shoes.

Nicole wasn't just another ninth grader—she was *the* ninth grader. During Parent-Teacher night, many a creep father had been slapped by their child's mother for staring too long at the "high-yella-heffa" in the Harbor School. I always laughed with pride, because I knew Nicole was mine.

Damn, what's wrong?

Hurt. Lost. She looked at me with the "I'm pregnant" glare, but I knew a baby wasn't possible because Nicole and I never had sex.

Unless a crumb snatcher could be conceived from masturbating to the thought of being with Nicole, my sock and I were safe.

The pain in her face pissed on my manhood. Not knowing the problem was only compounded by the very low percentage of my being able to help her.

As a limited teenager, I couldn't bare looking at the horror in her eyes.

Looking away, I noticed her neck, then her ears, and then her hands—something was very off.

"I've been robbed," she calmly stated.

"Oh no! Are you—"

"I'm fine," she said.

Oh my God! This can't be happening!

"They took ALL my jewelry Manzo!"

Please no!

"And..." Nicole said as she pulled my hand and guided me closer to her, placing my hand on her breast.

Removing my hand, I braced myself to the railing with both hands as she sat directly in front of me.

My weight tripled, and it was challenging to hold myself up. Looking down at her, I knew that I was the one in some real trouble.

Just say it! Say anything!

"And..." she repeated in a lower tone.

And what?

My strength weakened by my heavy anxiety and both hands hit the step between her legs. I placed my head on Nicole's lap and held her as she held me back.

Taking the deepest breath, I inhaled the air like courage was oxygen's main component, and I closed my eyes, waiting for the worst news.

Soft lips touched my ear and the cherry Chapstick parachuted the bomb.

"And your father knows."

* * *

I walked into apartment 13E with the biggest smile. Proud, I held both six feet trophies in each hand, respectively.

I had just returned with my basketball team, the Riverside Church Hawks, from New Jersey where we had won the Little Lad championship for boys thirteen years old and under.

Averaging twenty-seven points per game, I received the Mr. Little Lad award, the most valuable player in the tournament.

In previous years, Felipe Lopez and Stephon Marbury, the top ranked high school ball players in the country, had won the award. I finally had arrived as one of the best young talents in the country.

"Mommy, guess what?" I asked with excitement.

"Mommy?"

Two feet into the apartment, I saw my mother sitting on our couch. She was sobbing frantically with four big garbage bags on the floor in front of her.

Unconsciously, I dropped one of the trophies to the floor, and the golden child in the basketball uniform toppled and cracked.

Quickly releasing the other trophy, I sat cradling my crying mother's frail body.

"What's wrong Mommy?" I asked, feeling her tears against my cheek.

Rocking back and forth, she whaled in my arms and closed her eyes tightly.

Mommy's manic state caused me to cry. Her sorrow was my sorrow, and I no longer inquired about who caused *us* grief—because I could easily guess.

What the hell did Daddy do this time?

"Your father is a fucking bastard!" she screamed and broke free of my love. Hatred camped in the redness of her eyes, but the sobbing stopped.

Shaking her head, she began to explain what she had believed was my father's trail of lies.

"Have you noticed your father hasn't been here in at least a week?"

"Yes Mommy, but I thought he came home in the day and left out before we got in from school like he—"

"That motherfucker hasn't been here or called in almost a week!" she informed, never looking in my direction.

Mommy sat with her knees in her chest, and both her bare feet on the couch as she stared off while she talked. I listened.

"That bastard told me five days ago that he had to go to Virginia Beach with George and some friends to go fishing!"

Fishing?

"That lying bastard hasn't ever gone fishing in his life and can't even spell 'fishing' for that matter!" she continued.

"He just left me here with four goddamn kids and hasn't called or anything, like I'm stupid! I was born at night but not last *night*! I'm going to finally leave his cheating spic-ass!"

Mommy stopped talking, and I didn't ask for permission to speak. Pictures of our happy family covered the living room walls, and my mother seemed to study the photos.

Disney World. Puerto Rico. Christmas. My baby sister Sandy's two-year-old birthday party.

But the wedding pictures were the boiling point, and Mommy's silence fanned the fumes. She stood up and exploded.

"Manzo I want you to take all your father's shit in these bags and throw them in the fucking dumpster! I gave that asshole all of me and he's killing me inside! He's taking a knife and twisting it in my chest! Oh God! I just want to die!"

* * *

"Are you listening to me motherfucker?" Daddy screamed in my face before punching me in my chest, pulverizing the thoughts of the conversation I had with my mother just four days prior. The man demanded answers!

Caught completely off guard but refusing to display weakness, I stood my ground and cried a little inside.

At six feet tall, I was three inches taller than my father and outweighed him by twenty pounds, so it was going to take more than a punk-ass-sucker-punch to break me—but he did successfully gain my attention.

Shit didn't hurt!

"Where's your mind at Manzo?" Daddy asked.

Looking down at him at the center of the ring, I answered, "It's here."

"So tell me—what the fuck you were thinking about when you stole your mother's diamond ring and gave it to some whore in school?"

"I don't know. It was an accident."

"An *accident*?" he asked as he stepped back, looked around the room and waited for the imaginary audience to give him a real answer.

Daddy's antics were comical, and he was funny without even trying. I almost laughed but I knew better. I wasn't *that* dumb.

"What do you mean an accident?"

"Daddy, I mean—"

"Getting hit by a car is an accident! Dropping and breaking a dish is an accident!" He moved back into my face.

"Stealing a $1,000 diamond ring out of your mother's jewelry box and tricking the shit off to some little hussy ain't an accident—that's breaking and entering!"

Damn, just please don't mention the money in your briefcase!

"And another thing..."

Shit, he knows about that too!

"The bitch got robbed for all *her* jewelry! You think you were the only stupid little nigga to give her some jewelry?" he asked.

OK, he doesn't know.

"Yes, I was the only one. She's not like *that*," I replied.

"What the fuck you mean she's not like *that*?" My defending Nicole's honor infuriated my father more than *borrowing* Mommy's ring.

"You can't be my son! You ain't got no common sense!"

Shut up.

"Soooo...how are you gonna pay for another ring for your mother, lover boy?" he asked, slowly looking me up and down.

"I don't know," I mumbled.

"What? I can't hear you!"

"I don't know!"

"Of course you don't! Manzo you ain't nothing but a lying piece of shit!"

Just like you.

"Son I didn't raise you to be a criminal!"

Just like you.

"And I definitely didn't raise you to be no trick!"

Just like you.

"How could you deceive your mother, put her in so much goddamn pain, and take her trust for granted?"

"JUST LIKE YOU!" I roared.

Scowl for scowl, I stared at the man who was hardly around but always a part of me.

My bird chest filled with courage and I tilted my chin upwards, making me an extra inch taller than my father.

Startled by my defiance, he stared at the boy he loved with all his heart but did not recognize.

Confused on whether I would be on the attack, my father pumped his fist open and closed as the blood drained from his face.

"What did you say boy?" He inched closer. I started to lower my head and break eye contact, but I couldn't.

Picturing Mommy crying in my arms and begging God to die because of what this man was putting her through made me furious.

I loved my father to death, but I loved my mother beyond the grave. She was *my* mother.

She and I had our differences, but nothing that would ever allow me to not defend her honor when face to face with her oppressor.

The umbilical cord reattached, I stood solid.

Uninterrupted, I began to fill Daddy in on a few discoveries *I* had made on my own during the past week while he fished in another woman's pond.

"You didn't go fishing Daddy! You did go to Virginia Beach, but you went with your other girlfriend—Vanessa!"

The gangster's face quickly switched from "you ain't got shit on me pig" to "I will take the plea Your Honor."

Not giving him a chance to testify, I proceeded to read the charges—as he appeared to get even shorter in height.

"You've been screwing Vanessa for years, and she lives on 92nd Street on the Westside! She's light skin with long hair like my mother!

"You pay her rent and buy her anything she wants, and when you aren't sleeping at home, you're *sleeping* with her!"

No objections.

"You couldn't have gone fishing, because I checked your Ugly Stick and the fishing rod is brand new and unused! All Mommy had to do was check the shit herself!

"Because if she did, she would've seen not a trace of the rod ever being used in salt *or* fresh water for that matter! You could've at least rubbed a few goddamn minnows on the hook or something!"

No objections.

"And the same way you find out everything that happens with me and Nicole, is the same way I find out about you! Nicole's older sister is *Vanessa's* best friend! But you already know this!"

Small world, huh motherfucker?

"You lied to Mommy! Nobody in your *club* told you shit!" I said.

No objections.

"Mommy cried all week in my arms, and she packed all your clothes up! I convinced her to put your shit back and we did! I told her you were being good, and everything was all right!"

A look of pure gratitude stamped on his face, and Daddy moved his lips to talk but I continued my testimony, louder and more heartbroken.

"Don't thank me! I didn't do it because of you! I didn't tell her, because I didn't want to hurt her any more than your selfish ass already did!

"She's raising your kids alone—and you're killing her! There are some things money can't buy!"

Daddy pulled me into his arms, and I cried like a son who just had his first nightmare.

Although very painful, I could live without my parents being together, but I couldn't live without Mommy.

She also loved my father to death, but he was testing that theory. Daddy's secrets would always be safe with me if he kept my mother's heart safer.

I wasn't condoning my father's actions, but I wasn't going to rat him out either. He was still my dad.

"I'm sorry son. I love you," Daddy said, appearing to grow taller.

"I love you too Daddy! Just please be good to her!" I pleaded as he held the back of my head.

"I will son."

"And Daddy?"

"Yes son?"

"You really think Nicole is a hoe?"

Chapter Three

KIDS MEAL

"Yo Sammy what up?" I yelled to the back of Sammy's Pee-Dee Steakhouse green polo shirt.

I skipped two young Spanish girls and three West Indian construction workers in the line and headed straight to the counter. "I'm starving!"

"Yuh ah guh fi let him go first?" asked the dusty man with dreadlocks, a massive keloid scar across the side of his face and holding a yellow hard hat.

Sammy never answered or turned around as he threw two of slabs of ribs on the six-foot-long grill.

Tee and I, just kids with entitlement issues, acknowledged the man, and I attempted to apologize to *Mr. Marley*.

"Sorry sir—"

"Oh shit! Lil' Los...me cool...me cool!" Bob said remorsefully and tapped his right fist repeatedly over his heart. "Respect, respect!"

"Respect!" added Whaler number one.

"Respect!" Whaler number two followed suit.

"Respect," Tee said calmly with a slightly Caribbean accent.

"Uh, respect," I responded and mimicked everyone's peace sign. Tee was the faster learner.

I turned to face Sammy again without any worry. I needed some food.

I guess Carlos' son ain't waiting in no blood-clot-line after all.

"Them things looking really scrumptious today Sammy," I expressed.

"All the time Boss," Sammy responded.

Flames reached for Sammy's Jheri-Curl, and just missed his do, while swine sizzled and steamed out seasoned smoke.

The ribs' aroma was divine, and I thanked God my father's name wasn't Kareem, Abdul, or Jabbar.

The grill had a freeway of meats, steaks and chicken amongst them—but the pig was in the fast lane.

The smell of pork always zoomed through traffic and took the checkered flag waving in my nostrils.

"What's up Boss? What you and Tee having?" Sammy asked.

"We definitely want the ribs, baked potato, salad with French dressing, and two half lemonade, half fruit punches," I said.

"That's it Boss?"

"Oh, and please add two strawberry cheesecakes Boss," I said, automatically adding *Boss* like I always did after talking to Sammy for longer than thirty-seconds.

Yea, I will be a boss like my pops one day. Respect.

"No problem Boss."

"Thank you, Sammy," I said.

"Manzo?" Tee tapped my arm.

Ignoring Tee, I was lost in the barbecue Pop Art. The brush strokes burned as Sammy Warhol painted red happiness on our flesh canvas. My mouth watered.

"Yo Manzo?"

"What's up Tee?"

"Yo, I don't have enough money for *all* that," Tee whispered in my left ear. "My moms only gave me $3 today."

Hurry up Sammy!

"Nigga, you gonna have me washing dishes," Tee continued.

"Ha, ha, ha!" I laughed, because I pictured Tee scrubbing pots and pans with a filthy apron and a face full of barbecue sauce. I turned to face him.

Not on my watch Terrence.

"Relax Tee. It's my treat."

"It's always *your* treat."

"And *you're* always *my* brother, Tee."

"No doubt." Tee smiled and nodded.

"Ribs up Boss!" Sammy filleted the ghetto Hallmark moment.

Yes!

Sammy stood in a meat cloud of smoke like some sort of carnivorous God, offering two plates of eternal life with fire breathing behind him.

I almost bowed down to the dark-skin man with the potbelly and gold tooth.

On the counter, Sammy set both plates of the steaming, glazed swine on plastic trays.

Like twin wolves, Tee and I were ready to eat, even Kermit the Frog couldn't save these piggies.

We enjoyed lunch at Pee Dee's quite often, but each time our ferociousness had gotten a little worse. A growing boy must eat.

"Man, I'm gonna kill that shit. Good look Manzo!" Tee thanked me as he grabbed both trays and headed to our usual table in the back.

Rib Combo $6.99.

Cheesecake $1.50.

Large Drink $1.50.

Prices of the food were displayed on the walls above the counters, behind the grill, and on the menus by the cash register, but I never cared or attempted to add up anything I ever bought from there.

I simply reached into my Gap jeans and peeled off what I thought Sammy deserved—forty dollars.

"Here you go Boss," I said.

"Thank you, Boss—I always appreciate your tips young fella!"

"Anytime Boss! You are the man Sammy!"

Sammy humbled himself and showed gratitude in a very similar manner *everyone* that had ever dealt with my father had done.

Not fooling myself, I knew even at fourteen years old that I loved helping people, not for just the act of being generous, rather for the high it gave me.

I felt needed. I felt like my father. I felt like a boss.

Ready to destroy my meal, I snatched some napkins off the counter, gave the West Indians a head nod, and winked at the taller of two Spanish girls in line.

After discovering the black caterpillar above her eyelids, I speed-walked away with regret. I absolutely hated unibrows.

Sitting down, I did a quick rib count to make sure Tee hadn't swiped a couple like I always did when I arrived at the table first.

OK, still six ribs.

We good, Tee didn't take any.

"Yo, I re-apreshate dus Muhn-zo."

"What the fuck you just said Tee?" I asked with a chuckle. "Swallow your food before you choke B."

One rib already *muerto,* Tee had barbecue sauce smudged around his mouth, and had reminded me of a "Red Wings" conversation I had earlier with the school's janitor.

"Wuh?" he asked, irritated.

"Nothing man. Enjoy yourself."

Tee swallowed his food hard before starting the first topic of conversation always on our agenda—basketball.

"Manzo, dudes around my block told me how you dropped forty on the Gauchos the other day! Damn kid!"

"Hell no, nobody drops forty on them. It was only thirty-two points."

"*Only*? Ha, ha, ha, same shit! You be killing them!"

"No, *we* gotta kill Cam and Central Park East in the championship," I said.

"Hell yea, but Cam ain't fucking with you, and I got your boy Matthew and the rest of them bums—so we got this!" He cleaned his mouth with a toilette and grinned.

* * *

At five feet, ten inches, Tee was a solid basketball player with all the fundamentals to play point guard for our junior high school team, the Harbor Hawks.

Slimmer than I was by thirty pounds, he was very quick and could jump high. He was the best teammate, and he knew his role and made me a better ball player.

Handsome with the complexion of the center of an Oak tree, Tee lived in the East River Projects, but he wasn't "project-ish."

His parents were married, just like mine, and kept him out of the streets.

Tee was a good kid. The key difference between our parents was that both of his parents worked, legally, while my mom was a housewife, and my dad manufactured crack. Tee witnessed hard work. I witnessed hard coke.

Tee was my partner and we did everything together. Drama. Basketball. Chill. Inseparable, he and I ran Harbor, and either a girl loved me, loved him, or loved the both of us, at least in our cocky little minds.

Our freshness was impeccable. My designer clothes were purchased by drug dealing, and Tee's came from his mom's discounts.

Ms. Alice, one of the managers at Bloomingdales, kept Tee fashion-forward and looking sharp. Either way, Tee and I looked like new money every day, and we knew it.

Big James, Tee's dad, was an MTA Transit worker with great city-employment benefits and a decent paycheck.

He worked long hours and nights to provide for Tee and his older brother, Jimmy, but my father still made in a week what both Tee's parents made in a year—combined.

Tee wasn't poor but couldn't afford to splurge on forty-dollar lunches on the regular like I could. Shit, not many working adults could either.

My father always gave me money, and what he didn't give me—I just went in his pockets and took while he was asleep.

Money was always around, and Tee was my brother. If I ate, *we* ate—there were no questions about it.

Tee dished me the assist on the basketball court, and I returned the favor in real life.

* * *

"Listen, I'm not even worried about them bum-ass-niggas. We will win the District Four Championship," I said in between bites of baked potato, the melted butter *Vaseline'd* my lips.

"I hope so!" Tee said.

What?

"We don't hope Tee, we make shit happen. Hope is for the hope-less."

"True, true."

"But what I really wanted to know was...what do you think about this Woodberry Forest School stuff?" I asked.

Woodberry Forest School was an elite, all-boys preparatory school in Orange, Virginia.

Mr. McMillan, a recruiter for the school and friends with Principal Moore— had come to Harbor to talk with Tee and me about the possibility of us enrolling in September for high school.

Both of us were A-students, so Tee and I met all the prerequisites to be eligible for a full academic scholarship to the school.

We were intelligent, well mannered, respectful, had no criminal records, were involved in the arts, and could dunk a basketball.

Other than the Fresh Prince of Belair, we appeared to be the ideal Black students for any White school.

This is serious Tee.

"What you think?" he returned the question, cautiously gathering last night's thoughts.

"Kinda sounds good—I mean, *I* would go...even with the all-boys thing," I said and shrugged. "Just as long as no little fag tries to hump me, I'm cool."

"Ha, ha, ha!" we both laughed loudly and banged the table with our forks.

"You're stupid Manzo!"

"Seriously though Tee, we would be all the way in Bubble Fuck, Virginia with no pussy, homos spreading fairy dust on us, and surrounded by the moth-erfucking KKK!"

"Ha, ha, ha!" Tee almost choked.

"Shit, you're laughing—you ever saw that movie Deliverance?" I asked.

"*Squeal* like a pig boy! Oink-oink! I says you betta *squeal*—goddamnit —*squeal!*" I picked up a rib and put it in my mouth.

"Ha, ha, ha! Oh shit, I'm dying!" Tee held his stomach.

"For real—that's the shit we gotta really consider Tee!"

"Ha, ha, ha, I don't want this *shit!*" He tossed his rib back on the plate. "I ain't even hungry anymore!"

"But for real B, what you think?" I asked, tossing my rib next to his.

"I want to go Manzo." He put both elbows on the table, clasped his fingers together as he gazed off and stared at a better life. I just watched him and let him speak.

"The campus looks crazy beautiful, and I don't want to be here anymore. I live in a one-bedroom apartment in the projects. Jimmy and I share the living room B.

"I hate walking home and seeing crackheads and drug dealers and shit. No offense Manzo, but I don't know that life and I don't want to know that life.

"There's more out there for me, and if I stay here, I'm afraid that I will be just like the people I despise. I'm better than that. *You* are better than that!

"But if you stay then you might just fuck around and be a hustler like your pops or your cousin Hen-Dog—or some playground legend instead of a real legend like the dudes we read about in school.

"You love the energy of the fast life, and you're indirectly feeling the benefits, but if you stay, one day you might directly feel the consequences Manzo...and *that* shit would break my heart," Tee said.

A tear rolled down his face and got stuck on some dried-up sauce before continuing its journey.

A little embarrassed, Tee never looked at me, but I felt my brother's love, logic, and pain. He always made sense.

"Plus, I wouldn't want to go without you. It just wouldn't be the same B," he added.

My eyes watered, and it was my turn to look away. How could I not go after hearing my brother's heartfelt words? What type of man would I be? Woodberry was a great opportunity for *us*.

"All right, all right—you're making me cry and shit," I said, wiping my eyes. "We're going!"

"For real?" he asked in amazement.

"Yes for real!" I yelled. "I will tell Ms. Moore to set up a visit so we can see the campus."

"YES!" he howled.

"But don't get too excited. We still would have to interview down there...but I'm sure that's just some preliminary shit," I said.

"Maybe," Tee voiced, never wanting to jinx anything.

"Maaan, we're locked the fuck in!" I always believed we made our own luck. "We're not going to the sticks for nothing...they want us—GUARANTEED!"

The more I thought about who Tee and I were and what we would bring to any school, I no longer had a doubt that Woodberry Forest not only wanted both of us, but they *needed* us. We were the shit!

"Fuck yea B!" He smiled and slapped me five. "I can't wait to get outta Harlem—"

"Buuut..."

"But *what*?" Tee asked.

"Buuut—" I looked him in the eye.

"What Manzo? Come on—you got me all worried now!"

"But...no one better try and hump me or I'm fucking you up B!"

"Ha, ha, ha!" we both burst into laughter.

"Oh shit, what about *Tanisha*?" he asked.

The laughter stopped.

Tanisha, an eighth grader at Harbor, was my girlfriend, and we were in love. She was my first real girlfriend ever, which means we were having sex.

Nicole never gave me the pussy, so any vagina was an upgrade, and I appreciated not being a virgin anymore. I spent every chance outside of basketball and school with Tanisha.

Although I didn't put her into the equation when I told Tee that he and I were Virginia bound, I knew my decision would never change over a girl.

"Don't worry about her, I will tell her when I go over to her crib after basketball practice tonight. No sweat Tee."

"*Phew*!" Tee smiled. "I thought you changed your mind."

"Terrence, you're stuck with me." I firmly gripped his shoulder with my right hand, shaking him slowly. "We're going to VA-GINA!"

"Ha, ha, ha! You'se a dumb nigga, I swear! Your ass needs to be on TV!"

"Maaan, no bullshit! I wanna be on some shit like *In Living Color*!"

"You would be hilarious on that show!" Tee said.

Thanks, but on second thought, there's no way I'd be able to pay attention on that set Tee."

"Uuh, why not? Because you couldn't remember your lines or something?"

"Man, I'm not thinking about any *lines* Tee! I wouldn't pay attention... because I'd be staring at that that *fine-ass* Fly Girl all day! That Puerto Rican dancer-chick!"

"You talking about Jennifer Lopez. *J-Lo* or whatever they call her—"

"Tee that's my baby right there! I don't care if her name was *J-Lo* or *J-High*! I'd take anybody that even resembled a damn J-Lo! I'd even take a J-*Medium*!"

"Ha,ha,ha—crazy thing is, I know you ain't lying either Manzo!"

"Damn she's beautiful—but on some real shit though Tee...when did you become a Jamaican?" I asked as we both stood up.

"Shit, I will be Chinese, Dominican, or goddamn Irish if it stops us from getting our asses beat!"

"Ha, ha, ha, I hear that! Let's bounce B!" I said. "But damn, I really have to go over to Tanisha's crib and do something special before I let her know the deal."

"Good luck, and from that devilish grin, I hope it's not what I think it is."

"Oooh, I will think of *something*," I said as we walked past the Spanish girls' table.

"Hola!" the girl with the unibrow and white polka dot dress smiled and greeted us, but we strutted right out of the door.

No way Bert and Ernie.

* * *

Every time I came to the Martin Luther King Towers (formally named the Foster Projects) to visit Tanisha, I thought that I would bump into my older half-brother, Chink Peña, who lived in building Seventy with my grandmother, my aunt Helena, and my cousin Curly—all from my father's side of the family.

Chink and I were just two months apart—he was an "oopsie baby."

Believing that a "rubber" was just someone who felt women up on a busy train, my father had unprotected sex and impregnated another woman right before I was conceived.

On my parents' wedding day, July 18, 1977, I was in my mother's stomach, and the child who got his name because of his slanted eyes was born in Harlem Hospital.

Ingrid, Chink's mother, *did* know though that the man she was fucking raw had a fiancé, but Ingrid did not care.

I had guessed that when a woman got some good dick then a man's relationship status wasn't as important as the orgasm he provided.

Ingrid promised to keep her *love child* a secret, but my father wasn't going to take any chances.

Daddy didn't want anyone disclosing to Mommy that he had another family, so the day I was born, like a man, he did confess his first confirmed infidelity to her.

Enraged, my mother kicked my father out of the hospital right as he was about to sign my birth certificate.

She couldn't change the fact that her first born shared the same blood as his father and bastard brother—but she would never let me share their last name.

Scratching out *Peña* on my birth certificate with a number-two pencil, Mommy didn't want me to have *any* last name, because she said I was different, leaving me with the one name that came to her in a dream—*Manzo*.

Although my mother vowed to never take my father back after his latest betrayal, she still didn't have the courage to leave him. Daddy was all she had ever known.

Before my mother had even gotten her stitches removed, my father was back in the house.

When Chink and I were five years old, my father brought Chink into our home and asked Mommy to keep him with us because Ingrid was strung out on drugs, and my brother had no other place to stay.

Loyal to her husband, Mommy agreed to let Chink come live with us.

To my other siblings and to me, Chink was 100% our brother and we loved him as such.

I never knew what a half-brother was until Curly explained to me the difference between Chink and my other brothers, Alejandro and Javier.

The conversation opened my eyes, and soon after I noticed the pain in the eyes of my mother every time that she looked at Daddy's "other" son.

Mommy had no choice in harboring a child that was living proof of her sorrow, her stupidity, and my father's selfishness.

Compounding the disaster, Daddy was never home to share some responsibility in raising my older brother.

Mommy did her best to treat Chink as an equal, but he wasn't an equal. Chink wasn't her son.

Not being completely raised by my mother, Chink lacked the discipline and morals she instilled in my other brothers and me.

I could have only imagined the dilemma of trying to accept her husband, while also having to accept the side chick's offspring.

Embarrassed in public, Mommy used to tell people Chink and I were twins, so she didn't have to explain our proximity in age.

People in Wagner Projects used to give her looks that clearly said, "Bitch, you stupid," but Mommy endured the criticism daily, as well as Chink's peculiar and erratic behavior.

In 1989, after he vacuumed our little sister Sandy's finger by *accident*, Chink went into his room, picked up his toys and started talking to them while he pretended that they were real people.

Mommy feared that he had some deep psychological issues, and she worried about Sandy's safety.

On a very sad and rainy Saturday afternoon, Chink was sent to live at my grandmother's apartment in King Towers.

Mommy could no longer deal with the mental strain that accompanied my older brother, and I missed him terribly, but I understood Mommy's reasoning for not allowing Chink to live with us anymore.

My mother never trusted my grandmother after Chink was born, because my grandmother knew Ingrid and condoned my father's second life by accepting Ingrid the same way that my grandmother accepted my mother.

Alejandro, Javier, Sandy and I weren't allowed to go to my grandmother's house anymore, so for years I would only see Chink whenever we just happened to run into each other.

We would always make promises of seeing one another, but sadly we never followed through.

* * *

Right before I arrived at Tanisha's building, 1350 Fifth Avenue, to inform her of my plans to attend Woodberry Forest School, I told myself that I would detour to Lenox Avenue to visit my other family.

But the plan vanished, like it always did as the smell of pussy got closer. I could never just walk past Tanisha's building.

Thinking about my earlier conversation with Tee, I reached to knock on Tanisha's front door, but the door opened, and a French-manicured-hand grabbed my Riverside Church Hawks hoodie, pulling me into the pitch-black apartment.

"Hey what are you—"

"Ssh, be quiet!" Tanisha covered my mouth and whispered in my ear. "My grandfather is home. Just take my hand and follow me."

Blind, I held her hand and the Elizabeth Taylor's White Diamonds perfume led the way. Tanisha smelled delicious.

Familiar with Tanisha's two-bedroom project suite, I knew I had to turn left at the front door, take eight steps down the hallway, and make a *hard* right—walking straight into her room.

Mr. Berry, her 86-year-old-grandfather, always slept like a raisin in the moonlight—just two feet across from Tanisha's room.

A pro at tiptoeing out of the apartment while he was there, I was nervous about my first-time sneaking in the place.

Tanisha slowly opened her bedroom door and the light from her window exposed her silhouette.

Before I could activate my night vision, she pulled me into her room and gave me a slight tug to my chest with both of her hands.

The back of my knees hit the bed and I lost my balance, falling backward onto the mattress.

"Oh shit—"

"Ssh...stop making noise Manzo."

"OK," I whispered as I laid on my back.

What the hell am I doing?

Placing my hands over my face, I shook my brain to untangle the lust. I knew what I craved was very risky, also very wrong.

I wanted some *dome*—but without her granddaddy's eyes catching a dick go down his granddaughter's throat.

He would surely have a heart attack if he had gotten even a glimpse of Tanisha's skills, but I had already made myself comfortable.

So, I had hoped "death from watching granddaughter gag" was covered in Mr. Berry's good ole life insurance.

The fun was just beginning, and I loved a challenge.

Opening my eyes, I put all the weight on my elbows to sit upright, but a match being struck halted my efforts, and my eyes followed the sound.

Bent over a small table against a wall, a foot in front of me, Tanisha lit two scented candles as she looked back at me and smiled.

"Relax, he's asleep and never comes back here," Tanisha assured.

The twin flames burned; her unblemished mocha skin melted the darkness as her face glowed.

Tanisha's shiny *Indian* hair hugged her face, while the split ends rested on plump breast that set perfectly in a white-laced push-up bra.

My erection swatted away the butterflies, and there wasn't a chance of me leaving—I was no longer nervous.

I watched her light a third candle as she batted her almond shaped eyes while she pretended that I wasn't looking.

The Boyz II Men poster on her wall above her dresser came to life and shared the stage with the candles, a pink curling iron, a Revlon hair-relaxer box, and a tall white bottle of Cocoa Butter Lotion.

Tanisha stood up and thoughts of her family's Native American origins were quickly tomahawked.

Course pubic hairs, prickly and short, which had always been completely shaved, pressed beneath matching white-laced panties.

A garter belt sailed down young, thick, brown legs and docked onto thigh-high sheer white stockings.

Her thighs touched and enclosed around my appetizer. Famished, the thought of being satiated kept me on edge. More than excited, I rubbed on my cock and drooled a little.

"Ha, ha, ha—you want this pussy...don't you?"

I looked down at the bulge in my sweats and answered, "Yes please."

She stepped closer, but before I could stand up and slam her on the bed, my mind drifted momentarily, and I just stared at the neon green stars semi-glowing on her ceiling.

Feeling my sweatpants being slung down my legs, I just took deep breaths as we both watched the Big Dipper.

Slowly taking most of me in her mouth, Tanisha gave me head until I almost screamed.

To prevent shame and premature ejaculation, I had to imagine being on a spaceship—exploring the stars and fighting Darth Vader.

My Star Wars rendition worked until I lost my concentration and noticed her New Kids on the Block, Christmas poster.

Crept out by Joey, Jonathan, Jordan, and Danny in ugly sweaters staring at me, I sat up and gently pushed Tanisha off me.

"What's wrong? I ain't doing it right this time?" she asked.

"Uh, it's perfect. But it's your turn," I said.

"*My* turn?" she questioned.

"Yes, my turn to do you baby," I reiterated.

Never blinking, she held my hand and assisted me to my feet. Our faces inches apart, I could smell all two hours of basketball practice on her mouth, but I didn't care.

Tanisha removed her panties one leg at a time while she stared into my eyes.

After tossing the panties in my face, she jumped backward onto the bed, opened her legs and said one word, "OK."

Eating pussy was taboo in the Black community and had always been classified as something only nasty Puerto Ricans or dirty White boys had partaken in during sex.

I had never heard one of my friends, or any boy for that matter, talk about how he performed oral sex on a girl, but I knew from watching Emmanuelle, the French soft porn on Cinemax—that women lost their goddamn minds when a guy's head was between a woman's legs. I couldn't see *exactly* what occurred, but I could see one thing—the reaction.

Before tossing Tanisha's panties in a corner, I inhaled the satin.

With my Air Jordan's still on my feet and my Champion sweatpants around my ankles, I hopped on the bed with both ashy knees landing between Tanisha's legs.

Bending over, I closed my eyes and rested my forearms on the dingy comforter as my left hand looped under and over her right leg—cupping her thigh firmly.

Also following the technique that I had learned at 2:37 AM just two nights prior, I held Tanisha's left thigh with my right hand.

Transferring my weight to my elbows, I laid my legs and abdomen flat on the bed and propped her legs open even further.

"Mmmm..." Tanisha moaned.

My heart beat fast. The room smelled of vanilla, but I craved chocolate.

"Put your face in it Manzo."

Tanisha and I had sex plenty of times before, but I never actually *saw* what we did. The lights were always off, and the act itself never lasted longer than forty-five seconds.

The candles spotlighted her pelvic area, and I just stared at her pussy for a moment.

She had an abnormally large vagina compared to the girls I watched on cable television, and when I turned my head to the side—Tanisha's flower looked like a baby Audrey II from the movie, *A Little Shop of Horror.*

I didn't know whether I should kiss the big lipped plant or prick my finger and feed it.

Feeeed meee Seeeymoouur—

"What's wrong baby?" she asked.

"Uh...nothing."

"Then do it," she commanded.

"I'm about to baby."

Do it and then tell her that you are going to Woodberry for school. Do it!

Face to face with my new favorite alien, I pulled Tanisha's legs closer to my body, cradled my biceps under her thighs, and my hands clenched her quads.

"Mmmm, lick it now!" she demanded.

Sticking out my tongue, I moved in to devour the target, but right before I could taste greatness, the room shook.

BOOM!

"Tanisha, I know you in there with a boy!" Mr. Berry shouted as he unsuccessfully tried to knock down the door with his cane. "I'm going to kill that stanking muddah-fuckah!"

"Oh shit!" I said a little too loudly.

"Shut up." She covered my mouth.

"Open this goddamn door Tanisha!"

"Granddaddy there's no one in here!" she yelled before mouthing to me, "Get dressed!"

"Tanisha don't you lie to me young lady! I can smell little dick down the hallway!"

Jumping to the floor, I pulled my sweatpants up, and my boxers hadn't passed my thighs, but I didn't care.

"Granddaddy stop banging on the door—no one is here!"

"I'm going to kill that muddah-fuckah!" Mr. Berry threatened!

Tanisha hopped out of the bed and put on some shorts while screaming at her granddaddy.

Conflicted, I knew I could whip his ass, but I could never hit an old man, although the thought of being caned to death wasn't too appealing either.

"I'm going to let you in! Stop banging!"

"Are you crazy Tanisha?" I mouthed.

"Open this door you little hussy...NOW!" Mr. Berry persisted.

Now under full attack, I kissed her on her cheek and whispered, "I'm going to Woodberry Forest next year."

Quickly blowing out the candles and hiding behind the wall beside the door, I never saw her tears fall.

"Tanisha—"

"I'm coming granddaddy!" she hollered, walking in the dark toward the door.

A laxative couldn't have worked more effectively, as the sound of the doorknob unlocking almost made me shit on myself.

I clenched my ass muscles and pushed the turtlehead back in its shell.

"Where the fuck is that little nigga at?" Mr. Berry busted in the room but couldn't see anything, and he bumped into the bed.

"Turn the muddah-fuckin lights on!"

"The light is broken granddaddy!"

I slid out of the bedroom door, felt for the hallway wall and proceeded to creep and count eight paces while Mr. Berry interrogated Tanisha.

"Where that stankin' lil bastard at?" Mr. Berry asked. "Come on out'chea goddamnit!"

"Ain't nobody but me in my room—I was on the damn phone!"

"Then what's that goddamn smell?"

"I don't know! You're going senile granddaddy!"

"Senile my ass—I know sweaty balls Tanisha!"

"Stop disrespecting me! You taught me better granddaddy!"

"Taught you better, my ass! You *just* like your damn mama!"

"I am *nothing* like my goddamn mother!"

"Oooh really Tanisha? Then why in the hell your breath smell like Vienna sausages?"

Before Tanisha answered, I covered my mouth to not burst out laughing and was out of the front door, running down the staircase.

Once outside, the fresh air reminded me that I didn't die by the hands of a crazy old man with the nose of a bloodhound.

Surprisingly, I never gave it a thought that I had just told my girlfriend I was leaving the city indefinitely. I just wiped off the sweat on my face and laughed like a madman.

The motherfucker does know sweaty balls though!

Chapter Four

HOME SCHOOL

Creeping my eyes open, I yawned, scratched my twelve-year-old balls and rolled out of bed. The fuzziness of my New York Knicks area rug let me know I was standing.

Still drowsy, I stumbled out of the bedroom toward the bathroom without any need to look at the clock, because I already knew the time—7:30 AM.

We got 30 minutes.

"*KSH, KSH, KSH, KSH...*"

I love listening to Daddy count all that money in the morning.

After playing a game of "How much pee can I actually get in the toilet bowl?" I opened my eyes a little wider, so I could check my score, and it was obvious I needed more practice.

"*KSH, KSH, KSH, KSH...*"

Slightly bending at the waist, I flushed the toilet with my right hand while simultaneously pushing the door completely open with my left.

The natural light from my bedroom would be enough for me to find the crust in my eyes and the yellow on my teeth.

The sound of dollar bills scraping against one another grew louder, but I welcomed the friction. Daddy was home safe!

My father tallying up his night's earnings was just another sound to the beginning of a beautiful morning.

The birds chirped, the wind blew, cars honked, and my father counted *our* money.

A card shark couldn't even compete with the swiftness of Daddy's technique and style. Green, old White men shuffled from thumb to thumb, appearing to float with perfect form and symmetry. Daddy was quite the dealer.

My entire family grew accustomed to the rhythmic combination of our savings being deposited.

Mommy never awakened or moved as she slept only inches from the money machine. Firmly asleep also, my other siblings simply showed zero interest.

Opening the medicine cabinet, I snatched the red toothbrush and Colgate toothpaste. I mentally computed the length of the toothbrush because Javier's was the same color, except shorter.

The medicine cabinet closed, and the exhausted preteen reappeared in the mirror.

Mommy had told me not to watch the entire UNLV basketball game, but I couldn't resist watching Larry Johnson and his boys crush Long Beach State.

Basketball was my escape from our three-bedroom project apartment, although the bags underneath my eyes were my reality.

Screw it. I'll sleep in Spanish class before my game.

"KSH, KSH, KSH, KSH..."

I brushed my teeth and looked in the mirror, but I never even noticed the foamed-mouth-boy looking back at me.

I could only see the day and all its thrills, challenges, and commitments. I had a lot on my mind.

Alejandro and Javier better not take forever waking up! The bus should be on time.

Does Melody think I'm cute?

Oh man, I have to memorize those lines for drama!

I'm going to score thirty on Stephon next time!

I love Mr. Lorch, he's a great man.

"KSH—KSH."

Silence. The money machine had stopped.

The morning tones continued, but without its lead singer the single just couldn't go gold. The chirping birds just couldn't hit all the notes. Daddy discontinuing the money count scratched the record.

He never stopped when he was tired, he stopped when he was done, and there was never a remix. The subtraction of my favorite sound restored my cognizance. Instantly I knew that within seconds Daddy would blurt out, as he did every day, how much he had *earned* the past evening.

Prior to his announcement, I would guess the dollar figure based on the time he finished counting. My digital Casio watch with the calculator displayed 7:42 AM.

How much today?

Between twelve and fifteen minutes, sooo—twenty-two!

"Twenty-three," I heard him say through my parents' bedroom door, directly across from the bathroom.

I was getting too good at predicting the amounts. For eight weeks straight, I had never been more than a digit off either way.

Twenty-three thousand dollars was a good night's keep, but during a few consecutive days around the first of the month, Daddy's magic number was thirty-two, which he shouted a little louder—and I smiled a little wider.

Turning on the faucet, I dipped my left hand under the frigid water and scooped it into my mouth, while I listened to the crackling and popping of rubber bands being double looped around wads of drug money.

Here he comes.

Standing in the bathroom doorway, I wiped my mouth steadily with a hand towel and heard the loose screws on my parents' doorknob jingle. Withholding a nervous smile, I stood tall and waited to see my future.

Wearing only a green Polo shirt, Daddy opened the door and we stood almost eye to eye. The baggage under his eyes was a few pairs of pants heavier than mine.

He was exhausted and only five feet and nine inches in height, but he had a giant presence.

The three-carat diamond earring in his left ear sparkled almost as much as his jet-black curly Afro.

Before noticing his smile, I had eyed the diamond encrusted C hanging from his sixteen-inch, gold Herringbone chain that rested in the thick of his black chest hairs.

I loved seeing Daddy before I left for school, but I couldn't wait for the man to finally go to sleep.

Before bedtime, my father always placed his chain in Mommy's jewelry box, and I would steal it and sport it to school.

By the time that he woke up in the late afternoon, the bait would be back in the box—and I would've already caught a few fish. Girls of any age loved diamonds.

Daddy kept his beard trimmed and full like his pockets. He had small, slanted eyes, and from certain angles he appeared to be a perfect blend of Asian and Black, rather than Black and Puerto Rican.

His prominent *Peña* nose pointed slightly downward at the tip when he smiled, and his straight white teeth illuminated his full lips.

He was the type of handsome where most women could not even get angry or take him seriously when he attempted to display rage.

Positive energy soaked through his coffee-colored complexion, and his charisma could execute a woman's common sense.

Oddly, the best-looking guy in the room was often the funniest guy in the room. Daddy was hilarious.

If we were living during the Ancient Egyptian Dynasty, he would have been a king, but we weren't.

The year was 1990. The city was New York.

And although very unassuming, Carlos Peña was one of the biggest drug dealers in East Harlem.

Daddy always looked at me like he was looking in a mirror. I could never tell if he were proud or scared of his reflection—and I didn't care.

Growing up in a place where my friends didn't even have someone to call, "Daddy," I was always thrilled that he looked at me at all. I loved him and could always count on him in my time of need.

"Good morning son."

"Good morning Daddy. Can you buy me a new pair of sneakers?"

* * *

The childhood activities I gravitated toward never developed because of a natural love or passion. The affinity for the games I played were birthed from a greed for devotion from the spectators who watched.

Naturally, a Peña was supposed to play baseball and make his Puerto Rican heritage proud, but basketball was the sport of interest for most people in my neighborhood, especially the young hustlers and the women.

I was fascinated by the fast life, but Mommy was strict and ironically, forbade me from "fraternizing" with the young Carloses of the world.

She understood all too well how the risk of hanging with *thousandnaire* dropouts and *hoochie-mamas* outweighed the rewards. Being a thinker since conception, I found my loophole.

The basketball courts were directly behind my building and could be seen from our thirteenth-floor apartment's kitchen window.

Like a hawk, Mommy periodically peeped her head out of the window to confirm I was where I said I would be, and I was—faithfully.

I wasn't allowed to hang out on the corner of 123rd Street and Second Avenue with the older kids because that's where they gambled and sold drugs.

Even though my young spirit yearned for action, I was confined to the area around my building.

Unlike myself, the older kids could go wherever they pleased, but luckily for me—they loved playing basketball.

The *courts* would be my bridge to not only create friendships with the derelicts, but to also earn their respect and gain the attention of the girls who followed their every move.

Playing hoops was our chess. To be beaten in basketball was demoralizing to one's character and physical toughness. The most confident often out dueled the most skillful.

Taking someone's heart on the courts correlated to doing the same in the streets.

Add females to the equation and the stakes to the blacktop battles tripled. Girls noticed a winner, so the boys had to win.

Much stronger than all the kids my age, I dominated them on the courts with ease. The toddlers were just the opening act, and at some point, the fellas from the Avenue would be my main event.

Some days they wouldn't come because their day jobs didn't permit the time off, but I would still be on the courts practicing my moves and visualizing my terror of anyone who tried guarding me.

Jump shots. Crossover dribbles. Rebounds.

My game was steadily improving and although I held my own, the older dudes kept whipping my ass, but I welcomed the beating.

They schooled me, but the game of basketball wasn't *the* lesson. The lesson was learning how to be a man.

Every time I got knocked down, I got right back up. If someone blocked my shot, I would come right back and shoot again.

When someone talked shit in my face, I matched their banter, letter for fucking letter.

There was no quit or bitch in me, so fear or intimidation wasn't ever in my character, and the homies had begun to catch on quickly.

Soon word spread that *Los'* son was a baller, but in a completely different capacity than his father.

When I was thirteen years old, I was playing against guys up to ten years older than I was.

I had begun to catch the eye of the project cheerleaders who already knew who my father was, but with every battle won on the courts they began to whisper to each other that I was "cute."

Unlike the shy girls around my age, the young women were bold enough to speak to me directly, and with every compliment and wink of a fake eyelash—I became more and more of an attention whore.

Instead of just winning, I now wanted to embarrass my opponents.

I took bits and pieces of Larry Bird, Magic Johnson, and Michael Jordan's game, and combined it with Wagner's top street ballers.

Steve-Bo's trickery, June-Bo's tenacity, Craig's smoothness, and Cee-Town's mental maturity had helped me become nearly un-guardable in the projects.

My skillset surpassed anyone in my age bracket, but just as much as I was becoming a student of the game, I was becoming a student of the *game.*

Everybody at the courts was not there to play basketball, and everybody there to play basketball wasn't just trying to score by tossing a ball in a hoop.

When I was on the court, my focus was on winning and nothing else, but I didn't win every game and that meant I had to sit until it was my team's time to play again.

Each game took between fifteen to twenty minutes. If a team lost and had to wait for two games, then that team was basically part of the crowd for up to forty minutes.

There were criminals playing basketball, but there were even more roaming the sidelines, and when criminals talked, they didn't talk politics.

* * *

"We ain't losing to these bums today! Pass me the rock Kejo!" I demanded as I ran straight toward my teammate. "I got this bum on me!"

Kejo, a skinny brother with cornrows from my building who mimicked his game after Jordan and could jump back to Africa, was the most athletic and best player on the court at the time.

But, I had the obvious mismatch. With the game tied at thirty, the next team to score won the game.

Steve-Bo, an offensive terror, but the slowest defender in the game was guarding me. There wasn't a doubt in my mind that he was lunchmeat.

Any player defending me would need all his motor skills just to *try* and keep up, and Bo's eyes told me that he was either very high or had just finished swimming in Wagner's pool. But I didn't see any swimming trunks or arm floaties.

Tossing me the ball at half court, Kejo ran to the other side next to my other teammates, Jay Black, Tynell, and Junior. They cleared out a lane, so I could smoke Steve-Bo—one on one.

Before dribbling, I just held the ball for a moment and looked into my victim's eyes. Steve-Bo was three feet away in a defensive stance with his hands raised at his sides.

Being a shit-talker extraordinaire, he kept babbling something, but I couldn't hear him. I was in my zone.

He was giving me the jump shot and I felt I could make it, but I wanted to send a message to him and any other old motherfucker that ever tried to stop me.

The crowd stopped their conversations and began to pay closer attention to the next big thing from the Wagner Projects—me.

The court seemed to shrink as they moved closer, and my heart got bigger. Some rooted for either side and others called out bets.

"Manzo take that nigga Bo!"

"$100 the young boy drops another bucket!"

"Bet nigga!"

Not knowing who was for me or who was against me—I didn't care. It was my time. It was my moment.

I'm gonna bake your ass!

"You ain't shit lil' nigga!" Steve-Bo shouted in my face. Sweat dripped down my forehead as I curled my lips and gripped the ball tighter. I was angry.

Oh, I ain't shit, huh?

Proceeding to dribble with my left hand, I stared directly in his eyes and hoped he would try and steal the ball, but he didn't. The more I inched forward, the more he inched back.

"Shoot bitch!" he spat.

No way!

Switching the ball to my right hand, I continued to dribble and creep forward, but he kept moving backward daring me to shoot.

Steve-Bo was now at the free throw line and I was at the top of the key. The chants got louder.

"Shoot that shit Manzo!"

"You giving him too much room Bo!"

"You got him Zo! Let's get this money!"

Like a Harlem Globetrotter, I dribbled the ball back and forth between my legs, and I had Steve-Bo on his heels.

He was a foot in front of the free throw line and knew he had no choice but to stand his ground.

Right hand.

Left hand.

My toes touched the free throw line, and everyone in the park knew that I never missed from that spot.

He was giving me my shot and instead of forcing the ball to the basket for a layup and risking weak side defensive help, I had to play the percentages.

I could hit a free throw ninety-two out of 100 times, so I had no choice but to shoot.

I looked at Kejo and he gave me the nod to take the shot, because he had witnessed me drain buckets countless times from the exact spot I was standing.

Steve-Bo peeped the nod, and being a seasoned veteran, he could read our minds. But his psychic skills didn't matter—nothing was going to stop me from greatness.

I got your ass now Bo!

Looking at the basket, I bounced the ball, raised my shoulders, lifted my head, and used my left hand to secure the ball as I exploded into perfect jump shooting position.

Anticipating the shot, Steve-Bo lunged forward but never jumped to block the shot—instead, he slightly brushed my leg with his body and ran full speed toward the opposite basket.

What the...

The subtle contact handicapped my vertical tremendously but wasn't enough for me to call a foul, although the contact threw off my rhythm.

The ball rotated in the air, and I read the Spaulding print four times before the orange bomb appeared to hit its target as everyone anticipated my dagger.

"It's good!"

"That's money!"

In your face!

The basketball hit all net and then a pair of hands—at the *front* of the rim! Shooting an air-ball, I had missed badly.

Snatching the rebound out of the sky, Craig launched the ball to his teammate, Steve-Bo—who was waiting under their basket at the opposite end of the court.

The *cherry-picking* son of a bitch finger-rolled the ball into their hoop!

The game was over, my team lost, and people started to yell.

"Ah shit young blood!"

"Pay up motherfucker!"

"Maybe next time little nigga!"

"That was a fucking foul!"

"You will get them next time cutie!"

With both hands on the top of my head, I just walked to the nearest bench in utter disappointment.

Never looking back at my teammates or congratulating the crafty bastards who just embarrassed me, I sat down next to Gray-Eyed Greg and Jessie Frio— who were already engaged in serious conversation.

The basketball game was just an accessory to their daily pow-wow at the courts. I had no time to dwell on my schooling though, because the real lesson was just about to begin.

* * *

Gray-Eyed Greg and Jessie Frio weren't from Wagner Projects. They lived in one of the tenements on 120th Street between First and Second Avenue. I didn't know exactly which building, nor did I care.

The tenements were considered a downgrade from even the projects, so I kept my young ass away from the six story buildings with the fire escapes.

The duo from across the border were a few years older than I and spent most of their time in the projects playing basketball, chasing girls, or hustling.

Gray-Eyed Greg and Jessie Frio were considered just as much as a part of Wagner as anyone who resided there. Nobody fucked with them.

Jessie Frio, a chipped-tooth Puerto Rican with a vertical scar on the right side of his face, sported a stringy, unedged haircut.

With the panache of a *brother*, Jessie Frio was always wearing the latest sneakers and designer sweat suits from Harlem fashion designer, Dapper Dan.

Gray-Eyed Greg was fair-skinned with freckles and rocked a low-Caesar haircut. He and his Hispanic counterpart were inseparable.

Like most of the young men in the projects, neither *Gray Eyes* nor *Frio* sustained employment, but they always stayed fresh—gold chains, diamond earrings, and a pocket full of cash completed their daily attire.

I never knew exactly how Frio and Gray Eyes got their money, but I *knew*—so did the Housing Police.

Frio and Gray Eyes were harassed on the regular by the cops but never were detained. Word on the street was that the Houdini Brothers could make crack disappear right in front of an officer's eyes.

Always loving their rhetoric, I would laugh at their jokes, and I would even steal some of their material and use it in school like I had made the shit up myself.

After my failed attempt at being a star on the courts, I was glad that Frio and Gray Eyes were around.

Their performances were traditionally hilarious, but the subject matter today wouldn't be "Your Mama" jokes. The topic was a little *different*.

* * *

"That was some real bullshit!" I screamed as I sat on top of the benches next to Gray-Eyed Greg and put my feet on the cemented checkerboard table.

"Don't even sweat that shit Manzo. Them two niggas been pulling that move for years." Gray-Eyed Greg said before continuing his conversation with Jessie Frio.

"My moms was home, so I took the bitch to the roof of 2369," Gray Eyes said to Frio, whose brown eyes expanded with anticipation.

"We get to the roof and at first she started to front, but I remembered I had a couple of stones in my pocket, so I tells the bitch to suck me off."

"Word?" Frio asked.

"Word!" Gray Eyes said and then looked at me too.

"*Word?*" I repeated.

"Word," Gray Eyes answered.

"So, what happened B?" Frio asked, tapping his all white Nike Delta Force sneakers against the table.

"What *happened?*" Gray Eyes asked.

"Uh...you kissed her!" I replied.

"Ha, ha, ha!" they laughed.

What's so funny?

"Hell no! Nigga, I ain't kissing no motherfucking crackhead!"

"Oh yea...why would you Greg?" I spoke.

"I gave that bitch the rocks and she pulled out her pipe and smoked that shit!"

"Oooh shit, I ain't even know Rebecca smoked crack!" Frio shouted and stood up.

"Ha, ha, ha! Hell yea nigga!" Gray Eyes became more animated as his gold rope chain starting to swing.

Mommy's friend, Rebecca?

"So the bitch takes two hits of the glass dick then puts it down and starts piping this *real* dick!"

"You lying B!" Jessie Frio said.

"Hell nah I ain't lying—I tore that pussy up on Pebble Beach!" Gray Eyed said. "Man, after I finished with that bitch on the roof, my knees were all tore the fuck up! I had mad little pebbles jammed in my goddamn kneecaps!"

"Ha, ha, ha!" we all laughed.

"Shit, look at my knees B!" Gray Eyes demanded, rolling up both pant legs of his Gucci sweat suit.

His knees were bandaged, and the dried-up blood soaked through the two-day-old dressing of his love scars.

"You sure you weren't eating the box B?" Frio joked.

"Ha-ha—fuck you Frio!" Gray Eyes said and abruptly stopped laughing.

"Remember these two things Manzo," Gray Eyes said, Frio already nodding in agreement.

"One, always bring kneepads to Pebble beach..." he tapped my chest, with his gray eyes glowing in the sun.

"And two...you can fuck any bitch...if you got drugs *and* money. Any bitch."

Any bitch?

"*Any* bitch Manzo," Frio added.

Chapter Five

MARK 9:42

"You can't guard me my brother!" Stephon declared after draining a thirty-foot jump shot in my face.

"Lucky bastard!" I yelled.

"Game over rock star!"

Stephon Marbury wasn't lucky; the kid was great! A true Brooklyn point guard, he could do it all—shoot, dribble, pass, score, and jump.

Ask him who was going to be better than Michael Jordan, and he would reply, "Stephon Marbury!" in third person like he was talking about a current NBA superstar.

"You beat me this time, but I'm gonna whip your ass next time!" I said, pouring with sweat.

"Yea right Manzo! Maybe next time I will take off my boots!"

Practice had just finished, and I was shooting around while I waited for my meeting with Mr. Ernie Lorch, the director of the Riverside Church Hawks—to talk about my plans to leave New York for high school.

Other than to attend Oak Hill Academy, a basketball powerhouse, also located also in Virginia —Mr. Lorch didn't condone any of *his* boys leaving the state for school.

With my lack of interest in Oak Hill, Mr. Lorch offered to pay my tuition, but only if I went to All Hallows with Coach John Carey.

I had agreed to enroll at the Catholic school in the Bronx—until Woodberry became an option.

ped me grow as a player *and* a person, so I was extremely
se my intentions of leaving his program. Needing to collect my
the gym's wooden benches alone.

o minutes of peace, and *Steph* walked in the gym, tossed his black
leathe. , on the benches, and yelled, "One on motherfucking one, rock
star!"

His practice wasn't for another hour, but he always came early to work on his game.

Steph stepped on the court wearing baggy black pants, a polka dot button-up shirt, and black Timberland boots.

He sported a curly high-top fade haircut with a part in the middle and one gold hoop earring in both ears, respectively.

After Young Life dismantled its basketball program and merged with Riverside, Steph and I played for *the Church*.

Although we were the same age, he played in the Senior Division (eighteen years old and under) and I played in the Junior Division (sixteen years old and under).

We were the only two kids at the Church to play outside of our age brackets. Steph's basketball skills and fearlessness of defeat surpassed not just mine, but any fourteen-year old ball player on the planet.

Steph's confidence was infectious, and his presence always left me feeling stronger and more cognitive of my self-worth. He believed he could do anything, so I believed I could do *almost* anything.

"You pretty good...for a half-breed!" Steph joked.

"Fuck you, ha, ha, ha!"

"Hamilton!" Mr. Lorch summoned from his office, directly outside of the gym.

"I gotta bounce Steph! I'm almost next, and I don't want to run laps next practice for being late!"

"No doubt! Do your thing Manzo!"

We slapped five, and I turned to run out of the gym, but right when I reached the exit, Steph called out, "Manzo!"

"Yo!" I turned around, smiling and expecting a final joke—but he wasn't laughing.

"Manzo...don't ever let anybody make you do something you don't want to do," he said.

A little confused as to what the hell Steph was talking about, I looked at the sincerity in his eyes and just agreed, "OK, thanks B."

* * *

Riverside Church was an enormous gothic church built in 1926 and located on 120th Street and Riverside Drive—just a few blocks away from Columbia University.

The Church's main 392-foot-tall tower sat on a hill where the upper West Side met Harlem and could be seen from as far away as East Harlem, New Jersey, and even the Bronx.

Many kids stared at the Church and dreamed of being good enough to enter its doors, but no one aspired priesthood though.

The kids wanted to be a part of the clergy of supreme ballers, such as NBA players, Mark Jackson, Chris Mullin, Kenny Smith, Kenny Anderson, and Ed Pinkney.

Playing for the Church was a privilege for the privileged.

If a kid could ball then he was supplied with unlimited basketball gear, the best coaching, and trips around the world to play against the best competition.

The formula was simple, if a guy were great then he played for the Church or our rivals, the Gauchos—but if a guy were just good then he played for someone else.

Riverside Church's tryouts were held monthly, and ninety-five percent of the little devils who entered the Catholic church were told they weren't good enough, and to never return.

Showing no mercy for the meek, the ex-communicated kids were forced to settle for inferior basketball programs like Milbank, Aim High, Minisink, and Each One Teach One.

The gym itself was buried in the basement of Riverside Church, and just getting to the mecca of youth basketball replicated an Indiana Jones adventure.

The Church, always dimly lit and quiet, exhibited old paintings, relics, and sculptures that hid in secret passageways that led to the gym.

Only the eminent could enter, and I got my wings four years ago, when *Saint Lorch* deemed me worthy to wear the blue and yellow.

Mr. Lorch, a wealthy corporate lawyer, had a lot of power for a fifty-seven-year-old White man with no real basketball history.

He founded the team in 1961 as a program for underprivileged kids and turned his *non-profit* into an Amateur Athletic Union (AAU) phenomenon.

Riverside Church was a castle, and Mr. Lorch was without a doubt the king.

A bachelor, Mr. Lorch was six feet with a thinning black and silver comb-over. He wore large square, black frames that rested low on his droopy face.

Always clean-shaven, Mr. Lorch, with his bushy eyebrows, had a slight hunch to his walk, which made his big face seem even bigger whenever he yelled at us.

He was the nicest guy and normally soft-spoken, until it was time to play ball. Winning was everything, and if a kid messed up on the court, Mr. Lorch would give him quite the tongue-lashing.

He only coached the older teams with the college and professional basketball prospects, but he still kept a close eye on all age divisions. Mr. Lorch's name was synonymous with Riverside Church, so *Riverside* had to win.

Whenever Mr. Lorch was in the building, the ballers from every age were on their best behaviors.

Most of the kids were poor and looked to him not just for guidance, but also for shelter and security.

Like any coach, he paid special attention to the most dominant players, but there were special-needs-kids who weren't the best of the best but were always talking to Mr. Lorch.

He helped many kids' families pay their rents and keep on the lights. I never took or needed a single dime from him because my father provided everything I needed.

Daddy would've objected if I ever received a gift from another man but was OK with the kindhearted Mr. Lorch paying for my high school.

My father felt that I had committed years of service to the Riverside Church program, and out of principle alone—Mr. Lorch should fund my education as a sign of appreciation for my skills and loyalty.

"They don't make many whiteys like Mr. Lerch!" my father would often say, never able to pronounce my coach's name correctly.

Coming from the depths of the slums where no one helps anybody and blames the White man for all their problems, I loved what Mr. Lorch represented.

Here was a Caucasian reaching into the fire, grabbing the hands of young brown boys, and rescuing them from themselves.

When kids concentrated on school and basketball, the probability of them committing crimes or doing drugs drastically decreased.

The kids who played for the Church had a better chance at success than any random 100 who didn't. Mr. Lorch's program created opportunities on and *off* the court.

As a season ticket holder for the New York Yankees, Mr. Lorch took a few of us to our first professional baseball games.

His seats were right beside first base, so I always got to talk to the Yankees All-Star, Don Mattingly.

Mr. Lorch would buy us some peanuts and Cracker Jacks, and I would gratefully smile from the ceremonial first pitch until the end of the seventh inning, when he always stood, stretched his arms, and said— "Time for bed."

We never stayed for the entire game, but I was more than content by just being able to witness the energy of Yankee Stadium.

After the game, I was always the first player he dropped off in his silver Volvo 760 (my father had the exact same car in black), even though the other two kids lived closer to the stadium.

Grateful for the experience, I would say, "Thanks Mr. Lorch," and run upstairs to brag about how much fun we had.

Although I loved being a part of such a prestigious program like Riverside Church, I needed to go to Woodberry Forest School.

Having to tell Mr. Lorch was nerve wrecking, but I had to do what was best for my family...and *certainly,* what was best for me.

* * *

Set inside a dirty beige wall and resembling a utility closet, the rusted metal door of my coach's office, was four feet directly in front of the gym's entrance.

I've never been inside his lair, but I knew many kids who had—mainly to receive sneakers and money for various reasons.

Anxious to meet with my coach and mentor, I stood behind my friend, Keith, who was already waiting outside of the office.

"So Steph beat you too, huh?" the dark skin fifteen-year-old giant asked.

"Hold up! Not you too?" I responded.

"Yea the cocky little bastard beat me on Monday."

"Next time big guy," I said, and suddenly I heard the distant sounds of clapping but ignored it.

"Why do you have to talk to Mr. Lorch?" I asked.

"Shit, he told me to come by 'cuz he got a pair of Jordan's for me and a little change for my momz," Keith said with a grin.

"You know my momz can't afford rent *and* these size sixteens."

"Ha, ha, ha, you got some big-ass-feet B!"

"Ha, ha, ha—fuck you Manzo!"

CLAP.

Keith and I looked at each other and got quiet. The clapping noise stopped, but it was still eerie.

Random noises always occurred in the old church, and although I was curious, I didn't feel the need to play detective.

"There's some creepy-ass noises in this church B!" he said as he looked all around the ceiling like an exterminator.

"You ain't lying B."

"Ha, ha, ha, this place is haunted Manzo."

BOOM!

The office door opened and quickly slammed shut, startling us both.

Wearing a tight red hoodie like E.T.'s chauffeur, a slender boy jogged down the hallway—cradling a crispy pair of orange and blue Bo Jackson's in his right arm.

The office door had swung open toward the left side of the wall, where we stood—so I didn't get a clear visual of the kid's face. I didn't have a clue who had just zoomed away with his gift.

"Who was that?" I asked, very puzzled.

"I don't know, but the lil' nigga had some fresh-ass-kicks in his hand!" Keith said.

"Anderson!" Mr. Lorch summoned Keith.

"Hell yea! I'm about to shine on them when I get home!" he smiled.

"Go shine then B!" I said as Keith eagerly pulled open the door. I was happy for the future NBA star.

Alone in the hallway, I accepted the silence and contemplated whether going to Woodberry Forest School was the best option for me.

I played basketball in NYC for the best AAU team in the country, and we played against the best competition.

The Jamals in New York would keep my game sharp, as opposed to me easily punishing the Brandons in Virginia.

A bunch of prep school White boys weren't on my level, and the fact that I would be slaying a clan of overprivileged brats was appealing—but my growth as a ball player would ultimately suffer. Basketball was very important to me but so was becoming a better person.

At Woodberry Forest, I would be in a positive environment and around brilliant minded individuals with whom I would create lifetime bonds.

In New York, most of my friends were thugs and drug dealers. My father was *the* drug dealer.

If I stayed in the city, what would become of me?

Yes, I had a very supportive family.

Yes, I had a great man like Mr. Lorch willing to pay for my enrollment into one of the best Catholic school, All-Hallows.

I was blessed to be a part of a tremendous program like Riverside Church— but I lived in hell and the devil paid my rent.

Being the only positive male role model in my household, I knew my siblings watched me strive for excellence.

Alejandro, twelve, was valedictorian of East Harlem Block School, and Javier, nine, went to a school for the Talented and the Gifted (TAG).

Both were basketball phenomena and already played under Coach Dermon Player for Riverside Church's Biddy Division.

Sandy, four, was the only girl in the family and could already draw better than children twice her age.

Donté, two, had four pillars of achievement to hold him to higher standards when he finally blossomed.

If I left my family, would I be leaving them unprotected in the same pit I was running away from?

I wasn't a Peña on paper, but I was still the Peña shield—and my absence would strengthen my sibling's vulnerability to be devoured by our environment.

I had begun to feel ashamed that I would ever be so selfish and risk my family's quality of life for what seemed to be the quality of the moment.

Woodberry Forest would be a great opportunity for me, but at what cost?

Cut the head and the body will fall.

I *was* the head though, and I'd rather stay and give my siblings a greater chance at success by seeing me succeed rather than reading about it.

Anger set in and I banged the back of my head against the wall a few times in frustration. A river of guilt flowed from my eyes, so I closed them, wiped my face, and leaned my head against the wall.

I was hurt because I knew that I would never go to Woodberry Forest School.

I would never turn my back on the people who meant the most to me.

I loved Tee, but he would have to be on his own. There was too much at risk if I left.

Crazy thoughts entered my head and I let my brain absorb the insanity. I was everything to the Peñas, and without me they would surely perish.

Closing my eyelids, I let my assumptions drift away as a twisted movie played in my mind.

* * *

"Mommy, I'm home from school—what the fuck?" I yelled as soon as I entered apartment 13E.

I stepped slowly into my family's apartment and the rancid smell almost pushed me back out of the door.

I walked into the kitchen and the smell thickened. I covered my nose and mouth.

Flies controlled the sky while roaches foot patrolled the urine-soaked linoleum to and from the command center—a half-eaten box of Captain Crunch cereal on the floor beside the stove.

A tiny mouse ate dried egg yolk off the top of a pyramid of dirty dishes in the sink.

With its door opened, the refrigerator was filthy and absent of food, looking like an X-ray of the human body with missing organs. The kitchen table and microwave were also gone.

With her back to me, my mother sat in a blue plastic folding chair that we normally used for barbecues on Randall's Island.

She wore a thin pink-flowered nightgown, and I could count every bone in her spine.

The mustard colored scarf on my mother's head was tied into a small knot that rested in between the *number eleven*—formed by her protruding neck bones.

She looked out of the window at a beautiful day, but I couldn't see her face.

"Mommy?" I called out to her. Disturbed, I felt my stomach muscles tighten.

On the windowsill, I noticed a glass crack-pipe and a red Bic lighter next to an aluminum foil ashtray full of Newport cigarette butts.

"Mommy what's going on?" I hollered, moving further into the kitchen. "Where are the kids Mommy?"

"The kids?" she finally spoke. "Oh we *lost* the kids."

I dropped my WFS duffle bag, and I couldn't breathe. Looking around the dirty kitchen, I got lightheaded and my chest muscles tightened.

The mouse winked. The roaches marched. I still could not move.

Mommy reached for the crack-pipe, wearing oversized yellow rubber gloves. Never turning her head, she brought the weapon to her mouth, lit the barrel, and proceeded to blow her brains out.

"Stop smoking that shit Mommy!"

The sound of a twenty-foot giant slowly stepping on wine glasses echoed throughout the kitchen.

"Please stop Mommy!" I pleaded. "Where did you get that shit?"

The fire ducked back into the lighter and the crackling sound faded. She blew smoke out of the window.

"Ha, ha, ha," she wheezed a dry laugh and turned around, but—the woman wasn't my mother!

The nightmarish figure smoking crack in the Peña family's kitchen was Sandy, my little sister.

"Big bro...I got this *shit* from our Daddy!"

* * *

Back in the church's hallway, I opened my eyes in horror. I shook my head and used the bottom of my practice jersey to rescue the tears before they fell.

Totally distraught, I knew that I had responsibilities here in New York City that were greater than my own. I had to stay!

As the tears dried, I focused on the positives that would come by me not leaving home.

I knew that I was putting myself at risk for negative scenarios, but I had a solid foundation.

I had my family, my girlfriend, and I had Mr. Lorch.

Playing for Riverside Church was a complete blessing and would be a major part in keeping me out of trouble, so I could focus on my responsibilities.

Content with the decision to stay in the greatest city in the world, I was very grateful for Mr. Lorch's generosity, and I couldn't wait to tell him that I would go to All-Hallows.

Riverside was my second family, and if I had both, I was confident I would graduate high school with a full basketball scholarship to a big-time university.

CLAP!

Hoop dream interrupted; I was startled by the return of the clapping. I peeled my body off the wall and stood in the middle of the hallway.

CLAP!

My body tensed with a sudden paranoia as I sensed something sinister was happening around me.

Feet stitched to the floor; I closed my eyes to give my ears a boost.

CLAP!

CLAP!

Reopening my eyes, I turned around, staring at the wall in disbelief.

The clapping noise was coming from behind the concrete wall, which I found extremely peculiar—because there weren't any church groups or machinery behind it.

The only thing behind that wall was Mr. Lorch's office.

Ninja-like, I tiptoed a couple of steps and slowly turned my head parallel to the wall.

My breathing hastened, and I placed both hands on the wall with the sensitivity of touching my first pair of breasts.

Leaning forward, I rotated my head to the left while extending my neck to the right, in the wall's direction.

With my hands sliding down the wall from my sweaty palms, I looked down the hallway.

Quickly dismissing that I was insane, I planted my right ear on the wall. The cold sensation on the side of my face lasted only a second before the office door opened.

BOOM!

The loud noise frightened me!

I frantically pushed myself off the wall and stood up straight before the office door opened, completely closing again.

When the door shut, Keith stood in front of it—holding the pair of black and red Air Jordan VI's that he so coveted. I thought Keith would have been thrilled, but he looked unnerved.

"What's wrong Keith?" I asked.

His eyes watered, and his cheeks formed an attempted smile, but his half-squint pushed a tear overboard.

"I'm good B," Keith pretended.

His once jovial face was saddened, and his lips trembled. I knew he was hiding something.

He looked petrified like a child who had just wet the bed and was afraid to tell his parents.

Unsure of what to say, I watched Keith glance at his Jordan's before he turned and walked down the hallway.

"Manzo!" Mr. Lorch summoned.

I was so confused. I've played basketball with Keith for years, and I've never seen the big guy seem so little.

Keith may have gotten his Jordan's, but his soul gasped for air.

"Goddamnit Manzo, get your *ass* in here!" Mr. Lorch screamed again.

Keith reached the end of the hallway as I grabbed the office's doorknob, and he made a small gesture before turning the corner.

The movement was quick. The movement was subtle, but I noticed and almost gagged. Keith rubbed his butt.

It was NOT a scratch.

It was NOT a swipe.

It was a fucking rub!

With the doorknob in my hand, I got dizzy. The underworld heated, and the sweat followed.

My heart dribbled past my stomach and damn near slam dunked near my small intestines.

Shaking, I faced the door to perdition, and every comment, joke, or rumor I heard about Mr. Lorch blazed right in front of my eyes.

'Go get you some sneakers and let Lorch rub on them little cakes!'

'You know he like them young and Black!'

'I heard Riverside took y'all to Phoenix, and you slept in the bed with Mr. Lorch!'

'He'll pay for your school, but you gotta let him spank them buns with that paddle!'

"Manzo get your ass in here young man!" Mr. Lorch hollered.

Anger moved my legs. My fear moved them faster. I sprinted down the hallway and up the stairs.

Paintings of bearded White men with robes falling off their shoulders as they played with young children in the grass—smirked at me.

I ran through the Church's corridor and out into the dark night, worrying that I would lose sight—*but all things become visible when they are exposed by the light.*

My feet stopped when I got all the way to Wagner Projects, but my brain kept running.

I did not know exactly what happened in Mr. Lorch's office with Keith or any other player, but the unknown possibilities terrified my young mind.

Ernest Lorch was a man that I loved and respected as a father figure, but on my two-mile reflection, I did not shed a single tear for no longer having him in my life—I cried for Keith.

I cried for the boys who entered that dungeon whole and came out broken.

I cried for my brothers who would never play for Riverside Church again.

Lastly, I cried for my family who would have to fight life without me, because I was getting the hell away from Mr. Lorch and New York City.

I was going to Woodberry Forest School.

Chapter Six

ALMOST BROTHERS

'*Woodberry Forest School, a college preparatory school for boys, founded in 1889 by Robert Stringfellow Walker, a captain with Mosby's Rangers. The School was named for the estate on which it stands, formerly owned by William Madison, brother of President James Madison.*'

"They gonna hang our Black asses!"

The Madisons owned slaves!

"What'cha say there young fella?"

"Oh nothing sir!" I spoke loudly, thankful that Mr. Fur was eighty-seven years old and wore a hearing aid in each ear.

"Just wanted to say thank you for stopping and giving us the opportunity to read this great sign!" I said.

"Yes'sa, thank you, Mr. Fur!" Tee said. I almost laughed.

"OK young fellas, get back in the car please. We're almost there," said Mr. Fur.

One hour and thirty minutes was the estimated time needed to drive from Union Station in Washington, D.C. to Orange, Virginia. Being more than twice the age of the average driver, Mr. Fur took more than twice as long.

A wrinkled White man with big ears and a nose that belonged in a pot of collard greens, Mr. Fur wore gold-rimmed aviators with yellow tinted lenses, and I had guessed he was a marksman in World War I.

The oldest Woodberry driver and soft-spoken, Mr. Fur was grandpa nice. He smiled a lot and made me feel welcomed although I hadn't seen a Black person for miles. He expressed a genuine sincerity but seemed to mask a deeper pain.

Continuing my guessing, I assumed that he lost his wife some time ago and decided to come out of retirement to get out of the house and cope with his grief.

Lost in thought, I didn't pay attention to Mr. Fur's driving. Five miles into Interstate 66, I had dozed off, only to have been awakened by an elderly Asian couple driving a 1987 Dodge Caravan while honking their horn and yelling profanities. I knew something was off, and I had been awake since—for every crawl of the journey.

"We've been in this damn car for three hours Tee," I said.

"Ha, ha, ha, I know B, relax. We're *almost* there."

"Add the four-hour train ride to D.C. and that's seven hours man." I contorted my face. "This is some major bullshit."

"I know B." Tee shook his head. "Riding in the back of this National Lampoon wagon sucks balls."

"You guys wanna play ball?"

"Uh...yes sir Mr. Fur. Tee wants to play ball," I replied.

"Tee stop talking so loud!" I mouthed.

"Ha, ha, ha," he laughed under Mr. Fur's frequency, before putting his headphones back on with the rap group, Nice and Smooth blasting.

I smiled at my partner, and even though the batteries in my Sony Walkman had been dead for hours, I put my headphones back on to avoid another conversation about cows or football in 1945.

Rolling down the window, I closed my eyes and took a deep breath. It was the first time during the trip I embraced my reality.

The air smelled clean and fresh like right after Mommy cleaned the apartment with Pine-Sol. I loved the scent. It was home.

Suddenly, thoughts of my mother reached my conscience and I missed her terribly. The entire ride down the North James Highway, I did my best not to think of her.

"OK young fellas, we're here!" Mr. Fur said, saving me from my guilt trip.

"Oh shit, we're really here!" Tee yelled, and I quickly snatched off his headphones, but Mr. Fur had already homed in on Tee's station.

"Watch your mouth young fella," Mr. Fur said.

"Sorry!" Tee and I said simultaneously. I just looked at Tee in disgust and shook my head.

The wagon decelerated and floated left onto a narrow-paved road surrounded by tall beautiful oak trees.

A hand carved Woodberry Forest School sign was half covered by bushes and grew from the dirt on our right.

The gravel beneath us crunched through the calming quietness, as the birds alerted the forest of our arrival.

Light shined through the giant trees and pierced the bit of fogginess obstructing the view of the squirrels chattering and holding their nuts.

Dogs barked playfully in the distance while the branches waved, welcoming us to their green universe.

The wagon eased up Woodberry Forest Road, and I looked back just to make sure there was still pavement, almost expecting for the forest to enclose behind us.

"You hear that Tee?"

"Yea B," he replied looking out of the back-driver's side window. "No police sirens."

"Exactly," I said.

"You smell that Manzo?"

"Yea B," I answered. "No pollution."

"Exactly—it smells so fresh," Tee said.

Beginning to wonder if the school were in the woods, I felt the car slow down and noticed a tiny brick tollbooth in the middle of the road.

"This right here is the Grainger Gatehouse," Mr. Fur said.

As we got closer, I could see an empty seat through the gatehouse's glass window. The lights were on, but no one was in the outdoor office. Security must've been on break, but Mr. Fur still waved as we drove by.

"Who the hell is he waving at?" Tee leaned over and whispered.

"I don't have a clue," I replied.

"There's normally someone there, but they must be on break," Mr. Fur said as our eyes connected through the rearview mirror. "I ain't crazy yet."

Shit!

"Right up here is the beginning of the campus." Mr. Fur's liver-spotted-finger pointed the way.

"Are you serious?" Tee asked in disbelief. "This place can't be real!"

We had only driven a few feet in front of the green forcefield, but the sight of the campus flowing uphill was mesmerizing!

I mentally applauded the manicured lawns that appeared smoother than a pool table and laid the foundation to state-of-the-art facilities, a track, six football fields, a soccer field, a baseball field, and nine-hole golf course.

My body was sitting in the wagon, but my spirit was already participating in *most* of the activities the school had to offer.

"This sure beats Wagner Projects." I attempted to mask my jubilation. "This isn't a school, it's a country club."

"We hear that a lot young fella!" Mr. Fur spoke with pride. "If you fellas decide to come here then it will be *your* country club!"

"I don't need to see anymore, Mr. Fur. Where do I sign up?" Tee asked.

Inside I was more excited than Tee was. I was fronting for sure, and Mr. Fur, too old for my new tricks, knew it.

"How do you like it Manzo?"

"It's cool Mr. Fur."

"You think you could get used to this?" He waved his hand.

"I don't know yet sir. I guess I have to see more," I replied.

From the bottom of the hill, the sight of the campus was more than breathtaking.

Each field, each tree, and each structure were perfectly placed as if God were the architect and a Woodberry alumnus.

Only the good could come from such a place, and before we had even reached the track—I wanted to be a Woodberry Forest Tiger.

Mr. Fur cruised the wagon at eight miles per hour and rolled down his windows. Taking a deep breath, I sat back and looked up the hill at the different fields and buildings.

Even though I didn't see a microphone in his hand, I knew what was next—a very long tour of a very big campus.

"And on the left over here is the Finch Track named after the Finch family and built in 1987. They have track meets on it, or the kids just run by themselves."

"I'm going to run track Mr. Fur!" Tee yelled out of the window.

"I bet you are young-fella!"

"On my left is Palamar Field where the JV football and Bengal football team practice and play football," Mr. Fur continued, and the wagon trotted along as he talked.

"Do any of you young fellas play football?"

"I want to play! I think I would be a great running back!" Tee said.

"How 'bout you Manzo?" Mr. Fur asked.

"Me?"

"Yes young fella—*you.*"

I loved watching football and was the biggest Lawrence Taylor fan, but I had never given any real thought of playing the game. New York was a basketball city and I was one of the young kings.

Football seemed fun, and I'm sure I would be able to learn the game fast and compete on a high level here at Woodberry, especially against White boys—but I was a *baller*. So, I couldn't risk injury, considering I was destined for the NBA.

"No sir, I don't have any interest in playing football. I play basketball," I said.

"And over here is Gillespie Field where they play soccer." Mr. Fur continued the tour, ignoring my answer.

"You would dominate these kids," Tee leaned and whispered.

"...and if you look over here, that is the Barbee Center, named after..."

"Maybe I would dominate, but I can't risk it," I said.

"...there's squash, an indoor track, a swimming pool! Can you young fellas swim?"

"Yes we can Mr. Fur," Tee said and looked over at me.

"Yes Mr. Fur—Tee and I swim like fishes!"

Tee knows his Black ass can't swim!

"Ah, that's good! Over here on the right is Hanes Field, where *Tee* will be scoring touchdowns!"

"Fuck you," Tee mouthed in my direction.

"This is Murrell's field, where they play baseball..."

"Seriously, you need to play football with me when we get here," Tee urged.

"Last year the Tigers came in second in the Prep League," Mr. Fur yapped away.

I tried to pay attention to Mr. Fur and the beautiful structures he pointed to, but Tee began to bother me about playing football again.

We talked about my participation on the train and I adamantly said no, but he kept pressing the issue. My sport was basketball—to hell with football!

"I'm not playing shit but basketball B," I said.

"Yea, you say that shit now Manzo, but you're too great of an athlete to just—"

"Fuck a football Tee," I said.

"Yooo, chicks dig football players," Tee said.

"Motherfucker, this is an all boy's school."

"That's this school, but girls gotta come to the games."

"I'm not playing football Tee. Please stop asking."

"And over here is the Dick gym," Mr. Fur announced.

"The *what* gym?" I asked holding my stomach.

Mr. Fur stopped the car in frustration and looked back at us. I could tell he'd been through this foolishness before but expected us to surprise him with a higher level of maturity. Our Black behinds failed at being serious just like I had assumed the White boys did.

Besides a long white staircase that led up to the side of the brick building, the gym appeared normal to me.

Six enormous glass windows displayed the far-side bleachers, and the top part of four glass backboards.

I knew that once I entered the bland structure that I would be all the flavor that Woodberry needed to finally regain the prep-league's *basketball* championship.

"The gym is named after L.W. Dick," Mr. Fur explained.

"L.W. who?" Tee asked seriously.

"Young fella, can't you hear?" Mr. Fur turned and pointed out of the window before looking back at us. "Dick!"

"Ha, ha, ha!" Tee and I died laughing!

"The *Dick* gym?" I questioned. "Well, I guess I won't be playing basketball after all!"

"Ha, ha, ha!" we all laughed as a team.

Mr. Fur stopped the wagon ten feet in front of a police officer hosing down a white school bus with tinted windows, orange and white stripes, silver rims, and "Woodberry Forest School" written along the side of the bus.

Tee and I both stopped laughing mid chuckle when we noticed the cop.

We sat upright in the backseat and refused to make eye contact with the officer, because we had heard from the old-timers in our neighborhoods that Virginia cops were the most racist and beat up Black kids on the regular.

"What's got you young fellas so spooked?" Mr. Fur looked in the rearview mirror and asked, noticing us following our standard Harlem procedure for police interaction.

"Mr. Fur, we were just joking about the Dick Gym sir. We're so sorry," I apologized.

"Yes, we didn't mean anything by it," Tee spoke.

"What are you young fellas—ooohhh!" Mr. Fur glanced at the cop. "Wait, you guys think...ha, ha, ha!"

Tee and I didn't find anything amusing and kept quiet. The old man's laughter confused me, but he kept giggling until he poked his head out of the window and called the cop over to the wagon.

"Hey James, would you please come over here?"

"Don't say anything," I whispered to Tee.

"Yes sir, Mr. Fur!" the cop yelled back.

Dropping the green water hose, *James* stepped his pointed black python cowboy boots in a puddle and slithered toward us.

Although his light blue, short-sleeved dress shirt wasn't wet—his curly Afro was moist and glistened in the sun.

James' red neck matched the hue of his crater face, which resembled the back of a sunburned thigh with cellulite.

His cropped dark brown and gray beard smoothed atop his puffy cheeks, although one cheek bulged like he refused to swallow his lunch.

James was chewing tobacco, and his mildly purple, chapped lips never touched and served as a peephole to a bottom row of brown teeth.

The creases on his dark blue slacks were sharp and sliced from his boots up to his waist, where a large brass eagle belt buckle shined just as bright as the five-star badge on his chest.

If there were any doubt James loved his beer, his slender build and huge belly converted all non-believers.

"They got some funny looking sheriffs down—"

"Ssh! Chill," I said to Tee.

James reached the driver's side door and bent down slightly to position himself to be seen by everyone in the vehicle—just like a cop would. He looked at us and then at Mr. Fur who started his chuckling again.

Nervous, I just wiped the building perspiration from my forehead and remained quiet.

"Hey James, these two young fellas from *New York City* think you're an officer of the law!" Mr. Fur turned and looked at Tee and me. "Can you believe that?"

James' hairdo bounced as he and Mr. Fur laughed at the two paranoid Black kids in the back seat.

"Shiiid, I ain't no godt-dam cop!" James said. "You two big cidi boys come down to dis lil ole town, and y'all scerd as two puddycats in da dam junkyard— of a dam off-suh of da law?"

What the hell did he just say?

Tee and I glanced at each other and then slowly joined in on the laughter, "Ha, ha, ha!"

We didn't know exactly what James had said, but we knew there wasn't a cop in the land who spoke *that* language.

James had good energy and I liked him already, but I was relieved when he hit the top of the wagon two times and then walked off to finish spraying the school bus. I had to shake off thoughts of hammering rocks with a Virginia chain gang.

"See ya James!" Mr. Fur shifted the wagon back into drive, continuing up the driveway.

"Who was that Mr. Fur?" I asked.

"Oh, that's just James Moubray young fellas. He runs the Dick gym." He looked back for snickering, but Tee and I were a few minutes more mature and did not even smile.

"Why is he dressed like a patrolman?" Tee inquired.

"He drives the bus and that's his uniform. He's far from a cop."

"Good, I mean Tee and me just—"

"No need to explain young fellas." Mr. Fur stopped the wagon.

"Things are a lot different down here. I can tell y'all some good boys, and there's nothing to worry about here. You will always be safe at Woodberry...*always* fellas. Now let's go. We're here."

Tee and I exited the vehicle before Mr. Fur even had the opportunity to shift into park.

With the back doors winged open, we ran to the front of the wagon and stopped short of a brick walkway—before we stared at the four, thirty-foot, milk-white columns in front of us.

The *house* before us was mammoth. It was four stories high and the length of a project building. Santa Claus and his brother could've fit down the enormous chimney at the same damn time.

The raised patio rolled out fifteen spiral cement steps from each direction and was surrounded by massive perfectly trimmed bushes.

The brick fortress burned a Georgia dirt-red in the sun, against the vanilla molding. A solid structure, the fortress would've protected thousands of pigs from millions of big bad wolves.

"This is the biggest house that I've ever seen," Tee said.

"Well this isn't exactly a house young fella," Mr. Fur spoke, as he unnoticeably now stood right beside us.

"So what's this some type of *plantation*?" Tee asked.

"No young fellas, this here is the Walker Building." Mr. Fur removed his cap and rubbed his thinning gray head.

"This building was built in 1898 and was the original dorm and school building on this campus. Besides dorms, there are dining rooms, rec-rooms, and some more stuff that you will learn about on your next tour tomorrow. Y'all only seen a *fraction* of the campus so far.

"Leave y'all bags in the car and let's hurry and get inside. They're waiting to give you y'all interviews. We're running a *little* behind—follow me." Mr. Fur led the way, leaving the wagon's backdoors completely opened.

"And don't worry about your bags, nobody steals anything here at Woodberry," Mr. Fur stated proudly as he slowly climbed the steps of the Walker Building.

"I love this place already." Tee smiled.

I never saw Tee this happy.

"Me too Tee," I agreed.

We reached the top and I was very excited, although I absolutely didn't know what to expect once we went through the front door.

I just knew whatever was inside the Walker Building had to have been more fascinating than any door that opened for us in Harlem.

"Right through here young fellas." Mr. Fur held the front door open. "What y'all think?"

Holy shit!

The *living room* area was enormous and could fit both Tee's and my entire apartment right inside of it.

The space was symmetrical and split in half by two red, twenty-foot-long vintage rugs that ran vertical toward the opened doorway of what appeared to be a long dining room.

Each side of the living room consisted of a grand piano, fireplace, leather couches, and chairs that rested on top of another identical rug.

I pictured young Richard Nixons dressed in khakis and ascots sitting around conversing about issues I didn't give two shits about.

Light from two gold-tiered chandeliers intertwined with the natural light from bay windows adjacent to each other on both sides of the room.

A few oil painted portraits hung on the off-white walls between the bright white moldings. All the men in the portraits seemed to ask, "What is your Black-ass doing here?"

I had only seen rooms as elegant as the Walker Building's in movies where people who looked like me weren't allowed to sit around the fireplace and sing Kumbaya with the common folk.

"It's OK young fellas, y'all can come inside. This is your new school, *if* you like it." Mr. Fur laughed at our hesitance.

Looking down, I stepped into the doorway and onto the carpet very gingerly. Feet wet, I absorbed my future and breathed in the scents of old wood, leather, and a good life.

The house smell was different, but I loved it. Comfortable, I walked a few paces further into the Walker Building.

"This place is fly Manzo," Tee said.

"Who you telling? Where's Robin Leach?" I asked.

"Ha-ha, glad y'all like it," Mr. Fur said. "Come over here and have a seat."

Following Mr. Fur to the couch on the right half of the room, I felt one of the columns in the middle of the room and tapped my knuckles on it three times.

Looking back at Tee, I nodded my head like I was a real contractor inspecting the joint.

Tee, a graduate from the same school of bullshit, nodded back while Mr. Fur peeped the entire charade and chuckled once more.

"You two will fit right in," he said. "Please have a seat on the couches. Mrs. Grymes will come and get you one at a time for your interview."

"Who's going first?" Tee asked as we both sat down.

"If I'm correct, I believe…" Mr. Fur turned his head to the right and smiled. "Let's find out."

We couldn't see what Mr. Fur saw, but we did hear the distant sound of high heels marching on tile, so we knew the old man wasn't tripping.

Eight clucks later, a White woman with red lipstick, wearing a silk peach blouse with matching skirt suddenly emerged from a side doorway connected to a hallway.

"Hello Mr. Fur." The woman smiled and shook Mr. Fur's hand.

"Hello Diane." The old fellow smiled back, as his face and neck region turned light red.

Diane Grymes was a beautiful woman in her mid-forties with a short golden-brown haircut that accented her blue eyes. The lack of muscle tone in her legs and arms suggested she was naturally fit.

I had guessed she had only one child. She didn't look like the type of woman who wanted to tear up her body or share her husband's attention with a bunch of younger versions of herself.

She wore gold bangle earrings, a diamond tennis bracelet, and two-carat cushion cut, gold engagement ring and wedding band.

She smelled exquisite and kept looking down at her attire the way people did when they were extremely nervous or overtly conscious of their appearance.

"Young fellas, I would like to introduce y'all to Mrs. Grymes. She is Head-master Grinalds' secretary."

"Hello gentlemen," Mrs. Grymes greeted us with an adorable southern twang in her voice.

"Hello Mrs. Grymes." I stood and smiled, never making eye contact. "My name is Manzo."

"Pleasure to meet you Manzo."

"Hello Mrs. Grymes. My name is *Terence*," Tee said, gazing at her seductively.

"OK *Terence*," Mrs. Grymes stammered as she blushed and clutched her gold necklace. "How was y'all trip down to the country?"

"Beautiful," Tee said smoothly.

"Great! Well Terence, you can come with me. You're first to go in," she said before noticing Tee's left eyebrow raise slightly.

"Mr. Grinalds and Mr. McMillan are waiting for you. Come with me so we can move things along, so y'all can go watch the varsity football game at two O'clock."

"For real?" Tee asked. "We love football, right Manzo?"

"That's right, we sure do Mrs. Grymes!"

"Great! Manzo have a seat and when Terence is finished, he will come out and get you."

"Yes ma'am," I said.

"Mr. Fur, the boys will see you at the game. Thank you for the safe travels."

"No problem Diane, you are very welcome," Mr. Fur voiced.

"Good luck Tee!" I yelled to his back.

"So Mrs. Grymes, are you really married or..." was the last thing heard before the double doors closed behind them.

"He's not used to being around women, huh?" Mr. Fur asked.

"I don't know Mr. Fur. Ha, ha, ha!"

"Ha, ha, ha! I will see y'all after the game." He took two steps toward the Walker Building's entrance and then turned around like he forgot his keys or something valuable.

"It's the 1990s young fella, these ain't the old days. Forget what you've watched in the movies. Be yourself. Be the confident young man you are. It's OK to look *any* person the eye when you talk to him *or* her," he advised, winking his left eye and strolling out of the building.

Mr. Fur's words were very much needed, but I didn't know how much until I heard him speak them out loud.

I knew I didn't have any problems living with White people, but my beliefs didn't coincide with my practices.

Besides basketball, my life's experiences with different races were limited to my Black and Hispanic surroundings, and *the Color Purple*—the movie, not the book.

Only cohabiting with minorities, I understood that a culture shock was imminent, but I had looked forward to embracing and learning from the differences in ethnicities. I just wanted to be around good people.

Although I made immature jokes routinely, I didn't care about their races, their religions, or even their sexual orientations.

Not having seen a single student, I already felt that at the core we were all the same. Tee and I could have been the only Blacks at Woodberry, and it wouldn't have mattered.

I wanted to be a Woodberry boy, and the potential of what I could learn in four years at the school seemed limitless.

There was no chance I would ever turn down such a unique and blessed opportunity, and I couldn't wait for the headmaster to experience who I was.

Sitting down, I let my mind wander as I thought about Tee killing his interview just as I had planned.

I know Tee's in there speaking all proper—

"You're up B!" Tee burst through the side doors.

"What the hell? You were gone like five minutes!" I stood up and tucked the shirttails in my gray slacks.

"Yo Manzo—they want us sooooo bad B!" He couldn't stop smiling. "The interview is a formality! Trust me, they really want *us*!"

"Word?"

"Word Manzo!"

"No bullshit?" I asked.

"Come on now, they ain't bring our Black asses all the way down to redneck Virginia for nothing," Tee made a solid point. "Motherfucker, this is *us*! Of course they want Manzo and Tee!"

I loved when Tee started his cocky routine! He began bobbing his head and chewing imaginary gum with his mouth wide open for some strange reason. He looked like Mr. Ed, but he always got me hyped. I believed every single word that came out of his mouth.

"Hell yea Tee!"

"Yo they maaad cool...but there's one thing B." He stopped chewing, and my stomach flipped.

"What bro?" My heart pedaled faster.

"Yooo..."

"What Tee?"

"Yooo...the headmaster got a fucking red nose B."

"*What*?"

"The motherfucker got a red nose like Rudolph's little cousin or some shit." He still didn't crack a smile.

"*Rudolph*?" I asked.

"Yes Rudolph! You know...Santa's little fucking helper—Rudolph!" Tee explained.

"Listen, you will see for yourself—just when you see the shit, don't stare like I did...I wasn't ready B."

"Man, now is not the time to be playing so damn much Tee! There's too much at stake for us! Grow up...see you in a few minutes."

"*Oooh-Kaay*...whatever you say Zo. Good luck!"

"Thanks *Terrence!*" I smiled before shaking my head and rushing through the side doors.

* * *

The doors closed, and another world opened. Hardwood floors conceded to black and white checkered tiles speeding down a thirty-foot hallway, only stopping at Mrs. Grymes size seven Prada heels.

Two office doors on each side of the hallway separated the orange-framed pictures of the undefeated football teams throughout Woodberry's 108-year-history.

No basketball teams. No baseball teams. Just football and damn near just White faces. Like a fly in milk, each smiling brown speckle was submerged by fifty or so wholesome teammates.

"Right down here Manzo," Mrs. Grymes directed. "You can always look at pictures later."

"Yes I can—no problem." I walked a little faster but continued reading the names outside each closed office door along the way.

Mr. Huber, Dean of Academics—I bet he's a nerd.

Mr. Bond, Dean of Students—is definitely a stiff-ass.

Mrs. Hromyak—damn her perfume smells good.

Prefect Room? What the hell is a prefect room?

Who are these people?

Man, I'm too Black for this place.

A strange feeling of self-doubt and unworthiness shadowed my footsteps toward Mrs. Grymes. I abruptly felt like I didn't belong in such a *pure* school.

I didn't come from a family with a legacy of success and wealth. I felt like another unfortunate Black bastard destined for the slums of Harlem, the penitentiary, or death in those unforgiving New York City streets.

I finally reached Mrs. Grymes, her eyes summoned mine, and I damn near looked away. Remembering the words of Mr. Fur, I consciously returned eye contact.

"You will be fine." She grinned. "It's an honor for Woodberry to have you, not the other way around."

"It is?" I asked.

"Damn right it is Manzo. You belong right here." She pointed her index finger straight down to the floor.

"Yes ma'am, I do belong here."

Her words resuscitated my confidence. I didn't care if I were about to talk to an ex-marine or an ex-con. I brought something special to a special place.

There wasn't a face on those hallway walls, Black or White, whose presence would uplift an entire school, the faculty and the students.

I would attack life at a higher standard. I earned my position. Nobody was giving me shit! I deserved to be a Woodberry Forest School Tiger!

"Thank you, I needed that." I smiled.

"You're welcome. Let's go."

"Yes ma'am," I said before reading the silver-plated name on the door.

Mr. John Grinalds, Headmaster.

Door opened.

"Hey Manzo! Come on in here son! Mr. McMillan said, overjoyed. "Thank you so much Diane. Please close the door on your way out."

"You are more than welcome sir. See you later Manzo." She smiled and left.

Mr. McMillan stood at the far side of the room in front of a massive window as large as Mr. Grinalds' oak desk. Like a proud farmer staring at his prize stock, Mr. McMillan smiled as I entered the room.

He was six-feet tall with a dirty-blond, schoolboy haircut. Even twenty feet away I could see every tooth in his head. He was thrilled to see.

Mr. McMillan, as Waspy as a Princeton tennis coach, donned tan khakis, a blue sport coat, a dark brown braided belt, loafers with tassels, argyle socks, and a light blue monogrammed dress shirt with RMM stitched on the breast pocket. I couldn't remember what his initials stood for and never asked.

"It's a pleasure to finally have you here Manzo," he said and walked toward me with his arm extended.

"Yes, I'm so happy to finally be here Mr. McMillan," I responded, matching his strides with my arm extended as well.

"How was your trip?"

"It was great sir, thank you for the invitation."

"Our pleasure," he said, placing his hand on my shoulder and guiding me to one of the two gold-seamed, leather chairs at Mr. Grinalds' desk. "Have a seat please son."

"Yes sir, thank you."

We both sat and out of the many interesting pictures on the wall in front of me, my attention focused solely on an antique silver-framed, black and white photo of a beautiful White young woman wearing a sleeveless, long linen dress.

With Curly blonde hair flowing in the country breeze, she sat in an open green field and smiled side-eyed at the camera. I assumed the woman was Mr. Grinalds' wife, back in the *good ole days*.

I refocused my admiration away from the photo and toward the many other magnificent memories, while Mr. McMillan remained quiet for a moment and allowed me to enter the world of Grinalds.

Scattered across bricks, thirty-plus years of military service had commanded *most* of the room's attention.

Looking at the pictures, I was honored and overwhelmed with patriotic pride, even though I never wanted to join the military.

I got a secondhand look into the life of one of the "dumb bastards" my father had promised me to never become, but Mr. Grinalds didn't look too dumb to me. He looked like a badass from where I was sitting.

The photos of Mr. Grinalds displayed an extraordinary military career that any soldier would have been proud to have accomplished.

In one photo Mr. Grinalds was in a helicopter in the jungle, in another he was in a tank in the desert, and then the next, President George Bush was pinning a four-starred gold medal on his blue Marine uniform.

I didn't see any shots of him looking like anything other than a hero, and I had no choice but to genuinely respect him as such.

In Harlem, if a guy got shot one time and survived then he was considered a war veteran, and the entire neighborhood respected him.

Mr. Grinalds would have called all the shots in my hood with his resume, so I saluted him without even meeting him.

"So Manzo, we were all here wondering…why don't you have a last name, if you don't mind me asking?" Mr. McMillan questioned.

Oh boy, I knew this shit was coming.

For as long as I could remember, people asked me about my name, but I virtually never answered truthfully.

I had the bad habit of making a game out of people's *curiosity* by seeing what outlandish story I could make up on the spot.

To my knowledge, no one ever caught on to my bullshit and I highly doubted any guy who had to remind himself he actually owned the shirt on his back would catch on either.

OK RMM…let's play.

"Of course, I don't mind you asking sir," I said. "My father is a psychic, and he had a dream he was reading the newspaper's obituary section in the Harlem National Newspaper for Underprivileged Biracial Youth.

"He saw Manzo *Peña* listed with my picture...except I had a blonde Afro and a nose ring, *of course*—sooo, in order for me not to die in real life, he immediately went down to the courthouse and had my last name removed. It must've really worked, because I'm still here sir—ha, ha, ha."

"Oooh...yeeaa...uh...oooohh-kaay...thank you for that—sooo, what you think about the campus so far?" Mr. McMillan face was almost completely red.

Ha, ha, ha—still undefeated!

"It's amazing and has nice buildings sir"

"Glad you enjoyed half the campus."

"*Half*?" I asked.

"Yes, you still have to see Dowd-Finch, Taylor Hall, Turner Hall, Anderson Hall, Hanes Hall, and a few more I'm sure I haven't mentioned."

"Damn that's a lot—I mean dang that's a lot sir."

"Ha-ha, I know son," Mr. McMillan said, leaning back in his chair and crossing his legs. "Are you ready for your interview?"

"Uh, is it just you? Where's Mr. Grinalds?" I wondered.

"Ha-ha." Mr. McMillan disengaged eye contact, tilted his head upwards, and then grinned.

"I'm right here son," Mr. Grinalds had spoken, revealing his coordinates.

His words *surround-sounded* behind my chair and two huge hands pressed down on my shoulders, stopping me from rotating my torso or rising.

I peeped up for a clear visual, only to find the bottom of a clean shaved chin and a leatherneck.

"It's OK, don't get up son." Mr. Grinalds tapped my right shoulder two times.

"Sir-yes-sir," I answered.

"*Yes sir* is fine Manzo. This isn't a military school son," Mr. Grinalds informed.

I had begun to get nervous and the room caught fire. Sweat dripped down the back of my white Brooks Brothers button-up shirt, so I leaned forward to feel a draft and caught a glimpse of the side of Mr. Grinalds' face as he walked around his desk, facing the wall.

Mr. Grinalds looked like any other big eared, ex-military dude with his dark blue suit, gold-rimmed glasses, and high and tight haircut.

He was already taller than I was, but his energy and his presence made me feel like I was talking to an eight-foot Chuck Norris.

"You see this picture right here of me and Oliver North?" he asked, and suddenly got silent, seeming to transport to that moment in time the photo was taken. "I've known Ollie for many years."

"Do you know who General Oliver North is Manzo?" Mr. Grinalds quizzed.

Sure do...homie who lied to Congress—the Iran Contra criminal guy.

"Yes I do sir. He's a *mighty* fine man sir," I said.

"Yes, such an exemplary individual and a great friend." He paused again then continued, still without looking back.

"Ollie and I did everything together growing up, but there came a time in our lives where we needed to separate and do our own thing as individuals.

"There were some things he was qualified to do that I wasn't, and some things that I was qualified to do that he wasn't.

"We both had to take separate paths to get to the same place, and that's OK in life Manzo. We may not all take the same road, but if we stay diligent and live righteously, we will always create great opportunities...when *current* opportunities may not be available at the moment."

"Are you following me son?" Mr. Grinalds questioned.

"Yes sir...completely." I looked over at Mr. McMillan and although he gave a half-grin, he appeared more on edge than I was for some reason.

What is going on?

Tee wasn't in here this long.

"Like I said, Ollie and I have been friends for fifty years and we will always be friends. We have supported each other even during times where he may have been chosen to do something I wasn't, and vice versa.

"The important thing is that we both recognized when it was time to go our separate ways with no harsh feelings toward one another."

This guy keeps saying 'separate'—

Hold the fuck up!

A lightning bolt cracked my forehead, and I finally realized what all this bullshit was all about.

My heartbeat vibrated sweat from my brow and I got extremely paranoid and thirsty.

"You are a special kid, and there will be doors opened for you in many places in life that others won't be able to go. The hardest part sometimes is to let go and let someone else do what you thought was meant for you," Mr. Grinalds continued.

They don't want me! Oh no!

Tears welled up in my eyes, and my pride, getting weaker by the second, was the only dam. My soul strapped itself to my stomach for my gut not to be completely ripped apart.

Mr. Grinalds lynched my faith and I wanted to die. My hands tightly gripped the arms of my chair as I tried to listen to the assassin without having a mental breakdown.

That's why Mr. McMillan was nervous! You can't trust White people!

"You understand what I am saying son?" Mr. Grinalds asked and turned around.

They only want Tee!

Thoughts of life back in New York for the next four years almost made me get up and throw my chair through the dumbass' stupid photos on the wall. I felt like a corpse Mr. Grinalds had probably put in a body bag many times before.

I had nothing for me back at home and these people didn't give a shit about me. They didn't care if I ended up in jail or dead, but I couldn't let them win.

My anger turned to fury, and the only thing keeping me from acting like a real *nigger* was thoughts of Tee. My actions could jeopardize his standings with the school, and I would never forgive myself.

I was still very happy for Tee. The kid deserved *his* place at Woodberry, but I couldn't help but cry. The dam had broken. I was crushed.

I somehow squandered an amazing opportunity, and I would miss my homie who was more qualified than I was. Life would be different back in Harlem without Tee, but I had to keep fighting.

Shit, the chances were slim, but maybe we would end up in the same college together. Either way, I was still proud of my brother.

I sniffled a little and replied, "Yes sir, you don't want me...you only want Tee."

"*What?*" Mr. McMillan asked.

"What? No, no son—that's incorrect! It's the other way around!" Mr. Grinalds said. "We only have room for you Manzo...and *not* Tee."

"What?" I raised my head swiftly, and I could see Mr. Grinalds now sitting at his desk. He had both hands on the table and was smiling. Hard.

Wiping my wet eyes with sweaty fingers, I blinked a few times and just stared at Mr. Grinalds. I felt like I was at the damn circus. I put my head down in disbelief.

"Ha-ha," I laughed mildly.

"Ha-ha!" Mr. McMillan started laughing.

"Ha, ha, ha!" Mr. Grinalds also laughed.

"Ha, ha, ha!" I laughed the hardest, but I never took my eyes off my lap. I didn't know where else to look, *partly* because I was ashamed to be crying in front of two random men.

"I told you sir; Manzo would be OK!" Mr. McMillan said.

"He's a good kid Robert! I never doubted you!"

"You OK there son?" Mr. *Robert* McMillan asked. "We didn't mean to scare you like that. We apologize deeply."

"Yes Manzo, I see how you would be confused," Mr. Grinalds admitted as he put both hands on his desk and leaned halfway across it. "Son look at me please."

"Yes sir." I raised my head.

"I know you wanted Tee to come with you, but we only have an academic scholarship for you. I wish it were different but it's not," Mr. Grinalds frowned.

"Now, I need to know if you will accept a four year, full-academic scholarship to attend Woodberry Forest School in the fall?" Mr. Grinalds asked.

"Look out for your future son. Tee will be all right," Mr. McMillan said.

My emotions stretched to limitations my young spirit had never reached.

A few minutes earlier I would have sold my soul to George Burns for the chance of calling Woodberry Forest School my alma mater one day, but now I contemplated saying, "Fuck Woodberry!" to protect the realest bond with an imaginary brother.

I felt dirty! I wanted to run, go grab Tee, and keep on running until we were in a sanctuary—away from these monsters that were trying to *separate* us.

Caught between my future and my integrity, I sat and thought about my family back in New York. They would be so hurt if I didn't seize a magnificent opportunity that I not only earned, but could also open doors for the rest of my life.

Mommy's devastation would be incomparable to any disappointment Ms. Alice felt. Woodberry Forest School not wanting Tee would be an uncontrollable circumstance by some individuals who didn't want a boy to attend their school.

My turning down a full ride to a prestigious prep school would be summed up as some "stupid nigga shit."

My eyes wandered briefly to a small red cloth banner on the office wall, next to a photo of a young Mr. Grinalds with his platoon. The banner read *Semper Fidelis* in yellow.

I had recognized the Latin phrase from a *60 Minutes* special on Agent Orange. I knew the motto was a Marine *thing*. I also knew what Semper Fidelis meant.

'Always faithful.'

But to who?

"Well son?" Mr. Grinalds leaned a little further on the desk.

His stare was pure fire. I perspired heavily.

'God first and your family second Manzo. Don't ever forget.'

My mother's words cleared the smog and I could see again. Although Tee was *like* a brother, he wasn't my brother. I had to do what was right by my family.

If Tee were a good friend, he would just have to understand that I had an obligation to me and not to him. We were cool and all, but some things just had to be done.

Woodberry wanted me and not him, and I shouldn't have to suffer because Tee wasn't par the course. Mr. Grinalds was right about me being special, so I needed to be with others who were.

Obviously, Tee wasn't on *our* level here at Woodberry Forest School, so it was time to grow with some kids who were—no hard feelings.

Sorry bro, I love you, but you are on your own Tee.

"Yes, I will accept it sir!" I said emphatically, still lost in Latin translation.

"Atta-boy!" Mr. McMillan patted me on my back. "I told you he was a smart one sir!"

"Yes he is, and I'm proud of him too!" Mr. Grinalds agreed.

Looking at Mr. Grinalds, I suddenly was in a giddy mood and the stronger he smiled, the harder I laughed and couldn't stop.

I no longer thought about the most life changing decision of my fifteen years on earth, and I couldn't have cared less.

"Ha-ha. Thank you, sir," I said and attempted to control the laughter.

"Welcome aboard son!" Mr. McMillan patted my back again.

"*Ha, ha, ha.* Thank you, sir!"

"Ha-ha, glad to see you are back in a great mood son!" Mr. Grinalds' laughter deepened.

"Ha, ha, ha!" I couldn't stop laughing.

"Are you OK son?" Mr. McMillan asked and glanced at Mr. Grinalds.

"Yes sir—I'm fine," I answered, regaining a little composure. "I'm just so honored and grateful for this opportunity sir."

"It's nothing wrong with laughter—it clears the soul!" Mr. Grinalds walked around his desk toward a side office within his office.

"Robert let's pull up on the computer which documents we need to have Manzo bring home to his parents—one moment son."

"Coming sir!" Mr. McMillan popped off of his chair and accompanied Mr. Grinalds.

"Ha, ha, ha!" My laughter awakened my feet, and I couldn't help but stomp them a little. I covered my mouth with both hands to muffle my hysteria.

Tee was right—that motherfucker does have a red nose!

Chapter Seven

GRADY SMILED

"Gentlemen...today is a day that you will remember for the rest of your lives, right along with the birth of your first child and your first piece of ass," said Coach Jeff Davidsson as he started his final pre-game speech with smoke in his eyes. My teammates and I prepared for the blaze.

"We've come a long way men. We are 11-0 and we done it by always staying together and being committed to one another. You all are brothers.

"It doesn't matter who your parents are, where you come from, or the color of your damn skin. You all are brothers.

"Brothers stay loyal to one another, have each other's back, and always can depend on each other. That's just what brothers do. Anything less and you are a pussy! No one can separate brothers, and there is no two ways about it." He paused and his eyes landed on mine.

My linebacker coach and mentor, Jeff Davidsson, a fifty-four-year-old stout, blond-haired retired Navy captain with Hulk Hogan arms, possessed an old-school intensity that could be transferred with just a stare.

He was an ex-Naval Academy football and Lacrosse player who hollered and spat flames when he coached, but he never raised his voice at me—there was no reason to do so.

Coach Davidsson was a father to me and if we were fighting a war, I would have been collecting bodies for the man, rather than tackles. I never disobeyed him, and I always listened.

"Everybody close your eyes," Coach Davidsson demanded. "Think of one person in this world who isn't your blood brother, but you love him like one."

Each young man followed the order and closed his eyes. The locker room was completely silent, sans heavy breathing and the shuffling of football pads against metal lockers. Only one name floated in my mind—Tee Butler.

"OK, now open your eyes men. Now, although you consider that person your brother more than anyone else in the world, I need you men to fight for every single man on this football team like he *is* that person." Coach Davidsson began to pace back and forth and pumped his fist in the air after every few words.

"You're accountable for one another, and you will fight for one another. And if need be, you will die with one another GODDAMN IT!

"Today is the first day of the rest of your lives men! Today you will eat until your bellies are full, and then you will shit on these bastards and eat some more!

"For you seniors, there isn't a tomorrow! Your destiny is now and the only thing stopping you from football immortality is in that other motherfucking locker room!" Coach Davidsson roared as white foam collected at the sides of his mouth.

"Take a good look at each other!"

I rotated my head as much as the constricting shoulder pads allowed and filtered out my fellow seniors within sight. I could only see four of them, but each was sobbing, and so was I.

* * *

Every last game for any senior class in the world was emotional, but nothing could compare to the feelings felt for one another with kids in a boarding school.

We lived together. There was no going home after school or after practice. We were all far from our homes and family, and for four years all we had were each other.

We did almost everything as a unit, and this final game of our high school careers didn't just represent the last time we all played football together—it represented the dismemberment of a family.

Claiborne Johnston, the fiery second-string quarterback from Richmond who cried the hardest, looked at me and just nodded. Our emotional leader, he kept us energized and believing in ourselves.

Some plays, I wanted to slack off, but one look at Claiborne yelling and cheering and I knew I couldn't let my team or myself down.

Thank you, brother.

Bailey Dent, our six-foot, three-inch starting wide receiver, wiped the tears with the back of his glove and smiled. The kid was never in a bad mood, and when he wasn't keeping everyone laughing, he was in the mirror primping his blond hair like he was getting ready for a fashion shoot.

Woodberry didn't have any girls, but if we did the *Golden Boy* would've got his fair share of stink finger.

Thank you, brother.

Jay Kleberg, one of the three co-captains, always sat right next to me. At five-foot, eight inches, and 165 pounds, he was the hardest worker and most humble guy I have ever known.

His family owned, King Ranch, a *farm* in Texas about the size of Rhode Island, but he would never mention a word about his family's business.

Jay treated everyone equally and dealt with people based on their morals and actions, rather than money, color, or status.

I could see the side of Kleberg's face and watched the tears wash down his prominent chin, but we never directly looked at each other—we could feel each other's energy.

Two ultimate tough guys, we just playfully bumped elbows to let one another know we loved each other and would always fight for one another.

Thank you, brother.

Grady Cage, the coolest player on the team, rarely displayed any emotions on the field. He played center and I played middle linebacker, so he and I would battle almost every play in practice, every damn day. Grady only weighed 205 pounds but was Texas tough.

More athletic and a lot stronger, I used to punish Grady, but he never backed down or complained. He would just tighten up his chinstrap and keep attacking.

His tenacity made me a better player and taught me that no matter how big the opponent was, I had to give my all.

From across the locker room, Grady looked at me through drenched, red eyes, and did something I hadn't seen him do in a football uniform in four years —he smiled.

I wept stronger, then smiled back.

I will never forget you Grady.

* * *

The rest of the seniors were out of view, but I could hear their cries and sniffling all around me.

We were a tight group and we would truly miss each other, but we had one final battle, so I did my best to regain my composure and listen to our leader.

"It has truly been a pleasure to coach all of you men," Coach Davidsson resumed his speech.

"We have one more game to play—one more day to be warriors! Eleven and one isn't an option men! It is our destiny to be undefeated! We can't lose! Our team is strong! Our bond is stronger! Stand up men!"

Coach Davidson's complexion reddened, and he was cooking. Shit was about to get real! Whenever we were ordered to stand, we knew the taste of blood wasn't far behind.

The entire team stood up, metal and rubber cleats crunched against the locker room floor. The tears stopped, and the fangs grew. It was almost time to eat.

"Our team is strong!" Coach Davidsson repeated, as he always did right before the flames.

"But our team is strongest when our captains lead by example! Captain Jay Kleberg, you will annihilate anything that crosses your goddamn path!"

"Yes sir, I will!" Jay yelled.

"Your captains will die before they let us leave that field without a victory!" Coach Davidsson stopped in front of Jay and yelled, only inches from his face.

He rubbed Jay's matted brown hair with his right hand, and slowly touched foreheads with him.

Neither of them blinked or said a word before the lion walked away from the cub and the tirade continued.

"Your captains would rather be gutted like piglets at a meat market and served to the wolves than let EHS beat us! They will lead you to victory as we treat EHS like the whores that they are!

"Your captains will help you write a story that you will be able to tell your grandchildren, and they will tell their grandchildren, and they will tell their grandchildren!"

"Captain Manzo?" He stopped pacing and we stood face to face. Knowing the strength of Coach Davidsson's and my bond, the team didn't move or make a sound.

"I love you like a son."

"I love you too coach," I cried and stared into the soul of the man who for the last three years, helped rewire my morals and upgraded my standards of excellence.

"Before I met you coach, I thought I was average...but you showed me I could do anything I wanted to do with hard work."

"Manzo...you're as special as they come. You can do anything son," Coach

Davidsson spoke and then just watched me for a moment without saying a word.

Coach Davidsson swallowed hard and his face tensed. He would never cry in front of his men, so he wrestled his tears with success. Sentimental time over, he grabbed the numbers on my jersey and *coached*.

"You're the best motherfucking linebacker in this state, and I need you to take these men with you and bring back an undefeated season for Woodberry, for you, and for all these men in this goddamn locker room!" he screamed in my face, before relieving my jersey and slapping my chest.

"Do you understand me son?"

"Yes sir!" I howled.

"And for my last captain, you better run that ball all over them! You better stamp the record books today with your name all over it!" Coach Davidsson spoke as he walked through the standing bodies until he reached locker number thirty-four. The entire team watched his every step.

"You have had one of the best careers EVER running that ball in the state of Virginia!"

"Goddamn right he did!" Brunson DePass, our University of Clemson-bound placekicker, yelled from the far-right end of the locker room.

"Just like Jay and Manzo, I need you, *we* need you to simply do what you have done all year long." Coach Davidsson put both hands on the shoulder pads of the All-time leading rusher in Woodberry Forest School's history.

"You have been a pleasure to coach and watching you on that field for all these years has been entertaining and an utter joy young man.

"Today is the day that you put this offense on your back and show everyone what you are made of. We are going to win, and you *will* break the state record!" Coach Davidsson paused.

"In the record books, it's going to read, November 12, 1995, the rushing record for the Virginia State Private Schools belongs to..." Coach Davidsson raised one eyebrow and waited for the obvious answer.

The third captain stood up on a stool like a Greek god, opened both of his arms in the air, with his helmet in his right hand like a lightning bolt and replied, "TEE BUTLER!"

The team went crazy!

"Fuck yeeeeaaaaa!"

"Hell yea Tee!"

"Let's go kill these bastards!"

"We gonna kill those motherfuckaaaahhhhs!"

Players hit their helmets against the lockers and yelled uncontrollably.

Like a pack of wild animals, we growled and screamed until Coach

Davidsson succeeded to speak over of the insanity.

"All we have is each other, and all we need is each other to beat the shit out of EHS! We're going to terminate those fuckers with extreme prejudice!"

Like a sewing machine my feet tapped on the floor, and I wiggled my fingers. The more he talked, the more I had the urge to rip someone's head from his spine.

I was drenched in sweat, and manly tears of anger pushed the bitch ones out of my tear ducts for good.

Charged, I felt like someone was holding me, and I wanted to break free. I needed to be free. I needed to hit something!

"Put your goddamn helmets on and let's go win us a football game!" Coach Davidsson commanded.

"KILL EHS! KILL EHS! KILL EHS!" I chanted as the team joined the cheer and followed me to slaughter.

"FIRST DOWN!" the referee yelled from the one-inch yard line, as the Episcopal High School's faithful fans erupted in their home stadium.

"Come on! Let's go motherfucker!" I hollered fifty yards down the field at Marcus Wilder, who was in our end zone on his knees and shaking his head.

On the previous play, with the football at the fifty-yard line—EHS was down 28-24 and needed a touchdown to win with eight-seconds left in the game. The down and distance was fourth down and seventeen yards to go.

EHS had one timeout but chose to save it and run a play—which resulted in a forty-nine-yard Hail Mary pass to number twenty-four, Episcopal High School All-American wide receiver, Lamont Daniels.

At six-foot, three inches, Daniels was six inches taller than Marcus, whose outstretched hands had little to no chance to stop the acrobatic catch.

Making a remarkable play himself with one-second left in regulation, Jason Bailey, our starting cornerback, left his man to support Marcus, and tackled Daniels—only inches from the goal line.

Our school's undefeated season was on the line, and the very next play would decide the winner of the ninety-sixth meeting between rivals Woodberry Forest School and Episcopal High School, also known as *the Game*.

"TIMEOUT! TIMEOUT! TIMEOUT!" the EHS senior quarterback, Brandon Jones, repetitively jammed his left-hand's fingers into his right palm.

"Timeout—Episcopal!" The ref signaled for the game clock to stop, but the crowd continued its rowdiness.

"Hell yea EHS!"

"Beat those Woodberry faggots!"

"Not so bad now, huh Manzo?"

"Kids from the slums can't afford two goddamn names or something?"

All dressed in maroon and black, the 15,000 Episcopal High School fans rediscovered that their mouths could be used for more than sucking dick.

In an explosion of cheers and taunts, they believed that victory was only one foot and one-second away.

On the opposite sidelines, the Woodberry diehards, unbelieving mutes, had drowned in an orange sorrow of pity and self-doubt.

Negative energy ricocheted back and forth from player to fan, and the couple "Let's go Tigers!" weren't enough to spark energy or interest of a non-defeat.

A little White kid in the stands, with dirty-blond hair and a tiger painted on both cheeks—looked at me with tears in his eyes before turning away, hugging his father's leg, and weeping.

The father caressed the child's head and consoled him, while I read the dad's lips, "Damn...we had this game son!"

Completely drained, my teammates were scattered in the end zone and gasping for air. We had no idea on how not to lose, because not one of us had the energy to win.

They either were waiting for me to come and call the play, or for someone to shoot them and put them out of their misery. I really couldn't tell, as the EHS crowd continued to taunt.

"We got your Black-ass now Maahhhnnn-zooooe!"

"Y'all going down, you ass-bandits!"

"Who's your girlfriend in that all boys school Maaaahhhn-zoooe?"

"I wouldn't recruit you, you Yankee fuh-kang loser!"

I put my head down amongst the bashing and walked toward my teammates, not knowing what to say to the group of men who depended on my leadership for eleven wins without a single damn loss.

Jay Kleberg and Tony Brown were both on one knee with their helmets off, vomiting from exhaustion, and it had begun to sink in that we were going to lose the biggest athletic event of my life.

My legs lost strength and slightly lost feeling. Trotting to regain circulation, I passed the already huddled EHS offense, and never looked in their direction, but certainly heard the comments slung my way.

"Puerto Ricans should stick to *stick*-ball!" an EHS player yelled and they all laughed.

The laughter lashed across my back, and I contemplated unscrewing one of the metal cleats from my Nikes and showing those assholes another thing Boricuas were known for—cutting a motherfucker.

Stopping on the six-yard line, I was halfway between the EHS huddle and the goal line where the rest of my team pretended to be high school football players.

"Manzo!" Head Coach Bill Davis yelled my name as I looked toward our sideline. "Manzo let's go!"

"Manzo hurry up son!" Coach Davidsson added.

"MONSTER! MONSTER! RUN MONSTER!" our defensive coordinator Coach Andy Abbott screamed as he repeatedly flexed both arms in the air like a bodybuilder.

"Let's go Manzo! This is your team!" Coach Davis pleaded. "RUN MONSTER!"

"Monster" was a play where we lined up in a four-three base defense. My only responsibility was to use my instincts and make one of these trust fund babies use his good ole health insurance plan.

As a disgruntled Medicaid user, I enjoyed helping kids appreciate their privileged benefits. I aimed to teach and disfigure.

Coach Davis had called Monster a couple of times during the season to success, but he would never call the play on the goal line because of the risk factor.

My ability to read an offensive play from the defensive position was excellent, but no one was 100%. If I guessed wrong, then we were fucked for sure!

Calling Monster meant that my coaches believed in me—an ultimate sign of respect. We were 11-0 and whether we ended 12-0 or 11-1 depended on the Black boy from Harlem's ability to lead and play the game of football.

My body tensed with excitement. Being nervous wasn't an option because I was built for this moment. Forever hungry, I needed to eat!

Understanding the ramifications, I simply nodded to my coaches and ran to rally my team.

"Huddle the fuck up!" I sprinted toward my team.

The team bunched, faced me, and waited for me to call the play. I carefully stared into each tired eye before I called the final play of most of the guys' football careers.

Pride showered over me, and I was honored to lead such a group of warriors into battle.

I loved all of them and would have rather died than to have let these young men down.

"We're going to win this game right fucking now!" I yelled.

Each young man's eyes opened wider. They all began to stand tall. Their chests expanded and their appetites strengthened!

"We're going to win this fucking game!" I repeated my prediction.

"Hell yea!" Defensive tackle, Colin Auchincloss believed.

"The play is Monster!" I gave the order of destruction.

"Fuck yea homie!" Mark Briscoe screamed.

"We are going to kill those motherfuckers!" I vowed.

"Let's goooo!" Tony Brown, normally the quietest person on the team, yelled and pumped his fist.

"This is the last play the Psycho Ward will ever play together, so let's make our mark right now!" Jay Kleberg said, eyes watering.

"It's been an honor leading with you Manzo!"

"Yes it has Jay! I love all you country bastards! Now just stay with your goddamn man, and I will do the rest!"

"We believe you Manzo!" Reggie Beavan cried.

Reggie's ripped number eighty-nine jersey exposed the Riddell logo on his light green shoulder pads.

The once pearl white football pants were almost completely brown except for the grass marks on the knees.

His face mask chipped to the metal, while maroon stripes skidded diagonal across his helmet like a kindergartener used it during arts and craft.

Reggie looked *crazy,* the team felt crazier, and I was the craziest.

"Monster!" I gave the orders for the very last time.

"Ready...BREAK!" all eleven men yelled in a deep harmony, as we clapped loudly and could be heard over the heckling EHS fans.

"Fuck you Manzo!"

"Rick Ramsey ain't shit!"

"Let's go EHS!"

"Come on Woodberry!"

Just a lone Woodberry supporter could be heard randomly through the EHS uproar as the clouds shifted, and the wind blew the remains of my sanity out of my helmet's earhole.

The more the home team cheered, the more I needed to shut them the fuck up! I stomped back and forth in the end zone like Godzilla and watched the dinosaur egg resting a few inches away from my feet. I would die before I would let the football cross the chalk line.

"You will not move!" I chastised the football.

My teammates shuffled in their positions, anticipating EHS breaking their own huddle. No one talked or looked at me. We were all in our special places.

"BREAK!" The EHS players broke their huddle.

"Hey motherfuckers!" I taunted. "Hey you fat motherfuckers!"

Number fifty-two, the center, was a six-foot, one inch 260-pound chunk of bison.

He galloped to the football and stopped where I had been already waiting on the opposite side of the line of scrimmage.

A second later, the other appetizers filed in line on each side of him—but I paid no attention to any of them.

My eyes zoomed past the quarterback and the fullback, and fixated on the 230-pound running back, number thirty-three, Jim Toliver—the main course.

"Hey Jim! Don't get scared now motherfucker!"

"Hey watch your language Manzo!" a referee demanded.

"My bad, sorry Mr. Ref!"

"I'm gonna eat you alive BITCH!" I wasn't sorry. I jumped up and down directly in front of the center, and the referee just grinned and walked away. "These fat cocksuckers can't save you Little Jimmy!"

"EHS! EHS!" the Episcopal fans chanted louder.

"Run the ball down Manzo's fucking face James!"

"Send his Black-ass back to the ghetto!"

"Let's go Woodberry Tigers!"

"Kill those Tigers, Maroons!"

The noise pumped my heart, and I could no longer differentiate who rooted for me or against me. My jaw locked, and my nose flared as I snorted adrenaline and rage.

"Number thirty-five is the Mike!" Brandon Jones informed his team and stood behind the center who was already bent down with his right hand on the football. Jones had pointed at me to direct their blocking scheme, but I never noticed.

"Toliver?" I screamed. "Toliver? You hear me motherfucker!"

Jim Toliver just stood in his two-point stance with his hands on his thighs and knees slightly bent. He looked straight ahead without once moving his head or eyeballs.

The dude was disciplined and wouldn't respond or give me the tiniest hint which way he would run with the ball.

Infuriated, I began to move around to confuse the EHS offense and disguise where I would line up on the field.

"Down!" Jones yelled as all the offensive linemen and the fullback put their right hands on the ground, in the same three-point stance as the center.

Jones squatted and put both of his hands underneath the center's butt.

They were in attack mode.

"I am going to kiiiiillll yoooouuu Toooollliiivveeerrr!" I sang, but Toliver remained as stiff as Mr. Heisman, himself.

"BLUE FIFTY-TWO!" Jones screamed with his head on a swivel, never revealing which direction they would run.

"BLUE FIFTY-TWO! OMAHA! OMAHA!"

"READY! SET!"

'Always check the splits of the offensive line on the goal line!'

'The splits will tell you where they are running the ball Manzo!'

With only a moment to spare, I visually swept the feet of each offensive lineman like Coach Abbott preached every day in practice.

Although I had five defensive linemen obstructing my view, I could still see the transparent discrepancy in the offensive lineman's splits.

(Splits were the distances between each offensive lineman's outer foot in relation to the nearest outer foot of his teammate on the line of scrimmage.)

On the left side of the offensive line, the split between the guard and tackle, known as the *B-gap*, was approximately six inches wider than any other split between their linemen.

EHS appeared to be gunning for the B-gap, exactly where I was standing, because I was out of position with free rein to move around.

They had expected me to be directly over the center, in my normal position, but they forgot I was a fucking monster.

Oh shit—they're coming right at me!

Biting down hard on my mouthpiece, I salivated and staggered my stance.

I dug the cleats of my back-right foot into the dirt and leaned forward, placing my weight on my front foot that now toed the line of scrimmage.

In a race for legendary status, I watched the football for movement, with the concentration of a sprinter listening for the starter pistol.

"HUT!" Jones yelled loudly and jolted his body to draw us offsides.

The ball didn't move, and I flinched but no Woodberry players crossed the line of scrimmage!

Sweat dripped, my fists clenched, and my stomach turned. I was a gambler. I had bet my football legacy that these bastards were coming straight at me.

I took one final deep breath and waited for the dealer to flip the last card.

"HUUUTT!"

The football moved.

I moved faster.

Jones received the snap from the center, and I exploded, unblocked, through the A-gap with violent intentions.

Surprisingly, the fullback ran to the right side of the line with both arms opened over the top of each other, like he was going to be the one receiving the handoff, but I didn't care. I was not going to chase him!

Putting my head down, I gathered steam and sprinted straight for Toliver—who jab stepped to my team's right with his left foot like he would follow the fullback. Suddenly turning the other direction, he planted his right foot straight toward me.

Toliver had his arms open.

"FAKE!" Tony Brown screamed from his free-safety position, recognizing the deception also, but I didn't hear him.

Jones held the football securely with both hands and reverse pivoted toward the oncoming fullback.

But instead of jamming the football in the fullback's belly, he faked the handoff with an empty right hand.

With his back to the line of scrimmage, Jones reached out his left arm and handed the football to the reversing Toliver, but it was too late. The 240-pound savage's dinner was served!

"AAAHH!" I howled, as I catapulted off the ground and launched my right shoulder into the maroon "E" on the side of Jim's helmet!

SMACK!

"Ooooh shiiiitt!" most of the onlookers sang the same verse.

The football and Toliver's helmet raced each other to the clouds, before crashing back down into a dirt patch on the seven-yard line.

As my body completely laid over the moaning Toliver, I could see our strong-side linebacker, number fifty-five, Reggie Bloom, jump on the football and cradle it tightly like his freedom depended it.

A few EHS players jumped on him, but to no avail. Bloom almost hugged the air out of the damn ball.

"Woodberry Forest recovered the ball! GAME OVER!" the referee yelled.

"Fuck yea Woodberry!" players and the Woodberry fans began to celebrate!

"We did it!"

"We're undefeated!"

"Twelve and O!"

As our fans swarmed the Episcopal High School football field, I stood over the half-conscious Jim Toliver—and watched the snot bubbles blow from his nostrils without any sympathy.

My teammates patted my back, and I laughed before asking Jim his opinion concerning my peoples.

"Not too bad for a *Puerto Rican*, huh?"

Chapter Eight

WASTED VICTORY

"You played a helluva game today son," Mr. Michael Collins stated like a proud dad, which I appreciated hearing since my father couldn't make the trip to Washington D.C. because of work.

"How does it feel to be 12-0?"

"It really hasn't hit me yet. I'm just happy for the school," I said.

"Well, you still played a helluva game, and the school is just as proud as I am...you fellas did great!"

"Thanks. I hate Episcopal."

"I know you do Manzo. We *all* hate Episcopal."

Mr. Collins, or Dean Collins to the rest of the Woodberry campus, was an ex-marine from Chicago, with a medium build and a salt and pepper, military-style crew cut. Along with Coach Davidsson, he was my mentor and guided me into pre-adulthood.

Mr. Collins and his wife, Kerri, had two adorable little girls, Caitlin and McKenzie, and the Collins family made me feel like the kids' older brother rather than just another *brother*.

They loved me and cared for me like the big White son they always wanted, except I was Black.

Because my original counselor, Mr. David Doty, left after my freshman year, I had the rare luxury of choosing my next advisor.

Whomever I had chosen would be my advisor until I graduated, so I didn't take the process lightly.

Although, when Mrs. Grymes handed me the suggestions form—I had taken just four-seconds to write down my top three choices:

1. Mr. Collins.
2. Mr. Collins.
3. Mr. Collins.

He and I only had a few one-on-one conversations before my selection and each conversation was brief, but very honest. He didn't know how to bullshit, and I was too immature to accept bullshit.

Both of us, unaware how to play the phony-game, were a perfect match. The man told me what I needed to hear, not what I wanted to hear.

"The hotel is right over here on the right Mr. Collins," I said from the passenger's side of Mr. Collins' truck.

"OK, I see it. Y'all fancy tonight, huh?" he asked and smirked, noticing my hotel.

"The *Ritz Carlton*? You're moving up in the world big guy."

"I wish I could afford something like this, but I'm just a poor-Black-boy tagging along with some good ole White folks," I said.

"Tyler Beam and Costa Gogos got a little room for us."

"Ha, ha, ha...you're too much Manzo."

It was tradition, just as much as the Game itself, for alumni to come back and get hotel rooms for the current Woodberry boys to party.

Gogos and Beam were my teammates the year before, so it was only right that I roll with them.

Add the fact that they both loved my roommate, Reese Malone, and the quota of having two Black kids in the crew was filled.

Mr. Collins eased his 1982 navy-blue Nissan pickup truck behind a cream Mercedes Benz S600, directly in front of the hotel lobby.

The entryway's lights lasered from the gold-plated awning onto the Benzo's fresh wash and wax but sunk into the dull grittiness of the truck's thirteen-year-old paint job.

"Don't worry, you will have plenty of those types of cars if you keep working as hard as you do," Mr. Collins said as he shifted his baby in park, watching me glow with envy.

"The world is yours Manzo."

"I don't need any of that. I just need to take care of the fam," I said.

"Well keep them grades up and destroying kids on the field, and your mother will be kicking her feet up."

"I will do my best sir."

"You know there were scouts at the game tonight to see you and Tim Olmstead," Mr. Collins informed.

Tim Olmstead was our team's All-American Junior quarterback from Binghamton, New York. A six-foot, four-inch gunslinger, Tim could throw the football sixty yards deep—from his knees.

Many college scouts, including the University of Florida's head coach, Steve Spurrier, frequented our games, but I never knew exactly whom they were there to see.

I just played each game like a *crazed dog* and didn't worry too much about who watched.

At six-foot, one inch, and 240 pounds and running a 4.44 second forty-yard dash, I knew I couldn't be missed.

I figured if I tried to put someone in the hospital, then I was most likely to be remembered. My logic was effective.

"Yea, I figured. I get all these college recruiting letters every day, but I try not to pay too much attention right now," I said.

"I was in the stands, and me, Kerri, and the kids were sitting right next to the UVA and VT coaches."

"For real?"

"Yup."

Instate rivals, the Virginia Tech Hokies and the University of Virginia Cavaliers, along with the Penn State, University of Miami, and the University of Maryland, were heavily recruiting me.

But both Virginia schools had the most incentive and were determined to not let a "physical specimen" leave the Commonwealth of Virginia or play for its nemesis.

Charlottesville, Virginia, UVA's home, was only twenty miles away from Orange County and was where we Woodberry boys went to the mall and the movies on some weekends.

All the UVA students I'd ever come across seemed too square and preppy. Add the fact that not a single college girl I'd met would let me even smell the pussy, and I was turned off by just the thought of being a *Wahoo.*

I'd never visited Virginia Tech, but I heard, from a UVA coach, that in Blacksburg the VT students screwed their own cousins, and farm animals. Well, at least they screwed!

VT was in the lead over UVA by a little, but I knew that I would most likely end up at Penn State with Coach Joe Paterno.

"So what happened with the coaches?" I asked anxiously.

"Both coaches kept it cool and nodded at every play you made, *but*...."

"But what Mr. Collins?" My back had begun to perspire, so I sat upright.

"On the last play when you killed that guy, the UVA coach's face turned beet red, and he was piping hot at you son."

"Really? Why? What did I do?"

"Ha, ha, ha!"

"Why are you laughing? This ain't funny Mr. Collins!"

"OK, calm down son."

"Sorry sir." I took a deep breath.

"I can't believe you didn't know, but James Toliver just verbally committed to play for the Cavaliers next year!"

"Oooh shit!"

"Oooh shit is right son!"

Leaning back in my seat, I closed my eyes and banged the back of my head against the headrest a few times.

"Relax!" Mr. Collins yelled, bracing my shoulder with his right hand. "You will be fine!"

"How could you say that?" I asked.

"Well, for one, you're a great football player and student," he said.

"For two, the little VT coach was standing on his feet clapping, and yelling —*atta-boy Manzo!*"

"You're lying Mr. Collins!"

"No shit Manzo! He was cheering louder than anyone in the stadium!"

"Fuck yea! I mean, heck yea!" I pumped a fist.

"It's OK son."

"Coach Grimes really loved the hit, huh?"

"Loved it?" Mr. Collins looked at me with a bent brow. "Man, if you could have seen the UVA coach's mug, he wanted to kill Coach Grimes!"

* * *

Coach J.B. Grimes was Virginia Tech's offensive line coach. At five feet, seven inches, the country boy from Arkadelphia, Arkansas coached the nation's most monstrous offensive line, which averaged six feet, three inches and 333 pounds apiece.

Coach Grimes always wore a baseball cap over his balding scalp, and only laughed when something was funny. A straight shooter, he was responsible for recruiting me for the Hokies.

Many coaches from many different universities called my dorm every night but if I were busy studying, I wouldn't take the call—except if it were Coach Grimes. He was the only coach that would tell me to "play better" rather than kiss my ass.

Coach Davidsson and Mr. Collins liked Coach Grimes too. Coach Grimes was our type of guy.

My mentors would have a big influence on my decision on choosing a university, and I knew, without them ever admitting, they did not want me to go to UVA.

* * *

"Well, I'm happy at least Coach Grimes appreciated my *skills*—I really like that guy."

"Would you ever go to Tech?" Mr. Collins asked.

"Would I ever go to Tech?" I asked myself.

"I mean, it's a great program, and Cornell Brown went there so it must be legit. Yes sir, I would definitely consider Virginia Tech."

"He's their All-American, right?" Mr. Collins asked.

"Yeah, the big head dude from E.C. Glass high school in Lynchburg. Cornell Brown could've gone literally anywhere, but he chose VT."

"You still have some time to think about it Manzo." Mr. Collins shifted in his seat and reached into his front pants pocket.

"When are your recruiting visits?" he asked.

"I go home for Thanksgiving break next week, and the week after—I visit VT first, and then the following weeks I visit Penn State, Miami, Maryland, and then UV..." I stopped and looked over at Mr. Collins with his wallet in his hand.

"Well, maybe not UVA anymore!"

"I think you can scratch them off your list Manzo."

"You might be correct sir!"

"You talk to your folks yet?" Mr. Collins asked.

"Folks?"

"Yes Manzo, your *parents*."

I knew Mr. Collins would not let me out of his car without asking about my parents. I had avoided bringing them up, but it was inevitable, considering that the current discussion centered on the biggest decision of my life.

The back of my neck tightened, and I bit down on my bottom lip. The car began to shrink, and I couldn't breathe.

Turning my head, I rolled down the passenger side window, and watched the little Mexican man with the small feet, grab luggage from an ungrateful Persian couple. They didn't even say thank you.

The calm wind attempted to un-fry my thoughts but couldn't blow away my sadness. I gave a valiant effort, but my tears weighed too much.

I was an eighteen-year-old kid on top of the world, but my family had the uncanny ability to bring a person back to ground level.

Damn, why he asked about them?

"Manzo what's wrong? You can talk to me son," he put his hand on my shoulder.

Rolling up the window, I let the tears have their fun without interruption. Conflicted, I felt the urge to run out of the truck, but I also wanted to lock the doors and never leave.

The football game helped me bury my pain, but the game was over. There were no timeouts or referees in my life, and it was time to tackle reality. I turned and faced Mr. Collins.

"My parents are getting a divorce," I said.

His face paled as the blood drained, and his cheeks had risen with the squinting of his eyes.

Baffled, he slightly opened his mouth and re-closed it without delivering a single word, but the damage was evident.

"Shit happens, huh?" I asked.

"Manzo, I'm so sorry—"

BANG!

"Woooo—let's go Woodberry!"

Startled, I almost jumped out my damn seat! I turned to my right and saw a steamed window with a guy's face and lips mashed against it.

"Oooh great, I should've known you were hanging with this catfish." Mr. Collins pointed to the window.

"Manzo let's go par-taaay!" my classmate Reese Malone hooted.

I quickly wiped my eyes with the bottom of my Woodberry hoodie.

I didn't want to have to explain why I was parked in a pickup truck with a school advisor, crying in front of a hotel. I might have gotten my hood-pass revoked. *No Bueno!*

Sitting upright after a final cleanup attempt, I rolled down the window, and Reese peeled his face off the glass.

"Yooo, what you doing? Let's go upstairs!" Reese said, gesturing toward the hotel lobby.

"I'm coming; I was just talking with Mr. Collins."

"Oh shit, I didn't notice the truck." Reese backed away, his breath clearly smelling like Natty Ice.

Woodberry Forest School had a strict *no alcohol* policy, and a student could get expelled for taking just a sip of booze, on or off-campus.

EHS weekend was the only time where the faculty knew that most of the boys would get shit-faced, but the faculty still couldn't witness any part of the madness. Underage drinking was illegal, no matter how intense the rivalry.

Completely hammered, Reese just used his one pass—it was time for him and me to leave the premises.

"Reese go upstairs. I will be right there," I said.

"But—"

"Go dude!" I mouthed and pointed to the lobby.

"OK, bye Mr. Collins."

"Bye Reese," he said without looking in Reese's direction.

"I'm gonna go Mr. Collins," I said once Reese was inside the lobby and had one of the Mexican bellboys in a headlock, playing around as always.

"I will fill you in on everything when I get back to school sir," I promised.

"OK, no problem son," Mr. Collins replied.

"Sooo…what's going on upstairs tonight?" He turned around and looked me straight in the eye.

"Uh, just a fun time sir."

"Really?" he asked.

Woodberry prided itself on its Honor Code, and each boy pledged to never lie, cheat, or steal.

If the Honor code appeared to be broken in any degree, the student would have to meet with the Prefect Board, a group of twelve exemplary students selected by students and the faculty to uphold the Honor Code and overall rules of the school.

Each prefect oversaw an entire dorm and handled the functionality of that dorm. Ironically, I was a prefect. My dorm was B1-2, and Reese and Tee Butler were my roommates.

Mr. Collins asked a direct question and by rules of the Honor Code, I had to answer truthfully or face expulsion for my evasiveness.

"I'm just messing with you Manzo!" Mr. Collins laughed and punched my shoulder. "Get the hell out of here and go have some fun! We will talk when you get back. Be safe son."

"Thanks Mr. Collins!" I laughed before opening the car door.

"Wait a minute!" he yelled.

"Yes sir?" I sat back down.

"You need any money?" he asked as he reached in his old brown leather bill-fold and pulled out twenty dollars.

"Uuh, I'm good sir—"

"Nonsense. Here, take this and enjoy yourself. No sweat Manzo." He patted me on the back.

"Thank you, sir," I said and accepted the money. I would have insulted him if I didn't.

Stepping out of the vehicle, I snatched my backpack out of the truck's bed and walked toward the lobby's glass automatic doors.

I turned around for a final wave, but Mr. Collins was already peeling out of the driveway.

Chuckling to myself, I reached in my back pocket and pulled out the twelve crispy $100 bills my father mailed to me in a Con Edison envelope—which had "12-0" written in green marker across the top . I would rather have had my father at the game, but fuck it, the bread would do.

Twelve and O, bitches!

The Benjamins welcomed the lonely Jackson, and I stuffed the money back in my pocket.

Walking in the lobby, I greeted the concierge with a head nod, and got in the middle of three shiny gold-plated elevators.

Before pressing the "PH" button in the all-mirrored elevator, I examined the exhausted reflection critiquing my appearance and spoke to the MVP of the Game.

"Manzo, you need a drink."

* * *

The penthouse suite door opened; Reese stood holding two bottles of Jack Daniels. Clearly wasted, he smiled and then briskly hid both bottles behind his back.

Like a deer in the woods, Reese stuck his head out of the doorway and slowly looked in both directions down the hallway.

"You'se didn't bring Massa up here wit'cha now, did ya Mandingo?" Reese asked.

"Shut the fuck up! Mr. Collins left, asshole!" I laughed.

"I'm just fucking with you!" The *Jack* reappeared from behind Reese's back like magic. "Welcome to *mi casa*! Whiskey shots for the MVP are in order!"

"Damn, you don't waste no time, huh?"

"You only live once son! Come in!"

"This shit is siiicckk!" I yelled.

Walking into the penthouse, I dropped my bags on the marble floor. Smiling, I looked in awe at the pristine living room space that would be the headquarters for the weekend's fuckery.

I felt sorry for the staff responsible for cleaning up behind the animals after we bounced. The hotel room was about to be a zoo. I hoped Beam and Gogos had gotten insurance on the room.

At the far end of the suite, through one of the two patio windows, I could see the Washington Capitol lit in a distance, and I was drawn to the light.

My feet moved toward the window. I felt important. I felt presidential.

"Look at this place Reese!"

"Come on, you know Gogos and Beam had to set it out for us son!" Reese rapidly rubbed his thumbs across the fingers on each hand, respectively. "Money ain't a thang son!"

"Fuck yea, Beam and the Greek!" I sang.

"Long live tradition motherfucker!" Reese said as he placed the bottles of Jack Daniels next to two shot glasses on an island countertop in the middle of the room.

"You're loving that view, huh?" he asked.

"I've never saw D.C. like *this* Reese. Shit looks amazing."

Washington, D.C. twinkled in the night as the architectural royalty bounced its brightness off each other and onto a beautifully placed city, filled with life and protected by water.

Silhouettes of scattered trees cushioned the structures. I appreciated the city's beauty, but I knew what occurred daily across the river.

"You would never guess brothers get killed on the reg over there," I stated.

"Motherfucking murder capital of the world son," Reese said.

"Everybody smoking that *Boat* and them *Dippers*. Killing each other every damn day."

"*And* they have a mayor who smokes crack with hookers. Unbelievable." I shook my head.

"Come and take a shot with your boy." Reese started playing bartender.

"Hell yea! Pour it up! My muscles are a little sore from the game."

Before reaching the island, I continued to admire the suite. Everything was perfectly placed, and the room appeared to never have housed a group of drunk-ass vanilla boys, with a few chocolate sprinkles.

The couch's tan fabric looked as if I had to trim my dingle-berries just to sit on it. The pillows rested upright and firm. The Ritz Carlton was magnificent.

"This place has art on the walls and little lamps and shit!" I grabbed a shot.

"Manzo we gonna fuck this place up!"

"Fucking right bro!" I raised my glass to my mouth.

"Whoah, whoah, whoah son!" Reese pressed his hand against my forearm. "We gotta toast first lil' nigga!"

"Oh shit, my bad!" I apologized.

* * *

Reese was my *roll-dog,* and it only seemed right that he and I shared the first drink, before all the compressed boarding school rage had been released.

We had been best friends my entire four years at Woodberry and had grown to brotherhood since the day we met at Woodberry's summer school, prior to our freshman year.

Tee, Reese, and I were a trio, but there was no denying that Reese and I had grown closer over the years.

We had more in common than Tee and me, although Reese was raised in the sticks of Annapolis, Maryland, where most of the brothers called each other "son"—and mostly *dated* White girls.

Sports, pussy, and rap music glued us all together, but the other intangibles that Reese and I shared had weakened my bond with the more conservative Tee Butler.

Fearless and ambitious, Reese was six-foot, two inches but walked with hunched shoulders, so the kid could've been even taller if he had worked on his posture.

Although he used forced slang at times, Reese naturally talked proper, and sounded like a straight-up White boy over the phone.

Far from an Uncle Tom, he was raised by a proud Christian Black family that simply taught their kids how to pronounce their vowels and to treat people equally, no matter the color of a person's skin.

* * *

"Let's toast!" Reese said and lifted his glass.

That shit smells strong.

"Ha-ha—we're about to get twisted!" I said.

"No joking for a second son. This is grown man shit."

"OK, OK—my bad." I raised my glass.

"OK, you ready Manzo?"

"I'm *good.* You got the floor bro."

"Why thank you, good sir." He gave a nervous smile.

"For four years, we have been closer than brothers, and I'm going to miss you bro."

"I'm gonna miss you too."

"Manzo...I just want to say thank you for always being there, and good luck in college."

"That's the entire speech?" I asked.

"Yea that's it son!" Reese reached to tap glasses but suddenly stopped.

"Oh yea, I got a surprise for you in a few."

"*Surprise*?" I raised an eyebrow.

"It ain't *exactly* pussy...but you will like it."

"Damn it!" I pouted.

"You're silly son. *Salud*."

"Salud Reese."

He put the glass to his mouth and dipped his head backward. From his profile, Reese looked like a thinner version of his dad, Reese Sr., except with his mother's deep brown complexion.

"Aahh, that shit's good!" Reese howled after smashing the Jack.

"What the fuck?" I asked as the liquid smoke slid down my throat.

"You a man now boy!" Reese laughed, already pouring another round.

"What the fuck is that I just drank?" I asked.

"That's that Jack, nigga!"

"That shit taste like molasses that's been in the microwave too long!"

I closed my eyes and shook my head two hard times. Reese tried to hand me another shot glass full of whiskey.

"Another one so soon?" I asked and raised both hands in refusal.

"Man, sophomore year...you said EHS weekend you would get fucked up with me if y'all ever went undefeated. Well, twelve and O—it is motherfucker!" Reese reminded.

"Okaay, I remember—but don't after-school-special me. Just give me the liquor!" A boy of my word, I snatched the shot.

"Yessir! My ace—Big Man-zoooe!" Reese cheered. "Here's to White girls and cocaine!"

"White girls and *what*?" I asked.

"That shit is *good*!" he yelled.

"Fuck...aaahh!" I slammed the shot.

Shit burns!

"Hell yea son! That's the way you drink whiskey!"

The harsh smelling sweetness of vanilla ice cream roasting on burnt oak, soaked its way to my brain. I began to sweat.

My eyes watered, and I could no longer focus on being focused, so I sat down on a four-foot stool at the table.

My system survived the first round so far, but I wasn't prepared to go the distance. I prayed the bell would ring soon, but Reese poured another flurry of shots.

"Yoooo, I gotta chill Reese," I said.

"Nigga these for me!" he said before shooting another.

"Where's the beef?" he hollered.

"Where's the *what*?" I asked.

Although Jason Arwine and Kevin Rodriguez had warned me my sophomore year that Reese would blurt out crazy shit when he was drinking, the random comments he made still confused the hell out of me. I wasn't ready.

"Listen, I just want to say that I'm completely sorry—"

"Reese it's not that serious, I wanted to drink."

"No son!" He walked around the table and sat at the stool, two feet away from me. "I'm not talking about the booze son."

"What you are talking about then?" I asked.

"Manzo...I'm talking about your parents getting a divorce."

My body straightened, and I could see again. The D-word was the magic password to my sobriety, and sadness washed away the whiskey.

Unprepared for real life, I wanted to be somewhere else. On instinct, I tossed back another shot. The Jack Daniels now tasted delicious.

"Oh yea, the *divorce*," I said.

Last week when Alejandro informed me over the phone that our parents were getting a divorce, I ran to my dorm room and jumped in my bunk.

The room was dark and quiet, and I *thought* I was alone. Smothering my head with the pillow, I cried myself to sleep, and dreamt of happier times between my parents. There didn't seem to be many, but I found a few precious moments.

The next morning while Reese and I waited in line for breakfast, he leaned forward and whispered, "Did your parents get a divorce, or did Tanisha break up with you?"

"Parents," I replied, never looking back.

"You will be OK." He tapped me on the shoulder, and we never spoke another word about it—until now.

I'm truly blessed to have such a great friend.

"Thanks bro—shit happens." I jumped off the hotel's stool. "Hey forget that. Where's everyone?"

"Beams and Gogos met up with Bonneau and Sanders for a few. I believe Tennille, Ted Baker, and the rest of them went with their parents to dinner after the game. Everyone's coming to party here! Shit, even De Walker's country ass might come—so relax son!"

"Uuh, are Doug Winslow, Womack, Wolfe, and Richard Wright coming?" I asked.

"Yea Manzo! All the motherfuckers who name starts with an 'A' through goddamn 'Z' are coming! I just said *everyone!*"

"Well, *when* are they coming back?"

"Stop changing the subject!"

"What the fuck you want me to say Reese?" I shifted my weight from foot to foot trying to maintain balance.

"I'm hurting bro! The shit hurts bad!"

"I bet it does Manzo…I bet it does."

Reese looked downwards, and his demeanor dangled between drunkenness and sadness.

Although his parents never divorced, they had come close a couple of times during our years at Woodberry, and Reese was a wreck. He said he'd rather die than live without both parents.

"Reese?"

"Hey Reese!" I punched his arm. "You OK bro?"

"Yea I'm good!" He grabbed the bottle of Jack and poured two more shots.

"Let's be festive in this bitch!" he stammered.

"Great idea bro!" I agreed.

"How's your girl Tanisha?" He handed me the overflowing glass.

"Thanks, she's good. We're doing great. I love her, man."

"That's good. Y'all getting married and shit?" His eyes shut for a moment and then opened.

"Yes Reese…it appears so."

"Great! Let's toast to that!" he hollered.

While still seated, Reese used a humping motion to inch his stool closer to mine.

Like the drunken uncle at a Bar Mitzvah, he put his arm around my shoulder and professed his deep-felt emotions.

"I luh you bruh," he said.

"I love you too bruh."

"Here's to your wedding. Here's to us being brothers, and never, ever, ever fucking with each other's girls. That type shit ain't for us."

"Uh…of course bruh. I trust you with my life," I said, before Reese buried another shot.

"Aaaah…your go!" Reese removed his arm from my shoulder.

Man, I don't feel too good.

I covered my mouth with a fist and swallowed. The bile wanted to leave my body immediately and my stomach rumbled.

The sweat in my eyes made me close them tightly while the pain in my abdomen forced my breathing to be very rhythmic, short, and rapid.

"What the fuck, you having a baby out your ass or something?" Reese laughed.

"My stomach kills," I said.

"You better not throw up lil nigga!" Reese warned.

I will barf if I keep drinking this shit!

"Tighten up lil' nigga! Damn!" he ordered.

Swallowing repeatedly, I burped and tasted a remix of the team's pre-game meal as smoked-flavored spaghetti sauce flooded in the wrong direction.

Uncovering my mouth, I slowly stood up with my hands by my side like I was getting ready to draw a six-shooter from both hips. I was scared to even move.

"Ha, ha, ha! Billy *the fuh-king* kid over here is about to dial up *Earl!*"

"I'm cool bro… I ain't about throw up. I'm good," I said, and suddenly my stomach showed mercy.

"Now you *sure* you're OK?" Reese poured another shot.

"Yea I'm OK, but I'm not drinking anymore tonight bro," I said. "That's all you right there. My head is spinning."

CLICK.

BOOM!

Reese's apathetic moment was disrupted by the front door being unlocked and kicked open. The noise scared me, and the nausea returned as I forced a smile at our generous hosts.

Tyler Beam, six-foot, four inches, and slender, and Costa Gogos, five-foot, seven inches, and round—stood in the doorway for a few seconds before Tyler raised handles of Jim Beam in the air.

"I brought my uncles with me, and it's time to get fucking wasted my African American brothers!" Tyler Beam yelled as a village of White people behind him, boys and girls—raised an assortment of liquors, and rolled marijuana joints in the air. They all screamed at the top of their young Republican lungs.

"Woo-whooo!"

"Shit yea Beam!"

"Roll that shit! Light that shit! *Smoke* that shit!"

"We're getting WHITE BOY WASTED tonight Manzooooo!" Costa led the mob.

"Twelve and motherfucking ooooooohhhh! Meeooww!" the Woodberry Forest tiger mascot burst through the crowd and hollered.

"Twelve and O!"

"Twelve and O!"

"Twelve and O!"

As the crowd slowly entered the suite chanting, I quickly glanced at the clock and then back at Reese, who pumped his fist in unison with the mob.

I wanted to join the madness and greet my friends, but my stomach was the one preparing to give the people a very warm welcome. I squeezed my core and covered my mouth again to stop the eruption.

"Well Manzo, maybe I lied a lil' bit about the whole *pussy* thing! Surprise... meow! Ha, ha, ha!" Reese clawed the air before rejoining the celebration.

"Twelve and O!"

"Twelve and..." I attempted to join the mayhem before the climbing bile choked my school spirit.

Don't throw up!

Please God!

The mascot approached me, and I could smell the stench of cigarette smoke and garlic exuding from its tiny-screened mouth.

He playfully pawed my shoulder as he roared hot death up my nose. My nerves scorched while my body shivered.

I sweat. I shook. I prayed.

The furball knew English but spoke the wrong language. "Hey Maan-zooe! Good gaaaamme bruuuhh-thaa—"

"Aaaagggghh!"

Before blacking out, the big pussy puked on the little tiger.

Chapter Nine

FLUSHED DREAM

Stale urine resonating through the hallway smelled as fresh as it did when I was a child.

The graffiti on the stairwell's door had been painted a thick pale green, but the dent from my back when Daddy caught me tagging "Mayo" on the door remained.

Univision blasted from the TV in apartment 13G. The Puerto Ricans were still deaf.

Whistles and dribbling basketballs pounded its way through apartment 13A. Jay Black and Snookum still loved our Knicks.

The aroma. The sounds. The lessons. Everything that I smelled, heard, and saw seemed so indicative to the thirteenth floor of 2370 Second Avenue, except the energy.

The experiences lived in my head so vividly, but once the thought of my family living as a whole died—so did my emotional ties.

The energy crumbled, and the deep absence of my father could not be ignored. Daddy was really gone.

Thanksgiving is going to suck ass this year!

The same two Medeco keys I've had since my tenth birthday twirled in my hand but could no longer unlock the door to the same world.

Terrified to face the adjustments of apartment 13E, I stood for a moment's contemplation of whether to enter an unfamiliar place I used to know or go to Jay's and watch the Knicks almost win another game.

Maybe I should tell Mommy my flight got delayed?

"This is some real bullshit." I stomped my foot.

The top lock welcomed the larger key, forgiving my shaky hand. Although I hadn't missed curfew, I felt nervous like I'd done something wrong, and severe punishment awaited me on the other side of the aqua-bluish steel door.

"Fuck it." I turned the key.

CLICK.

"Come on." I rattled the key again, before extracting it for further investigation.

"Why won't it open?" I dropped my Woodberry duffle bag, forgetting my *football* MVP trophy was in it.

I held the key up to the light and inspected whether I'd snatched the wrong project apartment key from some other boy at school.

Simple deduction dismissed the theory, because Tee's key looked completely different, and the rest of the kids at school lived in mansions.

She changed the locks!

CLICK.

Door opened.

"Hey there son!" Mommy greeted her first born with a second-rate smile, before tightly hugging me.

"Hey Mommy!"

"I missed you so much!" She squeezed tighter.

"You OK Mommy?" I unattached myself from her embrace and examined her peculiar choice of wardrobe for the evening.

With disheveled hair; Mommy clutched the V-neck collar of an oversized Fruit of the Loom undershirt.

Surprisingly, she wore Chicago Bulls shorts which hung over a pair of giant red and black lumberjack slippers.

Daddy is a Knicks fan. Something ain't right.

"Oh I'm fine. You just startled me when I heard all that noise at the door." Mommy, never maintaining eye contact, continuously peeped behind her. "I thought you were coming tomorrow."

"Are you going to let me in Mommy?" I asked.

"I'm sorry, come on in here. I missed you."

She walked a few feet into the apartment, and I followed until the front door closed behind me. No further than the kitchen's entrance, Mommy stopped.

She then turned around to face me and bit her bottom lip, which she did often when she was nervous.

"The kids are at your Aunt Ree's for the weekend," she spoke, but all I could hear was the TV's surround sound blaring from the bedroom.

"And John Starks will go to the free throw line to win the game!" New York Knicks commentator Marv Albert jubilated.

"They won't be back until Sunday."

"What did you say Mommy? I didn't hear you."

"I said that the kids won't be back until Sunday!" she repeated and looked behind her again.

"And Starks makes the first free throw! The score is tied with one-second on the clock!" Marv added amongst the pandemonium of Madison Square Garden.

"Oh OK! Sorry Mommy—I couldn't hear you with the game on!" I said.

"How's school?" Mommy's face flushed as she put her head down.

Fuck school right now.

"School's fine!" I said.

"Chicago takes a timeout and when we return, John Starks will be at the free-throw line with a chance to put the Knicks up by one!" Marv informed.

The volume from Daddy's big screen TV drifted away as the springs in Daddy's mattress crunched a strange melody. The conductor was heavier and moved slower than the man of the house.

That's not my father!

"Manzo, we need to talk," my mother whispered to her twirling fingers, and I dropped my bag.

Excruciating pain shut my eyes as my thumping heart weakened its grip on the love for my mother. Anger soiled my spirit, and I was confused, but I wasn't stupid.

How could she?

"There's something you need to know son."

"Yes *Mommy*?" I asked.

"You know me and your father haven't been right in a while, and I haven't been happy in years?"

"Yes, I know...*mother*."

How could she?

"People grow apart, and it's time for a change." She finally raised her head and tears began to fall.

Watching Mommy cry over my father wasn't new to me, but her face appeared different from the last 100 times.

The brown eyes of a beautifully broken woman, frustrated by the crossroads of love and intelligence, weren't there anymore. Even with tears, she looked stronger and eager to fly.

Apparently, while in school, I missed the cocoon stage. The butterfly no longer cried for my father, or not even for herself. She cried for me.

"It's really over, huh?" I asked.

"Yes Manzo, it's over and you know I tried." Mommy placed her hand on my cheek.

"Give him another chance Mommy!"

"No I can't, it's over son! I tried!"

"Maybe you need to try harder?"

"Twenty-three years are enough! It's over!"

"You have to try for us Mommy!"

"Manzo, I'm sorry son! I can't and it's over!"

"That's bullshit!"

"Watch your damn mouth! You are still *my* son!" Mommy snapped.

"Hey is everything all right out there?" a man's voice shouted.

Who the fuck is that?

"It's OK Miguel, I'm just talking to Manzo, my son!" Mommy explained, as we stared at each other.

"Who's Miguel?"

"Miguel's my boyfriend."

"What?" I balled both fists, but not for solidarity.

"I've moved on. He's my...he's my man."

"What about Daddy?"

"It's over between me and your daddy!" she yelled as the vein in the middle of her forehead stretched two freckles.

"Is everything all right out there baby?" Miguel asked.

"Mind your fucking business nigga!" I hollered.

"Manzo watch your mouth in my house—"

"*Your* house?"

"Yes, my motherfucking house—"

"OK, let me meet my new stepfather who's chilling on *your* bed, watching *your* TV!"

"Not acting like that you aren't!"

"It's OK baby! Bulls about to get punched in the mouth anyway! I'm coming!" Miguel yelled.

The unfamiliar movement of an intruder rolling out of my father's bed continued until two thuds added to the disrespect.

I could hear Miguel standing and leaving the bedroom, but only to enter the bathroom directly across the hall.

The soft plastic toilet seat smacked against each other, and Miguel's slippers scratched against the tile.

His feet assumingly inched closer to the toilet as my mother and I stared at each other without speaking a word.

Both breathing slowly and silently, my mother and I awaited the conclusion of a shared thought.

No separation or divorce could unchain the link between our brains. Mommy was correct—I was still her son.

Miguel relieved himself with the bathroom door completely open, and the sounds of a man who had too many beers or just had sex, echoed densely off the solid project walls.

Hard urine hosed Daddy's toilet and Mommy's dignity as my heart boiled in a bowl of contempt.

"At least Daddy closed the damn door," I said.

"Son please be nice to him."

"If he washes his hands I will."

"Son be nice please. He's a nice guy."

"At least Daddy washed his hands."

"Don't ruin this for me son. Please." Mommy grabbed my arm with both hands and tugged for some support. "He treats me good," she said.

I bet he does.

"Please, just for me son. Please—please Manzo."

Fuck, I hate seeing her like this!

For Mommy, I have to give this guy a chance!

Frightened by the boy that she *taught* how to be a man, Mommy clutched my hand and placed it on her heart. Her eyes longed to be happy.

She pried her lips to smile as she did many nights that I held her firmly, killing the disease that Daddy's absence had inoculated into her young system.

Miguel had flushed, and my petulance followed his urine.

With a sudden change of attitude, I looked at my mother and realized she was my strength. She deserved a grateful and understanding son.

My father would always be my father, but the woman with the golden skin and high cheek bones— deserved a chance at a love Daddy just couldn't provide.

I couldn't blame my mother for finally breaking the chains. Any dude she brought home, whether he closed the bathroom door or not, would be susceptible to the eldest son's resistance.

But If I loved Mommy like I said I loved her, then I had to try, even if my efforts were forced.

"OK Mommy...I will be nice."

"Thank you, son—thank you."

She's had enough of my father's shit.

I must try if this guy makes her happy.

"Hey, how you doing? I'm Miguel." A deep voice interrupted my moment of sentiment.

Completely stunned by the presence of the six feet, four-inch, 250-pound Puerto Rican peering down at me, I stepped back to survey and absorb the Herculean Julio.

The anti-Daddy's head was clean shaved, and unlike my father's beard, Miguel sported a goatee.

He had tattoos all over his upper body; the most noticeable one on his left shoulder—a huge green Coquí frog.

Under his wife-beater wasn't any rugged muscle tone like he had done any hard prison time, but I knew that already from his pretty-boy tats. A guy in prison with a rose on his chest would have died with a dick in his butt.

Mommy's new flame couldn't have been older than twenty-eight years old. She was thirty-nine at the time.

As I calculated the age difference, my blood frenzied while my memory remained in the moment. Offended again, I began to convulse, and my eyes flickered.

I didn't hear this nasty motherfucker wash his hands!

"Manzo this is Miguel." Mommy watched as I stared at his hand, and she caressed my back, only to feel the fire.

"Manzo, this is *Miguel*," she repeated, sensing the meltdown.

Relax and shake his hand for Mommy!

"Hey Miguel." I extended my hand but cancelled the respectful introduction when I recognized his blue and orange basketball shorts.

What the fuck?

Miguel, a Chicago Bulls fan, wore a pair of official New York Knicks basketball shorts with the number thirty-four stitched on the left front thigh.

Daddy owned the same pair, given to him personally from Charles Oakley at a charity to keep drugs off the New York City streets. Daddy donated $10,000 just because people said he and *Big Oak* looked alike.

Calm down, it's just a coincidence.

My hand inched closer to Miguel's. Our fingers had touched as a signature in black magic marker on the left thigh of *Miguel's* shorts burst into my vision —"Charles Oakley."

Those are Daddy's shorts!

An unmanageable craziness punctured the hot molten in my heart. Beaten by betrayal, I commenced to torch any sympathy I had for Mommy.

Miguel's smirk doused gasoline on my savagery. He was too close. I had to burn him.

"You ain't my fucking father!" I howled before I instantaneously cocked my hand back and bombed a fist into Miguel's jaw, attempting to disintegrate his stupid-ass goatee.

Miguel smashed against the mirrored living room wall and flattened on Daddy's white carpet.

Pieces of glass coated Miguel as he laid motionless and blood slobbered from his mouth.

Unsympathetic, I discounted the shooting pain in my left hand, and Mommy wailing on my right shoulder.

"Manzo, what did you do?" she screamed as Miguel moaned. "Why the FUCK would you do that?"

She cried and continued to beat on my shoulder, but I didn't budge—while my breath thickened.

Oblivious to her disgrace, I enjoyed watching her boy-toy quiver and twinkle. A loyal son to a disloyal father, I smiled with false pride and callousness as the blood spew.

SMACK!

"How could you do this to me?" Mommy asked after she slapped me. "Why would you ever do something like this Manzo?"

SMACK!

Mommy slapped me again and cried, "How dare you put your hands on the man I love, because you'd rather take up for your piece of shit father than see your own mother happy for once in her life? You ungrateful bastard!

"I raised you by my damn self and you held me many nights when I cried because of that goddamn monster, and this is the thanks I get—you motherfucker?"

"Sorry Mom—"

"Don't you *sorry* me, you *sorry* motherfucker!" she yelled before stepping on broken glass with her bare feet.

"Mommy watch out for the—"

"SHUT UP MANZO!"

She sat and placed Miguel's head on her lap, stroking his face like she used to do me as a child, but I had never remembered her ever holding my father in such a way.

She had found a new reason to love with the semi-conscious man on the floor who loved her back.

Although I still felt the urge to finish the job and stomp Miguel the fuck out, I had no choice but to finally acknowledge Mommy's happiness.

"Are you satisfied now Manzo?"

"Mommy I'm sorry!"

"No you aren't! You're a monster just like your father and you don't even know it!"

"No I'm not! Don't say that!"

"Don't *say* that?" Mommy continued to cry.

"*Yes*, please don't say that!"

"Look at you! You think you're some big man, because you all on your own down there with those White folks playing football and lifting all those weights! You don't care about us anymore!" Mommy rocked, gently cradling Miguel's dome while blood soaked her t-shirt.

"You think you're big shit now, and you act like more your father every day!"

"Mommy that's bullshit!"

"Look at the way you talk to me! Just like him! You're arrogant just like him, you think your shit don't stink just like him, all you care about is yourself just like him, and..." Mommy buried her head against Miguel and kissed him on the cheek.

And what?

"And you make your mother cry...just like *your* daddy!"

"No Mommy!" I stepped toward her. "I love you! DO NOT say that!"

"Don't you come near me MOTHERFUCKER!"

"But Mommy!"

"Get out of my goddamn house and don't you ever come back here!"

"What?"

"Don't *what* me! You a big man! Get the fuck out of my house!"

"But Mommy, I—"

"I don't care where you go! Just get out of here!" she screamed, and Miguel moved his limbs.

"You're choosing this Goya-bean-eating-ass-nigga over your son?" I asked.

"I'm choosing to be *happy*! Now show me some *respect* for a change and leave before he gets up!"

"But—"

"But nothing!" She pointed toward the front door. "Go stay with that whore of a girlfriend you got!"

"*Whore?*"

"Did I fucking stutter? Yes, WHORE!"

"Don't say that! Tanisha's a good girl!"

"GET THE FUCK OUT!" Mommy screeched.

"What's going on Karen?" Miguel had awakened, speaking through a bloody mouth as she pressed his head back down in her lap.

"Nothing baby...Little *Los* was just leaving."

"Fine!" I said, and my mother and I exchanged lethal glares for a moment.

With my mother's love lost, I grabbed my bag and ran out of the door.

"FUUUUCK!" I wept once in the hallway, kicking the elevator door. "I have no place to go!"

Chapter Ten

SALTY REUNION

"Come on Tanisha, I need you! Answer the damn phone!"

RING.

"It's too cold for this bullshit!"

RING.

"Hello, you have reached the answering machine of Tanisha. I'm sorry—"

CLICK!

Where could she be?

With the wind cutting through Fifth Avenue, I snuggled in the phone booth on the corner of 112th Street repeatedly lodging coins in the phone booth with a swollen hand, but the talking slot machine never hit jackpot. I lost every time. Tanisha wasn't home.

My mustard colored leather jacket with the tassels was ideal for a Virginia night or scalping pilgrims, but the New York frigidness wiped out my fashion statement.

Closing my lapels, I kept peeking up at Tanisha's window until I finally saw her room light up for a brisk moment, only to darken again.

Is she up there, or is that her crazy-ass grandfather?

She always answers the phone.

I told her I was coming home today.

Fuck it, I'm going up there.

Over the years, Mr. Berry and I had become closer, but there had been various times where I knocked on his door, and he didn't have a clue who I was or what I wanted.

A cunning old fellow, Tanisha's granddaddy would smile and open the door just enough to stick his cane out and jab me in my stomach.

I almost punched him right in his suspender strap the last time he hit me but restrained myself when he called me "Randy" instead of the "Mabby" I'd become accustomed to hearing.

Although Mr. Berry was old and senile, I was reluctant to ever come unannounced to his apartment again, because that cane hurt like a motherfucker— but with nowhere else to go, I was ready to risk another shot to the gut.

The stoplight turned red, and two yellow cabs hankering to get back downtown screeched at the crosswalk.

After touching the sidewalk, I looked up and refocused on the thirteenth floor, seeking out Tanisha's bedroom window.

The darkness of her room charred my hope of getting out of the cold night and into some sweltering pussy.

Fuck it. I'm still going up. Please, please, please be home!

My right boot hit the first step leading to building 1350's entrance, and my loins heated with high hopes of practicing a few Peter North techniques I learned in my school's Audio and Visual Center. But before I could do a mental walkthrough of my porn star moves, someone yelled my name.

"Yooo Manzo!" The voice was somewhat recognizable, but I faked like I didn't hear it.

"Yooo Manzo, stop fronting! You hear me nigga!" the voice called again as my left foot dangled over the second step.

"Turn around!" The voice clearly came from across the street. "Look up, it's me *cuzzo!*"

Salt?

Oh shit! Salt!

Promptly turning around, I knew the exact location of my cousin Richard Salters, also known as *Salt* on the basketball courts. He lived at 1385 Fifth Avenue in the Taft Houses, which faced Tanisha's building.

Unlike most NYC projects, each floor in Taft had a gated terrace that the tenants could use for relaxing, enjoying the view, and smoking cigarettes.

But with privilege came abuse, and the terraces doubled as a place for kids to get their first blow jobs, smoke some bud, and to sip on some liquor. Some people even smoked crack, and shot heroin.

"Oh shit! What's up cuzzo?" I yelled.

"What's up Manzo? Come up for a second!" Salt demanded. He was light skinned, so I could easily make out his face as all ten fingers grasped the gate.

"The homies want to say what up! Tanisha ain't going nowhere cuzzo!"

The terraces were unlit except for the Fifth Avenue lights, making it impossible to see anyone sitting behind him.

I didn't see any homies, but I missed Salt and didn't care who was with him. I had to see the guy I loved like a brother and called my cousin—but had no official blood relation. Either way, Salt was my family.

Racing across the street, I beat the oncoming traffic and fought the stinging wind, which forcibly drove me in the opposite direction the closer I got to the building's entrance.

Exasperated from running up the steps, I reached the fifth floor and tiptoed over a puddle of urine that blocked access into the hall's entryway.

Once I crossed the booby trap and progressed into the hallway, I felt a gust of wind from the open terrace door.

Through the terrace's large bulletproof glass windows, I could see Salt smiling and gesturing for me to enter.

He wore a red Pelle Pelle leather jacket with a black hoodie underneath that covered his head, but the black do-rag was still visibly tied around his forehead.

He'd always been slim from playing basketball, but his cheeks seemed fuller than they were last summer. All that arroz con pollo was finally catching up to him.

Only eighteen years old, Salt looked older like most dudes from Harlem. We loved our beards.

A pretty boy at heart, he tried to downplay his Puerto Rican hair and hazel eyes by wearing oversized clothing and boots like the *Morenos*.

Although half Black and couldn't speak a lick of Spanish, Salt couldn't hide that cookie dough complexion he and his sister, Kimberly, inherited from their mom, Aunt Iris. Like my pops, Salt's father, Big Richard was brown skinned.

Before stepping into the terrace, I could hear murmuring, but I still couldn't see his company. I wasn't worried, but subconsciously my defenses were up until I knew whom I was coming to see.

Primo or no *primo*, the fact remained that any projects other than Wagner was enemy territory. Regardless if I were a schoolboy or not, the rules of being Black in Harlem didn't change for me.

"What's up cuzzo?"

"What's up Salt?" I entered the terrace and greeted him with dap and a hug. "Damn, it's cold as fuck out here!"

"You've been in Virginia too long nigga!" A deep bellowing voice glided through harsh winds into my right ear.

"Oooh shit, that's you Jim?"

Three indiscernible individuals sat in beach chairs against the wall, but even through the murkiness I singled out the lightest guy with the cornrows.

He stood up, and his bowlegged stance confirmed his identity, just as his scruffy face peered into the fluorescence of the hallway.

"Who else would it be nigga? I live on this floor," Jim said.

"My nigga! What up?!" I dropped my bag, we slapped five and embraced as a crude marijuana smell reeked from his sky-blue Pelle Pelle leather jacket. He always loved to get high.

"Shit, just chilling. What's up with you rock star?"

The other beach chairs squeaked, and I hesitated to respond after seeing two dark silhouettes progressing into the light, one after the other. Salt and Jim knew the entire Harlem, so I didn't have any inkling who was with them.

"Yo we would've beat y'all ass in the District Four championship if I'd been there!"

"Manzo don't you still owe me twenty dollars from that dice game in the back of Riverside Church?"

Cam!

Only dude I still owe is Mase!

"Oooh shit, what's up my niggas?" I repeated the greeting ritual with Cam and Mase, immediately noticing their identical fragrances.

"Y'all dudes smell like Cool Water and hippies!" I said.

"Daaaammmnn nigga, look how diesel you got!" Cam playfully punched me in the chest.

"I know riiigght, this nigga been eatin' da weights," Mase said with a slow drawl.

At five feet, nine inches, Mase stood three inches shorter than Cam, but both couldn't grow beards, so they appeared to be younger than Salt and Jim.

Mase wore a fitted Yankee cap over his waves, and Cam always kept his hair even all around and almost bald, a fresh *Caesar* haircut.

Pelle Pelle must've had a sale or were paying these dudes, because Cam donned a black leather jacket with *Pelle Pelle* written on the back, while Mase wore the same one, except he preferred green.

My coat didn't fit in with the quartet. I was different.

"Manzo you looking like a big fucking Geronimo right now in that coat B!" Cam clowned as Mase and Jim sat back down.

"Fuck you! Nothing has changed, huh?" I laughed and raised my arms to inspect my tassels.

"You look like you about to jump off the roof and fly away like a black crow dipped in honey mustard!" Salt laughed hysterically. Cam sat in his chair.

"Nigga, all crows are black—dumbass!" Jim corrected Salt and the laughing persisted.

"Oh yea, shut up! I'm high B!" Salt defended himself.

"Yooo Manzo...where the fuck did your mustache go B?"" Cam asked.

"Man shut up, they make us shave the shit off at school!" I said.

"This nigga Manzo got the *dick face* like he a motherfucking sportscaster now!" Jim joked, and we all laughed.

"Ha, ha, ha—man fuck your bow-legged-ass! It will grow back!" I said.

I hate Woodberry's shaving fucking rules!"

"But yo Manzo, I ain't see you since we all played ball with Derm." Mase doubled over in his chair, reached under it, and pulled out a few plastic cups that crowned a half-empty liter bottle of Hennessy.

"You too brolic to still be nice at ball B,"

"I'm aight Mase, but nowhere near as good as when we all played for the Church." I watched as Mase poured Hennessy into a cup and passed the cup to Cam. *"Football* is my shit now."

"Manzo be killing them White boys down South!" Salt smacked both his hands on my shoulders. "This big nigga gonna get a football scholarship to Penn State or some shit."

"Word B?" Jim asked before Mase handed him a cup of liquor.

"Hell yea B!" Salt said.

"I know you be fucking all those White bitches down there!" Cam shouted.

"Nah B—I don't because I go to an all-boys school," I said.

"What the fuck?" Jim almost dropped his drink.

"Nigga you lyin'." Mase half-raised out of his seat, passing another cup to Salt's outstretched hand.

"What? No *pussy* B?" Cam asked.

"This nigga backed-up like a motherfucker then." Jim frowned.

"Nigga I'm still alive! Jim is all in mourning and shit!" I said.

"Damn, I know your big-ass about to pound Tanisha into submission!" Salt pounded his free hand on the gate. They all laughed.

Oh shit, Tanisha!

Panic interrupted the happy reunion as the echoes of enjoyment faded. My senses, partial to sight rather than sound, thwarted my homies' giddiness and centralized on the resplendence of Tanisha's building .

Both hands on the gate, I looked up in search of her window. My eyes had not adjusted to the obscurity of the terrace, but love had a way of making a man see whatever he wanted.

There it goes!

"Manzo?"

Fucking light is still off!

"Manzo?" Salt called again.

"Yo what up?" I turned, and Salt was holding a cup of Henny in my face.

"Damn, you spaced the fuck out cuzzo."

"Oh-yea, my bad—"

"One mention of that girl name, and he start looking for that pussy like a fucking hound dog B!" Cam wisecracked. "That shit must be goooood!"

"That nigga went straight reee-tard!" Mase joined in on the roasting as everyone laughed.

"Y'all are silly B!" I joined the fun but kept peeping at Tanisha's window.

"Nigga would you stop stalking your girl and take this drink before my hand falls off? You gonna get the pussy—*chill*." Salt stared at me. "Relax cuzzo."

"Nigga take the drink and warm up!" Jim yelled. "I know you gotta be cold in that Pocahontas costume!"

"Ha-ha! Oooh shit! He said Poca-hontes."

"Shut up Mase! Give me that shit cuzzo!" I snatched the Henny from Salt's hand.

"OK, I knew my cuzzo had some balls!"

"What are we toasting to?" I asked.

"Whatever you want Manzo. You're the guest of honor," Jim said.

"Whatever I want?"

"Of course—whatever B," Cam answered.

"OK cool," I said, still undecided about what to say.

"Uuuh, here's to White girls and cocaine!" I raised my cup.

"Oh *hell* nooo!" Mase griped.

"This nigga trippin'!" Cam yelled.

"Maaan, you can't be serious—what the fuck wrong with your cousin, Salt?" Jim asked.

"I don't know Jim! He's been hangin' with those White boys too much!"

"Fuck you Salt!" I shouted.

"Maaan, let me make a toast," Mase volunteered.

"Fuck no! Lil' niggas be getting on the school bus by the time your slow-talk-ing-ass finally finished!" Cam joked, and we all burst out laughing.

Let me toast so I can hurry up and see Tanisha.

"OK, I would like to toast to Harlem, and may we all be a success at whatever we do." I raised my cup, and the laughing stopped. A moment's silence firmly established the approval of my first toast.

"Word…" Cam nodded.

"Word…" Jim rubbed his chin.

"Word…" Mase smiled.

"I like that shit cuzzo. Salud." Salt initiated the tapping of the cups, and we all drank to our destinies.

The cognac, smooth with a subtle sweetness, washed away another slice of purity. My belly thawed, and a pond of fortitude soaked my fears. I yearned for another drink. I felt invulnerable.

"Somebody pour me another one." I waved my cup.

"See, this nigga still Black! He like that Henny!" Jim covered his mouth and pointed at me.

"Ha, ha, ha! Fuck you Jim! The shit is good though!" I said.

"Manzo still a nigga—ha, ha!" Mase put a fist in the air. "He's back y'all!"

Suddenly, I looked at my right fist and thoughts of decking my mother's boyfriend earlier rushed my mind.

To my astonishment, I didn't feel a bit of remorse or regret. I felt like I was finally becoming a man, and men fucked shit up from time to time.

"Leave my cuzzo alone. Y'all know he don't be drinking and smoking in VA," Salt said.

Smoking?

"Where's *that* shit at anyway Salt?" Cam asked.

What shit?

"It's under your seat B," Salt replied.

"Stop playing and light it then," Jim urged.

Light what?

"Yea B. Light that chocolate!" Mase added.

What the fuck is chocolate?

"OK cuzzo! We gonna get you high B!" Salt said.

High?

"Yo Manzo…you never got high before B?" Cam grilled as a hush fell over my friends.

High?

Tell the truth.

Don't tell the truth.

Tell the truth!

"Well?" Jim asked.

Fuck, they gonna think I'm lame!

Tell the truth!

"Come on guys! Seriously?"

"*Come on guys!* Yup Manzo's White again." Cam did his stereotypical White man's voice while reaching under his beach chair.

"Fuck all y'all!" I didn't appreciate the mocking. "Y'all niggas *is* stupid!"

"Ha-ha—chill the fuck out cuzzo! We just messing with you!"

"I know y'all giving me shit...but pass that *chocolate!* You know the White boys keep me high!" I lied.

Fuck, why did I say that?

"Hell yea! I knew Manzo still kept it *real!*" Jim yelled.

Kept it real?

"Light that shit Cam." Mase rubbed his hands together.

"We about to get twisted cuzzo," Salt said.

Twisted?

"Yessir," Cam agreed.

No sir!

FLICK.

The terrace reddened as Cam connected the lighter's flame against the marijuana blunt dangling from his lips.

A box cutter and two White Owl cigars resting on an open spiral notebook with "Horse and Carriage" boldly written atop the scribbled page—briefly averted my attention from the pungency of my rolled-up digression.

The spark dissolved, and a crisp current permeated the terrace with a scent of chocolate-coated skunks burning in hell.

The smell, disturbing yet delicious, spiced the back of my throat, and I intuitively smacked my lips together.

Damn that smells so—

I can't smoke weed though!

"That's that chuuh-colate right there Manzo."

"No shit Mase, I smoke that shit all the time."

What am I doing?

Why am I lying?

"Pass that shit B!" Salt demanded.

"I know *Puffy* Combs!" Jim said.

"I just got this shit B!" Cam took more giant hits.

"Yoooo, you're steaming B! Puff, puff, pass!" Salt reminded Cam of the universal etiquette for weed sharing. I was clueless.

"*SWUUH...SWUUUH...*OK...damn...here Salt." Cam extended the blunt as Salt approached. "You terrible B."

"Yo...how you pass to Salt, and I'm right next to you?" Mase asked.

"Yea y'all fucking up the whole rotation," Jim said.

"This don't really count as my go...*SWUUUH*...I only got the blunt to pass to Manzo before he goes to see Tanisha. Looks like she's in her room now cuzzo." Salt pointed up through the smoke.

"Oh shit, that's a shadow moving! You right cuzzo!" I said.

"Yooo...hold the fuck up Salt!" Jim said. "How the fuck you know where this nigga girl's window is at?"

"Yea Salt, how your ass know that?" Mase interrogated.

"Fuck y'all niggas B!" Salt laughed.

"That's what I was thinking too!" Cam attempted to identify the window. "I don't even know who his girl is, and this peeping-Tom-ass-nigga knows the motherfucking window! Watch that creep Manzo!"

"Ha, ha, ha!" we all laughed.

Fanning the smoke out of my face, I returned my attention to Tanisha's window, and a shadow bounced from wall to ceiling and back to the wall. My manhood seemed to followed suit.

Just the thought of being in that warm room, in that hot box, hit a spot that the Henny had missed. I *had* to go. I needed to taste some *real* chocolate!

"Ha, ha, ha—man it was good seeing y'all—"

"Whoa, whoa cuzzo—hold up!" Salt blocked me from picking up my bag. "Chill and take a puff B! She ain't going nowhere!"

"Nah cuzzo. I got to go—"

"Just one puff cuzzo! Damn, let me find out you on some Bryant Gumble shit!"

"Ha, ha, ha!" Mase and Jim laughed while Cam still looked for Tanisha's window. *Leave now!*

"I gotta go B!" I said.

"OK, OK—my bad! *Listen*...just take a couple of pulls and chill with your niggas for a few minutes," Salt spoke with steam searing from his mouth and nostrils. The second-hand smoke clouded my thoughts.

"Come on cuzzo, we ain't see your ass in minute. Plus, that Henny *with* this chocolate will help you beat the pussy straight up."

"Yooo, I put the smack down on my bitch eeerr night Manzo," Mase added.

"No shit cuzzo—Mase is right." Salt winked a bloodshot eye.

"Beat the pussy up?" I asked.

"Yes cuzzo! Beat that shit like Mike fucking Tyson!"

"Damn, like *Iron Mike*?" I asked.

"First round knockout guaranteed. Straight out the fucking ring." Salt trapped the smoke in his lungs while he talked, and then held the blunt inches away from my cheek before continuing his pep.

"Go rock that shit, *rock star*. Show her that pussy belongs to you."

* * *

All my life I watched the *cool* kids in my projects smoke weed, and I vowed to never participate or indulge in the use of marijuana or any type of drugs, because I had no interest. I got my fix off of sacking quarterbacks and slam dunking basketballs. I was different.

I had to admit though, unlike the crack and heroin addicts, the weed smokers always seemed to fly high with a carefree disposition that provided harmless entertainment.

They laughed and told the funniest jokes while giving the deepest insight on shit they never even experienced. The potheads covered everything from Broadway plays to bocce ball.

Marijuana users weren't considered "lowlifes" and parents seldom told their children to stay away from the dudes preaching the ghetto gospel and eating barbecue potato chips.

On the project benches, there would often be at least one person smoking a joint within an arm's length of a child in a stroller, while the older children played and ignored the stench of the *special* cigarettes.

My father smoked weed in the privacy of his cars, or in his other apartments with his other women. But just like the smell of new pussy, sweet smoke spewed from his breath.

The mystery of his weed habit was solved much faster than identifying the whores feeding him all those vagina mints. Daddy drove his bitches right back home—but he left marijuana roaches everywhere.

Most schools educated their students on smoking bud and deemed the *drug* —super bad, but other than having the munchies, I couldn't figure out the negative connotations behind puffing on a plant that grew naturally from the earth.

Weed didn't break up families, and I never heard of anyone selling ass or giving oral pleasure *just* for a marijuana high—so taking a toke or two had to be terrific.

Plus, I lasted a solid ninety-seven seconds the last time Tanisha and I had sexual intercourse, and I needed to redeem myself.

Like a girl who could only put a dollar worth of fuel in an empty gas tank, Tanisha was frustrated with the quick pumps.

One night, I thought she would only feed me lettuce and carrots for dinner, because Tanisha even had the nerve to call me Roger Rabbit during an argument. The term was "a *big-ass* Roger Rabbit," to be exact.

* * *

"I ain't no rabbit, and I definitely ain't no Bryant-Gumble-ass-nigga B!" I snatched the blunt from Salt, shut my eyes...and the gateway opened.

My fresh lungs ingested the smoke, which seemed to drift down to my toes. I held my breath and an increased warmth encased my heart, generating sweat from every pore.

Smoke drifted from my nostrils, and insignificantly extinguished the bonfire smoldering inside my chest.

Opening my eyes, I tasted Hershey's Kisses, and a candy-coated-smog asphyxiated my depth perception. I felt woozy, my eyes watered, and my body craved oxygen.

Don't cough!

"COUGH! COUGH!"

"That big nigga took two *big*-ass pulls!" Jim laughed.

Still gasping for air, I was bent over with saliva running out my mouth.

"Aaaahhh, that nigga got the rabies!" Mase hollered and the fellas laughed madly.

"Fuck all y'all!" I pointed the blunt in the air. "Somebody take this shit!"

"Yea let me get that off ya! How you feel cuzzo?" Salt asked.

"Motherfucker...I feel like I'm dying!"

"Ha-ha—I remember my first time! You can't fool me nigga! Just breathe, you will be fine B," Cam said.

"Yeah cuzzo...breathe," Salt added.

Ears tingling, I stood tall and welcomed the uncertainty of my transgression.

A cool breeze swung a string of saliva from my mouth to my chin, and I sponged the spit with my right palm.

I shut my mouth and inhaled the Harlem night with hopes of cleansing my spirit, and exhaling the impurities wriggling in my brain. But as the oxygen bobbed from my upper lip to my nostrils and back, my sense of time and space depleted.

I felt like a child's last bubble floating in the sky, and my homies were watching, waiting for me to burst.

I was not a child though, and I was not a bubble, but I was surely floating. For the first time in my life—I was high.

"You OK cuzzo?"

Ignoring Salt's concerns, I closed my eyes and continued breathing steadily. I turned around and clawed the terrace gate with both hands.

I opened my eyes and suddenly Fifth Avenue looked unfamiliar. It looked magnificent!

"Y'all ever notice how the lights dance off the stars, to the buildings, to the cars—"

"Maaan—get the fuck outta here with that bullshit!" Jim yelled.

"This nigga bugging!" Cam couldn't stop laughing.

"I'm glad that gate is there B."

"Word Mase! Don't let him hit that shit no more Salt!" Cam pleaded.

"No seriously y'all, look at how the light just gleams off the sky to the street, and then back up top to the—"

Oh shit, her lights are off again!

Tanisha's blacked out window curtailed my appreciation for the ghetto's aurora. Oddly, I no longer distressed about her whereabouts or even if her grandfather would answer the door.

"To the *what* B?" Cam asked.

"To the what?" I turned and faced him, never letting go of the gate.

"Manzo, you just said the lights *gleamed*. Oh fuck it—this nigga is dumb high," Cam dismissed my commentary.

"Ha-ha, shut up Cam!" I quickly looked for something to joke on him about, only noticing his notebook again.

"Why you got a notebook? What are you in *special ed* or something B?"

"My man you've been gone waaay too long, I see." Cam picked up the notebook and placed it on his lap. "I ain't in no goddamn school—these are my raps B. I spit that fire Manzo."

"Word? You rap?" I asked.

"Word cuzzo! They all spit, and they dumb nice! Cam and Mase group is called Children of the Corn. Bloodshed is rappin' too—"

"Ooooh shit! There go that Ack-Vigor I told y'all about!" Cam shouted.

"That shit fi-yaah B!" Mase veered forward in his chair.

"Damn that shit is mean!" Salt added.

An all-black 1995 Acura Vigor with BBS rims and tinted windows coasted down Fifth Avenue and stopped directly in front of 1350.

The car looked to have been coated in melted licorice, freeze dried, and wiped down with baby oil. The paint job was immaculate!

A few kids walking by tapped each other and pointed as they goose-necked to see the driver through the smoked-out windows.

The mystery baller increased the car's volume, and Biggie Small's "One more chance" boomed. The nosey kids backed away.

"That sound system is crazy! Cam, who the hell is that?" Salt inquired.

"That's some Spanish cat from the Bronx. He's getting that dope money." Cam said, tapping the box cutter on his notebook. "When you're pushin' that heroin—you in a different fucking league B."

"Word, that's stupid bread." Jim stretched his arms.

"Maaan, niggas getting super paid fucking with that *her-ron*. That Sting Ray-Fuji dope from your block Manzo had niggas going bananas. Made that Purple City shit look like a welfare case.

"Lines was down the goddamn block! *And* you ain't fucking nothing but dime-pieces if you the man with that dope. Shit ain't even fair, blood."

"You ain't lying either Jim! Homeboy right there got some little baaaaad bitch he fuck wit in that building," Cam pointed to the Acura.

"Which one?" Salt asked. "I know every bad bitch in that building."

"I don't know the bitch name—I ain't from around here, but shorty got a *fat-ole-ass* and loves wearing red lipstick B."

"Damn, I bet she be sucking homie off, leaving his joint looking like one of those cherry pop-sickle sticks—ha, ha, ha!" Salt laughed, attempting to hold the smoke in his lungs.

"Word, I know what you mean. Tanisha wears red lipstick!"

"You a lucky dude then Manzo." Mase shook his head. "Yoooo Salt! Pass the motherfucking weed B!"

"Oh shit, my bad—here," Salt said.

Everything just seemed extra funny to me. The Hennessy and the weed mashed in my system. I felt incredible, without a care in the world.

My insides were scrambled, but my thoughts were lucid and honest. I enjoyed my time with my homies, but I needed to be with my future wife. I was also very hungry. My stomach kept growling.

"I gotta bounce and go see Tanisha, and I'm starving now."

"You got the munchies B," Jim said.

"I'm gonna munch on something else when I see my girl," I said.

"Y'all Puerto Rican niggas be eating ass and everything—yooo, there goes shorty right there!" Cam sat upright and pointed at the gate.

"*Her*?" Salt asked.

"*Her*?" Jim asked, even more surprised.

"Yea right there! Y'all motherfuckers blind or something?" Cam asked. "Y'all niggas don't see that bad bitch in the black walking towards the car?"

I quickly grabbed the gate with both hands and wedged my nose through an open hole.

I squinted my eyes and felt them thump with my crumbling heart.

Sweat dripped. Rage spouted. My soberness returned with murderous thoughts.

"Oooh shiiit!" Salt yelled.

"DIRTY BITCH!" Jim followed.

"I told y'all she was bad, right?" Cam asked.

"She's *thick*, and I know homie beating that fat-ass raw-dog B!" Mase stood up for a better view. "He prolly skeetin' all on her forehead and eer-thang!"

Nooooo!

To my overwhelming astonishment, Tanisha casually cat-walked down the stairs of her building, smiling hard, elongating her cheek muscles to the limit.

Gold dolphin earrings swam through her straight and shiny black hair, which shimmered down the side of her caramel face and ended atop the black mink jacket I bought for her.

I had saved five months of my father's *allowance* to purchase the bloodless varmints covering the heartless bitch.

This can't be happening!

Black denim stretched between her thick thighs and down her legs into a calf-high leather boot with two interfacing gold letter G's on the side of them.

Tanisha loved Gucci, so I had bought those boots for her on Valentine's Day with the money my father had given me for the straight A's on my report card.

I'm gonna kill that nigga!

My derangement heightened with the sight of her red lips singing along to *our* song, which had suddenly gotten louder.

The driver must've opened his passenger side window, because Tanisha stopped a few feet away from the car, put one hand on her hip and twirled around.

"Fuck that bitch cuzzo! You will find better!" Salt consoled.

"DIRTY, STINKING, BITCH!" Jim hollered.

"Oooh shit—that's *your* girl Manzo?" Cam asked.

A tear dropped, and I watched my future wife open the Acura's door.

Fuck this!

"Relax cuzzo!" Salt yelled.

"Fuck this!" I finally spoke as my grip strangled the gate.

"Relax Manzo...it's just a bitch!" Mase preached.

"Fuck that! I would go kill that nigga if I was…" Cam said, but before he could finish his thought, I had snatched the box cutter from his notebook and ran out of the terrace doorway and down the stairs.

I'm gonna slice his fucking head off!

BOOM!

Kicking the building's front door open, I spotted the Acura just as the car got in motion—immediately sprinting after the love machine!

Four steps into my stride, both Timberlands slipped off my feet—but I kept running!

"STOP!" I screamed. "STOP—YOU MOTHERFUCKERS!"

My tassels flapped in the air as I hotfooted in pursuit of *my* girlfriend, *my* best friend, *my* everything.

For a guy my size, I had out of this world speed, but launching into the unidentified driving object's sphere was impossible.

Fueled by extreme hate, I still kept running—because my soul would have hurt too much if I stopped.

"COME BACK! COME BACK!" I howled, watching the Acura make a right at 112th Street onto Lenox Avenue. "COME BACK! PLEASE! COME BACK!"

My legs pumped with hope, but there would be no miracle for me. Tanisha had vanished with a chunk of my heart that would never return.

Looking down at my two bloody socks, I knew I had to stop. I knew the chase was over. I let the pain run its course.

"COME BACK!"

"I LOVE YOU!"

I gasped and finding air for my strained lungs was a ragged torture.

No! No! God No!

Dropping to my knees, I stared at the box cutter in my hand and watched the blood run down my wrist and get absorbed by my sleeve. The blade had opened during the chase and cut deep into my palm, but it was my heart that needed the stitches.

I whimpered and before punching the pavement, I noticed the name on the Acura's personalized New Jersey license plate.

RANDY-1.

Chapter Eleven

PAINFUL DECISION

Standing on the tarmac of Charlottesville-Albemarle Airport, I looked up in deep confusion at the all-white G5 with *VT* written on the tail. Planes buzzed over my thoughts as the hissing of the jet's engine blared.

I looked back at Mr. Collins behind the steering wheel of his truck, only parked twenty feet away from the private jet, and I could see him smiling. He waved for me to keep walking.

Still in disbelief, I clutched the straps of my backpack tightly, turned around and advanced toward my twenty-million-dollar taxi.

The cloudy skies briefly opened, and the sun flashed through a mountain, across my face. A light breeze fluttered the smell of wet cement and jet fuel across the valley.

A Delta airliner landed in the distance, and its tires screeched a safe return. I pictured all the people clapping. Suddenly I felt special, yet vastly overwhelmed.

The airplane's door opened, and a row of metal steps unfolded onto the pavement. Stopping in my place, I observed the black hole and awaited the birth of my escort.

Uninformed of who was chaperoning me back to Blacksburg, I didn't know whether to expect Coach Frank Beamer or the Hokie bird mascot himself to stick his head out of the hatch, and I didn't care. I just wanted to fly.

Wait, where's the security and metal detectors? Do I just get straight on the plane?

"There goes that physical specimen!" a voice from within the plane yelled, a split second before a G.I. Joe advanced onto the leading step.

"The beast who only needs one name! Damn son, you are more jacked in person! Oh man, Bud Foster is gonna love your ass—you gonna fit nicely in our Up-G defense!"

Who's Bud Foster?

And what the hell is an 'Up-G'?

The cleanly shaven White guy with the spiked, dirty-blond flattop, and electric tiny blue eyes trotted down the steps. He tapped me on my right shoulder playfully and smiled like we were old pals.

I smiled back at my new friend with the youthful energy and demeanor of a player, and the crow's feet of a coach.

"It's a pleasure to finally meet you Manzo. I'm Coach Brent Pry." Coach Pry stretched out his right hand and I grabbed it.

"It's a pleasure to meet you sir."

"Shit, don't *sir* me, I'm not that old! I'm just a graduate assistant!" he said, with the firmness of his handshake matching the lean muscular build underneath his maroon Virginia Tech tracksuit. Coach Pry stood a couple of inches shorter than I.

"Graduate assistant?"

"Oh I will explain everything on the way to Tech!" Coach Pry said and then leaned forward and whispered. "Now say goodbye to Kevin Costner over there and let's get the fuck outta here!"

Turning around I bit my bottom lip in order not to laugh. Coach Pry and I simultaneously grinned and waved at Mr. Collins who was already backing his truck out of the gate.

I wasn't the least bit surprised Mr. Collins didn't get out and introduce himself—he wasn't ever one for the phony pleasantries.

"OK don't go getting all sad on me Manzo," Coach Pry stated after noticing my change of expression. "Trust me, you are headed to paradise. Follow me brother!"

As Coach Pry ran up the steps and entered the jet, I watched the back of Mr. Collins' truck blast dust down the service road.

Year after year, I told myself that I couldn't wait to get the hell out of Woodberry. Standing there and observing the man, who for the past three years was more of a father to me than my own—I realized how much love I had for my school and my advisor. I felt conflicted.

"Manzo let's go big fella!" Coach Pry ordered.

"Yes sir!" I yelled as I high kneed up the steps and entered the jet.

"Good-God son—those videos don't do your big-ass any justice!" hollered an animated fellow wearing an identical VT tracksuit and a white VT cap covering inch-long graying hair.

Red faced, the man was my height with a skinny frame, a potbelly, and spoke with one of those raspy *guy's guy* voices.

"Uuh...thank you, sir," I said.

"I mean, what the hell are they feeding you at Woodberry? Lil' White boys?"

"No sir, ha-ha!"

"You look like you're from Texas or some shit, not New York City!"

"Ha-ha, no sir. I'm def not from Texas."

"Coach Gentry is gonna love you son."

"Uuuuh...who's—"

"Shit, don't worry about that right now." The man smiled and caught me eyeballing the gap between his top two front teeth.

"Well I'm Coach Rickey Bustle, the Virginia Tech offensive coordinator and quarterback coach...and you can buy me some braces once you go pro."

"Uuuum..." I put my head down.

"Chill out son! I'm just fucking with ya!" Coach Bustle laughed and patted me on the shoulder. I raised my head and our eyes engaged.

"It's truly a pleasure to finally meet you Manzo."

"Thank you, sir. And it's a pleasure to meet you." We shook hands.

This guy is a caring asshole...my kind of coach.

"Well hell, come put your backpack down and have a seat and buckle up. We're leaving as soon as Coach Pry finishes taking a shit."

"I heard that!" Coach Pry yelled, closing his cell phone as he opened the rest room door located at the far end of the jet.

"I'm just kidding Manzo." Coach Bustle moved to the side and directed me toward one of eight open seats. "He's just letting Coach Beamer know you made it on the jet. Beamer is excited to meet you too."

"Uh...OK...thanks," I stammered.

"I take it you never flown in a PJ before." Coach Pry banked in the seat closest to the exit.

"PJ?" I asked and looked down at my Woodberry Forest sweat suit. Both coaches chuckled and looked at each other.

"Well I guess we have our answer!" Coach Bustle put his hand back on my shoulder. "PJ stands for personal jet, not pajamas. And today it's *your* personal jet. Sit down and relax son. You're the king today!"

"Yes sir." I placed my backpack onto my seat.

My muscles deepened in the supple leather seat cushions, while my neon-green Nike Air Max '95s slid forward against the slickness of the plush carpet.

The jet's entire interior was maroon, aside from an orange wood trim which ran above six sets of adjacent windows until reaching the exit door.

The eight seats were split into two sections of four, with each seat facing another with a pullout table in between them.

The table in front of me had a steak, a baked potato, sautéed onions, and some green beans which all smelled divine although trapped inside a steamed plastic-container.

Damn, all this just for my Black ass?

An open curtain exposed the closed cockpit door, and I could hear a woman's laughter sparingly.

Just the sound of a female's voice made my heart putter, and it finally began to sink in just where we were headed. Nervous, I fidgeted in my seat looking for a seatbelt.

I'm going to visit a college with mad girls!

"Are you hungry Manzo?" Coach Pry asked, as he and Coach Bustle sat down facing each other in the two seats across the aisle from me.

"No sir. I ate McDonald's on the way here."

"You damn young boys can eat whatever y'all want." Coach Bustle shook his head. "My fat-ass even looks at a Big Mac and I will gain weight."

"Well if you get hungry, that-there steak is for you." Coach Pry nodded toward the food.

"Thank you, Coach." I turned to my left to Coach Pry.

"Damn these seats are comfy. I just might fall asleep." Coach Bustle buckled his seatbelt. "I know you young boys need your rest too, so once we get going please feel free to rest."

"Thank you, Captain." A svelte White woman with shoulder length blonde hair, dressed in a blue miniskirt and a white short-sleeved blouse emerged from the cockpit, shutting the door behind her.

That's the stewardess?

"Hey guys. Y'all ready to go?" she asked as she pulled the hatch closed and locked it, hitting it twice to make sure it was closed securely.

"Yes ma'am. We sure are Susan," Coach Pry said with a half-cocked smile. He was in love or caught a stroke.

"Yes ma'am," Coach Bustle and I spoke simultaneously.

Damn, she's kinda hot for a White woman.

"And who is this big fella we have with us today?" she asked, walking in my direction.

Susan's fleshy red lips set fire to tanned skin, only cooled by icy-blue eyes.

The freckles on her face scattered perfectly, and my eyes did not know where to focus its admiration.

She couldn't have been a year over thirty, and my filthy young mind suddenly thirsted for the dirty old woman with the northern accent.

"Oh that's Manzo—next year's *starting* middle linebacker for the Hokies." Coach Bustle winked at me. "Ain't that right son?"

"Uuuh...yes sir, coach."

"Well, that's good to hear. Hold up one moment Manzo." Susan bent over and rubbed her thumb over the fresh scar on my right upper forehead, just under my hairline. "Looks like someone had an accident."

"Uuum...I hit my head playing basketball—I fell."

"Baby, you have to be more careful," she said.

As Susan played doctor, I peeped down the top of her unbuttoned blouse and happily choked on her Estée Lauder perfume.

A tiny gold crucifix trampolined off freckled silicone breasts, and I felt zero guilt. Jesus could've been Mickey Mouse, because I wasn't going to stop being a young pervert.

"Make sure you put something on that knot when you get back to Tech," Susan demanded over the jet's thundering engines.

Ha-ha...which knot?

The jet had begun to move.

"Yes ma'am. Thank you very much," I said.

"OK boys, we are taking off—so if you need anything just buzz me in the cockpit." She patted me on top of my head, walked away and entered the cockpit, closing the door behind her.

"Earth to Manzo!" Coach Bustle waved both hands over his head.

"Sorry Coach, I—"

"Ha, no need to explain. We understand. *Boy* do we understand!" Coach Pry put his right hand over his heart.

"Maaan, I can tell you gonna have a great time this weekend."

"Ha, I'm sure I will Coach Bustle."

"Manzo, what other schools do you plan on visiting before making your decision?" Coach Pry asked but aimed his question at Coach Bustle before focusing on me.

"Uh...uh, well sir...I *was* scheduled to visit Penn State next week, but that Coach Sandusky guy they got recruiting me kinda creeps me out—soooo it might just be Miami, Maryland, and..." I hesitated and looked to my right, unknowingly, we were already in the sky.

Damn, I gotta tell them.

"Uh, U-V...A sir." I continued to watch the clouds whisk by the Blue Ridge Mountains.

"Well you always have to trust your gut son—but those are some fantastic schools, and any one of them would be lucky to have you." Coach Bustle's approval eased my mind.

"Of course, we wouldn't want you playing for those sissies in Charlottesville, but that's another story!" Coach Pry joked. I turned to face them, and we all laughed.

"We're just joking, but we're serious. You got way too many damn tattoos for Thomas Jefferson's school," Coach Pry added.

Shit, Woodberry didn't approve of my tats either.

"How's your family life Manzo?" Coach Bustle asked.

Dysfunctional and totally fucked sir.

"It's wonderful sir. Everyone is happy and proud of me." I smiled.

"And ya dad?" Coach Pry asked.

He's a drug-dealing womanizer.

"Oh, he's a hard-working construction worker who has taught me so many valuable lessons. I'm very grateful for him."

"Oh that's great! I used to do construction back in the day." Coach Bustle smiled and tapped Coach Pry with his foot. "What type of construction does he do son?"

"Uh...he deals with bricks."

"There's a lot of money in laying bricks." Coach Bustle nodded.

Fucking right there is.

"So...let me ask you a very serious question Manzo." Coach Bustle sat up in his chair. "And I want you to be perfectly honest with me son."

"Uh...of course...yes sir."

"And however you answer, by no way will impact our decision to have you attend Virginia Tech...but we have to know the *complete* truth son." Coach Bustle rested both arms on the left armrest and leaned forward. He didn't blink.

Fuck, I know it's about Daddy!

How did they find out about my father? I can't tell them the truth.

I must tell them the truth. Will Daddy get in trouble?

"Uh...OK sir." My right leg had begun to jump spastically, so I crossed my legs. The steak's aroma curled my stomach.

What do I tell this White man?

Daddy will be so mad!

"I just would like to know, in all honesty..." Coach Bustle continued.

Fuck! No school is going to want me!

"I mean, me and Coach Pry can't figure out for the life of us..."

Be honest.

"Well...what I'm trying to ask is..." Coach Bustle covered his face with his hand, took a deep breath, and faced Coach Pry before looking back at me. "What in Heaven's name do you boarding school kids do for pussy?"

"Ha, ha, ha!" Coach Pry stomped his feet.

"Ha, ha, ha!" I laughed in relief. "You got me good Coach Bustle!"

"No seriously! What in the hell son?" Coach Bustle reached underneath his seat and grabbed a white deflated pillow, and a blue wool blanket. "My high school days were a *lit-tle bit* different."

"No wonder your damn grip was so tight!" Coach Pry joked.

"We have to make do some way. It's tough though," I said.

"Ain't that the truth. But listen, we have about thirty minutes left in the flight, so I want you to rest up because you have a long weekend ahead, starting with meeting Coach Beamer at Lane Stadium as soon as we get to campus." Coach Pry put his pillow behind his head and shifted toward his window.

"OK one more question and I will leave you alone," Coach Bustle said. "Well do you at least have a girlfriend back home son?"

"Well, it's complicated sir." I reclined my seat.

"When dealing with women, it always is, and it always will be son." Coach Bustle closed his eyes. "Get some rest big fella."

Pulling down the window shade, I flip-flopped in my seat and shut my eyes with hopes of sleep, but I was dreaming.

Coach Bustle conjured up images of the one person that I had thought I fooled myself of not having brought along with my baggage.

My final conversation with Tanisha replayed, and I couldn't press stop. The pain in my head was fresh, and the pain in my heart was forever. Fighting the memory was impossible.

* * *

"Listen Manzo, I never meant—"

"Don't you *listen Manzo* me, you fucking slut!" I screamed in Tanisha's face in the middle of Central Park.

"Manzo I'm sorry! It just happened! You were gone!" She cried through mascara stained cheeks while holding a twenty-four-ounce Mystic bottle.

"I was good to you!" I yelled.

"I knooow! I'm sorry, please forgive—"

"Forgive you?"

"Yes...please Manzo! I love you!"

"You *love* me?"

"Yes I love you so much! I made a mistake!" Tanisha placed her hand on my chest, and I quickly pushed her hand away.

"Don't you dare fucking touch me!"

"But it was a mistake—"

"*Mistake?*"

"Yes baby, it was a mistake! Oh God! Please...I swear on my life!"

"A mistake is going to the store and grabbing a head of fucking cabbage instead a head of lettuce!" I moved closer. My lips almost touching hers.

"A mistake isn't taking it in the ass constantly by some Spanish-ass-drug-dealer, God knows how many times!"

My slightly bent knees almost collapsed, and my stomach clenched as I almost vomited with the thought of Randy-1 slamming his cock into my girlfriend.

Drying the tears from my eyes with my palm, I looked down at the moving concrete and noticed two squirrels standing on their hind legs just a short distance away. Even those furry little bastards felt sorry for me—I was going nuts.

'*¡Toma lo mami!*'

'*¡Toma lo todo Tanisha!*'

"FUCK YOU!" my agony spat across her face. "Why didn't you just leave me?"

"I love you—that's why! I was just lonely! You were away at school and I was vulnerable, but I never stopped loving you! I just made a big mistake and got caught up, baby please listen! You have to believe me!" She hugged my neck. The Gucci perfume I bought her for her birthday challenged my integrity.

"Get the fuck off me you whore!" I shoved her away, and a middle-aged White couple by the pond quickly picked up their poodles and scampered in the opposite direction.

"It was a fucking mistake! I'm human!" Tanisha declared.

"*Human?*" I asked.

"Yes, I'm fucking human!"

"OK, if you're human and it was a mistake, then please tell me how many times you fucked this *Randy* asshole?" I stepped back and crossed my arms. "Please tell me Tanisha. Be honest for once."

"I dunno! I don't want to think about it—"

"No, answer me!" I stepped a couple of feet back.

"What's done is done Manzo—please stop!"

"How many times?" I asked again.

"Do you really want to know Manzo? This ain't gonna to make anything better baby!"

"If we will ever have a chance at getting back together, you have to just be honest with me and tell me everything baby," I spoke softly and advanced closer, took her beverage, drinking the last warm fruity sip.

"Come on baby, let's just move on please!" She clasped my hand and cried.

"Tanisha...let's just get this over with so we can move on baby." I pulled her closer to me and mildly kissed her wet lips. "This is me. Tell your man everything."

"OK, I'll tell you." She stopped crying, but I almost started, terrified of the words about to depart from those pretty red lips.

"Just relax baby," I consoled.

"OK, me and Randy probably had sex about...uh...about twenty times, I think." She watched a bird fly by and then put her head down. I wanted to be the bird.

How could she?

Be cool Manzo and keep her talking!

"OK, thank you for being honest baby." I swallowed and breathed deeply. "What else baby?"

"You sure you—"

"Yes baby, just continue. It's OK."

"And I gave him head a few times, and he ate me out every time," she said while facing the ground, her quivering hand had begun to sweat. "We never used condoms, but your sex is better than his!"

"It's OK baby. I believe you. Just keep talking."

Tanisha's voice was the score to a grotesque movie playing in my mind, and for some bizarre reason, not knowing how Randy looked, I kept visualizing the TV character "Ponch" on top of her.

I loved Erik Estrada in the show "C.H.I.P.S," but I was no less indignant about him fucking Tanisha as I would've been if I actual knew the identity of the real Randy.

¡Toma lo, mami!' 'Take it, mommy!'

My blood stewed, and I wanted to run. I wanted to disappear and transport to a universe where pain and heartache were just words, and love and trust were not just fiction.

When a partner has been unfaithful, all the magical times spent with the traitor disintegrated to dust against the mountain of betrayal, better yet—twenty betrayals and a handful of blowjobs.

There was nowhere to go and concentrating on the pleasurable parts of our relationship was pointless. I could never take her back. Tanisha killed our past and sucked away our future.

No longer constricting my tears, I allowed them to run freely, and when she looked me in my eyes, I awaited the final incision.

"*And...*" Tanisha looked down at her yellow North Face jacket and palmed her belly. "I'm pregnant."

Pregnant?

Unable to move or to speak, I watched *my* girlfriend steadily rub her baby bump as she cried, and I smiled impulsively.

Another man's seed called the inside of Tanisha's womb home, and I was permanently being evicted.

Lost between reality and insanity, I sobbed internally while tapping the Mystic bottle against my thigh.

"I'm so sorry Manzo! Please say something baby!"

Gritting my teeth, I tapped the glass bottle against my thigh faster and harder. The demons within my soul wanted blood.

Tormented, I hungered for violence. I needed to strike something—or someone.

"Manzo you're scaring me! Say something please!" Tanisha pleaded.

"Please Manzo, put that bottle down! You're scaring the shit outta me!"

"Bitch you're dead to me!" I scowled and dropped my eyelids before slowly hoisting the bottle in the air.

CRACK!

In a forceful blow, I smashed the Mystic bottle against the right side of my forehead. The glass shattered instantly.

The bottleneck dangled from my fingers. I never opened my eyes. I didn't make a sound.

"Manzo nooooooo!" Tanisha screamed madly. "Baby nooooo! Why did you do that?"

The warm blood leaked down my head right into the crease of my eyelid and slid down my cheek, depositing at the side of my bottom lip.

I couldn't hear anything or feel Tanisha yanking maniacally at my sleeves. The scarlet baptism absolved me of my naiveté, and I felt no pain. I was at peace.

* * *

"Manzo! Wake up son!" Coach Bustle pulled on my hoodie. "We're here big fella!"

"Huh? I'm up coach." I sat up and stretched my arms. "I'm up."

"Damn, you were knocked the hell out." Coach Pry chuckled.

"The car is waiting outside. You must've had one helluva dream son." Coach Bustle opened the plastic container and picked at my steak.

"I'm OK Coach. I'm cool." I yawned.

"Who's Tanisha?" Coach Pry inquired.

"Uuuh, no one. Just an old friend," I replied as I followed them out of the jet, rubbing my forehead—where the stitches used to be.

* * *

Lane Stadium. Home of the Fighting Gobblers.

"It looks like one of those Greek coliseums from back in the day!" I said after reading the words atop the entrance's fifty-foot high cement wall.

Wow, this shit is unreal!

"Yes, it sure does, doesn't it?" Coach Bustle patted me on the back. "One day, it will be home of *Manzo.*"

"What's up with that stone all around the base of the stadium? I noticed most of the buildings on Campus were built with it."

"Oh that-there stone is called *Hokie* Stone, and they call it that because we're the Hokies, and we use a ton of that shit!" Coach Bustle said.

"Well that sounds pretty logical Coach," I said.

"Can't get any simpler than that!" Coach Pry co-signed the explanation.

The Virginia Tech campus, destitute because of winter break, possessed great energy although all the students were gone, unlike the ghost town feel of Woodberry Forest during our vacations.

In Hokie-Land, nothing seemed completely off, rather on low and waiting to heat up. There were no bodies—just plenty of spirit. Lane Stadium was the soul.

The leaves had completely fallen, and from Spring Road I could see across Washington Street into a piece of the campus—just enough to view the names of a few dorms: Cochran Hall, West Ambler Johnson, and East Ambler Johnson.

Oddly, despite not seeing much, I felt like I had been enrolled at Virginia Tech for years.

"Damn, it's way colder here than it is at Woodberry." I put my hoodie over my head.

"You ain't lyin' son." Coach Bustle zipped his track jacket up to his chin. "It's December and we're deep in the mountains, but the cold lets you know you're alive."

"Shit, we better hurry and get him to the Beams." Coach Pry back peddled down the sidewalk. "Coach Beamer is already waiting for you stud!"

HONK!

A black Ford Explorer slowed down on Spring Road but didn't stop. The white-haired Caucasian man, wearing the exact tracksuit as my escorts, smiled and waved before speeding down the driveway into a building beside the stadium.

I couldn't see his face, but his sizable teeth and reddish skin tone was not what I had expected.

"Wave to Coach Hite, Manzo," Coach Bustle requested. "Coach Hite is the running backs coach and assistant head coach here. He's a great guy!"

"Oh, I thought that was Coach Beamer," I said, waving at Coach Hite.

"No way! Night and day those two, but let's go!" Coach Bustle broke into a light jog toward Coach Pry, who stood at a metal door, twenty feet away. I jogged nervously right behind him.

"OK buddy, are you ready?" Coach Pry asked.

"Uh...yes sir."

"OK my man, let's not keep the head honcho waiting." Coach Bustle pulled out some keys.

"I'm ready," I said.

"Just walk down the tunnel and you will see the field, he's right there." Coach Bustle unlocked and pulled the door open. A gust of cold wind rocked me backward.

Damn it's cold and dark in there!

"Now are you positive you're good big fella?" Coach Bustle asked.

Oh man, I'm really going to meet Coach Beamer!

"Ha-ha, just a little nervous about seeing the legend, but I'm fine sir."

"You guys will hit it off, so just be yourself," Coach Pry insured.

"That's what got you here Manzo."

Chapter Twelve

FAT MISTAKE

I could see the light. I could see the process, and confidently I marched toward both. The tunnel, tight and dark, squeezed my fears, leaving a passionate rage to be great in its midst.

Just a few feet away, a burnished portal awaited with the answers that only the experience within Lane Stadium could provide. My feet stomped in harmony, but the rhythm of the questions in my head sounded the loudest.

Could I be the next great Hokie like Bruce Smith?

How much will I play?

Will Coach Beamer be proud of me?

The pearly glow centralized with each stomp toward the open-gated entrance, and the stands began to stretch.

Following the football gods before me, I raised both hands and touched the slab of mounted Hokie stone before quickly reading the words encased in a hard-plastic frame at the center of the stone—tradition.

'For those who have passed, for those to come...reach for excellence.'

Peeping out of the darkness, I surveyed the insides of the state of Virginia's largest gladiator arena. My senses strangled from excitement, I watched the surrounding bleachers rise to the heavens and my eyes couldn't focus.

My heart pumped savagely, as blurred specs of orange, maroon, and white bounced in the distance. Only the deep green of the field interrupted the fun.

This is it!

Let's go Manzo! Man up!

Coach Beamer, just a few feet away, looked at me, smiled, and nodded his head. I nodded back. Sweat dripped from my face onto the concrete.

Removing his VT ball cap, he swabbed the tousled gray hairs on his forehead with his hand before putting the cap back on his head.

He turned and faced the football field, showing the infamous patch of skin graft, which covered the right side of his jaw and a portion of his neck.

Coach Beamer bared his imperfections proudly, and I had admired his confidence. The man exuded character. He *was* Virginia Tech.

"Are you ready to be great?" Coach Beamer screamed into the tunnel.

"Yes sir!" all seventy-four members of the Virginia Tech football team answered in unison.

"Well let's go!" Coach Beamer yelled and began running toward the football field with two male cheerleaders next to him. Each cheerleader holding giant, orange VT flags.

"And here are your 1996 Virginia Tech Hokies!" a shrilling voice ripped through the stadium speakers. A cannon blasted.

BOOM!

As the crowd of 50,000 stood in an eruption of cheers, our team ran in silence behind its leader onto the football field. Metallica's "Enter Sandman" blasted throughout the stadium.

The hairs on my arms raised, and the roars of strawberry faced fans vibrated the huge bowl of vanilla support.

Drunken White folks belligerently rooting for their team's victory let me know that I had finally arrived. Virginia Tech was my new home. I was now a Division-1 college football player.

"Let's gooooooo Hokies!" the student section chanted. "Beat Rutgers to death Hooookkkiiiieeesss!"

"We love you Jim Druckenmiller!" a young lady's voice professed her devotion for our six-foot, four-inch blond quarterback.

We veered to the right side of the field, headed to our sideline, but not before glaring at the Rutgers' sideline.

Intimidated, the players never looked our way, and many pretended to stretch or fiddle with the straps on their helmets.

The Scarlet Knights were whores we would pimp slap on our way to another Big East title. Everyone knew Rutgers would not leave Blacksburg with a victory, even the few Rutgers fans that made the trip from New Jersey.

"Let's go Rutgers! Do the best you can!" a white haired old Black man wearing a number seven red Rutgers jersey hollered from behind their benches.

The electricity Lane Stadium created amplified my craving to waste anyone with an "R" on his helmet.

When I reached the Tech sideline—I quickly realized though that my hellish intentions toward the university from the "armpit of America" was strictly in vain. Although I had dressed for the game, the coaches had no intentions of playing me.

A true freshman and third string linebacker, I didn't even travel to our first two away games versus Akron and Boston College.

We were deep at my position, and Coach Foster didn't want to play me for the entire year to save a year of football eligibility.

If I didn't ever step on the field, I would be considered a *red shirt* by NCAA rules and still would have another four years to play football.

I was completely in agreement with Coach Foster's decision because I needed another year to mentally develop. Coach Foster's complex UP-G defense proved to be too much for me to learn in only a couple of months.

However, physically, I was the strongest and fastest "*Mike*" linebacker on the team. I walked on campus benching 400 pounds and running a 4.51 second forty-yard-dash, all while weighing 245 pounds.

With starting middle linebacker Antonio Morrison out with an ankle injury, the coaches decided that I dress for the Rutgers game strictly for insurance purposes.

Steve Tate was named the starter, Michael "Dirty Mizzo" Hawkes was the backup, and I was the dickhead with the clean uniform filling up on Gatorade.

Coming out of the tunnel with my brothers was amazing but being the strongest cheerleader in the nation didn't sit well with me.

"Come on defense! Let's kick some ass today men!" Coach Foster rallied as the starting defense huddled around him.

"Myron, you make sure if that fullback comes on that side—that you take him on full speed, because Tate will have your backside help!

"Cornell, I know you want the sack, but stay home if you see that opposite side receiver swing your way. The play is coming to you son!" Coach Foster grabbed the metal, dented lunch pail from Cornell Brown.

The lunch pail symbolized the Virginia Tech defense, which came to put in work every day. We were a blue-collar bunch.

"Big Wave, if that guard tries to pull, you demolish his ass and Banks will come flying in for the kill!" Coach Foster turned his cap around and rubbed his thick, black mustache—signifying he wasn't messing around anymore.

The more he strategized the Hokie attack, the angrier I became. I wanted desperately to be a part of those eleven warriors, but I wasn't good enough to play with the men.

How was that the case? I was always good enough in any sport, and *never* sat and watched from the sidelines.

Instead of humbling myself and paying attention to one of the nation's top defensive coordinators, I pouted and lost all interest in the moment.

What the fuck am I dressed for? This shit is whack!

"Manzo! You so fine!" a girl in the stands screamed, and I immediately turned to investigate who my admirer was.

Who said that?

"*PHEEEP!*" the referee blew the whistle to start the game and everyone in the stadium stood up. I ignored the sound and continued my inquest.

Where is she?

"It's tails, and Rutgers elects to receive the ball!" the Voice of the Hokies, Bill Roth, informed the crowd. The Rutgers section cheered.

"That's right! Let's go score a touchdown Scarlet offense!" Terry Shea, Rutgers head coach, believed in miracles.

"OK Hokie defense, let's kick some ass!" James Crawford, one of our wide receivers, yelled almost directly in my ear.

"Manzo! You so fine!" the girl repeated her praise.

Taking off my helmet, I glanced over the middle right section of the bleachers. Behind our sideline there were thousands seated in the stands, designated predominantly for family and friends of the coaches and players.

Each player received four tickets to the game, but I didn't want my family coming to see me hand out towels.

Instead, I gave my tickets to Keion Carpenter, a close friend and free safety from Baltimore.

OK, I see Tala and her Northern Virginia posse, but I know it wasn't them calling me.

I see Yvette, but Big Wave would kick her and my ass if she yelled my name.

Melanie is too busy looking at Sully.

"Fuck yea Hokies!" The standing crowd burst with insuppressible joy!

"All right Cornell Brown!"

"Great sack number fifty-eight"

"One more stop Hokies!"

Brandi, Cook, and April would joke like that, but—

Oh shit—is that the girl right there?

The suspect blushed and through a profusion of outstretched arms, I could see her looking at me. She blinked and then I blinked.

Her golden bob clinched her temples, flowed down the corners of her eyebrows, and cut short at the top of her cheekbones.

Before my appreciation of her extravagant red lips concluded, she had risen out of her seat and joined in the ceremonious applaud. My cock did the same.

Not even fifteen rows of White folks could stop me from seeing that the young lady goggling at this jock had a bright future behind her.

For a moment, I thought she stuffed a pillow in her jeans to combat the discomfort of the hard benches, until she turned around and looked back at her own backside before she peeped back at me and smiled.

Where the fuck do they make White girls like that?

SMACK!

"Oooooh!" The crowd covered their mouths and a hush draped over everyone, but the eye-boning between the blonde Minotaur and me continued without restraint.

Her cutoff Orange VT tee shirt had shown a creamy flat stomach and a very delicate waistline. I wanted a poster of her bellybutton on my dorm room's wall.

For a point in time the fans floated away, relinquishing me to romance the first piece of White chocolate that I yearned to take a bite.

When she smiled, it was for me. Our eyes meshed and playing football was an afterthought but scoring remained the objective.

"Manzo!"

"Manzo!"

"Where's Manzo?" Coach Beamer yelled. His gruff voice was legendary and undeniable.

Huh...what?

"Get your ass over here Manzo!" Coach Beamer ordered.

Am I going into the game?

There could only be one reason Coach Beamer summoned me, and my intestines gyrated beneath my stomach and vibrated every single nerve.

Without warning, my body heated in preparation of being thrown into the fire. As steamed up as I was to finally play, I was confused about why my number was called, but there wasn't a moment to think.

"Yes sir! Right here!" I put on my helmet in between shaking and faced my team. Every single player appeared to have been just as surprised as I was.

"OK Manzo, let's go!" Coach Foster pushed his way between offensive linemen Jay Hagood and Derek Smith and tugged on the front of my jersey. "It's your time son!"

.   .   .

In his early forties with his combed back jet-black hair and thick black mustache, Coach Bud Foster could have passed more for a wise guy than a wise coach.

Handsome, in a 1970's Italian hitman sense of the word, he was tall and lean, and he walked like a horse soldier.

The dauntlessness of General Patton, Coach Foster trained young men to run through the field and life without fear. I would've jumped in real flames for my linebacker coach/defensive coordinator if he asked.

"Uh, I'm ready coach," I said.

"You better be son...Tate just got blindsided and your team needs you!" He pulled me onto the field past a clearly stressed Coach Beamer who patted me on my back.

"Yes I'm ready." I paused when I observed the trainers carting number forty-nine toward the tunnel. The crowd cheered when Tate finally moved his arms.

"You gonna be fine Tate!"

"Shake it off bro!" players on both sidelines shouted words of support.

"Look at me and listen Manzo!" Coach Foster yanked my face mask. "I got you out here because I believe in your ass, so don't fuck this up son!"

"Yes sir!"

"The down and distance is third and five, and these bastards are going to throw the ball!"

"Yes sir!"

"You love getting to the quarterback, and that's just what the hell we need right now!"

"Yes sir." Our eyes never disconnected.

"Rutgers got the ball at our thirty-yard line, so make a play and force these assholes to kick a field goal!" Coach Foster placed his right hand on my left shoulder pad and pointed to *my* defense huddled on the field.

"*PHEEEP!*" the referee blew the whistle. "Let's go Coach!"

This is really happening!

"Manzo just stay loose son! Ha-ha—it's the first quarter, no pressure," Coach Foster said.

"Yes sir!"

"OK, here's the play!" He pasted his exceptionally straight nose right on my face mask. "*Whip Dog*...OK?"

I know that play!

"Yes sir. Whip Dog." I almost smiled with relief.

Outside blitz with the weak side linebacker!

"You know what to do if the back goes in motion, right?"

I'm not a retard. I get the quarterback still.

"Yes sir, I know. I'm ready coach," I reassured.

"Glad you studied it, because we don't have time to go over it! Whip Dog! Now go make a play son!" Coach Foster tapped the side of my helmet and walked away casually.

"Replacing number forty-nine, Steve Tate, at linebacker is freshman, number fifty-four, Manzo!" Bill Roth introduced me to the world of college football.

"Let's go Manzo!" Coach Beamer pumped his fist.

"You got this Manzo!" Coach Grimes winked at me.

"Smash their goddamn teeth in *Young!*" backup quarterback Al Clark hollered. His funny Washington, D.C. accent eased my nerves a little.

As I ran from the hash mark to meet my brothers huddled at the middle of the thirty-yard line, the Blacksburg crowd rose to their feet and joined my teammates and coaches, who hooted for the defense to get a stop.

Our team mascot, the Hokie Bird, hopped around and flapped his wings upwards, urging the fans to scream louder.

"LET'S GO, HO-KIES, LET'S GO!" The cheerleaders evoked a chant to electrify the crowd who, in short order, joined the craziness.

I can do this!

I'm built for this!

Every member of the Hokies defense, bunched like bowling pins, faced the football except for linebacker, number fifty-five, Myron Newsome who affronted the defense with the football at his heels.

Decelerating my stride, I stopped and settled myself beside Myron, completing the huddle. No one made a sound.

What do I say?

"Uh, what's up guys?" I nervously asked.

"Ain't shit up, what's the motherfucking play Manzo?" Myron put his hand on the top of my helmet and smiled. "Practice is harder than this shit! You got this bro!"

"LET'S GO, HO-KIES, LET'S GO!" The crowd frenzied, making it almost impossible to hear my teammates.

"Don't bitch up now Harlem World!" Antonio Banks, number nine, shouted from the back of the huddle.

"What are we gonna do Manzo?" Cornell Brown, our All-American defensive end asked.

Cornell Brown, one of the best players in college football and to ever put on a Virginia Tech jersey, had just asked *me*, "What are we gonna do?"

His question alone was enough validation for me to believe that I belonged. I had a job to do and men to lead. Anxiety lifted; it was time to play football.

"Listen up! Let's stop these motherfuckers!" I thundered into number ninety-eight, Waverly "Big Wave" Jackson's face.

"Hell yea!" Big Wave squeaked back with his unusually high-pitched voice for a six-foot, two inch, 312-pound Black man.

With the binding attention of all ten padded beasts, I gritted my teeth and strapped on my helmet tightly. The need to punish was apparent in each man's eyes, and I wanted what they wanted.

We were a team. It was time to not only give, but to execute the orders. The wind shifted, and so did my attitude. Time to hurt something!

"The call is Whip Dog! Reeeaaaddyyy...BREAK!" I hollered and all eleven of us clapped, scampering to our respective positions.

"BREAK!" The Rutgers offense broke their own huddle, and the center, number fifty-two, was first to sprint to the ball on the line of scrimmage.

The other Scarlet Knights aligned in their formation a split second after he did.

Briefly, I glanced at my surroundings and for a moment I wanted to run away, but I knew my time had come to stamp my name in the minds of all who witnessed.

Taking a deep breath, I hallowed my vision to the players in front of me and pretended the world wasn't watching. Football was *just* a game.

"Tight end left! Tight end left!" yelled our *Rover* (safety), Pierson Prioleau.

"Switch Myron!" I yelled to Myron, who was already in route for the change. He tapped my helmet as we crossed paths.

"Good shit!" Myron screamed before split squatting in his Up-G defensive stance, with his right foot forward and his left foot back, five feet in front of number eighty-six—the Rutgers tight end.

OK, Myron has the tight end.

The Rutgers quarterback, number seventeen, Mike Stephans casually strolled up to the center, who was already bent over in his three-point stance, holding the football on the ground.

The lanky White boy quarterback stopped, extended two scrawny hairy arms, and pointed right at me.

"Number fifty-four is the MIKE!" Stephans informed his team.

"RED NINETEEN! RED NINETEEN!" Stephans hunched behind the center and set his hands under the center's butt. "RED TWENTY-TWO!"

We are going to kill these motherfuckers!

Defensive tackles, Nat Williams, number ninety-two, and Big Wave each had a hand on the ground—preparing to attack.

Cornell and John Engelberger, number ninety-six, our *strong* side defensive end—were last to get positioned as they watched the quarterback, ready to feast.

You gonna die today Stephans!

Hike the ball so I can kill you!

"BLUE FIFTY-TWO! BLUE FIFTY-TWO!" Stephans eyed the line of scrimmage up and down. Only a couple of feet away, I couldn't hear anything and had to read his lips. "CHECK!"

Check?

He's changing the play!

Stephans suddenly stood up and hurriedly backpedaled five feet and stopped at the *shotgun* position. The running back was number thirty-four, and he moved to the right of Stephans.

Fuck!

What do I do?

I don't know what to do!

Do I still blitz?

"OSCAR NINETY-ONE! OSCAR NINETY-ONE!"

With both hands preparing to receive the snap, Stephans lifted his right leg off the ground—bringing his knee toward his chest. The running back shuffled in motion toward the sideline.

Fuck!

Is that my man now?

"Let's go *God!*" offensive guard, Dwight Vick from Hampton, Virginia yelled from the sideline.

"Ty!" I hollered over to my right to Tyron Edmond, number two, our *Whip* linebacker. He supposed to rush the quarterback with me on a Whip Dog blitz, but he couldn't hear me.

"Ty! Ty!" I screamed again to no avail.

Fuck it, I'm going!

Creeping my way down to the end of the line of scrimmage next to Cornell, I planted my left foot and watched Stephans jerk both of his hands forward—signaling for the hike of the football.

The center snapped the ball and as it sailed in the air, I unrelentingly bulled straight for Stephans with plans of soldering my helmet against his ear hole.

SMACK!

"Uuuuughh!" Stephans wailed as I crossed my arms, ramming the side of my helmet and shoulder pad in his lower back.

"Oooohh!" The crowd could almost feel the blow.

"Woooo!" I proceeded to cheer while plastered on top of Stephans' limp body. "Fuck yea!"

Standing on my feet I wanted to give the Virginia Tech fans a chance to praise my performance, but my celebration would be short lived.

The crowd quieted, sans the top right corner of the student bleachers colored in red in the Rutgers section.

I was confused until I watched Stephans twist onto his back, and I listened to Bill Roth broadcast the bad news.

Why doesn't he have the football?

"TOUCH DOWN RUTGERS!"

What?

The Rutgers players were slapping high-fives with number thirty-four in the end zone while our players were gasping for air, already heading for an irate Coach Beamer's sideline.

Coach Foster's defense, number one in the nation, just fucked up royally, but he only stared at one player—me.

And even as he chewed his gum more violently and his face turned redder, I just had one thought as I approached Coach Foster.

Who the hell was that White girl with that fat ass?

Chapter Thirteen

SMOKING JUICE

"Ha, ha, ha, you thought you had a motherfucking sack didn't you?" Andre Kendrick asked from the driver's seat of his "Uncle's" 1993 black Nissan Sentra.

"Hell yea! Fucking dude was like a magician or some shit!" I replied, sitting fully reclined in the passenger seat.

"That shovel pass was crucial bro," Dre said.

"Dre man, I just knew I had his ass!"

"Yooo, he passed that shit like a damn hot potato to that bum-ass running back."

"When I hit Stephans, I was like 'Bruce Smith ain't got shit on me!'" I said as I sat up and reached my right hand underneath my seat, tapping the carpet until I found my brown paper bag.

"He looked at me on the ground like, 'Fooled you nigga!'"

"I know man...your face was priceless!" Dre said.

"I bet it was!"

"Beams could've killed your ass!"

"Shit I know!" I pulled out the half liter of Hennessy I had stashed in the bag and opened it before taking a swig.

"When Beams started cursing and walking with his head tilted sideways, *and* rubbing on that damn neck, I knew my Black-ass was in trouble B!"

"Ha, ha, ha...you a fool Manzo!"

"Ha, ha, ha!" I laughed with my best friend on the football team and leaned back in my seat again.

* * *

Andre Kendrick, a freshman running back, along with Cornell Brown and freshman defensive tackle, Carl Bradley, were the pride of E.C. Glass High School in Lynchburg, Virginia.

Dre and I lived a couple of doors down from each other on Cochran Hall and had become inseparable since the first day of training camp, when I went to his room unannounced and caught him watching a porno of himself with the local high school slut in his town.

Considering I went to an all-boys high school and hadn't had sex with anyone since Tanisha, I was in awe that a nineteen-year-old could've produced, directed, and starred in his very own fuck flick.

Immediately, the young Dre Spielberg was the coolest person I knew, and from a foundation of perverted vanity our friendship developed.

A muscular five-foot, seven inches with curly, jet black hair and a burnt sienna complexion, Dre was a pocket version of myself.

Often our teammates, Marcus Gildersleeve and Sean Sullivan, would call us Danny DeVito and Arnold Schwarzenegger from the movie *Twins*.

The comparison to the movie never bothered me, but of course, I wasn't the short and stubby, bald guy.

Livid, Dre would instantly retaliate with a plethora of standup-worthy, uncensored witticisms, and when Dre dropped the microphone—I would pick it up and continue the onslaught. When people messed with Dre, they messed with *us*.

Dre and I attended all the same classes, had the same humor, dressed similar, and even slept with many of the same girls.

A dangerous duo, we could damn near read each other's mind, which compounded the level of our mischief and fuckery.

* * *

"Shit, it was your first game. You gonna be an animal once you learn all the plays." Dre reclined his seat also and put his size nine, red on black Air Jordan XII's on the steering wheel.

"I know, but today I got in the game for one play and gave up a goddamn touchdown."

"Manzo I'm just happy we won the game, but only beating them bums 30-14 feels like a loss. Beams gonna whip our ass in practice like we lost too."

"I already know Coach Foster gonna treat me like my name is Kunta fucking Kinte."

"No bullshit. He whips the shit outta y'all," Dre said.

"Last time Dirty Mizzo fucked up in practice, he made that nigga run until his head got smaller!"

"Shut the fuck up Manzo!"

"Nah Dre, I'm serious!" I passed him the Henny. "You know Dirty Mizzo wears those small-ass hoops in his ears, right?"

"Yea, the gold ones," Dre said.

"Maaaan, Dirty missed a tackle against Brian Edmonds, and Coach Foster had the nigga running for like an hour!"

"OK, but what the hell that has to do with his head getting smaller?"

"Maaan, when Dirty Mizzo came back and took off his helmet—the nigga head was steaming like a pearl motherfucking onion!"

"Ha, ha, ha! What the hell is wrong with you?"

"Dre, I'm dead-ass serious B!"

"Stop! Stop—my side is hurting!" Dre was laughing as he held his right rib area with his left hand and the Henny in the other.

"Shit, either Dirty's whole head shrunk, or he switched earrings with Michael Jordan!"

"You are a fuh-king fool yo!"

"OK—you're laughing Dre, but when I come back to Cochran looking like that nigga in Beetlejuice, I don't wanna hear shit." I stuck my right hand back in the paper bag.

"Manzo you gotta be the funniest motherfucker I know—you ain't right in the head bro!" He reached into his jeans and passed me a green lighter.

Parked on campus at the Squires Student Center's parking lot, Dre and I were pre-gaming like we always did before a DJ Tony party.

Every Saturday night while the White students got shit-faced at bars like Arnold's, Big Al's, and Top of the Stairs—the minority students danced their Black and brown asses off at Squires until 2:00 AM.

Like any other campus event, there was no drinking allowed at Squires, so the kids had to get their minds right beforehand.

The tiny digital clock on the Sentra's dashboard blinked 10:45 PM, and normally we wouldn't have been in the parking lot so soon. But I had asked Dre to come smoke a blunt with me away from the vultures on the football team who were broke and treeless.

Although I loved to get high just as much as my little buddy, I just needed someone to talk to privately—away from the commotion of an apartment full of drunk athletes and groupies.

Dre was my main homie, plus he was smoking my bud, so he really had no choice but to listen to my bullshit.

"Yoooo, I wanted to holla at you about something," I said between pulls.

"Bet. You know you can talk to me about whatev..." Dre's right eyebrow lifted before he finished his sentence. "But it better not be no gay shit though, 'cuz I ain't with that ole dick-in-the-booty type shit."

"Stop acting stupid for a minute asshole!" I demanded before exhaling.

"OK but pass me the blunt before you start going all Morgan Freeman and shit." He jerked the blunt out of my hand right as I put the blunt to my lips.

"Gimme that. Niggas love having story time when they got the damn blunt."

"Nigga you lucky you're my homeboy." I corralled the Henny from his hand.

"Go ahead and continue Mr. Freeman. I'm all ears."

"All right, but no more fucking around—please Dre."

Like always the cognac, weed combo warmed my thoughts. I put my black on white Air Jordan XII's on the dash, rested my head against the headrest, and looked out of the window at the lames walking up the Squire's steps, arriving first to the party.

Conversing with Dre had been a daily occurrence, and we never discussed anything more serious than football, rap, and pussy, but I needed solid advice from a rock-solid friend.

"Dre...you ever get distracted?"

"From what?"

"From all this football shit," I said.

"Hell yea I get distracted. What type of question is that?" he asked.

"I mean to the point where you're on the field and can't concentrate on shit Dre?"

"You talking about, like one of those A-D-D motherfuckers?"

"I don't fucking know B."

"Man just say what you trying to say, because you're blowing my high B," Dre mocked.

"Ah man, here we go again."

"Y'all Harlem niggas kill me with that *B* shit." Dre exchanged his blunt for the Henny.

"I don't have time for all that Dre—listen! Here's what I'm trying to say...I really can't think about anything but pussy these days." I blew smoke out of the window and returned scoping at the early birds.

"Nigga that's natural. I wanna fuck all day."

"Yea, but the difference is that I don't just *want* to—I *do* fuck all day B."

"We all get pussy Manzo—"

"Yes we do, and that's exactly my point B—I mean *Dre*." I rolled up the window. "I take shit a little too far."

"What, you into some kinky type shit?" His right eyebrow hoisted again.

"That's not the point—"

"Well get to the point Mr. Marcus!"

"Man I'm not trying to be no porn star like that dude, but...but I'm terrible—I fuck like three different girls a day Dre." I hung the blunt in front of him, but he didn't take it.

"*What*?" Dre dropped his feet to the floor. "You lying?"

"Hell no I ain't lying!"

"Maaaaan, they really do need to start calling you Mr. Manzo! Goddamn! You know how much pussy that is?"

"Yea I know how much pussy that is!"

"When the hell do you go to class?" He finally snagged the weed.

"I don't," I answered.

"You don't?"

"No, and obviously neither do you because we're in the same goddamn classes Dre."

"Oh yea...I be sleep."

"And I *be* fucking." I drank the Henny.

"Manzo I be too tired for all that class shit. Just give me the damn test."

"I mean, it ain't hard to pass the test, but I know I would have better grades if I actually went...but I'd rather drill some ass than walk across the damn *Drill* field!"

"Ha, nigga you high!" Dre blew a cloud of smoke in my direction.

"Nigga, *we* high!" I rebutted.

As Dre smashed the tip of the blunt in the car's ashtray, directly underneath the stereo, I capped the bottle of Hennessy and stuck the liquor back in the brown paper bag resting on my lap.

I was twisted. My mind looped over words, causing our current topic to fry in a skillet of confusion.

"Yea, like I was saying...what the fuck were we just talking about—oh yea, oh yea..." I finally recollected my thoughts and replaced the paper bag under the seat. "I fuck all the damn time, and that's why I can't learn my plays."

"I thought you be studying your plays with Nick Sorenson, Midget, Ike, and Lorenzo in the commons area?" Dre asked.

"Hell no, I try—but I can't."

"You can't?"

"Nope."

"Why not?" he asked.

"I try but those track girls walk by with those little-ass shorts on, and I go missing every single damn time."

"Word?"

"*Word*." I said.

"Which one?"

"What you mean Dre?"

"Which damn track girl Manzo?"

"The Black one with the fat ass."

"Nigga, they *all* Black with fat asses!"

"Exactly my little buddy. None of your business."

Scratching his head, Dre blankly stared at the steering wheel with his mouth opened slightly.

After a few seconds of contemplation, he lifted his head and turned to me wide-eyed. I had been already looking at him.

"You're a stone-cold *savage* B," Dre said.

"I know nigga."

"Woodberry messed you up, didn't it?"

"Hell yea! You called it," I said.

"You ain't never been around this much ass in your life, huh?"

"Never, and the shit drives me crazy every day."

"Shit, I bet."

"You see, all y'all had mad bitches around y'all in high school, so all this isn't so shocking to you, but having all this freedom *and* bitches is fucking up my concentration with football and the classroom. I can't think about shit else but bitches."

"I guess beating your dick for four years in the mountains could have that effect on a nigga," Dre said.

"Exactly, so now you understand what I'm going through in this motherfucker on a daily basis."

"I see." Dre nodded. "But what about the smoking and drinking?"

"The what?" I asked.

"The smoking and the drinking!" he spoke louder. "What are you deaf now?"

"Man, what the fuck does that have to do with anything?" My body temperature had risen. I rolled down the window.

"It ain't that *Dre!*"

"Damn I'm just asking! Don't kill me!" He rolled down his window also.

"Everybody we hang with smoke and drink and they're cool. I'm telling you it's going to that all-boys school that's messing me up. A lil' smoke and drink ain't doing shit. This is college nigga!"

"I'm just saying Manzo, shit effects people different." Dre reached into the console and pulled out an eight-ounce blue bottle of Polo Sport cologne before spraying it on his red Polo shirt. "Just think about it."

"And you know what else motherfucker?" I *tapped* Dre on the shoulder, and my face stiffened.

"What?" he asked, matching my attitude, our faces now only a foot apart.

"I need to know something right fucking now Dre!"

"What the fuck your bipolar ass need to know?" His body tensed, and he moved closer, wheezing Henny up my nostrils.

"Say what you gotta say nigga! I'm trying to help your crazy ass, but I ain't scared of you Manzo! Don't let the small size fool you!"

"You ain't gotta be scared, but you will answer this goddamn question for me —and you *better* keep it 100 with me! I need to know...how are you so little...and your nose is sooooo fucking big?"

"Fuck you! Ha, ha, ha, ha!" Dre's face delicately transformed, obviously relieved.

"No seriously though! Your nose looks like an appetizer at an African restaurant—"

"Ooooh shit! Look at your boy Tee Butler bringing a *White* girl to a Squire's party!" Dre yelled and pointed out his window.

"Where?"

"Manzo don't act blind now!" Dre extended his finger further. "The only nigga across the street with a turtleneck on, holding a White girl's hand!"

"That's not..." I leaned closer to the windshield. "Ooooh shiiiid, that *is* Tee!"

And Monica!

"Your roommate, *the Frenchman*." Dre shook his head.

* * *

Tee Butler.

Yes, the same Tee Butler who attended junior high school *and* high school with me was currently my roommate on Cochran Hall—and my football teammate.

Surprisingly, he didn't receive any Division-1 football scholarship offers out of Woodberry Forest and decided to attend Virginia Tech with me as a "walk-on," a player who made the team through a tryout.

Even though we were roommates and had known each other for most of our lives, Tee and I had begun to grow apart from the first moment we stepped on campus.

At Woodberry there were only a handful of minorities, so we almost had no choice but to socialize and grow as one, but Virginia Tech was an entirely different situation.

Naturally, I gravitated to the more popular arrogant misfits of the team who dominated the football field as much as we did the social scene.

We called ourselves the Boyz Club, because about twenty of us hung out in bottom adjoining-apartments at 1215 Progress Street.

Daily, we would run through girls as fast as we did liquor and weed. We were lunatics and without question—the most fun.

Tee, much more straightedge, didn't smoke weed and only drank on the weekends. He descended toward the dudes on the team I considered super lame.

Just for kicks, I would fuck his friends' girlfriends and then compare notes with other Boyz Club members who had done the same.

But no one messed with Tee or his girl, Monica, because he was an extension of myself. Plus, Tee was cool and harmless. Everyone liked Tee Butler.

Tee was dubbed "the Frenchman" when one night I had invited him over to 1215 to drink, and he showed up wearing a blue and white striped shirt, a Tam, and a scarf like a Black Vincent Van Gogh or some shit.

Not keen on the names of the many French artists, someone shouted, "Introducing, Lé' Tee Butliér—the Frenchman!" and the name stuck.

* * *

"Yoooo, the nigga really holding her hand!" Dre smacked his forehead. "Now that's crucial!"

"That *is* a turtleneck." I rubbed my eyes.

With his long sleeve black turtleneck tucked in his blue Tommy Hilfiger jeans, Tee clutched his girl's hand—galumphing his black Timberland boots up the Squire's steps and through the glass double doors.

He smiled, although the few African American young women on the front benches did not.

Monica, squeezed in a mini black dress, exposed the top of her bountiful, posture-altering tanned breasts, while her toned legs sank into black high heels.

A thin build with curves, she pinned her dark brown hair in a bun and wore no jewelry. Monica was very hot and very *White*, although she was actually Hispanic.

"OJ fucking Bum Juice," I muttered.

"OJ—*what*?" Dre asked, instantly turning toward me.

"What?" I asked.

"What did you just now say Manzo?"

"You mean OJ Bum Juice?"

"Yea, what the fuck is that?"

"Oh shit, I never told you what an OJ Bum Juice was?" My eyebrows dropped.

"Nah, why you call Tee that?"

"Because that's what the fuck he is Dre."

"But why?" He placed the cologne back in the console.

"Oh shit, you really don't know?"

"Hell nah, you never told me!"

"Man, it's just something I made up with my brothers." I shrugged my shoulders.

"But why?" he asked.

"Shit, our cousin Crisco was the only one in our hood to mess with a White girl, so one day I was high as fuck and I just called him OJ Bum Juice."

"Ha, ha, ha—for real?" he asked.

"Hell yea, and the shit just stuck—because you know how OJ only messes with them White bitches."

"So why you didn't just call him *OJ*, or the *Juice*?"

"Nigga that's OJ's name! I put the *bum* in there to show that the person was like a low-budget O.J. Simpson."

"So, any person who messes with a White girl...you would call them OJ Bum Juice?" Dre asked.

"You almost got it right, except it ain't *any* person—it's any *Black* person."

"Yooooo, that's funny as a motherfucker!" Dre curled over the steering wheel.

"I know, but it was just some inside shit. I'm not trying to make a nigga feel bad for dating outside his race. I don't have any beef with that—not my business."

"I know, but it's funny as shit bro!"

"I know, but down here y'all love them goddamn juices!" I said.

"Now what the fuck is a *juice*?"

"Nigga...are you not listening?" I asked. "A juice is a White girl Dre."

"I see now, ha, ha, ha!"

"Are you sure?" I asked.

"Yea, yea—so, the dude is an *OJ Bum Juice,* and the White girl is simply a *juice*." He tugged at his chin hairs and nodded.

"OK, OK...I get it now Manzo."

"Oh, and one more thing Dre."

"What?" he asked eagerly, resembling a kid waiting for the ending of a bedtime story.

"If a Black dude is seen with a White girl...that means that he's *juicing*," I explained.

"Huh?"

"Like if you see *Jerome* with a White girl at the bar...then you would say, 'I just saw Jerome *juicing* at the bar.'"

"Ha, ha, ha—I get it! I get it!" Dre couldn't stop laughing.

"The shit is stupid as hell but makes total fucking sense!" I admitted.

"Yooo...so that means almost our whole damn team is a bunch of OJ Bum juices then?" Dre asked.

"Bingo my little friend."

"Manzo, let's name and count the OJ Bum Juices on the squad." Dre sat up and grasped his left index finger.

"Man, we will be here all night trying to count the juicing motherfuckers on our team," I said.

"Come on B!"

"All right, all right Dre—you name the player, and I will confirm if they fit the OJ Bum Juice criteria!" I straightened up in my seat.

"OK let's go! Rob Adams?" Dre scanned the car's roof for names.

"Juice," I answered.

"Shawn Scales?"

"Juice."

"Aaron Layne?"

"Juice."

"Cory Bird?"

"Juice—but name them faster Dre!"

"Ken Oxendine?" He quickened his pace, and I began to answer almost before he could even finish the name.

"Juice."

"Todd Washington?"

"*Big* juice."

"Corny White?"

"*King* juice."

"Danny Wheel?"

"*Major* juice."

"Antonio Banks?"

"*Primetime* juice."

"Cornell Brown?"

"*All-American* juice."

"Ha, ha, ha! Yoooo—OK damn, you made your point nigga!" Dre said. "The Hokies are *juiced* the fuck out!"

Yup, y'all sure are Dre.

"Manzo—maaaan your bud is always crucial! I'm high as a motherfucker!"

"I always get the best shit...I love smoking weed B."

I loved smoking weed, and for the first time I had admitted it out loud. The words resonated through my fogged mind.

Getting lifted made me happy and full of laughter. I took great pleasure in deep conversations and bonding-experiences with friends like Dre, as we let problems and pressures freewheel to the distant land of "I just don't give a fuck."

Drug experimentation was synonymous with college, and I had no reason to be troubled. I was just being a kid.

"What were we just talking about though?" I asked Dre.

"Juices...nigga, you're fried!"

"Oh yea, my bad! As I was saying, I told you y'all love them White girls down here!"

"Shit, not me!" He opened his door. "Come on let's go, people are going in now."

"But you are correct, I'm fried." I opened the passenger side door.

"I love my Black sisters—I mean, I've fucked a few pink toes back in the day... but I promise on everything I love, I don't mess with them juices no more," he swore.

"Shit, I believe you Dre," I lied.

"How 'bout you Manzo?"

"Nah, I've never been with a juice...at least not yet." A revitalizing burst of wind aligned my footsteps as we walked toward the party.

"Now this is what I'm talking about—look at all those fine Black beauties across the street!" I said.

A lovely cocoa crowd of the sexiest young women Virginia had to offer developed on the steps to the Squire's entrance, and I could taste the sweetness in the air as Dre and I approached College Avenue.

"If I Ruled the World" by Nas, trumpeted each time the tinted glass doors opened. The hunt was under way.

"Damn, them bitches looking thick tonight. Hold up a sec," Dre said before he stopped in the middle of the street, dipped his head back, and poured Visine in both eyes. "Here, you want this?"

"Man I don't give a fuck who knows I'm baked—let's go!" I said. "I want to party, go to Hardee's, and then go beat on something!"

"Hell yea Manzo! I hope that—"

"*SCREECH!*"

"What the fuck?" Dre yelled as we both frantically jumped further onto the curb.

"Somebody wants their ass beat!" I shouted.

Just as our Jordan's tiptoed onto the sidewalk, a speeding 1994 orange Honda Accord slammed on its breaks, only inches from us.

The campus' bright lights veiled the Honda's windshield, masking the driver's identity.

Although I couldn't outright see the maniac, there was some familiarity about what my eyes captured through the open sunroof—short, blonde hair.

Nooo! Could it be?

"That White bitch is crazy!" a Black girl hollered from on top of the steps.

"Yo bitch, you better watch where the fuck you're going!" Dre wolfed, making his way up the steps. "Come on Manzo, let's go!"

Is that her?

"Hold up one sec Dre!" I anxiously moved closer to the Honda and bent over just as the passenger side window opened.

Fuck, it's her! The girl in the stands!

My stranger wore a white VT basketball t-shirt, blue jeans, and no make-up. With the sight of her sparkling blues eyes, my heart sped faster and faster—I felt like ripping the motherfucker out of my chest and handing it to her.

That juice is so fucking bad!

"You gonna go with your midget friend, or are you gonna get your sexy-ass in this dang car?" she asked and looked through me. "I don't have all day *Manzo!*"

And she knows my goddamn name!

"Weeell?" She unlocked the door.

I looked back at Dre waiting with one foot on the fourth step, and the other on the fifth—slumped against the banister with a bewildered expression on his face, and both of his hands in the air.

The gathering crowd of African American princesses, who just moments ago I had lusted for, looked as confused as Dre.

Everyone awaited my decision whether I would stay and party—or leave with the reckless driver?

"Shiiid...sorry lil' homie!" I shrugged and got in the Honda, closing the door.

"Sellout!" someone blurted.

"How ironic? OJ Bum Juice!" Dre shook his head.

How ironic?

I completely understood why Dre would be upset that I ditched him for a random White girl, but his antics were comical—as well as hypocritical.

Dre, a pint-sized juice himself, would sneak off to Terrace View Apartments to spend every night with a big butt White girl of his very own, but he didn't think that I knew.

By no means was I a detective though. Blacksburg was just too small, and I was just too smart.

My blonde companion put the Honda in drive and before she hightailed down College Avenue, I stood on my seat and looked out of the sunroof.

The mortified look on my little buddy's face was priceless after I yelled, "HEY ANDRE BUM JUICE! GIVE ASHLEY HER GODDAMN CAR BACK!"

Chapter Fourteen

ROLE PLAY

"Damn, what the fuck am I doing out here?" I asked myself.

"Dude, what the fuck am I doing out here?" the tall freckled-faced White boy with a red curly Afro and Birkenstock sandals questioned also.

"I guess we both know why we're out here," I said and blew into my hands. "It's getting a little brick out here."

"Brick? What's that?"

"Brick means cold. You're lucky you got on those thick-ass socks and corduroys." I pointed to his feet.

"Oh yea bro. It is kind of nippy out here." He put his hands in his pants pockets and looked around.

"This bitch better hurry up and open this door, because I'm ready to fuck something."

"Ha-ha, oh shit!" I said.

"I'm serious brother."

"Ha-ha, I know you are!"

Getting into West Ambler Johnson through the front door was impossible after 10:00 PM. There was always a security person at the front desk making sure outsiders like me and my new gangster Jewish homie wouldn't infiltrate the co-ed dorm.

But West "AJ" had two unguarded side doors that funneled ambitious horny college kids to and from their destinations.

Although I was impatient, I was very familiar with the alternative route, and the exact four minutes it would take for a young lady to get on the elevator, reach her floor—and then run down the east exit stairs to push open the locked door.

I banged quite a few girls in West AJ, but they all saved me a trip and came to Cochran, except for Toya.

* * *

Toya, a freshman from Fredericksburg, Virginia, lived on the fourth floor of West AJ with her hometown homegirl Kadesha, and I would sneak to their room whenever Kadesha stayed at her boyfriend's dorm.

I had met Toya at a Squire's party and the girl was lovely in a raw, countrified type of way.

She had a beautiful figure and gentle face, and her only scent was from her lotion. Toya wore bright white Reebok Classics, and all her clothes were simple and safe.

What Toya lacked in fashion she made up in sweetness, but from the first introduction I knew that there was no way I ever would see her in any romantic capacity, not even for a blowjob behind the library.

She had the complexion of a week-old banana, a Tweety Bird head, and long straight black hair. Although she was very attractive, I didn't come to Virginia to find another Nicole or another Mommy.

During our first encounter, I respectfully attempted to dismiss myself from Toya's presence at a Delish Promotions party, but the young lady, tipsy and persistent, held my hand and whispered in my ear, "I am a virgin."

Finding a virgin in college was rare, but I had been unicorn-lucky, and I *had* to be Toya's first—and she knew it.

After months of playing *just the tip*, she finally let me deflower her, but not until I said that I loved her and that she was my girlfriend.

A big lie and a little blood on the sheets later, Toya and I were hitched, although I never sanctioned our union publicly and continued fucking other girls.

* * *

"My name's Jed? What's yours bro?" My new friend extended his right hand.

"Manzo. Nice to meet you Big Red." We firmly shook hands.

"Ha-ha, I said Jed not Red."

"I know, but I like Big Red better."

"Ha, OK. Red...like your eyes?"

"What are you talking about B?" I rubbed my eyes. "I'm just tired."

"Shit, I wish I were *tired* like you brother."

"Ha-ha," I chuckled.

"I'm just joshing with you bro." He playfully hit my arm.

"*Joshing?*"

"I'm messing with you. Joshing means joking."

"Oh yea! I know what joshing means. I went to boarding school with nothing but White boys." I stretched my arms and dramatically yawned.

"Don't mind me. I'm *tired*, remember?" I said.

"Who are you waiting for?" he asked.

"A girl."

"Shit, I would hope so Big Black. She got a name?"

"Of course bro. It's uuh..." I looked to the stars for help. "Uumm."

What's her fucking name? Damn I'm high.

"Uuuuh..."

Crystal?

Kathy?

"Uuuuh...hold up...I know it Big Red."

"Ha, ha, ha—it's OK bro...it happens," Jed said.

Brittney?

Yes!

"Yes, her name is Brittney."

"You sure?"

"Ha-ha, yea, I'm sure Big Red." I pulsed my fingers in front of me, gripping the air. "Roundest ass I've ever seen!"

"Oh man, she sounds like a very *special* young lady," he said.

"Damn right she is! You know Brittney?"

"Nah, I don't know that bitch."

"What the fuck Big Red?"

"Oh sorry bro. I didn't mean to offend you." Jed stepped back a foot.

"I'm not offended, you just caught me off guard!"

"I guess I listen to too much Biggie!" he said.

"Man, you might be the coolest Jew I know Big Red, and I'm from New York City."

"Does this mean I finally got some street cred?" He smiled.

"Yea Big Red. I'm vouching for you."

"If only my mother were here to witness such a monumental moment." He gestured prayer hands and looked at the moon.

"Sarcastic motherfucker! I thought you were serious!" I laughed. "You were just joshing with my Black-ass, huh?"

"Nah, I was just fucking with you that time."

"Aight—you got me bro." I nodded. "But anyway, you never told me who you were here to see."

"Oh yea, my bad. I'm here to see my *slow-ass* girlfriend." He glanced at his Timex. "Her name is—"

BAM!

What the—

"Ooooh, I see you made a friend," Brittney said after bursting through the metal side door. "You ready?"

"Yea, but you scared the shit out of me!" I replied.

"I thought it was just me bro," he said. "Scared the shit outta me too!"

"Aaaaw, I'm sorry buddy." She forged a smile at Jed. "Come on Manzo. Let's go handsome."

"OK, let me just—"

Don't let it close!

Before vanishing into the exit, Brittney gave the door a mercy nudge, granting me a desperate second to catch the door just before closing.

Although I played linebacker, I moved with the blazing agility of a wide receiver and grabbed the door within a tenth of an inch of smashing my fingers.

Pussy possessed the power to make any player switch positions.

"Hold up!" I yelled into the stairwell. Brittney had already run up a flight.

"Damn, you almost lost your whole hand chasing after that ass!" Jed said.

"Wait a second!" I hollered again before turning to Jed.

"What the fuck is her problem?" I asked.

"Man, I don't know. That's *your* bitch—you better go get her bro."

"You aren't coming up?"

"Nah, I'll wait right here. My bitch will be here in a second."

"You want to come grab the door?" I asked.

"Nah I'm cool. If you keep the door open for too long an alarm will go off."

"Oh shit, well I better get the fuck outta here." I held the door with my left hand and attempted to use the other to give Jed a classic handshake, but he clasped our thumbs together, and we slid our fingers against one another before locking hands and letting go.

"OK, I see you dapping it up Big Red!"

"Later bro. See you around," he said as I pivoted to enter the exit, and the side door shut behind me.

Oh Shit!

"Big Red!" I pushed the door open and reached into my pants pocket.

"Yo?" he answered.

"Here you go bro! Shalom!" I tossed him a quarter ounce bag of bud. "Enjoy your night!"

"Oh shit Manzo, you are the fucking man! Shalom!" He inhaled the plastic, closed his eyes, and rapidly stuffed the bag into his front pants pocket.

"Hold up, you might need this!"

"What?" I asked.

"Here you go bro!" Jed *Frisbee'd* a tiny, lustrous gold object, which I caught with both hands.

"Ha, ha, ha—thanks!" I held his gift in the air in disbelief. "This ain't a White boy condom, this shit is a Magnum!"

The unwieldy door, heavy and steadily closing, pushed against me, and my feet inched toward the remainder of my night.

Before the door shut completely, I planted the left side of my face against it—catching a glimpse of Jed flexing his right bicep as he grinned and said, "I may be a Jew, but I ain't *all* Jewish."

* * *

"Dang, you guys having a real bromance out there!" Brittney looked down at me from the fourth floor of the burnt-orange staircase. Her yellow hair swung like boiled spaghetti.

"Are you coming or not?"

"Yea, I'm coming." I slid the Magnum in my back pocket.

The trail of fresh paint festered in the air and cautioned me not to touch the walls or banisters, even before I spotted the red-on-white *Wet Paint* sign on the floor with masking tape adhered on each of the sign's corners.

Picking the sign up and sticking it back on the wall, I began my sprint up the steps.

"Wow, you're such a nice boy. Your mama taught you well," she said. "Don't touch the walls!"

"Ha-ha, thanks for the advice babe." I swiftly reached the third floor and suddenly stopped.

Third floor...oh shit!

"Why are you stopping baby? You scared or something?" Brittney asked.

Yes!

"Uh, no...but do you live on the fourth floor?"

Please don't live on Toya's floor!

"Why?" She tucked her hair behind her ears.

Because Toya's gonna kill your ass if you do!

"Uuuh no reason. Just curious," I said.

Fuck, she does!

"Well for your information Mister Manzo, I live on the fifth floor." She casually progressed up the stairs. I could've counted every Levi's thread stitched to her perfect ass.

Thank you, Jesus!

"Oh OK, just wondering." I reached her as she held open the fifth floor's exit door.

"After you." I smiled.

If you don't get your ass in this goddamn door already.

"Why thank you, kind sir."

CLICK!

BAM!

Oh shit!

"Giiirrrll, I almost forgot all about..." a girl's voice followed the fourth floor's door being popped open, and in a flash, I sidestepped inside Brittney's floor and slammed the exit door.

BAM!

"Fuck dude—you trying to wake up the dead?" Brittney asked.

That was close!

"Ha-ha, no. My bad babe."

That didn't sound like Toya, but it definitely was a Black girl.

"You looked spooked. You scared of getting caught or something?" Brittney inquired.

I knew that I was on the fifth floor, but the eerie resemblance to the fourth was unmistakable and almost maddening.

Ten wooden doors, five on each side, continued down a thirty-foot cucumber-green hallway, which stopped at a cement wall, connecting another perpendicular hallway.

The coalescence of Bath and Body Works, Pantene, and Hot Pockets lingered in the air, as Natalie Merchant's "Wonder" competed for dorm supremacy with Sheryl Crow's "If It Makes You Happy."

"Scared of getting caught? Ha-ha, I'm cool—what are you talking about?" I played dumb.

"Don't worry hun...security will never find you in my room." She walked two feet, stopping at room 521 and glancing down at the floor. Toya lived in room 421.

"I didn't mean to make so much noise, that's all. Guess I'm just a little too strong," I said.

Is this a setup?

Does she know about Toya?

"Well save your strength big fella. You might need it." She jammed her key into the doorknob, and her eyes wandered to my crotch and back into my eyes.

"I think I have enough strength to—"

"Shut up and come fuck me." She cracked open the door.

Brittney's demands were direct and something that I had never experienced —like being with a White girl.

She didn't play coy or play games, she asserted her intentions and chopped the part out where the guy had to finesse his way to the pussy.

I didn't care or had given any thought to what color she was, where her ancestors originated from, or how, out of seventy-eight football players, I had been selected to entertain such a hot piece of ass.

And if she were purposely trying to get me busted by Toya, Brittney chose the right six words to trap the right Black beast.

Staring relentlessly, she smoothed her top teeth with her tongue as I stared back, matching her keenness to devour one another.

Brittney's five-foot, five-inch body squirmed, and my eyes roamed to piercing nipples and thick muscular thighs.

Wearing no bra, she had perky breasts that would fit into a kid's bowl of cereal without the milk.

Her meaty vagina *camel-toed* against light blue jeans with a seemingly darker blue discoloration in the upper groin area. She was wet, and I had seen enough.

I charged Brittney and pressed my mouth against hers while cupping the sides of her delicate face with my coarse hands.

Her cherry lip balm smoothed my dry lips as our tongues danced together in a synchronization of violence and passion.

With my eyes closed and my neck slightly bent to the right, I pushed against her as our pelvic regions collided, and her upper back and butt launched open the door.

She quickly backpedaled, and moans of warm and choppy breaths blew life into my erection. The door bounced off the wall and then slammed shut, securing the lust in the room.

She reached underneath my arms with both hands and clawed my back through my long sleeve DKNY t-shirt. I kissed her harder.

Brittney's backside crunched on a solid structure, halting our momentum. I tasted her tonsils and opened my eyes.

The overhead light was off, but the room illuminated from the brightness of a thirty-four-inch computer monitor which set behind Brittney on a biscuit colored wood desk, the length of a skateboard—while the back of her upper thighs mashed the black keyboard.

The desk, packed between two unmade twin-sized beds, was positioned in front of an undressed window that faced another dorm room's opened window, equally as bare, loosely fifteen feet away and seemingly vacant.

Brittney dislodged her talons from my back and grappled with my braided leather belt, unbuckling it with one hand.

This is really happening!

I shut my eyes and exhaled fiercely as her cold and tiny White hands explored my warm big Black cock.

"Ouch!" I abruptly shoved Brittney's face off mine, and my hands inadvertently dropped to her throat. "What the fuck?"

She fucking bit me!

"Choke me Manzo!" she ordered.

What?

"Choke me!"

Is she serious?

"Choke me, you big pussy!" she challenged while tightly stroking my meat to the downbeat of her heaving chest. Her spiritless blue eyes never batted an eyelash.

"I can't." Blood assembled on my bottom lip and I licked it off. The pain was gone.

"Choke me! Do it, you big pussy!"

"I'm not a pussy!"

"Do it!" She brought in the reserves. Both her hands were now pepper grinding my cock. I compressed her neck with more force.

"Harder!" she demanded.

"No...aaah...nooo—"

"Harder, you pussy!" she spat. "Are you big for nothing?"

"OK!" I clenched heavily and felt her larynx shift from one thumb to the other, sweat tumbling below my skin and down my face.

"Yes...*COUGH, COUGH*...yes...harder..."

"Aaaaahhh...mmmm...OK!" I moaned and squeezed.

"Yaaahs...*COUGH, COUGH*...yaahs." Her eyes closed; veins sprouted from her forehead.

Brittney's body slumped to the left, enough to uncover a consequential portion of her computer monitor. The screensaver's passion loosened my grip.

"*COUGH, COUGH*...why...you...*COUGH*...stopped Manzo?"

Paying no mind to her question, I sidestepped a few inches and leaned forward to get an unimpaired view of the marvelous moment captured underneath twenty or so scattered computer icons.

Brittney losing her balance, *tug-of-war'ed* my cock for her not to spill backward onto the desk as my hands still tenderly braced her throat.

The Dell's monitor displayed life-sized profiles of Brittney and a yellowish, Black gentleman with a low-cut fade haircut, a pencil-thin mustache, manicured eyebrows, and a posse of razor bumps terrorizing both of his chins.

Their lips locked as she eyed him with a sky-blue twinkle of young rapture while he stoically focused on the camera.

The lovebirds were matched in white Kobe Bryant jerseys, and I hated the fucking Lakers. Ironically, the guy wearing the jersey hated me.

Jermaine Gibson.

Jermaine, a damn near seven-foot freshman for the Hokies basketball team, always smiled and greeted me and the other football players with respect. He *was* cool.

Besides a couple of classes and parties, I never had any dealings with the pretty boy, and I was stunned when Tala, my only non-sexual girlfriend, told me that he detested me because I thought that "I was the shit."

Well, I didn't think, I *knew* I was the shit. Either way, Jermaine did not have a good reason to hate me.

I'm gonna make your bitch-ass really hate me now Jermaine.

"Manzo—"

"Shut up!" I clamped both of her nipples through her t-shirt. "You like that?"

"*Mmmm*...twist them off...*mmmm*."

"You're a freak!" I said, still staring at the monitor.

"I'm *your* freak now...*mmmm*."

"You want this Black cock?" I unbuttoned her jeans.

"Yes daddy...*mmmm*...give it to me!" She flapped my manhood over my white boxer briefs, petrifying my erection.

"Pay attention to *me*! Give me that big Black cock!"

Your girl screaming for it now Jermaine!

"*Mmmmm*...give it to me Manzo!" She jerked faster and harder.

"OK Brittney!"

Taking a fistful of denim in each hand, I elevated my elbows and yanked her jeans' open fly in opposite directions as if Coach Gentry were in attendance.

Buttons *flying saucer'ed* across the room, and her 501s shredded to her calves.

A tang of lemon and rosewood, with a plastic under-scent deluged my palate but never stopped my munchies for the *other* White meat.

"Grrrr...come here!" I grabbed her midriff with both hands and tossed her onto her stomach, her forearms demolishing the keyboard. A few letters raised hell on the desk before plunging to the floor.

An unblemished plump, vanilla-peach with a rare ripeness, halved by a pink satin ribbon, wiggled for help—and my tool was ready for assistance.

Brittney's ass, the size of my Sony Trinitron, removed the cotton from my mouth. I drooled, but I was still thirsty. I needed that juice.

"Yes daddy! Take it!" She arched her back.

White girls not supposed to have ass like this!

"All right...you want this Black cock?" I tore her thong and flung it over my shoulder. Her bald vagina could've cured apartheid.

Totally shaved!

"Mmmmm...yes daddy!" She parted her legs farther, as I bent and pulled my jeans and underwear down to my ankles, hurriedly springing back to full height. "Put it in me daddy!"

I'm really going to fuck a White girl!

Positioning my pelvic area precisely eight inches away from her contact, I clutched God's blueprint for happiness, and my chocolate hands swirled into her skin. I pulled her toward me.

My canoe streamed into Brittney's canal and drifted down a wonderful warm river, halting at the bank of her soul.

"Aaah...damn Manzo." Her body tensed.

"Relax...you're with daddy now." I said.

"Mmmm..."

"Feels good?" I pushed her casually away before refilling her belly.

"Aaah...fuck yea daddy!"

OH SHIT!

A light shimmered through the window and sparked my attention, and I could see two brown haired White girls walking into the neighboring dorm room, both in VT sweatshirts and Pokémon pajama pants.

The taller chubbier faced one held a red plastic bowl of popcorn, while the girl with a monster nose and heavy acne held a six-pack of Mountain Dew. It was movie night.

They gonna see us.

"Don't stop...mmmm." Brittney backed further into me.

We should close the blinds!

The two girls, trancelike, approached their window, stopped, and took a gander at my situation. Gravity got the best of their jaws.

Nose placed her beverages on their desk, elbowed *Chubs*, and both of their mouths moved, but neither dared to look away. The awkwardness started to chop my wood. I wanted to hide!

"You better not be a pussy and stop!" Brittney screamed to the window. "Let those bitches watch!"

Satisfying an unexperienced sexual conquest had suddenly replaced my momentary shyness.

No one had ever watched me have sex. No girl I had ever had sex with, to my understanding, would enjoy someone watching us.

I had never been with a juice though, and the first of anything was normally the most memorable, whether good or bad.

I was born to perform. I was born to shine. I was a rock star. It was showtime!

"You want them to watch me fuck you?"

"Yes please!" Brittney squeezed her vagina.

"Yes what?" I asked.

"*Mmmm...*"

"Yes, *what?*" My hands elevated to her waist.

"*Aaaah* damn."

"Yes, *what?*" I penetrated deeper with more accuracy, hitting her spot.

"Yes *daddy!*"

"Say you love this Black cock!"

"I...*aaahh...ooohh*...love...*aaahh*...this Black cock!"

"*Grrrr...*this my pussy now!" I pumped ferociously, and the Magnum condom fell out my jeans and onto the floor.

"YES...YES...YES!" Her arms flared erratically across the rocking desk, toppling a bottle of Elizabeth Arden sunflower perfume.

"You like them watching?" I grabbed a fistful of hair and raised her head as if I were displaying its dismemberment to my tribe.

"*Aaaah*...YES, YES! Oh God—YES! I fucking love it! Pound this fat white ass Manzo!" Brittney watched Chubs eat popcorn, while Nose had both hands tucked into the front of her PJs.

"This is my pussy!" I pumped even harder.

I'm Jermaine tonight!

"This my pussy...*grrr!*" I pushed her head into the monitor, smearing her lips against her boyfriend's.

"Whose pussy is this?" I asked,

"Yours...YES!"

"Whose pussy is it?"

"*Aaaah...*YOURS DADDY!"

"Whose pussy is it?"

"YOURS DADDY!"

"Call me Jermaine!"

"*Aaaah...ooohh...*it's...YOURS!"

"Call me fucking Jermaine—I said!"

"Jermaine! Yes Jermaine...*ooohh*...take this pussy! Fuck me Jermaine!"

"Louder!"

"FUCK ME JERMAINE!"

"Louder!"

"FUCK ME JERMAAIIINNNEEE!"

"I'M ABOUT TO COME!" I hollered and shoved her face into the *real* Jermaine's forehead, and the computer monitor fell to the floor—dragging what was left of the keyboard and her relationship.

"ME TOOOO!" Her vagina vibrated liquid fire down her legs before her body convulsed and went limp on the desk.

"AAAAAHH!" The pressure in my loins built to a radiating tingle.

My knees buckled and touched as I crossed heaven's threshold with *Bambi-legs*—releasing inside of Jermaine's girlfriend.

"Shiiiit...*aahh...*oooooh, shit...goddamn...Brittney!"

Fuck—I see why all these dudes juicing.

Pussy got a nine-volt battery in that motherfucker!

I planted on top of her as we panted in harmony. I spotted an alarm clock on the windowsill before noticing the empty bowl dangling from Chub's hand, and the mound of popcorn at her feet.

12:21 AM.

"Manzo?" she asked softly.

"Yes Brittney?" My head rested on her back. Her heart pounded against my cheek.

"Can I ask you for a favor?"

"Sure, anything babe."

Let me guess, don't tell anyone, huh?

"Next time we fuck...can you call me Toya?"

Chapter Fifteen

SHITTY CHOICES

Crippled from last night's entertainment, I unlocked my eyelids. The blurred numbers on the alarm clock disappeared and reappeared in rhythm with the pounding in my head.

I made a feeble attempt to sit upright and a slender porcelain arm skidded down my chest, and stopped at the crease between my abs.

I rested my head full of wavy hair back on the pillow, and my eyes returned to its happy darkness.

6:35 AM.

Five more minutes and I'm good.

What's today?

Hold up. It's Wednesday!

Wednesday morning workouts! Oh shit!

"FUUUUCK!" I muscled a thick ivory leg off me and launched out of the bed onto the hardwood floors.

The red satin sheet sailed before delicately landing back onto my company who remained unconscious.

I'm fucked!

Scavenging for my clothing with only a silver morning's light, I found my gray VT sweatpants at the foot of the bed and jumped into them without trying to find my underwear. The cotton snagged briefly to the dried pink substance pasted to my inner thighs.

What the—

Where's my—fuck it!

Unable to locate my shirt, I nabbed my gray VT hoodie draped to the back of the wooden desk-chair.

I tossed my favorite garment over my head and put my arms through the sleeves before yanking the bottom of the hoodie. The fabric chafed the stickiness of my back.

What the hell is that stuff on me?

6:37 AM.

Shit, I gotta bounce!

My keys?

My cellphone?

I slid my bare feet into the black Nike sandals with "fifty-four" magic-marked on both white checks. Scraping across the bedroom to an extravagant, mirrored cherry-wood dresser, I discovered my belongings, amongst other random shit, resting next to a silver jewelry box and an old bible, the King James version.

What happened last night?

OK, there's my weed. Damn, I wanna smoke.

6:39 AM.

No time to—

Oooh shit, what the fuck are those for?

While rushing to find my cell phone and car keys, I managed to inspect the accompanying items and was left in an abysmal state of confusion. I remembered with whom I left Impax with but could not recollect explicitly what happened after leaving the club.

There wasn't anything considerably puzzling about the bitty bottle of KY-Jelly, empty liter of Aristocrat Vodka, half-smoked blunt, pack of Gummi Bears, and even the melted pint of Haagen-Dazs strawberry ice cream was par the course. But the last object was a straight bogie—a red, rubber butt-plug.

That's that shit in the pornos!

Man, juices are some freaks!

How I forget all this crazy shit?

Yooo! I look like death!

"What's wrong Manzo?" Adriana lifted her head from the pillow and black curls fell from across her face to her shoulders.

She spoke through the mirror, "What happened?"

"Nothing baby, I gotta go."

6:41 A.M.

"Don't leave daddy." She smiled.

"Babe I wish I could stay, but I gotta bounce. But I will be right back." I swiped my keys and my cell phone.

"Please stay," she said.

"I can't babe."

"Are you *sure*?" She perked up, the sheets hooked to her aroused nipples before dropping, freeing two pearly blimps.

Goddamn!

Maybe I have a lil' time. 6:42 A.M.

Shit!

"Listen, stay right there! I have to jet to campus, and I'll be back to give you all this dick!"

"Me too?" Simona popped her head from under a pillow like a hungry meerkat.

"Ha-ha, of course! You can have some dick too Simona," I replied.

What happened last night?

Roommates, Adriana and Simona lived in Hunters Ridge Apartments, off of North Main Street in Blacksburg. Although unrelated, the stallions, both with long and curly black hair—had bodies like *sisters.*

They were mobsters' kids from New York City and had befriended me after I caught them passing notes to each other during a biology exam. I just winked and never spoke another word of the incident to anyone.

Before long, they were more than just my two favorite White girls at Tech— they were my two-favorite people.

They would cook for me, do my homework, let me cheat off them in class, and provided an occasional room and board when I needed to escape from campus.

In return, I gave my juices football tickets for every home game, smoked my weed with them, and provided all of their books, because scholarship-athletes never had to pay for any school supplies.

Of course, the equation wouldn't have been complete if there weren't any fucking involved. We had plenty of sex, just not all together.

While Simona and I played "Hide the Snickers" in one bedroom, Adriana and her boyfriend, Big Howard, did the same in the other.

But when Big Howard, a teammate of mine, broke Adriana's heart—I got to break her back. Hey, I couldn't let my homegirl suffer.

Jump back in the bed!

6:43 AM.

Shit, later!

The sheets drowned between Simona's Big-Apple-ass, but I watched in disappointment, unable to recall being the prosciutto in this Italian sub.

We kept no secrets in the house, and neither young lady gave a damn that they were sharing me. We had never enjoyed each other's friendship at the same time, although we had discussed a threesome a few times while we were high and joking.

Intertwining our lust seemed like a natural progression because there were many times that I would come over plastered and not know whom I was inside of until I heard, "Gimme that big Black *cack*." Simona had the thicker Staten Island accent.

"We have a lot to *discuss* when I get back." I picked up the sex toy by its base with my right index finger and thumb and shook my head. "Y'all some damn freaks up in here."

"Ha-ha, *we're* some freaks?" Adriana put her arm around Simona and pulled her closer, as they both faced one another and laughed.

"Nooooo...*you're* the freak!" Simona pointed at me. "We do have a lot to discuss young man! Next time don't pass out on us! We had to teach you a lesson!"

6:45 AM.

Fuck!

"Y'all crazy!" I tossed the butt-plug on the dresser and ran out of the room.

"Byyyeee!" I heard as the front door closed.

Crazy-ass juices!

Damn it's brick out here!

Oh shit! I still got Brittney's car!

I knew that I had Brittney's Honda, but it wasn't until I saw the vehicle that I even thought about her—or the fact that I was supposed to bring the car back to her, roughly ten hours ago.

I know she blew my phone up.

The bustling November air whiffed through my sweats and between my toes as my shaky right hand pulled, both, my keys and cell from my hoodie pocket.

The numbness restrained the sensation in my fingers but didn't alter my ability to read the electric blue Nokia 909.

6:47 AM.

Eighteen messages. Sooo annoying!

Fuck! I only have thirteen minutes!

Opening the car door, I jumped inside and threw the phone on the passenger seat before closing the door and shoving the key in the ignition, turning the key quickly.

The frozen leather interior reached into my soul and straightened my posture.

I shifted the car into drive with no time to warm the engine, eased off the break, and pressed on the gas pedal with increasing force until I was out of the parking lot—making a right onto North Main Street.

Once on North Main Street, almost a straight shot to Lane Stadium, I zipped past Food Lion doing eighty miles-per-hour before reaching for my phone to listen to my messages, skipping the ones I deemed unimportant.

'You have eighteen new messages...message one...'

'Manzo, I miss you. Where are you baby?'

BEEP.

'Are you OK baby, I'm getting worried?'

BEEP.

'I wanna fuck. Come back daddy.'

BEEP.

'OK where the fuck are you?'

BEEP.

'Oh you think you're slick motherfucker—'

BEEP.

'You better not have any of your bitches in my fucking car—'

BEEP.

'If you don't come back right now, I'm calling the fucking cops and telling—'

BEEP.

'You said you were going out to get you some hot sauce, and that was five hours ago! WHERE IS YOUR BLACK ASS?'

BEEP.

'I know you with that bitch Toya, or that fucking A-rab bitch you pretend to just be friends with—'

BEEP.

'You are a piece of shit, and if I ever—'

BEEP.

'OK I'm sorry I called you a piece of shit, just come home. I won't be mad. I just need to know you are safe baby. I love you so much.'

BEEP.

Fuck, let me call Brittney back and—

'Oh are you ignoring me? Fuck you, you bitch! You ain't a real man! I hope you *catch AIDS from one of those sluts you fucking! I'm gonna find me a real man, you COWARD!'*

BEEP.

Well, maybe not.

6:51 AM.

I'm here! Made it!

Hold up! Where are they going?

I created my own parking space and parked the car on the grass between the Jamerson Athletic Center and Lane Stadium, while I watched my teammates, Jamel Smith and Keith Short, steam across Stadium Road in soaked sweat suits. They unmistakably had just finished an intense workout.

6:53 AM.

But why are they here so early?

I guess it's just me and Lambo at seven o'clock then.

Upon opening the car door, a gust of wind heaved the stench of dirty baby diaper throughout the vehicle.

I had noticed the odor during the ride and paid little attention to the smell, considering Blacksburg was full of manure infested farmland.

Hopping out of the car, I tossed my phone and keys into the console and popped the trunk. I needed my cleats and socks.

What? Ooooh man! Noooo!

Just as I motioned to shut the car door and retrieve my gear, Anthony Lambo, a 300-pound freshman defensive tackle from Newark, New Jersey, trudged out of Lane Stadium's unbolted side door, which led directly to the football field.

The sight of the six-foot, three-inch Italian with the spiked black hair under a dusty, wet, white headband made me nauseous, and I could taste *almost* everything I ate the night before. I knew I had fucked up royally!

But it's not even 7:00 AM yet!

Lambo, Short, Jamel, and I were absent last week when Chris Roberson, a graduate assistant in the football office, came to check the attendance of the players in Dr. Baffey's 8:00 AM Health 101 class.

Lambo overslept, Short was too drunk to drive to class, and Jamel just didn't feel like coming.

To my defense, I had been in class before the roll call, but I had just left to *use* the bathroom. Either way, a Wednesday morning workout was the standard punishment for skipping class, and there was no way in hell my three codefendants were assigned a different time than I had.

"Manzo—what the fuck bro? Where have you been?" Lambo raised both arms, and sweat plummeted down his face and neck, submerging into his hoodie.

"I've been home bro! What are you talking about?"

"Home?" He stopped in front of me and closed the car door.

"Yea home!" I repeated.

"Hey wise guy, how the fuck were you home and you live two doors down from me bro?"

"Come on Lambo, you know what I mean!"

"No I don't know what you mean bro! Those bitches you be with ain't home bro!"

"How the fuck I was supposed to know y'all were gonna start early?"

"Early? Are you fucking kidding me bro?" He scratched his cheek, his five o'clock shadow glittered with the flicker of sunshine.

"Hey dumbass—it's called *6:00 AM* workouts for a reason!"

"I thought it was called 6:00 AM *and* 7:00 AM workouts, just depending on the hour you—"

"Do you fucking hear yourself right now bro?" He chuckled. "Are you high right now bro?"

"Heeeellll no!" I denied. "Listen, this is my first time and I didn't know the time, so it ain't my fault—"

"Manzo it's never your fault bro! That's what you said when Chris marked you absent—"

"I was in the bathroom—"

"Geeett the fuck outta here! Everyone knows you were fucking Suzie Wong in the Burke Johnston bathroom bro!"

Suzie got a big fucking mouth!

"Aight Lambo...I was—but I had to, so the bitch would let me cheat off her in psychology class!"

"It's always an excuse with you bro!" He shook his head and spit on the ground.

"Listen, I am not your father bro. I'm your friend and your teammate. All I'm saying is that you're a special talent, but you will never go nowhere doing the dumb shit you doing. You and Myron are the most athletic linebackers we got, but you don't play at all.

"Dirty Mike ain't better than you! Steve Tate or Tony Mo ain't better than you! They just work harder and take this game and *life* more seriously than you do!

"And if you keep getting trashed and fucking everything walking then you ain't neva gonna see the field! In these people's eyes, you just gonna be another *nigga* from the projects...who *could've* gone pro!"

Damn that hurt, but he's right.

Lambo put his paw on my shoulder and his positive energy upraised my common sense. I nodded steadily.

His eyes, small and obscure, ironically carried warmth that appeased my worries, although he had the stare of a John Gotti debt collector.

Lambo cared, and I valued his friendship and ability to respectfully express a truth I desperately needed to hear.

"Thanks bro. That was real," I said.

"That's the only way we will ever be bro," Lambo replied.

Oh shit, Coach Gentry!

"Where's Coach Gentry? Is he mad?" I asked.

"I mean, he ain't happy—"

"But did he say anything?"

"Manzo calm down bro!"

"Look at me Lambo! I look like I've been smoking rocks!"

"You ain't lying bro, and you smell like *shit*! What the fuck you were doing last night?"

"Really that bad bro?" I pinched the front of my hoodie and sniffed it. "I can't smell anything."

"Trust me, you stink bro. Go back to the dorm to freshen up—"

"I don't have time bro!" I pinched another area of my hoodie and inhaled deeply.

"Manzo just go see Gent bro! You already know how he's gonna be! You gotta just man the fuck up tough guy!" Lambo pointed to the entrance of Jamerson, the home of Virginia Tech's weight room, and college football's best and meanest strength and conditioning coach, Mike Gentry.

* * *

KNOCK. KNOCK.

Be calm.

"Manzo that better be you," Coach Gentry spoke from inside his office, the door halfway open.

Damn, I'm fucked!

"Yes sir—it's me sir."

"Well come on in here son."

"Yes sir." I stepped inside.

"Shut the door please."

"Yes sir—no problem sir."

"Well have a seat Manzo."

I am in fucking trouble! He's being too nice!

"Thank you, sir," I said.

Rolling the black leather office chair away from the desk, I sat gently on the landmine and awaited the detonation.

Gent sat peacefully forking chunks of white tuna straight out of the can and into his mouth. He chewed and stared.

Nervous, I felt like the chicken of the sea as his thickset mustache wiggled atop a hidden upper lip.

Coach Gentry, a stocky five-foot, ten inches with short, muscular, hairy arms and a belly—wasn't a big man.

But even with him seated, he and his presence *King Kong'ed* the tiny window-less office and put a blend of fear, love, and respect into the unlucky player sitting across from him.

Gent's rattail-less mullet helmeted onto a square red face, and his chin and wide neck lacked a definitive separation. Although he could've been on the Simpson's, there was nothing comical about the man.

"You like Harlem?" he asked.

"Uuh, yes sir."

"Do you love Harlem, Manzo?"

"Uuh, yes sir. I love Harlem."

"Describe it to me son." Coach Gentry scraped the last of the tuna into his mouth.

"Describe what sir?"

"Describe...*Harlem*." His breath turned my stomach, and he knew it.

"OK sir," I said, observing the drabness of his office.

Other than a black-stained, faux wood desk with no drawers, and a ceiling-high bookshelf packed with only huge volumes of fitness related books in all six rows—Gent's office contained no proof of life except for the coach himself.

He had a wife and son, and many academic degrees and accolades, but when he came to work, the players and his craft were the focus. No pictures. No awards. No games.

"Harlem is a nice place I guess, if you are from there. But there's a lot of crime and shit, I mean *stuff*. It's where all my family and friends are. Oh yea, the Apollo Theatre is there and—"

"Sounds like an amazing place." Gent placed the tuna can on his desk.

"It's home so I'm used to it—"

"You love it? Do you love home Manzo?"

"Yes sir, I love where I'm from." My lips curled the beginning of a smile.

"Well that's where you gonna be if you keep fucking up!" Gent screamed deafeningly, and I tasted his disgust.

"Miss another goddamn 6:00 AM WORKOUT, and you gonna be the fastest linebacker on 125th street!"

I don't want to go home!

"Sorry Coach!"

"Don't you sorry me Manzo!" Gent shook his head. "You weren't sorry when you were giving it to Suzie Wong in the bathroom!"

Fuuuck! Somebody snitched!

"Uuum sir...I don't know—"

"Manzo don't sit there and even begin to lie son!"

"But sir—"

"The next time you have sex with a girl in the bathroom, please make sure nobody can hear you genius!"

"But sir, anybody could've—"

"Son you better stop lying to me!" Gent's face reddened more; a vein thickened in his neck.

"Don't you ever lie to me son, I am God—I know *everything!*"

Bullshit, he's bluffing.

"But sir, how can you—"

BAM!

"Enough!" Gent crashed the bottom of his fist on his desk. I stopped talking and breathing for a moment.

As Coach Gentry looked at me in disappointment, I stared right back, and I could see that he cared about me—a lot.

Like Mr. Collins, he was a man of honor and did everything to instill his integrity into the young men who crossed his path.

I was nineteen years old and getting into a *little* trouble was age appropriate but being dishonest and not taking full responsibility for my actions were not acceptable.

Without a doubt, I knew Gent had known the truth about Suzie and me, but I just didn't know *how* he knew, and any unknown variable will keep a liar lying to the end.

Before I could continue embarrassing myself, he showed me exactly how much he cared about the undeserving young man sitting across from him.

"You had Ms. Wong yelling 'fuck me Manzo' into a bathroom vent, which happens to lead straight into the faculty lounge—but you didn't hear that from me."

Shit!

I told that stupid bitch to stop yelling! Chinese girls can't take no dick!

"Damn Coach." I put my head down.

"No one ratted on you but yourself son. Next time choose a girl that can take a little more dick." Gent joked, and it took the willpower of a monk not to burst out in laughter.

That's what I just said!

"Son get your shit together. And speaking of *shit*..." Gent paused, and I looked up immediately. "Don't EVER come in this office looking the way you look and *smelling* the way you smell! Have some respect for this program and yourself!"

Do I stink that bad?

How?

"Yes sir," I said.

"You smell like you've been wrestling in dog shit!"

"Sorry sir."

"Stop being sorry and be great! Everyone seems to believe in you, except you!" Gent pointed at me.

"Yes sir."

"Now, I want to see your ass every Wednesday morning at 6:00 AM *sharp* for the next four weeks, and if you are even late to one, we are shipping you back to *El Barrio* on the first thing smoking! This is your last shot Manzo!"

God no!

"Do we have an understanding son?" Gent asked, extending his right hand.

"Yes sir." I shook his hand.

"Now get the hell out of here and pull yourself together before going to class son." He nodded toward the door, grabbed a notebook off the desk labeled, 'Lift or Die,' and swiveled his chair toward the back wall.

"Yes sir. Thank you, sir." I left the office.

* * *

Standing outside, I felt blessed to still be a Virginia Tech football player, and I let Gent's words sink in before walking to my car.

I was at a great university with an amazing opportunity, and I had almost blown my college career by being an immature dumbass. I could have fun, but I had to make school and football a priority. Fun would always be there.

Time to get serious.

I was ready to change my life, but before I could think about some character and life adjustments—another cool gust of wind blew in my face. I could smell the horrid stench that had followed me from the girls' apartment.

Suddenly, I forgot about my meeting with Coach Gentry and could only think about what Simona said before I left the girls' bedroom.

'No, you're the freak.'

'We had to teach you a lesson.'

Hold up...

Wait a minute...

No fucking way!

Standing just a few feet away from the Honda, I shivered with a demoralizing anger as I stared at the driver's side window.

Something just wasn't right, and I could almost feel it, but prayed I was completely wrong. I kept shaking my head as I unsuccessfully attempted to remember last night.

Frustrated with my *imagination*, I couldn't help but speak to my haggard reflection.

"They better not have touched me with that motherfucking butt-plug."

Chapter Sixteen

DUMB LUCK

"Good job Hokies!"

"It's OK Hokies, we will back next year!"

"Nebraska sucks ass!"

"Hold y'alls heads up high men!"

The parking lot was foggy and damp from a late evening shower that spiced the air with wet concrete and defeat. Victory was a smell from the past, washed away in the Miami night.

Outside of Pro Player Stadium, hundreds of Hokies' faithful cheered as our team solemnly trudged through the gauntlet of support, and onto the team bus.

We just had been battered by the University of Nebraska Cornhuskers, 41-21 in the Fed Ex Orange Bowl.

"Go Virginia Tech—go!"

"Good game Shayne Graham!"

"Way to go Loren Johnson!"

"Way to keep fighting Manzo! Harlem kids are never scared to take a chance!"

A short, middle-aged, black haired Hispanic man with a white Virginia Tech t-shirt, fitted blue jeans, and silver toed, black leather cowboy boots yelled and patted me on the back as I stepped onto the team bus.

After glancing at his diamond Rolex, the man winked at me before I watched his spiked, faded haircut parade coolly back through the crowd. His Stetson cologne kept his spot warm.

'Way to keep fighting'? 'Scared to take a chance'?

I didn't even play amigo!

Both feet planted on the top step, I felt the air on the back of my neck from the bus's doors shutting.

Unintentionally the last player to enter, I gripped the front railing tightly and began my breaststroke to my seat at the far end.

Mildly embarrassed for delaying my comrades a prompt departure from a forgettable memory, I sidestepped up the aisle with my head down, through seated silhouettes of misery. Everyone was quiet, sans the strum of the engine and a few recognizable whispers.

It's like a funeral in here.

"We have a lot of talent returning so we should be top ten next year," Coach Foster spoke as I moved through the aisle and held onto the back of every other headrest for balance.

I hope he's talking about me.

"Shit, the guy I might hire told me I'm going fourth round or better. What about you?" Antonio Banks asked someone.

"I haven't talked to anyone yet, but I'm sure it's about the same." The Florida accent undeniably belonged to Torrian Gray. "I hope we get drafted by the same team but what are the chances, huh?"

Reaching the middle of the bus, I lost my balance and plopped into my seat just as the driver made a hard left out of the parking lot.

My elbow slammed flush against the metal armrest, and I grimaced in embarrassment awaiting my teammates' laughter or some silly comment, but everyone remained lost in the intimacy of his own thoughts.

Fuck, that shit hurt!

Corey Moore, the right side of his face pasted against the window, never moved or spoke. Every time we passed a streetlight, the sheen of tears lubed across his cheeks had become more visible.

He had been crying since the seniors' emotional farewell speeches in the locker room. Only Cornell and Brandon Semones' words pushed out a few droplets from my eyes.

I loved the seniors, but I needed them out of my way. Plus, I couldn't wait to take Brandon's jersey number next year.

I'm finally gonna get number twenty-one—

"PSSST..." Someone behind me apparently wanted Corey's or my attention.

"PSSST...Manzo?" he muttered between the seats. "Hey it's Bird."

"Yo?" I replied.

"PSSST...Manzo?"

"I said *yo* Bird."

"Oh my bad."

"What's up Bird?"

"Manzo?"

"Maaan, what the fuck do you want Bird?"

"Oh OK...you can hear me," Bird said.

"Yes, I can hear you bro."

This dude sounds mad nervous.

"You OK bro?" I asked Bird.

"Yea I'm cool."

"Well say what you want to say homie. You know we can talk about anything."

"Aight...cool," Bird said. "Manzo get your shit together so this could never happen to us."

"Huh Bird?"

"Just let me please talk and listen for a minute. This shit is serious Manzo."

Ah man, what the fuck does he want now?

"No problem bro. I'm listening," I said.

* * *

Cory Bird, a fellow member of the freshman class, was from Mays Landing, New Jersey. He was a five-foot, ten inches, 195-pound wide receiver with unsurpassed strength and athletic ability—and a high football IQ.

Bird appeared to be just another self-absorbed light skinned dude with muscles and hair from the White side of his family, but his wide nose, cauliflower ears, and tattoo of a monkey on his right shoulder toughened his look from Prince to the Rock.

Although Bird and I took many of the same classes, lived on the same dorm, partied at the same bars, and pollinated the same juices, we never took our friendship to the level of Dre and mine, primarily because Bird had more sense than I did.

He didn't smoke weed and could compartmentalize when it was time to be a student, a football player, and a douche bag. I only had one speed—*full speed.*

* * *

"It's like this Manzo, you see how everyone on this bus is sad and shit?" Bird asked.

"Yea bro, it's like someone died."

"You right, and that's because it is kind of a death for a lot of these dudes?"

"Man it ain't that serious. It's just a game Bird."

"Just a *game*? Bro you are buggin'. Some of these dudes will never play football again and just lost the last game of their careers."

"Well, you can't win them all."

"Your attitude about this game ain't right bro." He reclined his seat like he was done talking, but fleetly snapped forward and continued softly speaking between the chairs.

"This is exactly why we needed to talk."

"Ha-ha, because I think football is a game? Cut the fucking jokes Bird."

"You need to take this opportunity more seriously Manzo."

"I am."

"Really?" he asked.

"Yes...really."

"How bro? Please fill me in, because you haven't played a single down in six games bro."

Damn, it's been six games!

"Uh, that's because the coaches don't like me."

Do they like me?

"Ha-ha, shut up bro. *Everybody* loves you or you would be gone by now," he said.

"But I changed Bird."

"Dude, you haven't changed shit. You just got a little slicker."

"I'm not perfect but—"

"Yo Manzo, you still can't remember your plays, you still not going to *all* your classes, you still chasing juices before and after practice. And you always still smell like weed when we hang out. You better thank God your name hasn't popped up for a random drug test by the NCAA."

"OK I'm working on some things, and I still have to make a few changes."

"You think?"

"Listen, don't be a dick Bird."

"You wear condoms?"

"*What* the fuck?" I asked.

"Answer the question bro," he demanded. "Do you wear condoms with all these girls?"

"Condoms?"

"Yea, condoms Manzo. The shits niggas steal from Kroger's."

"Motherfucker I know what a condom is."

"OK, so answer the question then bro."

When was the last time I wore a condom? Was it with...?

No, it was with...

Nah, Julie only gave me head that time. What year is this again?

"Dude, I could feel your brain working through the seats. You can't remember when the last time you wore one, huh?" Bird asked.

Fuck, I can't remember!

"Man all my girls are clean anyway. But what the fuck does condoms have to do with football?" I challenged.

"Everything! You're reckless in every aspect of your life nigga."

What?

Damn...fuck...Bird is right! I need to change!

I had no words for Bird, he was on point with his assessment of my life and I couldn't deny the truth. Living recklessly, I never thought about the consequences of my actions, nor did I care.

In my mind, I really wanted to change my ways, because I understood that I would never reach my goals of graduating college and being drafted into the NFL if I continued living the way I did.

So, each morning I would make a promise to myself to be a more responsible and a more committed student-athlete, but by 1:00 PM—I had already fucked two girls, drank three beers, and missed four classes.

"Listen Manzo, I know Lambo and some of the others talked to you—so I'm not going to beat you upside the head anymore with this, but know that I'm only talking to you because I care bro. You're my homie."

"You're my homie too Bird, and I appreciate you."

"We have a chance to do something special here at Tech. Shit we might be playing for the National Championship one day," he said.

Could we?

Oh man, I never thought about that.

"Ike, Midget, Keion and Prioleau locking shit down, Carl Bradley and Nat on the line, you running the middle, and Corey Moore coming off *that* edge bro— we'd be unstoppable on defense."

"Shit you're right," I said as I glanced at a snoring Corey Moore. "Nobody would be fucking with us."

"I'm telling you Manzo...*Ssh,* hold up." Bird leaned back in his seat as someone walked past us and entered the bathroom.

CLICK.

SLAM!

"That was Coach Wiles. You get the point though. We need you. Get your shit together please bro," he said.

"No doubt Bird. Good looks," I replied, illuminating the time on my Nautica watch.

12:05 AM?

It's 1997 now!

What the fuck, we missed New Year's?

Since birth I have spent every New Year's Eve with my family, and as I sat on the bus staring at my watch, I missed them and wondered if they missed me.

Each year we would all get together like many other families and count down the seconds to the start of a new beginning, but there was one instance that I remembered when we weren't all together as a family when the ball dropped to a new year.

As the team bus turned onto Collins Avenue, I couldn't help but relive the moment.

* * *

12:05 AM.

"It's OK Karen. Carlos is probably just in traffic, but he will be here," Diana said to my mother, who stood with her back against the living room wall with her eyes shut. "Wait until he sees how you look."

Where are you Daddy?

Hurry up man! I want to start eating that fried chicken I smell in the kitchen!

"Tell your mother how good she looks Manzo," Diana requested from her loveseat.

"Uh...yea...Mommy...you look so pretty!" I said from the damaged green leather sofa, adjacent to a thirty-five-inch floor model TV with "DDD" carved diagonally on the side of it.

Distracted, I didn't compliment Mommy like I normally would do, but she looked stunning—Mommy stayed runway-ready.

She adored high end fashion brands by most of the top designers—no matter their origins.

* * *

Beck when I was just a *leettle* boy, I watched my parents shop numerous times, and I developed an obsession for the merchandise—not the labels.

In Wagner, I saw addicts passing a plethora of green paper to Black people looking like my father.

On Fifth Avenue, I saw Daddy dish identical dollars to the well dressed "whiteys" who sold exactly what his woman wanted.

The managers even served my mother glasses of Dom Perignon from silver trays, with crackers and Brie cheese.

As I openly stared at the mannequins' breasts, and Daddy slyly took the sales clerks' phone numbers—*Mommy* bought dresses, furs, and even cool-furniture.

My parents feigned to possess their purchases like if they just copped some hard powder, and I knew right then that the popular pieces had supreme *powers*.

Intrigued, I would sit with my mother at home and read Vogue magazines on her bed while she showed me the latest trends and styles from all around the world.

She gave me an appreciation for detail and quality. I was the teacher's pet, developing an affinity for the first-rate-fabrics and exquisite designs.

But I wasn't interested in the fashion, I was fascinated with the product—which seemed more profitable than the Now & Laters candy I sold in class.

* * *

"Guuurl, that outfit is slamming! Carlos is gonna love it!" Diana said.

"Thanks." My mother dryly replied.

Mommy wore a Dolce & Gabanna short black mini-skirt, Fendi thigh-high black leather boots, and a Saint Laurent black deep V-neck sweater, while her black hair *straight-combed* from under a black top-hat with "Happy New Year's" sparkled in silver across the front.

Her bright powder-red MAC lipstick sealed two perfect lips that popped madly, in contrast to her biscuit colored skin.

Set atop a minimum of cleavage, was an eighteen-carat gold chain which supported a chunky medallion and read, "Los loves Karen" in diamonds.

The chain had been my father's most recent addition to her jewelry box.

"*Relax* Karen, everything's gonna be fine—"

"Mommy!" Diana's eight-year-old daughter, Dironna, *tattletale'd* from the kid's bedroom. "Javier and Alejandro keep picking on Sandy and Donté!"

"Dironna leave me the HELL alone and play with the kids!" Diana answered. "I'm going to tell your father when he *decides* to come home if you ain't being nice!"

Diana, my mother's oldest and dearest friend, grew up with her in Wagner Project's building 2375, along with Diana's sister Latisha and their mother Ms. Bernice.

Diana was a smallish, dark skinned woman with a short, slicked, comb-over hairdo, large eyes, and longish teeth.

She had as much fight in her as she did comedy, and Diana and my mom would be on the phone for hours either laughing or contemplating which bitch's ass from the neighborhood they would kick if the bitch "kept acting up," even though they both never had a fight in their lives.

Traditionally, my family would celebrate New Year's Eve in the madness of our own apartment, but Diana's husband, Jack, got caught with his Lee's around his ankles, karate chopping their next-door neighbor's face with his cock in Diana's bedroom one afternoon.

Diana grabbed a knife before the neighbor ran to the roof, and Jack three-legged-raced out of the front door and down Madison Avenue.

My mother, the great friend she was, insisted on traveling to Lehman Village, because she did not want to leave Diana and Diana's three small children, Dironna, Donald, and Douglas alone on New Year's Eve.

KNOCK! KNOCK!

"Come in! It's open!" Diana hollered down the hallway as she muted the TV with the remote. "See Karen, everything is OK now! Carlos is here!"

Yes, Daddy's here!

Without speaking, Mommy slowly stepped away from the wall, and turned to face the doorway, just ten feet away. She squinted her eyes, twirled her necklace in her right hand, and shook her head.

"Happy New Year's everyone!" my father greeted while he tapped his sky-blue alligator loafers down the hallway. He held two bottles of Dom Perignon champagne in both hands, respectively.

"It's 1991! Let's get this party started folks!"

"Hey Los!" Diana loved my father. "See Karen, everything is—"

"FUCK YOU MOTHERFUCKER!" My mother ripped off her necklace and threw it in Daddy's face.

CRASH!

A bottle of Dom Perignon dropped from my father's hand and shattered on the floor. "What the hell is wrong with you woman?" Daddy yelled.

What the hell?

"What's wrong with *me*?" Mommy asked.

"Yea, what the hell is wrong with *you*?" Daddy asked again while he rubbed his right cheek, the bottoms of his pants, and his gators were swamped.

"Are you fucking serious right now Carlos?"

"What was that Mommy?" Dironna hollered from the room.

"Just an accident baby! Stay in the room and mind your damn business!"

Diana sassed over the chatter of fizzling grapes.

"What? Calm down! Damn! It was mad traffic, and I ain't even do shit!" Daddy protested.

"You ain't do shit?" Mommy walked two paces toward my father.

"Karen No!"

"Mind your business Diana!" Mommy side-eyed over her shoulder at Diana.

CRUNCH!

Mommy stepped on pieces of glass and nudged my father on his neck. "What is this then nigga?"

"What's what *Karen*?" Daddy took a step back.

"That shit on your neck motherfucker—stop acting stupid!"

"I can't see what you are talking about. What...what shit?" Daddy pinched his nostrils and sniffed before touching the spot on his neck.

"*And* you're coked up too? Wooow." Mommy asked.

"Manzo let's go in the room and—"

"No Diana, *my* son needs to see what type of man NOT to be!" Mommy stepped closer to my father.

I thought he quit using.

"Come on Karen, you're being irrational!" Daddy nervously looked down and brushed the front of his black leather pants.

His five-karat diamond pinky ring shimmered against a 100-Watt light bulb screwed into a shade-less lamp sitting on a milk crate filled with cassette tapes beside the couch. "I ain't on nothing—you buggin'!"

That shit must be really good if Daddy keeps doing it.

"Oh am I?" Mommy leaned forward and put her nose inches from the collar of his black leather jacket. "*SNIFF.*"

"Why are you smelling me? You trippin' woman!"

"Ha-ha...Coco Chanel, huh Manzo?" Mommy shook her head.

"Yea that's *your* perfume on me that you're smelling, so don't even try no bull-shit right now!"

"Coco Chanel is the perfume I *used* to wear. I only wear Dior now, and have been for the last four months." Mommy smiled.

"If you gonna have your other bitches smell like me...then at least get the scent right—you dumb motherfucker!"

"But Karen—"

"Don't *but Karen* me *Los*! You're a pathetic excuse of a man and I'm tired of this shit!"

"But I can explain!"

"Don't try and explain shit to me Carlos, it's too late!" Mommy waived away my father's attempt to hold her.

"Don't you *dare* fucking touch me!"

"OK now you're embarrassing me in front of people?" Daddy peeped at Diana.

"Oooh, you worried about Diana motherfucker?" Mommy placed both hands on her hips.

"Diana already knows you're a piece a shit! You need to be worried about your fucking son!"

"What the hell you talking about? My son knows I'm a good man!"

Yea Daddy's a good man!

"That's the problem right there Carlos, but you too dumb to see what's going on!"

"Stop calling me dumb!" Daddy yelled.

"Why should I stop, huh? You are dumb, and you just don't get it!"

"Don't get what?"

"You don't get that your son idolizes you and worships everything you do!"

"He should, I'm his goddamn father!"

"So he should want to be like you, huh?" Mommy pointed to Daddy's chest.

"Hell yea!" Daddy swatted away Mommy's finger.

"I provide for this entire family and make sure that my children and my ungrateful fucking *wife* has everything they need!"

"*Ungrateful*?" Mommy asked, placing her hand on her chest.

"Yes, *ungrateful*!"

"I am supposed to be thankful that my *husband* shows up late on New Year's Eve smelling like pussy and perfume and is all coked the fuck up—with a hickey on his goddamn neck?"

"You don't know what the hell you're talking about woman—I fell!" Daddy flipped the collar of his baby-blue silk shirt and resumed staring at the floor.

The apartment went completely silent, which meant that there were seven nosey little Black kids in the back room absorbing every single word hollered, and I wanted to get up and make sure that they were all right.

I also wanted to get up and hug my mother, but I couldn't move because the person I felt the most compassion for at that moment was my father.

I was not a fool and I knew my father was still slanging coke, fucking hoes, and keeping his nose dirty, but it shredded my soul to see the man standing in my presence with a sense of vulnerability and defeat that I've never witnessed.

It hurt me to see him hurt, even though every ounce of emotion I had should have been for the victimization of my mother.

"Carlos, it's not about you or me right now. I know who I married and I'm here by choice, but these kids don't have a choice who their father is.

"It's not about what you can buy them and all that bullshit, but it's about the type of example you are showing them, especially Manzo." Mommy pointed at me and her eyes dampened, while Diana quietly walked to the kids' room and closed the door behind her.

"If you don't *show* your son a better example of what type of a man to be, he is going to be just like you.

"He's going to disrespect women, walk around like his shit don't stink and believe that easy money and fast living is the way to live...but he might not be as lucky as you.

"*Sins of the father*...you're Catholic motherfucker. You should know the rest."

* * *

"Washington Avenue!"

Huh?

"Washington Avenue!" the bus driver announced again over the loudspeaker.

"The coaches said there's no curfew tonight, just be safe and make sure you guys are in front of the Eden Roc at 2:00 PM *sharp* if you are flying back to Christiansburg tomorrow."

No curfew?

Serious?

SMACK.

"Let's go Zo." Sean Sullivan hit me across my back.

"Shit, you don't have to tell me twice." I immediately got up and followed the couple of bodies that passed me through the darkness and out of the bus's front door.

"You never gonna learn," Cory Bird murmured, and I ignored him.

"Last call for Washington Avenue!" the driver repeated.

"OK boys be safe!" the bus driver yelled before shutting the bus doors and making a hard-right down Espanola Way.

"Hold up! Wait, it's just us?" I said, noticing that Dre, *Sully* and myself were the only players to get off the bus. "Why these niggas ain't get off?"

"Maaaan fuck them! Look across the street!" Dre yelled.

"Holy shit!" Sully nudged my arm and pointed.

As foreign cars cruised in both directions down Washington Street blasting a fusion of Latin music and rap, I looked through the *palm-tree'd* intersection at the short white building on the corner.

The structure blazed sky-blue, orange, red, and pink fluorescent lights from a huge awning, which set thirty feet high over the entrance.

The place looked like an old-school movie theatre but couldn't have been. Not even a flick co-starring Wilt Chamberlain and Julio Iglesias would've had *that* much ass in a line.

Tonight Poison Clan.

"It says Poison Clan is here tonight. Who the hell the is Poison Clan?" I asked.

"Poison Clan? Who gives a fuck who they are? Look at them bitches! We in there!" Dre said as he started crossing the street without a vote. Sully and I followed.

"Well actually, Poison Clan is a rap group with J.T. Money—"

"Okaaay Sully!" Dre interrupted.

"Ha-ha!" I laughed.

"Yo fuck you Dre! Your lil' Webster on steroids-looking-ass!" Sully trotted to keep up.

My foot reached the sidewalk in front of Club Cambiar and I almost tripped. Hundreds of sculpted-ass young women in four-inch heels, white tight mini-dresses, with side boobs and extra cleavage bouncing—chewed gum, chatted, and patiently waited to be added to the club's menu.

Most of the curly haired brunette goddesses were tanned to a golden crisp, with a few brown beauties scattered amongst them.

"Man this shit looks crucial bro. I hope we can get in this piece," Sully pointed to a line full of guys adjacent to the girls.

"Oh shit, I didn't even see those Ricky Martins over there!" Dre yelled over the base thumping from *Cambiar's* double door entrance.

"What the fuck? I haven't seen so many white shoes and chest hairs since my family reunion," I joked.

"Is this Spanish night or some shit Sully?" Dre asked.

"Nah dog, it's just Miami. Every night is Spanish night, and you gonna see a bunch of metrosexual Tony Montanas running around too."

"Y'all sure we can get in here because—"

"Hey, you three!" an unidentified voice interrupted my question.

"Someone is calling us?" Dre asked.

"Man I hope not. I don't feel like fucking up none of these Jon Secadas tonight," I said.

"Hey! You three in the black! Y'all deaf or something?" the voice continued, and everyone in the area had begun to stare. "Come over here *por favor!*"

Who's that?

"Someone wants us," Dre said as we all looked at each other.

"Man fuck that, don't be scared. Come on," I said and walked in between the small crowd. Dre and Sully marched behind.

"What's up bro?" I asked the *smallest* of the three mammoth, baldheaded African American bouncers dressed in cheap black suits, standing behind a velvet rope.

Goddamn these Milk Dud head niggas are big!

"Watch out Kong," the voice spoke again, and the bouncers sidestepped making a lane.

Kong?

A man, no taller than Dre, filled in the space like a chipped tooth amongst giant molars.

The man's hair was slicked back into a ponytail, showing a flawless, radiant diamond stud earring in his left ear. His navy-blue suit was impeccable and tailored up to the gold Rolex Daytona on his right wrist.

The lights from the awning overhead dropped on his baked face, which made it difficult for me to determine his age. But no matter the era he was from, there was no question, he was the boss.

"What's up guys? I'm Santos." Santos looked up at Sully and back at me. "And I have a question for you my friends."

"What's your question my friend?" I asked.

"I just wanted to know." He smiled with perfect veneers.

"Know what my *friend*?" I asked.

"I just wanted to know...ha-ha..." He looked at Sully and me from chin to toe. "Are you fucking guys, *brothers* or *lovers*? Ha, ha, ha!"

Clenching my fist, I glanced at Sully, whose pale face had begun to deluge with blood.

He was a straight Caucasian out of Boca Raton, but like most White boys who hung out with brothers, the six-foot, five-inch 280-pound tight end was battle-tested and never backed down from a fight.

I will hit Kong.

Sully will hit the one closest to him.

Dre will—

"Whoa, whoa...I'm totally giving you shit about your matching tracksuits. Don't beat me up!" Santos turned to Kong and winked. "I know who you guys are. Tough game tonight against Nebraska, but it's OK—let's have some fun muchachos."

"Kong give the Virginia Tech guys my table. Buenos suerte con las chicas gentlemen. Enjoy your evening." Santos walked away, and a bouncer briskly followed to hold open one of the doors and both entered.

"What the fuck just happened?" Dre asked from three feet behind me.

"Right this way gentlemen, and I wish you a fine evening." Kong unhooked the red velvet rope. His voice was a total surprise.

Oh shit, this big nigga sound White as fuck!

"Thank you, tío Tom. We will indeed enjoy the festivities tonight. Let's go Sully." I said before looking back at Dre.

"Bring your scary-ass on."

* * *

Tupac's "All Eyez On Me" electrified the club with thug life as alternate egos bopped their heads and swayed their arms to the beat of a street tale that many knew, but even more pretended to know.

Standing alone on the balcony level, Dre, Sully, and I preached in unison Pac's gospel down to the *believers* on the dance floor. Some held their drinks high. We held our bottles of Cristal higher.

Red lights burned the sky, flaming a giant strobe light in the center of the club that parted the posers from the posers.

Four blonde-wigged girls in black leather thigh-high boots, fishnet stockings, and white two-piece thong bikinis dangled from a single stripper pole at the far end of the room beside the bar, but no one seemed to notice the human shish kebab. All eyes were on us.

Euro-grapes trashed my reality with each bubbling sip while floating marijuana smoke, secondhand sizzled the *self* from my consciousness and doubt.

If even temporarily, we owned the moment, but the most intoxicating substance was the attention. Attention could absorb baking soda better than cocaine. Tupac rapped but we performed, and I never wanted to leave the stage.

"All eyez on *us* motherfuckers!" Dre shouted.

"Hell yea, we are living fellas!" I raised my champagne bottle in the air. Sully and Dre touched their bottles against mine.

"We are living like fucking kings!" Sully bobbed his head to the beat.

"Man when we go to the league, we gonna do this shit every single day!" I said.

"Fuck yea! But look! Who's those bad-ass bitches at our table?" Sully asked.

"Where?" Dre turned his head.

"Chill Dre!" Sully grabbed Dre's arm. "I know your midget-ass can't see over my shoulder but don't blow up the spot!"

"Man fuck you Sully!" Dre spat back.

"Oh shit, they are bad too!" I peeped the girls through my peripheral. "I'm trying to fuck something tonight!"

"Fuck y'all waiting for then?" Dre pulled out his bottle of Polo Sport and sprayed himself indiscreetly.

"That smells good! Good call Dre!" Sully reached out his hand. "Dre let me get some of that Polo *Short!*"

"Short? Oh shit! Ha, ha, ha!" I laughed.

"Get your own damn cologne, dirty White boy!" Dre joked.

"Man, fuck you Arnold!" Sully scowled.

"Y'all always going at it. Let's go!" I headed toward our table, approximately six feet behind us.

Advancing a few paces, I had finally gotten a chance to get a complete look at the three smiling women dressed in identical black mini dresses, sitting on a black and white leather couch the length of an adult cow.

The club's lights trooped up smooth brown athletic legs, dying subtly in the shadowy bunker between them.

The ripeness of six coconuts, augmented to perfection, momentarily froze my scanner in cleavage-mode until the woman in the middle spoke, encouraging me to go to the next level.

"Helloooo...hola señor!"

Oh shit. I love that accent!

"Hola señoritas!" I said and finally looked her in the eyes, glancing at the other two women who were giggling toward each other.

Fuck, they are hot!

All three women had their black hair slicked back into buns, wore red lipstick over full lips and identical small diamond encrusted crosses around their necks.

The woman directly in front of me appeared a little older than her slender-faced counterparts, all smelling sweet as if they bathed in warm papaya oil.

I want to bite these hoes!

"Hello big guy. I'm Rosa." The woman smiled while extending her small hand to me.

So pretty! Her eyes though!

"Hey...what color—"

"They are green and hazel...and jes, they are real." She laughed. "Like jour muscles, no?"

"Ha-ha, jes...I mean *yes*, they're real too," I said.

How much did I drink already? Be cool nigga.

This bitch is super bad though!

All three women chuckled, and I noticed the one to my left had a hickey on her neck that she attempted to conceal with makeup.

Yep, these hoes fucking!

"And who are your friends?" I asked.

"Ha-ha, my friends?" Rosa made eye contact with both women and nodded. "My friends are now friends of *jour* friends."

"Aaah shit, Sully and Dre..." I said and turned to my left, expecting to see my teammates by my side.

They had remained standing next to the banister, bobbing their heads to the music—pretending not to pay attention to *mis amigas* and me.

"Don't worry about the shy ones. Ju will be muy bien," Rosa promised. "Come sit down with me. This is jour table señor...no es mío"

After not so discreetly taking something out of Rosa's hand and grabbing champagne glasses, the Latinas wiggled their way off the couch and around the table. One of the carafes of orange juice almost toppled over but I didn't notice at all.

Looking at their bodies, I almost dropped my bottle of champagne. I've never seen such shapely creatures in my life!

Although excited, I didn't fully comprehend what I was seeing but *never* wanted to look away.

Holy shit!

Look at those asses!

"Byeee," the taller Latina with the tattoo on her left shoulder of Jessica Rabbit said as they sashayed toward Sully and Dre.

The women's waistlines seemed trim enough to wear a Cabbage Patch Kid's belt, but their *culos* needed suspenders.

Either everything that the Latinas ate went straight to their behinds, or they were kin to an alien breed of South American ants. I fantasized of stuffing my face in their mounds until Rosa brought me back to earth.

"*Manzo?*" Rosa said my name as no one ever did.

"Huh...yes...yes...I'm here babe," I said.

Hold up! How she knows my name?

Oh shit, Hokies got me famous already!

"Come sit down with me, no tienes miedo guapo." Rosa patted the couch before uncrossing and crossing her legs again.

"I'm not scared of you bonita." I sat beside Rosa.

Fuck she smells so good!

Lord please forgive how bad I want this pussy!

"I'm not gonna lie Rosa, they don't make asses like that in Blacksburg. It's out of this world. Is that...*real*?" I pointed.

"Ha, ha, ha...*real*?" Rosa pointed also. "Real fun is all that matters, no?"

"Fucking right that's all that matters babe."

"Ju friends having fun it seems."

"Fuck yea, they're loving your sisters." I pointed to Sully and Dre smiling blissfully, each pouring champagne into the girls' flutes.

"They no me hermanas *Manzo*." Rosa put her hand on my lap while I poured her a glass of champagne.

"I'm the hostess here at Cambiar and they *work* for the club."

"Oooh OK, cool." I said.

"Let me ask you something Manzo." Rosa slid her hand further up my thigh.

"Uh...sure...ask whatever." My cock gained weight.

"Ju want a bump?" she spoke into my ear.

"A bump?"

"Jes, like a bump of coke muchacho."

"Yes I know what a bump is. My daddy sold plenty of *bumps*. No, I'm good though but you can do whatever you like."

"Ju sure guapo?"

"Yes babe I'm sure. We play football, we smoke a little weed and drink, but we don't do bumps or lines or mess with blow."

"Well...tell that to ju big gringo friend." She pointed.

"Huh?"

Following her finger, I watched Sully bend his head down, put his right index finger on his right nostril, and snort powder off *Jessica Conejo's* left breast that she held with two hands as if she were feeding a grown infant.

Even through the darkness of the club, I saw him swiftly lick her nipple and stand up straight like he didn't just commit a class-C misdemeanor.

Oh shit! Them Florida boys get down I see!

"Well to each his own Rosa. But I'm good on that babe," I said.

"No problemo guapo." She turned and dipped her head slightly away from me. "*SNIIIIFFF!*"

Fucking vacuum!

"Aaah, está bien." She squeezed the bridge of her nose and looked into my eyes. "You like to fuck Manzo?"

"Uuuh, what?" I asked.

She said 'fuck'?

"Jes, do ju like to fuck Manzo?" Rosa replaced her left hand further up my groin.

"Sí Rosa...absolutamente," I replied.

"Of course, what boy jour age doesn't?"

"Shit I don't know any *boys* my age—"

"I love to fuck too, *especially* on cocaína." Rosa said.

Oh God!

"But anyway Manzo, can I ask ju a question?" She moved her face closer to mine.

"Por supuesto Rosa."

"Ju like money?" She smiled.

"Money? jes, I mean yes. Me encanta el dinero." I answered.

"Do ju college fútbol players make any money?"

"We make a little money." I grinned.

"Well I like ju...I like ju a lot, and I'm gonna help ju make plenty money if ju like?" Rosa nodded toward her amigas who were licking Sully's neck as Dre just watched, bopping his head to Sisqo's "Thong Song".

"How you gonna help make me some money?" I asked and took a huge swig from the bottle. "Ahhhh."

"Easy. Muy fácil." She wiped my bottom lip with her thumb.

"How?" I asked.

"Ju interested Manzo?"

"Yes."

If it means I can fuck you.

"Bueno." Rosa's little fingers brushed the tip of my bulge. My VT windbreakers left nothing to the imagination.

"Ju fly to Miami on a private plane, no?" she asked.

"Yes, we did."

"Ju fly back on a private plane, no?"

"Yes, we do."

"Ju go through no security, no?"

"Nah, we never have to go through security when we fly." I raised an eyebrow.

"Sooo, if I gave ju a package to take back for me—ju could, muy fácil, no?" She scratched *my* package slowly with her thumb.

"Yes I could babe." I drank from the bottle again, keeping eye contact. "Yes, muy fácil."

"OK guapo, ju take a package from me...and I will give ju $10,000, no?"

Hold up!

What?

Drugs?

"Hold up! Please tell me that you don't want me to take drugs on a fucking plane?" I reluctantly brushed her hand off my lap.

This bitch is buggin'!

"Guapo, I never said *drogas*."

"Rosa, I'm not stupid so please don't play me like I am."

"No, no, listen Manzo, tranquilo guapo—"

"I'm calm babe but come on—"

"I never said drogas."

"So OK, tell me what you're talking about then?" I said and placed my bottle on the table.

Lady thinks I'm stupid.

"OK, escúchame por favor."

"I'm listening babe." I laughed, leaning back into the soft leather couches.

"Ju team take a private plane here, no?"

"Yes."

"Ju walk right on the plane no security check, no?"

"No security, correct."

"Ju get off the plane—no security, no?"

"No, we got right on the bus."

"So no securidad, no policía, no nada—no?"

"No, we just get right on the bus."

"Nobody check jour bags, no?"

"No, nobody ever checks my bags babe."

"And going back will be lo mismo, no?"

"Yes, it's the same routine every time we fly." I picked the Cristal back up.

"Soooo, if ju had a bag ju could give it to me when ju got off the bus at a hotel, no?"

"Yes...no...I mean, I could...but I'm not a transporter. Hold up, hold up...you said *me*?"

"Well not me...*us*." She pointed to her to friends who were already looking at me, paying no attention to Sully and Dre.

This can't be fucking happening!

Is this bitch trying to set me up?

"Wait babe. I bring the bag to you three...at a *hotel*?"

"Jes and we celebrate for a few." Rosa gently squeezed my cock.

"Mmmm...ju *are* Black." She kissed my neck.

"Aaaah...mmm...but what if I get caught?"

"El último cosa ju will catch is mucho dinero...and this pussy, por supuesto." Rosa stuck her wet finger in my mouth. I tasted nothing.

God, I want her!
You can do this...
You can't do this...
I'm going to prison...
This is easy money...
God I want her...and her friends.

Closing my eyes for a moment, I felt embarrassed and highly disappointed in myself that I even considered to take a package from a stranger, bring it on the team plane, and then deliver the package, which I knew had to be drugs, to three hookers in a hotel room.

Rosa's plan seemed very simple, but I was no drug dealer. $10,000 was a lot of money, and I would be the goddamn man on campus, but I wasn't willing to risk my freedom, my education, my football career, my family, and my reputation for any amount of money. I just couldn't. I was different.

I'm not doing this dumb shit!

"Soooo Manzo?" Rosa put her hand in my pants.

"Oooh, mmmm..." I moaned.

"Sooo?" She smiled.

Goddamn I want her!

"Toma el dinero and let's have some fun guapo." She looked deeply in my eyes, and suddenly I remembered where I had seen *Rosa*.

Archie's barbershop! The Jamaican poster girl! They could be twins!

As a kid, around eight years old, I used to get my haircut across the street from my building at Archie's Barbershop on Second Avenue, and every time I went in there the old timers debated about everything from Plato to politics, but I would never listen.

Archie had a bunch of posters on the wall of sports legends like Muhammad Ali, Sugar Ray Leonard, and Dr. Jay.

I idolized all the icons of the era, but there was one poster that I would sit, stare at, and fantasize from the minute I entered the shop until the moment I left —the "Jamaica" poster.

The girl in the poster, with her baseball bat complexion and carven cheekbones, had her jet-black hair slicked behind her ears as the sun showered her freshly dipped body, wet from the ocean behind her.

Eyebrows edged by the razor of Jesus gave way to magnificent mono-lid eyes, which jousted for attention with her sharp nipples piercing through a soaked, red, almost body-painted t-shirt with "JAMAICA" written across a handful of perfect breasts.

I dreamed of holding my barbershop companion's waist and eating Skittles out her bellybutton before swimming to anywhere other than Wagner Projects.

* * *

Rosa was my childhood fantasy in the flesh. I had dreamed of one day getting my moment of reality with this unreal woman, and I wasn't going to risk not conquering my obsession because of something as minute as being busted by the cops or losing my scholarship to play football.

I was a jerk, but I wasn't a chicken.

At that instance, getting on a plane and crossing state lines in the friendly skies with a bag of mystery seemed easier than finding another Rosa. I had to have her.

The money, and the other Latinas weren't factors and only would make a better story to never tell.

Pushing her hand from around my cock before I came on myself, I panted for air and gave my final answer.

Fuck it!

"OK, OK...damn—I will do it!" I conceded.

"Really?" she asked in disbelief.

What am I doing?

"Yes, I will do it...but I have this red t-shirt I want you to wear."

"Ha-ha, OK. Anything for ju guapo." She kissed me on my cheek.

"Here call this number when ju get back to jour hotel—Eden Roc, no?"

"Uuh...yea." I hesitated to grab her card.

Rosa...305...555...4040

But how the fuck does she know my hotel?

"OK Harlem World! I see you getting the digits!" Dre yelled, but Manzo was gone.

Who wrote this?

What's that smell?

Reminds me of the team bus for some reason.

My nerves prickled as I attempted to process the white business card with only the phone number and name written in blue ink.

I could've just been confused by the champagne swirling in my mind, but I could swear the card was written in a man's handwriting and reeked of a very strong, but all too familiar scent—Stetson cologne.

Chapter Seventeen

CHAIN SMOKING

June 16, 1997 was the first night I had been back to Harlem since I had left for college last August. I was excited to see all my friends around my father's new neighborhood on Lexington Avenue before trooping to my original stomping grounds, Wagner Projects, just a few blocks away.

I couldn't wait for the warm welcoming because I loved my hood, and I knew they all loved me back.

I couldn't wait to describe Virginia Tech, the games, the juices, the parties, as well as show off my new chiseled physique.

While at school, I had told stories of how great Harlem was and tried to give some insight of the bond that we all shared growing up in such an amazing city like New York.

Of course, all of the stories weren't pleasant considering the amount of childhood buddies lost to senseless killings, but my pain made me the fighter I was, and I would never forget my roots.

Being from Harlem was a badge of honor that I wore with the utmost pride, everywhere I went.

Stepping off the front steps of building 123 of the M.S. Houses, I was dressed and ready for the night. I felt and looked like new money.

I had just popped the tags off my navy-blue Nautica sweatpants and white t-shirt.

A New York City staple in any weather, my crispy Timberland boots were a deep blend of yellow mustard and raw honey.

The eighteen-karat-gold, diamond Jesus-piece-medallion I bought in Atlanta a week after the Orange Bowl hung from a Cuban-link-chain and set perfectly between brand new pecs.

My hair, wavy and trimmed sharply by my longtime barber, Ellis, shined with the streetlights. Staring at my head for too long would make a motherfucker seasick.

Versace Blue Jeans cologne exuded invincibility from my pores as I ran into my homie D-Rugs at the corner of 129th Street and Lexington Avenue.

Stressing over classes, and the grueling football practices were over—summer vacation was underway.

"Goddamn homie, what the fuck is that around your neck?" D-Rugs pointed to my chain. "Fucking Jesus got diamonds all around his head and shit! You gonna give the nigga brain freeze kid!"

"Ha-ha, shut up D-Rugs!" We gave dap and embraced. "What's good bro?"

"Damn kid, you built like a fucking Mack truck now!" He beat my chest with his fist. "What they feeding y'all niggas down there—snow bunny sandwiches?"

"Ha, ha, ha!" we both laughed hysterically.

"Nigga you still crazy as ever!" I said.

"But seriously, I need to play football! You got on a chain like you motherfucking Jay-Z or some shit! Daaamn, what this shit cost nigga—about twenty g's?" D-Rugs lifted the medallion again. "This shit is heavy! What you had to do for *this* monster?"

"Maaaaan stop talking about this piece of junk!" I said.

"But yo, I'm about to go to Wagner to holla at Dirt and Wayne-God. Who can I cop some bud from around here?" I asked.

"I can hit my man up in Lincoln in a sec...but you know I stay strapped college boy!" He raised both hands, one held a blunt and the other held a red lighter. Like magic, the smoke session had started.

Still mesmerized by my Jesus piece, D-Rugs couldn't keep his eyes off my chain as we walked down Lexington Avenue hitting the blunt in the humid Harlem summer night.

Watching him admire the sparkling rocks hanging from my neck, I knew what the first thing I would buy him when I made it to the NFL.

My friends and family would have anything they wanted. I would make sure that if I ate, we ate.

"Damn, it's hotter than the devil's ass out here bruh!" D-Rugs yelled after taking a pull. "I need to find me a bitch to smash in the AC!"

"You ain't lying brother. A shorty with an air conditioner sounds divine right now, but I'm really trying to finally stay loyal to my girl.

"So I'm gonna just get off this damn block with all these thirsty bitches and skate to Wagner. Plus, if my pops drive by and see me smoking with *your* crazy ass—I'm fucked bro!" I said.

"Shiiiitttt, Big Carlos ain't coming around! He prolly bangin' on some coke-head bitch right now his damn self!" D-Rugs laughed.

"Stop being scared young nigga and hit this blunt again! Coach Beamer ain't in no Harlem tah-niiight!"

"Aint nobody scared bro!" I said. "Gimme that shit and stop being a fucking clown!"

D-Rugs reached his arm out to pass me the blunt but stopped in mid-air. His expression changed, he no longer laughed.

He just smirked, nodded his head up and down and said, "Yea aight nigga. Whatever."

Immediately, I knew that he did not appreciate me calling him a "fucking clown," but I did not care. Still annoyed by his comment about my pops, I stared directly into his eyes.

I extended my hand and waited for the weed, but he withdrew the blunt and took another puff while maintaining eye contact.

D-Rugs' midnight eyes seemed to shrink. Smoke breathing out of his nostrils and mouth, the dragon spoke.

"I'm gonna bounce and try and holla at one of those Spanish-Haitian sisters in Wilson Projects—them bitches is bad! You should come with me and try and bag the young one, Tuta. She would looove you my nigga!" he said as his smile reappeared, passing me the blunt.

"Shit, you aint lying—they some bad bitches! I met April and Charlette when I was hangin' with Salt and his aunt Michelle at her spot on 105th, but I'm good bro. I'm tryna be faithful to my shorty back at Tech."

"OK-OK, I hear that playboy! I'm outta here though, you can have the rest of that blunt though—but oh yea, let me make that call for you real quick Manzo. I know you still need that bud."

"Oh shit, I almost forgot! Good looks bro!" I thanked him.

"No doubt Manzo. You know I always got you."

Man, I love my niggas.

I watched my homeboy cross the street and pull out his cell phone, and I was content with having a moment alone.

Suddenly, I was missing Brittney and listening to his conversation would not have remedied my illness. I had my thoughts, and I had my medicine.

Putting the blunt to my lips, I took another dose and was happy that D-Rugs was getting me some more bud. He was a good friend to have.

I have been acquainted with D-Rugs for years, but I did not *know* him.

We were around the same age and from the same hood, so naturally, we have had many interactions: pickup basketball games, late night smoke sessions in the staircase, and arguments about sports in the park, but oddly—I didn't even know his real name, and I never asked.

His features, his reputation, and his jail time were the only things I was sure about.

D-Rugs was five-foot, ten inches and fit from working out during his many minor stints in Spafford and Riker's Island.

His mocha brown complexion, tiny dark eyes, and jet-black curly Afro made him appear to have some "Indian in his family" for real.

Looking at him, one could easily make the mistake of assuming that he was a pretty boy—a softie. D-Rugs was neither—he was a killer.

He was not the type of guy anyone fooled with or called, "a fucking clown," but I didn't know any better. I was twice his size and fearless. Plus, nobody dared to touch one of Carlos' kids.

Glancing across the street at D-Rugs, in between pulls, I noticed that his hand gestures seemed too animated for a conversation with a weed dealer.

He constantly moved his arms and nodded his head like he was giving directions, until our eyes met—he grinned and put up one finger.

Extremely baked, I looked away and thought about Brittney who I had officially made my girlfriend since Toya found out I was creeping to the *fifth* floor of West AJ nearly every night.

Jed, the Jewish fella I befriended, was actually waiting for Toya's roommate, Kadesha, the night I had first met Brittney.

When Kadesha asked Jed about the Kind Bud he had, the putz told her the story, and then the yenta immediately told Toya. Oy fucking vey!

After a week of lying to Toya about Brittney, I finally let Toya go, and my teammate Angelo Harrison picked her up. Our squad was very *green*—we loved to recycle.

What is Brittney doing?

Why doesn't she answer her phone? Damn I miss her.

"Yoooo my nigga—stay right here!" D-Rugs yelled while already seated in a Day & Night cab.

"I'm just gonna grab that smoke from my homie in Lincoln and come right back! Gimme five minutes, tops!"

Before I could speak, the cab rolled away, and I threw up a fist.

The chariot's red eyes faded into the darkness, leaving me high and alone on the corner of 126th Street and Lexington Avenue.

I took a final toke, and the weed tackled my confusion.

My mind huddled and decided it was a better play to think about Brittney rather than to worry about D-Rugs' whereabouts—but the inexperienced coach should have been fired immediately.

* * *

"Why can't I go with you to New York, Manzo?" Brittney asked as she began to cry.

"Listen, I'm going home to spend some time with my family and friends," I said, looking out of the passenger side window.

"I will see you in a week when I come back. Brittney *please* leave me alone about this and just take me to the airport—"

"FUCK YOU! You're just embarrassed because you're in love with a White girl!" she shouted and took her eyes off the road.

"For the last time, I'm not embarrassed—"

"Yes you are! You show me ZERO attention and affection when Black people are around!" she sobbed. "You would die if I treated you like that!"

"You're buggin', and please watch the goddamn road babe," I demanded.

"All I want to do at home is hang with my family and friends—"

"*Friends*? *Friends*? Those people are not your *friends*," she said calmly.

"Manzo...they're all jealous of you and don't want to see you do good. *You* better be careful up there. *You* go to college. *You* play football. *You* have a lot to lose—not them. Don't be a fool baby. I love you and I worry."

"OK babe...you're right," I spoke softly, matching her tone. "I just need to be around my family right now—"

"Family? I *am* a part of your family—you bastard!" she yelled.

"Well at least I am when you're fucking me, using my credit cards, and driving my car to see your other bitches! I'm not as stupid as you think, *my brother!*" she shouted as my heart jumped.

I had no reply. I had no rebuttal.

Her heart ached. She cried harder.

I just sat in silence as I looked out of the window and counted the trees.

420.

* * *

Pulling out my cell phone to call my girlfriend, I noticed that the block, normally full of life, in front of the A.K. Houses was uncharacteristically serene.

It was midnight on a Saturday and normally the street was flooded with men in cars, and the sidewalks with half-dressed women trying to get in those cars.

No hoes. No tricks.

I was on my *own* block and enjoying my high, so I did not worry. Never looking up, I began dialing Brittney's cell phone number.

757 484...

What the hell?

Halfway through dialing, I had noticed two small, untied Air Force Ones a little too close for New York City comfort. Someone was clearly invading my three feet of personal space allotted by God.

The streets were empty. I had been in Blacksburg for a while, but I did not forget the drill. Senses barking, I knew what was next.

Fuck!

My blunt, my phone, and my high dropped instantly! Looking up, I grabbed two little arms just as the robber attempted to snatch my chain.

He held my Cuban link firmly in his hands as I tried to squeeze blood out of his wrists. His grip was tight, but there was no way that a little Puerto Rican dude was going to overpower my big Black ass.

Not possible!

I'm gonna kill you!

We waltzed a few seconds. Adrenaline spiked, I looked at the amigo's face and I did not recognize him—but his widened brown eyes told a story, so I listened.

"Check this out homie. I don't know you either. I'm just trying to make a dollar and make a name for myself in these streets. I'm struggling to survive, and you're standing on a corner in *Harlem* with that big-ass-diamond-Jesus-piece on your neck. I know you're mad diesel, but I have kids to feed, nothing personal— but guess what?"

Both his eyes shifted to my left for a split second and said, "I am not alone!"

Shit!

Quickly, I picked the pocket-gangster up by the arms and tossed him several feet into the air. My chain popped. Jesus landed on the pavement, the amigo on a Ford Explorer.

I turned suddenly, only to find myself staring down the barrel of a black Glock 40. Powerfully, I open-handed smacked the gun!

Hurdling over the hood of a Chevy Malibu, I started to sprint down Lexington Avenue. I heard three separate clicks before I reached the corner.

The gun was jammed. God was good.

I ran at a record best speed, only slowing down on 124th Street and Lexington Avenue to make a left.

The impossible had just occurred; one of Carlos' kids had just been robbed at gunpoint. Logically, my next stop was only a few blocks away, 124th street between Third and Second Avenue.

In twenty-five seconds, flat, I had reached my safe house, Club 232, my father's bar.

* * *

Frantically, I mashed the buzzer a dozen or so times. I was hyperventilating and sweating profusely.

Paranoid, I paced around in a circle as I looked up the block and wondered if I had been followed. No one answered the door.

"Fuuucccckkk!" I yelled, still pacing and keeping watch.

Daddy please be here! I need you!

Mouth extra dry, I wiped the foam from my lips and proceeded to buzz. The last four attempts were more forceful and desperate as I pleaded for help.

BUZZ.

"Open!"

BUZZ.

"The!"

BUZZ.

"Fucking!

BUZZ...

"Dooorr—"

"OK all right! Stop—" a man's voice screamed as the door opened. "Manzo!"

I had expected to see my father standing in the doorway, but it was not him. The man looked like my father, except twenty-two years younger with a lighter skin tone.

Refocusing my eyes, I realized that the man who stood in front of me was my older brother, Chink.

We both sobbed immediately without me explaining what had just occurred, and I guessed that Chink somehow could sense his little brother's horrific experience.

Chink represented security, hope, and comfort—family. I was no longer alone.

It would have only taken one Peña for me to feel safe, but with Chink I felt safer. He held me, and we cried while he whispered his intentions in my ear.

"We are going to kill those motherfuckers," he said and released his embrace, grabbing both of my cheeks firmly.

Pressing his forehead against mine, he looked into my spirit and reprogrammed my soul. Tears flowed from my eyes. Electricity shot from his.

"We are going to kill those motherfuckers," he repeated his mantra.

"We are going to kill those motherfuckers," I finally repeated out loud in a dark tone, not recognizing the speaker.

The voltage from his eyeballs intensified as he slightly grinned.

Understanding the situation at hand, I grinned back. Suddenly, Chink grabbed my t-shirt and pulled me inside the doorway.

"Let's go, Daddy's upstairs!" he yelled as he began running up the stairs, and like a good little brother—I slammed the door behind me and followed.

My anger gradually climbed as Chink and I stomped in unison up the steps. By the time we reached the top, I wanted what Chink wanted—murder. Big brothers always knew best.

The club was empty, and the bright overhead lighting irritated my eyes. An industrial fan blowing was the only sound.

Empty plastic cups lined the bar top, and chairs rested upside down on the eight small tables. A few crumbled dollar bills were scattered around the mini stage located at the front of the room. Friday night had been Los' *world-famous* stripper night.

"Go to the bathroom and clean yourself up little bro," Chink demanded. "We don't want Daddy seeing you like that. Come to the office when you're done OK?"

He did not wait for a response and headed toward the back of the bar to the office. As I watched him, I never felt more love for Chink than I did at that moment.

He had my back. All Peñas had each other's back, but I was still mystified as how he knew the severity of my ordeal.

He never once asked me questions about what had happened. Knowing Chink, I understood that the names, or the actual event was irrelevant. Only the result mattered, not the route we had taken to get there.

Someone violated his little brother and he wanted blood. But how did he know? I chalked it up as brotherly intuition and entered the bathroom to wash up.

Lights.

Nooooooo!

Looking in the mirror I had begun to cry. My entire mouth area and t-shirt were covered in blood.

I had not recalled getting my red wings, or eating a gazelle for dinner, so my Halloween costume had me perplexed.

Fuck, I got shot! Where's the wound?

I looked down at my body and proceeded to hysterically pat myself down like I couldn't find my wallet.

During the frisk, I felt a sting in my right palm, and I had discovered that my right hand bled. I raised my hand to my face and stared at the cut briefly before recollecting what had happened.

My hand jammed the gun. I wiped my mouth.

Mystery solved.

Grabbing the bar of soap, I washed off the blood as well as I could before I opened the door and headed to my father's office.

I still had blood on my shirt and looked like I had been bobbing for apples in a bucket of ketchup, but my cleanup would lessen the sting. My father would still be horrified, nonetheless.

I entered the tiny office, and I had noticed the twenty-one bottles of Hennessy on the shelves before I noticed my father sitting at his desk.

Chink sat motionless in a chair with his head between his legs, and his hands on his head. He never looked up.

"Manzo! Oh God son—are you all right?" my father asked as he got up from his desk and hugged me, before he rubbed his hands across my bloodstained shirt and examined my body for any wounds.

"Who the fuck did this? What the fuck happened?" he asked angrily.

"I am OK Daddy, I'm not hurt," I said looking down. "Just a cut on my hand from the gun."

His eyes widened, and he started to tear up. "Tell me what the hell happened son, please!"

Picking his head up from his lap, Chink looked at me and I could almost read his mind. His face told me to start from the beginning and don't leave out a damn detail.

Dramatically blowing out air and wiping my forehead, I started the sad, common, ghetto tale from the very beginning.

Throughout the five minutes, my father shook his legs uncontrollably and stared blankly at me as Chink cried.

I told the story as if I were just the narrator and not the main character, because I could have not relived the fresh nightmare otherwise.

I was fine personally but empathizing for the listeners killed me. Only my Sixth-grade spelling bee could have matched the intensity at which anyone had ever listened to my voice.

"D-Rugs—that motherfucker!" Chink yelled just as the narration concluded. "He fucked with the wrong ones this time! Come on let's go find these niggas and *murder* them!"

We are going to kill those motherfuckers!

"Shit, let's go—"

"Whoa Manzo! Hold up a goddamn minute Chink!" my father yelled.

Both Chink and I looked at each other for a second before we had decided to be quiet and let our father speak.

We knew that his plan of execution would be more thorough and foolproof than our "Wild, Wild, East" tactics.

Carlos was thirty years deep in the game, and we respected him more than we did the Jesus with the thorns, not the one with the diamonds.

Assuming he killed a couple of niggas and a few spics in his day, we shut up and waited for the coach's orders.

"Let's try and get your chain back somehow. You think they would give it back?" my father asked. "There's no need for this to escalate any further."

Huh?

We are NOT going to kill those motherfuckers?

Completely baffled, I looked away from my father and then looked at Chink, who shook his head and put it back in his lap.

Chink never questioned our father's decisions. Speaking the unspoken had always been my job. Livid, I wanted a promotion.

"Daddy are you kidding me?" I asked. "What the fuck are you talking about—"

"Watch your mouth Manz—"

"No, you watch *your* mouth!" I screamed at my father for the second time in my life. "Them niggas just tried to kill *your* son and *you* are more worried about some fucking piece of shit chain? Give me a break!"

"All I'm saying son is that we do not need any more trouble! Let's try and work this out without anyone getting hurt!"

Who is this pussy?

I looked at my father up and down to make sure that was really him. *My* father would never back down when someone attempted to hurt his child, nonetheless, kill one of us.

He was the man in Harlem. How could he take my almost being a corpse so lightly? Furious, I asked a question no son should ever ask his father.

"What kind of man are you?"

SMACK!

I never saw his hand hit my jaw, but I sure as hell felt it. The sound of an old hand on a young face awakened Chink from his trance.

Completely shocked, I just stood there and almost smiled. Getting slapped like a bitch sucked but knowing that my father still had some fire excited me.

I had attacked his manhood, and I struck a nerve that lied dormant for years. Looking at his eyes roasting, I knew that the man we had heard stories about was dying to escape.

"You remember who the fuck you're talking to son!" Daddy advised, spit flying in my face.

"I have been putting in work since you've been swimming in my mother-fucking nuts! I would die before I let something happen to any one of my children—but it's a way you do things!"

"Daddy?" Chink asked and stood.

"WHAT?" my father snapped.

Chink quickly sat back down before saying, "Daddy, if we don't do something right now then we're opening free rein on our entire family to be fucked with. Everyone knows who you are—and *what* you do."

Chink stood back up and looked my father in the eyes.

"We must punish these niggas tonight, or any one of us could be next—even you," Chink spoke sincerely as he reached up and held the $92,000 *platinum*, diamond encrusted Jesus medallion hanging from our father's neck.

Daddy looked down at the target on his chest, but it was now someone more sinister who looked back up at me.

Noticing the look in my father's eyes, I knew he had suddenly transformed into his alter ego—*Los!*

"Don't fucking move!" Los demanded, almost running out of the office.

Both confused, Chink and I just looked at each without speaking. We knew who our father was and his capabilities, but we did not have an exact understanding when it came to that other guy, Los.

All our lives our father kept him away from us, although the old timers told us many a tale about Los, but when confronted, our father would just laugh and say, "If you believe that, then I have some land in Mexico to sell you."

My brothers and I would still listen to the entertaining stories, but as soon as they ended, we would laugh and say, "Those old niggas are full of shit!"

* * *

I never believed a word anyone had to say about my father until that time Daddy went on his "fishing trip" for a week.

Mommy packed all of his things, but after reconsidering asked me to help her unpack his shit. Like a good son, I did.

Refilling his closet, I noticed a black leather Prada briefcase and I opened it. The hue from all the green $100 bills snatched my vision until I placed his briefcase back behind his fur coats.

I thought I was seeing things, until later that night when I had *cat burglar'ed* into my parents' bedroom and pulled a record heist for a twelve-year-old.

As my mother slept, I counted the $499,900 in my room before opening a Manila envelope, which contained a deed for six acres of land in Vera Cruz, Mexico.

My chubby cheeks grinned because my father was not a liar, and I had fallen in love with *Los*. (I *borrowed* $100 from his stash, which was small fee for cheating, and of course, he never noticed the missing bill.)

* * *

"What the hell you think he's doing?" I asked right at the three-minute mark.

Before Chink expressed his opinion, Los walked in with a black duffle bag on his right shoulder and a cell phone in his left hand.

"Let's get some air," Los spoke as he walked out of the office and headed downstairs.

Oh my God, what is happening? Where are we going?

What are we gonna do?

"Nobody will ever mess with you again lil' bro," Chink promised as he yanked my arm and pulled me toward the door. "You or any *other* Peña."

Walking down the stairs of the bar, I could not feel my legs. I knew exactly *what* we were going to do. I knew *where* we were going. My body tensed. I started to bitch-up.

Sensing my hesitation, Chink never let go of my arm and guided me. My anxiety nearly paralyzed my limbs, but I managed to *Handi-man* down the stairs.

Once at the bottom, Chink opened the front door, looked back at me, and then released my arm.

No words were spoken, but I knew immediately that my big brother was giving me the option to either go back upstairs or leave out of the front door with bloody intentions.

What do I do? I can't do this! I'm scared!

Turning my attention away from Chink's piercing eyes, I peeped out of the door and noticed a black S600 Mercedes Benz.

The tinted passenger side window was halfway down, and I noticed a Puerto

Rican gentleman behind the steering wheel before I noticed Los staring at me. Los' expression mirrored Chink's

What do I do?

I shouldn't go!

I'm scared!

I was not a murderer. I was not a gangster. I was not a thug.

I was a boarding school educated, Division-I student athlete who should've been in school instead of the streets of Harlem contemplating revenge, but the fact remained that someone attempted to kill me.

People plotted my demise in my own neighborhood. How could I back down now? It was possible the savages could return to murder me, or a family member if I did not retaliate.

What type of man would I have been to walk away from my family in their time of need?

I was not a murderer. I was not a gangster. I was not a thug—but I was not a coward either, and neither were Los and Chink, who awaited my decision.

In my delusional state of mind, we were protectors of the Peña clan, so my choice was crystal.

My limbs regained their strength, and I was no longer scared. I stood up straight and looked back at Chink.

Slowly speaking, I said, "We are going to kill those motherfuckers."

Prior to running to the car, Chink replied, "Damn straight lil' bro!"

We scanned 124th Street. The block was desolate and not a soul lurked.

Chink entered the car behind the unknown driver. I sat behind Los who ordered the driver to take off even before my door had been completely closed.

The driver, not saying a word, just flicked his Newport out of the window and sped off. There was no introduction. We asked no questions. We did not care.

The quiet streets seemed to await our arrival, but when the ghetto's gates opened there would be no trumpets and no horns, only gunshots and sirens.

East Harlem was no stranger to revenge. Word always traveled fast; a hood-wide curfew had been in order.

"Pull up to 126th Street—and park the car on the left side of the block," Los instructed the driver. "Keep watch Eduardo. This will only take a moment."

My nerves unraveled, but I was more eager than afraid.

As Los began rummaging through the duffel bag, the sound of metal on metal sang a song of redemption.

Entertained, I was hell-bent on making the pussies who robbed me hit the high notes. Chink's words repeating in my head served as the lyrics.

We are going to kill these motherfuckers.

"Here take this Chink," Los ordered, handing him a P89 Ruger handgun. "Do you know how to use that?"

"Of course," Chink said while he cocked the gun back, releasing a bullet into the chamber. "Thank you."

It reminded me of those Christmas Days when my father would hand out gifts, and I just wanted the best present as usual. For some reason, he would get me the biggest and most expensive gift. Some things never changed.

The bad Santa handed me a chrome long-nose .357 Magnum. I felt like the Joker, ready to kill a fucking clown.

"Do you know how to use that Manzo?" Los questioned in a more nurturing tone.

"Of course. I point and I kill." I said, even though I had never shot a pistol in my life. The sight of the cannon itself terrified me. "Thank you."

"Pull up the block and stop at the corner over there on the right," Los instructed, pointing his chrome Smith and Wesson .38 snub-nosed revolver to the exact spot he wanted the driver to park. "And then turn off the lights Eduardo."

The car sat idled under a broken streetlamp on the Northwest side of 126th Street and Lexington Avenue. Silent, everyone remained on guard.

The stores were closed and only a few crackheads and transgender prostitutes walked the streets. The hood was on *Orange Alert*.

After three hours of "Was that the guy?", reality set in that our attempt on finding the assailants was futile. No one knew where D-Rugs lived, and I did not even get a clean look at the gunman.

Four minorities riding around with guns in a Mercedes at 1:00 AM was not an option.

We were left sitting in a tank waiting for a little Spanish dude to come back to the scene of the crime—before the police did. Not so smart.

Adrenaline gone, we were wasting our time and I wanted to leave. My brother's whispers needed a remix, but there would be none. I was scared.

The longer we waited, the more I feared dying. Being in a car with weapons of Black-ass destruction suddenly put the fear of God in me.

I didn't want to be the hunted or the hunter—either six-letter-word increased the probability of me dying as just another sucker.

I wanted to fuck the oddsmakers and live a full life of endless positive experiences and opportunities. Death, normally, the easy money, would never get my bet.

Dead, I would be just another nigga swallowed by his environment, an animal eaten by an animal.

I would have my name spray-painted on some pissy wall, and my face airbrushed on t-shirts worn mostly by people who did not really care about me. My best friend would bang my girl, and life would go on.

Fuck that!

Tapping Los on the shoulder, I looked at my father and said, "Daddy I want to go home."

Chapter Eighteen

NO OFFENSE

"I understand Coach, but this can't be happening now. This my fourth year on the team, and I am just supposed to accept this bullshit?" I said to Coach Foster over my house phone.

You piece of shit!

"Well, aren't you my position coach? How don't you have any say?" I asked.

"It's not your call? Then who fucking call is it Coach?"

KNOCK.

KNOCK.

They're trying to fuck me!

"Excuse my language Coach Foster, I have nothing but the utmost respect for you, but can you blame me for cursing? Look at what the fuc...the *hell* you're telling me?" I covered the phone and took a hit of the blunt in the ashtray on my coffee table.

"*SWUUUUH...FHUUUUUH...*" I closed my eyes.

"So basically, it's Coach Beamer's call and you can't do shit about it?" I asked.

"Weigh my options? Weigh my options? What the hell is that supposed to mean Coach?"

Is he fucking serious?

"Why do I need to talk to my family? There's nowhere else I rather be than—"

BANG!

BANG!

"One-second Coach, please." I smothered the cordless phone against my Iceberg jean-shorts and walked down the hallway of my Terrace View townhouse.

Who's banging on my motherfucking door like that?

"Who the fuck is it?" I yanked the door open.

"It's me bro!" My teammate, Michael Vick, smiled and shook his head.

Oh shit, I almost forgot!

"Nigga just come in! Don't knock," I insisted and pointed to the phone.

"Oh my bad Manzo," he whispered.

"I'm here Coach, sorry that was the mail lady," I continued.

"So the decision is final, huh?" I walked back to the living room, sat on my green leather couch, and just shook my head. "This is so messed up! I'm going to need a day to think about my *options!*"

My life is over!

"Yes sir, I know it's not your call. I will talk to you tomorrow."

"All right, have a good day Coach." I hung up the phone and bit my bottom lip.

"You OK Manzo? What's good?" Mike asked while standing in the living room entrance.

"Good?" I asked dryly. "You gonna be up for the Heisman and be the first pick in the NFL fucking draft—that's *good.*"

I can't believe this is happening to me!

"Stop saying that—I haven't even played a damn game yet." Mike sat on the matching green leather recliner.

"Seriously bro, what's going on Manzo?"

"I told you, you will be the first name called at the draft. That's what's going on." I faked a smile.

"Cut the bullshit Manzo-man. What's going on?"

Just tell him.

I gazed at the wall with my number twenty-one Gator Bowl jersey hanging unevenly in a glass frame before returning my attention to Mike, who leaned forward in the recliner.

With his black do-rag tied in the front like his forehead was a gift, Mike donned heavily worn, untied Timberland boots with each lace tied in a little knot hanging out of the top holes.

His sleeveless, white t-shirt with "Bad News" spray-painted on the front in kale green, represented the false pride he and many other young brothers had in their hometown of Newport News, Virginia. Violence and crime plagued most of its African American community.

Mike, a generous six feet and 215 pounds, had glossy, snuff-colored skin, comparable to looking into a clear glass bowl of French onion soup set on a plate made of pure dark chocolate.

Like many guys on the team, Mike rocked an even, low haircut with waves. A fine textured, jet-black semi-unibrow matched his sharply edged goatee, and enclosed full and moisturized lips, the exact undertone of his face. Although he didn't smoke weed, he looked like he ate blunts for breakfast.

The starting quarterback on our team, Michael Vick, was a redshirt freshman with freakish athletic ability, superlative speed, and a weapon of a left arm.

If he threw a football at someone's face, the Commonwealth of Virginia would give Mike the gas chamber without a trial. He wore number seven. The young man was godly.

"Fuuuuccck!" I tapped the back of my head on the *Scarface* poster behind me.

This is bad!

"WOOF...WOOF!" My outburst had awakened Champagne, Mike's four-month-old, Teddy-bear-brown Pit bull I'd been babysitting.

Great, this crazy little bitch is up.

"You want me to go get her?" I asked. "She's on timeout upstairs in her cage, because she ate the tongue off my brand-new Jordan's."

"WOOF...WOOF!"

"Nah, I want you to tell me what's going on. Champagne be quiet please!" Mike looked up and hollered, the barking ceased immediately. "Good girl!"

"How the fuck you do that—"

"Come on Manzo stop stalling."

"Aight nigga...fuck." I snatched the blunt from the ashtray and took a long pull.

Damn, just tell him.

"That was Coach Foster on the phone." I replaced the blunt in the ashtray.

"What did he say to you?"

"Just some bullshit my nigga."

"*What*?" He asked.

"Maaaaan...these motherfuckers talking about moving me to fucking *fullback!*"

"Ooooh shit—for real?" He smiled.

"What the fuck is your Black-ass smiling about? This shit ain't funny!"

"I'm smiling because I play offense and I was just telling Ronyell how *you* should play offense.

"Now I'm going to have one of the best athletes on the squad in the backfield with me. That's why the fuck I'm smiling."

"But I'm a *linebacker*, I don't want to play no offense—"

"Manzo you aren't a linebacker bro! You ain't shit, I hate to tell you! You haven't played really since you been here and that's not because you don't have the talent. You just have never taken football seriously."

"I know, but this year was going to be different! I'm not trying to change positions and have to compete with that lil' tank-motherfucker Jarrett Ferguson!" I hit the blunt again.

"This year gonna be different, huh...really?" Mike looked at me, looked at the blunt, and then back at me again. "Really?"

"Man don't judge me nigga—you supposed to be my homie!"

"I am your homie Manzo!"

"Then why you on my back?"

"Because I'm not gonna see you sit here feeling sorry for yourself like you can't see how much you fucked up here!" he yelled.

"Nigga fuck you!"

"*Nigga* fuck you!" Mike cloned my ignorance.

"*WOOF...WOOF—*"

"Champagne be quiet!" Mike hollered, never disengaging from our stare-down.

Since I'd known Michael Vick, he never had gotten upset or raised his voice off or on the football field. The definition of cool, Mike kept a steady demeanor, even in the most social settings, he never said too much.

His barking at me only meant that he cared, and although I was higher than a research monkey, I could see the love in his eyes.

His scowl represented a cutting frustration from a brother not getting through to another brother, but his words had legs and I was tired of running.

My heart drummed as my saliva seemed to evaporate toward my forehead and form beads of embittered denial that descended the sides of my face.

The perfume of every puddle of puppy-piss passed on my carpet had cultivated my peevishness. I drew together my fist, but never to throw a punch, more so, to squeeze the stubbornness from my soul.

I knew Mike was right. I knew I had to listen.

"Man, what are we doing?" My muscles relaxed with my attitude, and I relaxed back into the softness of the couch.

"Don't put your craziness on me. What are *you* doing? You're my ace and I'm never gonna lie to you Manzo."

"I know Mike...I know. I'm just mad confused."

"As you should be, but don't run away from this situation. Embrace the challenge."

"Maybe I should just quit and transfer to another school or some shit?" I asked.

"Hell nah Manzo!"

"Why? These people don't want me here."

"If they didn't want you here then they would've gotten rid of your crazy-ass a long time ago."

"They're moving me so Ben Taylor and the rest of those White boys can play."

"They don't need to do that so they could play. You're doing more than enough to push them in front of you."

"You really know how to cut a nigga deep." I shook my head.

"You're just being real emotional right now which I can understand, but you need to look at it from another angle Manzo."

"What angle?"

"This is your fourth year and you still haven't grasped the defensive schemes. So maybe the coaches are trying to finally utilize your abilities and make the game easier for you." Mike leaned forward and rubbed his hands together like he was in a huddle.

"Offense is proactive, so you have to think less."

"Nigga, I ain't dumb!"

"I know, but that shit you smoking screwing with your brain."

"So I need to change positions because I'm a fucking pothead is your advice?"

"Ha-ha, naaaah man," Mike said.

"Then what are you saying?" I asked.

"Manzo you get the ball and run someone over like you did in high school, and you go destroy someone when you block them. That's it!"

"I still gotta learn an entire new play system—"

"Man those simple-ass plays Coach Stinespring runs—a damn retard can understand them."

"Oooh...so now I'm retarded?"

"Stop fucking around Manzo!" He shook his head. "You know what I'm saying. Think about it bro."

"I know what you mean, but damn bro...*offense*?"

"Yes, offense...*my* offense," he said as he stood up. "But think about it, and I hope to see you at practice in a few rock star."

"Aight nigga, my brain is spinning. I will think about it." I had risen and gave Mike dap and a hug. "Thanks for listening. Love you, bro.

"Love your crazy-ass too bro. Don't think too hard, you gonna be OK." He walked to the front door, grabbed the doorknob, and then turned around.

"FYI...dudes on offense get waaaay more pussy than y'all defensive assholes."

"Ha-ha—shut the fuck up Mike!"

"Do I need to go upstairs and get Champagne?" He opened the front door.

Oh shit, I almost forgot about this girl.

"Nah, hold up Mike." I stepped a couple of feet closer toward the stairs.

"Baaaaabbbyyy!" I yelled.

"Yes baby?" my friend answered.

"Please let Champagne go love!"

"Ok my love!" she hollered.

"You stay hitting something—who's *that*?" Mike whispered and pointed upstairs.

"Ha, ha, ha...just a friend Michael."

"*WOOF, WOOF, WOOOF!*"

"Wait a minute—ooooh shit...I recognize that ride outside!" Mike's detective skills proved supreme, as a blur of brown fur darted down the stairs and out of the door.

"Mind your motherfucking business please, good sir." I insisted.

"Ha, ha—oh shit Manzo! You are officially a scumbag!" He shut the door behind him.

"Hey, it's a free country! Later *Ookie!*" I called Mike by his nickname.

As Monica, Tee Butler's ex-girlfriend, shuffled upstairs putting on her clothes, I sat thinking about what Mike said, and I now had a more positive outlook of my possible new beginning with the team.

Playing fullback would be so easy to me if I could just take football more seriously and make it a priority in my life.

Moving to offense was my last chance to get on the field and finally show the world that I could not only play football, but I could play football at the highest level—the NFL.

I'm going to be on the field scoring touchdowns with my homie...

Going the league will be really easy now...

I'm going to run me a bitch over like motherfucking Christian OKoye...

Shyrone and Dre gonna score mad touchdowns running behind me!

If I stop smoking and fucking with all these juices, I'm going to break records my last year...

My mom's going to get that house I promised...

I know I'm making the right decision...

I got this!

2:32 PM.

After peeping the time on the cable box on top of my TV, I had twenty-eight minutes to drive from Terrace View, get halfway dressed for practice, and make it for the start of our position's meeting with my new running back coach, Coach Hite.

With the speed that I normally had driven, I knew I had plenty of time, so I reached in the ashtray and re-sparked the blunt that had been begging me for a celebratory toke.

Five minutes is all I need.

"*SWUUUH...SWUUUUH...PHUUUUUU*." I blew smoke in the direction of my jersey and leaned my head back on the couch.

Man, I'm going to miss Coach Foster, Dirty Mizzo, Mel, and Ty...

Rest of the linebackers I don't give a fuck about for real—Ben Taylor's a cool-ass White boy though.

Fuck, I'm hungry as hell.

They think they are real slick asking me to change positions...

That's that bullshit...

They don't really like me...

Every time I blew out smoke, I shook my head a little more.

I am not a fullback, I'm a fucking linebacker! They don't want me here!

They are moving me so the White boys can get a shot! Coach Foster is wrong!

I thought he had my back!

Beamer is probably a racist!

He's not giving me a chance because I'm a nigga!

2:40 PM

Fuck it I will just be late. I don't care.

Standing up with the blunt in my right hand and the phone in the other, I walked to my closed patio glass door.

Stop talking silly!

Coaches are doing what's best for the team!

I love Coach Foster!

Beams is absolutely not a damn racist!

Everything will be fine...

Go to practice Manzo...

A new beginning!

Opening the patio door, I welcomed the rare August breeze against my face, and I shut my eyes briefly with the afternoon sun giving me life.

My eyelids fought gravity, and I watched the leaves whisk along bending branches that refused to break or split.

Blacksburg was beautiful, and I wasn't leaving my home that I had spent four years building the man that I was.

Making mistakes was a part of anyone's early adulthood, and I had a chance to make things right again, which consisted of me not running away from the adversity that I was singularly to blame.

If I had been as productive playing football as I were partying, I would still be a linebacker—*the* starting linebacker.

But I was not productive, and I had to be honest with myself that I was not going to ever be the young man that I destroyed.

The way my collegiate career was going, it appeared that moving to fullback was the final chance that I would get to *ever* get on the field.

Considering how I royally fucked up so far, I owed it to the coaches, my teammates, and myself to either give 110% effort or not bother playing football entirely.

I couldn't conceive quitting the team as a viable option, but the more I thought about what truly made me happy in life, the easier it was to pick up the phone and dial Coach Foster's number with a smile.

540...555...3200...

"SWUUUUH...PHUUUU—"

Fuck it.

"Hey Coach Foster. Yea it's Manzo again...I quit."

Chapter Nineteen

MOON STRUCK

"Manzo, how do you quit the damn team and not even holla at your boys first?" Dre asked after taking his third shot of Bacardi 151.

Let's talk about something else please!

"Manzo practice wasn't the same without you," DC added. "Every time I caught a pass, I expected you to be right there trying to bat the shit down."

Damn, I miss playing already!

"The entire team was kinda fucked up the whole goddamn practice. You're the life of the locker room for-real for-real," Dre said.

What am I going to do?

"Man, I hate this place on a school night. Why y'all choose this redneck-ass-bar to meet? Big Al's sucks." I knocked back my third shot of 151. "*Ahhhh...shit burns your goddamn soul.*"

"Oooohh, here we go with this bullshit again." Dre threw both his hands in the air. "Stop fronting, you chose to meet here remember?"

Big Al's, located on 201 North Main Street in Blacksburg, was right across the street from Preston's but worlds apart in character and atmosphere.

Unlike the hip-hop friendly Preston's, Big Al's was a hometown sports bar where anyone could come enjoy a tall Blue Moon with a game of darts or shuffleboard while getting a history lesson of past Virginia Tech teams.

Awaiting at the top of the stairs to the bar's main entrance was a neon red sign that hung from the ceiling and blazed "Big Al's" with an unlit arrow pointing into the main doorway.

The arrow used to illuminate with the same pride as the owner's name, until kids started tapping the arrow on their way in like they were suited up to play the Miami Hurricanes. Where there's plenty of alcohol, there's plenty of tradition.

Entering Big Al's, there was a bar, set at the far wall, with ten stools aligned in front that separated the bar from the fifteen or so small tables and highchairs in the establishment's main area.

Wide but not long, Big Al's had a lone co-ed bathroom that, along with a stuffed six-foot black bear who had a missing right eye and a twenty-four-ounce Natural Light can glued to its right paw, on the far-left wall.

Two pool tables, a shuffleboard table, a dartboard, and the football team's designated tables, hidden from plain view, dominated the right wing.

Bruce Smith, Cornell Brown, Antonio Freeman, Jim Pyne, and Jim Druckenmiller were among the VT football gods to have their jerseys framed and hung throughout the bar—which had no DJ and a 1950's jukebox that played only Pop, Rock, or Country music.

Although many of the icons who were immortalized through pictures and sports memorabilia were Black, catering to a mixed crowd was not a high priority.

The combination of the bar's rustic décor with Fox News continuously playing on its one non-sports TV, screamed *stay out niggers*, which, on the contrary—was why some of the Black guys on the team frequented the place so often.

We could squeeze a juice at Big Al's without much competition, and without the full-clipped-eyes of disgusted Black girls shooting us dead.

"We're your brothers Manzo. You don't have to front like you don't give a shit 'cuz we know you do so talk to us. That is why you wanted to hang tonight, right?" DC asked.

"I'm good DC—"

"No, you're not—"

"*Yes*, I am." I responded.

Damn, I hate I have to leave these guys!

I couldn't look at DC without thinking of how much I would miss the six-foot, three-inch, 280-pound tight end from Smithfield, Virginia. He had been the closest thing to a brother to me, even more so than Dre at the time.

Often people even had mistaken me and DC for brothers, considering we both were bald headed, brown skin, massive, and sported a goatee.

Derek Carter came to Tech a year after I did, but from his very first day we were homies, and he immediately had become part of our Boyz Club.

A natural fit, DC loved getting high, fucking juices, drinking, an occasional fight or two, and playing football—my twin.

With Dre always going back to Lynchburg on the weekends to visit his girl-friend, Ne-Ne, I had become closer with DC even though we would all still hang together during the week.

"So you *cool*?" Dre asked.

"Yea man, I'm cool."

The smell of cotton-candy, Exclamation perfume, cigarette smoke, and whiskey-permeated-wood conjured up memories of legendary times at Big Al's —until a middle-aged blonde woman with bad skin, pink lipstick, and wearing a blue Christiansburg High school t-shirt popped a quarter in the jukebox.

Journey? Fuck!

Not now!

The piano at the beginning of Journey's "Don't Stop Believing" crept its way through the speakers above the bar, and although we sat at a table at the end of Big Al's—I could hear the riff clearly amongst the frivolous chatter of the devoted Tuesday night's drinkers.

Was the song a sign that I shouldn't have quit the team? Or was I just another dramatic drunk college kid getting nostalgic about *old* times and drunk nights?

No matter my disorientation, Steve Perry had a song to sing, and I had four shoulders to cry on.

Almost the entire bar, about fifty people, were on their feet singing, raising their drinks, and pointing at one another.

"Sing it Beth! Woooo!" the bartender with the mullet, crusted acne, and faded maroon Hokie-bird t-shirt screamed.

Damn I fucked up!

"Manzo you want to bounce?" Dre asked when I put my head down. My right hand hooded my eyes, and my body stirred.

I want to die!

BANG!

CLINK!

"Fuck!" I pounded the table and the empty shot glasses jumped along with the crowd. "What did I do fellas? What did I do?"

Removing my hand, I let the tears swell and fall from wet eyes without shame or worry or judgment.

Only DC and Dre witnessed my distress since we were tucked away behind two untaken pool tables. The crowd kept singing their favorite song, and I kept crying to my favorite people.

"I mean I came here with good intentions and I fucked it all up, because I'd rather fuck juices and get high! I'm a fucking disgrace to my family, Woodberry, and the team!"

"It ain't too late Manzo—"

"Yes it is Dre!" I cried. "Yes it is man! I haven't played at all and that's a shame, because if I would've taken this shit seriously, I would have left a couple of years early for the draft! But I'm a fucking bum! I am a bust!

"I'm a *complete* waste of talent, and I can't blame Beams for wanting to get rid of my Black-ass! Beams and Coach Foster are the best! They have been great to me! They gave me chance after chance, and I haven't done shit with those chances!"

"Don't say that—"

"Why DC?" I put both hands in the air.

"Because—"

"Why DC?"

"Manzo, if you'd let me talk, I could tell you *why!*"

"OK, I'm listening." I slid my chair closer to our table as the Caucasian karaoke continued. "Let me hear this."

"Because you got mad talent and pride, and I know that if you really wanted this shit that you can go get it. You letting this situation get to you.

"But Manzo—you gotta face the fact that just because you have the talent to go far in football, football may just not be for you. You don't love football.

"You love being the man, love the bitches, and the money that you can get if you went pro. But you don't love the game itself.

"You grew up playing basketball and got scholarships for football after just two years of starting at Woodberry. You're a great athlete who wound up playing football, but you don't love this shit.

"You're the most headstrong guy I know when it comes to something that *you* want to do. Now you can blame anything and anybody you want, but I do all the same shit you do, except when it's time to ball—I show up and ball, because I love the game...and you don't!" DC said and wiped the corners of his eyes. Dre followed suit.

DC's words stung and then scored.

We all sat silently absorbing the truth that I had run from and didn't want to face, but those close to me had plausibly already noted.

I didn't have what it took to be a legend of the fall, because I just didn't give a fuck—period.

Football was just another hustle—a hustle to get into school, for attention, a hustle to be loved and adorned by women, and a hustle to be looked at as the man by my peers and *friends* back home.

My main objective was to get paid one day for playing, but there would be no money—because there was no love.

"You're right DC. You are so right," I said.

"He is Manzo." Dre placed a hand on my shoulder.

"I'm just keeping it real with you because you my nigga Manzo." DC smiled, and I braced myself to the stool to not fall over.

"But let me ask y'all two something." I said.

"Go ahead!" Dre leaned forward.

"Are you motherfuckers as drunk as I am?" I pointed to the empty shot glasses.

"Ha, ha, ha, ha, ha!" they both laughed.

"Hell yea! I'm twisted! I was like I hope this motherfucker gets what I'm saying, because I don't know how much more Joe Clark I got left in the tank!" DC wobbled on his stool.

"Man them shots got me fucked up too for real," Dre said.

Hold up.

Is this lil nigga's hand still on me?

"OK Dre, you can get your little dick beater off my shoulder bro!" I said. "I ain't with that ole dick-in-the-booty shit y'all do in Lynchburg!"

Our outburst of laughter occurred just as Journey's song ended.

"Fuck you Manzo! I ain't consoling your dumbass no more!" Dre threatened. "Next time you're crying, go to Brittney!"

Oh shit, Brittney!

"Fuck, I still have to tell Brittney and my family I left the team!"

"When are you going to tell them?" Dre asked.

"I don't know. When I figure out what I'm going to do next."

"What are you thinking?" DC signaled to the waitress to bring another round.

"I don't have a clue. I could stay and finish school here or try and transfer and play football at another school like Syracuse or some shit."

"But if you transfer to another D-1 school, you gonna have to sit out another year unless you enroll now, and that's almost impossible. It's already August 31st, and most classes start in a few days," Dre informed.

"Damn, you're right! I didn't think any of this shit through!" I shook my head.

"Bro, what the hell you been thinking about then?" DC asked.

"Besides missing the team, oddly nothing that concerned football.

"I thought about what I'm going to do in the future with my life. How am I gonna get rich now that football is gone? I can't work for anyone. I gotta be a boss like my pops.

"Picture me having some White man tell me when I can eat and how long I can eat for. I can't do that shit, and it scares me to even think about having a job. Fuck a job!

"I need to get millions on my own. If it's not football, then I'm cool, as long as I'm getting major paper. Can't get major paper working for the next guy."

"Well can't you work for your dad at his club until you get your own *club*." DC smirked.

Damn, he knows what my father really does for a living.

"I have no interest in being like my pops or owning a *club* DC."

"Manzo you stupid 'cuz if my pops owned a club, I would be there right now with the bitches, having fun, and getting that money." Dre rubbed his hands together.

OK good, Dre doesn't have a clue about my pops!

"I know Dre, but I don't think I will go that route. Thanks," I said.

"Would Britney be mad if you left?" DC asked.

"Shiiiid, of course she would be mad, but I truly believe we would be all right. I love her with all my heart, and I know that things would work out. She would still be faithful like she's always been if I left," I said, but swore I felt DC tap Dre's leg with his knee under the table.

"She's the only one for me fellas."

"I guess you're right Manzo." Dre looked at D.C. before speaking to me.

Hold up, what's going on?

"Why are you two motherfuckers acting so strange all of a—"

"Here you go gentlemen...another round of Bacardi 151 for you big *strong* men. *SNIFF, SNIFF,*" the waitress interrupted and placed three shots of the brown venom on the table before pinching the tip of her nose.

"Enjoy studs."

The chubby-armed-waitress winked at me before leaving as I watched the back of her jean-skirt lift just enough to see the red pimples glowing right beneath pale, plump butt-cheeks.

Her dark roots on her head sprouted into a wet blonde bun, magnifying her glass-studded VT earrings.

She had a rural Virginia prettiness with cement colored eyes, a semi-potbelly, and DD breasts scantily hidden under a white Big Al's tank top.

If she weren't sick, I would have given her the dick. My standards had dropped 151 notches.

"Oh shit Manzo. I think that juice is in love with you," Dre teased.

"Hell yea, she wants to gobble your Hokie bird," DC added.

"She wanted you to suck a zit off her ass," Dre joked.

"The juice *was* all extra friendly to me. I would beat the pepperonis off that pie if she wasn't all sick and shit," I said.

"Ha, ha, ha...*sick?*" DC curled his lips. "Yea, that bitch sick aight. You crazy Manzo!"

"I'm going to take a piss before we drink *that* shit." I stood up.

"Great idea," DC said.

"Hell yea fellas!" Dre raised out his seat.

What the fuck?

"Yoooo—look at that line for the bathroom!" I pointed to the opposite end of the bar. "Them bitches waiting for government cheese or some shit?"

"Damn man!" Dre peeped the eight fidgety college girls standing behind one another, and he sat back down. "Juices always trying go to the moon."

"The *moon?*" I questioned Dre and sat. "You VA cats call the bathroom *the moon?*"

"Nah nigga!" Dre hit DC on the shoulder and gestured toward me.

"This New York *City* dude really don't know what the moon is DC?"

"I guess not Dre," he replied.

"What the hell is the moon then Dre?" I snatched the shot of liquor in frustration and smacked it against the back of my throat.

The dripping acid smoldered my organs to a crisp as the room tilted in one direction. My mind tilted in the other.

The 151 made dust of my sobriety's remains and crumbled my spirits. The shot burned with the fury of sucking on rubbing alcohol ice cubes.

Woozy, I lost my bearings for a second, but the energy of the moment kept me on course. I refused to tap out of our discussion.

"OK Manzo! That's what the fuck I'm talking about! Let's go Dre!" DC cheered before they both drank, thwacking the shot glasses on the table once they finished.

"Aaahh—now please let's tell this guy what the moon is 'cuz I'm not drinking no more of that shit. Jesus take the wheel!" Dre consecutively touched his forehead, his stomach, his left pec, and then his right—the sign of the cross.

"Damn, that 151 turned this lil' nigga into T.D. *Fakes!*" I held my own chest laughing.

"Yooo, that shit was mad corny. Now I know you're drunk," Dre rebutted.

"Fucking right I am," I said. "My head is spinning, and I have to drive. Tell me about that moon shit, so I can bring Brittney's worrisome-ass her car back."

"Yooo, you seriously don't know what we talking about Manzo?" DC's laughter subsided. "Like no bullshit?"

"Nah DC—I don't have a clue."

"I thought if anybody knew then *you* would know." DC pointed to the bathroom line, now ten-girls-long.

"Oh you're being funny now, huh?" I asked.

"Just chill for a second and look at those girls moving around all funny on the line," DC said.

"Yea I see them bitches. They're shaking a little. So they have to pee. What's the big fucking deal?" I shrugged my shoulders.

"Sooooo, all ten girls have to pee *that* bad...at the *same* damn time Manzo?" Dre asked.

"How the fuck should I know lil' guy?"

"Nigga...all those White bitches are going to the bathroom to *powder their noses.*"

DC tapped the tip of his nose twice. "¿Comprende?"

Powder their noses? Ooooh shit!

"Come on bro, I ain't slow. I know what that means," I said.

Those juices are doing coke! Get the fuck outta here!

"Good, because my moms said I can't hang with slow motherfuckers," DC stated.

"Ha-ha...shut up." I studied the movements of the girls.

"Sooo, that nerdy juice with the glasses and orange Tech tank-top fucks with the powder too?"

"Absolutely Manzo." Dre nodded.

"But how y'all know?" I asked.

"Because we just know." DC jabbed my shoulder and then pointed to the girls in line.

"Manzo...watch when the bathroom door opens, three juices will all go in at the same time. Just watch."

"Watch Manzo," Dre urged.

These dudes drunker than me.

Like magic, just under ten-seconds from DC's premonition, our waitress storms out of the bathroom door pinching her nose again, and the next three blondes dashed in before the door shut closed on its own.

I couldn't see their faces clearly, but the orange leggings did little to conceal soccer-ball-sized asses sculpted beneath the shiny fabric. I knew exactly who they were.

"Oh shit, y'all were right!" I blurted.

"Told you! And from the look on your face, you know who those girls are don't you?" Dre asked.

"Hell yea, those-them High Tech bitches," I said.

The High Techs were the official dance team of the Hokies, and they performed at football games, but their main stage was halftime at the basketball games.

Unlike the cheerleaders, comprised of short armed, Mary Lou Retton-looking juices, the High Techs each had the build of an Alvin Ailey all-star.

The High Techs were taller, thicker, and absolutely more seductive. They didn't do back flips, but they did touch their toes, and apparently—a few of them loved cocaine.

"I don't know any of their names, but good-gracious they bad as a mother-fucker." DC bit his bottom lip.

"I want to put the beats on any one of them!" I said.

"Don't talk so loud nigga," Dre said.

"You can do whatever to them bitches if you got some blow," DC said. "But stop staring over there y'all. We don't want them knowing we're talking about them."

"OK." I pulled my chair even closer. "But how do *y'all* know so much about it?"

"Yooo, stop looking over there!" Dre ordered.

"My bad, my bad," I apologized.

"Manzo shit is different here in VA than in New York. We may not live in NYC, but we're from the hood too—and we see shit just like you do.

"All my homies back home in Smithfield slang coke, straight powder. And mad people sniff that shit, especially the dealers and the young White college kids," DC said.

"Maaaaan if you got caught snorting the shit, people would call you a fucking crackhead in my hood."

"Shit, I know Manzo, but down South it's waaaay different." Dre swooned in his stool. "Damn...I'm a lit-tle fucked up fellas."

"So all these people at Tech sniff coke?" I ignored Dre.

"Damn near bro," DC replied.

"Get the fuck outta here."

"I wouldn't bullshit you Manzo. Motherfuckers love that P here," DC said.

P must stand for powder.

"Is that shit any good down here like it is in New York?" My palms had begun to itch.

"Heeelll nooo!" Dre shook his head. "It's OK, I heard, but everyone knows that NYC got that rocket fuel."

"How you know Dre?" I asked and side eyed.

"Nigga don't look at me like that. I never done P. That's word to everything I love." Dre put his hand in the air like he was on the stand.

Oooh man!

"Don't look at me like that, I ain't lying!" Dre put his middle finger up. "Cats from Lynchburg drive all the way to New York all the time for that *raw*."

"Shiiiiid, my niggas drive from Smithfield too. And the shit be fire I heard, but making that trip without a steady connect is hell for them. So they just be coppin' their shit from local dudes." DC informed.

I know mad drug dealers.

"How much is that shit in y'all hoods?" I asked.

Can't cost that much more than the city.

"I don't know about wholesale, because I try not to be *all* in their biz like-that like-that," Dre answered first.

"Yea I really don't know the price my Smithfield homies get their shit for. I stay outta their business—but I hear shit because we all fuck the same girls, and you know how dudes love to pillow talk."

"Shit, y'all niggas have to know some type of price. I mean they *are* your homies. And I know y'all don't fuck around, because most my homies back in Harlem slang these days.

"And I can tell y'all all about anything from Heroin to PCP, but I've never done it. So no judgement over here, I'm just drunk and curious. Damn, all we're doing is *talking* fellas. How much?" I leaned back and waited for an answer.

"You talking about an eight ball or a gram?" DC lowered his voice.

"A gram, I guess. I never even heard of an eight ball," I admitted.

"Well a gram of some good shit is prolly like a c-note all day," DC said.

"A fucking *c-note*?" I shouted.

"Yea, a c-note Manzo." DC looked around. "Keep your voice down nigga."

"I know what a c-note is, but you have to be bullshitting me. No fucking way!" I crossed my arms.

"No bullshit Manzo, that's what it cost in Lynchburg too." Dre nodded.

"Dre...$100 for *one* gram of *cocaine*, right?" I asked.

"Yea motherfucker, a gram of coke—Yayo, Powder, P, White Horse, White girl. Yes, fucking cocaine," Dre said.

"$100 for a gram is like $100,000 for a kilo on the breakdown," I said.

"Now this nigga is a mathematician all of a sudden," Dre laughed and glanced at DC for comical support but there wasn't any.

"Yea Manzo, they're killing it in VA. This ain't *New York City*," DC said.

$100,000 can be made on a key?

"A key ain't shit to get off down here. My boy Cool Willie can bust down a key in a week," DC said nonchalantly.

"My nigga—a fucking *week*?"

"Hell yea Manzo. My homie Slick in Lynchburg can do the shit in like four days," Dre added.

"Four days!" I began to sweat. "Y'all motherfuckers are bullshitting me. Cut the jokes man. I'm too buzzed for games."

"Do you see me laughing?" DC rubbed his goatee.

Oh shit, he's serious!

"You're acting all super surprised at shit Manzo. Well how much it cost up there in the Big Apple B?" Dre inquired.

"Maaaan, if I told y'all...you would think I'm lying."

"Spit it out," DC requested. "Stop playing. You got us all curious and shit now."

"Y'all not gonna believe this shit," I said before I slanted closer. "Fifteen dollars."

"*What?*" they asked together, pulling their stools closer to the table.

"Fifteen measly-ass dollars. I shit you not fellas," I said.

"Pesos or *real* dollars? Because that sounds unreal," DC asked.

"DC...did this big head nigga just say fifteen dollars?"

"Yea Dre-Vito...I said fifteen dollars. Not motherfucking *pesos*...dollars. Fifteen dollars a gram."

"$15,000 a kilo. Fifteen dollars." My palms itched again.

"Good-gracious that's a crucial price Manzo. How you know?" DC asked.

Besides my father being the biggest coke dealer on the East side?

"Man the same way you guys know. I'm from the projects, and everybody and their momma know the coke price like the stock market.

"My homie Dirt is like my brother and sells hella-crack. He's always either happy when the coke price is low or mad when it's high.

"I never touched that stuff, but mad niggas in the hood sell coke just like VA, except we have a thousand times more people *and* apparently, the shit is stronger and *a lot* cheaper than—"

Music blared from above, surprising all three of us and momentarily disrupted the narcotics rant of three student-athletes who had no business fact-sharing about the intricacies of the drug game.

Intrigued, we were just drunk kids, old enough to recognize the classic lyrics of "Hotel California," yet young enough to ignore the signs. The conversation should have definitely ended.

"Finally, somebody picked some chill shit out that jukebox, Hotel California is my shit." Dre said.

"Anyway, finish what you were saying Manzo," DC urged.

"Hold up, let me say something. Bottom line is that whoever comes down here with a boatload of that shit will be an instant millionaire," Dre said.

A millionaire?

"Now that's a fact! In like a few months too," DC said.

A few months?

"How is that possible?" I asked and brushed the sweat from my brow. "How —in a *college* town?"

"Nigga are you crazy?" DC contorted his face.

"Manzo this is a college town. All these rich White kids here do blow, and guess who's paying for it?"

"Shit DC, I dunno—" I asked.

"Their parents!"

Fuck, he's right!

"Their parents are sending them the bread, and they're spending it on drugs and alcohol—Dre, how many students here at Tech?" DC asked.

"At least 30,000," I answered.

"Plus the townies in Blacksburg, Christiansburg, Radford, and surrounding counties—a motherfucker would make a killing," DC elaborated.

"So you're saying a person could make millions, huh?" I placed my unsteady hands under the table.

"*Millions*," Dre answered.

"*Millions*?" I looked at Dre.

"*Millions*," DC replied.

The usual starters had now walked in Big Al's and the energy of a Blacksburg's Tuesday night had been released with the striking aroma of grilled hot dogs, beer, and cigarettes.

The Virginia slims at the next table threw winks in my direction that normally I would have *Derek Jeter'ed*. But my mind had been hit with dreams of scoring in a different field. DC, Dre, and the Eagles battled for my attention, but I could not be reached. Nobody was home.

$100,000 per kilo I can make...

Shit $131,000 is the NFL league minimum...I could kill this shit easily...

$100,000 minus the $15,000 per key I would make a profit of $85,000 every week...

Fifty-two weeks in a year times $85,000 equals abooouuutt...eighty-five times fifty-two...oh, shit!

$4.4 million and some change in a year!

More than the average fucking NFL player easily!

"But for-real for-real Manzo, a nigga would be crazy to bring some powder down this motherfucker. I don't know about New York but these dudes snitching like shit in Virginia," DC said.

"Hell yea Manzo! That's why it's good we're in school and doing the right thing, 'cuz if this football shit doesn't work out then we at least have something to fall back on.

"Selling powder def not the way to go. You can make crazy money, but you gonna go to prison, or a motherfucker gonna peel your cap back for sure. You best believe that," Dre said.

"No bullshit Dre! I would never sell no damn P! These dudes out here ain't playing fair! You would have to be dumb as hell! I would get a job before I ever sold drugs!" DC said.

I could buy my moms a big house and my entire family would be straight for life...

Brittney would never have to work again.

"... gave my cousin Phil thirty goddamn years for selling keys. Virginia is a Commonwealth State and they hang niggas for three things—crack, driving charges, and motherfucking child support," Dre warned.

"Shit, when my uncle got sentenced...guess what the judge told him?" DC asked.

"What?" Dre raised both hands.

"The judge told my uncle to look outside the courtroom at a tree, and the entire courtroom did. The shit was like a baby tree, like some Mr. Miyagi, Karate Kid type shit.

"And the judge said, 'You see that-there tree?' My uncle said, 'Yes sir.' And then the judge said, 'You don't get out of prison until that tree is fully grown!'" DC said.

"Oooooh shiiiiid! It takes like fifty years for one of those shits to get my height!" Dre spoke. "What the fuck did he get caught with?"

"An eight ball of crack and a pocketknife." DC shook his head.

What about the police? Virginia police are slow...I won't get caught...

Daddy never got caught...

I'm gonna need a partner...

Dirt would come down here for sure...

I will still go to school...

fuck school...

Nah, I gotta go to school...I can do this!

Hustle for two years and quit cold turkey...

By the time I'm twenty-three, twenty-four I'm out—

"Yoooo!" I yelled after *safely* landing back at Big Al's.

"What Buzz Lightyear?" Dre answered. "This guy was on Pluto. I'm not drinking wit this crazy fool no more DC."

"What's today's date?" I asked as I scoped the newest additions to the ever-growing bathroom line, the same damn three High Techs.

"Today is August 31ˢᵗ I think." DC pulled his cell phone out his pocket, glanced at it, and then stuffed in back into his gray sweats. "Yea, the thirty-first...why?"

I'm going to make it snow in Blacksburg.

"I know what I want Santa to bring me for my birthday," I said.

"Maaan, this dude drunk! Your birthday ain't on Christmas asshole! The shit is in two days!" Dre reminded me.

"Exactly my little buddy. *Exactly*."

Chapter Twenty

C17H21N04

"My nigga, I ain't see you in too damn long. What the *fuck* are they feeding you down here?" Dirt asked while seated at my dining room table rolling a blunt. "You easily the most diesel dude from the hood now."

"Ain't nothing but fat dudes and crackheads in our hood, so that ain't too hard," I replied from my chair across from his.

"I'm saying though, you left with titties, now you're lifting White girls with one hand and shit."

"Ha, ha, ha! Fuck you Dirt!"

"And speaking of hood, why you never come back to Harlem anymore my nigga?" he asked.

Fuck—he knows I got robbed!

"I don't know. No time I guess," I said to the floor.

"We miss you in the projects. Anyway Manzo, I'm serious about losing weight. I'm ready to get on my workout shit while I'm down here." He rubbed his protruding belly.

Good, I don't think he knows!

"Seriously Dirt?"

"Hell-nah I ain't serious! Bitches just care about the bread in a nigga's pockets, you can keep them muscles." He licked the edge of the blunt paper, giving it a final twist at the end.

"You got a light?"

"In front of you, in that ashtray." I pointed.

"Yooo, you got a VT lighter inside a VT ashtray?" He sparked the blunt.

"Ha-ha...yea...so?"

"*SUUUUUH.* Y'all motherfuckers gone VT craaaazzzyy down this bitch."

"Well, this *is* Virginia Tech," I said.

"As soon as I hit I-81, all I saw was VT eeerr-thang." He reached under the table, placing on it—a black duffle bag, just large enough to fit four of my textbooks and a pair of socks.

"*SUUUUUH.* I think y'all bitches even got VT tramp stamps and shit."

"Oh shit, how did you know?" I asked.

"Different campus...same shit bro." He slid the bag in front of me.

"Oh yea, happy birthday! Twenty-two! Getting old nigga!"

"Thanks Dirt!" We slapped five. "Now pass that damn blunt. We share in Blacksburg!"

Is this shit really happening? Am I really going to do this?

If I can't trust Dirt, I can't trust anybody.

* * *

Dirt and I grew up together in Wagner Projects and had been friends literally since we came out of the womb.

We were just two months apart and his mother, Ms. Stephanie, and my mother had also been friends since childhood.

Ironically, Dirt's father—Victor, was also a big-time, Puerto Rican drug dealer with a sweet tooth but was murdered when Dirt and his older brother Leslie were little boys.

Matthew Santiago was Dirt's birth name, but his nickname seemed to come from God himself, because as a teenager—he was just always involved in some sort of criminal activity: Gambling, fighting, stealing, and eventually drug dealing.

Ms. Stephanie did all she could to keep Matt out of trouble, even enrolled him in Catholic school, but he took bible lessons in the day and did the devil's work at night.

A high school graduate with a knack for rackets, he was always into what he did best—Dirt.

Looking at him sitting at my table, I couldn't help but laugh to myself. Behind his mangy beard, Caesar haircut, and blackish-brown lips—all I could see was the boy I used to play with on the monkey bars.

Dirt was still the little dude that people had confused for my fifth brother. Even our mothers understood the mix-up.

He and I shared the exact same skin tone, Black and Puerto Rican infused hair texture, Michael Jackson-in-the-Wiz-nose and lips, and dinky eyes.

Our key physical differences were that I had my mother's cheekbones, a humongous head, a receding hairline. I was also six inches taller with a seventy-pound weight advantage.

But if I ever needed someone to play me in a movie when I was in junior high school, Dirt was the guy.

Wagner Projects was the office to many crack entrepreneurs, but Dirt always led the Fortune 100 companies in the quality of product and number of workers willing to man the trenches for their thirty percent of ghetto royalties.

Dirt did not limit his corporation to local endeavors though. He would get on the road and set up shop wherever his expertise was needed.

Having hustled in towns and colleges from Boston to Charlottesville, Dirt followed the protocol for maximizing an imported investment. He specialized in taking the proper routes and precautions for a safe and easy arrival. Dirt was *my* guy.

* * *

"I like this townhouse you got here. I like how it's mad space. And you know I'm loving that *Scarface* poster." He nodded a few times. "What's the name of this complex?"

"You know I had to get the joint of Montana sitting in his office. Glad you like my place. This complex is Terrace View apartments. I got three bedrooms upstairs."

You ain't fucking in my bed!

"That couch woulda been good enough, but that's love my nigga, thanks. But let's get on the same page real quick." Dirt tapped the blunt against the ashtray, passing me the weed.

"I know we discussed this shit like crazy over the phone, but you sure you want to do this because it's no sweat to me. I can just head back to C-Ville with this shit and get this off with Outlaw and B-Move."

"Come on Dirt. I told you I'm all in and I'm a man now. Stop asking me if I'm in, because I can do this shit easily. It's in my blood to get money."

If my pops could do it then I could do it.

"Nigga I know, but I just want to make sure." He began unzipping the duffle bag.

"UVA or VT…I don't really give a fuck where this paper comes from, but I will say your situation seems a lot sweeter than over there in Charlottesville."

"Hell yea it is. Fuck UVA! I love Outlaw and B-move, but the homies will be OK," I said without knowing, caring, or fully understanding what operation Dirt had going on in Cavalier country with two of my other childhood buddies from Wagner projects.

"OK Manzo, say no more, but just know that this shit ain't a game—"

"Blah, blah, my nigga—just open the bag. You are blowing my high."

"You're still a fucking asshole I see." Dirt reached into the bag.

What the fuck is that smell? Ooooh shiiiit!

CLUNK!

"How's *that*, muscle-head?" Dirt tossed a hard, vacuumed-sealed bag onto my glass dining room table. The ashtray jumped for joy.

Holy shit!

"How you like that, *college boy*?" He snatched the blunt from my lips.

Having watched too many movies, I expected Dirt to pull out a giant sandwich bag filled with a substance as white and soft as baby powder, or slightly denser like flour.

But I was completely wrong and proved more ignorant about my potential career path than I had ever believed.

The package was rectangular and about the height and width of a 200-page notebook encased in ice.

The hard plastic's luster appeared magnetic and capable of electrifying an alien mothership or giving a blind man's sight back with a single touch.

There was no white, and no powder—only cornmeal-flaked concrete glistened beneath the package's restraints.

Super high, I expected the yellow intruder to fly, spin, and shoot rainbow sparks across my apartment.

That's more than three ounces! Is that a real brick?

"How much is in that shit Dirt?"

"Did you get the scale?" he asked.

"Yes."

"Well, where is it?"

"It's right there under your chair in that white mesh bag with the clothes in it." I pointed.

"Oh shit, I thought it was laundry day or some shit." He passed me the blunt before grabbing the bag.

"Manzo, this shit is mad heavy. What the fuck is in here?"

"Everything you asked for, and some clothes from my football locker that I packed when I left the team."

CLANK!

He dropped the bag on the table and asked, "You got everything I asked for?"

"Dirt just pull everything out."

That's a lot of fucking coke he got! What if I get caught with all that? What if I can't sell it fast enough?

"Good Lord, where did you get this from my nigga?" He pulled the gigantic scale from the cocoon of soiled VT shorts and sweats and held the scale like a pet, as its cord and plug dangled in the air.

"This shit is bananas!"

"I borrowed that shit from Chemistry class."

"Damn Manzo, you taking Chemistry?"

"Well, not really, but my home girl Adriana is, and she took the shit for me. I'm borrowing it from her."

"These White girls will do anything for y'all football niggas."

"How you know she's White?" I asked.

"Cut the fucking jokes!" He shook his head. "Black girls wouldn't steal air for a nigga to breathe! My sisters ain't stupid!"

"Ha-ha!" I laughed. "Man you're terrible!"

"Facts my nigga! Facts! Where's the outlet?" Dirt sat up in his chair.

"Too funny! It's behind you—plug it in."

Dirt set the scientific scale on the table and plugged the contraption into the wall, giving the scale life.

The face lit "oo.oog" on its tan, bike-ramped base which sloped upwards onto a keyboard-sized square metal platform.

The visual of the coke and the scale together gave me anxiety, but my drug lord starter kit was almost complete.

What the fuck am I doing?

"This shit is a monster Manzo." Dirt swiftly waved his hand over the metal, and the numbers frenzied to oo.17g and then back down to oo.oog.

"Yoooo, this shit can even measure the motherfucking air!"

"Hell yea Dirt! It's the best!" I blew smoke at the machine and watched the numbers dance.

"And you can put like ten keys on this bitch," he said.

"We won't need that much though, will we?" Sweat beads formed on my brow.

"Nigga, we might need two scales in a couple of weeks."

God I don't know if I'm ready for this!

"I can feel your knee tapping against the table." Dirt snatched the trembling blunt out of my lips.

"Calm down and take a deep breath my nigga. You about to be a twenty-two-year-old millionaire. Stop being pussy. You scaring me."

"I'm saying though Dirt—"

"You saying what?" He reached into the mesh bag and extracted a box of Gemstar razor blades, a box of latex gloves, a box of Glad sandwich bags, and a hammer—all items he asked me to get.

"What are you saying? You nervous? You have *anxiety*? You second guessing? All the questions you have, every nigga who ever got money has had. So chill out. You either with this shit or you ain't!

"Big Los ain't gonna keep his titty in your mouth forever, and you're not going to the NFL. I hate to piss on that dream. I know you miss your team and don't want to talk about it, but it's a wrap for that Beamer Ball shit.

"Now how you gonna survive? What you gonna do? Get a job working for the next nigga? You gonna have half hour lunch breaks and eat a fucking cheese sandwich at your desk? It's time we get ours Manzo.

"So, are you with getting millions, fucking the baddest bitches, buying err-thang you ever wanted for you and your fam? Or you scared of these slow-ass Virginia crackers locking you up? You're from Harlem. It's time to start acting like it. It's our time my nigga."

Dirt didn't say anything that I had not told or asked myself for the last few days. I just needed to hear it. I needed him or someone to stamp that I was indeed making the right decision.

He would never let me put myself in a situation that he wouldn't put himself in, and I felt confident that success was the only option for the *brothers* from Wagner Projects.

No longer worried about the Barney Fife's of Blacksburg, I was ready to do something *special* and get more money than any NFL contract could ever provide for me. I was ready to be a legend, and no one was going to stop me!

He's right!

Let's get this money!

"I'm saying though Dirt...how's that hammer gonna help us get these millions?"

"You gonna see. So this means you're in my nigga?"

"Fucking right! Can't let you have all the fun!" I replied.

"Smart man! Now go close those blinds please and let's get this shit poppin'."

"Bet!" I pulled my seat out, walked into the living room to the patio window, and peeped out of the window before closing the blinds.

"It's mad people walking around for it to be this early."

"They young and White?" Dirt asked.

"Yes."

"They got book bags on?"

"Uuh yup." I returned to the table.

"Maaan sit your scary-ass down nigga. It's 8:23 AM. They going to class."

"Oh yea, that's right," I gave a nervous laugh.

"Here put these on and chill." He tossed me two rubber gloves. "You know what they're for?"

"Dirt stop trying to play me. I saw New Jack City." I shoved my right hand in the first glove.

"You'sa funny nigga Manzo. I kid you not."

"You think we can eat before we do this?" I asked.

"Bruh, we already punched in the clock. Should've thought about that earlier." He removed the cardboard sleeve from around two razors and slid one of the blades across the table.

"And absolutely no liquids around this table. You get thirsty go in the kitchen, but DO NOT, and I repeat, DO NOT have any water or juice or any liquids around this table—*ever* my nigga."

"Damn Dirt, I ain't slow!" I shook my head.

"Aight...hope you listening. Put the ashtray on the floor too." He put his second glove on and tore open the box of plastic baggies.

"When the fuck you become such a goddamn Nazi?" I put the ashtray on one of the two vacant chairs.

"You ready to get this money Manzo?"

Shit, I hope so.

"Hell yea I'm ready!" I stared back at Dirt, noticing the tiny scar under his left eye from a softball game when we were nine years old. "Let's do this brother."

We got this.

"It's you and me my nigga. We can't lose." He pinched the cocaine tablet by one of its corners and sliced free an inch of plastic with the razor. "Welcome to the first day of the rest of our lives."

Holy shit!

That smell!

My eyes watered before my nose singed with joy from an invisible smoke of heaven fuming a weird jungle taste, both chemical and organic.

I had smelled and even tasted cocaine before, and I expected the common scent of gasoline arm-wrestling with ether, but this cake came from a different bakery. The scent of success filled the air.

What in the world?

We gonna be rich!

Dirt outlined the tomb with the razor, decorticated the thin layer of protection, and pitched the plastic on my hardwood floor.

The block, paved with a glittered Dove soap smoothness, seemed to make his face glow, highlighting a satisfaction that I had never witnessed from Dirt.

The piece had the extravagance of a relic, well deserving of a surrounding velvet rope and laser beam security.

The excavation complete, he rubbed his thumb across the claws of an engraved scorpion, life-sized and dead center of our glossy, pale-yellow artifact.

"It's beautiful," he professed his love.

"A *scorpion*?" I asked.

"Yes, a scorpion my brother."

"Where that shit come from Dirt?"

"Mexico, *Colombia*—who gives a shit?" He never looked up and trailed his thumb to the right top corner of the block, stopping at a square indenture—approximately a quarter of an inch.

"You see this right here?" he asked.

"Yea what the fuck is that?"

"These marks are from its twin that sat on top of this shit like a Lego." The petrologist pointed to the four corners of the slab. "You don't get any better than this my nigga."

"Ooooh shit." I cautiously moved in for a closer look.

"Ha-ha...Manzo you can touch it. It's *yours*."

"Well, ours," he corrected. "Go ahead."

"This shit is mad hard...and *shiny* too!" I caressed the coke and then tapped it with my knuckle.

"How somebody gonna get this hard shit up their nose?" I asked, genuinely concerned.

"Nobody snorting this shit like this. We have to break this shit down." He picked up the hammer and then placed it back on the table.

"I thought we were gonna hang a picture or some shit when we finished!" I laughed, but Dirt continued massaging the slab.

This dude is in a trance.

"How much is that?" I asked. "I've never seen no shit like that before Dirt."

"This baby right here is 500 grizzies."

"500 grams?"

"Yup, half-a-fucking key. And this how they come too. Bricks come in 500-gram slabs like this when it's pure. You see most niggas don't know this because they watch too many goddamn movies.

"Also because the shit they get in whole bricks been stepped on so many times by them Dominicans in the Heights and then re-rocked."

"Yooo, I said to bring like three ounces or something like that—"

"I wasn't coming all the way here for no three motherfucking ounces! Stop worrying Manzo. We *actually* gonna need more."

"*More?*"

"Yes...*more.*" He picked back up the hammer. "Is this table real glass?"

"Hell-nah, this some cheap-ass shit Wayne Briggs got from home," I lied on my roommate. I had bought the table from a Christiansburg thrift shop.

"Good 'cuz it's actually perfect for what a nigga try'na do." Dirt tapped the table with the hammer.

"Yea, we good money," he said.

"Where's Wayne *Briggs*? You a country bumpkin now too, by the way," Dirt said.

"Hell nah! Why you say that?"

"Only down South motherfuckers call each other by their entire government name!"

"Yoooo, you right about that too!" The light conversation eased my nerves.

"*Wayne* is in class and then football practice—I told him to stay at Vicki's for the night. That's his girl."

"Let me guess, *Vicki* is a White bitch too?" Dirt tilted his head to the side.

"Fuck you Dirt!" I shook my head.

"Y'all love them bunnies down here!"

BANG!

"What the fuck?" I yelled after Dirt smashed of the slab with the hammer.

"You scared the shit out me!"

"Relax and come look at this *perfection.*" He picked up the slab's broken corner, no larger than an ice cube, and held it up to the overhead light—leaving on the table, the world's most expensive chipped tooth.

"Man warn me next time! That looks like the side of one of those Grand Canyon shits!" I moved closer.

"Yessir. It's a rock just like them shits. Look how it's layered Manzo."

"I see, I see. I'm looking for a little White motherfucker with a rope hangin' from that bitch!" I said and instinctively licked my lips.

"You see how the edges are sharp like the side of a mountain?" he asked and pointed.

"Yes."

"You see how it's a lil' yellow and not milk-white like the movies? This is what you call that *flake* or *fish scale.*" He maintained twirling the rock in the light.

"*Flake? Fish scale?* Why they call it that?" I asked.

"Hold up and watch this." Dirt lowered the coke inches away from the slab, tightened both hands around the rock, tucked both his lips tightly together while his cheeks raised—and twisted his hands in opposite directions for relatively three-seconds until the rock separated.

SNAP!

"Goddamn, that shit is mad hard!" I blurted.

"I know, but take a look at this my nigga."

Holding both pieces of pureness in each hand respectively for me to examine, Dirt moved the precious stones from left to right like a cocaine jeweler.

Scaled rainbows swayed with the light, shimmering a wealthy coruscation. The rock's color scheme resembled a beautiful capiz shell.

I didn't know if I wanted to eat, snort, or sell my new obsession, either way, I wanted the cocaine to be a part of my life.

"No bullshit—it looks just like motherfucking fish scales for real Dirt."

"I know but now watch this, kid." He chucked both rocks back onto the table, made the peace sign with his right hand, swiped his two fingers across the top of the slab—raising his hand to the light. I immediately noticed the frosting.

"You see that Zo?"

"Oh shit, it's not real powdery on the glove. It's shiny and oily too," I said.

"Now you're learning. That means the shit is official." He nodded his head.

"Man...that shit looks so good. I can see why people like doing it. It looks so *good*," I spoke under my breath as my eyes amplified.

"Hold up, *what* did you say?" he asked.

"Uh, what are you talking about?"

"You sound like you want to try this shit."

"What you are talking about Dirt?"

"Don't play with me, because I will pack this shit the fuck up and bounce before I let you try this shit!" he threatened.

"What the fuck? I would never try this shit! I ain't no crackhead! Come on, you're tripping now!"

"Trippin'? I hope I am, 'cuz you sound all *enamored* by all this my nigga." He folded his arms.

"Hell no, I wouldn't do no damn blow...ever! You trying to play me Dirt!"

"Listen I'm not trying to play nothing. We here to make money and I love you. You're my brother, and I've seen mad people get turned out on this shit, and I'm not gonna let that happen to you. That's why we always wear these stupid-ass gloves, so this addicting shit don't ever get in our system.

"Now let these White kids spend *their* daddy's money coppin' from us.

These White bitches gonna try and get you to snort this shit and get all freaky with them, but you gotta leave these devils alone that fuck with this shit.

"I know how you love pussy, and you already fucking every Amber that comes your way, but you absolutely can't fuck with this! No Bueno Manzo!"

"OK Dirt, stop beating me upside the head like I'm some baser or some shit! I want money! I'm not in this shit to party!"

"You sure?" he asked.

"Yea I'm sure!"

"Let me ask you this then...what's up with your White shorty?" he questioned.

"Uuuh, which one?"

"Your main one—what's her name? The White bitch with the mean short haircut you showed me a pic of, with the Black girl ass?"

"You're talking about my girl Brittney?"

"Does this *Brittney* do coke?"

"*Coke*? Hell no! She doesn't even smoke weed Dirt."

"You sure?"

"Hell yea I'm sure. I'm not even telling her about this shit I'm doing. She would leave me in a minute!"

"Good Manzo. Don't tell her nothing you don't have to."

"I'm not stupid like you think." I shifted in my seat.

"I know you not, but I'm still gonna look out for you. And what about school?"

"What about school?" I asked.

"You still going, right?" He opened the box of plastic baggies and yanked a wad out, placing them next to the digital scale.

"Hell yea I'm still going. I graduate this summer. I'm not playing around."

"That's good because all you have to do is introduce me to the folks that wanna cop this shit, and I will take it from there. You don't have to sell shit. Just keep going to school and getting this money."

"But you took a *cab* here from Charlottesville. How you gonna get around with no damn car?" I wondered.

"Maaaan it's mad White bitches here, *and* we got all this fucking blow—I'll have a fleet of Rav-4's outside this motherfucker ready to drive me to Africa. Watch your boy work!"

"You'sa a fool Dirt!"

"We gonna be rich fools soon. Stay focused." He extended a gloved fist, and I bumped it with mine.

"How much money are we going to make, and how does this shit work from a money standpoint?"

"Bout time you asked. We gonna make a shit load." He bounced his head up and down before continuing.

"I got the 500 grizzies from my amigo at fifteen bucks a pop, so that's $7,500 that we don't have to pay until we are done with the shit. It's called *consignment*. My amigo gave it to us on consignment."

"And *consignment* is cool?" I asked.

"Hell yea my nigga! It's every drug dealer's dream to get a connect to credit you some shit. We can get whatever we want. I just chose to go small and take it slow."

Small?

"Listen Manzo, we will make at least fifty racks minus the $7,500, soooo...thaaat's—"

"$21,250 a piece after giving your amigo his bread," I answered.

"Yup! Is that a good start for you Brainiac?" He grinned. "I almost forgot how good your ass is with them numbers."

That's mad paper!

"But how *long* do we have to pay him? And will he come kill us if we don't pay in time?" I questioned apprehensively.

"Stop worrying. This isn't the movies. First off, no one knows you, and I will pay him when we finish. I have this chump change in my stash if shit went sour. We good my nigga."

"OK, shit that sounds mad sweet!" I said.

"That's because it is college boy. You already got people lined up for us though?"

"I got my lil' Asian broad I been banging. She sniffs mad blow, and she's gonna bring me to a party at a house on North Main Street tonight to meet a dude named Freddy. Freddy is the man around here with the ecstasy pills. He's gonna connect me with the *in* crowd as she calls it."

"What the fuck is ecstasy?" Dirt asked.

"Some pill that makes girls horny and want to get pounded in the ass, and apparently guys too."

"What type of fruity shit is that?"

"You stupid Dirt! The guys don't want to get pounded. Well, at least I don't think so. Shit does make dudes horny though, I heard. But for real I have never done it—so I really don't have a damn clue what the shit does." I shrugged.

"Shiiiid, the *in* your-ass crowd can keep that freaky shit. What's your China-doll's name?" he asked.

"Shorty name is Jane."

"Damn nigga, you eating General Tso chicken too? You trust her?"

Not falling for this trick.

"I mean…she got a tight lil' pussy, but I don't know about trusting her 100%. It's a start though."

"OK bet…but watch her and be careful." He peeled off a single baggie and opened it. "You need me to go with you?"

"Nah you might scare them looking like you just escaped from fucking prison," I said.

"Ha-ha…you might be right. Aight let me show you how to bag this shit up my nigga."

"I'm ready." I unfolded my arms and scooted my chair closer to the table.

"Aight Manzo, this shit is mad easy—especially for a smart college fella like yourself."

He picked up one of the already broken rocks and tossed it on the scale.

CLANK.

0.98 grams

"OK that's a gram." He reached for the rock.

"No it's not! That's .02 off, *right*?" I asked. "We don't want to cheat them do we?"

"I see what you're thinking but that's not cheating them. We just rounding up. You see nobody has a scale like this, so if they put this on any other scale it will read one whole gram.

"Plus we don't have time to be worrying about small shit like that. So if it's 0.9 or better, just throw it in the bag and keep it moving." Dirt opened a baggie and held it up in front of his face.

"And if it's over a gram Manzo—you just take the razor and slice that motherfucker until it is a gram, or little under, preferably."

I'm not cheating my customers.

"And then you take the rock, drop it in the baggie like so, slide it to one corner of the baggie, hold the rock while twisting the excess plastic mad tight.

"And then you tie the plastic into a tight knot firmly against the rock like this, leaving no extra space in the bag for air.

"Then you take your razor, cut the excess plastic off and ditch it, aaandd *voila*, you just made the easiest 100 bucks you will ever make in your motherfucking life." Dirt handed me the product discreetly.

"Damn bro, can I hire you to make balloon animals at my lil' brother's next birthday party?" I asked and laughed.

"Yo, you not putting any cut or anything in this stuff Dirt? Will it be too strong? I ain't trying to kill none of these college motherfuckers."

"Nah, nobody gonna die. But the shit suppose'ta be potent. We're giving it to them raw."

"A-yooo...*no homo*! Give it to them *raw*?" I laughed.

"Cut it out! Playtime is over! Grow the fuck up—quick!" He chastised. "Now look at how I did that shit! Can you do it exactly like that?"

My smile vanished with the rest of my jokes, and I held the coke in front of my face, examining the rock while twirling it in my fingers.

My blood pumped dollar signs as I squeezed the perfect piece of cocaine with immense pressure, but not even a speck of dust flaked off.

The rock's strength ran through me.

The supreme powder had supreme powers.

Although failing to conceal the smell or energy, the tiny knot stuck to the blow like a fuse. If the coke were black and ignited, the Mario brothers could've tossed the bombs around for a high score. I was going to toss the bombs around Blacksburg for a high price.

This is gonna make us millions! Fuck the NFL!

"I can do *this*. I can do this Dirt. Let's get this money!" I said.

"Good, that's what I like to hear Manzo." He stood up and outstretched his arms until his gold Versace belt buckle said hello.

"Only 499 lil' rocks to go. I'm going upstairs for a motherfucking nap."

"Go get some rest. I got this shit. Not a problem." I assured.

"And Manzo?"

"What's up?" I threw the coke on the table.

Before going up the stairs, Dirt snagged his bag from under the table, reached inside, pulled out a chrome Smith & Wesson .45 with a pearl handle, and then made a promise.

"And that little *situation* in Harlem with your chain will be handled accordingly my nigga. Your problems are my problems now."

Chapter Twenty-One

JANE DOUGH

"Aaah yea! Don't stop! I'm about to come! Aaaaaaaahhhhhhh...fuck!" I pushed the back of Jane's head deeper into my lap. "Get all of it!"

Jesus Christ!

"Aaaaahhh...OK stop!" I yanked her ponytail, but she wasn't finished the job. "Stop!"

"OK, now I'm done." Jane released my cock.

"Fuuuck!" I struggled to speak. "That's not...that's not funny Ms. Pac-man Junior!"

"Only for you, Mr. Manzo."

Her Head is on 1000!

"Hope you got all of it babe. Don't need Brittney finding nut stains in her car."

"You know I got skills, aaaaalll gone. CSI wouldn't be able to find shit, love." She wiped the corners of her lips.

* * *

Jane was a star. At times I couldn't believe that the state of Virginia could have birthed such an exotic little woman.

At just four feet, eleven inches and 125 pounds, she was slender with an unassuming thickness, considering her small stature.

With 36D breasts, twenty-four-inch waist, and thirty-five inches of ass and hips—It didn't take one of her cousins to understand Jane's curvature ratio.

With flawless makeup beneath eyebrows etched to perfection, Jane had a minuscule wide set of smoky eyes that always looked closed but saw everything.

Her face, smooth like butterscotch ice cream on a cone after seven licks, made her appear seventeen-anime-years old, although she was actually twenty-one.

She had lustrous straight hair, a few shades blacker than her heart, that whipped across her ass like carwash brushes when she walked.

Jane's veneered mouth harbored an enlarged tongue, double pierced like her whisker-less cat.

A tremendous golden-eyed, red and orange coy fish tattoo covered the right side of her back and butt, with the fish's tail ending at her thigh.

A perfect combination of couture and goth, she was dressed in a Vera Wang black mini-dress with spaghetti straps, high top, size-six, black patent leather Christian Dior sneakers and a black Gucci spiked choker.

A rebel with a cause, Jane did almost anything to displease her diplomat father who, ironically, would spoil her with even more gifts the more she acted like a complete brat.

After she scored 1510 on her SATs, her father brought her a C-340 Mercedes Benz, and Jane got upgraded when she flunked spring semester and had gotten arrested for possession of marijuana at a Fairfax, VA checkpoint. She now drove a black 1999 Maserati Quattroporte.

Sophomore year I met Jane in Economics 101, and we used to stare at each other the entire class but never said a word to one another, until one day she arrived late, and the only seat available was next to me.

The lights went off for a video presentation, and I went off from Jane's hand job. It was quite the introduction.

A few days later Jane was riding me, until Brittney knocked on my door unannounced, and I hid Jane in the dryer in my kitchen.

"The Last Dragon" DVD had just started, and Brittney walked into my crib extra horny. Brittney and I fucked in my living room from the beginning of the flick until Leroy "got that glow."

When Brittney left, almost two hours later, I cautiously opened the dryer expecting a burst of fire, instead Jane jumped out sweating, ran to my couch, bent over and yelled, "Fuck me like you just fucked her!" I was in love.

I did love Jane almost as much as I loved Brittney, and in my head, we were one big happy family, although Brittney was clueless about us.

For home football games, I would get Jane and Brittney seats right next to each other, because it made life simpler for me to wave to both, rather than having to find each one in the crowd independently.

Oftentimes Brittney and Jane would talk extensively during the game, and they even exchanged phone numbers and made plans to go hang out, but Jane never followed up on the offer.

I never worried one bit that Jane would expose our relationship to Brittney, even if they did go for a drink or two.

I continued my sexual conquest with many other girls at Virginia Tech even though I essentially had two girlfriends, but I could never take my situation with Jane seriously. The girl loved drugs and partying too much.

The nights I had to spend with Brittney, Jane was out with her friends doing blow until the early mornings.

There was no way I could trust a cokehead, but like the truly selfish, manipulative, douche bag I was—I led Jane to trust in me and believe that I was going to end things with Brittney *very soon.*

* * *

"Sooo glad you've been eating pineapples like I asked." Jane opened the sun visor on her side to check her face, and the light came on. A picture of Brittney and me kissing at Busch Garden's was lodged into the side of the mirror.

"Aaaaw so cute. This is my favorite photo of you two."

"*Ha-ha*, thanks," I said dryly, as she reapplied her red lipstick.

"Brittney's one hot bitch, but ain't *nobody* fucking with me." She closed the visor.

"Of course babe. Nobody's hotter than my Lady...*Jane.*"

"I love when you call me that Manzo."

"I love you more than I love my Mary...*Jane.*"

"Aaaw you're so sweet. Please just one more baby!" She blushed.

"Uuh...who has the best sloppy-toppy? Motherfucking...*Jane.*"

"Oh fuck you Manzo! You always know how to ruin a good moment!" She pouted and crossed her arms. I pulled up my Polo boxer briefs and jeans.

"Ha-ha! I was just kidding babe! OK, OK...here's another one—"

"Just stop! You already killed it asshole!" She turned and faced the window. "I'm just a little Asian slut to you."

"Come on baby, don't be like that. I was just kidding. Lighten up. You make me so happy. I *love* you." I held her little hand on her lap. "I'm lost without you ma-ma."

"Really?" she spoke to the passenger side window.

"Of course my love," I whispered in her ear.

"Aaaww OK, I love you too." She turned around. "When you leave Brittney, we gonna be together right?"

"Of course, it's me and you forever." I released her hand and leaned back into my reclined seat as she tried to kiss me. Either she ate a whole Callery Pear tree, or I smelled the semen on her breath.

No way I'm kissing a nut-mouth!

"You're an asshole Manzo!" She pouted again and re-crossed her arms. "Just make sure you give me some fucking blow when we get inside, is all I know."

"Of course—chill babe. Stop it please. Hey which house are we going to?" I pointed ahead while quickly switching topics.

"We better get going to see your homie. What's his name again? *Franky*?" I asked.

"Freddy asshole! Stop smoking so much and remember this dude's name! It's kinda important, you know!"

"Damn babe chill! My bad Jane. I got it."

Franky...shit...I mean Freddy! His name is Freddy.

"OK where am I from Manzo?" Jane asked.

Oh fuck!

"Uuuh...what are you talking about babe?"

Fuck! China?

Is it Thailand?

Damn she just told me earlier.

"You don't remember, do you?" she asked.

Come ooooonn, think!

"Of course I remember."

Fuck! Maybe I do need to stop smoking weed.

"Where then?" She sat up and stared at me as I pretended to examine the cul-de-sac, looking at the two-story, white freshly painted houses with the porch lights on, surrounded by dark forest—twenty yards in front of Brittney's Honda.

"Answer me! Where am I from asshole?"

Don't say China!

"Uuuh...you're froooom... *Asia* my love."

"Just forget it! You pothead motherfuckers are all the same!" She picked up her Valentino red beaded tote bag off the floor.

"The house is the one on the left at 519 North Main like I told you—ten goddamn minutes ago!"

"Oh yea! Wait!" I yelled as Jane opened the car door. "Fuck, I'm sorry!"

SLAM!

"Wait!" I hopped out of the car. "Hold up babe!"

"Fuck you!" she hollered as the moonlight guided her through the thirty or so vehicles parked erratically on the front lawn.

"You ain't shit Manzo!"

"Hold up I'm com—" I said right before closing the door, noticing a bright light on the driver's side floor.

What's that? Is that my cell phone? Oh shit!

Happy that I didn't forget my cell phone, I reached toward the light and picked up my Nokia. A deep panic filled my body, and my nerves writhed under my skin.

I could hear the bass booming through the woods from the house on the left, but my anxiety muted the sounds.

I couldn't hear shit, but I could still see. I held the cell phone to my face and wanted to vomit when I watched the seconds tick away.

Wifey Cell...22:09...

22:10...

22:11...

22:12...

Fuck!

What do I do?

"Oh my God," I mumbled as I accepted the fact that I had butt-dialed Brittney's phone.

22:31...

22:32...

Say something!

"Uh...*hello*?" I apprehensively placed the phone to my ear and spoke. "Hello?"

Is she listening?

Is this her voicemail? No one is there.

"Hellooo—Manzo!" I flinched by the sound of own my name, but the voice was Jane's and not Brittney's. I quickly turned the phone off and shoved it in my pocket.

"Manzo!" Jane repeated.

"I'm coming babe!" I replied and closed the car door.

She wasn't listening.

She would've said something.

That was her voicemail!

Hold up!

Her voicemail is not set up!

Thank God!

By the time my red, black, and white Jordan 1's minced through damp grass up to Jane, who stood on the front porch of 519 North Main—I had convinced myself with certainty that Brittney had not been listening, and that I would be just fine.

Musical beats with no lyrics clobbered through four blacked-out front windows, and my anxiety turned into excitement.

Whether it had been the weed, my ambition for wealth, or the sight of my number one side-chick, I was in complete chill mode—having a pocketful of the best coke on earth also helped.

Damn she's so sexy when she's mad.

"Listen, I don't want to fight with you tonight in front of these people babe." Jane grabbed my hand.

"Tonight is important for you if you seriously wanna make some money, and I won't let you fuck this up...but we *will* revisit your bullshit later," she said.

No, we're not. I'm going home to my girl.

"OK my love. Thank you," I said to her cleavage.

"Why the hell are you sweating so much? It's only seventy degrees." she asked and thumbed perspiration from my forehead. "Are you *nervous*?"

"Uh a little, I guess. I'm new to this."

"Stop worrying babe, I got you." She smiled.

"So here's the plan, I've been to these parties a few times, and I already know it's packed in there, but it's only 12:30 and people aren't complete zombies yet so be cool. You're bigger than me, so you go first, and I'll hold your hand and follow."

"But I have no clue where—"

"Manzo let me finish!"

"My bad. Go ahead babe." I shut up.

"When you first walk in, go straight toward the back, toward that big black-light with the tank sitting underneath."

"*Tank*?" I had to ask.

"Yes, a nitrous tank that Steven always brings to these parties—"

"*Nitrous*?"

"Yes nitrous. Aww, I forget you're so innocent. Just make a left at the black-light, and Freddy's gonna be in the first room on the left."

What the fuck is a nitrous tank doing here?

"OK, blacklight—first room on the left. Got it babe," I said.

"And be cool. Everyone here might stare at you because they know who you are from the football team." She placed my hand on the rusty gold-doorknob and stepped behind me.

"*And* because you'll be the biggest, sexiest Black motherfucker in there."

I got this. Let's go.

"Let's have some fun and make some connections babe." She winked and nodded for me to enter. I opened the door.

* * *

Ear-splitting harmonized electronic dance music with extraordinarily low-pitched, super heavy bass tones welcomed us. Immediately I bopped my head with the beat while I blinked from a hybrid haze of marijuana and cigarette smoke.

DOOSH, DOOSH!

A mundane, medicine-like mist with a menthol base instantly tingled my eyes and cleared my nasal passage.

I could smell every fruity mall-lotion with exceptional keenness but couldn't pinpoint the other scent, which somehow reminded me of my childhood.

What the fuck?

This is insane! Is that smelling salt?

Icy-Hot?

I stepped inside the new world and secured Jane's hand. She closed the door behind her.

With nowhere to move because of the roughly 150 people gridlocked in front of me, I stopped to absorb the scene before I plowed our way through the house's sweet spot. The bass was enlivening.

The whole place illuminated bright purple from the neon moonbeams flashing throughout the house from hanging blacklights the length of baseball bats.

I felt as if I were in another universe or inside a giant grape being health inspected with a flashlight.

Although dark, the space capsule was conspicuous. Almost everything could be seen clearly—just *differently.*

The crowd at first glance appeared to have been a perfect split of jelly glazed, fluorescent girls and boys, all sucking on an assortment of Charm's Lollipops.

The kids' fist-pumped in accordance with the beat and direction of a bare-chested, body-painted, *White* DJ with a rainbow striped face.

He was set up between two tan couches against the wall in the far-left corner of the spacious house.

The DJ's wavy shoulder length hair, the color of a neon yellow highlighter, swayed with the barrage of pre-adults bouncing all around him, and his booth made of graffitied wooden crates. The windows behind him were covered with a black comforter.

Somewhat twenty feet away from me, on the couch to the right of the DJ, were four drippy-juices in a massage-chain, rubbing baby oil on each other.

Each blonde sat stacked, one behind the other, in between each other's toned legs, respectively. They were clothed in just plum-laced bras and lavender boy shorts with four-inch-long Greek symbols going down the seams.

The sorority girls humped to the swing of the song's deep organ chords and trance-inducing blended sound.

While most of the male invaders within a splash, displayed their appreciation by unpretentiously watching—two shirtless guys on the opposite couch were inattentive to everyone, except each other.

Directly under a blacklight, the two sky-blue dudes were on their knees facing one another in a bewildering closeness.

The less imposing figure, the guy on the right, was petite and model-frail with a hairy chest, and a purple ponytail tied with a rubber orange glow-in-the-dark necklace, which matched the red and green accessories around his wrists and neck.

A left thumb ring and gold hoop earrings that I could fit two fingers through finished his look.

He was freshly shaven with a wide nose, soft, dimpled chin, and shapely, manicured eyebrows with an arch that would make Mariah Carey jealous. The little guy's *friend* was definitely appreciating the company.

An athletic physique, the young man on the left had no body fat with grooved muscles that flexed with profound separation.

The length of the pomegranate hairs on his face kept pace with his fuzzed scalp, but, without trouble, lapped his hairless upper body.

He had an aristocratic smile with hooded eyes, a narrow, freckled nose, and straight, radiant teeth.

But all I needed to see was the tattoo of the VT logo in the middle of a Celtic cross on his right shoulder to recognize who he was. I used to line up next to the guy every day in practice for three years. He was fellow linebacker, Jay Douglas.

Oh shit…that's Jay! What the hell is he doing?

With his arms by his side and his eyes shut, Jay teetered to the beat, maintaining balance while his homie gently thumbed a clear cream on Jay's eyebrows, cheekbones, and the bridge of Jay's nose—without a single protest from my ex-teammate.

The little guy's nose was a couple of inches from Jay's lips, and I, for a bit, thought they would kiss.

But the half-pint Steven Segal reached into his skinny-legged-jeans back pocket and pulled out a white-tipped, blue plastic tube that I thought was Chapstick, on first glance.

Jay seemed to know the protocol and propped himself up in expectancy of the next steps of this bizarre process, entirely foreign to me.

The little guy placed the tube in his mouth and appeared to blow a smile into Jay's face.

Jay's eyes battered, as the little guy breathed good spirits from the magical instrument.

Careening his head back, Jay rotated his face with the counterclockwise movement of the wand and twirled his hips like a doped-up hula girl. The toughest guy in the locker room was in bliss.

What is he blowing?

That smell—

Oh shit—

I should had recognized the Vicks odor a lot faster since my mother used to knead it on my chest when I was sick as a kid.

Also, Emma Vicks, some kin of the owner of the product, was a student at Virginia Tech and gave me head once in the Preston's parking lot.

After we were done, I sobered up with one look at her lack of upper lip and leathery skin. She tanned way too much.

Emma was not the cutest sweet potato pie in the oven, but she was funny and brilliant. She gave me a Vicks Inhaler Stick, so I wouldn't forget her last name.

That's that Vicks vapor shit!

Abruptly, Jay disarranged my nerves with a snappy turn of his head, and I grabbed Jane's hand tighter, wishing it were a cross.

I was packed away behind the crowd, so I didn't believe Jay could see me, but something about his eyes said he could feel me.

He looked wide awake, yet extremely sleepy and incoherent.

His huge dark-circled eyes pulled in counter direction of his bouncing forehead as he bit his lips, after opening and closing his mouth every two-seconds.

Picking up a bottled water off of the couch, Jay drank the Smart Water and before he tossed the bottle back down, I caught on to what I *hadn't* smelled —alcohol.

Water?

Is this a dry party?

The music paused momentarily, and people screamed and chugged water or deep-glowing plastic cups of orange juice—but no booze.

Not believing that I could ever witness a college party without its popular substance of choice, I scanned the rowdy crowd from left to right.

I assumed to find, at a very minimum, a can of beer, but I would find no such metal or liquid—only zombified, overprivileged White kids enjoying life at a level we Black kids deemed crazy and taboo.

On the right side of the house, there was a roomy, dark indigo kitchen with a steel, sapphire stove and range, a navy-blue refrigerator, and a surfboard-length island in the middle.

Resting on the island were a desk lamp with a purple bulb, unopened bags of Doritos, four cartons of Tropicana Orange juice toppled on its side, and five untouched gallons of Aristocrat Vodka next to a giant clear bowl of semi-melted ice.

Why isn't anyone drinking alcohol? What's in that orange juice?

A guy my height with dark, long, gel-spiked hair, sporting a sky-blue tank top, who reminded me of every Staten Island kid I encountered—squeezed past me, from my right to left side, and our legs scraped awkwardly.

Blocking my line of vision, *Vinny* turned to me and said, "My bad bro! I ain't one of these fags in here!" and continued pushing through the crowd, after raising a tattooed arm toward Jay.

My mouth dropped. The homophobic hedgehog rustled by the next batch of people, but I couldn't move because I was in shock!

I was tremendously disturbed by the gay bashing, but Vinny's words bothered me less than something I perceived as more disconcerting—Vinny's eyes.

Beneath a threadlike Caribbean Sea-blue canvas, jittering pupils with a shiny eight ball hue were completely dilated under partially closed eyelids.

Aimlessly, Vinny's eyes watched everywhere, but nowhere, blinking confidence and wonder simultaneously. The micro planets eclipsed any sign of a soul.

Wagner Projects bred, I was too familiar with the eyes of drug addicts, but never witnessed such demons as the ones camped inside Vinny's face.

He was completely nonchalant with a blissful awareness like the devil granted him immunity from all human bullshit. No man of flesh was that *cool*— except on Ecstasy.

All these kids have the same eyes! Is everyone here on goddamn X?

DOOSH, DOOSH!

The party ignited with the return of the bass, and an uncontrollable pandemonium spread electricity through the crowd.

People jumped and fist-pumped without a care for personal space or sensibility.

After a juice wearing an orange wig, and extra-large denim overalls with no shirt or bra nearly elbowed me in the face, I pulled Jane's hand and spearheaded a shallow gap between the two bodies in front of me.

People screamed all around me as I trekked through ten sets of dancing Garfield-faced college kids making the most of their age appropriate experiences.

They all held orange and green glow sticks—*Bruce Lee'ing* them in the air to the beat like nun chucks.

Pushing my way through, I kept my head down and out of the laser show, and an animal, which looked like a baby black panther, darted across my shins. Startled, I paced more ferociously.

"Go Portia!" the crowd yelled.

"Work that shit girl!"

Too freaked out to give two shits about whoever Portia was, I ignored the shouts from the left side of the house and trudged a little further before I raised up to check my position.

We had shoved our way to the back of the zoo—just ten feet away from a stocky, shaggy-haired White guy directly under the longest blacklight in the house. He was posted in front of a screen door with a six-foot missile by his side.

Roughly five-feet, ten inches and 215 pounds, the guy had thick muscles under a hot-purple wife beater, with chest hairs going up his clavicle.

With almond eyes pinching the top of his nose, which started between smoothed eyebrows and ended at a subtle upper lip—the young man looked alert like he was ready to run at any given moment.

A shadowing cowboy-like stub, combined with his apparent time in the sun, made him look of a Mediterranean decent.

But his torn khaki cargo shorts, and hanging, braided-belt exposed he was a good ole boy—and I knew him.

Blacklight—

Nitrous tank—

Steven fucking Haynes!

When Jane mentioned her friend Steven, I thought she was talking about one of her random homies, and not the Hokie ex-communicated from the team a couple years ago, for violating most of the rules in the Student-Athlete Handout Book.

Steven was a wild boy like most of the team, and there was never any solid evidence connecting him and any of his menacing activities.

But when a graduate assistant on the team, who turned Steven in for cheating on a test, was found one Sunday morning on the Lane Stadium fifty-yard-line naked, hog-tied, and unconscious with an apple crammed in his mouth—the coaches thought it was in the program's best interest to amicably part ways with the running back from Richmond, Virginia.

"Yoooo Steven!" I hollered as I elbowed a lovely Arab couple, both wearing black shades and tongue kissing passionately—melting with the sound.

"Steven!"

He can't hear me.

Steven laughed and orally engaged with a skinny juice wearing shades, leaning against a wall, that connected the kitchen with a closed room door—probably a bathroom or a closet.

The girl's long, curly hair draped most of her face and stopped right above the letter D on her front-tied, black t-shirt which read "I Would Fuck Me" in bright-yellow lettering.

With tight, denim shorts folded to her crotch, she had sculpted thighs, and a "200 sit-ups a day" midriff. She was an unbreakable juice.

Stationing both hands on the metallic nozzle poking out of the top of the navy-blue, rusted, six-foot, Nitrous tank—the carnival worker twisted his left wrist, and a basketball-sized purple balloon sprouted from his right enclosed fist.

Never tying the balloon, Steven handed it to the outstretched claw of the girl on the wall, eager to claim her prize.

Why do these people want a Nitrous balloon?

I'm gonna ask the fool.

"Yo Stev—"

What the fuck?

I advanced two steps toward the reunion, and the door to my right popped open, forcing me to instinctively lean back.

The first Black dude I saw at the party trooped out of the unlit bathroom drying his hands with a paper towel, the toilet still roaring.

Our faces inches from another, we stared at each other with unquestionable recognition, although he knew me better than I knew him.

* * *

Gerald or "Townie Gerald" to all the Virginia Tech students, because we put *Townie* in front of all non-students that lived in the area—was a low-level pot dealer who lived with his sister at College Park Apartments.

Gerald had a warm, coffee-regular complexion, with twenty fine bristles of hair that comprised his black goatee.

Five wide braids cornrowed down the back of his pint-sized head, stopping between a Cuban-link gold-chain, and his sharp shoulders.

With a hard, indented jaw like he chewed on plastic straws on his off time—his face appeared untrustworthy and squirrelly.

Extra bony without a mark on his skin, he was five-foot, seven inches and appeared even younger than his baggie outfit suggested.

Gerald and his crew of misfits frequented Squires, Preston's, and the rest of the bars. The *tough* townies partied as much as the football players or any other students. I mean; Blacksburg *was* their hometown.

Unlike many of the townies that had a pilgrim-like disdain for the students, Gerald always showed love for the Hokies, giving the players discounts on weed —even buying rounds of Hennessey for the freshmen when he saw them downtown.

I never accepted a drink from him or bought his weed, because I drank for free, considering I was screwing most of the female bartenders in Blacksburg. I only smoked Kind Bud—not that bricked-up shit he sold.

Gerald and I never had a reason to talk or even say hello to one another, until I saw him in Sharkey's eating wings with his girlfriend, Nancy—a pale, petite, squinty-eyed juice with flowing golden-brown spiral curls, a flat-chest, and a doughy little-ass.

Nancy spilled her drink when I walked in the bar, and Gerald immediately knew his girl's big secret, although she told me she was single.

He may have looked seventeen years old, but Gerald was in his early thirties, and no fool. The *man* was sharp.

When I left Sharkey's, Nancy told Gerald everything, from how her and I met in biology class, to how our first time having sex was outside on the grass...at night...in the Westview Cemetery! Man, that was some scary pussy.

A month ago, which had been the last time Nancy and I ever talked, she told me that she explained to Gerald that I never knew anything about their relationship. Nancy said that he never raised his voice or got angry about the news.

He only said, "Tell Manzo we cool—hoes will be hoes," and kept eating his wings.

Although I knew Gerald had a stable of juices, I was surprised by his response. I would've reacted a little *differently*.

After she finished disclosing the details of her confession, I walked Nancy to her car and decided to never talk to her again.

No way was I trusting a juice that ran her mouth that much.

Plus, I actually respected and admired Gerald for how he dealt with the situation. He was a cool character.

* * *

"Yo Manzo! Yo Jane!" Gerald shouted, bounced his head to the beat, and scooted in the direction of the DJ booth as the bathroom door closed behind him. The fit juice with the shades was no longer standing against the wall.

"Hey Gerald!" Jane yelled and pushed me forward.

Gerald doesn't seem mad about Nancy—

Oh shit, there she is!

"Kristy get up! Get off the floor Kristy! Stop it!" Steven, a foot away and kneeling on one knee, screamed to the winner on the floor as she squirmed on her belly while holding a deflated balloon.

"Get out of my body!" Kristy pounded the floor with her fist and feet, her ass cheeks jiggling with every kick.

"Get up stupid!" Steven attempted to assist Kristy, but she vehemently resisted. "Stop fighting me and get up!"

She's buggin'!

"Drugs...I command you...get *out* of my *body*...noooow!" Kristy threw the balloon and pretended to swim with both arms and feet.

"Drugs...I order you...get out...of...my...booooodddyy!"

"What the fuck Kristy? You ain't in no pool bitch!" Steven hysterically laughed, and people trudged around both of them without a care.

"No more Nitrous for you!" Steven said.

Nitrous? Man, we outta here—was that a pussy?

A White, naked body zoomed past the backyard's screen door and I caught a glimpse in the purple rays of what I believed to have been a hairy vagina.

Waiting a couple of seconds for confirmation, I gawked at the screen door, ignoring Kristy's performance, and another White body flew by— except it had a dick.

Fuck this! Jane said the door on the left!

'JANE AND HER BIG BLACK STUD'

After reading the *welcome* sign written on the door, three feet away, I knew we finally were about to meet Freddy, unless he had expected another *big Black stud* to accompany Jane.

Worried about another flying wiener, I yanked Jane past Steven, hurriedly opening the room door without knocking.

"Hold up! Knock—" Jane tried stopping me, but I had already pulled her in behind me.

Holy shit!

In a bedroom, barely sizable enough to fit its unmade king-sized waterbed with three white pillows, and a twelve-ounce Smart Water bottle set on top of a white down-comforter—a little Caucasian fellow was huddled over the middle of a four-foot-long mirrored dresser that completely pressed against the room's right wall.

He sported a black-mesh Von Dutch trucker cap, a blue Superman t-shirt, and faded blue jeans that bell-bottomed over his green *used-to-be* suede Pumas with fat green laces.

The back of his locked, trembling right knee rested on the corner of the bed's wooden platform as the guy's shaky right-fingers pinched white pills individually from a pile, the circumference of a can of peanuts.

After briefly inspecting each pill, the guy chucked the pills into a pink plastic pillowcase-shaped bag that set on top of a piece of scribbled notebook paper at the dresser's edge.

"425...426...426...I mean...427..." The guy never acknowledged our presence as my eyes adjusted to the overhead light.

Does he see us?

"432...433...434..." he kept counting, and I tapped Jane who shifted to my right side while she covered her mouth from laughing.

Is this a fucking joke?

This lil' blind motherfucker blowing my high!

Man, fuck this! I'm gone—

"Freddy...heeeellooooo!" Jane yelled.

"Ooooh shit!" Freddy raised his head before looking at me, then to Jane, then to me, then back to Jane. "How long y'all been standing there?"

He's trashed!

"Long enough to see you've been...getting...this...monaaay!" Jane stepped toward Freddy with open arms. "Heeeey Fred—"

"Hold up! Stay right there!" Freddy stood up fast and lifted both palms to Jane.

"What Freddy? It's me, Jane...and this is my boyfriend Manzo...*remember*?" she stopped and asked.

Boyfriend?

If he reaches for a weapon, I'm gonna punch him!

"You two...don't fucking...move!" he demanded through a clamped jaw.

This guy is on another planet!

Freddy twisted his mouth and chewed slowly on his bottom lip while dilated, gray-lined pupils watched my every move. I watched right back.

His black sideburns slicked from under his cap and cut sharply at the bottoms of his earlobes. He had no facial hair, and a mildly fanged *grin*.

Not counting the pills in his stomach, Freddy weighed around 140 pounds and stood a wimpy five-foot, seven inches, with a nose as straight as his posture.

Handsome, in a Ben Affleck hadn't slept in a month type of way, he rocked his body from side to side and alternated steps non-stop but never advanced. With a waltz of paranoia perfected, Freddy perspired heavily.

"OK Freddy, we're not moving. Stop acting weird babe," Jane pleaded. "What do you want us to do now?"

Say something.

"Yea Freddy, what's good bro?" I asked.

"Don't move and look up," he requested.

"So we can move?" Jane asked.

"Yes...only to look up. Move...to look up." Freddy pointed up.

"OK bro...but what's—"

"What's *that*?" Jane hurdled my attempted question. Freddy chuckled.

"That's one of those Christmas things Freddy?" Jane asked.

"Oh shit, it is Jane," I confirmed.

This man is nuts!

A foot beyond the front door, hanging from the twelve-foot ceiling on a strip of Scotch tape—two brownish leaves, stuck together with chewed pink bubble gum, dangled within an arm's swing directly above Jane and me.

Freddy watched the leaves in a child-like reverence, swaying his head with the light draft, before realizing Jane and I were still in the room.

"Yea that's my mistletoe. Y'all don't like it?" he asked Jane.

Why does this crazy fuck have mistletoe?

"Hell yea Freddy, we love it," Jane replied.

"OK...if you love it...then kiss your...*big Black stud*. I mean...kiss your boyfriend then," Freddy struggled to say and opened his mouth three times like he was yawning but made no sound.

I'm not her fucking boyfriend!

"Hold up Freddy. You want us to *kiss*?" Jane asked.

"Yes...French style." Freddy pointed to Jane and then to me.

This lil bastard on some real freaky shit.

"Freddy quit playing all the time! How many pills did you eat already babe?" Jane asked.

"Uuuh...I'm fine. But if you must know...I ate...number 115...uuh...number

290...number 291...uuum...and number 375...because...number 368 was chipped a lil' bit," he said.

"Sooo, so far...one...two...three...four...I *only* had four beans...and a chipped bean. I'm perfectly fine."

Four beans?

"Uh, isn't that a lot Jane? Shouldn't we get this dude to a hospital or something?" I asked.

"Nah Manzo, Freddy can eat ten triple-stacks and still make it to 7-11 and back. He's OK."

"Listen...enough...of the bullshit Jane. If your boyfriend...ain't a cop...then y'all must kiss. If not...then nice...knowing you guys." Freddy gestured a lazy hand to the door.

"Freddy I'm not a fucking cop bro! I go to school here! I *played* football here!" I lifted my arm. Jane pushed it downward.

"Chill babe! Freddy you're embarrassing me!" Jane shifted her bag to her right shoulder.

"Kiss her." Freddy's eyes sunk lower and then bug-eyed.

"An informant is not allowed...to kiss a cop. If you guys want my business... then kiss. Now...under the mistletoe...or there's nothing...to talk about, folks. I mean that is...your *boyfriend*, Jane."

Just kiss the bitch and get this money!

"OK! OK Freddy! We will kiss! No big deal! Fuck it!" I looked up at the leaves, and then looked down at Jane, her mouth already opened in astonishment.

"OK...fuck, I will kiss my *girlfriend*," I said.

What looney has mistletoe in damn September?

Fuck it! We about to get paid!

Cupping Jane's slender face with both hands, I parted my lips and guided our faces along the same path, my thumbs melting in her beauty. Her Burberry Weekend perfume, sweet and inviting, ignited my lust.

I yearned to devour Jane, and I no longer cared who watched. Our lips merged with gentle force, and two tongues, thirsty to joust, collided with each other.

As delicate arms wrapped around my waist, I pulled Jane closer and kissed her—hard.

My manhood, Great Wall of China solid, pressed against her stomach with malicious intent, the longer we kissed.

I pursued our passion with pride and thought of punishing her pussy with prejudice.

Jane's nectarous saliva seemed to give me strength, but the sudden flashback of Jane's *dinner* made me weak.

"OK that's enough!" I pushed Jane away from me. "I'm not a cop Franky!"

"Manzo you really are an asshole and can't help it, can you?" Jane's red lipstick was smudged around her mouth, so I wiped my own mouth with my shirt.

"Babe what are you talking about?" I asked.

"You know what the hell I'm talking about—and I told you 1000 fucking times that his name is *Freddy*, not Franky!"

I gotta get this nasty taste out of my mouth!

"Freddy, Franky...whatever your name is, I'm not a cop, so can we talk business or I'm outta here!" I stepped past Freddy to pick up the bottle of water on the bed.

"Noooo!" Freddy yelled and hit my hand.

SMACK!

Did this crazy White motherfucker just hit me?

"Oooh, because I'm *Black* I can't drink your water now?" I asked.

"Ha, ha, ha...naaah...bro." Freddy opened the bottle, poured enough water to fill its cap, and quickly threw the liquid in his mouth, gulping hard through shivering lips, with his eyes shut. "*Aaaahhh!*"

"Ha, ha, ha!" Jane laughed.

"Bitch why are you laughing?" I asked Jane.

"Because that's not water asshole!" she replied.

What?

"This...not...water...bro." Freddy's speech slurred even more.

"What? What the hell is it?" I asked Freddy.

"It's...G bro. Fucking...G."

"G?" I asked.

"Yes G—you fucking goody-two-shoes! GHB! You really have a lot to learn Manzo!" Jane pulled me back to her and rubbed my head.

"Aaaww, I will teach the little fella—"

"Get off my damn head! What the fuck is GHB Jane?"

"You don't need to know yet, but if you would've drunk that bottle with *those* big ole lips, they would've had a barbecue every summer back in Harlem for your dead Black-ass!"

"*Word.*" Freddy opened the top drawer of the dresser, shoved the bottle of GHB in it and pulled out a magazine.

"Real funny Yoko. Just keep that GHZ shit away from me," I said.

"Hey...here's your twin." Freddy pointed to the magazine in his hand.

"I knew you...I knew you weren't a cop bro...ha-ha."

A Hokie Huddler? He's playing games!

Freddy held a Virginia Tech football program folded to the page with the team's defense, and there was a smiling headshot of me right between the photos of Jamel Smith and Michael Hawkes.

Because of my Batman hairline and crooked goatee from my local crackhead barber from Philly, Michael Lanier—I knew the Hokie Huddler was from 1997, but I didn't care to guess which game. A moment of nostalgia had set. I missed my team and playing football.

What am I doing with my life? I don't have to do this!

"Freddy you are such a dick! Why did you make us kiss then?" An irritated Jane quickly took me off the field but put me back in the game.

We gonna get this money! Fuck football!

"Yea motherfucker! Why are you playing games *Freddy*?" I asked.

"I figured...if your tongue...was in her mouth..." At a pace a dope fiend would lap, Freddy inserted the program back in the drawer.

He reached in his right pants pocket and pulled out a rolled up $100 bill. Digging in the other, he withdrew a blue and yellow Blockbuster's card and carefully set both on top of the dresser—inches from the hunk of pills.

How high is this dude?

He can't even finish a sentence!

"If your tongue...was in her mouth...Jane would finally shut the fuck up...ha-ha," he continued.

"HA-HA! Oh shit!" I laughed.

"Fuck you Freddy!" Jane grumped.

"Just playing, love. Moment of truth. Put your blow...put your blow on the dresser...please." Freddy fanned his hand toward himself.

"Oooh shit! This is what I'm talking about! Love you Freddy!" Jane cheered.

"Uuh Freddy...you sure you want to do this shit in your condition? It's super strong bro?" I asked.

He's gonna die!

"Hey, if you're scared...then get a dog." Freddy gestured again for the blow.

"Your girlfriend speaks...highly of you. Don't waste my time...*Manzo*."

"Yea Freddy's a fucking monster! Give him the blow!" Jane said then leaned forward to whisper in my right ear.

"Don't forget my shit either *boo*."

"Man are y'all sure?" I asked.

"Yes!" Freddy and Jane answered together.

What if all that shit doesn't mix well in his system? I could go to jail!

An antsy Freddy rocked back and forth in place, continuously nodding with the drowned beat echoing through the walls.

His cheeks drooped, and a frozen expression of surprise fought to pry open dead eyelids.

Freddy, tired and alert, looked a mess. I knew with conviction that I shouldn't give him any blow, but I was thinking like a college kid. I needed to start thinking like the coldhearted hustler that needed to get paid.

Either I would give Freddy the blow like a man and become a little closer to making my plan with Dirt come to fruition, or I could walk out of the door and get my resume together for McDonald's—but the fence straddling had come to an end.

Fuck his health. He's grown.

Get paid!

"OK Freddy, this shit will send you to the moon bro. So if you die, I hope you have a will and it's signed and in the hands of a good attorney." I pulled out a tightly wrapped eight ball of coke, one solid piece of rock, holding it in front of Freddy's face—Exhibit A.

"What the...fuck? Is this...is this real Manzo?" Freddy asked as I handed him *his* coke. "This motherfucker here is harder than a 1955...I mean...a 1956 Chevy fender."

"I told you Freddy!" Jane clutched her invisible pearls.

"Yup Freddy-Spaghetti, harder than a fender . Put that in your pocket though please. That's yours to play with later," I requested.

"But...I want to—"

"Aaannd, that's what this is for homie." I pulled out a second eight ball, all powder, untied the red twisty and poured an inch-high-pile on the dresser next to the $100 bill.

"You would need a hammer to break that Freddy, and nobody has time for that shit right now," I said.

"Shit...thanks." Freddy licked his lips and started rolling the bill for blastoff. "Smells strong and...and fucking clean bro."

It does smell good.

I love that smell now.

"Daaamn...that stuff smells potent as *fuck*!" Jane eased her way behind me and gently scratched my back, watching the coke on the dresser like a hound.

"Here, ladies first—"

"No!" I nudged Freddy's hand from offering Jane the bill.

"This is not for her! It's for you! If *you* are scared—get a fucking dog *Freddy*."

"Never scared...my brother." Freddy placed the bill to his nose.

Please don't die motherfucker!

"Hold up Freddy, you're not gonna make a line? That's a mountain dude!" Jane asked as I slipped my last eight ball behind me into her opened handbag. She peeped my move.

"Fuck it, you're grown. Please proceed. Myyy bad," Jane said.

"Jane...don't stop me again...babe," he said.

Corkscrewing the tip of the bill into his right nostril, Freddy planted the end of the bill at the base of the mound of cocaine—the size of a mini-Reese's Peanut Butter Cup .

"Like your boyfriend said...I'm Freddy...mother-fucking *Spaghetti*...I got this shit."

"*SNIIIIFFF! SNIIIIFFF!*"

Wiping the pyramid from the face of the earth, Freddy double-inhaled a gram of the flakiest blow known to man. Not a grain was spared.

Freddy's nose needed its own infomercial!

The only remnant of coke was a thin powdery spot where the assassination had taken place, and the rest of the white proceeded with the gentrification of his brain.

Holy shiiiidd!

"*Aaaaahhh...Loooooorrrrddd! Eat me raaaaaww!*" Freddy yelled at himself in the mirror after throwing the bill on the dresser.

"Holy fuck Freddy!" Jane hollered.

"Woooooo this is some A-1 shit! This is some top-notch product! Fuck my life —this is some great shit here folks!" Freddy's shuffling in place quickened, and his eyes were now fully opened.

"Are you OK Freddy?" I asked.

"Am I OK? You just gave me the best blow I ever had in my fucking life, and you ask me, 'If I'm OK?' You bet your ass I'm OK, my new best friend!" He patted me rigidly on the back.

"You're gonna be a rich man! Because I tell you this shit you got here is A-1 to the motherfucking max son-son!" he shouted.

"I told you Freddy! I told you my man don't play! Manzo has that fire!"

"You sure did, you beautiful little China doll!" Freddy hugged Jane, picked her up, and twirled her around twice.

"Weeeeeee!" Jane's dress had risen, brandishing her rice cakes before she landed. "I can't wait to try this shit!"

He's fucking jacked now! Is this the same guy?

I'm gonna eat her until she screams later.

Freddy's demeanor transformed from incoherent to super alert right before my eyes. He was a totally different person and unrecognizable, from his speech to his motor skills.

No longer annunciating through clenched teeth, he spoke with an acuteness of an English professor and moved with a fluid confusion—his brain cylinders anticipating thoughts birthed by a blizzard of bliss.

His face froze in an open-eyed yawn without a blinking interruption, while the cocaine crumbled his vegetative calm—leaving no evidence of any other substances. Freddy was cured!

"OK first thing we gonna do is let all my people know that you have the very best shit in this dumbass Commonwealth, and we gonna have all of them buy from you and you gonna have all your people buy beans from me, OK?" He stopped moving.

"Uuh...OK," I said.

"OK, so how much is a gram?" he asked.

"$100 a gram, and I'm not taking a dollar less." I shook my head.

"OK no problem son-son." Freddy re-started his dance.

"OK this shit is heavy—real heavy. And clean, waaaay better than Gerald shit. Real clean."

"*Gerald*?" I asked.

This nigga Gerald selling coke now!

"Yes Gerald, the only half Caucasian brother out there! His black pit bull is running around out there—Smitty. You know Gerald?"

"Nah Freddy. I don't know any Gerald bro," I answered and gave Jane a soft nudge.

"Nah Manzo don't know Gerald, Freddy." Jane smiled and caressed my back.

I love this girl.

"Well either way—fuck him and anybody else that sells blow because you gonna kill them! Nobody has this quality shit Manzo!" He patted both front pockets.

"My friend Portia knows everyone and can help you get this cheddar son-son!"

"Oh yea Portia, my home girl. Told you baby, you gonna have all the money!" Jane squeezed my ass.

"That's right love birds—oh here they are." Freddy snatched two pills off of the dresser.

"Goddamn—the drain from your blow got my throat feeling like I sucked Frosty the Snowman's cock!"

A-yoooo!

"I'm just kidding! I'm not gay my brother. I'm joshing with you. Here take *this* and give Jane a good ole Mandingo shellacking!" He dropped two of the pills into my palm.

"I need a good ole *Mandingo Shellacking*! Thanks Freddy!" Jane kissed the side of my neck, marking her territory with a bright red lip print.

"Sorry Freddy—I don't fuck with this type shit bro." I handed the pills back to him. "Thanks, but no thanks."

"Aaaaw Maaan-zzzooooe," Jane wined.

"No Jane—don't peer pressure the motherfucker! He will be back for that goddamn Mitsubishi, *double stack*!" Freddy threw the pills on the dresser and patted his pockets again.

What is a double stack?

"Fuck! *Those* are soooo bomb!" Jane exclaimed.

"Where's my list?" Freddy turned in a complete circle.

"What *list* bro?" I asked.

"Yea Freddy—what list?" Jane asked also.

"My money list!" He checked his back pockets and looked to the ceiling.

"The list with the names of people who owe me cash at this party. I need my list!"

He's losing it!

"OK, well, ask the motherfucker who lives here?" I tried reasoning.

"Yea ask Leo," Jane remarked.

Who the fuck is Leo?

"I would but the Korean motherfucker is outside in the backyard with some sorority bitches playing Naked Olympics!" Freddy opened the top left dresser drawer.

Oh shit, the paper is right on the dresser!

"Where is my list? I need my fucking list?" he asked again and ripped back the bed's comforter. Freddy's eight ball flew off the bed and hit the closet door.

"Is this it?" I snatched the piece of paper from under pink plastic bag.

"Yea is that it Freddy?" Jane helped.

"Bingo bitches! Hells yea!" he shouted as I handed him the paper scribbled in red ink, after I scanned to the bottom number. "Goddamn, you saved my life son-son!"

$3,700!

For one party? That's paper!

Somebody gonna rob this little motherfucker!

"Who you got watching your back Freddy?" I asked and watched him walk to the opposite side of the bed.

I won't let nothing happen to him...ever.

"Steven, but you see what type of job he did. Y'all walked right in. I need another line. I want to cheat death tonight folks."

He's gonna die!

"He-he, if Manzo lets me, I will do one with you—"

KNOCK!

KNOCK!

Shit!

"Calm down big guy. It's just Steven for this list," Freddy reassured after catching me flinch. "Open the door please Jane—before this dude shits his pants!"

"Relax my love. I got it Freddy." Jane turned to her right, and I turned with her, grabbed her waist and pulled her closer to me.

Harder than the eight ball in Freddy's hand, I pressed my cock in between Jane's ass and nuzzled my chin on her shoulder, her choker gently pricked my neck. Aroused from the delicate pain, I nibbled on her neck.

"I love you Manzo!"

"I love you too *Jane!*" I mimicked her tone. "Stop yelling—I'm right here."

"Aaaww." She stretched her arm and twisted the doorknob, pulling the door open.

"Come in Steven and stop scaring my boyfriend—oooh my fucking God!" Jane screamed.

WHAT THE FUCK?

"Get all that shit Steven!" a female's voice cheered from outside of the room.

"Suck that nitrous motherfucker!" a guy encouraged.

"Steve! Steve! Steve!" More people rooted madly for Mr. Haynes, but we couldn't see the crowd, nor could we see Steven. *Someone* was blocking our view!

Fuuuuck! What's she doing here?

In my orange, VT workout t-shirt and shorts, Brittney stood in a purple glow with tears in her swollen eyes and mascara streaming down her face.

With her bottom lip tucked under her top teeth, Brittney had a runny nose and capital-murder-stare.

Her skin flushed with pain.

Her eyes iced with contempt.

Dropping both hands from Jane's waist, I wanted to go hide in a dryer or jump out of the window, away from the agony I caused my real girlfriend, my life, my best friend.

She heard everything on my phone!

Fuck drugs! Fuck money! I wanted to hold Brittney! I wanted to tell her how sorry I was and that I only loved her.

But before I'd been given the opportunity to lie to her, Brittney shook her head after reading the sign on the bedroom door and noticing the lipstick on my neck and all around my mouth.

Heartbroken, she forced a smile and then with all her rage—Brittney punched Jane in the *goddamn* face.

Chapter Twenty-Two

CAT NIP

Outside of Preston's on a frigid February Saturday night at 1:05 AM, I was on my way to check on Brittney and her stomach cramps, and I bumped into Portia who was headed home from working a double at Sharkey's.

Our first opportunity to talk without Jane's watchful eye, I kicked it with Portia and her wing-sauce-splattered overalls for a moment on Main Street.

I had been slamming cocktails for the past couple of hours with Bruce Garnes while Nat Williams punished seventeen O'Doulles. My mind had been on my pregnant girlfriend until Portia came along.

Portia told me she was tired of being broke and had some customers for me if I were still interested.

Appreciative for the new customers, I told her to call me Sunday and I'd have whatever she needed.

She mentioned that her night was very stressful and that she needed an immediate sample to vouch for the product, although I knew for a fact, Jane already *briefed* her on the potency of my cocaine.

Before I could call her out for playing games, Portia invited me to her place to *chill*, do some blow, and to spend the night, if I were free.

Spend the night? Bitches ain't shit!

Fuck, I have to check on Brittney and the baby!

"Sounds amazing, but I will have to pass until tomorrow babe. I have to get up early," I explained.

"Aaaww, you suuure you can't spend some time with me tonight?" She placed her hand on my shoulder. "I won't tell Jane. It will be our little secret. Could be fun."

Oh God, I want to fuck this broad right now!

Stop! Go home to your pregnant girlfriend asshole!

"I wish but I gotta go babe." I reached in my jeans slyly, tucked my hard cock against my stomach underneath my hoodie—and proceeded to walk to the Honda, parked a block away in front of the Army and Navy store.

I gotta be good this time! Damn man!

Brittney said if I cheat again it's over!

"OK party-*pooper*. If you change your mind, come to University Terrace, building-one, apartment twenty-three. I will be up!"

"OK beautiful! Have a good night!" I hollered back to her while I trotted and hugged myself, attempting to keep warm in the icy winds.

Opening the car door, I watched Portia get into the passenger side of a 1994 white Ford Bronco, wave to me, before the truck hightailed down South Main Street.

Because of a glaring streetlight and black tinted windows, I couldn't identify the driver but had recently seen the Bronco parked outside Cassell Coliseum. For all I knew it could've been OJ Simpson himself.

Sitting in the Honda, I jingled the car keys in my pocket without ever sticking them into the ignition.

I knew I should go, but the alcohol parked my thoughts on Portia and doing blow for the first time. I was stuck.

Normally, I would've sparked the half-blunt in the ashtray to clear my thoughts before going home, but for the first time I had no desire for marijuana, and I wasn't the least bit surprised.

Smoking weed had gotten mundane, and I had gotten envious of my customers and their stories of wild late-night parties and weird sex with coke-head young sluts, willing to do positively anything for a good time.

Whenever I saw three hot girls at the bar go to the bathroom at the same time, I had fantasies of them being in my bed naked—snorting lines of coke off my cock as we talked about fashion and literature.

With weed, all I did was eat shitty food, get sleepy, and lazy-fuck a girl screaming I was the best she'd ever had, while I thought about how to make more money.

My life needed a jolt of energy with individuals who had the voltage to match my zeal. Blunts and Squires' parties were no longer my spark plug.

Need to try new shit!

I can see Brittney tomorrow. You going to be a dad soon! Have fun now!

After ten minutes of deliberation, I opened the glove compartment and swapped my cell phone for bags of blow. I stuck the keys in the ignition and twisted my fate.

Looking in the rear-view mirror, I smiled at myself before speeding into the wrong lane. Bored with the Honda, I needed a Portia.

* * *

Feeling the effects of the three Long Island iced teas and two glasses of Hennessy, I lumbered up the stairs to Apartment twenty-three. For a moment, I just stared at the gold-plated digits.

Face to face with the iconic number, I conjured up images of Michael Jordan slam-dunking on Patrick Ewing. I wondered if Big Pat, when facing MJ, was ever as nervous as I was at that moment.

I knew that if I entered the apartment that my nostrils' virginity would be stripped away just like the New York Knick's title hopes. Even intoxicated, I was afraid and unsure if I wanted to snort cocaine for the first time.

What the fuck am I doing? Leave Manzo!

As I stood in front of Portia's apartment door contemplating whether to leave or knock, I put my hand in my right pants pocket.

I rotated the three eight balls in my palm, only stopping to squeeze one out of frustration. Hard as a rock!

I couldn't break, crumble, or even make a dent in the boulder. Only the plastic baggie suffered damaged.

The cocaine's jagged edges pierced through the suffocating plastic. Now, the blow could breathe. The White girl exhaled, and I stole her breath.

I looked down at my pocket and began to pull out the coke when the door suddenly opened. Quickly, I shoved the drugs back in my pocket.

I picked my head up to find the number twenty-three replaced with Portia's tanned face, blue eyes, and blonde hair. A little startled and confused, I squinted my eyes and grabbed my chin.

Without saying hello, Portia just smiled and shook her head. She noticed the expression on my face and sighed, "I saw your car's headlights through the window and heard your drunk self, stomping like a mad man silly."

Admiring herself, Portia put her left index finger in her mouth and asked seductively "You gonna come in?"

The words were pushed out, almost scripted. My eyes followed her eyes, and I no longer cared if she had spent hours in front of the mirror practicing her grand reveal. Bravo young lady, bravo!

Her white, lace, see-through bra tightly hugged her 36F breasts like they were long-lost family reuniting. I told myself I wasn't a breast man, but her dime-sized nipples called me a liar.

Portia had the type of breasts that could get her a raise or out of a speeding ticket, or in this case, the best cocaine in the country.

Good thing she was wearing a pair of Virginia Tech football, practice shorts. I don't think I could have restrained myself if she didn't.

On autopilot, my penis headed in the direction he wanted to go. The consequences of going inside Portia's apartment were no longer relevant. I wanted to navigate new land.

"Yes, I do want to come in...my *dear*," I said.

"You're so silly. Come on in love," she summoned and grabbed my hand.

"Wow, this is nice!" I complimented, not even completely inside the dimly lit apartment.

Leaving me standing by the front door, Portia, let go of my hand and scampered a few feet to an oversized lamp on what appeared to be a stack of textbooks. I was eager for her to turn up the lights, because I wanted to see those melons in HD.

Lights.

Yes!

The lights got a little brighter, but it wasn't until she started to reverse pivot that I had begun to look around. I didn't want her catching me staring at her ass. Chivalry wasn't dead.

"Is *this* better baby?" she asked. "What do you think?"

Scanning the apartment, I hesitated on answering. Being rude wasn't my intention. I thought I was having an extreme case of déjà vu though, and the hair on my arms stood straight up.

I lifted my head and straightened my posture like if I were an inch taller, I could solve the mystery.

Everybody's apartment looks the same. Have I fucked this girl before?

College apartments often resembled each other, because most students could not afford to hire Eddie Ross or Martha Stewart for interior decorating.

Kids had to stretch those dollars, and the best place to ball on a budget was shopping at Walmart.

From the looks of things, Portia had "made it rain" a few times in the Mecca of bad taste: Walmart vases. Walmart area rugs. Walmart prints. Walmart lamps.

"This is nice. This is *soooo* you." I nodded.

"Thanks!" Portia pointed. "Do you like the table?"

"What tabl—oh shit!" I blurted.

In the middle of the living room sat a mirrored coffee table. Five feet long and rectangular, the table was covered by scattered college football magazines.

At the far end of the table rested a half-liter of Jameson, a pack of Parliament lights, a dusty Visa card, a bottle of Windex, and a roll of paper towels.

Either she was a cokehead bookie studying the point spread, or she had been pre-gaming with another avid football fan.

My admiration for such a functional piece of furniture was quickly replaced by feelings of anxiety and nervousness.

I have sat at many glass tables with disciples gathered around me, but I have never participated in their last supper.

I had vowed to never use coke, and I had never been tempted, but tonight was different! The universe hiccupped, and I could feel the change in the air.

No longer did I desire to just hold sermon, I now yearned to be a part of the congregation. I wanted to be like my almighty father.

* * *

"Manzo?" my younger brother, Alejandro, whispered as he tapped his knuckles on the bottom bunk.

"Manzo—"

"What?" I answered, annoyed that he woke me up.

"I thought Mommy was in Long Island visiting Aunt Bernice?" he asked, leaning over the top bunk.

"Yea, she is stupid," I whispered. "Leave me alone and let me get some sleep."

"Big bro listen," the seven-year-old pestered. "I hear a lady laughing in the living room. Listen."

After a few seconds of silence, Tina Marie's voice could be heard singing faintly through the walls.

"Lil brother that ain't nuttin' but Daddy listening to the record player—"

"Los your sexy-ass is a fucking fool, I swear!" A woman clearly spoke while laughing. "Let me *taste* that shit nigga!"

Who is that?

"I told you big bro—"

"Shut up Alejandro!" I said as I reached up and put my hand over my little brother's tiny mouth.

Alejandro was right! There was a woman in my *mother's* living room, but she was not my mother. And if we could hear them, they could possibly hear us.

"Lick the powder off, Sheila," my father ordered. "Ooooh that feels like heaven, doll."

Aunty Sheila?

What is going on?

Sheila or Aunty Sheila, as we called her, was my mother's best friend—her absolute best friend. They would do everything together: Shop. Party. Eat.

My mother and Aunty Sheila could have been sisters for real!

They were so much alike: same shape, same height, same high-yellow skin complexion, and the same long black hair. Now, they apparently had the same man—my father.

Earlier that evening, Alejandro and I witnessed a *sick* Aunty Sheila tell my mom in the elevator that she would not make the trip to Long Island with my mother.

Aunty Sheila had a raspy voice, a terrible cough, and fucking tissues. There must have been a miracle on 122nd Street because Aunty Sheila was suddenly cured.

Alejandro's breathing got deeper, and I could feel the warmth of his breath in my palm. The air fuming out of those little lungs was intense. I felt like I could close my fist and throw a fastball of hot oxygen.

"Ssh," I whispered. "Go back to sleep, it's going to—"

Before the lie reached the end of my tongue, I felt a liquid run down my hand and in between my fingers. Snot didn't flow like that, but tears did. My little brother was crying.

Aaaah man, Daddy why?

I looked up at Alejandro's little face and saw the pain in his eyes. One half of his face was pitch black and the other half had an eerie glow and was sparkling from the moonlit tears. He did not make a sound.

The voices in the living room began to fade as the volume of the music steadily increased.

Inching my neck toward the door, I closed my eyes and raised the level of my supersonic hearing.

The soulful voices of Rick James and Tina Marie singing "Fire and Desire" jammed my frequency.

As the song continued to play, Alejandro's tears hit third gear and sped down my wrist through a maze of goosebumps and hair. I could not think of any words to combat my little brother's pain.

At that moment I knew that my little brother knew exactly what our father was doing behind those walls.

Alejandro was only seven years old, but he was not dumb. Children growing up in the projects were more mature than average kids.

The innocence of a ghetto child was stripped away early in life by the everyday struggles they experienced in a poverty-stricken *do what you gotta do* society.

Alejandro was twelve in *project* years—that had made me fourteen.

"Fuck this," I said to myself as I released my hand from Alejandro's mouth and jumped out of bed.

"Wait, where you—" were the last words I heard before I was already out our bedroom door.

Standing in the dark hallway, I could see light creep from the bottom of the living room door, and I was extremely nervous—but the soft three-inch carpet underneath my feet was oddly comforting.

I did not know what I would see if I continued on my mission, but I had to keep moving, so I slowly advanced a few steps toward the door—my target.

I was a moth drawn to the flames, and although I might've died if I reached it —I didn't care.

I would have rather died trying to get to the light than to have lived in the dark any longer. I took a deep breath, and gently grabbed the doorknob.

I wish my mommy were here!

Eyes closed, I began turning the doorknob to the right and pulled slowly, stopping when I heard Rick James warn me about the fire.

Open your eyes Manzo.

It's going to be OK.

Staring at the back of the door, I pictured my dad and Aunty Sheila sitting on the couch playing cards, four feet apart and fully clothed.

On opposite sides of the coffee table, they each had a glass of orange juice that sat on a coaster. Aunty Sheila was eating a powdered donut.

Normal. Innocent.

It's going to be OK.

The lyrics to my parents' favorite song tried to tell me to take my young ass to bed, but I did not listen, and I pulled the door completely open—the music got louder.

Standing in the doorway, I squinted my eyes and wiped the crust from the corners. The living room's bright light had blurred my vision.

Blinking twice, I regained focus. My smile vanished, and my heart stopped. I wish I had been blind.

Eyes shut and naked, my father was sitting on the couch with his head tilted completely back.

One hand rested at his side, while the other hand had a firm grip on the back of Aunty Sheila's head.

Naked herself, Sheila (I would never call her "Aunty" again after that night) was on her knees and between my father's ashy legs.

First, I noticed the mismatched tube socks on my father's feet.

Second, my father's cock in Sheila's mouth.

No cards.

No juices.

No donuts.

Just coke.

Suddenly, I could hear footsteps coming from the kitchen, and before I had the chance to process exactly what I was seeing—another naked woman had appeared.

Wearing only red high heels and holding a large circular mirror full of cocaine, the woman was statuesque and wore too much make up. She looked me in my eyes and gave me a smile that was far too familiar.

Confused, I returned my attention to my father who still had his eyes closed as Sheila continued to stroke to the beat.

I looked back at all that blow on the mirror, and then at the woman holding it. I couldn't think straight.

Turning and sprinting to my bedroom, I quickly closed the door and locked it.

Jumping back in the bed, I pulled the blanket over my body, desperately trying to control my breathing. I started to sweat. My mind raced.

What's going on? Am I in trouble?

Alejandro's snoring put an end to the questions, he had cried himself to sleep.

His peacefulness calmed my anxiety, but did not clear my confusion, and I would stay up all night staring at the top bunk—surprisingly asking myself only two questions:

1. Why did Pam, Sheila's *real* sister, have Daddy's name tattooed on her breast?

2. If I had some coke...would girls suck on *my* penis too?

With my mind back in Portia's crib, I took a deep breath, and my uneasiness faded. Still conflicted, I decided at that moment to relax and let the night progress into something unnatural.

I tossed my black Avirex leather jacket beside the coffee table and put my hand back in my pocket just to feel the coke—making sure my friends still had my back.

"Table's pretty hot Portia," I said coolly.

"Word?" she *Vanilla-Iced*.

"Ha-Ha, yes—*word*. Let's sit down."

"OK." She grinned.

Making our way to the couch, I felt Portia's hand trembling. There was no doubt that she was already jacked up, but I really didn't give a fuck that she had already blasted-off.

My coke was the best around, and I was confident that Ms. Dolly Parton Jr. would soon be humming country songs from here to the moon and back.

We sat down and her erected Nipsey Russells immediately transformed my cock into the Tin Man. Now thoughts of sucking her breasts filled my head, and my manhood aggressively pressed against my jeans.

Suddenly shoving a white, powdery substance up my nose wasn't a priority to me.

I put both hands on her huge tits, closed my eyes and leaned in for a kiss. But instead of feeling soft lips, I felt ten fingers and two slimy palms slip under my hoodie and push against my chest.

"Whoa, whoa, whoa!" she said before scooting back on the couch.

"Take it easy big boy. We're not in a rush. Let's party a lil' bit while it's early."

"Oh my bad babe!" I apologized. "I understand totally. Great plan."

Curious to see how *early* it was, I glanced up at the cat clock on the wall. Only after being distracted by the *You're Puuurrfect* written on the enormous cat's tail, I noticed the time—1:47 AM.

It seemed damn late to me, but in the cokehead time zone, 1:47 AM was the equivalent to 5:47 PM. Technically, it was just dinnertime for Portia.

"Trust me Manzo, you are *never* gonna forget tonight," she promised while brushing her golden hair away from her face, exposing her baby-blues.

"What you got daddy?" she asked as she stroked my forearm.

Standing up, I began to dig into my pocket. Portia's eyes widened as she goggled at my jeans with her mouth opened.

My reputation preceded me, so she anticipated me pulling out something big, hard, and white, but I really wanted to pull out something big, hard, and Black!

Removing the coke from my pocket, I spotted an opening on the table and placed the golf balls gently on it because I didn't want to crack the mirror.

I looked down at Portia, and a beam of sweat rolled down her forehead. She was desperate to tee-off. Amazed, she eyed the coke and never blinked.

"Ma...Manzo...c'mon those can't be real, can they?" she stammered.

With the eight-balls finally in my court, I arrogantly said, "You obviously didn't do your homework on me.

"Go get me a cutting board, two one-dollar bills, and a hammer. And stop asking stupid questions babe."

As I began ripping the baggie off of the first eight ball with my teeth, Portia darted off the couch. She moved so fast, I thought Crockett and Tubbs had knocked on the door.

Before I could even finish, she was back standing in front of me with a cutting board in one hand, a hammer in the other hand, and her teeth clamped down on the dollar bills.

Good girl.

"Thank you. Please sit down," I requested.

I didn't even wait for a response or see her sit down before I placed the cutting board on the floor and proceeded with the following *coke-structions*:

STEP ONE: Place an open dollar bill on the cutting board.
STEP TWO: Take the second dollar bill and wrap around eight ball.
STEP THREE: Place wrapped coke on flat bill.
STEP FOUR: Position hammer over the coke and hold steady.
STEP FIVE: Hit the coke with the hammer. Repeat if necessary.

BANG!
Fuck this shit is hard!
BANG!
One more time!
BANG!
Jackpot motherfucker!

Picking up the deflated bill, I stood back up and unwrapped my present, pouring the snow over the table. Off-white flurries danced across the mirror; each flake doubled in perception, as Portia *Christmas-Day*-smiled.

Repeating the hammer-time process, I made two more mini frosted-mountains. All that was missing were tiny log cabins and, of course, Caucasians to create a miniature ski lodge. Time to hit the slopes!

"Oh my God Manzo! You're trying to kill us!" Portia exclaimed. "Like there's nooooooo way in hell we can do all that! Shit looks like a science project!"

"Manzo—you totally think you're Tony Montana!" She laughed and shook her head.

"*I didn't come to this country to be no dishwasher, Chico,*" I mimicked my favorite movie character and sat down again.

"You brought all that—I know it can't be *that* good Manzo," she said.

Using the credit card, I sliced the first structure in half and slid the debris a few inches away.

The *pedico* still had pieces of pebble amidst the pure powder, so I placed the dollar bill on top of the rubble. It was now time for the heavy machinery, courtesy of Mr. Jameson.

Grinding the coke with the bottom of the Jameson bottle, I flattened the *rockettes*. Such a hard nut to crack, the cocaine finally crumbled.

I lifted the bill and the mountain had been reduced to a small hill of Gypsum sand. Tight. Smooth. Sparkling.

Not even thirty-seconds had passed, and the blonde tornado wanted to make her presence felt.

"Cut that motherfucker up already!" she commanded, grabbing the bill and tightly rolling it up. "It's getting late!"

'You're puuuurrfect'

1:58 AM...

Oh now it's late?

"Go for it babe," I authorized.

Portia scraped the coke back and forth with the rhythm of a violinist and the concentration of a surgeon. She was in a trance.

Only an artist could have rivaled the accuracy of her stroke, and I studied her every move.

Portia was the conductor of our cocaine train, and the white rails would lead us deeper into our journey. All a-fucking-board!

My nervousness was replaced by jealousy, because Portia forgot I was in the room. The odd man out in our threesome, I just watched with envy.

I wanted both White girls. My juices were having fun without me, and I wanted to be included.

After sculpting more lines of coke with her card, Portia looked over at me. Suddenly realizing I was still in the room and wasn't dead, she almost looked annoyed.

She smiled and asked, "Do you want me to make you one?"

She can't be serious!

"Sure, if it's not too much of a hassle babe," I said.

She *Picasso'ed* another massive four lines, and I didn't know if she expected me to snort the lines or park Brittney's car between them.

Heart pumping rapidly, I wasn't concerned about how the coke would feel going up my nose, or even getting hooked on the drug—I was worried about having a heart attack!

Simply trying to impress Portia is why I brought so much *yayo*.

Ten and a half grams is a lot of damn blow, and I had never seen two people finish such an amount in one sitting.

Not one pair of J. Edgar Hoovers that I knew could vacuum even two grams of my shit in a night. Believing that there wasn't any chance of us snorting all the coke, I relaxed a little.

Portia doctored a mere eight lines total, and the first eight ball was in the ICU. Knocking over a saltshaker would have produced more residue than what had remained.

Eager to see stars, she wiped away the dust with her index finger and rubbed the blow across her gums. Slightly sucking on her fingertip, she made a smacking sound.

"What the fuck? Freddy and Jane were right!" She chuckled, shaking her head and rubbing her brow in disbelief. "Get outta my way Manzo!"

Like a machine being assembled, she jammed and rotated the dollar bill in her right nostril—click.

As I moved over on the couch, she bent down over the mirror and held the bill steady—placing the tip of the dirty money at the edge of the third line from the left; the biggest line of course.

On instinct, I reached over and pulled her hair into a ponytail with both hands and did not let go. I didn't want the masterpiece on the table ruined.

Ready to score, Portia relaxed her diaphragm, emptied her lungs, then inhaled violently and the line began to disappear.

She.

Could.

Go.

All.

The.

Way.

"Fuck...my...liiffeee!" She abruptly jumped up and scared me.

"Ooooh shit!" I yelled for two reasons:

1. I never witnessed someone *Charlie Sheen* a line of that magnitude.

2. I still had her blonde hair extensions in my hand!

"This is the best blow I have ever, ever, ever had!" she said rapidly, picking up the Jameson and taking a giant swig. "New York blow fucking rocks! It kicks ass man!"

Placing the bottle back on the table, she snatched the pack of Parliament lights and sprinted to the kitchen. I looked at the hair extensions in disbelief and tossed them on a nearby chair.

She came back with a lit cigarette in one hand and the pack in the other. She was too whacked to notice that half of her hair was seated a few feet away.

Portia had been upgraded from a coke-whore to a *working* girl, but I preferred her new look. The transformation turned me on, although she wouldn't even be quiet for a single moment.

"Oh Manzo I love you so much we need to hang out more because I always tell people how great of a guy you are and how you are not a bad person it's just that Coach Beamer gave you a raw deal so what else were you supposed to do I would've quit the team too..." she continued with the verbal assault, in between pulls of her cigarette.

Deep in my own thoughts, I could only stand to listen to a few words at a time.

Please God make her shut the fuck up!

"...my mother is a Cancer I bet you are a Scorpio, but you seem to have a Gemini rising because of how calm you are and how attentive you are..."

I'm a Virgo...nausea rising.

"You ever played that game? It was fun when I lived in Abu Dhabi but I didn't like how the kids would ignore me and only pay attention to the Emirati girls because they were considered the prettiest girls in our class..."

What game?

And where the fuck is Abu Dhabi?

"...the bees stung my brother and we ran soooo far without shoes on, my feet hurt but all I could think about was how grandma showed me..."

The coke had Portia's tongue doing jumping jacks, and I had refused to stay for the rest of the workout. She superset subjects without taking a breath, and I strongly believed she wouldn't break for water—or for *me*.

I stared at her beautiful breasts for a few more reps and then decided my training session was over.

Rest in peace, chivalry!

To hell with this, I'm out!

I was upset that I wasn't going to get laid, but I was also relieved to not have tried cocaine.

Ready to get up and collect the rest of my coke and jet, I tuned back just as Portia asked, "...so can we screw? My pussy's jumping boy!"

"*What* did you just say about your pussy?"

"What do you mean, *what*?" she asked as our eyes met.

Finally, silence.

"Hurry up and do a line my brother! My *pussy* is jumping—that means it's time to screw!" she *bobble-headed* while pointing at the table.

Normally, I hated when a White girl said, "my brother," but if "pussy" were in the conversation, I loved every rocket-fueled word that exploded out of her mouth.

Looking at the table of blow, I anxiously wanted to get my nose dirty, but looking at Portia, dirtying my cock was the objective. My tank of emotions on full, I was nervous, yet excited.

I felt like I was in the tunnel of Lane Stadium before a football game again! I wanted to win, and I knew I could win. I had only wished that I had a Coach Beamer pep talk to push me to victory.

* * *

'Now I want you to man up! Go out there and do the things that you know you can do! It's OK to be scared! But as men we face adversity head on—and as men there is nothing we can't overcome! I believe in you! You worked hard to get to this point! There is no substitute for victory! We're remembered for what we do, not by what we attempt!

'Offense—hold on to that ball tight! Don't let it go! It's yours!

'Defense—crush 'em good! Blow that line up! Fight, fight, fight!

'Even if you get a bloody nose—you still fight, goddamn-it!

'Even if you're paranoid and your nerves get unedged—you try harder!

'You're a Virginia Tech Hokie! Act like one, goddamn-it!

'Now bring it in! Hokie, Hokie, Hokie...High, High, High!'

* * *

"Hellooo Manzo? Let's get high!" Portia repeated, snatching me out of the tunnel of Lane Stadium. "What planet are you on baby?"

"Oh man, my bad babe," I said while looking around for my teammates and 50,000 cheering fans.

"Here take this and put it in your nose and inhale but don't inhale too hard! You're going to feel something but keep going it will feel good and then switch to your other nostril for the rest!

"I'm sure you have seen it done a million times but be careful because your stuff is super-duper strong!

"When you're finished I will bang a couple of lines out and then I wanna give you a blow job because I love doing that right after a blast off—OH MY GOD you're gonna die Manzo!" she raced through her instructions as she stood and removed her shorts—exposing her slender, yet meaty, bald vagina that could have replaced the cat on her clock.

Portia's pussy was *puuurrfect*.

She had me exactly where she wanted. I melted just looking at Portia. I would do anything to please her and even more to have her. Touch her. Taste her. Conquer her. My blue balls where no match against her blue eyes.

In my mind, I was about to win; not realizing I was a loser as soon as I got out of my car—the fix was in.

Officially becoming a slave to my passions and desires, I grabbed the bill.

Jamming the bill in my right nostril, I bent over the mirror and placed the bill on the biggest line of coke.

Peeping my reflection in the mirror, I expected to see a different face, an older face. I had expected to see my father, but all I saw was a different Manzo.

At that moment, I had taken full responsibility for my actions, understanding that the choices that I made were my own. Yes, I wanted to be cool like my pops, but only I was responsible for my decisions.

My father wanted me to go to school. I wanted street credibility.

My father wanted me to play football. I wanted to sell bags of death.

My father wanted me to stay away from drugs, and now, I wanted to abuse drugs.

Using my own judgment, I was going to stick a filthy piece of paper up my nose and ignite a mind-altering chemical in my brain, so I could have unprotected intercourse with a promiscuous coke-fiend—and then blame it all on my father?

No fucking way!

On my own free will, I closed one eye and snorted half of the line just like I saw done for the first time, in the movie—*Scarface*. I was five years old.

SNIFF!

Face. Numb.

On my own free will, I closed one eye and snorted the other half of the line just like I saw done for the second time, in the movie—*Superfly*. I was five and a *half*.

SNIFF!

Fucking. Jacked.

The cocaine ambushed my nasal passage, leaving behind a frosted pit of false pride. A jolt of confidence magnified my faith in my decisions.

As my reality deconstructed, my fears became my passions. I had transformed into a different person and immediately fell in love with him.

I was not my father—I was better.

Standing up, I felt my heart pounding. I began to sweat from my hairline to my *taint*.

Words mingled in my frontal lobe, but not one word dared to leave the party. Although I was speechless, I felt alive for the first time—I could do anything!

The world is mine.

"Damn, that does feel amazing!" I said.

"Fucking right it does big boy!"

"What the hell babe? I could get five root canals right now—" Before I could finish my sentence, there was a rumbling in my stomach, I farted loudly!

Being around many cocaine users, I was not surprised, embarrassed, or disturbed by my gas passing. Gas happened—often.

Just the sight or thought of cocaine could cause a user to fart or even need to crap. Farting was protocol. Shitting on myself was taboo.

"If I got five root canals and three teeth pulled, I wouldn't feel a thing," I continued, ignoring the aroma of rotten eggs.

"I feel like a God!"

"You *are* a God! You're so hot right now!" she screamed as she stood, unfazed by my flatulence.

Portia stood directly in front of me smiling, and I smiled back, although I was not certain if my mouth even moved—my entire head was an igloo.

She put her hands on my shoulders, and I did not know who was shaking more.

We were two coked-up thespians on stage for the final act, but I was not seasoned enough to take the lead.

My emotions intertwined, I didn't know whether to kiss her, run, recite a poem, or pull out my cock.

I was horny—but I wasn't.

I was happy—but I was concerned.

I felt deeply—but I didn't give a shit about anything.

I was confident—but I was unsure.

Sensing the disturbance of our drug connection, Portia kissed me.

"Don't you want this pussy?" she asked, gripping my cock with her trembling hand. "Just relax and take what you came here for Manzo."

Oh God yes! Finally!

Without hesitation, I grabbed the back of her neck with my left hand and her face with my right. I packed my tongue between her lips, as we ate each other's mouths until we found our rhythm.

Drool escaped down the side my chin. Portia stopped stroking and grabbed my face with both hands. She licked the saliva that had crept down my neck and began working her way to my face. Just as I noticed that I could not feel anything, her teeth crunched down on my cheek.

"Aaaah!" I yelled, feeling each single fang. "That shit hurt—"

"Shut the fuck up," she whispered in my ear.

"You're too big to be crying." She bit my neck harder.

Aaaah—

Oooh shit—

Yes ma'am!

I cried a single tear, but the pain was liberating, and I welcomed it.

I wanted the pain.

I needed the pain.

Portia was taking me on a sexual pilgrimage that I had never experienced, and I was an eager traveler.

With every bite, she silenced the righteous and awakened the wicked. She was a bad girl, and now I was a bad boy.

Closing my eyes, I moaned and yearned for her to take another nibble, but Portia had decided that lunchtime was over.

She pushed me on the couch, and before I knew what was happening, she violently yanked my jeans down to my ankles, jumping on top of me.

This pussy is in trouble!

Eyes closed and body numb, I felt her hands doing *something* in my underwear.

"I need you to hit bottom *big* guy," she demanded.

Hit bottom? That's what I do.

I know Jane told her how I get down.

"How bad do you want this wet stuff?" she asked. "Don't be scared. Relax."

"I can't feel shit!" I said as my body trembled, hearing my heart beating.

What's going on?

"It's OK Manzo," she ensured in a very low and nurturing voice.

"You're just jacked up...and that's OK love. Take deep breaths and think about all the things you're going to do to me and this wet stuff."

"OK babe," I complied.

Calm down! Breathe!

Inhale. Breathe. Exhale. Breathe. Inhale.

The trembling lessened, and I began to picture Portia's soft lips against mine. I then imagined her on top of me, riding me.

* * *

The rhythm was slow and steady and gradually became faster and more violent. Her breasts bounced up and down as our bodies became one. Portia's vagina was so goddamn wet.

Breathe. Inhale. Breathe. Exhale.

My imagination continued and with each pelvic thrust I entered her deeper and deeper. Grabbing her ass with both hands, I squeezed harder and harder.

I could feel the bottom of her vagina, and I wanted to go through it. Portia tilted her head back as sweat began to slide down her neck, aiming for the gap between her breasts.

Breathe. Inhale. Breathe. Exhale.

I pictured Portia moaning in delight as she tightened her legs around my body. She placed her hands under my hoodie and dug her nails into my skin. The pain was so good.

She pounded on top of me like she had something to prove. The bed beat against the wall with a melody that almost had me snapping my fingers and tapping my feet.

I thought I could actually feel the moisture from her insides dripping down my legs. Nothing seemed virtual about this reality.

Breathe. Inhale. Breathe. Exhale.

* * *

As the fantasy concluded, my body calmed, and my heart stopped pounding. I was now ready for the real thing. I was going to give Portia the fuck of her lifetime!

I had heard that coke sex was the absolute best sex, and she would not be disappointed. My imagination had nothing on all the filthy, disgusting things we were going to do for real.

Ready to transform my mental movie into live TV, I finally opened my eyes to see my co-star.

"What the fuck?" I shouted.

"GET. THE. FUCK. OUT!" Portia yelled.

Oooooh shiiiittt!

Either Portia had a fight with some shrimp-with-lobster-sauce, or I just ejaculated all over her—in real life!

Mortified, she couldn't wipe my mistake from her face—it was too much. I couldn't wipe Steve Urkel from my mind—I was too silly.

'*Did I dooo thaaat?*'

"What the hell happened?" I asked as my only comeback.

I didn't feel a thing!

"What the fuck do you mean what happened?" she asked.

"When I get out of the goddamn bathroom, you and your limp dick better be gone—ASSHOLE!"

Portia stood up and glared at me like she wanted me executed. I had never, in my life, seen an *angrier* grill. She looked at the coke on the table, and then she looked at me.

"And you better leave me some goddamn blow...you...you... *motherfucking*— PREMATURE EJACULATOR!" She rolled her eyes and hastily ran to the bathroom.

Paranoia parallel parked in the middle of my mind, and I started to shake. I wasn't sure if Portia were calling the cops or getting a gun.

I sure as hell wasn't going to stay to find out!

Listening to the shower running, I was nervous about what she was plotting in that bathroom. I had to get my high ass out of her apartment before the water stopped.

I jumped up like the couch was on fire and immediately swiped the two untouched eight balls. I was scared, but I wasn't stupid.

Although the night didn't end *exactly* how she had planned, Portia couldn't complain about the amount of cocaine I had left her. There was still enough powder on the mirror for an entire sorority house.

I *incidentally* spread my love on her face.

I left her $300 worth of blow.

Fair exchange was no robbery.

Scrambling like a mad man, I put on my jeans and stuffed my feet inside my sneakers.

I stopped moving and listened, and I could hear splashing water—but I knew time was running out! Soon, the rubber ducky would come out quacking.

OK, good she's still in there!

Drenched in sweat, I looked down at the coke.

My heart beat faster.

My mouth got drier.

I shook a little more, and then I farted.

Damn, I *needed* another line! Did I have time? Of course, I did!

There was *always* enough time to do another line—was part of the lesson I had just learned.

Fuck it!

Man, I grabbed that bill and rolled it so fast!

It was halfway rolled and almost too big to fit in my nostril, but my snot lubed the bill inside of my nose perfectly.

In one-point-two-seconds, I had snorted the largest line on the mirror!

Dropping the bill, I closed my eyes super tight, leaned my head back, and grabbed my chest with both hands.

I felt like a baby horse tried to kick a field goal with my heart!

Jeeeesssssuuuuussss Chriiiiiiissstttt!

The water stopped running.

Oh shit!

With one hand clutching my bruised heart, and the other attempting to hold up my unbuckled pants, I snatched my jacket off the floor and ran to the front door.

I grabbed the doorknob with my sweaty palms, almost unable to open the door.

Freedom!

Standing at the doorway, I could feel the night's breeze. The air was cooler than I was, and my heart immediately stopped hurting.

I looked down just as I was about to exit the front door, only discovering Portia's Virginia Tech Football shorts wrapped around my foot. Quickly unraveling them from my sneaker, I almost tossed the shorts immediately, but my curiosity overpowered my jacked-up-ness.

There it was, written in black marker on the left leg—number seventy-seven.

Damn!

I knew that was your Bronco big fella!

"I hope my homie lasted longer than I did," I mumbled, before jumping in my spaceship and flying to the moon.

Chapter Twenty-Three

THE EXPERIMENT

"Freddy!" I yelled. "Open up bro. It's me Manzo!"

I hear him in there!

BANG! BANG! BANG!

"All right, all right, already! Don't break my fucking door!" Freddy hollered from inside of his Terrace View townhouse, a minute walk from my place.

"I thought you were the po—goddamn Manzo! What the fuck happened to your eye?"

"Glad you're home—don't even ask." I walked in holding an ice pack pressed against my left eye.

"I see you finally caught that Miami flu going around. But whose girl you fucked this time though?" he asked while sliding in his white and orange VT flip-flops down the wooded hallway. I followed.

"Not right now Freddy. I need a drink!"

And a fucking line!

"You sure that's *all* you need—you, *premature ejaculator*, you?" Freddy died laughing.

"Portia has a big fucking mouth, I see," I said. "And is that *Steven* sleeping on your couch?"

"Bitches will be bitches son-son. And forget Steven—have a seat and tell me who beat the ass of the baddest motherfucker in school?" Freddy threw aside some clothes off the tan recliner, and I sat down, keeping the icepack on my eye.

"Good look," I thanked.

This place is a mess!

Positioned in the middle of the living room, there was a rectangular wooden coffee table with the same poster I had of Tony Montana, seated with his arm in a sling, set underneath the table's glass surface. Freddy built the table by hand.

On Freddy's prized creation, eleven empty Natural Light beer cans were scattered amongst a white Bic lighter and a porcelain saucer with four and half massive lines of coke settled next to a rolled $100 bill.

Between the coffee table and a dusty fifty-inch, black Sony Trinitron television against the left wall, laid a dusty orange area rug with *Virginia Tech* written in white—a pair of dreggy, red Chuck Taylor's slumbered on the letter V.

Four six-inch Bose wireless speakers hung on each of the four corners of the living room walls, while the stereo system was tucked in an entertainment center behind a watermelon-sized woofer in the far-left corner of the room.

A gray wool couch, the current bed of a shaggy-haired Steven Haynes wearing maroon shorts and white, V-neck t-shirt—extended long ways against the right wall while a brown La-Z-Boy served as an addition to the Bob's Discount special.

In the kitchen, to the left of the front door, filthy dishes spilled from the sink to the counter, another *Natty* Light hangout—while an unplugged grease-covered George Foreman grill expanded its charred mouth.

An open cabinet filled with canned goods, Ramen noodles, and seasonings suspended above a cruddy refrigerator with stacks of papers, and a liter of Jägermeister at the fridge's top.

I'm so glad I have a housekeeper! Smells like death in here!

"Y'all have a party last night and didn't invite me?" I asked.

"Every day's a party Manzo." Freddy sat at the end of Steven's feet.

"Steven move the fuck over dude!" Freddy ordered.

"Uhh," Steven grunted.

"Wake up! Manzo's here!"

"Uuuhh." Steven turned his head around. He wore a pink pair of Oakley's.

Why does this asshole have on shades?

"What up Steven?" I greeted.

"Uuuuh." Steven raised his head, looked at us, and then the plate of blow before leaning over the coffee table—ripping an entire line of cocaine and going back to sleep.

"What the fuck?" I asked. "How is that shit even possible?"

"Ha, that's just Steven. You want one?"

"For real Freddy...I'm going through some shit right now bro.

"I need to get fucked up ASAP! I need whatever you got in here!" I swiped a tear forming in my right eye. "I'm going through it!"

"Damn Manzo! What dude hit you?"

"Freddy, it wasn't a dude. It was Brittney, but I don't want to talk about it bro. I just need to get wasted. But I don't want any more blow right now!"

"Shit, OK bro! I got you! That's what I'm here for my man! What you want to do?"

How could she do this?

"Everything in the house!"

"Manzo, you obviously don't know my house."

"I don't care! Everything you got! Come on bro! I need you to help me! I'm already jacked but the blow is not helping! I'm stressing like a motherfucker!"

"OK, no problem big fella! But let me see your eye though!" Freddy requested.

"Aight." I removed the ice pack and careened my head in his direction.

"Goddamn! Somebody whipped your premature-ejaculating-ass!" Steven popped up his head and blurted.

"Go back to bed asshole!" I said.

"Fuck, Brittney got you kinda good bro!" Freddy winced. "You haven't seen it?"

"Nah, by the time I came to my senses she was gone, and I jetted over here. But I don't feel shit though. My vision is a fucked up. Is it *that* bad though? Give me a mirror."

"Nooo!" Steven and Freddy snapped together.

"Are y'all fucking serious?" I unsuccessfully scanned the place for a mirror. "I'm going to the bathroom."

Brittney killed our future!

"Relax bro!" Steven pulled my arm. "You're with your homies now! You gonna be *cool.*"

"You've been *crying* bro?" Freddy probed. "Your eyes all puffy and shit!"

"Hell no! I ain't no pussy!" I replied and threw the icepack on the floor.

"Just stay right there! We're getting fucked up!" Freddy stood, tucked in his white t-shirt and tied the string at the waist of his yellow Washington Redskins sweatpants.

"Steven please do the honors of moving the beer cans, good fella. I will be right back," Freddy said.

"Aye-aye captain!" Steven sat up as Freddy skipped down the hall and up the stairs, across from the kitchen. "Time to visit another galaxy Manzo! Shit's about to get real up this motherfucker!"

"*SNIFF*, another *galaxy*?" I asked.

"Yup, another galaxy," Steven confirmed, removed his shades, and placed them on my face, my life becoming darker. "*Our* troubles are about to be over."

CRASH!

Shit!

"Strike!" Steven howled after swiping all the beer cans off the table in one swing. "I hope your day is clear...*tomorrow!*"

"Tomorrow? What's Freddy getting?" I asked timidly.

"Oooh, you gonna see bro." Steven nodded as Freddy thudded down the stairs.

"You're getting scared yet Manzo?" Freddy shouted.

A little!

"I'm good. Let's go bro!" I returned, watching him walk toward us.

"Fuck yea dude!" Steven pumped both fists.

Oh shit!

I'm going to die!

"Dinner is now served!" Freddy hollered before placing a two-foot-long mirrored-serving-tray on the coffee table.

The serving tray's frame was an antique silver mixed with bronzed gold, and had a pearlescent, crocodile skin-like design running along the perimeter.

Extravagant arrowheads, pointing outward at each corner of the frame, linked the artistry—while two sculpted, adjacent handles held the oversized tray's beauty in place.

On the tray's upper-left corner, a crystal grenade of Patron Silver towered the mirrored war zone.

Like a tank flanked by six rows of single-filed-soldiers, a chunk of carved coke and yellow-flaked lines, two inches in length—protected the fort below the tequila.

Anchored on the tray's middle-left border, a twin pack of Parliament Lights, favoring carcinogenic battleships, fired six missiles of fine white powder—toward its jaundiced opposition. A pod of twelve Blue Dolphin ecstasy pills had rolled port-side for safety.

At the top-center of the tray, three sandy Carolina-blue bazookas aimed at three bitty, deflated army-green balloons, subordinate to Dean Smith's powder.

The balloons resembled vegan fish snacks and settled overhead an alloy cylinder, no larger than a shotgun bullet.

Six chrome mini Hydrogen bombs bunked at the mirror's upper-right region, just above a twelve-ounce bottle of Poland Spring water.

Under the *water*, a Mason jar, exploding with Kind bud nuggets, was planted beside five cannons of chalky-white substance, too fine to have been cocaine, at the bottom-right corner of the tray—completing the board-game from hell.

"Holy shit! Y'all really trying to kill me! I'm gonna get a heart attack Freddy!" I said.

"You wanted *everything* in my crib! So here's eerr-thang! Let's go to another motherfucking dimension boys!"

"Fuck yea! Let's rock boys! Wooo-hoo!" Steven slapped my leg. "You're with us Manzo! The *professionals*!"

"Yea this ain't shit bro! We did more than this two nights ago!" Freddy disclosed.

"Ain't shit, huh?" I questioned.

These White boys are crazy!

"Yooo, you with Freddy *goddamn* Spaghetti and Steven the motherfucking *real deal* Haynes now! You in or you out, 'cuz I'm ready to fuck an alien in her ass?" Steven thrust his hips twice from his seat.

Of course I'm in!

I'm not a bitch!

"Fuck yea I'm in! The blow I did earlier got me a little skittish, I guess," I said.

"*Skittish*?" Steven laughed and pointed at Freddy. "Did this big Black motherfucker from the *pro*-jexx just say...*skittish*?"

"Damn son-son...you think you in Woodberry Forest, huh?" Freddy patted my back.

"Fuck you! Don't touch me! Let's go to the moon, you crazy-ass White boys!"

"That's what I'm talking about! Manzo don't be akkin' all *skittish* 'round your homies!" Steven said.

"Aight asshole, I get it! I'm down, but somebody please explain what I'm looking at. This shit is bananas." I arched forward on the recliner, gesturing toward the tray.

I will do anything except heroine or crack.

"Well—"

"Whoa, I got this Steven," Freddy interrupted. "Let me fuck this cat—you just hold the tail."

This dude just stole my saying!

"Ha, ha, ha! OK, *fuck the cat* then bro!" Steven nodded.

"OK, but I ain't mentioning the obvious shit you do know Manzo," Freddy suggested and positioned himself on the edge of the La-Z-Boy, at the opposite side of the coffee table.

"OK bet," I agreed.

These dudes are crazy!

"These are the infamous Blue Dolphin beans I told you about the other day. They're way more clean and stronger than the Mitsubishis. You will roll your fucking face off dude. Here, we're taking two right now." Freddy gathered six of the e-pills, dropping two in each of Steven's and my right hands.

I thought we need bitches to do E.

"Yeeeaa Buddy!" Steven tossed the Blue Dolphins in his mouth and helped himself to a swig of Patron.

"I've never done E fellas. But Fred—don't we need some bitches?" I asked. "I'm not getting all horny around you motherfuckers!"

I'm not with that fruity shit.

"Ha, ha, ha!" Steven cracked up.

"Don't worry! Your booty hole is safe around us—ha, ha, ha! Plus, if you get too horny...just go home and eat a steamed dumpling out of Jane's pussy!"

"Ha, ha, ha! Fuck you Steven!" I laughed.

"But on the real Manzo, ain't nobody here gay or touching nobody. This is E, and those are lines of Molly—MDMA," Freddy pointed and explained.

"And right there, in front of those Parliaments—don't even ask yet. I will explain in a sec. *That* shit just gonna add to the complete mind fuck! And if you get all weird, then I'm kicking your ass out myself bro! This ain't an episode of *Oz!*"

Molly? MDMA?

What the fuck?

"Don't go all *Adebisi* on us crackers Manzo!" Steven laughed dramatically and passed me the tequila. I threw the pills in my mouth and took a swig.

"You're officially a fucking retard bro! I've never been to jail and ain't ever going! Let's get twisted!" I said.

Shit taste bitter!

"In about twenty minutes, your life's gonna change forever Manzo." Freddy grabbed the Patron and followed suit.

Please Lord, don't let me die tonight with these fuckers!

"Yooo, beside the GHB in that fake-ass water bottle, what's the rest of that shit on there?" I inquired.

"I forgot you're hip to the G," Freddy uttered.

"Wait until you take a cap of that shit!" Steven shook his head. "Wooo-wee!"

"Don't scare the dude, asshole!" Freddy yelled and waved his hands in the air like a pharmaceutical meteorologist, continuing his presentation.

"Anyway, these lines you asked about right here are Special K or *Ketamine.* These green balloons are to huff the Nitrous from these metal bomb looking things called, *whippets.*

"This cylinder here is called a *cracker*—this is what we're gonna use to take the Nitrous from the whippets and inflate the balloons. Your brain will be fried silly, you will see."

"Last time I did whippets, I couldn't remember my mom's name for a week dude!" Steven confessed.

"No fucking way!"

"He ain't lying Manzo," Freddy validated.

What am I doing? Why did I come here?

I need to forget about Brittney! She's the devil!

Be cool!

I need a blunt to calm my nerves.

"I'm not messing with them cigs, but I see y'all White folks got that good ole Kind Bud. I need to smoke baaaad, but where are the blunts?"

"Ha-ha, *blunts*?" Steven asked.

"Man we're not smoking any blunts!" Freddy declared.

"*Grape Ape* motherfucker!" Steven hollered at me.

"Steven you bumped your goddamn head or something?" I hopped out my chair—irate and towering over him.

"We supposed to be boys—you racist bastard! I should kick your White-ass for calling me a mother-fuckin' purple *monkey*!"

"Whoa...whoa...ha, ha, ha, ha, ha...whoooaaa...ha, ha, ha, ha!" Steven put both hands up but couldn't stop laughing.

"Ha, ha, ha, ha...oh...my...fucking God! Ha, ha, ha, ha! Classic!" Freddy ran around the coffee table and plopped next to Steven on the couch.

"Shit ain't funny! Why the fuck y'all laughing? You condoning this shit Freddy?" I asked.

"Hey asshole, I wasn't calling *you* Grape Ape!" Steven said through tears while Freddy got out of his seat, drifted to the hallway closet next to the kitchen's entrance, opening the closet door.

Where's he going?

"Grape Ape is the name of *this*!" Freddy reached in the closet, and carefully extracted a purple water bong, a few inches taller than he.

"Meet our friend, who gets us hella high, and who definitely is *not* you Manzo...or any other *Africaaaaan Americaaaan*!

"Introducing, from parts unknown...the one, and the only...Graaaaaappeee Aaaaaaaapppeee!" Steven announced like "Mean" Gene Okerlund.

"This is so classic! I shit you not fellas!" Freddy laughed so hard on his revisit to the coffee table, Grape Ape damn near plummeted to the floor. "Oh shit, I got you! Not ever gonna let you go big fella!"

I'd smoked weed out of many water bongs before, the tallest having been a blue four-footer named Poppa Smurf—but nothing could compare to the mammoth that Freddy situated in front of me.

Grape Ape, thick and with a mall's fluorescent light bulb length, was a piece of blown-glass-sweetness—a giant's Jolly Rancher.

Grape Ape pipelined like a waterslide into its softball-sized base where an inch-long silver rod poked out angularly with a connecting *bowl*, only the tip of my thumb could fit.

"This dude was 'bout to call the United Negro College Fund on us!" Steven joked.

"Fuck you Steven! Y'all was about to get punished in this motherfucker!" I joined the fun and sat down.

"Steven you're a fool bro!" Freddy said.

"Yea, you're a goddamn idiot! Don't you mean the NAACP asshole!" I corrected.

"Oh yea, ha, ha, ha. Same difference," Steven said.

"Man let's get high fellas!" Freddy pulled a yellow Washington Redskins lighter out his hoodie pocket.

"Yea let Rosa Parks over here go first!" Steven suggested.

"This shit is tooooo funny," Freddy said. "Manzo let's go! You need to calm your ass down before the blow makes you think we're in the KKK or some shit."

"Pack that shit! I ain't scared of Grape Ape!" I said.

"You sure?" Freddy asked.

"Yea let's go bro! I need to get fried! No more fucking around!" I urged.

"Steven move over and let Manzo stand on the couch. Shit's about to get riz-zeal."

"Stand on the couch?" I asked.

"Dude, this motherfucker is six feet. The water will spill if you try and smoke it just leaning the shit that far back," Steven rationalized and scooted over.

"Oh shit, my bad. Makes sense. Pack that shit Spaghetti. I ain't scared."

Damn...six feet?

I can't do that shit!

"Yessir!" Freddy plucked a nug out of the Mason jar and squished the weed into the bowl with his left thumb. I kicked off my flip-flops and hopped on the couch.

This is crazy!

"Yo, grab the top with both hands and slowly tilt it forward, and just put your mouth on it like a small bong and keep pulling until I pull the bowl out," Freddy instructed.

"Timeout, timeout—aay-yooooo! That sounds gay as fuck!" I snapped as I shook my head and made the letter T with my hands.

"Freddy please say *pause* before I do anything," I appealed.

"Pause, pause, pause! Myyy...baaaadd fellas! Now come on son-son, stop stalling!"

Can't fool Freddy!

"Man let's go, this ain't my first rodeo!" I informed. "Hold up! But does it have enough water in it?"

"Yea goddamnit! Hurry and go so we can go!" Steven commanded, exasperated from my stonewalling.

"Put your mouth on it, so Freddy can light the motherfucker! Just go already!"

"OK, OK...aite, aite! Light motherfucking Grape Ape's monkey-ass on fire! I got this shit fellas!" I said.

Grape Ape gonna Donkey Kong my Black-ass!

"OK I'm lighting it. You got this son-son."

Freddy kneeled to one knee and on his second attempt, the lighter sparked and flamed as I steadily inhaled and kindled the sizzling marijuana.

Ivory smoke drifted and spiraled up the bong like a lost ghost, while bouncing bubbles boiled and crackled, crawling up the throat of the purple beast.

My nose was too stuffed with cocaine, so I couldn't smell the pungency of either the bong water or the Kind Bud itself—simply breathing was problematic.

Exhaling out of my nose was impossible, so I stopped pulling when the smoke reached just three feet into the experience.

Covering my mouth with my right hand, I capped Grape Ape with my left—ensnaring a couple gasps of *fresh air* before continuing the process.

Damn, Freddy needs to do something about those cobwebs.

In the right corner of the ceiling, a house spider took pleasure in a weaved refreshment, whilst Freddy re-roasting the weed and regaining my attention.

Swiftly replacing both hands around Grape Ape, I crammed my mouth into the bong, dissevering my lips partially, and the inhalation commenced.

Driven on ravaging the first course, I disregarded my lightheadedness and continued inhaling. My collarbone and chin met, hiding any sight of my neck.

"Oh shit Manzo, you almost got this shit! Keep pulling!" Steven coached.

Hunting for death, the smoke snaked to Grape Ape's Adams Apple like a penetrating acid fog, while my toes clawed the couch for oxygen, and sweat scattered between my eyebrows.

Come on, you got this!

My body trembled in distress, and I no longer could fight. Seconds away from passing the hell out, I blew out of my nose in desperation, and the air in my left nostril drilled a gateway to the high life. I could breathe.

"Pull!" Steven ordered.

Oh shit!

"Go!" Freddy snatched the bowl, and its metal tail slid out of the bong— leaving behind a hole the circumference of a pencil.

I strongly inhaled, and the apparition crossed into my soul as the cloud disappeared—loading my lungs.

"Fuck yea!" Steven applauded.

"Hold it in bro! Hold it Manzo!" Freddy shouted.

Hold it!

Don't blow any out yet!

With every second I held my breath, my chest grew a welcoming warmth and thawed a coat of cocaine in my blood, but something more down-reaching stewed a tinge of paradise, foreign to any high I'd ever felt before.

Inside, I smiled and emotional barriers sank with my feet into the plush wool, my heart beat a perfect rhythm.

Letting go of Grape Ape, I removed the sunglasses and my world refined. Riveted by the overhead light, I blew out smoke like a wolf. At last—I was alive.

"Fucking animal!" Freddy yelled and sprouted to his feet. "You got all of it!"

"You already know bro! Shit...I gotta sit down though," I said. "Take this shit. Who's next?"

"Uuuh...*next*?" Freddy asked, already walking to the closet with Grape Ape.

"Hold up, you and this nut aren't smoking?" I asked.

"Hell no! Fuck weed! We ready for the real shit! Ain't nobody got time to mess around with Grape Ape son-son." Freddy sat next to me, and Steven *musical-chaired* to the La-Z-Boy.

"You two assholes tricked me to smoke that shit?"

"Nah bro, you needed it. You were too coked up," Steven explained. "How do you feel now?"

"How does he *feel*? Look at his eyes bro!" Freddy beamed a finger in my face.

"I told y'all my eye does not hurt!" I said.

"Relax, he ain't talking about your *boo-boo*. We're starting to roll!" Steven said.

"*Roll*?" I asked.

"Yea the beans got a foot in my ass right now," Steven said.

Oh shit, their pupils are dilated as fuck too!

"Y'all looking like two European rats right now," I said.

"We need some beats ASAP!" Freddy dug in between the couches, extracting a remote.

"Freddy play Victor Calderone."

Who?

"Great call Steven!" Freddy mashed the remote with his thumb, the bass gradually hitting a soothing level.

"Yea that's my shit bro!" Steven bopped his head and grabbed a tall bottle of Fiji water from the floor.

"Shit all sounds the same to my Black ass," I said.

I can't stop moving my jaw.

I don't feel the blow anymore.

"Victor's the DJ! Take a gulp of water! Sit back and feel the beat and relax bro! We about to take the fuck off!" Steven handed me the water and reclined his chair.

"Thanks. Why are we drinking water though?" I asked.

Damn that taste so good.

Glad it's not G!

"Let me get that son-son. Thanks." Freddy took a swig, setting the water at his feet.

"This shit will intensify your roll, and you have to stay hydrated, so you don't pass the hell out. Now sit back for a few minutes—feel the beat like Steven said and relax. We're just getting started, K is next."

Freddy boosted the volume, and we all drooped in a serenity of accompanied solitude.

Slightly squirming in my seat with a happiness brimming on euphoria, I felt my eyes enlarge under collapsed lids as I devoted myself to the rhythm.

Strings of liquid-cooled-heat enmeshed in my body, and the song's bass morphed my ears into tongues—I could taste the music.

The drums. The machines. The beat. I licked the rhapsody to the core with a rabid smile.

The melodic tones weakened my social defenses. I bounced with a plastic spirit and a retreated ego into an incomparable state of existence.

The music zoomed me to a world where the beat had been the only language articulated.

Lost were the street poets of imaginary fortunes, sexual conquests, and *felonious capers*—because men lied, women lied, but the beat didn't.

The cotton fibers against my neck feathered my skin like a massage from an angel wing, and I itched for more.

Leaning forward, I slung the hoodie over my head and brushed the fabric along the sides of my face.

Through a clenched jaw, I gnawed tolerably on my juiceless lips and could feel my intestines strangely vibrating.

What is that?

"Freddy!" I shrilled. "Freddy!"

"Yo what up?" Freddy lowered the volume on the music, crumbling the reverie.

"That noise, what's *that*?" Steven asked before I could.

"Manzo you're so wasted. You're humming my brother," Freddy said.

BUZZ. BUZZ.

"So I'm not bugging, am I? Freddy? *Steven*?" I hunted for an answer.

"Hey asshole, It's your phone dude!" Steven tapped my stomach.

My phone?

BUZZ.

"Oh yea, it's my phone." I inserted my right hand in my hoodie pocket and felt the vibration. "Who is it?"

"You have to answer the shit first dude." Steven stuck his right thumb to his temple and extended the pinky to his mouth, shaking his head. "Duuuh."

Fuck, it's Jane!

"What the—"

"Let me answer that for you Manzo." Steven snatched my phone.

"Don't answer that Steve—" Freddy tried to help.

"Hello...oh hey Jane, it's Steven."

"Fucking asshole," I mouthed without making a sound.

"Yea he's here. We're getting trashed. You should come say *hello* to him... nooo, Brittney isn't with us." He sank in his seat.

"Steven you gonna cause a bitch war," Freddy struggled to speak.

"Jane said, 'You're a violent fucking sociopath, and you need to get help immediately.'" Steven smirked and put a thumb up in the air.

Why is this asshole giving me a thumbs-up?

"She said, 'Never talk to her again, and when is Dirt bringing back her car?'"

Ah man, I want to fuck her so bad right now!

"Tell her he just went to 7-11—stop tripping," I replied and then whispered to Steven. "Hang up asshole—"

"She said, 'It shouldn't take two hours to go to 7-11. Which one did he go to?'"

"The one up the road," I said.

"She said, '*Which* one up the road?'"

"Tell her the *one* up the road...in Charlottesville," I answered honestly.

We all laughed furiously as I snatched my phone, shutting off the power and placing it back inside my pocket.

"She called you every *Black son-of-a-bitch* in the book bro." Steven shook his head.

She's still not more upset than Brittney.

"It happens bro. Manzo take some K. You need to mellow out. Time to get serious." Freddy handed me the $100 bill.

"*Serious*? I'm rolling my face off! You're sure I'm gonna be aight?" I accepted the *Big Face* hundred.

"Stop asking that and fuck the cat's tail bro! Just fuck the cat and show it who's...who's the real boss bro." Steven stared at me.

"That's not the saying dickhead!" I loomed over the coffee table.

"I know. It's the remix fool," Steven said.

"Get your boy, Spaghetti. Which is the K?" I asked.

"On the tray—above the bottle of Georgia Home Boy."

"I see it. Thanks Fred," I said.

"No prob, but just take a little—*holy* shit!" Freddy shouted and vaulted to his feet.

Damn that burns more than coke!

"What the fuck bro? You ripped two rails of K?" Steven questioned and ascended from the La-Z-Boy. "You *did*! They gonna send you back to Africa in a goddamn box bro!"

"Fuck you! I live Harlem, not Africa!"

"Gimme that bill!" Freddy kidnapped Benjamin. "You supposed to only take *this* much."

"But that's just a half a line, *total*," I rebutted.

I did four times as much.

"Thanks for the math lesson. We know Manzo," Steven added. "Pass me that bill Fred!"

Am I gonna OD?

"Am I going to die? Do I need to drink milk or some shit? What do I do? Why y'all ain't tell me?"

They trying to kill me!

"Reeee-laaax dude and have a seat on this thing! Breathe motherfucker!" Steven yanked my arm toward the La-Z-Boy, and we switched seats before he snorted a half a line of Ketamine.

"So am I going to die or what?" I struggled to ask, my vision onset to smudging.

Fuck I can't really focus on shit!

"I'm going blind guys! Oh shit, I'm going blind! Freddy? Steven? Where are you?" I screamed.

"Ha, ha, ha, you're not going blind! Just blink a few times dude!" Freddy burst out laughing with Steven. "You're about to be a real K-tard!"

"Just be cool. You're not going blind. You're going in a *K-hole*. You're not going blind—ha...ha...ha," Steven rendered a drowsy explanation.

Did he say K-hole?

"A fucking k-*what*?" I pressed.

A speedy rush of paralysis had sewn my body to the La-Z-Boy, although my mind seemed normal.

Freddy and Steven's mouth moved, but my mental jabbering slurred over their lesson in K-nometry as an encompassing dark beat strummed heavily.

I couldn't move or fend the overhead light's lasers from softening their faces to a putty of pallid flesh as they persisted to chatter, point, and chuckle.

What the fuck they laughing at?

Why can't I move?

Can they hear me?

Freddy?

Steven?

Am I in a K-hole?

How do I get out?

Help guys!

Is this real?

Am I hallucinating?

Watch out Freddy!

Freddy's jaw flapped loosely with each head movement, barely missing the spider's cobweb strand adhered to the tray's nest of cocaine that shrunk with each of our newest guest's violent pumps.

Steven lit one of the Parliament Lights, took a drag, and blew three giant circles of smoke around me like a Hula-Hoop.

Wearing an orange do-rag, the Hokie bird mascot snorted the rings before flying into the cigarette's embers—now situated between the gills on Steven's neck.

As Steven's nose wiggled and flared, he leaned forward and rapped his thoughts.

"Yoooo...yoooo...yoooo...yooooo...Maaaanzooooo...I knooooow...thiiiiis iiiiis geeeetting oooold...buuuut... yoooou aaaaare...iiiiin aaaa Kaaaay-hoooole... yoooo...yoooo...yoooo!" Steven crossed his arms and *Beastie-Boy'ed* his head to the side.

Why is he rapping?

God make him stop rapping!

Freddy say something!

Do something!

I need you to call Brittney!

Tell her I'm still fucking hurt, but I understand!

And then call Jane, Freddy!

Steven?

What's that light?

Hey guys, what's that fucking light?

A mild panic flushed my high when the overhead light fixture dislodged from the ceiling, hovered over my head, increasingly plunging with a scintillating force.

Freddy and Steven faded with the ambience, and all I could see was a moonlit cemetery with milky-white, blue-eyed kangaroos with limp black roses overhanging their pouches—hopping from wet grave to wet grave.

A kangaroo splashed water on a small nameless headstone, and a rush of warmth lathered my face with irrefutable realness.

I shut my eyes to reclaim vision, but when I opened them, the Kangaroos had vanished.

An obscure Freddy stood in front of me holding a pink box of Kleenex in his right hand, and a Poland Spring water bottle in the other.

"Freddy!" I cried out. "Freddy can you hear me?"

"Yes, I'm not deaf motherfucker!" he reminded.

"Why are you yelling?" Steven asked.

Oh shit, they can hear me!

"Dude, you're out of the K-Hole. Take a fucking chill pill or have some GHB." Freddy shook the bottle.

"And wipe your eyes bro. Damn cry baby." Steven handed me a few tissues out of the box. "I've never seen someone cry in a K-hole!"

"*Cry?*" I patted my face dry.

Are they messing with me?

"Yea dude, you just sat there crying like a fucking mime—crying with no expression!" Freddy said.

"No shit? For how long? Two minutes?" I asked.

"Two minutes?" Steven asked and tapped Freddy. "Try twenty-one minutes dude!"

"No way! Twenty-one *minutes*?" I asked.

"Yup, I don't think you need any more drugs bro," Freddy suggested.

"Yea it's OK to be *lame!*" Steven laughed.

"Nah, we not stopping bitches! What's next?" I twirled an index finger at the tray. "I ain't no pussy-ass-bitch! Let's go!"

"Woooo!" Steven yelled. "And *that's* why I believe in Affirmative Action...I love you, Tysheem!"

"*What?*" Freddy plunked back onto the couch.

"Fuck you, *Mortimer!* My name ain't no Tysheem, asshole! You had me for a second!" I cracked up and hit Steven with my tissue.

There was a Black guy named Tysheem Martin at Woodberry though—

Oh shit—my Creative Writing exam!

"What's wrong dude?" Steven asked.

"What time is it?" I questioned.

Maybe I have time?

"It's...it's 3:10 in the afternoon. You have a date?" Freddy checked his maroon Washington Redskin's watch.

"Nah but I have a quiz at 3:30 with Nikki Giovanni. Fuck, I forgot! I need to go!"

"Ha-ha bro. You ain't goin' nowhere like *this.*" Steven gripped my shoulder, pulling me back down to my seat.

"You show up all whacked, and they're taking you to jail or to the hospital for sure." Freddy said.

"But I never missed a quiz! I got twenty minutes!" I contested.

I must go!

"Man take a sip of this and pass it to Steven...and *chiiiill.*" Freddy handed me the water bottle.

I am thirsty—

That's not water! That's fucking G!

Gamma Hydroxybutyrate, clear and odorless, with the zest of a metal-based detergent, was warm and salty.

There was no harsh acidity or sting to the taste, just an impressive load of disgusting bitterness deluging the senses.

The Robot soap scraped sections of sanity from the top of my esophagus to the bottom of my stomach. As my mind pre-heated—sweat and panic flowed with the temperature.

Tastes like death!

I am going to die for sure!

"This is your classroom today bro! Pass that Georgia Home Boy!" Steven snatched the bottle and took a swig. "No school today—you La Costra Nostra mother-fuckeeerrrssss!"

La Costra Nostra?

"Thanks Steven. Shit never gets easy though...this taste suuucks!" Freddy grabbed the bottle from Steven, took a sip, and then placed the bottle back on the tray.

I feel sick!

"Aaah...and Steven, *Miss* Nikki Giovanni ain't Italian asshole! She's Black!"

"Ha, ha, ha! Oh, OK Freddy—I thought that was Gotti's peoples, my bad," Steven retracted.

"I'm getting nauseous guys! I feel like I need to throw up!" I shouted.

"Relax and breathe!" Steven coached.

"Relax Manzo—breathe dude!" Freddy detained my right shoulder, stopping me from standing.

I must get out of here!

"This is that date rape shit! Y'all trying to fuck me!" I yelled.

Run!

"Dude...stop...breathe...nobody's trying to fuck you bro. Relax and breathe. Just breathe dude. We're your boys." Steven came to Freddy's aid and braced my left shoulder with both hands.

Run!

Relax!

Breathe!

Run!

"Manzo this is *me*—Freddy. Relax and breathe big fella. You got this bro. Master the G motherfucker. Control that bitch bro. Breathe and relax. Yes, that's it. Relaaax dude."

Relax! Breathe! You are OK.

"Feel the beat and breathe bro. We...got this. We...got...this...bro..." Steven's speech garbled, as he and Freddy's gripped loosened concurrently. I dwindled back into the La-Z-Boy.

Breathe—

I'm oooh...kaaay...

My thoughts dribbled. My words flattened.

I trudged through the oncoming lights and punched bolts of fire skyrocketing for my face, the bass walloping with each blow.

I swung and sweat to an angelic blend of funk-infused sound and rapture. The music was king, and I was its slave.

The Ketamine relinquished control to the new substance, and the GHB's base of floor stripper mixed with drain cleaner spewed euphoria over my intellectual gifts. I was clumsy with a magical drunkenness.

I wanted to dance.

I wanted to do more drugs.

I wanted to get some pussy.

I wanted to read a book and have two Brazilian girls suck on my toes.

I wanted to do anything that I could have thought of because everything seemed amazing. I felt unstoppable.

Best song I ever heard!

I could be President—

I know I could fuck J-Lo—

I'm gonna be rich—

Oh shit! How did I get here?

* * *

In the middle of a packed Lane Stadium on a sunny spring day, I danced on stage in a black graduation gown, the maroon and orange tassels on my cap flapping with each move.

At the podium, ten feet away, a six-foot spider, dressed in its own cap and gown, held a rolled diploma tied in an orange ribbon between two of the spider's prickly legs.

The spider, auburn with specs of gray, untied the ribbon and spread the diploma—*Manzo* written backward in white had appeared in each of the spider's eight eyes, identical to magnificent pieces of whittled onyx.

Enchanted, I smiled and paced a single step but could no longer continue. I was stuck.

Looking down at my bare feet melting into the wooden stage, I struggled to move through the stench of burning tobacco.

Disoriented, I scanned the crowd of unrecognizable people garbed in black, seated in folding chairs.

I noticed Brittney cloaked in a silk red sheet, breastfeeding a baby skeleton. Milk discharged into the baby's mouth and trickled down its bones onto Brittney's lap.

To the right of Brittney, Jane, veiled in a black wedding dress and no makeup, cried as she photographed herself with a Polaroid camera. Jane flicked the photos in the wind after each take.

The Polaroids transformed into doves with quarter-sized emerald eyes, soaring above freely, flapping toward the sun.

The doves flew and rejoiced until the sky gloomed with hundreds of stocky blue jays, closing over the white-feather performance.

Still unable to move, I watched the blue jays fly over as the crowd stood up, clapped and cheered.

Flames blazed from the blue jays' beaks as they swooped down, attacking their feathered foes with ferocious accuracy. The doves darted in all directions but could not outwit the fire.

Burning embers trailed through the air as charred bones plummeted around me. I grasped a blazing quill and felt the heat between my fingers.

Mesmerized by the glow, I neglected the scent of scorched carbon and paper.

My hand traveled to my mouth, and I placed the base of my compulsion between my slightly divided lips before inhaling the foreign fog into my lungs.

My mind relaxed and sank beneath the distasteful enjoyment of nicotine swimming in my blood. I shut my eyes and exhaled the smoke.

* * *

My eyes opened, and Steven was slumped on the couch with sunken cheeks and a sweaty t-shirt as he held three inflated balloons by the tips.

Freddy swiped the cigarette from my hand and mashed it in the ashtray with two other butts resting on the coffee table.

Slurring his words and struggling to give instructions, Steven managed to pass a balloon to Freddy and me for our next phase of flight.

Where are the birds?

Where are Brittney and my baby?

"Wow...man. I don't know what's good. But where are we? OK, just keep the... balloon pinched. Until you sucked...all the nitrous. Just inhale. That's called huffing. Breathe in and out...the balloon. Slowly.

"Wow, uh, yea...if you must stop, just pinch. Pinch the shit—again. And then huff some more...until it's gone. OK, that's it—uuuh, oh yea...rock on," Steven mumbled.

"I am fucking *crushed* dudes. I think I saw my dead grandmother, playing chess...wi—with Batman...ha-ha." Freddy patted me on the back.

"Ha-ha, the G...got me...trippin' too. Kangaroos, birds...*Batman*. What's next? Let's keep going," I prompted.

"Welcome to our world...son-son. It's...it's...hippie-crack time. Let's go." Freddy smiled and nodded.

Hippie crack?

"When do we...do we go?" I asked.

"Now," Steven answered, and he and Freddy placed the balloons in their mouths and proceeded huffing. I copied.

Looks easy.

Palming the balloon with my left hand, I clamped the rubber neck between my teeth before unclenching my jaw and steadily inhaling Hell's flavorless vapor.

Between the fingers of my left hand, the balloon expanded and contracted with the rise and fall of my chest.

The temperature in my lungs rapidly cooled. My brain squeezed hot oxygen from both nostrils—freezing my face as a billion insects ice-skated underneath my scalp.

The Nitrous Oxide asphyxiated my train of thought with a vice grip tightness. With each inhale, years of education leaked from my ears until only a pool of stupidity remained.

My body panicked, but when I saw an unfazed Steven and Freddy on the couch huffing away in pleasant delirium—I channeled my inner trailer-park teen, knowing I had to finish the balloon.

Oh my God!

What's going on?

It hurts—

It feels good—

Am I going to die?

I clutched a tingly ball of rubber under my numb fingertips and huffed with deathly force until I absorbed all the invisible poison deep into my character—without having the ability or IQ to conclusively make sense of who I was, where I was, or what I was doing.

With fresh oxygen resurfacing in my body, I gasped, slung the balloon, and celebrated a puerile victory with my new teammates, already waiting for me at the finish line—wriggling in their seats.

"What...the fuck...du...du...dude?" Steven stuttered.

"Where's the...Forest Whitaker?" Freddy pointed to the tray. "We have...to...do...we have to do...the Forest Whitaker."

"Forest...Whitaker?" I asked, squeezing the sides of my head with both hands.

"I...can't...can't...brain...fri...brain fried," I informed.

"Forest Whitaker...is the...sky-blue lines...under the...un...under da weed jar," Steven responded.

"What's in a...Forest Whitaker? And...why y'all call it...a...a Forest Whitaker?" I pressed for an explanation.

"Molly...X...K...and...what else Steven?" Freddy snatched the bill off the tray before relinquishing the rolled-up money on my lap.

"What *else*?" I asked.

"Yea Steven. You remember?" Freddy asked again.

Yea what else?

"Fucking *blow*...you...re...you...retards." Steven snickered. "And it's called...a Forest Whitaker...because—well...you wait and...and you tell us...ha, ha, ha."

Blow?

Forest Whitaker? What the fuck?

"Is...is Mr. Whitaker...going to kill me...Freddy?" I asked, poking the bill into my right nostril.

"We're...beyond questions. So...let's finally...get to the...fucking moon. So...I can go...I can go see...*my* Melinda...Freddy can see...his girl...

"And Manzo...you...can...get...knocked out again...from one of...your *bitches* again...ha, ha, ha. My red rocket...needs some...Mel-love," Steven responded.

"Word," Freddy consented, stood, and replaced the sunglasses on my face. "There you go...a true...goddamn...rock star."

I want the biggest line!

That one in the middle definitely looks like mine!

I ended the rhetoric, and impulsively *slayed* two lines, and felt my back pound against the couch, whip-lashing the sunglasses off my face.

With my head in the blue, I felt the chemicals spiking their way to my brain, gradually dripping a numbing tingle in the back of my tonsils.

The sound faded with my sense of taste and left me in a muted wasteland of blandness.

My heart beat fast, then slow, and then fast again.

A bead of sweat wandered along a cold black brow. My back arched as a fevered shiver crawled up my spine.

I watched the overhead light burn through never-ending bouncing red dots.

My right eye enjoyed the game, but my left eye refused to watch—no matter how adamantly I tried to keep it open. I could have been a stunt double in the movie *Ghost Dog*.

Forest...fucking...Whitaker!

A symphony of drugs harmonized—the highs, the lows, all playing its part and becoming one in my system.

The narcotics complemented one another with a sensual rotation of insanity. When the cocaine reached for the stars, the Molly and Ecstasy snatched the blow back to earth, and then the Ketamine clawed everyone into a burrow—before the melody repeated.

My mind was held inactive until I blinked, and a naked infant dawned in the distance and waved goodbye.

Genderless and chubby, the beautiful baby had seven black curled hairs on its crown, my father's nose, Brittney's blue eyes, Mommy's cheekbones and the sweetest smile.

I already loved *Little Me* more than life itself and would have done anything to protect my child.

The infant ascended further into the light, fading away as I desperately raked both my arms above my face in a psychotic sorrow.

Don't go!

Come back!

I'm sorry!

I love you!

Come back!

Please!

A sobbing one-eyed madman, I allowed the pain to sting through the drugs while disregarding Freddy and Steven suspended over me in bewilderment, before I dashed out of the townhouse and back to my place.

I was *gone*, and my baby was gone, along with thoughts of ever seeing it again.

I had the best education.

I had a million dollars, plenty of women and new bad habits.

My enemies respected me.

My friends and family loved me, but I had no children.

Fatherhood would have to wait though, because without my knowledge or consent, earlier that morning—Brittney had an abortion.

Chapter Twenty-Four

WHITE LIE

May 5th, 2000 was the last day of school before exams, and although I didn't attend many of my other professor's classes, I seldom missed Creative Writing with Nikki Giovanni.

In need of filling an elective, I signed up for her class only because most of my friends on the football team had enrolled.

I never realized that Nikki Giovanni was one of the most well-known African American poets, writers, and activists in the world.

I had always attended the first day of classes in a semester just to show my face and pick up the test and assignment schedules.

But after meeting Ms. Giovanni, feeling her energy, and witnessing all the students hang on to her every word—I was intrigued to experience more of the iconic figure who wore men's suits and ties with effeminate grandeur.

Ms. Giovanni, a graceful fifty-six-year-old with a sandy complexion, was lean with short, fine blonde hairs spinning away from her naturally receding hairline.

Delicate eyebrows situated above charming brown eyes laden with graciousness and life. Her freckles dotted the creases encircling her eyes down to her prominent cheekbones and full nose.

Her laugh lines fenced an elongated chin, and lips that housed perfectly straight teeth and a dazzling smile.

Standing not much over five feet, she had a fragile appearance in her oversized ensembles, but the woman epitomized fortitude and was a pillar of strength for all Black people during the Civil Rights Movement.

A few words into her first-class lecture, I knew that Ms. Giovanni had been through a lot. I didn't need to read all of her credentials to understand that my bullshit was easily detectable and unwelcome.

So, besides the debacle in March with Freddy and Steven, I abstained from using drugs on Thursdays before Ms. Giovanni's afternoon lessons. At no point would I ever allow her to meet the demon.

Clear minded, I participated in class frequently with an unexplained genuine affinity for any subject matter Ms. Giovanni presented.

English had been my most powerful subject at Woodberry, but Ms. Giovanni didn't teach me English, she taught *life* and how to structure it in words.

With her, I gathered knowledge in bulk and learned to write and correlate my personal experiences with gorgeous force.

My street wisdom fused with a premier education, transformed my writing into something *different*.

After each class, I would rush home to write her assigned paper in its entirety, with a celebratory mound of cocaine beside my laptop.

After typing my last line, I snorted my first—freezing my genius.

Even though Ms. Giovanni handed my papers back with corrections, I felt I had been excelling, so it was surprising when she asked that I stay after class for a consultation.

* * *

Ms. Giovanni's Shank Hall classroom, windowless and cozy, was painted white and had twenty metal desks aligned in four rows of five that faced her desk—adjacent to a white marker board covering the entire right wall. There were no pictures and no plants.

She stood beside me in a gray suit, white dress-shirt, and a loosened canary tie, while I slouched in my seat, closest to the front door, fixated at *Manzo* written in red at the top right corner of the marker board.

"Mis-ter Manzo," Ms. Giovanni spoke.

Fuck! I shouldn't have missed that quiz!

I hope she's not failing me!

"That's my name Ms. Giovanni."

"Relax, I'm not failing you Manzo."

"Wow, thank you so much Ms. Giovanni." I rose from my desk to shake her hand.

"Sit down Manzo. I'm not doing you any favors young man," she asserted.

"Yes ma'am." I sat back down.

Then why did she ask me to stay after class?

"You missed a useless, but mandatory quiz. But I can't fail you."

"Ma'am I'm confused. I thought you said you weren't doing me any favors?"

"Like I said Manzo, I'm not doing you any favors. I'm passing you because you really can write."

"Uh, you like *my* writing?"

"I gave all your papers A's. I never put a grade, because I don't want you kids getting gassed."

Ha-ha, did she say 'gassed'?

"You gave *me* all A's ma'am?"

"Any professor would have. You have a lot of potential Manzo. Your writing is actually brilliant."

"*Brilliant?*"

"Young man look at me when I'm talking to you and stop acting all coy with me. You know you *think* you're brilliant, and that's precisely why I asked to speak with you after class."

"Uh, yes ma'am," I abided.

"And stop '*yes ma'aming*' me. Got a sister feeling all old and stuff." Ms. Giovanni shuffled her black wingtips. "I still got a lot of dancing left in me."

"No disrespect Ms. Giovanni."

"I know you can't help it Manzo." She smiled.

"Two things those folks at Woodberry Forest School showed you were how to be a gentleman and how to write."

"Yes Ms. Giovanni. Thank you. I guess they did. A.P. English still remains my hardest class ever." I smiled back.

"Yes, they did...but Harlem taught you some more *advanced placement* stuff that you brought back with you; I *hear*."

Wait.

What did she say?

"Harlem?" I asked.

"Yes, *Harlem* Manzo."

"Ms. Giovanni, I never played football in New York. I learned how to ball in Virginia, not Harlem."

"Manzo I'm not talking about any sports young man." Ms. Giovanni dropped her smile.

What the hell is she talking about?

"I don't know what you mean Ms. Giovanni."

"Oooh Ok, well it's good that you don't know what I mean then." She placed both hands on my desk and made direct eye contact.

"Because if you did—it would be my duty as a faculty member of Virginia Tech to go to straight to the proper authorities."

Oh my God! She knows!

Who's snitching?

Lie to her! Play dumb!

"Ms. Giovanni, I...don't—"

She subtly touched my quivering hand, and her cold gold rings rested between my knuckles.

My words flushed along with the blood from her face, leaving her pale with a mother's disappointment.

Her cheeks drooped down with her heart, and I was thoroughly riddled with shame and embarrassment. My eyes focused on her diamond stud earrings.

The scent of Oud dipped in strawberries obliterated my lies before they left my mouth. She was Nikki Giovanni, the woman I loved and respected as a teacher, leader, and a mentor.

I could *never* lie to Ms. Giovanni, but I couldn't tell her the truth either.

"Ms. Giovanni...I just want to get my degree and get far away from Virginia," I said.

"And when are you finished school Manzo?"

"I can attend the graduation ceremony next month, but I don't get my diploma until after I'm finished my second Summer session in August," I answered.

"Are you going to walk?"

"No ma'am, I mean—*Ms. Giovanni*. I'm not walking across anybody's stage. Makes no sense unless I'm done all the way. Not walking and then still have to take classes. Shit is, excuse me—*stuff* is lame."

"No, what's lame is for a bright-minded student to concentrate on *stuff* besides him or her attaining a college degree," she stated.

"What do you expect me to sit here and say Ms. Giovanni?"

Don't admit to shit!

"Oh young man, I don't expect you to say anything, I just hope that you listen."

Keep your mouth closed!

"So now what Ms. Giovanni?" I asked.

You are talking too much! Who ratted me out?

"Nothing I suppose. If I repeated every campus *rumor* I heard about students then I might as well be a damn parrot and not a professor. Kids love to talk about nonsense." She walked to her desk, put both hands in her pockets, and turned around.

"Now, if you had admitted to anything, then yes, I would be obligated to do the right thing *immediately*—but you didn't."

"I just want to get my degree and get out of Virginia." I shook my head.

"I hear that and that's a great idea—but on the flip-side young man, if an *old* lady who minds her business like me has heard some *stuff*, then chances are many others have also."

"Why do you say that?" I fidgeted in my seat.

Only my friends know I sell coke!

"Well this is a conversation I'm not going to have with you since the rumors aren't *true*. Just know Manzo, that this is Blacksburg, and everybody knows everybody's business. So if only one person knows your business, then that's one person too many in this town."

Shit! She's right!

I must leave town!

"Why are we discussing these rumors then Ms. Giovanni?" I asked.

"Besides me doing my just-duty to protect the students of this great university, you remind me of another beautiful Black boy we lost not too long ago who was dear to my heart.

"And I think that if someone may have talked to him like I'm talking to you, just maybe he would've changed his life and made some different decisions." She wiped the dampness from the corner of her eyes and started rolling up her left sleeve.

I thought she didn't have kids. Is she wearing a wire?

Is Ms. Giovanni the police?

"Who Ms. Giovanni?" I asked.

"You know him—well...you *knew* him." She pointed to the tattoo on her left forearm. "Tupac Shakur."

"*Thug-life*! Oh man! You have 'Thug-Life' tattooed on your forearm!"

I love this woman!

"Yes, I got it when that beautiful Black boy was assassinated."

"I love Tupac. He's my favorite rapper of all time and I listen to him every single day. But why do you say he was assassinated Ms. Giovanni?"

"You just told me why," she said.

"I did? How?"

"You just said that you listened to Tupac every day, and he's been gone for three years." Ms. Giovanni caressed the tattoo with her fingers. "He's still teaching us from the grave, just like Malcolm and Martin."

"So true, but I'm not on either of those guys' level," I admitted.

"And this is very true Manzo, but you see, sometimes it takes a bad situation to help a person find his way and his true calling. We make mistakes to find ourselves."

"But we all make mistakes Ms. Giovanni, but that doesn't mean we all are great men like Tupac and them."

"Again, you are correct, but you forget that I'm only talking about you. I've read your papers and observed you in class. You don't see how you affect the people around you. They listen—and they follow you.

"Just look at how the fellas dress in class. They all copy *you*, down to how you skip a hole with your shoestrings when you tie your tennis shoes." She grinned, and I looked down at my Jordan's."

Relax. Breathe.

You gonna be OK.

"Some people got *it*, and *it* you can't teach. God gives us gifts, and some are more transparent than others. Besides writing, your gifts are your charisma and charm amongst other things—the girls stare at you all class Manzo. Trust me, I'm a woman. I see them little hot-in-the-pants girls watching you.

"Young man, you have a calling and it's not too late to tap into that potential. Be a writer. Be anything you want—just be positive.

"Just know there are consequences for your actions. This is the wrong place to be playing with these people.

"Shoot, just sixty years ago, they were lynching folks here. These folks aren't going to let anyone come in this town and be a Cancer to these college kids— and they shouldn't.

"So please listen when I tell you that *if* you are doing anything you're not supposed to be doing, then please stop. You are too bright. Break the cycle Manzo. Because there's too many young gifted brothers like yourself wasting their talents chasing a bunch of nothing. You have powers. Use them for good. Use them *only* for good Manzo."

Chapter Twenty-Five

SICK DAY

Summer Session had started a couple of weeks earlier, but I had yet to attend any classes because of my paranoia after my meeting with Ms. Giovanni. Everywhere I went, I looked over my shoulder, and I felt like I was being watched.

Every White person I saw, I thought was a cop. The more money I made, the more I was afraid of everyone, and my drug use had become out of control.

With Dirt having to stay in New York for a while to maintain his Harlem operation, I delegated the day-to-day business to Aaron and Biscuit.

They were two Roanoke dealers that I met at Big Al's, who had been buying coke from me for the past few months.

Aaron and Biscuit were hungry, so I let them control Blacksburg and the surrounding counties as I expanded my business to Roanoke where they knew all the dealers in their area.

Business was doing extremely well, and I had a solid team—but I still needed Dirt.

Dirt and I would talk every week on pre-paid cell phones that we would destroy after each conversation.

We would send our new numbers in a typed letter to a P.O. Box in the Bronx, and another in Christiansburg, Virginia.

We bought a house in Northwest Roanoke to hide the drugs and money, that only Aaron, Biscuit, Dirt, and I knew about.

I never kept any coke at my place in Blacksburg beside the *small* quantity I kept for personal use.

Every two weeks the *connect* would send a different Spanish girl to Roanoke with twenty kilos, and I would give her $300,000 for the *connect* and $50,000 for Dirt, and after paying the workers—the rest went to me.

Dirt's percentage had decreased since he wasn't around, but he never complained. $50,000 was a nice payout for just pushing buttons.

Although I enjoyed the extra money and had splurged on a few luxury items, I would have rather had my partner in the trenches with me.

After losing my baby and my girl, manning a million-dollar cocaine enterprise while chasing a college degree was becoming too much to handle.

Since the abortion, Brittney and I met once, had farewell sex, and never talked again. She graduated last month and moved to Arlington, Virginia, to manage the Nordstrom at the Tyson's Corner Mall. I missed her dearly.

Jane had been my support system, but she moved back home for the summer, leaving me with a few choice head-monsters for sporadic blowjobs just to break the monotony of masturbating to porn during my isolated cocaine benders.

I would cry for hours thinking about Brittney while one, two, or sometimes even three girls at once snorted blow off my cock. The girls took turns, while home movies of Brittney and me projected on my living room wall.

Friday nights were normally when I started my shenanigans with the girls, but I was too afraid to open my front door for anyone.

So, I locked myself in my townhouse with an ounce of blow, ten packs of Newports cigarettes, an ounce of Hydro weed, two liters of Jack Daniel's, a lighter, blunts, a loaded chrome .44 Magnum, and absolutely nothing or no one to eat.

It was now Sunday, and I had been up for two days straight.

With both cell phones, a Nokia and a Motorola, on my kitchen counter next to the party supplies and my gun, I had everything I needed downstairs—because I spent most of the weekend on my kitchen floor.

Too unhinged to go upstairs, I crept around my home in a pair of maroon VT shorts, and barefoot like a thief—jumping at every single noise, searching the same three closets for intruders, watching for shadows passing by my blinds, and staring out of my peephole for hours at a time.

The .44 Magnum remained either in my hand or within arm's reach, and I didn't answer my phone or talk to anyone until Dirt called.

RING. RING.

Fuck its Dirt! Don't answer!

RING. RING.

You have to answer!

He's gonna know I'm coked up!

RING. RING.

Answer the fucking phone! Act normal!

Breathe!

"What's up Dirt?" I spoke into the Motorola after pressing the speaker button.

"What up my nigga?"

"Everything good," I replied.

"Them thangs should be over there tomorrow and that should last us for a couple of weeks. It's a little more," he said.

You hear that?

"Cool Dirt, because we *definitely* need more. I got the 300 racks here for your peoples, and the fifty money orders—a rack a piece for you."

What's that sound?

"Great shit. A nigga needs that!" Dirt said.

"All day bro. You know you can count on your boy until you can get back down here." I lit a Newport. "We still killing shit."

They coming to get me!

I can't get locked up!

"Manzo...you OK my nigga?"

"I'm good—why you asking?"

He knows! Act normal!

"You don't sound like yourself. You sound hoarse as hell. You *sure* you OK?"

No, they're coming to get me! What's that sound?

"No worries Dirt."

My throat kills!

"You sound congested and you sniffing like a motherfucker. You better not be down there fucking with that shit my nigga. You know we don't get down like *that* bro!"

"*Me?*" I pressed mute on the phone and snorted one of ten lines next to the half-drank liter of Jack Daniels, and an astray on my kitchen counter—between a black stove and an empty chrome sink.

Fuck, my nose is raw!

"Yea you! Who else would I be talking to?" Dirt asked.

They coming to get me!

"I'm good. Stop worrying. It's June. You know I get them allergies," I replied after unmuting my cell.

Someone's at my door!

"Aight, if you say so. August is around the corner.

"You get that diploma, and we heading the fuck outta Dodge, and then you can kick your feet up. Don't get caught up and get a habit, *no bueno* Manzo."

Who's that at the door? You hear that?

"We only smoke weed. No cancer sticks. No blow. We got this," I assured and muted the phone again, ripping another line of cocaine.

Check the front door! No stay right here!

"OK good my nigga. That's what I like to hear. How's Aaron and Biscuit?"

Check the front door!

"They good bro. They're keeping these fools in check over here and doing crazy numbers in Roanoke," I replied. "Our new spot was brilliant."

"Hello?" Dirt shouted.

Un-mute the phone!

"I'm here! Sorry, just drank this Theraflu."

"I thought you disappeared," he joked.

What's that noise upstairs? They're coming!

"I'm here." I mashed the Newport into the ashtray with the other fourteen or so butts. "But like I said, Aaron and Biscuit are killing it. The new spot was perfect. Smooth sailing from here."

What's that sound?

Who's in my house?

"Good shit. I know I haven't met them yet, but do you really trust them though?"

"Yea, they're official. They're making mad money. Glad I made them a part of the team. Aaron is my nigga, and Biscuit may be White, but she's hood as fuck. She's that bitch. No question, I trust them," I said.

Who's there?

Tiptoeing out of the kitchen to my front door, I slowly pressed a twitching right eye to the peephole, and again, no one was there.

As I listened to a mixture of my heart thudding and cars riding by, I stared at the only visible object, a townhouse ten yards away.

Sweat dribbled down my forehead and into my eye, but I didn't dare blink. I feared that the second I unclouded my vision that *someone* would knock down my door.

Show your fucking face! I know you there!

Oh God help me please!

"OK that's dope! As long as you're vouching for them, then I'm good, but don't sleep on them niggas. Stay on point 'cuz this a dirty game bruh. One minute they're your homies and the next they're pointing a finger at you in court," Dirt ministered, instilling a deeper panic.

They're coming!

Calm down!

"Uh...we cool Dirt. Uuuh, I will hit you after our peoples drop by. Love you bro," I uttered and finally blinked.

Save your brother Dirt! They're coming to get me!

"Cool my nigga. Take care of that cold and be safe. Two more months Manzo —oh yea and wait until I show you *my* new whips. Love you. Later." Dirt hung up.

Don't go Dirt! I'm in trouble!

They're coming to get me! Go turn off the phone!

Cautiously backing away from the door, I turned right and took three steps to the kitchen counter, pressing the power button on the trap phone.

My heart beat faster than I had ever recalled, and I briefly feared getting a heart attack, but I feared being sober more. I grabbed the $100 bill and inhaled another line.

What's that noise? Somebody's at the door! My heart hurts!

Fuck your heart! Check the door!

Placing my right hand over my heart, I returned to the door as my hand attempted to smother the palpitations.

Drenched in perspiration and stench, I wiped my face with my soiled wife-beater and positioned my left eye on the peephole.

Instantly, I saw a bald, middle-aged White man with a long, straight nose, shaggy goatee, and wearing a pair of black Oakley sunglasses—look at my door momentarily before passing.

Impulsively, I dropped to the floor with my back against the door and clutched both legs against my chest with fastened fingers.

Who's that?

I told you they were coming! I gotta get outta here!

They're here! Oh God no!

My chest heaved, and I wheezed pure agony from lungs lacquered with thick layers of mint smoke.

Fighting for air, I blew my nose on the tail of my wife-beater—discharging a heavy gel of white death and blood clots.

The homeless smell steaming from my underarms and loins viciously snapped my snout, and I tasted a mixture of cigarette soot, and a Port Authority bathroom-stall.

I gotta leave! You can't leave! Call Dirt!

No don't call Dirt!

Call Mommy and say goodbye!

Laying on my stomach, I slithered to the kitchen like a snail harmed from a hiker's heel.

I left behind a trail of snot and blood, and crazily clawed the counter for the first cell phone I could reach.

Weary eyes, red and lit with ether watched the window while the coke calcified the fear in my suffering heart. I was out of breath and almost out of time. My sodden right hand finally trapped my phone.

718...

Please God! Mommy be home!

555...

God I need my mom!

1225...

Make her answer this motherfucking phone!

Please oh Lord in heaven!

Please don't let them take me!

RING. RING.

Your little boy needs you!

RING. RING.

The Nokia slipped through my slimy trembling fingers and fell on my lap. Quickly, I picked up the phone, pressed *speaker*, and positioned the phone at the edge of the counter.

Forgetting that I had just used my wife-beater as a Kleenex, I dried my face with it, streaking blood and mucous across my forehead and mouth.

Oblivious to the tang of iron and anguish, I waited to hear if God was listening.

RING.

"Hello?" Mommy finally answered, and I wept from the sound of her voice.

"Hey...hello," I spoke through a clenched jaw.

"Uuh, who's this?"

"It's me Mommy."

"*Manzo?*" she asked.

"Yes Mommy."

"What's wrong son? And who number is this?"

"This is my other phone Mommy."

"Talk to me son. What's wrong? Why are you crying baby? Did someone hurt you?"

"Mommy...they're coming to get me."

"*Who's* coming to get you?" she asked before yelling to her new husband. "Eugene turn that motherfucking TV down! It's Manzo, my son!"

Please help me!

I'm worse than my father!

"Mommy I'm scared! There's a man coming to take me away!"

What's that noise? It's him!

"Son stop crying and breathe. I can't help you unless you talk to me."

"OK I will try!"

"That's right Manzo...just breathe. It's going to be OK. You don't sound good, and you sound far away. Where are you?"

What's that noise?

"I just want to make you proud and graduate," I cried.

"You do make me proud baby. I'm very proud of you, but I need to know where you are Manzo?"

"I'm in hell Mommy...and I can't get out."

The phone went silent and even as fucked up I was, I knew Mommy had begun to cry, but she didn't want to show the agony I was putting her through.

She was a rock. She was *my* rock, but there's always a point when a mother's tears would fall.

After a few seconds, with a voice struggling not to crack, Mommy proceeded to walk me through the fire with hopes that the young man she had raised would rise again.

I can't go to prison!

She needs me!

"Manzo, how much drugs have you done?"

"I don't know Mommy."

"OK Manzo. I need to know where you are son. You are alive and have air in your lungs and can survive anything. You are not in hell. Where are you, *my* son?"

"I'm on my kitchen floor Mommy. I don't want to let them in! I can't go to prison! I just can't!"

That's him at my door!

I can hear him breathing! Oh shit, I have to run!

"OK just breathe. I need you to stand up and look out of your window son."

"Noooo—I can't! I have to run from *him*!" I screamed.

"Breathe Manzo. Nobody's coming to get you. I understand you're scared. Just stand up for your mother and look out your window. I'm right here."

Don't do it!

He will see you!

Get the fuck up!

"OK...I'm getting up for you Mommy."

"And when you get up...just go look out of the window and tell me what you see son. Just tell me what you see. I'm right here baby."

"OK, I'm standing up Mommy."

I glanced at the lines of blow, impulsively licking blood from my lips before half-turning left and peeking through the blinds. The natural light momentarily blinded me.

I squinted to refocus and find out whether the man I saw, or any other enemy was outside of my home.

I don't see anything. But he could be hiding!

"OK baby, what do you see?" Mommy asked.

"I just see grass and a red Schwinn bike on the grass, and the other town-houses in front of my crib."

But they're out there waiting Mommy!

"OK, look to your left son. What do you see?"

"I see a parking lot. A parking lot with just two cars. A black Escalade...and a Benz...oh, and a motorcycle—a yellow Ducati. That's it Mommy."

"Manzo...do you really see *those* vehicles?"

"Yea Mommy, they're right in my parking spots."

Mommy didn't speak for a few moments, and I didn't have a clue why not. She could've either been crying again or assessing the situation better from her end to help me get through this ordeal.

Brain fried, I couldn't think straight and never realized that I had just given Mommy a visual of *my* new whips.

As far as my family was concerned, I didn't own a car and had been riding a bike to school since Brittney and I ended things. A hustler's ex-wife, Mommy pieced the puzzle together in a matter of seconds.

She's right. No one is there. Breathe and relax.

Do another line. Now!

"Son, I want you to listen to me...and listen to me good. OK?"

Do the line!

"Yes Mommy," I agreed while rolling the $100 bill tightly as I spoke. "I'm listening."

Left nostril? Right nostril? Both!

"I don't know exactly what you're doing, but it doesn't take Perry Mason to figure things out. You're sending Matthew over here with all this money for me, and I appreciate it.

"But I know where it comes from and I don't want any of it. Your brother Jason is only three years old, and I don't want him witnessing this mess.

"Eugene has a good, *legal* job, and I love that Jason can see hard work from his father, because my other kids only know fast money.

"Y'all were too damn spoiled. And now you're using and selling that shit. *Come home*, because this mess you got yourself in will only get worse son.

"I'm begging you my child—you're *not* your father. You're better than him —*and* you are setting a terrible example for Javier and Alejandro.

"They follow whatever you do, and I'm scared for them. They already spending the money you send them like water while fronting for these no-good niggas around here.

"Manzo, I love you, and I need you to listen to your mama. Those White folks aren't playing with your Black ass. You need to pack your shit and get the hell out of Virginia. Leave immediately son!"

I snorted two rails of blow, guzzled some Jack Daniels before placing the liquor bottle back on the kitchen counter.

"Manzo stop putting that shit up your nose and listen to meeee!" Mommy wailed.
They are coming!
I can hear them! They are back!
He's back! Run!
"It's my medicine Mommy—I need it! They're coming! I can hear them!"
"No they are not son! The drugs are killing your brain!"
My heart hurts!
"I want to die! Mommy, I want to be with my baby!"
"What *baby* son?"
Do another line!
"Get out of my fucking head! Aaaaaahhh!" I roared.
Do another line!
"What baby? Who's in your head Manzo?"
I want to die! Do another line! Kill yourself!
"I'm not going to prison! I'm going to hell to find my baby!" I snorted another two lines of coke.
"Manzo! Stop! Please stop!" Mommy cried hysterically.
Grab the gun!
Kill him when he comes!
"I can't stop! He's after me Mommy!" I cried with her.
"Oh my God son, I let you down—"
"Mommy I'm ending all this!"
Grab the fucking gun!
"No son—"

"They're not taking me!" I tossed the bill and lifted the .44 from behind the liquor bottle.

He's at the door!

"Eugene come help me please!" Mommy shouted.

"Bye Mommy—"

"Manzo nooooo—"

"Sorry Mommy...I tried—"

"Wait...wait! Son don't gooo—"

SMASH!

I pitched the trap phone into the wall, shattering the phone into several flying pieces.

Wounded tears skid down my cheeks, and crimson spots speckled the top of my wife-beater. The cocaine had scooped my organs, hollowing my trembling soul.

Defeated, I hoisted the .44 and pushed the cold, long-barrel under my chin. A bucking pulse pushed back, but I felt nothing.

I tickled the trigger with no fear of making the gun laugh.

I'm not gonna let them take me away! I gotta do this!

Too late Mommy!

I love you!

BUZZ.

My Motorola vibrated, and I had immediately thought it was my mother until I remembered that she only had my home number. I ripped the house phone out of the wall the first day into my bender.

I was a suicidal savage, but I was still curious. I needed to know who was calling before I splattered my brains all over my kitchen's walls. I grabbed my phone with a free left hand, holding the gun *steady* in the other.

BUZZ.

Brittney?

BUZZ.

Answer the phone! Then shoot yourself!

BUZZ.

"Hello Brittney," I whispered.

"I'm just a little *sick* right now. How are you?"

"OK cool. Let me call you back Brittney. OK...bye."

Did someone call her?

At first, I thought that Mommy or another family member may have called and told Brittney of how severe my derangement had become, but no one could've possibly contacted her. No one knew Brittney's information.

There were no worries or concerns in Brittney's voice or tone. She seemed genuinely disappointed in having to hear me breathe.

The nature of her call was purely informative, sans passion or interest, and I knew she wished she didn't have to contact me.

She *tried* living a life without ever seeing my face again, but her new affliction doubled as my savior. I had to keep living. The stakes of my existence had just been raised dramatically.

The irony of life guided my hand, and I gently lowered the hunkering metal and settled the gun and phone on the counter.

Cocaine still flourishing in my system, I sat on the kitchen floor chugging liquor, smoking weed and cigarettes until my high mellowed enough to call Mommy, to apologize, and to repeat Brittney's message verbatim.

"I'm pregnant—and I'm keeping it."

Chapter Twenty-Six

LAST CRUMB

August 6, 2000, a week away from my last final exam *ever*—I was on edge and nervous. Although nearing its end, our operation was soaring, along with my neurosis and the cocaine up my nose.

I only trusted Dirt and had begun to think that Aaron had been stealing from me, but I had no proof or justification as to why I would think that about him.

He was a good kid, and an outstanding earner—but he had a little too much ambition.

Aaron had expressed his disapproval of my plan to leave Virginia without having introduced Biscuit or him to the *connect*, so I said they could have the Roanoke house when I left school as consolation.

I paid $174,000 in cash, under an alias to a crooked realtor in the area; therefore, I had zero concerns about the home being traced back to Dirt or me.

I figured Aaron would've appreciated the gesture as much as Biscuit did, but he *needed* the connect and the bitching persisted, so I sweetened the deal and gave Aaron my Escalade to keep.

I would have given up all the materialistic items I had, before I vouched for a single soul once I left town. Plus, unknowingly to Aaron and Biscuit, Dirt was my connect.

As soon as the last deal was done, Dirt and I were done. Never wanting to return to Virginia, Dirt would go back to New York. I would only return to take my final exams, and then I would go back to Brittney and the baby. Game over.

Brittney was four-months pregnant and living modestly in a discreet two-bedroom apartment, in Oxon Hill, Maryland, just outside of Washington, D.C.—not too far from Reese Malone and his family in Annapolis.

I moved her in the vicinity to the Malone family, because I needed someone to look after Brittney while I was away working.

She had become really close with them, and I truly appreciated how my extended family adored Brittney and supported me.

No one knew me in Oxon Hill, so I figured Brittney and I could lay low until she had the baby. With a Virginia Tech degree and a shit load of paper, we could move anywhere in the world.

I had found beautiful homes in Paris, Los Angeles, and Austin, Texas—all within my financial means, but I should've included drug rehabs in my search for a new place and contentment.

A *functioning* addict, I figured that my drug habit would die naturally when I no longer had *easy* access to cocaine. If I weren't around people with blow, I couldn't do blow.

Although cocaine could be bought in any city, the plan seemed logical, but my priorities weren't.

More attentive to my pockets than my sobriety, I thoroughly planned my escape from the Commonwealth while I envisioned a better life for not just myself, but also my loved ones.

The *connect* had already received his final payment, so the only business left was for Dirt and me to split the final profits after paying Biscuit and Aaron, and we would all go our separate ways.

My mother and siblings wouldn't have to work for anyone again, my pops would retire, and my drug dealing days would be just another entertaining story to tell around the campfire.

$189,800

$189,900

$190,000

That's it?

"Aaron, what the fuck is going on?" I asked as I threw rubber-band-stacks of cash in a duffle bag. "It supposed to be $200,000, it's ten-fucking-racks short. Where's the rest?"

This is my last run!

Shit can't fuck up!

In my West Vale Road, duplex home in Northeast Roanoke, Aaron took a swing from a bottle of Hennessy in between pulls of his Marlboro cigarette.

Coked-up, he fidgeted in one of four red La-Z-Boy recliners encircling a glass coffee table in the living room, ten feet to the right of the kitchen.

Never making eye contact, Aaron replied, "Chill Manzo! Biscuit got mad work left at her crib! It will all add up, trust me!"

Glaring at him, I gritted my teeth and shook my head. I immediately pinched the mini straw off the glass coffee table and punished a line of blow.

Images of me cracking Aaron's skull with a bat, a hammer, or any blunt object flashed across my mind as my nostrils burned with vengeance.

Fucking liar! Trust you?

Nigga, I will bash your peezy-ass head to a pulp!

"Whatever! Get up and roll a blunt while I pack my shit!" I demanded. "Biscuit will be here any minute, so hurry the fuck up!"

"Aight *Boss*," he muttered, but I was already in the kitchen with the duffle bag.

Standing in the center of the kitchen, I had forgotten my purpose for being there. The coke cuddled my rationale as my mind sprinted through the possibilities.

My eyeballs oscillated until I discovered a thick piece of metal sticking out between the wall and the refrigerator.

Three swift steps and I yanked the crowbar from the refrigerator's side. Paint chips fell to the floor. The fifteen-pound key was mine.

Turning around, I bent down on one knee and jammed the crowbar in between the center marble tile.

I pried the tile open, slid it over, exposing the Secure Paragon safe. I was sweating like a thief.

The safe's neon blue security numbers watched me. Normally, I would get excited and eager to make a deposit in *El Banco De Manzo*, but I felt extremely nervous and anxious.

Normally, I wasn't coked up either, so I quickly dismissed the notion that anything was abnormal besides my heartbeat.

Everything is OK.

What's the code?

"Nine...twenty-five...fifty-five," I whispered to myself, Daddy's birthday.

"The blunt's rolled! What's going on?" Aaron yelled from the living room. "It never takes you that long to—"

"Would you please shut up?" I screamed. "I'm opening the shit now!"

Nine...twenty-five...fifty-five—

CLICK.

The safe hissed as the door popped opened.

The serpent's belly was empty except for a few fake ID's with my face on them, in the event I ever had to go on the run from the police.

Feeding time; I dumped the cash inside and closed its mouth. Stuffed, the cold-blooded monster had no room for dessert.

Tile returned; I stood up and was face to face with Aaron. My heart stopped.

No one was ever to be near me when I opened the safe. Only Dirt and I knew the code, and we changed it every week.

The parts of my brain soaked in blow told me to pick up the crowbar, the other parts said to chill. Aaron spoke before I counted all the votes.

"Relax my brother," he said calmly. "I know you're jacked up, so I brought you over the blunt."

Stare down.

How long was he standing there? Did he see the code?

Aaron's eyes shifted from left to right as if my eyeballs were a computer screen and displayed my thoughts.

His trembling hand had held the marijuana in front of my face, but I never noticed. All I smelled was ether. All I saw was deception.

The white horse galloping around my mind demanded I kill him, and I never disobeyed an order.

You can't trust him!

I glanced down at the crowbar. Aaron glanced down at the crowbar. I looked back up. Aaron looked back up.

Kill him!

Aaron was more than my lieutenant. He was the Godfather to my entire operation. If something ever happened to me, he was responsible for the welfare of my *baby*. Could I really trust him though?

He made plenty of money, but he wasn't making *my* type of money, and I was the six feet, 250-pound roadblock between him and the startup money for a million-dollar business.

Friendship could last a lifetime. Greed lasted a little longer.

Looking at Aaron, I had begun to examine the face of my *friend.*

He had thick, dark eyebrows, and a scar on his forehead that matched a scar on his cheek, which he got when he was ten years old in a car accident.

His lips, never fully closed, exposed a chipped tooth from a fight when he was twelve—while his perfectly even hairline and lack of facial hair were contributions from his father.

The cocaine controlled my calculations, and my brain didn't compute that Aaron's closeness was how I knew so much about him. All I saw was the genetic make-up of a human being.

Humans couldn't be trusted. Aaron was human. Aaron couldn't be trusted. Aaron must be terminated.

Kill him now before he kills you!

Grab the crowbar and bash his head, now!

I smiled.

He smiled.

Picturing Aaron's split forehead spewing brain matter, I began to breathe like a midget sprinter, short and fast.

I couldn't speak a word. Death locked my jaw, and murder widened my eyes shut. I had to kill him.

My right hand reached up for the blunt as my left arm covertly inched toward the crowbar. His eyes said *don't try it*, but his sigh of relief said that he knew he was almost lunchmeat.

You can't trust him! Either him or you!

I grabbed the blunt and unlocked my mouth to say, "Sorry Aaron."

Now!

I didn't wait to see Aaron's confused expression before I turned to swiftly pick up the crowbar, but suddenly there was a loud bang that granted his stay of execution.

BOOM! BOOM!

"Open up the goddamn door y'all!" Biscuit blared. "I know y'all hear me!"

Oh shit, it's Biscuit!

Walking to the door, I didn't know if the hard pounding came from my chest or the door. Biscuit scared the hell out of me.

Being just seconds away from rearranging the structure of Aaron's forehead, I perspired heavily, and my legs tremored with each step.

When I reached the door, I felt 20/20 vision drilling the back of my head. I turned around and Aaron looked very disturbed and confused, almost childlike.

Either someone had just told him that there was no Santa Claus, or he knew his turkey almost got stuffed. Lucky bastard must have been nice that year.

"Why did you say that you were sorry Manzo?" Aaron had *Tiny-Tim'ed*.

Feeling awful, I just shook my head and said, "It's nothing bro. The blow got a nigga a little paranoid—"

BOOM! BOOM!

"Open up this motherfucking door Manzo!" Biscuit demanded.

"Calm the fuck down Biscuit!" I ordered as I unlocked the door.

Before I turned the doorknob, I peeped at Aaron who hadn't moved.

Water filled his big eyes, and I could see he was a blink away from officially crying. He wasn't a fool—there was no Santa Claus.

Turning the doorknob, I watched Aaron hit the blunt, and I apologized, "We good homie. I'm just fucked up–"

"What the hell is going on?" Biscuit burst through the door, nearly knocking me to the floor.

"Get your shit! We only have twenty-one minutes until your train leaves, and I have to run to my crib real fast to get my license!"

In tight blue jeans, a pair of white Reebok Classics, and a black cotton t-shirt that stretched out at her breasts, almost as far as at her protruding belly—Biscuit had appeared very disheveled.

She was pink-faced and sweaty, with her dark yellow, frizzled micro-braids cornrowed to the middle of her broad back.

Her fleshy cheeks were covered with new acne, and her Green Jolly Rancher eyes, were now apple-cider brown.

She loved to rock green contacts, gaudy gold bangle earrings, a gold nose ring, diamond rings on her thumbs, and a chunky herringbone chain between chunkier chins—but all her accessories were missing, including her platinum Rolex Sea-Dweller and Coach bag.

Heavyset with a countrified flare, she never left home without the flashy distractions from her weight. Biscuit's rawness was exorbitantly odd.

Extremely insecure, she had rather people focus on her style than her stout body and pale "she has a good personality" face.

Biscuit detested being overweight, almost as much she did being under-colored, and if she were granted three wishes—they would've been to be Black, skinny, and Black.

Cognizant of how much Biscuit lived to impress, I was surprised by her appearance, but I passed on playing fashion police because I was too high and thrown off by her unusual behavior.

I needed to get the hell out of Roanoke as quickly and safely as possible without any fuckups, and her idea of going home didn't seem like a bright one, although Biscuit always triumphed under duress.

I was confused, and I needed her to clarify her moves.

"License? Hold up. Why do *you* need your license Biscuit?" I asked.

"Manzo, I don't want to get stopped by the cops and not have it on me," she pleaded.

"What sense does it make to drive seven minutes to your place when the Amtrak station is in the opposite direction, *five* minutes from here?" Aaron interrupted.

Biscuit eyed Aaron, sucking her teeth. His question obviously annoyed her.

Opening her mouth, she looked back at me—but no words were spoken.

A few seconds had passed, and the mute still had not spoken. I took a toke of the bud, inadvertently blew smoke in her face, and waited for Biscuit to say something.

Bitch, you better say start talking.

Fanning the smoke, she began her testimonial, "Uh, listen I still have to drive home from the train station, and I ain't trying to get pulled over on the way back!"

What the hell is going on tonight?

For months Manzo's *Law* had been obeyed without compromise, and within thirty minutes I already had both, Aaron and Biscuit, attempting to rewrite two commandments:

1. Thou shall stay the fuck away from Manzo when he's at the safe.
2. Thou shall drive Manzo straight to the train station.

Simple.

Rules had to be followed.

There were millions of people in prison or dead simply because they did not stick to the designed plan. I had a family to feed and land to conquer, so there was not the slightest bit of room for mishaps or negligence.

"Biscuit you know the rules!" I said. "You supposed to be on point and have your license and be ready to take me *straight* to the train!"

"Manzo I know, I'm sorry—but we still have time babe! Let's go before—" she pleaded.

"Fuck that, I will drive you Manzo!" Aaron demanded.

"Nooooo!" she shrieked.

Silence.

What's happening here?

My mind raised its hand. Instantly, I felt *something* was off and my gut had all the answers.

Always punctual and very efficient, Biscuit had remained the one constant in our organization. When Aaron and I were off getting high and screwing strippers from the Gold & Silver Club, she was bagging coke, calling dealers, and counting dollars.

She never made mistakes, and her value was in her precision. Her precision was our foundation. Without Biscuit, our cake would crumble, and Aaron understood the severity of the situation.

"Yoooo Biscuit, you're scaring me. What is going on?" he asked as he began rubbing her back.

"I...I..." she stammered in between sobs.

"You better fucking say something!" I barked.

"I got my fuckin' *period*—you assholes!" she roared. "I have had the day from hell!"

"My hormones are going bonkers shawty, and all I want to do is get you safely to the *damn* train station and I lost track of time, so I am a lil' fuckin' hard on myself! I would die if anything ever happened to you Manzo!" she continued to protest.

"Aaron is all whacked and cannot get you there with the quickness like I can! So please grab your bags and give me a fuckin' break before I lose it shawty!"

Period?

Oh shit.

Of course.

Biscuit was a solid performer who always put the team first. I could always trust her to do the right thing when no one was looking.

I believed her. I believed in her.

Only the mystical powers of a woman's period could explain her uncharacteristic behavior. We solved the riddle. She was not being shady. She was just being a bitch. Women.

Shaking my head nonchalantly, I caressed my temples with both hands and glanced at Aaron. Our disgruntled expressions steadily transformed into smiles, our smiles into laughter. We laughed, hard.

"Fuck you cokehead-ass-motherfuckers! This shit ain't funny!" she said, before giggling to herself. "Y'all ain't shit!"

Relighting the hydroponics, I puffed and passed it to her before I snatched my Prada suitcase off the couch.

Normally the sweetest, she was very bitter when she bled. I had hoped that the weed would bake the monster, and only my Biscuit would remain.

I didn't want to travel alone with a crazy lady, but it was already too late for her to leave the village.

"Let's go Manzo!" Biscuit said as she passed the blunt to Aaron. "Move ya ass shawty!"

"OK, OK!" I said.

"And Aaron, don't forget to tell Dirt to give us the combo to the safe when he gets here tomorrow!" she reminded.

Damn, I almost forgot!

"Oh yea," I added dryly as we walked out of the door, never saying goodbye to Aaron.

Guilt handicapped my paranoia, and I felt bad that I didn't trust Aaron—but I still did not trust him.

Before opening the door to her candy-apple-red 1987 Oldsmobile Cutlass Supreme, Biscuit smirked and asked, "What would you ever do without me?"

Placing my suitcase on the back seat, I replied, "I don't know. You're the only one around here I can trust babe."

* * *

The Virginia breeze always smelled fresh with a hint of a better today, and a smidgen of a greater tomorrow. Optimism in the state for lovers was not a choice —it was the way of life.

Nothing ever seemed to go wrong, well, for me at least. The most juvenile plan could be executed without fault and earn thousands daily.

Far from a mastermind, I just followed the instructions which read, "Step 1: Shoot fish in barrel," but for some reason—I felt like I was out of bullets.

As we cruised down Orange Avenue and headed to Sixteenth Street Northwest, I opened the window to get a whiff of hope—the odor of dead skunk killed my dreams. I closed the window and slightly lowered the volume on Project Pat's "Cheese and Dope."

I was nervous and needed affirmation that I was just a coke-filled wreck, and nothing was actually wrong. My ace, Biscuit, always had the answers.

"Biscuit," I called as I tapped her leg twice.

"Wassup Manzo?" she replied after sucking her teeth.

"Why you turned down the song?" she asked, restarting the song and raising the volume.

"All right, All right, that's loud enough!" I said. "I want us to be able to talk without screaming at each other!"

"OK my bad. Is that good right there?" She asked.

"Yes—perfect babe. You know Pat's that nigga, but you gonna give me even more fucking anxiety."

"Ha-ha, *and* you know we ain't tryna do that my nigga."

Why this bitch always saying 'nigga'?

"Let me ask you a question, but first stop saying nigga," I demanded. "Shit ain't cool at all. Talk like you have some goddamn sense babe."

"Oh my bad shawty!" she apologized. "Talk to me. You know it stays right here. You are *my* baby."

* * *

Biscuit and I were more than just business associates. We were partners bonded by our common greed to own the Commonwealth.

Yes, she worked for me, but I totally considered her an equal.

In Roanoke City, almost no one knew that I supplied most of the cocaine pumped to the streets. I was the heart. Biscuit was the blood.

Our tandem, combined with the quality of the product—made us unstoppable.

Besides selling cocaine by the gram, we now sold weight—anything from an eight ball to entire kilos could be purchased at *wholesale* prices.

The blow was so pure and affordable that fiends, as well as, dealers from as far as Tennessee trekked to the Star City for a taste of my Manhattan medicine. Nurse Biscuit helped heal the suffering, while I counted the money.

Perfection.

Aaron had always been jealous of her and my relationship, and never quite grasped why she outranked him. He assumed that when a woman got a promotion over a man, she was fucking the boss.

Biscuit and I NEVER had sex or had ever been sexual, but Aaron was a typical male and believed otherwise.

Aaron's ignorance and envy outpaced his intelligence as he insisted on referring to Biscuit as my *girlfriend*—until one night while we were blowing rails, and I corrected him.

I put my SIG Sauer P320 to his neck and said, "Nigga, get it right. Her name is Biscuit!" Aaron agreed. *Biscuit* would suffice.

Spending most of my time with Biscuit, I understood his assumption of my friendship with her. Aaron was far from being wildly inaccurate—he was just inappropriate.

A good soldier kept his opinions to himself, followed orders, and never challenged the decisions of a higher-up, especially a general. The penalty could be death.

I didn't want Biscuit; I already had a girlfriend. Brittney's dedication to our union branded my heart.

Knowing I was miles away and ushering demons to hell, Brittney complied with my sins—although she never agreed with them.

With every moon Brittney prayed for my protection and food on our plate. Torn, she enabled my madness, because she knew to challenge my insanity would lead to my disappearance.

I was going to do what I wanted anyway, and it was less torturous to support me and pray than to dismiss me and weep.

Faithful and stupid, Brittney personified countless women in love.

Her love attempted to glue our destinies, while my love only stuck to the bread. The more Brittney yearned my warmth on the dead side of the bed, the more money I burned to reheat her happiness.

She complained about my absence, I apologized with another designer bag. My father taught me well.

Week after week, Brittney waited sadly with a growing belly as she conjured up thoughts of the end of my lack of a career.

Brittney knew deep down that I would never quit, which left prison or death as the only retirement options.

Swallowing her common sense, she dreamt of me coming home after working a nine to five and *living* the American dream.

But I was a drug-pushing-animal who gambled with his life—the African American nightmare.

My coin collecting crippled the construction of our commitment. Each trip to the Commonwealth was critical and chipped away at the core of our connection.

Brittney waited for Manzo, but Lil' Los continuously came back, and he never cuddled or caressed her. He was cruel and crushed coke by the caseload.

Careless, I even began to creep to the car constantly to call and converse with Biscuit—the captain of my crew.

The two days I played house made me miserable. It was difficult to get high and chill while a woman on the cusp of exploding screamed in my ear.

Feeling useless, I would frequently get up to *urinate*. My numerous trips to the bathroom infuriated Brittney.

She knew that I didn't have to do number one or number two that fucking much. My vegetative state, and my chain smoking snitched on me. I was snorting uncut cocaine—*number three*.

"I know what you're doing in there, you goddamn crackhead!" she would holler. "Stop sniffing that shit and come out here so we can talk!"

Assuming my position on the couch, I would take my lashing as my mistress whipped me with words of changing my life, being a great father, and getting a job. Like a good slave, I never talked back to Brittney and tried to block out the pain.

Submissive, I only spoke when ordered. The session always ended when I said the safe word "OK," and me thinking, *I want to go home.*

During my last visit, just a few hours in, I did not want to be around Brittney. She started complaining about my lack of intimacy and thought I did not find her attractive anymore because she was pregnant. But my lack of fire had nothing to do with aesthetics.

Getting an erection was *nearly* impossible without some sort of visual aid. The coke tied my cock in a noose—making love was a chore.

Although I still thought Brittney was beautiful, I knew I was miserable and in the wrong place when an entire afternoon had passed, and I didn't even notice that Brittney was in the room. She might as well have been a lamp.

I finally admitted to myself that my mind didn't make the train ride. My lights were on, but Manzo was far from home.

Hustling was my life and my favorite pleasure. My family was my work and a burden.

In Roanoke, I did drugs, counted money, and pressed buttons.

At home, I got reprimanded and fucked my pregnant girlfriend on her side, while staring at a picture on the nightstand—her younger sister, Amanda, wearing a college softball uniform.

In Roanoke, I was alive and happy.

At home, I was braindead and homesick.

In Roanoke, I had riveting conversations with Biscuit.

At home I wanted to duct-tape Brittney's mouth shut.

I knew where I desired to be, and I could no longer deny with whom. The sad truth never hid.

Biscuit was intelligent, believed in me, stroked my ego, and always said, "yes." After executing orders without flaw, she would come to the house with a bag full of money.

As I counted *Manzo, the third's* college fund, Biscuit would roll a blunt and talk about almost anything: Art. Entertainment. Flowers. Anal.

No subject was taboo, and the conversations were honest and enlightening. We were physically platonic, but our brains pounded every day.

Sometimes I was on top. Sometimes I was on the bottom, but regardless the position, an orgasm was guaranteed.

Pumping paragraphs proved to be more powerful than pumping pelvises. I never had sex with Biscuit, but often I sprawled across the bed thinking about our mental intercourse.

Many times after we talked, I would call back minutes later—wanting more insight on a discussion that made my brain ejaculate.

Mentally, I was fucked.

Biscuit seduced my intellect, always leaving me wanting more. When I began to confide in her about personal matters between Brittney and me, I knew that I more than liked Biscuit—I loved her.

If I were attracted to her, she would have been my wife, but the lack of attraction stunted our friendship from evolving into an intimate union.

My relationship with Brittney frustrated Biscuit at times, because Biscuit wanted me all to herself. But despite our deep connection, she could never be more than just a friend.

Superficial, I would always choose a big ass and a pretty face over a big girl with a beautiful mind.

* * *

"I wanted to talk to you about how funny Aaron's been acting, because I know I could talk to you about anything Biscuit. But I might just be paranoid—I'm a little jacked up," I said, continuously tapping my feet.

"A *little* jacked up? Shit, you tweakin' like a motherfucker," she said.

"Aaron's a good dude Manzo. Let's wait until tomorrow to kick it though. I know you ain't coming back to Roanoke, but I still can call you...*right*?"

"Of course you can call me. I'm getting out of the game, not getting out your life. But you ain't lying though babe, I'm a fucking wrecked. Let's wait—no big deal."

Is Aaron plotting on me?

Is he a rat?

What is he, goddamnit?

"Yea 'cuz I don't like talking to you when you've been sniffing *co-caine* all damn day. You get too paranoid and shit. Just breathe baby—you aight.

"And you know I'm coming to see your fine-ass...but let me ask you this though—are you and Brittney having a boy or a girl?"

Everything is cool. She's always right.

Breathe. Almost free.

"I don't know. Want it to be a secret, but I'm praying for a little Manzo for sure babe," I answered. "But I would love a little girl just as much."

"Aaaw, that's *nice*," she said.

"Thanks Biscuit."

"I don't know how you get so fucked up and still pass your classes at Virginia Tech. You excited about finishing school?" she asked.

"Hell yea babe. I can't wait to get that degree, get out of here, and start a new life. Be a father. Go legit, you know."

"You gonna be a great dad Manzo. You're an amazing man."

"Thanks babe. You're amazing too Biscuit."

I'm gonna miss her. I really love her.

"Manzo it's good you're stopping this shit, but what you gonna do with *all* that money you got?" Biscuit asked.

"I know it's the perfect time to be done. I'm gonna invest in some shit with my Jewish friends. Change my name to Manzo *Rosensteinbeckburg.*"

"Manzo—you crazy shawty! I'm gonna miss your ass when you go away!"

"You act like I'm dying or something. You can always visit me; you're my homie for life."

"Yea, I'm your *homie.* But Manzo...can I ask you something?" Biscuit questioned with the softness of a little girl, never taking her eyes off the road.

"Of course babe, you can ask me anything. Go ahead," I said.

"I know we're homies now, but you think that you could you ever love me... love me like *your* woman?"

Ooooh God not again! Not right now!

We already had plenty of talks on how we were best friends, and how an intimate relationship would only complicate and ruin our special bond, so I didn't feel like having another discussion. Plus, I was jacked-up and worried if I would make my train to Washington, D.C.

Processing a conversation about *love, like,* or even the weather was impossible. She knew my condition, so how could she ask me anything that remotely made me think?

You have got to be fucking kidding me!

"Look Biscuit..." I turned to face her and answer, but before I spat out a venomous reply, my thought faded.

Her crying instantly warmed my cold blood. I was speechless.

With every passing streetlamp, I could see the tears trailing down her cheeks. Unsure if it were her body or my eyeballs shivering, I grabbed her hand. She quickly jerked back as if my very touch was lethal.

"Listen Biscuit," I said gently. "I *do* love you so much, and our love is stronger than any married couple, but we're friends and that's why what we have works so much. You don't want a guy like me. I will never be faithful to anything but my business.

"You deserve better baby. I honor what we have, and I would rather die than deceive you. You're my soulmate, but I know me. *You* know me Biscuit. You would HATE me if we were anything more than what we are now. Trust me."

"Yea...I know you. I know you, aight. It's cool Manzo. You *keep* trying to play a bitch like I'm dumb though. Don't worry about it shawty. It's cool...it's *real* cool."

Biscuit's sobbing intensified, and she gripped the steering wheel with both hands as she stepped on the gas pedal harder.

Making an abrupt right onto Sixteenth Street Northwest, she slammed on the breaks right outside of Eureka Park.

What the fuck? Why are we stopping?

She doesn't live right here.

While Project Pat continued to play through the stereo, Biscuit's eyes blazed in the darkness as her stare murdered my rhetoric.

With a demonic calm, she clenched her teeth and squealed words that would haunt me for the rest of my life.

"Manzo, if I can't have you...no one will!"

Wait—what the hell is that noise?

"Biscuit is that a...a *helicopter*?

"Oooh shit—Biscuit it's the fucking feds!"

"Drive-Biscuit-drive!"

Her eyes steadily dropped.

"Drive goddamnit! DRIVE!

Her car never moved.

"Noooo!" I hollered.

Bright lights.

"Oh-shit, oh-shit, oh-shit!" I hyperventilated.

Sirens.

"I can't go to jail! I have to graduate!"

Bull horn.

"BISCUIT—YOU FAT FUCKING RAT!"

Chapter Twenty-Seven

SHELL SHOCKED

Jumping off the couch, I dropped the plate of coke on the floor and dashed to my front door, not caring that Jane was upstairs naked on my bed snorting lines and watching our latest *home movie*.

Without looking through the peephole or asking who it was, I turned the doorknob and yanked open the door with all my might. The back of the door plowed into the sidewall and melted into the plaster.

Face to face with a killer, I breathed deeply. Brittney covered her mouth with the sleeve of her Virginia Tech hoodie and wept.

"What the fuck are you crying for bitch?" I yelled.

"Manzo I am so sorry, I just thought that—"

Grabbing her matted blonde hair and tossing her onto my living room floor, I was on top of her with my left hand around her throat before the butcher had a chance to complete her thought. I was *mad*.

Let's see how you like dying!

Our noses touched and sweat dripped into her deep blue eyes. She never blinked as my saliva bridged our faces.

As Brittney gagged and attempted to push me off her, my grip tightened with blossoming rage. I was killing my girlfriend.

Die, you murderer!

Her eyes rolled back, and her nails dug deep into my abdomen but couldn't reach my soul.

Die bitch!

Grip. Tightened.

Fuck you!

"You had an abortion behind my back!" I growled.

"You killed *my* fucking kid!"

"Tell my baby daddy loves him!" I cried.

Brittney's face turned blue as I attempted to send her life out to sea, but at that moment a heavy breeze sailed through my living room window, parting the red curtains.

A heavy beam of sunlight anchored onto an object to the left of me and glimmered brightly. Even the Lochness Monster had peripheral vision. I took the bait.

What is that?

Squinting teary eyes, I immediately recognized the shattered picture frame on the floor resting against the wall.

The rays from the sun prohibited me from fully viewing Brittney and me kissing on a rollercoaster, but I knew what the photo was. I had just gotten Jane's favorite picture of Brittney and me blown up and framed yesterday.

My grip loosened.

Oh man, that was a fun day.

Homicidal spell broken; I smiled a little. Suddenly, I was not enraged anymore.

I was remorseful.

I was embarrassed.

I was concerned.

I was still super coked up—but I was still in love.

Oh God, what the fuck am I doing? I killed my girlfriend.

Looking down, I expected to see my lifeless soulmate, but instead—I saw a pale blur zooming toward my face.

* * *

BANG! BANG!

"Huh?" I said as my eyes barely opened, awakening from a *dream.*

"Manzo, meat or no meat?" an unrecognizable voice hollered, calling my name like we were friends.

"What?" I asked.

Who's that?

Can I ever just get some damn sleep?

Shutting my eyes, I drifted back into unconsciousness and pressed the snooze button on real life. I thought I had time to spare, and in a sense I was correct.

BANG! BANG!

Instantly raising my head off the frigid metal bench, I willed my left eyelid to open.

Only three feet directly in front of the dried-up tears on my face, was a rectangular opening, slightly large enough in width and height to fit a birthday gift from the Macy's sweater department.

What?

Right eyelid opened.

What?

I squinted terribly. My eyes adjusted to the yellow overhead light. The buzzing sound stung my judgment as a mouth seemed to float horizontally on the opposite side of my hive.

Suddenly, I knew where I was, and I missed my queen. I desperately needed my honey. I had to call Brittney.

Stay calm. Breathe.

"Manzo, meat or no motherfucking meat boy?" the mustached mouth asked through the door's opened *food*-slot.

Chow time? Oh, shit!

I fucked up!

Is Dirt OK?

"God-damn-it, are you hard of hearing boy?" asked the correction officer.

Boy?

A jolt of anger propelled my body off the bunk. The thin white sheet, which once hugged my shoulders, flew in the air.

Channeling all my strength into my right foot, I kicked the steel door—leaving a huge dent.

Simultaneously, the potty-mouth-officer checked out, and my insanity checked in.

Quickly bending down, I jammed my mouth into the hole. The metal sandwiched my cheeks and squeezed out a language foreign to Mr. John Reimers—one of my favorite high school professors.

The digression of a gentleman had been completed.

"Who you calling boy, you motherfucking redneck? Let me out this motherfucker and I will show you who the boy is, you punk bitch!

"Let me out this motherfucker! I ain't do nothing! I have to get out, so I can get my college degree! Oh Gooood...nooo!" I yelled.

I watched the guard drop the food tray and sprint down the hall. His keys jingled the background music to my lyrical lunacy. Before I reached my second verse the officer had already turned the corner.

"Come back you FUCKING COWARD! I need to make a phone call, YOU PUSSY!" I screamed to the faint sound of footsteps running down a second hallway.

Standing back up, I had begun to pace back and forth from one side of the cell to the other.

Halfway thinking, halfway talking out loud, I walked two paces and then touched one wall, before I turned around—repeating my manic mambo.

"It's going to be OK, I'm going to get a phone call and call my girl to go to my safe, and then get me a lawyer, and then bail me out and, and then I'm going to collect all my money from my stash houses, and I'm going to get Brittney and move her and my son to another country and never come back."

You are delusional.

You are never getting out.

"Yes I am!" I yelped as my steps quickened and expanded, my hand gestures became more animated.

In my jail cell, there was a fool trying to convince a crazy man of a master plan for living a happily ever after. But I wasn't Snow White, and those White folks with the stars on their badges were more powerful than the Magic Mirror.

A counsel of seven dwarfs could have come up with a more feasible fairytale than what I concocted.

"My bail will probably be like $50,000, so I will have my girl give my mother the money, and she will come bail me out, and then I will go straight to the airport without telling my family, and it will be good for my son, because he can learn another language, and on Christmas my mother can come visit with my brothers and my sister, and I won't be able to get extradited, so I will be OK. It's going to be OK—no worries."

Lord please get me out of here!

I will never sell drugs again, I promise! I will be good!

Wait, that rat bitch!

Biscuit set—

"Manzo, it's going to be OK brother," a deep voice with a heavy southern drawl had spoken.

Although the voice confused the hell out of me, I knew it didn't come from God—He would never have been from the South.

My eyes refocused on the slot, and it was very apparent that the speaker was wearing a black helmet with a clear, protective visor.

He looked like he was ready to play a game of hockey, and I had a feeling that my Black ass was going to be the puck.

"Relax brother. We just want to bring you out here with us, so we can talk to you," the good cop said.

We?

Us?

Kneeling a little further, I inched my head closer to the opening, and I could see just the torsos and legs of three more individuals.

But these officers were not wearing anything remotely close to a standard correctional officer's uniform. They had on riot gear.

Helmets?

Check.

Shields?

Check.

Boots?

Check.

Red necks?

Check.

The goddamn *Turtles!*

Turtles, as inmates on Dateline called them because of their Teenage Ninja Turtle-like padded armor—were highly trained officers who specialized in defusing extremely violent or hostile situations.

A massive African American with tattoos, high on drugs and in a rage—I was *that* violent or hostile situation.

Shit!

"Listen Manzo," the good cop, *Donatello,* said. "All we want to do is process you and get you out of this tiny cell and in a pod with some other people, a shower, TV, and a phone—but you have to cooperate and let us in."

The calmness of his southern accent had its desired effect, and I began to feel a little calmer. I knew that I was in a no-win situation.

Deep down, I still had some good boy left in me to realize when it's time to do the right thing. Wrestling with four Turtles would not only have been wrong, it would have been painful.

Don't fight them.

I just want to go home.

"What it's gonna be Manzo?" Donatello questioned sincerely. "You gonna be cool and let us in brother?"

God I just want to go home. Don't be stupid.

Standing back up, I put both hands to my face and rubbed my head, dragging my hands to my chin.

I looked up at the light and saw Mommy. I missed my mother. Lil' Manzo really fucked up this time.

Be good Manzo.

Be good for Mommy. She taught me better.

"OK, all right!" I shouted. "OK come in! I don't want any problems!"

"Great Manzo," spoke a higher pitched, *Leonardo.* "Now just turn around for us and put your hands on the wall. You're a hoss of a fella, so your arms will not fit through the slot, which means we gonna have to come in and cuff ya, partner. Be cool. Let's get this part over buddy."

Be easy.

This will all be over soon.

"OK, I'm putting my hands on the wall," I stated evenly, not wanting the Turtles to sense any signs of aggression.

As promised, I turned around and placed both hands on the chipped paint of the heavily dense, brick wall.

My hands were steady as I took deep breaths. Understanding the circumstances, I knew that complying was the only option.

Relax.

Going home soon.

They not gonna hurt you if you be good.

"OK Manzo, you're doing good," Donatello said. "Keep your hands on the wall and DO NOT, I repeat, DO NOT make a single move. Are we clear?"

Just do as he says.

"Yes sir." I said.

Be good for your baby.

"OK hoss, we're coming in! Don't you motherfucking move big fella!" *Raphael* yelled, finally adding his voice to the summit.

Raphael's vulgarity incinerated the peaceful energy Donatello and Leonardo had created.

Internal temperatures surged, and I was certain that I was not the only one who experienced the fire. The sound of the keys against the metal door microwaved my anxiety.

My body convulsed with nervousness, and my hands began to slip down the wall. My palms drenched with fear.

The sudden smell of cocaine re-flavored my nostrils and shocked my system. The electricity *Frankenstein'ed* my coke boogers back to life. I felt jacked and tried hard to contain the monster.

Be good.

Come on motherfucker! Don't lose it!

The cell door opened.

"OK-now big fella. Just relax," Donatello said slow and softly as if he were talking to an animal at the zoo. "It's just me coming in. No sweat boy."

Boy? Again?

The word "boy" infuriated me, and my legs began to shake while my teeth chattered.

The crusted coke in my nose melted and dripped toward my upper lip. I could taste the power.

Don't move!

Be good!

They will hurt you!

Donatello carefully grabbed my right arm, put it behind my back, shackling my right wrist.

The clicking sound from the handcuffs somehow had a calming effect as I took a deep breath.

One more arm and I didn't have to worry about the heroes in a half-shell putting me through a shredder.

Almost over.

No one's gonna hurt you.

"One more arm big fella and it's over," Donatello said and then let out a sigh of relief. "Nice and easy. Nice *and* easy."

He secured my left arm firmer and swifter than the right. The slight pain from the cold metal pinching my wrist proved that I was still alive.

My heart slowed, and my nerves settled. My legs regained its stability. Cuffed, the creature was captured.

"OK, now turn around big fella," Donatello peacefully requested. "It's almost over."

Turning around, I had expected to see just another average sized, five-foot, ten-inch correctional officer; the scrappy White guy who played Junior Varsity football but lacked the size and tenacity to play with the big boys—but Don wasn't him.

Goddamn!

Don was three inches taller than I was and just as wide.

Looking up at his freshly shaved face, I could see through his mask that he didn't have any hair on the sides of his head. He was either completely bald or had a military style crew cut.

His little-boy-gray eyes did not match the amplitude of his stature, and I could not guess the age of the giant man-doll.

"You see that wasn't so hard now was it...*boy*?" Don asked without any resemblance of a smile.

Before I could think, before I could speak, or process my *new* name any further—Don coiled his arm back into his shell, snapping his knuckles straight into my mouth.

Rest in peace, bottom tooth. Turtles never took any chances.

Chapter Twenty-Eight

BEAT MACHINES

February 12, 2001

Hey Manzo,

Hope all is well, and you're hanging in there, big guy. I finally spoke with Assistant United States Attorney Sharon Rogers and DEA Agent Pete McMurtry again, and they are still adamant on not giving you a bond unless you cooperate.

If you played ball, they would suggest to the magistrate a $500,000 cash or property bond, and you would have to wear an ankle monitor and live with Brittney in Maryland.

They would consider it absconding if you left outside your permitted area, which obviously means you couldn't go back to New York or Virginia under any circumstance, or you would be in violation. And then you would go back to Roanoke City Jail and lose the money and/or property.

I know you have no interest in cooperating, but as your attorney it is my duty to share this info with you, so we can weigh our options.

As you can see from the Motion of Discovery I dropped off, Katherine Jones is the only confidential informant and the only drugs you have been charged with so far are the ones found in her Oldsmobile. The $200,000 Ms. Jones claimed to be at that house still has never been found, nor have the two kilos of cocaine she said you stashed at her place, so that's great news for us.

A trial date of May 18th has been set tentatively with United States Judge John Burke presiding. We lucked out because he's the fairest judge in the Western District of Virginia. Although we still haven't heard any plea deal yet, I'm continuing with our case like we are going to trial.

Manzo, as you already know please call me if you have any questions. I will be by with your family next week to visit so keep positive and remember, it's imperative that you do not discuss our case with anyone in there. ABSOLUTELY no one!

Take care,
  Mitch J. Hudson, Esq.'

On the inmate's side of Roanoke City Jail's visitation room, I read my attorney's letter that Officer Ferguson handed to me before I took a seat.

It had been six months since I got locked up and charged with two *federal* felonies: Possession with Intent to Distribute Five Grams of Crack Cocaine, and Possession with Intent to Distribute Seven Grams of Heroin.

The drugs were found underneath the passenger's side seat of Biscuit's car—where I was sitting.

Considered a *flight risk* with *no ties to the community*, I had been denied a bail of any kind, which left me in the custody of RCJ until my trial date, or until I had agreed to a plea bargain, received my sentence—and shipped off to federal prison for drugs that I didn't sell and weren't mine.

Confused, I didn't know whether to have felt blessed or a faultless sense of injustice because I was guilty, *real* guilty—just not guilty of the crime I had been charged.

My clientele didn't do heroin, and the thought of needles and dope fiends leaning over gave me the creeps.

Yes, I'm sure that some clients cooked my cocaine into crack, but it wasn't presumable for me to have been the chef. I couldn't even cook a steak. I sold cocaine and no other drugs, but I did know a young lady who did—Biscuit.

A real go-getter, Biscuit dabbled in *whatever* would provide for her family, and I understood her hunger. She had been candid with me from the start about her side dealings.

As long as Biscuit's ambitions didn't impede our operation, I didn't mind her side hustle. I wasn't her father or her husband—I couldn't tell her how to eat.

A stellar employee and even better friend, she raised no suspicion that anything she participated in would harm me or my workers—especially Aaron, who had never been arrested or even found.

Aaron stole my $200,000. Aaron stole my two kilos of cocaine. Aaron *unwittingly* did me a favor.

Aaron swindling my potential third and fourth felonies was the only logical explanation of the missing money and cocaine—Biscuit having been an accomplice was the only unknown variable, although she had passed a polygraph denying her involvement.

No one had entered Biscuit's home the day of my arrest except Aaron. I wholeheartedly believed he watched me punch in the code to the safe—carrying out an applaudable heist before federal agents had time to detain me and double back to my house. But I couldn't prove Aaron did anything, and I honestly didn't care.

No matter what occurred, I fearfully needed that thieving bastard to hotfoot to the end of the earth while snorting every damn gram of coke, spending all the loot along the way.

Without Aaron, the blow, or the money, the DEA was left with a case that should've been conducted by the Virginia State authorities.

Twelve total grams of *anything* were petty by most federal guidelines. However, the DEA would never relinquish my case over to the state, in any way, and risk further embarrassment.

The feds had a ninety-three percent conviction rate, and I wasn't delusional about me facing anyone other than the big boys, because the government wanted me badly—but they *needed* Aaron.

If he were arrested and charged with virtually anything, the feds would bank on him cooperating, along with Biscuit, against me for a lesser sentence, and then I would have to deal with something uglier—conspiracy.

Under United States law, all Biscuit and Aaron were required to do was give the feds a verbal layout of the quantity of drugs I supplied during their time in my organization.

The drugs and money then would be tallied, and I'd be prosecuted for the total amounts of narcotics and cash *mentioned*—without a piece of physical evidence provided.

Luckily for Dirt, he had never met Biscuit or Aaron, but I was confident that when Biscuit sold her soul to the feds that Dirt's name was on the receipt.

The only link to Dirt and Roanoke was I, and ratting on my childhood friend was preposterous, even though I knew the assistant U.S. attorney would attempt to squeeze a confession out of me, with a potential conspiracy conviction acting as the fist.

To the Assistant United States Attorney, I was just a "college kid over his head," who would do anything to avoid a twenty-year-prison bid and be there to raise his newborn daughter—but the A.U.S.A could not have been more incorrect.

Sharon Rogers knew my academic level. She knew of my aspirations to be a great father—but she did not know my pedigree.

* * *

A visit in August from my father and Uncle Henry had given me supreme insight, and I listened studiously. Both helped me consolidate my scattered thoughts.

I turned my focus from my case to my *actions* after listening to the eldest Peña men. Daddy's sermon of wisdom to his saddened son played in my mind every single day.

> 'Son don't be stubborn like your cousin Chris. Naturally you will sit in here and try to figure out every loophole in the world to beat your case, but if you did wrong and you are guilty—then you are guilty.
> They offer you a good plea then you take it.
> Arrogance will get you life in prison. Don't wreck your brain on what-ifs. That's what you paid a lawyer all that money for. Pay more attention to the words that come out of your mouth from here on.
> People don't think about the consequences for saying too much. They don't think about their family's safety or where they gonna live after their bid.
> You're a young man with a lot of respect and can handle whatever God brings your way.
> And when you come home, you can hold your head high and get back to living. You tried your hand, but shit didn't work out the way it does for some.
> I love you. You are a fighter. You are a survivor. And you cannot be broken.'

Daddy's advice and encouragement had been major in aiding me through the days in jail when my body craved cocaine, and my mind rejected reality.

Although the drug withdrawals, and the initial shock dissolved in a month, the pain remained.

Like all the other inmates, I missed my life and would have rather been any place in the world besides RCJ, but the uncertainty of my fate was the most excruciating. Not knowing when or if I would ever come home kept me up at night.

When I finally closed my eyes to sleep, after a prayer to God for forgiveness and the ultimate mercy, the shrieks of Brittney and Mommy's reaction to my first phone calls—haunted me.

I had killed a huge piece of both of their hearts, and there wasn't anything I could possibly have done from my cell to birth new hope.

With a heart full of remorse, and eyes lathered in regret, I would rest and dream about life in the real world—only to wake up and relive the nightmare again.

Thanks to the front page of the Roanoke Times, news had spread fast that a *former Hokie football player* had been arrested on federal drug charges.

Strangers, friends, former classmates, and high school coaches reached out to the newspaper to obtain my lawyer's info.

With my permission, Mr. Hudson provided my new address to whoever asked, and the letters instantaneously followed.

Too embarrassed to write back, I just read the letters and silently thanked all that had time to support me with their pictures, their prayers, their well wishes, and although I didn't need any—their money.

* * *

I was housed in D-Pod and everyone treated me like a celebrity. The inmates never made me wait in line to use the payphone, and the correctional officers gave me extra time in the Law Library and on visits.

Roanoke was still Virginia Tech country, and the people from the Star City loved their football team. I had been the closest most of them had ever gotten to a *real* football player, criminal or not.

Sergeant Lawson, head of inmate recreation, moonlighted as a referee for Big East Football games and had remembered me from a special team's play I made as freshman against Miami. So, of course, D-Pod got more gym time than any other unit.

I preferred being alone in my cell listening to *Jammin* JJS, 104.9 FM on my Walkman, or reading any book I could find written by Sidney Sheldon. But I always appreciated leaving the pod, which was cramped with no ventilation.

Each pod, painted relish green, and the square footage of an average daycare, had eight, two-man cells.

There were four cells on the top tier, and four on the bottom.

The cells had red, thick, metal doors with a vertical rectangle of plexiglass embedded at eye level.

A steel table, the top shaped like a hexagon, had five circular seats attached along the table's perimeter.

The table set under a single row of metal stairs, a few inches from the pod's left wall.

Two tables, identical to the one under the stairs, were positioned in the middle and right side of the room, respectively.

Tucked away in a right nook, parallel the tables, was a communal bathroom with one shower and a chrome toilet, missing a seat.

Living up to jail standards, the bathroom reeked of *SUS*—semen, urine, and shit.

To the right of the doorless bathroom, the lone payphone was bolted solidly to a wall—and a twenty-four-inch Hitachi television sat in a limp, white plastic-chair, to the left of the payphone.

Simultaneously, an inmate could watch television and take a shit—while other inmates watched him.

There was no privacy. Someone was always watching.

In addition to a security camera over the entryway, most of the pod's front wall was bulletproof glass.

A guard could stroll by and scope our behavior effortlessly. Our tendencies were being studied just as much as we were being monitored.

Hordes of *unfamiliar* middle-aged White men and women in suits, bifocals, and clipboards peeped into the pods each week.

They scribbled notes before scratching their chins, conversing amongst each other, and exiting out of the gate. After a couple of weeks, I had barely noticed they were even there.

Only the inmates who had something to hide concerned themselves with the movements of the guards and staff. Criminals were like children, always attempting to get away with something—just for the rush.

I committed a crime but still didn't consider myself a criminal, so I followed the rules, concentrated on myself, and lived for Tuesdays—visitation day.

* * *

A trivial gray area of congestion, the visiting room at Roanoke City Jail had four booths that were separated by five-inch-thick alloy dividers that protected inmates from eyeing another inmate's visitor.

On the left partition of each booth, dangled a black phone that suspended in front of a large square of thick clear glass.

A single narrow burnished-metal arm-table, running the length of an SUV —rested beneath the dividers, connecting all the booths together.

Under the table, four circular stools were screwed into a semi-waxed, brown floor that were smudged with footsteps of woe.

Slouched uncomfortably in the first seat on the left, my normal visitation booth, I waited anxiously while an inmate who had been called out first—sat next to me with his head resting between his arms on the table.

All I could see when I first walked in were his blond mullet fluffed over his red neck, and RCJ written in black letters on the back of his orange jumpsuit.

Besides smelling horrendous like many Joe Dirt's in city or county jails, he incessantly drummed his left slipper on the floor.

The annoying sound interrupted my reaction to Mr. Hudson's letter, and thoughts of seeing my one-month-old daughter in person—for the first time.

I'm not taking any meeting! Cooperate—my fucking ass!

Good Aaron, stay far away! Keep working Mr. Hudson!

TAP. TAP.

This asshole is really getting on my fucking nerves!

But later for that shit—

I'm really gonna see my baby in a minute! Will she know I'm her father?

I wish I could hold her!

TAP. TAP.

Will she like the name Ruby Skye when she grows up? Damn, why won't they let me hold my baby?

TAP. TAP.

Does she look like me for real?

TAP. TAP.

I wish this stink motherfucker would stop beating his feet!

"Visitor for Manzo!" a man's voice boomed from the overhead speaker. "Seat one!"

Oh shit, she's here! My baby's here!

"Visitor for Cunningham! Seat two!"

Oh shit, I'm really to see my kid!

Breathe.

Relax.

"Well it's about goddamn time," the guy next to me said, lifting his head.

Oooh, that's dude who was cursing at his mom. Crater-face.

I almost didn't recognize the only other inmate in the room, because when we were at visitation together a week ago—he sported his mullet bobby-pinned to the back of his head.

To myself, I nicknamed him Crater-face because of his dreadful skin, resembling pink snow after a pigeon gathering.

Cunningham was bony with squinty, saffron eyes, and hallowed cheeks that cuddled his robotic jaw, like a famished rock star on methamphetamines.

Puss, ready for detonation, peeped through the tops of pimples that pushed around his blond goatee and up to beefy, blushed nostrils.

His scent was ungodly, and he stunk as if someone put him in rolling paper with a bag of onions, and a pound of Bugler tobacco—smoking him for a week.

Last Tuesday, when his mother came to see him, Cunningham argued with her—because she wouldn't sell her car to pay a lawyer, claiming that he could get Cunningham's charges dismissed immediately.

In front of two other inmates and myself, Cunningham threatened to cut his mother's head off and "skull-fuck" it before sending her brain to George Bush for alien observation.

Busy with my own *situation* at the time, I blocked out his further verbal lashing as the guards summoned him outside of the mesh gate entrance.

Cunningham had problems, but I hoped he wouldn't start his crazy bullshit while Brittney and my little girl were visiting.

Better be cool, Crater-face.

TAP. TAP.

Where are they?

CLICK.

"Heeeeey big sis! How are you?" Cunningham slung the phone off the receiver and began talking, wrapping up the feet music. "How's Mom and Dad?"

OK it's his sister, I think. Good it's not his mom.

Where is my family?

Apart from my arraignment in August, Brittney had not set a pink toe in Roanoke, because I asked that she worry about the baby and not me.

Oxon Hill was a four-hour drive, and I wasn't worth the anxiety from traveling or the risk of her having a possible car accident.

Her family routinely frequented our home, and her father despised my *Black ass*, so I only called once a week to avoid any altercations.

Our communication was limited to letters, and messages through my attorney, but Ruby was out of the womb, and the time had finally come for me to see my babies.

Oh my God!

They are here!

Standing beyond the glass in a delicate low-cut spaghetti-strapped red silk dress, with a rouged mouth, and impeccably tanned—Brittney gracefully slid the baby bag, all white with pink polka-dots, from her right shoulder onto the table.

Her spiked nipples punctured my thoughts as she swept her golden bangs while cradling our baby in a pink cotton blanket.

I miss sucking on them lil' titties!

I'm gonna beat the breaks off that pussy when I get out of here!

Oh man, Ruby's so beautiful!

Spreading the baby's covering, Brittney finally smiled and the heavens unlocked. My angel laid snug with her eyes shut and her little fingers curled at her chin.

Ruby had a resounding paleness with a brown-sugar complexion, and rosy cheeks that coordinated with her lips. Her sweet-tea-colored cowlicks waved finely across her forehead.

Ruby appeared peachy-soft while she rested graciously and panted with a pureness only a baby could have done.

I love her so much already! I wish I could touch her!

I need to get outta this place! She needs me!

The more I watched Ruby, the more I loved her. The more I loved her, the crazier I was becoming.

I wanted to punch through the glass and touch my child!

I wanted to hold her and let her feel my warmth.

I wanted her to inhale my energy.

I wanted to whisper in her ear and let her know that Daddy would always protect her and nurture her.

I wanted to put her on my knees and play Horsey like my daddy did with me, but I couldn't.

Just when I almost lost control, Brittney picked up the phone, and I did the same. My future wife knew me so well.

Placing the phone to my ear, I pressed an open right hand on the glass at eye level and spread my fingers.

Brittney lifted her phone and securely positioned it between her ear with her shoulder, uniting her right hand with mine. We couldn't touch, but we could feel.

Less than an inch away, we embraced mentally, and our souls wandered together—refusing to be segregated.

Her blue eyes, cold and heavy with misfortune, carried blackened bags of grief and presented a lovely haggardness.

She's so stressed right now! I need to be home!

"Hey beautiful. Damn, that dress was made for you babe. Your hair looks amazing too. I see it got longer," I said.

"It did, I guess. You need to get your tooth fixed," she dryly replied and slid her hand away from the glass. I removed my hand also.

"I have to wait until I get out to get it replaced. Damn Turtles got me good." I smiled, poking my tongue where my bottom tooth used to be.

"Yea...that's not cute," she said.

Damn, she's being a real bitch!

"It'll be OK. Ruby's a doll! Wow, I can't believe we made that Britt!"

Hope the smell of the wax on the floor isn't bothering the baby.

"Yes she's a doll, and *we* did make that, but I'm the only one out here raising her since the Daddy's not around."

"Hold up, what's with the attitude babe?" I asked.

"*Attitude*? Are you serious Manzo? I'm out here all alone taking care of her while you're in jail, and you have the nerve to ask me why I have an attitude?"

"Please relax a little. I understand, but can we talk without the anger? I really can't take all this right now."

"It's all about you as always, huh Manzo?"

"What are you talking about? I'm just asking we talk like adults. You haven't even been here five minutes, and you're already beefing with me."

"Of course I'm *beefing* with you. Your daughter is twenty-five days old, and you haven't been with her or us for a single day of it.

"And you have no clue when you're getting out this place, and I'm supposed to just sit here and act like everything is just fine, huh?"

"No, you aren't, but giving me attitude isn't helping the situation, and I need you to try and be positive. I'm not locked up for murder," I said.

"Be *positive*?"

"Yes Brittney—positive."

"You have no idea how you have hurt and embarrassed me and my family. You weren't even there when your own child was born. My mom and Amanda had to be there. Do you *know* what my mom said in the delivery room?"

"No, you never told me. What did she say?" I questioned.

"Well, my mom looked at Amanda and said, 'Don't you make the same *mistake*'...is what she said." Brittney choked on her words.

"Your *mom* said that shit?"

"Yea she said that, and now I'm here and these people got dogs sniffing my baby like I'm bringing a bomb in this place. All because you want to trust some... lard-ass-wigger-bitch who you were probably screwing!"

"Don't say that Brittney! You know I would never fuck a girl like her!"

"I don't know shit! You fuck everybody else!"

"Are you serious right now Brittney?"

"Yea I'm serious! You are too nice to these hoes! And now you're sitting behind a glass and can't touch your daughter, and I must suffer too!

"These bitches have and *always* will be your problem...always! You're just like your dad!"

"I'm just like my dad, huh?"

"No, no, you're right—I take that back. *Your* dad never got taken away from his family for twenty years—"

"*Twenty years?* What the hell are you talking about?" I asked.

Who's telling her this dumb shit?

"My dad's friend is a lawyer, and he said that you're *definitely* going to get twenty years."

"Well, tell your dad and his lawyer to *definitely* suck my big Black dick."

"Real fucking mature Manzo. Grow up! You're never gonna change!"

"Listen, my charge is federal. There are guidelines the judge must go by, and I studied my case in the law library *a lot*. The amount of drugs they're saying were mine only carries a mandatory minimum of five years to ten years on the higher end—"

"*Only?*"

"Yes *only*...considering if I do take this to trial and lose, I would get twenty years. Or if I wait too long to take a plea after they finally offer one, they gonna get some more people to rat on me, and then I will face conspiracy, and I don't even know how much time that shit brings. Feds don't play fair babe."

What the fuck is that noise?

"Is this what your *lawyer* is saying, or is this just some jailhouse bullshit you and your poker buddies came up with?" Brittney grilled.

"Brittney you must really think I'm stupid."

"Well you're in here aren't you?" She shook her head.

"Listen, so basically I'm going to have to support *my* daughter alone, and you aren't coming home, and you're abandoning us for at least five years?"

Abandoning you?

You knew what I was doing! Support?

I left you with enough bread for 100 fucking years!

"I'm not speculating about anything right now," I said. "There are too many variables."

"And you're definitely not getting a bond?"

"No babe, it doesn't look like these people are gonna give me a bond."

"And what about school Manzo?"

"What about school?" I questioned.

"Is Tech going to let you somehow finish school in there?"

I wish!

"No, my mom called and talked to my counselor. They're not letting me grad-uate because I didn't take any final exams, so I'm stuck for now with 122 credits and no goddamn degree."

"But you only need 120 to graduate though," she stated.

"I know babe—but without the final exams I'm fucked for now."

What's that sound?

Is this dude beating-off right now?

I thought that was his sister visiting him.

Before a visit with their lady friends, inmates would cut holes in their jump-suit pockets to discreetly masturbate without being spotted by the guards or another inmate.

Most inmates were silent and *respectful*, never making too much noise, or ever bringing any unwanted attention.

Adhering to the unwritten protocol of visitation, I had no right to say anything to Cunningham, although I wished he wasn't seated right next to me.

Thank God, with the metal dividers, Brittney couldn't see Cunningham, so I had to just ignore his moans and mind my own damn business.

"Just great, my baby's father will be a jailbird with no degree," she spat.

Baby's father?

"Yo Brittney, who the fuck do you think you are?"

"A *single* mom is who the fuck I am!"

"Do you love me?" I asked.

"Of course I love you Manzo, but—"

"Aren't you my girlfriend?" I further interrogated. "I mean...aren't we together?"

"Listen, let's just concentrate on what's going with your case before we start worrying about us. Anyway, what's that letter?"

I can't believe she's doing this to me! I love her so much!

"I'm going to marry you as soon as I get out. I promise," I affirmed.

"Manzo just stop please. What's that letter right there say?"

"It's from Mr. Hudson—"

"Saying *what* Manzo?"

"Saying some shit about the DEA and that US Attorney bitch wanting a meeting with me. They said I won't get bail unless I *cooperate*—"

"*And* you will get a shorter time in prison?" Brittney pried.

"It doesn't say that, but yea that would be the case—"

"So when are you meeting them?"

"*What*?" I asked.

"Manzo you *heard* me. So...when are you meeting with them to cooperate?" she shifted in her stool.

"Brittney I'm not taking any meeting, and I'm *not* cooperating. I have nothing to say to anyone...period."

Biting her bottom lip, Brittney made a strange face in the direction of Cunningham's sister for a few seconds before laying eyes on Ruby, and then staring at me.

Inhaling emphatically, Brittney bent forward and raised Ruby closer to the glass.

After catching a glimpse at Brittney's expanding cleavage, I watched my daughter yawn and wiggle in the comfort of her mother's clutch.

Ruby never awakened, while Brittney grinned with unconvincing compassion. I awaited the lecture.

My angel was born on the twenty-first.

My lucky number.

I need to be home.

"Manzo, I want you to listen to me clearly OK?" she spoke with a low pitch, and at a slacked pace—over-articulating every single word.

"Are you listening to me?"

"Yes Brittney, stop talking to me like a child and speak your mind," I said.

"Just want to make sure there's no misunderstanding, OK?" she asked.

"Yes babe."

"I want you to take a good look at your daughter, because if you don't do *whatever* it takes to get the hell out of here, you won't be a part of our lives anymore.

"She needs her father, and if you want a future with me—you need to be *out here* with me. I don't care about money or anything. I want *you* home.

"Now, I'm not telling you to rat or snitch or anything like that on your friends, but you're going to have to make a choice—it's either gonna be us or them.

"You have chosen the streets for too long so think about what I'm saying, and if I were you, I would take that meeting or risk—"

Brittney abruptly stopped talking and unexpectedly swung her head to her left and screamed, "Hey bitch—stop fingering your damn pussy next to me and my baby!"

"Oh shit—sorry miss! Ssssh, stop yelling please!" I heard the woman say through the phone.

"What da fuck Manzo man? Dis some buuull shiiid! You know our rules dude!" Cunningham protested, sweat zipping through his zits.

"I know bro, my bad." I lifted both palms in apology. "Just chill, won't happen again bro—just be cool."

Oh shit!

Please don't say another fucking word!

"Why are you apologizing to *him*?" Brittney roared in my ear, but all my focus remained on Cunningham.

Cover the phone—

"Ain't nobody say shit last week when ya lil' Oriental slut was fingering *her* yella slanted-eyed-twat—while YOU was beatin' YOUR goddamn meat!" Cunningham recollected.

Ah man.

Too late.

Both sides of the visitation room silenced, and my heart kept stride with the room's rising temperature and Brittney's breathing.

Panic restricted my neck from making eye contact with Brittney, until I summoned the inner courage to eat my ignorance and infidelity.

I'd preferred going to trial with an all-White jury from Mississippi than looking at the pain in the mother of my daughter's face, but I had to accept the circumstances.

I really fucked up this time!

Brittney, already on her feet, sustained her composure, even though her skin was not far from the color of her dress.

Stunned, we both peered at one another without a voice, but I would have bet our thoughts overlapped.

I knew the sequel to Jane's and my adult film played vividly in her mind. Same characters—just different scenarios.

Yes, it was possible to cheat on someone while in jail, and I did, every week with Jane for six months straight, but Cunningham only needed to witness one scene to take the stand.

When Cunningham had been escorted out of visitation last week, he walked behind me to the awaiting guards while my right hand semi-pumped away in my pocket. Jane shivered like she was coming, and she did come—nine times.

Jane and I were savages together on the streets, and jail just intensified our lust for one another. Other inmates were invisible to us, but certainly, Jane and I weren't invisible to Cunningham.

Cunningham was a moronic inbred, but he wasn't a liar, I was.

And I knew Brittney had been prepared for me to jabber a bunch of dishonest verbiage—but I didn't.

There was nothing I could have said at that moment to console her, so I remained quiet and watched her pick up the baby bag. I had disappointed her again. My misbehavior was essentially predictable.

"Happy Valentine's Day Manzo," Brittney cried and strutted out of sight with the biggest piece of me.

Chapter Twenty-Nine

BATTERED LOYALTY

"So, how you are holding up big fella?" Mr. Hudson asked.

I want to get the fuck out of this jail!

"As good as I can be, I guess," I replied.

"You know Manzo, I really admire that about you."

"Admire what about me?"

"You never complain, not once in the eight months you've been in this shit hole have you ever complained," he praised. "My other clients won't stop whining about something...the food, the guards, no fresh air. But *you*? Not a peep."

"I mean, this *is* jail. Shit sucks but what's the use of complaining. This place isn't supposed to be home. I'm ready to get the hell out of here though, but as long as that clock moves each day, I can handle the rest."

"Yes, that's exactly the attitude we need right now! Some things will get you angry, but we must stay positive big fella," Mr. Hudson said.

He's being too nice.

Please God, he better not say they got Aaron.

Tell me the what's going on!

In a cramped *office*, three doors down from the law library, devoid of inmates, I rested in an aluminum chair at the head of a cot-sized pine-table, with my back nipping the yellow wall, parallel to the room's entrance.

My attorney, Mitch J. Hudson, sat to my left, across from the two empty chairs on my right—while a fifth chair tucked lonely at the foot of the table.

Shackled in handcuffs and leg restraints, I clasped my hands together on the table, and thumb wrestled restlessly as my handcuffs chimed and tinkled.

I didn't want to be anywhere near the feds, but after a few D-Pod inmates openly discussed their sentence reductions, *and* the special treatment at their *proffers* (meeting between criminal defendant and the government)—I called my attorney and agreed to a sit-down.

Although, I preferred not confronting my oppressors, sharing a table with the feds didn't scare me, but my attorney, needing to discuss some new developments in my case—had me spooked.

* * *

Mr. Hudson, with his luxuriant mustache and narrow blue eyes shining behind tortoise-rimmed glasses, wasn't just my attorney, he was my friend— and the only person I really talked to since Brittney blocked me from calling her collect.

Mr. Hudson and I would talk about life, love, big tits, and even tell jokes.

Usually the shit starter, I would clown Mr. Hudson about his gray Beatles haircut, lack of an upper lip, and only owning the one navy-blue suit, white dress shirt, black tie combination that I've ever seen him wear.

His favorite comeback was pulling up his sleeve to flash his silver Rolex Presidential, before pointing at my handcuffs and saying, "Mine says 9:00 AM, but I think it's a little fast. What time you got big fella?"

No matter what we said to each other in jest, nothing was ever taken personally, the raunchier the humor—the better.

Mr. Hudson could say I washed Michael Vick's jock straps at Tech, and I could say that his wife had to pull his stomach up just to see his pecker—no big deal. We both genuinely laughed.

I considered it a luxury to have a great attorney who worked diligently for me, but also one that helped me decompress. He was worth every rack out of my stash of cash.

Despite being in his early fifties, Mr. Hudson had a youthful vibe, along with a Woodberry Forest charm that won over my mom when my parents hired him for my case.

My attorney never made promises he couldn't keep, nor just told me things that I wanted to hear.

The same man who disclosed on our first encounter that he was a republican and didn't care too much for Tupac or Biggie—was the same man who I entrusted with my freedom.

So, when an uneasy Mr. Hudson small-talked while he shuffled through documents, I knew I wouldn't enjoy what he hesitated on reporting.

* * *

"I'm trying to stay positive, but your face is red. You know you White people can't hide your emotions." I stopped fidgeting.

"Let's talk before these people get here," he said, finally looking me in the eyes. "Do you know Michael Lanier?"

My barber?

"If you're talking about my barber, then yes," I answered.

I hope he's OK! I really liked that dude!

"Do you know Darren Macon?"

"You know I know Darren Macon, Mr. Hudson. We played on the football team together."

I haven't talked to Darren in a minute.

"I know Manzo, but I have to ask again." He placed the paper he held back in the folder and picked up another document.

"Oooh kaaay, last one. Do you know a Timothy Henderson?" he asked.

"You know I know Timmy. That's my homie from Connecticut I played at Tech with. I think he just quit the team recently."

Hold up—Wait—

Please say it ain't so!!

"Oooh kay...well—"

"What did they say about *me*?" I needed answers.

Come on, not them! No way!

"Well...the thing is Manzo—"

"Just tell me what they fucking said!" I slapped the table. Mr. Hudson jumped in his seat.

No fucking way! No way!

"OK Manzo...just take some deep breaths and listen to *everything* I'm about to tell you before you flip out. Trust me. Just listen. Can you do that big fella?" Mr. Hudson placed a hand on my forearm. He trembled more than I did.

Calm down.

He's on your side. Breathe.

"I'm listening to you. Excuse me for yelling at you Mr. Hudson."

Those fucking rat bastards!

"No problem Manzo. Just relax. Here's what we have right now." He removed his hand from my arm, thumbing through the next set of documents.

"So, Michael Lanier, your *barber*, and his wife Deanna got caught writing bad checks in March of last year, so in return to drop the charges, Mr. Lanier became a confidential informant with the Blacksburg Drug Task Force. Allegedly buying drugs from you numerous times. Twenty dollar-pieces of crack between April and July of last year."

"*What?*" I asked loudly.

God no!

This can't be happening!

"Hold up Manzo. Just let me tell you everything. We only have a few moments before DEA Agent Pete McMurtry, and Assistant United States Attorney Sharon Rogers get here. Of course, you can say whatever you want at the end, OK?"

I never sold crack! Lying motherfucker!

"OK go ahead. My bad," I said.

"Michael Lanier isn't saying he got it directly from you. The Task Force set up the *buys* with Mr. Lanier to get drugs from you—drugs that you sent via Timothy Henderson, and Darren Macon.

"When Mr. Henderson and Mr. Macon got arrested on the conspiracy for these controlled buys of crack cocaine, they cooperated *completely* with the Task Force for whatever deal they were promised, and they agreed to testify in court.

"But we haven't talked about you hiring me for this case, so I can't officially ask for the Motion of Discovery. I don't have a clue how strong a case they have against you.

"But either way, as of now, you're going to be charged by the Commonwealth of Virginia with twelve counts of Conspiracy to Distribute Crack Cocaine. Each count is punishable from three to ten years in prison, state time...not federal. Apples and oranges big fella."

Twelve counts?

Of Conspiracy? Oh God, no!

That's 36-120 fucking years! I'm never going home!

After eight months of bandaging the stress and depression of my federal charges, I had sunk back into a black hole of regret.

Why did I ever sell drugs in Virginia? The state for lovers didn't love me.

My sweat pooled with fear under the rusted metal on my wrists and ankles. Inside a beige wastebasket in the corner of the room, rancid tomato sauce, smirched on a greased white paper plate, suctioned bile to my tonsils.

A final slice of betrayal from a couple of rats disguised as Fighting Gobblers, just about caused me to vomit.

My body poached with mistrust under my jumpsuit, and perspiration stretched down my spine, itching with hysteria.

Gasping for peace, I gulped the jail air and exhaled cowardice.

I wanted my mother, a holy savior—or a machine gun to blast my way to freedom, because fighting twelve counts in front of twelve Whites was a death sentence anyway. No jury in the Commonwealth would acquit me.

My trial would be a savage's funeral and a cage-opening experience for three cheese-less rodents of the African descent.

Mr. Hudson momentarily sat in silence and let spending a football number behind bars resonate in my mind before I decided to comment on my association with my accusers. Guilty or less guilty, I would need his counsel.

Hiring someone else wasn't a possibility, considering a DEA agent and an assistant United States attorney were coming to talk to me in minutes. My trial date was next week, May 18th, and I was terrified.

I need this motherfucker!

Ruby will be grown when I get out!

"Mr. Hudson you are my attorney, period." I pinched tears from the corners of my eyes. "What are *we* going to do?"

"Smart man you are Manzo. First, let me let you know that for me to take on these *new* charges. I'm going to need $25,000 more than what I charged you for the federal case since it's—"

"OK—so seventy-five racks?" I reaffirmed.

"Yes, a $75,000 retainer," he answered.

"OK done! The bread will be down here tomorrow. Just tell me what the fuck is going on? I'm losing it! I'm like freaking the fuck out right now! Tell me something Mr. Hudson...*please!*"

I'm not doing all that time!

"OK Manzo just relax. I have my office working on these new *complications* as we speak. Forgive me for assuming—"

"Thank you. No need to apologize. Get to the point," I demanded.

"Yes sir. Sooo, here's what we are going to do...just relax and listen for a moment." Mr. Hudson discarded the papers in his hand, and removed a stapled document titled Manzo *Action Plan* from his folder before proceeding to read.

"All right Manzo. So as of now...we are facing a sixty month mandatory minimum sentence, which is five years, of course, for the five grams of crack cocaine found in Ms. Jones' car because, *lo and behold*, exactly five grams of crack comes with a mandatory minimum. Four grams would've been considerably less time to face.

"Oh what a coincidence that there were five grams. The seven grams of Heroin really is insignificant and will be run concurrently. You with me so far?"

Biscuit, you dirty bitch!

"Yes, I learned this in the law library. I'm with you. Keep going," I responded.

"Now we both know that Ms. Jones set you up with the drugs. Shit, the feds probably know, even though, I don't believe they had any involvement in what she did.

"But she did it to save her own ass, and everyone must live with it, especially because the *mystery* money and cocaine never showed up. Thank heavens on that." He chuckled and flipped the page.

Thank God...and Aaron.

"So Manzo, here's the options we have, not in any particular order. We can take the plea of sixty months that I, nor even F. Lee Bailey for that matter, could get you a day under if we decided to go the plea route.

"The only way to get under sixty months on a mandatory minimum sentence is to cooperate and give the feds some pertinent information leading to the arrest of someone of interest that you may know.

"And your sentence would be up to the judge, after hearing a recommended sentence from the U.S. attorney—and a counter recommendation from us.

"And you would have to do *at least* eighty-five percent of your sentence, which will include a period of probation once you completed your time in prison.

"We could get what's called a *5K-1*, which is basically the legal code for a time reduction for your assistance in prosecuting another suspect—and usually cuts your prison sentence at least fifty percent.

"And you could get more time deducted, depending on the info provided, and how big of a fish you fried. You would be looking at a maximum sentence of two and a half years if the person takes a plea and is convicted.

"And if the person you cooperated against decides to go to trial instead of taking a plea, you will have to go to court to testify against him to get any type of reduction.

"But you would receive a bigger time cut for your testimony which has to lead to a conviction, of course. And this is called a *Rule-35* when you go back to court from prison to testify.

"A Rule-35 guarantees more reduction than 5K-1 to your sentence. Everything depends on the route the suspect or suspects take to see which one you would qualify for."

All these euphemisms for ratting.

"Biscuit is basically getting this 5K-1 thing for helping them bag me?" I asked.

"Weeell, actually no. Ms. Jones' case was state, not federal. Everything I'm saying now is federal laws, not state. She got caught with two grams of cocaine.

"She would've been sent to a drug or diversion program, somewhere like Chatham, Virginia...for like four months, tops!

"But she cut a deal to set you up with the feds because of the whole out-of-state element *and* the amounts of drugs you were *allegedly* moving—"

"*What?*" I hollered.

"She would've gotten four months in a motherfucking program? Are you fucking serious Mr. Hudson?"

"I hate to say so big fella, but yes, and I just learned of this a couple of days ago. The feds are some tricky bastards, but couldn't keep it a secret anymore, with our trial set for next week."

"So she's going to walk free?" I asked.

"*Walk free?*" Mr. Hudson raised his eyebrows, steadily shaking his head. "Walk free? Shit Manzo, they might just give the bitch the key to the city. Oops, did I just say bitch? I meant, Ms. Jones."

"That's some bullshit!"

"Yes it is. But that's the system Manzo, which brings me to my last point about our federal case before we continue with the state." He turned another page.

I better not ever see Biscuit again!

"Manzo, we have a great chance of beating your federal case as it is now, even with Ms. Jones' testimony—because there's no wiretaps or recordings with you saying anything about *selling* drugs.

"Although, she did record you basically admitting having 'all that money you got' and being high on 'co-caine' as she said on the tapes.

"But you didn't have any drugs or *guns* in your possession, which would've been devastating on many levels.

"But we're OK big fella. There's no Aaron, and as of now, this Dirt fella, who the feds *really* want you to help them get—is just a fairytale.

"You have nothing in your name. No cars. No houses. No money, besides the $1,215 in your pocket, was found.

"Your main cell phone was clean, and your other phone was a day old and only had a couple of calls to one unidentified number.

"And, to boot, you're accused of being in possession of drugs that the feds are going to have to testify that Ms. Jones never gave them information about, although the drugs were in the car with you. She explicitly said that you dealt 'mountains of cocaine'...nothing else."

"But this new bullshit fucks everything up?" I asked.

"Well, it does make things complicated, but not impossible Manzo."

"I'm never getting out, am I?"

"Hold up Manzo don't jump the gun. Things aren't as bad as they seem."

"So what's the damn plan, because as of now all you've given me are fancy terms to rat my way out this bitch? I haven't heard shit on how you are working for *me*!"

Maybe I need a new lawyer!

"I understand your frustration—"

"No you dooon't! Nobody does, *Mitch*! This cunt Biscuit—she set me up!

"I got two ungrateful sons-of-bitches, who I fed and treated like fucking brothers snitching on me! I let those dudes stay in my crib! I did everything for them! I thought they were my friends!

"And this fucking Michael Lanier? I knew he sniffed blow, so instead of giving him money for haircuts, I used to give a gram of *co-caine* at a time! That's $100 dollars to him!

"He *did* call me, and I *did* send Tim and Darren to him, because I didn't need that money! They said they wanted to go and make some extra bread, so I let my *brothers* eat! I didn't consider it selling drugs!

"I was just looking out for my *friends*! And yes, it could've been twelve times —at least! I used to call Mike from my crib for haircuts before I started hustling, so he had my home number and I liked the guy!

"He was cool! They *all* were cool! Darren and my *homeboy* Tim got greedy and started cooking the shit I gave them!

"I used to tell Darren to chill and play football, but he wanted to hook up that stupid-ass green Buick of his—so he started going out on his own! I couldn't stop him!

"He was a grown man! They all were grown!

"Now all these fucking rats are pointing a finger at me like I'm a bad person when I'm not! I just wanted to be the first person in my family to graduate college and now I have shamed my family!

"My girl hates me because I can't keep my dick in my pants! I have a baby girl who will grow up not knowing me and will probably hate me too!

"Woodberry is probably ashamed that I had ever gone there! I got little brothers and a beautiful little sister who I let down! I'm not supposed to be here!

"I should be sacking quarterbacks on Sundays! I had NFL athletic ability— but I fucked that up! This shouldn't be my life!

"When *my* team played for the fucking National Championship, *just* like Cory Bird predicted—I was with those High Tech bitches in a goddamn penthouse suite in the French Quarters!

"But I should've been on the field with my brothers and helped them beat Florida State's ass—but I let them down! I'm a quitter! We...*they* lost the biggest game of Virginia Tech's history!

"I'm no better than any other *NIGGA* from where I escaped!

"And let's not forget—I am highly...and I mean *highly* addicted to drugs! I'm a motherfucking junkie loser who won't ever get out to enjoy a penny of my money...*and* I'm guilty as all hell!

"So we aren't going to anybody's fucking trial!

"Not in Roanoke! Not in Blacksburg! Not *anywhere* in Virginia!

"And now I'm in a room waiting for a meeting with the feds, who are expecting me to be the same filth as these other cocksuckers, and snitch on my best friend—my *brother!*

"You don't have a fucking clue what's going on in my head, and that's fine! I just need you to do your *goddamn* job!

"So...*Mr.* Hudson...you will have gotten 125 *fucking* THOU-SAND DOLLARS from me! Not my family...*me!* Now...what are *you* going to do to help me get out this nightmare?"

Unapologetically, I snapped with a malicious monologue of self-condemning failures check-listed from my famished soul.

The words, true and bleak, cleaved my heart, but I no longer felt sorry for myself. I had finally faced a mirror and couldn't deny who I've become and what I was up against.

I had the means for the best defense possible, and I required a fighter by my side. I had enough of absorbing blows from the government. My attorney had one last chance to start swinging with me.

Mr. Hudson's expression had gradually stiffened with each word, and the pain within my cries seemed to anger him.

Placing his papers onto the desk, he removed his glasses, wiped them with his tie, and then placed the glasses back on his face.

I had challenged his competence and skillset, and after a six-figure stare at the ceiling, he gazed at me before speaking about our new approach.

"Manzo thank you for being honest with your feelings. No trial. This *is* what's going to happen. No more fucking around with these people!"

"I'm listening Mr. Hudson," I said.

"We're going to take the plea for the sixty month mandatory minimum. This state stuff is laughable, because state conspiracy and federal conspiracy are two different things.

"A state conspiracy charge has the exact same punishment as a regular distribution charge.

"There are no *enhancements* like a federal conspiracy charge, so don't get too worked up about the twelve controlled buys that added up to a measly seven grams.

"The state knew that if we wanted to go to trial that we would have to fight against all twelve charges individually, which means that even if you were convicted on just one that you could get jail time. You with me so far?" he asked.

"Yes sir."

"OK good. Now, the feds normally do NOT run any prison time concurrent with state prison time, but I can get the state to run whatever time we might agree to with them—with the time the feds give you.

"So this means that if you get sentenced to five years federal first, and we would get five years *or* less with the state after—you would only serve five years in a federal prison.

"No state prison time, *but,* you most likely will be on two probations when you got out. But absolutely no additional state-prison time! Still with me?"

Now we're talking.

"Yes sir." I nodded.

"So it's important like hell that we get this federal stuff over before taking a state plea, and you won't have twelve counts of anything. I can get it dropped to probably three.

"And I'm only speculating because I have not seen the evidence against you, but with you telling me you're guilty, *and* with at least three cooperating witnesses, *and* you already taking a federal plea, it's going to be hard to convince a jury around here that you are innocent, especially when we you know damn well you are not.

"And then we are playing with fire, because you would be at the judge's mercy if we lost in a trial. I've seen people get twenty years for a single gram of crack after losing in a trial."

Fuck that!

No trial!

"Now Manzo, everything I've just said isn't *definite,* but I'm confident I can make this happen. I just want us to be on the same page that there are no guarantees. But I will work my ass off to this make happen.

"Also, I don't know how much info you plan to give up today, but if you are letting the feds know how and *who* you got your drugs from, you will get a substantial time cut.

"I might even push for the state to totally drop their case. And you probably would be getting out once the person you helped them prosecute pleaded guilty."

"That means if I *cooperated*, I could go basically go straight home?" I asked.

"Yes, I would ask for time served and you would at most go to a halfway house for thirty days or less, and then you would go home, be on probation for a little while, and then be done with this stuff.

"But of course, if *Dirt*, and I'm only saying his name because that's the only person they said they wanted.

"But if *whoever* you testified against decided to go to trial, then you would have to stay here until you went to trial and testified against him, *and* he was found guilty."

I would have to point a finger at Dirt in court!

"I don't know any Dirt, Mr. Hudson—"

"I know Manzo. I'm just telling you our options. It could be Dirt, it could be someone else, but they are going to want to know *who* your supplier was—and every detail of your relationship with this person. How the drugs got here, how much money you made...*everything*.

"And if you withheld anything and they found out, then they could take the deal off the table. And before you even ask...the answer is *yes*.

"After you told them whatever it was you already told them, they could snatch the deal right from under us big fella."

"These people are the *real* gangsters," I interjected.

"Yes, I can see your comparison Manzo, but you are with the big boys and they do not bullshit.

"So, you think about all this before you do, or you don't say anything, but either way, after this meeting you will be taken to Christiansburg for arraignment, processed there, and then brought back here.

"And we aren't asking to see the magistrate, because asking for a bail is useless. Even if you got a bail, you wouldn't get out of jail because of your current federal detainment.

"But the wheels would be moving, and we can get this *nightmare*, as you say, over with as fast as possible."

Thank God!

I like what he's saying now!

"Sounds like a plan Mr. Hudson. I feel a lot better," I voiced with a genuine appreciation while my stomach growled.

I'm starving!

Man I hope these federal assholes bring me food like everyone said they did!

"We got this Manzo. You gonna be—"

KNOCK.

KNOCK.

That's them!

"One moment please!" Mr. Hudson hollered, before wrapping up our private discussion.

"OK Manzo just relax. Only say what you feel comfortable saying. If they ask you something that you're confused about then just ask me, or say no comment, and if *we* need a moment to think some things over then I will ask them to leave for a moment.

"But make sure you don't lie to these people. If you cooperate, then remember to not leave anything out...OK?"

"OK, no problem," I said.

"So, we're good big fella?"

I smell that fried chicken!

"Yes sir. Let's get this shit over with please," I urged.

Please have food!

"You are the boss. All righty then, let's do this." He patted me on my back. "OK come in!"

The door pushed open, and Assistant United States Attorney Sharon Rogers walked in the room in a charcoal skirt-suit, hemmed just above her knees.

She had gray-rooted, straight, rich mahogany hair fanned atop her single-buttoned jacket, shawl–collared with a double face.

And her white, crewneck, cotton blouse was buttoned to the ashen overhang of skin between her chin and throat.

A flat, gold cross, held on by a prayer to a petty Figaro chain wedged between the loose skin on her neck.

A minuscule American Flag was pinned angularly on her right lapel. She wore her gang sign proudly.

Mrs. Rogers, a zaftig in her forties, was tallish and had podgy cheeks with a bulldog sag like she shot spitballs out a straw on her free time, with her two smashed earthworms for lips.

She never wore perfume or makeup, except for a strip of eyeliner on each of her hooded brows, veiling a set of outspread ginger eyes.

The bridge of her nose ramped in the middle with a broken accuracy of an Eastern European nanny, but Mrs. Rogers was a widow from New Orleans.

The deceased *Mr.* Rogers had been a cop, shot dead in the NOLA's Third Ward...by a young Black drug dealer.

A step behind her, DEA Agent, Pete McMurtry, tapped his brown, ostrich-skin cowboy boots into the meeting in the same tucked, lime Lynyrd Skynyrd t-shirt, and ragged-denim Wrangler's he wore when he arrested me.

A belt, matching Agent McMurtry's boots, even secured an empty black leather gun holster to his right hip in identical fashion.

At our first introduction, his Glock .40 was in his hand though, and pointed at my temple while I sat unarmed in Biscuit's car. I had thought about him every day since my incarceration.

In his late thirties, stocky, with a belly and broad shoulders, Agent McMurtry had a sleek, egg-shaped head set on once-athletic shoulders. If he had a micro-inch of hair, we would've been the same height.

His clean face, full and soft, seemed above suspicion, exempting his viperish eyes, and an invariably fixed sneer.

The sight of him exacerbated my anxiety, until I noticed the name on the white paper bag in his hand—*Bojangles.*

I hate that dude—

Bingo!

They really brought fried chicken!

"Hey Mitch. How are you?" Mrs. Rogers greeted after the door closed.

"Hey Sharon. I'm good. How are you?" Mr. Hudson stood.

"I'm doing well. You remember Agent McMurtry, don't cha?" Mrs. Rogers asked.

"Of course I do. Hey Agent McMurtry." Mr. Hudson shook their hands.

"Hey Mitch, please call me Pete."

That shit smells good as fuck!

"OK *Pete*, you two go around the table and have a seat in those chairs next to Manzo, if you don't mind?" Mr. Hudson asked.

"Oh sure, no problem. Thank you," Mrs. Rogers obliged.

Bitch is ugly, but I'd still hit.

"Sure Mitch. Don't look like the big guy can cause us too much harm." Agent McMurtry pointed to the handcuffs.

Fuck you, redneck!

"Manzo's a nice young man and—"

"Mitch, Sam Simmons from the Blacksburg Task Force will be joining us in a moment, if that's OK?" Mrs. Rogers interrupted my attorney.

Who the hell is Sam Simmons?

"No problem Sharon. He can sit down there." Mr. Hudson pointed to the chair at end of the table that faced me. "It's like a family dinner."

These people ain't my goddamn family.

"Speaking of *dinner*." Agent McMurtry placed the Bojangles bag in front of me. "I know you must be hungry big guy. I sure hope you like *fried chicken*."

"Yes sir, I sure do. You have no idea how much I *love* fried chicken. Thank you, because I haven't eaten all day. Thank you, sir."

Take these cuffs off and I'd beat your motherfucking ass!

"Hold up, let me take those darn cuffs off so you can eat ya suppa." Agent McMurtry unshackled my wrist with his key, sliding the handcuffs to Mrs. Rogers. "OK now you can enjoy ya suppa."

Lucky I'm hungry asshole.

"Thank you, sir. This is much better." I caressed my wrist, and reached into the bag, placing the contents on the table.

A breast and a thigh!

I'm gonna fuck this biscuit up!

I haven't had a Coke in so damn long!

"Did I get what *you people* eat Manzo?"

"Yes Agent McMurtry, it's perfect. Thank you again sir," I answered.

"Good, so while Manzo eats, let's start Mitch," Mrs. Roger requested.

"Yes, that's fine Sharon. We're listening," Mr. Hudson consented.

"Manzo remember, anything you don't want to answer or talk about then you don't have to, and at any point you want to stop the meeting then we can stop," Mr. Hudson advised.

The fellas in my pod weren't lying about them getting fried chicken!

"Manzo are you listening?" Mr. Hudson kneed me under the table.

"Yes sir. I'm good to go. I'm ready," I acknowledged while drizzling hot sauce on my chicken.

"OK, this interview is being recorded Mr. Hudson," Mrs. Rogers specified after pulling out a handheld silver Sony recorder from her jacket pocket.

"Saves us from writing things down," Agent McMurtry added.

"That's fine—" I tore half the chicken breast with one bite.

The tender rush of crisped poultry and spiced fats saturated my tongue with a cayenne kick of happiness. I was chewing and smiling.

The grease coated my palate powerfully and I reveled in carnivorous bliss. Indiscriminately, I inhaled meat and gristle with unapologetic haste and enjoyment, as my dinner guests watched with an annoyed wonder.

I shut my eyes to the spectators and opened my ears to my jaw's fragmentizing explosions of flavor, until all the chow was gone.

Wiping my hands and face with a napkin, I finally lifted my head, and everyone in the room silently focused on me with a wide-eyed glare of amazement, and I did not care.

Jail food was the worst, and I'd spent eight long months eating the *Woo-Woos* and *Wham-Whams* all day from the commissary.

My body had been suffused with sugar and preservatives. Only at night or while watching a sporting event did we jazz up the menu.

* * *

Inmates made *Shing-Dings*, a jailhouse nacho concocted of potato chips, sliced beef sausages and pickles, with squeezed cheese and pickle juice dumped into a soda bottle—then dropped into a halved soda bottle of water, that was heated by cut wires connected from an electrical outlet.

We would take the empty chip bags and rip them completely open to form a flat, rectangular base, before we placed all the chip bags side by side on a table.

After spreading the chips on our shiny silver platter, we poured the melted cheese-blend on the chips, followed by sprinkling tiny cubes of *1800 watt-grilled* beef sausage and pickle. We had no utensils. We all ate together with our hands.

Every Sunday, I provided a buffet of Shing-Dings, covering all three tables, for all twenty or so inmates.

Most of the inmates were indigent, and couldn't afford to buy commissary at all, so I would purchase a clear garbage bag full of food, and sodas to share with everyone during football games.

Never expecting anything in return, I relished seeing the guys in D-Pod enjoy themselves, even if for a moment.

Unlike some of the other federal inmates, I never bragged about my finances while I ate alone—laughing at the struggles of the less fortunate.

My mother raised me to help others, *and* to not eat like a pig. I never said I was perfect.

* * *

"Mr. Hudson, now that your client has eaten, can we *please* start now?" Mrs. Rogers requested, evidently irked.

"*Yes*, let's start," Mr. Hudson agreed.

"Damn hoss over there sure can eat, I tell ya," Agent McMurtry spoke. "Told you Mrs. Rogers that this boy would love the chicken."

"Mrs. Rogers, *please* ask your questions," Mr. Hudson said.

"OK thank you, Mr. Hudson. Manzo, for the record, I'm Assistant United States Attorney Sharon Rogers. I'm here with DEA Agent Pete McMurtry.

"I would like you to state if you are here by *force* or any *threat* to the well-being of you or anyone in your family?"

Is this ugly bitch serious?

"No ma'am, I haven't," I answered.

Except y'all threatening to put me in a box for twenty years.

"OK good. Now Manzo, has anyone...including law enforcement or the United States Government paid you for your cooperation?"

"No Mrs. Rogers. I have not been paid."

Does Bojangles count?

"OK good. Moving right along." Mrs. Rogers twirled her gold cross between her fingers.

"OK, so you know you're facing a maximum of twenty years in federal prison if you take your case to trial and lose Manzo?"

"Yes, I know Mrs. Rogers."

"OK, and for the five grams of crack alone that you were charged to having been in possession with the intent to distribute, you're facing a sixty month mandatory minimum, with no possibility to do a day under eighty-five percent of it. Four years and ten months with good behavior. I'm sure you know this."

"Yes Mrs. Rogers, I know."

My lawyer's sitting right across from you. Of course I know.

"OK, so you're facing some very serious charges, and the government appreciates your earnestness to cooperate and help yourself. I promise you that for your *substantial* assistance that we will do everything to get you home to... uuuh...hold up...I have it right on my tongue—"

"Brittney, Mrs. Rogers," Mr. Hudson interjected.

"Thank you, Mr. Hudson. My apologies...Brittney."

"Yea and she fine too. That big booty gal you got there is really fine, I tell ya." Agent McMurtry licked his lips.

What the fuck did he just say?

"*What?*" I stared at Agent McMurtry. Mr. Hudson punched my leg this time.

"Don't get your panties all in a bunch. I'm just joshing with you brother," Agent McMurtry said.

KNOCK! KNOCK!

"Come in!" Mrs. Rogers summoned the person.

"Hey guys—sorry I'm late," a bald, middle-aged White man apologized.

Hold up—

"Hey Sarg! It's OK, come in!" Agent McMurtry greeted.

I know that guy from somewhere.

"Hey Sam, no worries. You are just in time," Mrs. Rogers said.

Where do I know him from?

"Hey Sharon. Hey Pete. Got caught up in Blacksburg with work. I guess I'm sitting right here," Sam explained after shaking Agent McMurtry's hand and having a seat at the end of the table, opposite of me.

Wait...is that him?

"Sergeant Sam Simmons meet Mitch Hudson...Manzo's attorney," Mrs. Rogers said.

Oh my God!

"Hello Sergeant Simmons." My attorney waved. Sergeant Simmons returned the gesture.

That's the guy!

Sergeant Sam Simmons' deep saffron U.S Polo Association shirt fit him snug around the midsection and had a splotch of ketchup on his chest, under the shirt's signature emblem like the horse was on its period.

In perfect attire to coach a high school football away-game, he was dressed in gray slacks with creases that ended slightly above his white sneakers.

Simmons' goatee, clearly edged with the same razor he shaved his head, was bushy, non-symmetrical and encompassed almost the entire area from his chin to his bottom lip. His mouth resembled a 1977 vagina.

His head, the texture and color of a raw pork chop, had thin tan lines running from the corners of his eyes to the backside of his earlobes.

A brawny man with retired offensive tackle height, Simmons set his folder on the table but wouldn't dare to make eye contact with me.

Our energies merged with strife, and I had believed he knew from my shocked reaction that I recognized him.

On many a night, I descriptively told stories about him to anyone that joined me around the coke-fire, and people said that I had been *losing it*. Eventually, I believed I was seeing things.

Sam Simmons wasn't a ghost or some sort of apparition, and when he placed his black Oakley's next to my chicken boneyard—the hairs on my body perked with terror.

Sergeant Sam Simmons, without a doubt, *was* the guy I had told my mother about that I had seen through my peephole as he snooped around my house.

Told y'all I wasn't crazy!

"And *hello* Manzo," Sergeant Simmons addressed me while he smirked at a picture of my mug shot in his folder.

I would've blown that look off your fucking face if you came inside my crib!

"Hello Sergeant Simmons. Pleasure to meet you sir," I said.

Rats are the only reason I'm here asshole, not you.

"I thought you two knew each other," Agent McMurtry spoke.

"Well...we *sorta* do." Sergeant Simmons heaved a few chuckles.

"I know that's right!" Agent McMurtry laughed.

"OK Agent McMurtry, let's continue please," Mrs. Rogers suggested.

McMurtry really thinks these people like his dumbass.

"Let's get right to it. We know what the charges are. I've explained *all* of them, so no more beating around the bush folks.

"We need to hear from Sergeant Simmons, and we need to hear what my client is being offered, *collectively*, from the state *and* the federal Government," Mr. Hudson said.

About time he's acting like my lawyer!

"You are correct Mr. Hudson. Sergeant Simmons please begin, and I will follow," Mrs. Rogers agreed.

"OK, first off, let me start by saying, as you know, you are going to be charged today with twelve counts of conspiracy. And I'm sure Mitch told you that, so let's just cut to the chase.

"Your client is a *Kingpin*, and we all know that he's way bigger than this petty crap we got him on, and me and DA Powell are going to recommend to the judge that this fella gets his time to run *consecutively*, not concurrently with the federal time he will serve.

"So if he gets five years with the feds, and eight years with the state, we want Manzo to do his punk-ass five years with the feds, *and* then go straight to state prison and do the remaining eight years.

"The boy deserves at least thirteen years for the amounts of drugs he was pushing, and the amount of fortune, I know *for a fact*, he made down here," Sergeant Simmons sermonized.

Hold up!

Can they do that?

And why is he not looking at me when he speaks? Fucking coward!

"OK, now you're jumping the gun here, but your position isn't surprising, and I expect you and *District Attorney* Powell to do everything that you're saying, *especially*, it being an election year.

"But you're talking strictly speculation. My client is being charged with a total of, oh what a coincidence, thirteen grams...*total*. And that's both cases—give me a break Sam!

"You want him to serve a year *per* gram? Good luck with that, pal. So instead of trying to scare us, please just tell us the damn plea, and what you guys are offering for my client's cooperation because we don't scare easily."

Love my lawyer!

"It's not about scaring anyone, *Mr.* Hudson. It's our position," Sergeant Simmons said.

"OK *Sam*, so what's *your* position, considering DA Powell was too busy, it seems, to bless us with his presence?" Mr. Hudson asked.

"Well, that's where we come in Mr. Hudson," Mrs. Rogers interjected.

"If your client helps us, then it's also helping the state, and the state will *piggyback,* for lack of a better term, with the federal government. So basically your client would be helping both causes by cooperating."

"And if he doesn't Mrs. Rogers?" Mr. Hudson inquired.

"Well, you already know our position. He will get the five-year mandatory minimum. *Unless* Manzo goes to trial, and he *will* get twenty years. I will see to it."

"And I will see to it he gets at least eight years added on from the state," Sergeant Simmons promised.

"Sergeant Simmons you're just a detective and have no power for such a thing...simmer down, sport. Soooo, tell me the grand total here Sharon, we're listening," Mr. Hudson said.

Yea what's the plea?

"Ten months, and five years of supervised release with the federal government, the state would dismiss *all* of the counts, except for one count, that would be dropped down to a simple possession.

"No prison time with the Commonwealth, just five years of probation also. That's the final deal for Manzo's cooperation. *And* if need be, his testimony in court, of course."

Ten months!

"And the jail time he has already done will count toward the ten months, I'm assuming?" Mr. Hudson asked.

"Absolutely Mr. Hudson," Mrs. Rogers confirmed.

This can't be real!

"And we can get this in writing?" Mr. Hudson asked.

"Yes, if we agree and Manzo play's ball, then Judge Burke would go with the government's recommendation of sentencing."

Two more months and I could be back home to my family!

"And how long do we have to think about this plea?" Mr. Hudson asked.

"You have until the end of this meeting Mr. Hudson," Mrs. Rogers stated.

Goddamn she's not playing!

"Shoot, well that's not much time for us to think this young man's future, is it?" Mr. Hudson asked.

"Maaan, that's a sweet deal! Y'all better jump up on that-there!" Agent McMurtry spoke like a backwoods car salesman.

"Mr. Hudson let's speak reality for a moment. There is going to be a line of people willing to cooperate against your client, including your football *pals,* Darren Macon and Timothy Henderson.

"Eventually the right persons will come along and tell us everything that your client could've. And then I'm going to charge him with conspiracy... *federal* conspiracy.

"And your client will be facing a lot longer than twenty years, and there will be no more meetings between us.

"I'm going to just listen to all the people point the finger at your client, add up his involvement, and throw the damn book at him. The choice is yours." Mrs. Rogers foretold her version of the future, with absolute certainty, and I'd believed her.

Oh shit! They trying to give twenty *years or better!*

I can't do all that time! Oh God!

What do I do? Say something Mr. Hudson! This bitch ain't playing!

"You make some valid points," Mr. Hudson admitted after hitting my thigh with his. "So *what* would you like to know, Mrs. Rogers? You have our curiosity."

"*Weeeelll,* I for-one would like to know where you hid all that damn money, but I know we will never get that answer, huh boy?" Agent McMurtry pressed.

Go fuck yourself!

"That's enough Agent McMurtry!" Mrs. Roger chastised before calmly making her demand. "It's not a *what,* Mr. Hudson—it's a *who.* The only person we are concerned about is your client's friend Dirt."

Dirt? No fucking way!

I'm never turning him in! Fuck these people!

"So my client gives you everything he knows, his involvement with Dirt, the amounts of drugs *allegedly* they sold together, and he does just another sixty days or so in jail and he's free. Is that what you're saying?"

"Yes," Mrs. Rogers answered.

But he's my brother!

"And what if my client can help you with someone else?"

"Fuck everybody else Mr. Hudson! Excuse my language Mrs. Rogers." Sergeant Simmons steamed.

"We want Dirt! We don't want *Mud* or *Dust* or *Sand* or any other of the filthy fucking street-named animals you know! We want Dirt! And this boy either gives us Dirt in the next five minutes or deal's off the goddamn table—and we're walking!"

Simmons wants to bury me!

What? Twenty years or Dirt?

God no! I can't do all that time!

"Listen up, *rock star*. We know that you ain't *da man*, and we know that Dirt's the middle supplier. We know that Dirt has an amigo somewhere, and that's who we want, not you. And when we get Dirt, and we *will* get the bastard for sure, he's gonna roll over on everyone too—even *you*.

"It's how the game is now played. Loyalty ain't nuttin' but a tattoo son. Dirt's going to get caught anyway. Y'all all get caught. You might as well get the damn credit for it son. So don't be foolish Manzorini.

"Give us Dirt and go home in two months to ya beautiful girlfriend and baby girl. It's simple. You have to do the right thing son. You're smart, so be smart.

"Or you gonna sit in jail for twenty years, and a big buck just like yourself gonna be riding Brittney's plump, juicy White-ass while your baby girl's watchin' Nickelodeon in the livin' room, listenin' to Lee-roy split momma—like three scoops of ice cream and a goddamn banana. And I know that ain't what'cha want, so use your brains *brother*," Agent McMurtry added.

What?

Nobody's going to fuck my girl!

I have to get out this motherfucker now!

"Yes Manzo, you're highly intelligent. Use those brains. So...what's it going to be Mr. Hudson?" Mrs. Rogers asked for a final answer.

I can't stay here!

I need to go home!

"Now Manzo, it's your call. I would never advise a client to cooperate or not. My job is to help put you in the best position *after* you made a choice on what *you* wanted to do.

"Sooo, take a couple of minutes to think about it. If you would like for everyone to leave and we discuss some stuff in private, then that's what we will do.

"But it's *totally* up to you big fella, whichever way we're going. Whatever you decide, that's the way *we* are going. Your call."

Fuck man! What do I do?

With everyone waiting impatiently for my decision, I sat with a puzzling disbelief of how profoundly my life would change with the next words I uttered.

I knew ratting on my best friend was wrong, just as I knew my not being around for twenty years to raise my daughter was also wrong.

The five-year plea I could do and be home before I turned thirty years old, but when presented with the option of doing another sixty days or doing sixty months, I was unsure.

I didn't want to go to prison. I didn't want Dirt to go to prison either. I also knew that if I brought a case against him that I could never show my face in New York again, but I would be free to raise my daughter anywhere else.

Striving to be the perfect father, I would teach Ruby valuable life lessons, take her to school and her pageants, help her with her homework, and guide her.

I would love her, and protect her, all while Dirt wasted away for years, and his kids, Heaven and Keion, grew up without *their* father.

Was his family worth more than mine?

Didn't I owe it to *my* family to sacrifice anything to be with them—even my respect, reputation, and friendship with a guy I had known for my entire life?

Why should I lose my girl and baby when I had the opportunity to make things right?

Agent McMurtry was accurate about another guy having sex with my girl!

Five or twenty years was an eternity for a human, man or woman, to have gone without affection or companionship.

Brittney was a good girl, but I knew that if I went to prison that someone would slide up in her, just as I would slide up in a plethora of women if the roles had been reversed.

So, me not cooperating was essentially escorting at least one cock down the throat of the woman that I loved and planned on marrying.

After the fiasco at Brittney's last visit, I had $32,000 delivered to my sister, Sandy, to purchase a three-karat, cushion cut engagement ring from Jacob the Jeweler in Manhattan.

He did an incredible job replicating the ring I had first seen in a Dupont Registry Magazine.

I instructed Sandy to put the ring in a safe deposit box at Chase bank until I was sentenced, because I had planned the perfect prison proposal—but my scheme would be moot if I snitched on Dirt.

My brain ached.

My morals conflicted.

The clock ticked.

I hated Roanoke City Jail and had zero desire to spend another day behind bars. I would have done almost anything to get out of my legal quagmire but cooperating with the very people who incarcerated me just didn't feel right.

Loyalty was not "just a tattoo" for me. My allegiance to my close friends had *always* been honorable and unswerving.

Surpassing Sergeant Simmons' sinister scowl, I watched the wall suddenly play a picture of the last time I had to choose between my brother and myself—the admissions interview at Woodberry Forest School.

* * *

"Robert let's pull up on the computer which documents we need to have Manzo bring home to his parents—one moment son."

"Coming sir!" Mr. McMillan popped off of his chair and accompanied Mr. Grinalds.

"Ha, ha, ha!" My laughter awakened my feet, and I couldn't help but stomp them a little. I covered my mouth with both hands to muffle my hysteria.

Tee was right—that motherfucker does have a red nose!

I'm really gonna miss Tee's funny ass though!

Thinking about Tee and how we always laughed at the same things caused me to panic. What was I doing?

Tee would be beyond mortified when he had found out that I was leaving him behind.

Knowing that I had left the one person I cared about just as I did the five other kids who shot out my father's penis, I couldn't feasibly have enjoyed a single day at Woodberry.

Tee's and my brotherhood had been built on loyalty and trust, and we always had each other's back.

Friends like Tee were rare, and I would've died for the guy, lied in court under oath for the guy, and taken an ass whipping for the guy.

At Harbor, nobody messed with Tee, because they knew that they would have to deal with me, and the *entire* Wagner Projects. In my hood, kids my age killed because they were bored.

Tee's East River Projects, a lot smaller and without the as notorious reputation and body counts, were closer to our junior high school, but Ms. Alice, Tee's mom, only let him outside to play basketball at the courts right outside their first-floor window.

The only way he could have even stayed outside past 8:00 PM was if his older friends, Big Dee and Larry, watched him.

Tee was far from a punk though, I was just overprotective of him because my father raised me to always be there for my friends, if they were genuinely friends, and Tee was my friend in every sense of the definition.

Daddy told me to never let money, girls, or opportunity severe the link between an ace and myself.

Tee *was* my ace, and I couldn't see God dealing me the hand I needed to win without Tee.

I was sure that the boys at Woodberry Forest School were great kids that, in time, would become like brothers.

But I had no intentions on finding out, if Tee wasn't there to continue the journey that we had started together in 1990 on 109th Street between Second and Third Avenue.

Most fifteen-year-old boys would've jumped and ditched their friend, but I wasn't just any fifteen-year-old, and Tee wasn't just any friend.

I had to speak my mind. I was different.

These people are tripping!

No way I'm leaving Tee! Not a chance!

"OK Manzo, we have papers right here to give to your family!" Mr. Grinalds said as he and Mr. McMillan walked back into the main office.

"Yes, so happy to have you son!" Mr. McMillan expressed his delight, extending out the contracts.

"I don't need those sir," I rejected.

"*Excuse me* Manzo. Did you just say you didn't need these son?" Mr. Grinalds asked peacefully.

"No sir, I won't need those. I'm not coming to Woodberry Forest School," I answered apprehensively.

"What's the problem son? Did we miss something?" Mr. McMillan asked after he and Mr. Grinalds exchanged glances. "Have we upset you? If we did, we can make it right!"

Just tell them.

Don't hold back! Speak!

"Yes son, just speak up. We just want to make you happy with coming here. What changed in a matter of minutes son?" Mr. Grinalds asked.

Tell them!

"Sir, I love this school and it's beautiful. You and Mr. McMillan have treated me like the White folks in Africa that you see in those missionary commercials, but I am not leaving Tee behind. I will not come to Woodberry Forest School.

"If Tee isn't good enough, then I'm not good enough.

"So, either Tee comes with me to your school or Tee can have my place. But I will not come here without my brother. Thank you for the opportunity, but I just can't. Either way, thank you for the amazing opportunity," I disclosed passionately.

"Manzo, I totally understand what you're saying—but it's not about being good enough. It's about funding, and we only have money for you and not Tee," Mr. McMillan explained their predicament.

"I'm sorry, but there's nothing that's going to make me change my mind," I said.

"I really think that you're making a mistake—"

"Fine son! Tee will come with you!" Mr. Grinalds interrupted Mr. McMillan.

"But sir...we don't have—"

"No *buts* Robert!" Mr. Grinalds said. "Call Roger Wilson and tell him about Tee Butler. Roger's looking for another kid besides José Vasquez to sponsor, and we just found one *worthy* of his scholarship!"

Roger Wilson?

Oh yea, the alumni dude from Porky's!

Damn, how much did he make from that one movie?

"Yes sir! I will call him immediately!" Mr. McMillan ran to the other room.

This is really happening! Oh my God!

Tee's going to be so happy!

"*Seriously* Mr. Grinalds?" I asked with a huge smile.

"Yes son...*seriously.*" Mr. Grinalds smiled back.

"Thank you...thank you...thank you...*thaaank yooou*! We won't let you down! We will work hard and go beyond what is asked! We will represent Woodberry... and we won't lie, cheat, or steal *stuff*! I'm so happy right now!"

"I know you guys will be a great addition!" Mr. Grinalds said, putting a heavy hand on my shoulder and continued his praise.

"I like you Manzo. You remind me of a Marine. We leave no man behind. You are a leader and we need leaders here. Go get Tee Butler and bring him back here please. Young man...welcome to Woodberry Forest School!"

Back in Roanoke City Jail, the picture on the wall faded, but the man who I was remained.

Although I had helped to destroy lives and families for self-fulfillment and monetary gains, I wasn't going to compound my transgressions by sending my brother to prison.

I trusted the wrong people, and my dumbass got trapped in a game that I had no business playing.

Dirt didn't get caught, and he would *never* get caught if any type of law enforcement were banking on my testimony. Not a chance!

No, I didn't want to go to prison with the murderers, rapist, and crooks.

No, I didn't want to leave Brittney and Ruby.

No, I didn't want to be taken from my family, especially my younger siblings who needed me, but when I made the conscious decision of breaking the law—I had known the risk and the ramifications.

I wasn't a coward who wouldn't take responsibility for his own actions, and I was now finally prepared to live with *my* choices!

After channeling strength from Daddy's wisdom, I was groomed to bear my first hardship of becoming a man.

'*You are a young man with a lot of respect and can handle whatever God brings your way. And when you come home, you can hold your head high and get back to living.*

'*You tried your hand, but shit didn't work out the way it does for some. I love you son.*

'*You are a fighter. You are a survivor. You cannot be broken.*'

"I don't know anyone named Dirt, and I will *never* know anyone named Dirt," I announced, and then turned to Mr. Hudson.

"I have nothing more to say to *these people*—I'm ready to go back to my cell."

"Well folks, no more questions! See you good people in court!" Mr. Hudson spoke, looking pleased.

BAM!

"Hold up! Wait a goddamn minute boy!" Agent McMurtry barked after he pounded a right fist on the table.

"You not as smart as we thought you were, I see! You got us down here—wastin' our goddamn time! You had plenty of time to think about this! Just why in the hell did you meet with us in the first place if you didn't plan on cooperating boy?"

As Agent McMurtry talked, I had become repulsed by just the mere sight of him. If I had closed my eyes and just listened, I would've thought that anybody at the table besides Agent McMurtry was speaking.

But my eyes and my mind were open, and I could undeniably see the self-hating man on my left. We could've been related.

Agent McMurtry had voluminous lips, a widespread nose, a high butt, and a brown-gravy tinted mask.

Even though he identified with the good ole boys, he could never be one of them. He tried hard, but he just couldn't. He was the wrong color.

Agent Pete McMurtry was African American.

Livid because I would not send another Black man to prison, Agent McMurtry was the only one who displayed any emotion concerning my stance. Sergeant Simmons and Mrs. Rogers never flinched.

Look at this fucking Uncle Tom.

Agent McMurtry had put a pistol to my head and cuffs on my wrist, and I was positively on my way to federal prison, but he needed more than my conviction. He needed my integrity, but I would never let him, or anyone get it.

There would be no pats on the back over rounds of Coors Lights, or "attaboys" from his peers for Agent McMurtry.

There would be no pay raises, or promotions, or quotas met at the expense of me ratting on Dirt.

I had done wrong and deserved whatever punishment the courts felt suitable. But my case ended with *my* case.

Unbeknownst to everyone, including my attorney—cooperating with law enforcement had never been my purpose for the proffer agreement in the first place.

"Why did I take this meeting?" I repeated Agent McMurtry's question.

"Yes, *why*? Why the hell did you take this meeting boy?" Agent McMurtry asked.

Grabbing the can of Coca-Cola, I took a gulp of the refreshing soda and washed down the last of the Bojangles—before looking Agent McMurtry directly in his eyes and saying, "You should already know why I took this meeting."

"I loves me some fried chicken...*brother.*"

Chapter Thirty

FREE TRIP

"I am United States Marshal, Dennis Webb, and welcome to the Justice Prisoner and Alien Transportation System, or better known as Con Air!" Marshal Webb yelled over the all-aluminum Boeing 727's revving engine.

Like the movie?

"Yes, Con Air...just like the movie—*except* ain't no Nicholas Cages getting on that-there plane with you gentlemen, *and* ladies!

"And if any one of you gentlemen, *and* ladies, try to run, try to cause a panic, try to incite a disturbance, or try to physically harm any one of my Marshals— you will be gunned down, just like in the movies!

"And If you can't tell who's a Marshal, them the folks with the big guns, and *United States Marshals* written on the back of their jumpsuits!" he explained, pacing back and forth under the plane's nose.

Marshal Webb was around fifty years old and had the coral complexion of a schoolteacher who recently returned from vacation.

He wore wire-rimmed oval glasses, khaki pants, child-sized black boots and a navy-blue polo with an encircled yellow star stitched on the left side of his chest.

Small framed with a Napoleon backbone, Marshal Webb had stringy, lemon-curry-hair cut sharply above his collar, and his sideburns ended where his ears had begun.

He spoke with a Midwestern-general's authority, and the hairless corners of his mouth sagged into laugh lines, which extended from the fringe of his nostrils.

His face had a wrinkled innocence, but the AR-15 assault rifle in his hands didn't, so I had no qualms about following the man's directions.

"As you can see, you have been separated and are standing in two groups—the men and the women!

"Not only can you not talk to a person from a different group, you can't even talk to the person beside you!

"So, I better not hear a word from any of you! So men, you can think *whatever* you want in those pretty little heads of yours, *but* I better not catch any of you men fraternizing with the female inmates, and that goes the same for you women!

"When you get on the plane, you will sit *exactly* where we sit you! You will be quiet! You will eat the two sandwiches and drink the bottle of water we give you!

"Y'all get some rest, but keep quiet, and if you need to go to the bathroom, please wave! *Trust me*, someone will see you!

"We will be in the air almost two hours, then landing safely to Harrisburg, Pennsylvania! You will get on your designated buses, and off to your next spots!

"Fuck your questions and concerns and thank you for flying Con Air!"

* * *

On the tarmac of Hartsfield-Jackson International Airport in Atlanta, Georgia—Marshal Webb explained the rules to the awaiting eighty shackled inmates that stood aligned in eight vertical, single-filed lines of ten.

Facing the aircraft, we had been separated by gender and were evenly split to the left and right of the plane's nose.

Nine other dispersed U.S. Marshals, all Caucasian and uniformed in tactical gear, gripped assault rifles. One of the Marshals at the plane's tail held a German Shepherd by a leash.

All the inmates, in orange jumpsuits and blue slippers, seemed drained with an intermixture of boredom, depression, and exhaustion.

No happier than slaves getting on the Amistad, we were dirty and un-groomed with crust in our eyes, and agony in our hearts.

Along with our plain-faced female counterparts, who many had grown mustaches and unibrows—tattooed men with coarse-grained lips, and wild facial hair gazed into the June sky, admiring a bird's liberty.

Some of the women were natural beauties. Most weren't, but I didn't care.

I liked the young Black girl with the hazel eyes and cornrows just as much as I did the one-eyed Hispanic grandma in the third row.

I would've given a year's commissary for two minutes alone with any of them, and the feelings were apparently mutual.

Like lions that haven't eaten, the men *and* the women snuck glances filled with hunger and fantasy.

We were all chained to our mistakes, but we were still alive. Lust blew with the musk of boiled onions and jet fuel.

With no toiletries on our individual journeys, we all stank from mouth-to-ass, naturally, some more than others, depending on the route taken.

* * *

After leaving RCJ, deputies drove me in a van to Lynchburg City Jail, where I stayed for five days.

Most of the inmates in LCJ showed me love, because they knew my ex-teammates from the town: Andre Kendrick, Cornell Brown, Carl Bradley, and Robert Adams.

The inmates gave me food, snacks, magazines, and plenty of phone time. I didn't want for anything, but when I got moved to Petersburg, Virginia, the hospitality differed.

In Federal Correctional Institution-Petersburg, I was placed in an isolated cell for my entire stay without a hint of a shower, soap, or a toothbrush.

The only food I could eat were the turkey and cheese sandwiches pushed through the door's slot three times a day.

I wasn't allowed to make any phone calls or read anything besides a half-torn magazine with a five-page-spread of Christina Aguilera.

More bored than horny, I masturbated to the songstress' photos while humming *Genie in a Bottle*—for eight days straight.

My first time in solitary confinement, I'd gone a little batty, and when the Marshals had come to transport me to Atlanta, I was famished, depleted of protein, and reeked of mayonnaise.

During the eight-hour bus ride to the Atlanta airport, I pretended to sleep, so none of the other inmates would talk to me.

I didn't want to indulge in frivolous conversations about how much money an inmate made, or how many *bitches* he fucked, or which rapper his cousin's *baby-daddy's* sister went to the middle school prom with in 1989.

Instead, my thoughts were filled with appreciation and gratitude to God, my family, my real friends, and my attorney for keeping his promise.

* * *

Last month, the Honorable Judge John Burke sentenced me to the sixty-month Federal Mandatory Minimum for *Possession with the Intent to sell five grams of crack cocaine*, and *Possession with the Intent to sell seven grams of heroin*. Both counts running concurrently, which, of course—was the plea agreement.

During my sentencing, Assistant U.S. Attorney Sharon Rogers attempted to get a continuation on my case, but Mr. Hudson argued diligently that she had no grounds to impinge on my Constitutional Rights for a quick and speedy trial—and the Honorable Judge Burke agreed.

No one with any substantial evidence had emerged, and without the disappearing Dirt and Aaron, I couldn't have been charged with anything further.

No new witnesses.

No new developments.

No new federal case.

Outraged about the five year prison sentence, and the *four* years of supervised release I had received in federal court—DEA Agent Pete McMurtry took the stand for thirty minutes at my state sentencing, where I pleaded guilty to three counts of Conspiracy to sell crack cocaine, totaling three grams.

Agent McMurtry's testimony was deemed *personal*, and the court even erupted in laughter when he repeated my "fried chicken" punch line. The *brother* must've forgotten that White folks loved a *good* fried chicken joke.

After the Honorable Judge *Stanley* Burke, ironically, the nephew of the judge on my federal case, dismissed Agent McMurtry from the stand—Mr. Hudson brought in Daddy, then Brittney, and finally, Mommy as character witnesses to testify on my behalf.

Each gave heartfelt accounts about their relationships with me, my upbringing, and how I've changed.

Never feeling so loved, I cried with each word, and silently vowed to live up to the potential of the young man they all described.

Unlike my federal hearing, where no one could've said anything to influence the judge's decision, I emphatically believed my family's support helped me in my state hearing.

I was sentenced to five years in prison, with five years of probation, both running concurrent with my federal sentence. Mr. Hudson was the best, and I was more than happy to pay for his daughter's first year tuition at Harvard.

Two weeks later, I was out of RCJ and in transit to my first choice of prison, Federal Correctional Institution-Cumberland, in Maryland—only two hours away from Brittney and Ruby.

* * *

A Delta plane leaped into the stratosphere, and I had envied every single person aboard, even the one's flying coach, and the caged dogs next to the landing gear.

With the sun barking fire, I wanted to be with the cool passengers who had the luxury of soaring willingly, and without chains.

The 747 flew into the bowels of the heavens, and the clouds absorbed my aspirations of independence.

My *diesel therapy*, a term used by the Marshals, had begun with a fresh fondness for the rule-following squares I prided myself to never have been.

Nice guys *didn't* finish last.

"OK people, the women inmates will enter through the front of the plane, and the men will enter through the back! Let's go people!" Marshal Webb commanded.

"Right this way men! Follow the man in front of you slowly! Don't go until the man to your left goes and follow him! Don't stop until you reach Marshal Anderson at the stairs! Let's go!" a raspy voice behind me shouted. "Ladies go right there to Marshal Leftwich! Move people!"

The third person in the front row, I didn't have to wait long to start walking. I trailed just inches behind a heavyset Latino with a crew cut, and three teardrop tattoos under booth eyes—signifying he had murdered six people.

He limped, foot for foot, behind a slender Black kid with mini-dreadlocks and a tattoo on his forearm of a lion with a mane full of dreads.

The leg restraints cut into our bare ankles, but we had to keep trudging ahead to a ramp of stairs at the plane's tail.

The overseers patrolled beside us with keen eyes and itchy fingers, as a serenade of chains jingled to the first steps of a federal prison bid.

I dared not look at any marshals in the face, in fear that a reckless eyeball could end with a senseless death. Instead, I focused on the word, *Peligroso*, inked on the back of the gang-banger's neck in front of me.

When my amigo stopped moving, I would stop moving. An arm's length from a serial killer, I was more terrified of the goggled White faces than the tattooed brown one.

Just keep moving and looking straight. Don't stop looking straight.
Almost there.

An overcast momentarily shaded me from the penetrating heat, while a deafening mechanical hiss bit further into my brain, and I knew we were under the plane's wing—only a few feet away from the stairs.

An easy breeze blew, and I grinned inside with the whiff of jet-fuel and burnt rubber. The smell proved that I was alive.

I had only done ten months, but I knew that with patience, perseverance, and the grace of God—I would be home one day continuing to live. But I had to get through this plane ride first!

Four more years and I'm back.

One day at a time.

This plane is long as shit though.

"Stop right there Ziggy!" a deep voiced Marshal Anderson ordered, while mounted at the foot of the stairs with a German shepherd. The burly man grasped a leather leash in one hand, and a rifle in the other.

"Go up the steps slowly! Don't want you hurting yourself!"

Ziggy?

Racist bastard.

"OK *Guadalupe*—your turn! Nice and slow!" Marshal Anderson sustained the renaming.

"Fuck you cabrón! My name ain't no stinking Guadalupe—it's Hector, puto!" the amigo corrected.

"We have a hos-tile one here!" Marshal Anderson yelled, and two unseen marshals, equal in girth, appeared miraculously from behind the stairs.

"Aaaaaah! Get off me, you fucking gringo pigs!" Hector screamed as one marshal put him in a headlock, and the second marshal boosted the amigo's feet in the air.

The marshals carried Hector up the steps like a sack of pinto beans, into the plane's open door.

"Aaah! Fuck you! I know my rights! I know my..."

They're not playing!

How did they just man-handle him like that?

"How 'bout you, *Santo Domingo*? You know your rights too?" Marshal Anderson asked me. The stench of cigarette and pickle blew in my face.

Don't say anything!

I'm not Dominican you stank-mouth-bitch!

Wish I could knock those goggles off your stupid face!

"A platano of little words I see! Smart man, you are—Santo Domingo! Go up the stairs and be careful big fella! Don't want you hurting yourself!"

Waddling up the stairs, I endured the agony of steel gouging my ankles with each stride.

As I leaned forward for balance, the chain around my waist, which looped between my handcuffs, pressed cruelly against my Lumbar spine.

Oh God, how can they do this to us? Shit hurts!

I felt like I was being sawed in half each time I raised a knee.

Once reaching the last step, I clenched my jaw and wouldn't dare to blink because my eyes had filled with tears. I would rather have died than give the marshals the satisfaction of seeing me cry.

* * *

Immediately entering the plane, I passed by a locked gun rack on my left with eight shotguns, before walking through a caged doorway.

And I noticed Hector detained, with six Velcro body straps, to a solitary seat that faced outwards. He was sleeping.

I carefully kept moving toward Marshal Webb, fifteen rows ahead, standing in the aisle at the middle of the plane, while the female inmates entered an adjacent caged doorway.

He pointed to his right at the inmate with the dreads, already settled in a windowless window seat, which meant I was stuck in the center.

Worried, I hoped no one as big as I got the aisle seat. Being shackled and tight would've been unbearable.

"Right this way hoss! Better to be stuck with the bitch seat in here, than be *stuck* like a *bitch* in the joint!" Marshal Webb joked.

Fuck you!

Finally, I get to sit down!

Resting silently, the dread nodded at me, and I nodded back just as another inmate plunked into the seat next me.

Snuff-colored with gray hairs flaked in the thick of a curly Afro, with an untouched mustache that grew frenziedly over his top lip—the inmate had spotless skin, and a slender nose.

The willowy fellow had blackish lips like he smoked rolled up cigarettes all day in the city jail.

His weasel eyes wandered with worry, suggesting he had never been to prison, or at very least, never been on a plane to one.

He wasn't Hispanic, but he wasn't all African American either. We could've been kin. From his face to his mannerisms, he reminded me of my little brother, Alejandro.

Damn I miss my brothers! I hope they be OK without me!

"What up bull? My name is Boo," he acquainted himself, but I didn't reply.

This dude trying to get us put to bed like the amigo.

"Shit, my bad," he apologized, lowering his voice.

Please don't talk any more Boo!

Surprisingly, despite the inside of a kennel feel, and flight attendants with artillery, the plane was no different from any other commercial airliner.

Minus the coffee and hot food aroma, the plane even had the same blend of lingering smells: Stale air that re-circulated from the outside through the engines to the cabin, cleaning chemicals, plastic, and ass-sweat permeating from the cushions.

After a few minutes, the plane suffused with musty convicts, and I thought there might have been actual beasts on-board.

My nuts are humming.

Man, why they had to have an empty row between us? I can't see any of the girls' faces.

Hold up, I can see a couple of chins. Damn, she got almost a full fucking beard! They sure that's a woman?

Man, if she got a pussy, I'd fuck her hairy ass. Cooch probably smells like death though.

Shit, I don't care. Would I eat it?

Nah. Hell no.

Man, I'm lying.

I'd eat that box like an Ethiopian at a Chinese buffet!

"Ladies and gentlemen, we're about to take off! Once in the air, we will give you lunch! Try not to make a mess!

"Remember, nooooo talking period! Oh yea, put on your seatbelts please! That's it! Enjoy the ride folks!" Marshal Webb informed and headed to the back.

"Motherfucking devil," the dread whispered with a West Indian accent, while seatbelts had begun to fasten.

CLICK. CLICK.

Why the hell do we need these?

"How are we looking up there marshals?" Marshal Webb hollered.

"All ready to go Webb!" a female's voice answered.

Damn, I didn't see any lady marshals! Sounds sexy!

Wonder what she looks like.

"OK tell the captain we are secured and let's go!" Marshal Webb authorized, as the plane continued in motion.

No emergency exit spiel or nothing, huh? If we crash, then we're all just dead!

We gonna be in the fucking air with jailery on and can't move! We will drown instantly if we land in water!

And if we crash on land, survive, and run, we will be shot!

God, if you're listening—don't let me die like this! I have too much good in my heart, and too much good to offer the world! Thank you. Amen.

"Jah, let cha boi feel dah ganja runnin' tru mi lungs one mah time, my-yute—Amen," the dread spoke quietly.

Did he just call God, 'my-yute'? Ha-ha, Jamaican niggas.

"Lord, I'm too pretty to die in this jawn, thanks," Boo prayed.

'Jawn'?

Ha-ha, Philly niggas.

The 727 dashed down the runway, and the gears shifted powerfully. I prayed silently, but the mumbles of devotion to a Higher Power could be heard throughout the cabin.

The Marshals, showing they did have a heart, didn't complain or reprimand anymore for breaking the marshals' vow of silence.

The plane slashed through the shuddering winds that wiped out the voices, but just as we bounced to the air—a *passenger* in the front could be heard expressing her overwhelming anxiety.

"HELP! AAAHH! God get me off this plane! I don't want to die! I have four children! How could they take a mother away from her babies? I'm innocent!

"My husband put that shit in my bag and said I wouldn't get caught! I can't go to prison! Nooooo! I can't do thirty years! Oooh God, why? Whhhyy?" the woman shrilled, and I rubbernecked to identify the troubled soul—but I couldn't see a thing from my position.

"Ma'am just relax! It's going to be OK! Just relax and breathe!" the female Marshal said, attempting to control the situation.

Please stop and listen!

"Noooo—it's not! I need to go home! Get me off this plane!" the woman cried, spastically yanking at her restraints. "I don't belong here!"

Please stop! You can't win!

"Andrew she's hostile!" the female Marshal cited.

"Okie-dokie!" the Asian marshal replied.

"You bitch! Do you have kids, you bitch? I hope they fucking diiiieee! Oooh God! GET ME OUT OF HERE!" the inmate screamed louder. Her outrage gave me goosebumps.

"OK, this will pinch juuusst a bit!" Andrew warned.

"Aaaah—fuck you! Fuck yooou! Fuuuh..." the inmate's voice faded.

"OK, she's out!" Andrew said. "You want to strap her up in the back with the Mexican?"

"Nah, just let her sleep it off! By the time she wakes up, she'll be in a prison cell...for the next thirty *years*!" the female marshal joked.

"Good one Tina!" Andrew approved of the insensitive satire.

Tina, you are a cunt!

"All good Webb!" Tina shouted.

"Roger that!" Marshal Webb yelled from the plane's rear.

"And for that outburst, ladies and gentlemen, there will be no food or water on this-here dang flight! Next time, there will be no bathroom privileges either!"

The low-pitched grumbles spread row by row, and many inmates sucked their teeth in protest, but most, like me—never verbalized any dissatisfaction.

Challenging federal agents with guns, while shackled 30,000 feet in the air was not intelligent and wouldn't produce a favorable outcome for anyone.

We were at the mercy of the Con-Air authoritarians, who would certainly cause any one of us bodily harm then go have a burger, and giggle at our suffering.

After months of sitting in solitary confinement for inciting a riot, we would wait to hear how much "good-time" we lost from our sentence.

Obviously, I had never been to the feds, but I learned enough in jail about the system from guys who had—to understand to keep my opinions to myself, do my time, and come home.

Other than the principle of having another man dictate if I could eat or not, I didn't really care about missing the damn sandwiches! My tummy was full of sadness.

The sedated mom had four little kids, and thirty long years. Swallowing the prisoner's predicament was painful.

I listened to her pleads for exculpation *outside* of a courtroom, and I could feel the decay in her heart.

I thought of Mommy, who could've easily been in the same situation, although Daddy always protected her from his street life—never revealing any parts of his business to her.

But there were still risk for anyone receiving benefits from a drug dealer—especially a drug dealer's wife.

That lady could've been Mommy.

How will that lady's children grow up without their moms? Shit is fucked up!

She got thirty joints! And I'm here complaining about a punk-ass five years.

Woman would cut her hand off to get my time.

So glad Mommy never got in trouble.

I wouldn't know what to do if something ever did. Thank God, she's always been safe!

We always have been safe.

I didn't like Eugene at first, strictly because he wasn't Daddy. Eugene is great for her though.

Now I see, he's great for her.

A great father and an honest man.

Money doesn't mean shit sometimes.

My dumbass had to learn the hard way.

My thoughts fluently roamed from hypothetical to reality, and I didn't obstruct the lane that my mind yearned to wander as the plane cruised with the gentle sounds of sleeping inmates.

I didn't have to ever sell drugs, but I had become obsessed with the allure of the lifestyle—the money, the girls, and the respect.

I was a smart kid with ambition to achieve positive goals, but I was stubborn and arrogant. I insisted on conforming to what I saw, but was never meant to be.

This shit is crazy.

I'm supposed to be playing in the NFL or something. I regret ever trying weed.

I was a good boy before the drugs.

I lost my way.

When I get out, I'm following the rules.

I got greedy. I would trade all the money I've made to be home with Ruby.

If I had listened to my parents instead of watching the streets, I would not have been sitting in a last-class seat on Con-Air.

Long before selling my first gram of coke, I had thought about being a drug dealer, but my family's wise words stopped me from indulging in the ignorance.

Although I remembered a few times that I took heed to positive advice, the one moment that I didn't listen was impossible to forget—my first conversation ever with Coach Frank Beamer.

* * *

"Hey Manzo, I'm coach Frank Beamer. Pleasure to meet you." Coach Beamer, in his maroon VT windbreaker suit, shook my hand as we stood on the fifty-yard-line of a vacated Lane Stadium.

Oh man, it's really him!

"Pleasure is all mine sir," I greeted and smiled.

"So you had a nice flight with Coach Pry and Coach Bustle?"

"Yes sir. Great guys sir. And thank you for sending the jet. A van would've been fine by me sir."

"Oh, nonsense son. Here at Tech, we take care of our guys," he said, slapping my shoulder.

"Yes sir. Thank you, Coach Beamer. Virginia Tech is a quality program. I have heard nothing but great things about this place."

"So have you been on any other recruiting trips yet Manzo?"

"No sir, this is my first one."

"OK good. Well, you will enjoy this one. I have the brothers, Todd and T.J. Washington, as your guides for the weekend.

'They will show you the campus, and I'm sure they will get you out on the town. I know you're looking forward to that after being in your all-boys school."

"Ha-ha, yes sir—I can't deny that at all Coach."

"Woodberry Forest is a mighty fine school. One of the best, and Coach Grimes tells me you received an academic scholarship there, which is outstanding! So, if you can handle the academics at Woodberry, then you won't have any troubles here Manzo."

"Yes sir." I nodded.

"So would you go to class if you came here?" Coach Beamer inquired.

"Yes sir, I wouldn't skip a single class."

"And I believe you Manzo, because here class is important, and not just for eligibility purposes—but for life *beyond* football."

"Yes sir."

"Now it's pretty clear to all the coaches that you have what it takes to play here—to play *anywhere*. But we need good character guys who will stay out of trouble, get an A-1 education, and work his tail off, on and off the field." Coach Beamer clarified his program's expectations. "You understand son?"

"Yes sir, I absolutely understand."

"In life, I have a simple rule that I live by, and that we here at Virginia Tech demand from our young men. And that rule is to *always do things right*. Just do things right and you will make your parents, the university, and your friends proud," he explained.

"The guys who want to take short cuts in life will have a harder time and live with a bunch of regrets. I can promise ya that son."

Always do things right.

"Now Manzo, that doesn't mean you have to be perfect. You might make a mistake or two while you're here, just like any young man your age, but if you make doing this right part of who you are, the mistakes you make will be limited. And when you do make a mistake, you take responsibility for it, and grow from it.

"Mistakes are a part of life, but it's the people who learn from them, correct them and don't repeat them—are the ones who are successful.

"And you seem to be one of those guys who are destined for success...if you, *just do things right*."

* * *

Coach Beamer never mentioned the actual game of football. He never mentioned the wins or the losses, or how the Hokies upset the University of Texas in the 1995 Sugar Bowl.

Not a word was spoken about the many players drafted into the NFL each year either.

He talked about the fundamental principles of being a good person, which would ultimately translate into the type of football player Virginia Tech wanted on their team.

From reading the newspapers and watching ESPN, I had known about the dozen or so players on the team that had messed up, just as I'd known about the many chances that Coach Beamer had given them to change their lives.

Some kids listened, some kids didn't, and the ones who failed to reform were removed from the team.

The university and Coach Beamer's reputation had been scrutinized for the perception of being undisciplined, so I comprehended completely that the program needed a change, and I would be part of that change.

After meeting the legend, I had decided that I would attend Virginia Tech, and I didn't even bother going on another recruiting trip.

Honored that I was deemed worthy to fight with the Hokies on Saturdays, I pledged that I would live my life by Coach Beamer's motto.

He talked to me like a father—like he cared.

His influence and energy reached my core values, and my entire time playing for one of the greatest college football coaches of all time, Coach Beamer remained consistent with his expectations, his morals, and his love for each guy who had put on a uniform.

But somewhere I changed, and my life changed when I ignored Coach Beamer's wisdom and *stopped* doing things right.

* * *

I would not be on this damn plane if I'd just did things right!

Why didn't I listen to Coach Beamer?

Just look at me in chains like an animal! I'm better than this! God didn't bring me to this earth for this shit! Fuck drugs!

Fuck coke! Fuck the cars! Fuck the money!
Should've never took that first pull of weed!
Jay said that shit gonna lead to other stuff!
Why didn't I listen? I wanted everything so fast!
I'm a Woodberry alum on a fucking federal plane to prison!
I will be a good father!
It's not too late. The world will see.
Starting right now, I gotta do things right...

With genuine remorse in my heart, I dozed off and slept without any interruption until we landed in Harrisburg, Pennsylvania.

Starving and stank, I had a headache, yet I was overjoyed to get off Con-Air, and onto *Con-bus.*

My ankles bled, but my soul felt cleansed with a new sense of purpose and priority. I knew I couldn't live without error, although, even in prison, I planned on living as righteously as possible.

Sadly though, my carry-on of promises was left on the plane and would not travel with me, the 139.9 miles to my new home, and one of the most dangerous prisons in the federal system, FCI-Cumberland.

Chapter Thirty-One

FRESH MEET

"OK Manzo, you got ya prison identification—keep that with you at all times. Here is your prison handbook, ya cell number is written on top—cell number six.

Damn, I look like a real thug in this pic.

"You can keep those slippers, the t-shirt, and pajama pants things you have on that I gave you, but in the sack that you're holding—there's three khaki pants, three khaki shirts, one short sleeve, two long sleeve, and ya belt.

"Please keep ya shirt tucked in at all times. Here's ya size-thirteen boots, five white boxer shorts, five pair of socks, size-thirteen shower shoes, a pair of white sheets, one wool blanket, one pillow, a toothbrush, toothpaste, soap, deodorant, and small comb...but noooo partridge in a goddamn pear tree," Officer Stewart listed the items as he sat behind his desk, stuffing my property in a white mesh laundry bag."

Damn, this shit reminds of me Lester Karlin handing out equipment at Tech.

"Ha-ha—thank you, sir," I said.

"OK, so, sign right here would ya big fella?"

"Yes sir," I obliged, signing the first of three-forms on his desk.

"OK, for the visitation—you must see the counselor in your unit for the forms to send to your visitors that they must complete and send back directly to the counselor.

"Other than your immediate family, they can't be convicted felons, or they will get denied, so don't waste your time," Officer Stewart explained.

Damn, that's most of my peoples!

"You understand that son?" he asked.

"Yes sir."

"So Manzo, the people should be people that you know will come. Besides immediate family, you can only have ten people on ya visitation list at a time, so don't waste a spot for a *maybe*—because it takes a few days to check ya folks out and get them approved and in the system. Don't want to have your *homies* stuck outside. You got that?"

"Yes sir," I responded.

I'm going to get to hold Ruby!

"OK, sooo, outside of your *wife*, siblings, parents, and children—who do you want on your list son?"

"Um, I would like Reese Malone, Nat Williams, Michael Starke, James Crawford, Tyron Edmond, Cornell Brown, Tala Shalavi. *Tala*...spelled, T-a-l-a. Shahlavi...S-h-a-h-l-a-v-i. Freddy Hollins, Melanie Burgess, and Sean Sullivan... spelled, *S-E-A-N*—"

"Wait a minute son! You just spelled it wrong. That's *sean*...like, 'I *sean* him get stabbed'."

That's 'seen' asshole!

"No sir, it's spelled correctly. *Sean*...S-E-A-N...is pronounced the same as—"

"What crazy son-of-gun names their kid, *Sean*?" He ignored my English lesson.

"Anyway...anybody else you want son?"

I wish I could see Dirt!

"No sir, that's already ten. Thank you."

I just want to get the fuck outta here!

* * *

The last of six incoming inmates at the Receiving and Discharge Building in FCI-Cumberland, I waited in a bench-less holding cell for an hour before Officer Stewart had taken my fingerprints and snapped my picture.

Because of an incident on the compound, most of the officers working the prisoner intake had to run out of R&D, leaving Officer Stewart alone to process the class of June 19, 2001, and he was not in a rush.

Uniformed in a pressed, brown, short-sleeved button-down shirt, and tan slacks with dark-brown stripes down the side, Officer Stewart, a bearish man in his forties—poked his chest out unsuccessfully past his gut when he walked. He had a natural skinny-legged drag to his step like he was an actual giant.

His face was pudgy, and his right eye twitched after six blinks.

Beneath the nine slicked-over, flaxen hairs on his balding scalp, a colony of monster moles swelled as if pink Gremlins would pop out of his skull after a quick dip in the pool.

He had tobacco-lathered ragged teeth, and forearms that bulged with the impenetrable density of a dairy farmer.

Officer Stewart seemed like he enjoyed being the biggest guy in any room, just as much as he did to watch wresting with a cold beer.

I had heard stories from the guys in the Roanoke City Jail about most the Cumberland officers being racist, but it was natural for people of color to assume that White folks in the mountains weren't fond of our kind.

Add the fact that we were convicts, and most assumptions were considered fact, but I would never pass judgment on individuals based on the opinions of others, even though Officer Stewart's *satire* went beyond political incorrectness.

I hoped the first guard I met wasn't a representation of them all.

Earlier in the holding cell, I was discussing with Boo, the Philly dude from the plane, how Jay-Z and the new kid, 50-Cent, were my favorite rappers.

Simultaneously, the other three Black inmates, Denis Cole, Marvin Hill, and Kareem Solomon—conversed with Vincenzo Federico, a mobster from California, about how Italians *loved them some Black pussy.*

Vincenzo cried out in laughter, and Officer Stewart tossed his half-eaten Arby's roast beef sandwich on his desk, and ran to the cell bars, scrutinizing the situation.

Once discovering that no harm had been done to Vincenzo, Officer Stewart snickered and commented as he walked away, "Glad you five brothers weren't raping the guinea. I would've tossed a basketball in there, so you guys would stop."

After the officer's remark, a hush hung over the cell, but I was the sole inmate to display any animosity for the despicable comment—I merely shook my head.

Officer Stewart smirked and removed the top folder from a stack on his desk, tucking the folder at the bottom of the pile.

Once he called Denis *Cole* out of the cell to be processed first, I was well aware I would be last to leave R&D, since *Manzo* was always first in the alphabetical order because I had no last name.

Finding Officer Stewart's pettiness comical, I returned a smirk without a worry, because the clock on the wall still ticked, and I had nothing but time.

With patience, I wished each retreating inmate a safe prison bid, and waited my turn.

* * *

"OK, Maaaan-zo...hey, why don't you have a doggone last name?

I knew this bullshit was coming.

"My father was a Black Panther and didn't like his slave name, so he ditched the shit."

"Oooh...OK...uum...all righty then. Sooo...lastly, right over here on the bottom of this last form, sign, saying that your money did follow you from the Roanoke City Jail.

"And it says here, in your prison account...you haaavve...you have... *$9,899!*" Officer Stewart screeched, jerking back his neck.

"Damn son—you a big time *motha-fuhckah,* I see. But you know you can't spend but $250 a month at the commissary here?"

"Yes sir, I was informed. Thank you," I said.

"Good thing it ain't $10,000, I wudda had to report you to the doggone IRS. You a lucky one son," he said.

Not lucky. Smart.

"Yes sir. How strange? I guess I am, ha-ha," I *agreed,* scribbling my initials where he pointed.

"Did Huey P. Newton leave you a little something-something in his will?" he inquired.

Real piece of fucking work, this guy.

"No sir, my mother sold her car and gave me all the money. She said she didn't mind the two-mile walk to and from work. My mom is 300 pounds, so the exercise should do her well," I lied.

"OK...well...shit...uuh...OK—let's get you out of here."

Good, because I can do this shit all day buddy.

"Oh yea, almost forgot. You can only move from building to building on a ten-minute-move, which means when you hear that horn go off, every hour, on the *half* hour.

"You have ten minutes to get from A to B. After the ten minutes, all the doors will be locked, and you will get a shot for being in a restricted area.

"A shot is a write-up, and getting too many shots, depending on the severity of the type of shot you receive, could lead to loss of visitation for an extended period of time.

"Also, you could lose ya commissary, spend some time in the hole, and even lose some good-time...but you do have the right to appeal the shot with ya counselor." Officer Stewart had risen to his feet.

"Your counselor's name is Mr. *Britt* by the way. Like your boo-thang, so don't go catching flashbacks and try and poke him in the ass or anything. He can't have babies."

What?

"I'm just fucking with ya Baby Huey—but let me take that pen from you killer. Thaaank you, follow me please.

"Don't forget your sack. You might need that. Don't want you selling ass for soap.

"Let's go big fella. Come with me. It's *show time*," he ordered.

After grabbing my belongings, I caught a fleeting glance of President *Dubya* on the wall before following Officer Stewart down a hallway—which extended twenty feet to a laurel-green painted door, opposite the building's front entrance.

Officer Stewart waved his left hand at the security camera that angled directly at us.

The door buzzed, and he heaved it open before letting me pass, firmly shutting the door behind him.

Oh shit, I'm about to go on the compound! This is it!

Side by side, we walked several ivory tiles to another door, identical to the previous entryway, except for an eye-level, egg-shaped glass window, which shared some natural light.

Officer Stewart repeated his hand movements at the second, yet bulkier security camera, screwed to the top left of the wall.

My nerves shook with the high-pitched clearance to the compound as Officer Stewart unblocked the final lane toward my new life.

* * *

The door opened with the essence of picnics on Randall's Island wafting through the air.

The astringent musk from freshly cut-grass mellowed my mood, bringing to mind, a filthy-footed boy scampering through the meadows. The nostalgia was pleasurable and compelling.

Although a mob of Mister-*not-so*-Nice-Guys awaited me on the other side of the law, I felt enlivened with the opportunity to encounter the unknown, like a child on his first day of school. I had no fear—just great promise.

Damn, it's bright and hot out there!

Mommy always made the best barbecue ribs. This is a prison?

The only prisons that I've ever seen in my life had been the hardcore penitentiaries filmed on dreary cloudy days in the movies or on *60 Minutes*, but FCI-Cumberland was not one of those prisons—*aesthetically.*

Looking out into my new neighborhood, I was taken aback by the landscape and architecture of the compound, with its manicured lawns, thriving beech trees, and untarnished red brick buildings.

As the sun shined brightly, my eyes followed the paved linear path at my feet. The path spanned fifteen yards to a square of cement, the size of a kiddy pool, planted in the middle of the prison.

Connecting to the square, five more avenues of concrete diverged from around the platform like octopus tentacles, unraveling throughout the compound.

Excluding the path leading to a group of buildings on my left, each walkway sloped three hundred feet, and ended at a set of triangular, two-story complexes that resembled Billiard racks.

Place looks like a college campus!

"OK hoss, as you can see the pound is empty. It's 2:24 PM and the ten-minute-move starts at 2:30, so I'm gonna let you out a few minutes early to beat the rush," Officer Stewart said.

Damn that's mad nice of him.

"Don't want anyone plucking ya off before you had a chance to shower." He giggled.

"Lighten up Manzo. I'm just busting your balls, but anyway...right there... that ole square thing in the middle, right there. Ya see that?"

"Yes sir, I see that," I answered.

"OK, once you get to that square, which we call, Times Square—like the one in *Nuu Yawk*, so you should feel right at home big fella.

"But anyway, once you get to that-there square, go down the road to your right...not the hard right...the wiggly one to the left of that one, but on the right." he explained and snaked his hand in the air.

I'm not dumb!

"You got that big fella?"

"Yes sir, I see the one you're talking about, thank you."

"OK, good. Once you go all the way down there, your new residence is B-1, which is the palace on the right, not the left. The left is *B-2*. You're in *B-1*. Sooo, the left is B-2...and the right *is*?"

"B-1...got it," I answered.

This shit is crazy, my dorm at Woodberry was B-1.

"Good! You're a smart one, I tell ya! OK, lets fly out of the nest, crow. Good luck and don't drop the cocoa butter!" Officer Stewart made a parting quip, and placed a hand on my back, lightly guiding me out of the door.

Did he just call me a crow?

SLAM!

CLICK!

Oh shit, this is really happening! I need a cigarette!

Some weed!

A drink!

Something!

Mesmerized by the scenery, I hefted my bag over my shoulder and advanced up the walkway.

The compound was desolate sans two White officers in dirty-pigeon colored uniforms, sporting navy-blue caps and shades, and standing in front of a building, west of Times Square. One officer appeared to be holding an airhorn.

Inmates' banter, along with basketballs pounding, could be heard in the distance, and I assumed that the *yard* was behind the structures, in the opposite direction from my unit.

I hope these guys have some skills on the court. I need some real sneakers for real though.

I reached Times Square and stopped before surveying the trail to B-1. I was supposed to be receiving punishment for my two counts of drug distribution, but nothing so far about prison seemed unlike my last two institutions.

The serenity of FCI-Cumberland matched that of Woodberry Forest School and Virginia Tech.

As I listened to the birds lullabying and watched the squirrels playing, I couldn't fathom anyone housed in these units, other than students and scholar-athletes, but, of course, I was wrong.

"BRNNNEHHHHHHH!"

Amidst a heart-thumping flinch, I twisted around to find a trim, White officer with a red beard that complemented his ruddy complexion and freckles, three-feet away and holding an air horn to the sky.

He held his silver Timex to his face, and even though I didn't see any sprinters yet, I knew that the race had started—I already identified the tracks.

"TEN-MINUTE-MOVE!" the officer hollered.

What the fuck?

"You better get a move on big guy," the officer suggested.

An outpour of inmates burst out the doors of every unit, rapidly spilling up the path that led to where I stood next to a government employee.

From all angles, men stampeded tightly together, swarming the compound in haste and with purpose, while in conversation with others, or in the solitude of their own thoughts.

Like a game of Space Invaders, they charged in rows, but there was no zapping these creatures. We belonged to the same colony.

Walk asshole!

Like Fritz and Hen-Dog's old crew—No Fear!

You got this!

Accepting that I was one of them and there was nothing to be afraid of, I entered the thoroughfare confidently, and teetered where grass and cement met.

Twelve steps into my odyssey, I *brushed* shoulders with the leader of the pack, a baldheaded gargantuan with a lazy eye, shaved face, and an immense keloid scar—sliced from his left ear to his chin.

In a sweat suit that barely fit, he had patent-leather Black skin, and was the width of the walkway.

His huge quad muscles separated with each stomp of the all-white Air Force Ones on his feet.

I ignored the physical contact and kept moving, but the couple of passing remarks grabbed my attention.

"Oooh shiiid! Big John gonna get some freessshh meeeaat!" someone with a Spanish accent hooted.

"I dunno amigo—da new fishy is kinda swole too! Watch-out-dere-now Big John Stud!" an inmate squealed, sounding totally like a woman.

"Ha, ha, ha—tell 'em Big John! The bigger, the *better!*" a scratchy voice added.

Keep walking!

They're bugging!

I'm nobody's fucking fish! I need to find a shank!

Riled up by the commentary, I hightailed down the walkway with sweat soaking my t-shirt to my belly, sidestepping the assemblage of figures flashing by my left peripheral. I could see everything, but I wanted to see nothing.

Americans. Arabs. Asians. Dread-swinging-West-Indians. Gang bangers. Gays. Indians. Italians. Jewish men. Latinos Muslims. Native. Nerds. Old timers. Rednecks Rednecks. Tattooed skinheads. Transgenders. Young boys.

All the faceless faces of a convict were attired in a mélange of prison couture.

The inmates wore khakis, sweatpants, gym shorts, white t-shirts, gray t-shirts, construction boots, wife-beaters, and sneakers from Kmart's "my momma can't afford Jordan's" section.

With the rush hour of transgressors passing, I slipped by a few inmates smoking Black & Mild cigars outside of B-1, before opening the doors to my unit.

* * *

Relinquishing my bag on the floor, I placed both hands on the Smurf-blue banisters and marveled at the boxed, open spaced, multi-leveled unit.

The common's area, set inside a pristinely waxed and narrow footpath, submerged three feet like a sunken living room—stretching horizontally with a thin red carpet that ran from baseline to baseline.

In the right nearest corner, a black thirty-two-inch-television, hanging from a pole that was bolted to the bottom of the second floor's walkway, played the movie *Lethal Weapon* soundlessly.

Wearing headphones and watching the move, three Caucasian inmates, in gray sweatpants, white t-shirts and flip-flops—lounged in beige plastic chairs with numbers inscribed on the back in magic marker.

Twenty feet behind the movie buffs, a frail, elderly man in a khaki uniform, with a lizard face, and jerk-chicken skin tone—dealt cards on a square table covered with an unwashed blanket, the color of a seven-year-old's shoestrings.

A sunburnt surfer-type with shoulder-length sandy-hair, who looked like he soaked his face in crystal meth, sat facing the fast-fingered reptilian who whisked cards to all four sides of the table.

On the opposite end of the common's area, an inmate with a torn white t-shirt sleeve squeezed around his exposed yellow head, incessantly did pull-ups on the back of the row of stairs that led to the second tier. His accessory flopped with each repetition like a daisy in a windstorm.

Clothed in gym shorts and an altered sweatshirt that fit him like a football jersey, he had an Olympic swimmer's physique, and sculpted calves that were accentuated by his black ankle socks.

Man, I need to work out with homie. I can't wait to lose this gut.

In a lone chair facing left, a few feet from the home gym, a pint-sized gentleman donned a brown suede Kufi over his Caesar haircut.

He bopped his head to the Beanie Sigel rap video playing on a television, which suspended from a pole like the other TV.

The avid BET fan's New Balances flashed a virgin-white, and his oversized khaki uniform seemed to have been creased by Allah SWT, Himself.

The Muslim brother had citrine-pigmented aboriginal features, with a thick-set, seal-brown beard masking his age and race. He could've passed for Arab, but I knew my people.

The youngster was surely Puerto Rican and in his early twenties. No older man could remember that many damn rap lyrics.

Yooo, I haven't seen a video in mad long!

I need to get some headphones immediately!

Damn, whatever big boy cooking over there must be bangin!

B-1 had the zest of a Spanish restaurant, and I could taste the Sazón and Adobo seasoning in the air.

For a moment, I thought there was a kitchen in one of the rooms, but I quickly nosed out the origins of the Sofrito aroma.

A microwave beeped sequentially on a table resting on the left outer half of the unit's bottom floor, while a knock-kneed husky inmate with the standard t-shirt, shorts, and black Nike flip-flops—stirred a long green spoon into a tan plastic *bowl*, resembling the base of a big flowerpot.

He had an unnatural sepia tinge to his chubby face like he had been sunbathing, and the tattoos that sleeved his arms and legs were as indiscernible as his light beard.

Opening the microwave, the chef pulled out a rectangular Tupperware dish, and emptied the steaming contents into his mixing bowl as a pale tubby officer strolled out of the office, which was entrenched in the center of the outermost wall—parallel to B-1's entrance.

The guard, with a drill-sergeant's fade and a snowy-haired five o'clock shadow, stroked his belly and lifted his snout in the air.

Snooping at the microwave, the guard simpered, looking delighted by the cuisine, before returning to the office.

That shit smells good as a motherfucker! How you cook chicken in a microwave?

What's in those back rooms?

Throughout the first floor, men walked casually around the perimeter, entering and exiting glass cubicles at the top-left corner of the unit that I perceived as more television rooms, since everyone who entered or exited the room had on headphones—some men carried chairs.

Each time the door opened, I could hear hints of an animated discussion about who was the better college quarterback, Michael Vick or Peyton Manning?

The inmates argued with the conviction of a classic barbershop debate, and I knew before long that I'd be sharing my knowledge with B-1's premiere sports analysts, but I understood I would have to be careful.

Proving that I was right could turn out so wrong.

People generally got heated when defending their teams or favorite players.

Considering that many of my ex-teammates played in the pros, like Super Bowl XXXV champion, Cornell Brown—I had no desire to have to defend my friends or my school over an inmate's disrespectful comments.

That's a no brainer...Michael Vick.

It's mad cells upstairs!

This place is big as shit! Where's the showers?

The second tier, approximately twenty feet overhead the base of the unit, consisted of neighboring prison cells in rows of fifteen, on each of the three walls in my range of vision.

With exception to the sea serpent paint, the cell doors were interchangeable with the ones at the Roanoke City Jail.

A few of cells even had their rectangular windows blacked out, of course, universally signifying *Do Not Disturb.*

Outside of the cells, a confined balcony, also safeguarded by banisters, doubled as a passageway that linked along all four walls—elevating the unit to a loft residency.

* * *

"BENNY!" the old timer at the card table had arisen from his chair and hollered. "Has anyone seen dat godt-damn Benny?"

"Yea, and where the fuck is Juan at?" the flower child at the table asked.

"JUAN!" the old timer screamed again, looking around the unit. "Y'all get y'alls asses out here!"

CLICK!

BANG!

"We right here Skid! Hold the hell up!" a Tuscan brown heavyset young man with jet-black, wavy hair demanded after storming out of a cell, four doors down from where I stood.

His sweatpants and t-shirt were offensively filthy as if he had just run from third base and slid into home plate.

Fat-necked and jolly, the brother had a chubby-cheeked innocence as if he always covered his eyes with his hands during the brief nudity of a movie.

The feds didn't lock people up for being saints though, so I reminded myself that appearance meant positively nothing in prison.

"Goddamn, Skid Row! You try'na blow a nigga spot up, champ!" a second brother said with a slack-jawed, Washington, D.C. diction.

He rocked a knotty beard, dingy wife-beater and khakis, and ear-length dreads that needed another five years of growth for anyone to contemplate his ethnicity.

Exiting the smoky cell, the guy closed the door behind him and hopped over the banister to the common's area as his portly sidekick traveled the long and less physical route, all along dragging his untied, scraped government-issued boots down, then around the walkway.

Damn, is that weed I smell?

"Benny hurry ya fat-ass up! Y'all youngins always slowing down my damn game!" Skid Row persisted. "Y'all try'na play Spades or what?"

"We here Skid! Stop all that yelling!" Benny said.

"Juan, I'mma drag you by one of dem lil' nappy-ass dreads—you keep playing wit me!" Skid Row threatened.

"Fuck you Skid! Your old-ass ain't gonna do shit!" Juan laughed and sat in the chair that faced the unit's doorway, while Benny plunked in the chair across from him.

"Ooooh shit Skid, you better be quiet before them young boys put them hands on you!" the chef at the microwave added.

"Zane...are you outta ya rabid-ass mind?" Skid asked.

"I don't know Skid. They might jump your old country-ass!" Zane taunted.

"Zane now you know betta! I wud put my foot so far in dis fat motherfucker's ass! *And*, this fake-ass Maxi Priest...*Juan*...or whoever da nigga think he is!

"And somebody please tell me...why in da *hell* dis nigga's momma name his Black-ass after a Mexican coffee maker?" Skid roasted.

"Fuck you! And that coffee nigga is *Columbian* not Mexican, dumbass! Ya ole James Earl Jones in Conan, python-face-looking muhfucker!" Benny snapped back, coming to Juan's rescue.

"Fuck you, ya dirty...Arnold Drummond's fat, retarded uncle-looking-summa'bitch!" Skid clowned.

Ha, ha, ha! These dudes are crazy!

"Hey Skid!" a voice roared from an opened door at the back of the B-1, and in a flash the unit had gotten eerily quiet.

Who said that?

"Uuh...yea...yea...Big Ed," a soft-spoken Skid Row answered.

"Cut all that damn noise out! I'm try'na watch Serena beat this bony Russian girl's ass in here!" the voice ordered.

"Yes Big Ed! No problem!" Skid Row complied and sat down.

Oh shit, that dude is big as fuck!

Pinpointing the center of attention, I doubtlessly understood Skid Row's rationale for not arguing with the monster filling the TV room's entire doorway.

Loaded with melanin and muscles, and with a glorious beard that rivaled Popeye's nemesis, Big Ed had stringy cornrows hanging from under his black beanie.

The man had to have been at least six-foot, five inches and 270 pounds without an ounce of body fat.

His massiveness strained every cotton fiber of his V-neck t-shirt like he had to coat in olive oil before he got dressed.

Big Ed's chest, like bushy bongos, set atop a half-dozen abs that protruded like he had swallowed an ice-tray.

Top heavy, he possessed giant arms that exceeded the girth of his wimpy legs, and his age could've been a legit reason he didn't train his lower extremities.

Although smooth-skinned and gray-less, Big Ed looked to be in his forties, which told me he was most likely over fifty years old.

Serving time was the closest thing to the fountain of youth.

"Hey fellas, is everything all right out here?" the guard patrolled out the office and generally asked.

"Everything is cool Jenkins! I got this!" Big Ed said.

"No problem Big Ed!" Officer Jenkins moseyed on back to his happy place.

Damn, Big Ed runs shit in here!

"Now Skid, you interrupt me watching my baby Serena again, and I'm gonna have to take you upstairs and spank ya!" Big Ed smiled.

"Ha, ha, ha!" the unit erupted in laughter.

"Ah-man, go 'head wit dat bullshit Big Ed!" Skid picked up his cards.

"Big Ed be careful—ole Skid might start tap dancing and playing the drums in front of your motherfucking TV room!" Benny said.

"Ha, ha, ha, ha!" I howled irresistibly, my amusement peeling around the building.

The players at the table dropped their cards, and an awkward silence cleared the unit of its exuberance. I wanted to run away from all the stares.

Absorbed in the unit's high-spiritedness as I waited for Mr. Britt, I had not made a sound, but Benny's buffoonery had really reached my tickle box.

Unable to disappear, I knew that I couldn't just sink my head like some bitch, so I chose to focus on the one man that seemed to demand the most respect —Big Ed.

Ah man, he's looking right through me!

Don't look away!

Lord please don't let that big nigga come over here!

"Hey slim. Where the fuck you from?" Ed hollered.

Fuck, I don't want any shit from him!

Probably got a machete in those big-ass boots!

Speak!

"I'm from New York City!" I answered unflinchingly, and Zane looked up, ceasing to slice the beef sausage sizzling on a lid placed on top of the microwave.

"Another *bama* from up top, huh?" he *asked.*

Fuck!

Why did I come here?

Niggas in Roanoke told me they don't like New Yorkers here!

"Yes, I'm from up top!"

"Nigga, who's your favorite football team...the Giants or the Jets?" Big Ed recommenced.

Come on!

What's with all the questions? It's a test! Everything is always a test in prison!

Be cool!

He's making assumptions! Don't say the Giants!

Say neither!

"I don't like any of those teams!" I replied.

What team do I say?

"So who's your team slim?" Big Ed asked again.

"My Daddy's favorite team!" I lied.

My daddy doesn't even watch football! Pick a team!

"*Nigga*...and what team is that?" Big asked, noticeably irritated.

Think! Hold up!

'Slim'...

'Champ'...

'Bama'...

That's D.C. slang!

"*Nigga*...my team is the mother-fucking Washington Redskins!" I shouted.

"Goddamn right brother!" Someone cheered from inside *Big Ed's* TV room, and then others eavesdropping on the top tier added to the jubilation.

"Hell yea, tell 'em again New York City!"

"Skins taking it all this year!"

"It's our year Zane! Fuck them Giants!" Big Ed hollered.

Oh shit, the chef is from New York!

"Fuck them Skins Big Ed!" Zane defended *our* team.

"Zane listen to your homeboy! I fucks with that bama! Holla at you later Big New York! Not you Zane, you're little New York now!" Big Ed teased Zane and raised a fist toward me before re-entering his TV room.

I reciprocated the hand language as the inmates reestablished minding their own businesses.

"You'sa funny nigga Big Ed!" Zane spoke and placed his plastic knife on the tray of meat.

So far, so good. Where's the counselor?

"Big homie!" Zane hollered in my direction.

"What's up homie?" I asked.

"Who are you waiting for?" Zane inquired.

"I'm waiting for the counselor, Mr. Britt!"

"You don't have to wait for him! Stay right there!" Zane inserted his bowl in the microwave and galloped down the steps into the common's area, making his way to me.

He's from the city but stay on point!

"Pardon my hands, they got food on them. I'm Zane," he gave his obvious alias.

"Man that's cool. I see you doing your thing. I'm Manzo." I said and reached over the banister, tapping my right fist against his.

"Where in the city you from Manzo?"

"I'm from Harlem."

"Another *Harlem* cat—OK, that's what's up son. I'm from Brownsville."

"Oh OK...a *Brooklyn* nigga." I smirked.

"This ain't Rikers Island son. It's all love in the feds. Harlem and Brooklyn brothers are one."

"Shit, I'm not on that type of time anyway Zane, but I know what you mean homie. There's strength in numbers."

"You ain't never lied homeboy. Where you from in Harlem?"

"I'm from the east-side...Wagner Projects. You know where that's at?"

"*Do I know where Wagner is*? You can't be serious son. Y'all Manhattan cats the ones that don't leave Manhattan. BK dudes go everywhere. Hell yea, I know Wagner. I got mad peeps there!"

"Yooo, Zane you ain't lying homie! We ain't going to no fucking Brooklyn. I bagged mad bitches in the Tunnel with my homies Deeda and Jim.

"But the minute one of them bitches said they were from Brooklyn, shiiid, I would tear that bitch's phone number up in tiny little pieces and throw the shit right on the club's floor."

"Harlem niggas not crossing that bridge." He shook his head.

"Shiiiid, if someone told my moms when I was a kid that I was in BK, she would've gone to Gracie Mansion with a bullhorn and made Mayor Koch come get my Black ass. Dead-ass-serious homie."

"I tell the other homies here that shit, and they front all the time," Zane said.

"No fronting over here Zane—but who you know in Wagner Projects?"

"Shit, I know Fish. I know Pee-Wee, Craig, Boo-Black, B-Move, Tynell. Let me see, who else I know?" He squinted at the roof.

"Oh yea—Zah...Outlaw, Ted Smooth, Skittles, Reddy-Red...uum...Smokey Suarez, D-Papers...uuuh...Kenny and Bill Bazemore, Pookie-Duke, Johnny Fresh, Lefty Dave, Green-eyed Tone, Rod, and Mel...uuh-uuh...Delli, Tom Black.

"I know uuuh...Sean-Boogie, C-Town, Z-Black, Barry-B, Theo, Kenny Hutch and E-G...rest in peace...uh...uh...Pop, Ron O'Neil, Blair, Maine-Tain...that funny lil' nigga Jarvis.

"I'm gonna stop right there though, but I know mad niggas Manzo."

"Ooooh shit! Yooo, you named all my niggas!" I spoke in amazement. "How you know all my peoples?"

"My older brother Jack used to play ball with a lot of them dudes, and he did some other things that we don't even have to discuss.

"But I used to be with Jack all the time, and then I grew up—and you know how things go Manzo. But yea, I'm hip to your hood. Wagner's serious son."

"I'm twenty-four. How old are you Zane, if you don't mind me asking?"

"I'm twenty-six. I'm just a bald-headed young nigga, son."

"We must've just missed each other, because after my peeps moved out, I went to boarding school and then college.

"So I wasn't in Wagner anymore like that, or we definitely would've known each other. Small world, huh?"

"Yessir Manzo, small world—but I know you need to put your stuff away, so come to my cell after you drop off your shit, and we can kick it where all these dudes out here ain't listening. Birds be picking up seeds in this joint. What cell you in?"

"I'm in cell six," I answered.

"Oh shit, that's right over here, two cells from mine. I'm in cell four." Zane pointed to the cell that Benny, and Juan had departed just a moment prior.

"Juan, the dude with the *wittle*-ass dreads, is your celly. He's from D.C. like most of these shiesty cats, but he's cool."

"OK, so we're close," I said.

"Hell yea son," he said and waved his arm at the brother exercising with the head garb. "Yoooo Daf!"

"What's up Zane?" Daf removed his headphones after a set of diamond push-ups.

"Come here real quick son! This a homie right here!" Zane hollered.

Daf from New York too?

"Oh man, OK," Daf spoke with a modest interest and tiptoed toward us.

Fuck, I'm interrupting the man's workout.

"Daf, this is Manzo. He's a homie from Harlem. Manzo, this is Daf, our homie from Brooklyn," Zane introduced.

Am I the only asshole who gives his real name?

"What's up Daf?"

"Hey brother Manzo," Daf greeted and we exchanged a firm handshake.

"Yea, we were just kicking it a second before Manzo dropped his things off in his room. Give him the scoop on a few things. You know we gotta look out for the homies," Zane said.

"Most definitely brother Zane. We take care of our own in here. It's not many of us, but we have some quality brothers in the unit. There's a couple we don't rock with—but for the most part, standup brothers," Daf spoke.

The sweat slipped under the sealed cotton on Daf's forehead, and arched under his eyelids, all while he maintained a militant focus.

The opposite of Zane in expression and energy, Daf, bald-faced with dimpled cheeks, had an impassive demeanor, and he perfectly annunciated every syllable to every word—without slang or cursing.

There were no traits of New York City or premature love in Daf's rhetoric.

Communicating in a tactful even tone, he seemed to speak deliberately in a language that flanked passive aggressiveness and assertiveness.

Knowing that every day that I had spent in prison would be a test, I prepared myself, well before I had arrived at FCI-Cumberland, to *listen* meticulously to any and everything another inmate said or didn't say.

Status and, possibly, survival could depend on my vigilance just as it did in the streets. If I failed, there might not be a retake.

Just as in Roanoke City Jail, an inmate's reputation in prison correlated with whom he was associated with, and Daf was no-nonsense. He wasn't going to risk his character and values for anyone, homeboy or not.

And with a mere forty words—Daf had given me three options:

1. Confess I was a rat or a homosexual.

2. Ignore his comments, whether purposely or because of my simple ignorance.

3. Acknowledge the severity of his remarks, either honestly or dishonestly, and ideally with a viable solution if my response could be detrimental to my health.

"Daf, first off, I love pussy more than air, and if the warden of this joint agreed to give me a piece of pussy every month, I would let him add ten more years to my sentence—that's how much I love some pussy. No fake *butt*-pussy either. Real *woman* pussy," I said.

"Good to know my brother. Good to know," Daf applauded.

"Second, lastly, or *whatever*—my pre-sentencing report should be here in ten days, and as soon as it gets here, I will show it to you, Zane, and any other homie that wants to see it," I proposed.

"That would be very much appreciated, and I commend you on the offer brother Manzo, but inmates can no longer get their pre-sentencing reports.

"The officers who check the mail will just confiscate it and send it back to the sender, so don't even waste your time my brother." Daf briefed.

"Yea Manzo, those pre-sentencing reports were exposing these hot niggas too much, so they put a stop to it," Zane further explained.

'Hot'? Oh yea, that means snitches.

"Yes, I know, and I'm aware of the new bullshit going on in the feds, so I had my lawyer give mine to my moms, and she's sending my pre-sentencing report, page by page...in eleven different letters.

"The guards won't let the entire thing through, but they will let a page through that's mixed in some other legal shit," I said, and Zane and Daf glanced at one another with raised brows.

* * *

During my stay at RCJ, the guys who had already been to federal prison had given narratives of inmates who were stabbed, raped, and even killed because of information written in an inmate's pre-sentencing report.

A pre-sentencing report (PSI) was a court document that provided all components of a guilty defendant's case and criminal history, to determine the severity of the sentence.

The PSI could work for *or* against the defendant, and had every detail, including if the person had cooperated with authorities in any degree.

Before the government passed the rule to prohibit pre-sentencing reports, a federal prisoner had to have his forms available in a moment's notice for full disclosure, if asked by a fellow inmate.

If the prisoner in question didn't oblige, he would have to leave the compound, and "check-in"—which meant asking the officers for solitary confinement housing until being transferred to a *safer* institution.

The absence of *paperwork* equaled an admission of guilt, so, after months of city-jail-tales, which were always horrific in nature, I devised a way to transition into prison life with a sign on my back saying I *did* live my life right.

I had to protect myself from any doubts or false accusations.

* * *

"Ooooh shit! That's fucking brilliant Manzo!" Zane exclaimed. "Daf why didn't *you* think of that homie?"

"I don't know why. It's a logical solution to filter out all these *hot* dudes pretending to be men of character," Daf concluded.

"Damn, I feel like I'm going to get a lot of people hating me now," I worried.

I don't want anyone getting hurt and blaming me!

"Man, we would never put you in any harm's way. As far as I'm concern, this ain't your idea. My word homie," Zane attested.

Please don't!

"Don't worry brother Manzo. You will be fine." Daf nodded. "You are a smart brother, I see...but can you play ball?"

"*Basketball?*" I asked.

"Yes, basketball brother," Daf replied.

"Maaan, brother Daf, I'm from Harlem and I played for Riverside Church. *And* I was All-Prep for four years straight in high school—of course I can play!"

"Oh yea, you have to be nice then. Next ten-minute-move, I want you to play with me in a two-on-two game on the yard for some money.

"You don't need a dime either. Zane and I got it covered, and we will split the books with you. You with it my brother...or is your game weak?" Daf challenged.

I'll dog these country niggas! Books?

Oh shit, books of stamps are really money in here!

"Man, hell yea I'm with it, but I don't have any sneakers and shit though," I said.

"No worries. What you about, a size twelve or thirteen Manzo?" Zane asked.

"Yea, I'm a thirteen homie."

"OK, I got kicks and shorts for you Manzo. Go get changed Daf, and meet us in my cell.

"Hell yeaaaa, them D.C. niggas gonna be sick we got another baller from up top! Let's get this money son!"

"Bet Zane! See you brothers in a minute." Daf turned and headed for stairs.

"OK Zane! I see you got a brolic homeboy on the pound!" the Latino enjoying the music videos hollered.

"You already know, Lil' Junie! Get your Philly homies and come to the yard on the move and watch my big homie whip Big John's ass!"

What?

I know he's not talking about that big Black motherfucker who bumped me!

Please don't be that dude!

"Follow me Manzo—yooo, you OK son? You look like you saw a goddamn ghost."

"Shit, I'm cool Zane. Let's go," I said

"OK cool. Let me grab my food at this microwave, and I'll walk around. Meet me right there in cell two." Zane trotted to retrieve his dinner as I dragged myself to his cell.

I just got here! I don't want any problems! Don't play!

I will say my stomach hurt! I will say I need some rest!

"Manzo?" Zane spoke.

"What's up Zane?"

Damn that food smells good!

"You're talking to yourself. Come in son," Zane invited while balancing three stacked bowls of food in his left hand as he turned the doorknob with his right.

"Just rappin'," I concocted.

CLICK.

"Oh shit, you spit?" he asked and pushed into his cell. I followed.

"Nah, just rappin' some 50-Cent shit," I lied again.

SLAM.

Holy shit!

Before treading timidly into the gleam of his spotless floor, I thought that his cell would've been similar to the few that I resided or had seen in movies, and in documentaries—but I was incorrect.

With irreproachable tidiness and organization, Zane's *house*, the hue of Pina Colada mix, had twice the room capacity of my college dorm room and simulated a Kansas bunker more than a pad for convicts.

Cases of Pepsi, Sprite, Coca-Cola, and Ginger Ale stockpiled beneath a cream-coated steel, double bunk that ran crosswise against the back of a cinder-blocked wall.

The bedding of both mattresses was tucked and folded with a midshipman's attention to detail.

Mesh bags, filled to the brim with a collection of canned and packaged food, including beef sausages, tuna, mackerel, sardines, clams, crabmeat, octopus, salmon, and chicken chunks—suspended from both bedposts like protein punching bags.

Underneath the bottom bunk, six pairs of footwear, individually sheathed and tied inside clear trash bags, were aligned in front of the sodas.

Even through the obscurity, I easily recognized the black Nike boots, construction Timberland's, Jordan IV's, white low-top Air Force Ones, and the Air Max '95—because I had all them myself, but at home.

Unlike state prisons, the feds didn't allow inmates to receive any type of care packages from any outside sources, therefore I wondered how Zane swindled so much contraband.

In an opened, four-feet-high, metal locker fixed to the left wall—boxes of Famous Amos cookies, Little Debbie cakes, and honey buns were stacked efficiently in the lower cubbyhole.

An array of chocolate bars, crackers, and peanuts were stuffed between bags of UTZ potato chips in the top and middle slots.

Atop of a matching locker, Master-locked and placed inches away, an overabundance of Ramen noodles, bags of white rice, including bottles of honey and squeeze cheese—rested behind four green peppers and five onions.

The cell had the organization and smell of a mini supermarket.

"Oh-OK lil' Fiddy, you can put your bag down and have a seat at the desk son," Zane said as he walked past the toilet behind the door. He set the food on the wooden desk across from the lockers.

"Thanks Zane, but I'm good standing...if that's cool?" I denied the comfort for my wearied legs.

"Yea, no problem son, but let me ask you something...are you really a fucking Skins fan?"

"Hell no Zane! I'm Giants all day, but Michael Strahan and Tiki Barber can't help me up in this bitch!" I admitted.

"Ha, ha, ha...I knew it! Don't worry about Big Ed. He's mad cool Manzo."

"Shiiid, that big nigga had me under pressure Zane! Better safe than sorry. Is everybody in this place named *Big* something?"

"Yooo, I asked the same shit when I first got here! Yea, there's a lot of big dudes here. Ed is just the OG to these D.C. dudes in this joint," Zane clarified, twisting the combination into the locker's lock.

"Oh, OK—I figured," I said.

Don't ask about Big John.

He gonna think I'm scared of the nigga.

"You know how things go here Manzo. I've been in this bitch two years so far and shit goes down here, but you won't have any problems son.

"You a big nigga yourself, and as long as you not doing a bunch of wolfing, on some fake tough guy shit—you will be fine," he reassured.

"Yea, that's not my style. I want to do my time and bounce," I said.

"I hear that. I just take care of my business, workout, kick it with a few our homies, and mind my damn business.

"Here goes a pair of shorts for you baller. Don't lose in my shits son." He handed me the gray gym shorts.

"Good looks Zane. I will wash them and give them back."

If Big John don't kill me in them.

"Nah son, those are yours—keep them," he said while pinching an empty mesh bag from his locker. "Let me get your kicks."

"Man, thanks Zane."

"Here, these should work." He unwrapped the black Jordan's and tried to hand them to me.

What?

These damn near new! I can't take them.

Something's up!

"Yooo Zane, I couldn't possibly take these from you—"

"Manzo let's get something straight son. You're my homie, and we all we got in this place. I'm not gonna come by your cell tonight asking for *repayment*.

"No funny business son. You will represent all of us in a few when you get on that court. We can't have a homie out there in a pair of zips.

"I'm not gonna ask what your charges were, but I'm sure you're in here for getting money like the rest of us. We lived good out there and we gonna live good in here.

"So please take the sneakers. No sweat. My pleasure...no homo. And besides, I have two more pair just like this in the homie Cowboy's locker upstairs."

Damn, this dude seems sincere. He does have a point.

Take the kicks, but still don't sleep on any of these dudes.

"Man, thanks again homie. I hope I didn't offend you."

"Nah son, you on point and that's a great trait to have, and playing it safe is the way to be, but sometimes people actually do shit out the kindness of their hearts...even in prison homie.

"But I will advise that you don't take shit from anyone that ain't a homie.

"But shit, you're in the unit with me and Daf—we got everything you need son!" he spoke, commencing to dump every type of food and snack into the bag.

"Word, I appreciate the generosity Zane. But damn homie, you do have a damn bodega up in here."

"Ha-ha...that's because it is, Manzo. It's a store."

"A *store*?" I asked in astonishment.

"Yea son, like a real store!

"Dudes come in here and pay with stamps for whatever they need. I make a crazy profit, and the ones that don't have stamps, I make them go to the store for me on commissary day and buy things I need to sell.

"You know, just like restocking—like a supermarket," he broke down his operation.

"Oh shit, that's dope bro! And this is legal in here?" I pried.

"Not really, but the prison doesn't trip...it's not like I'm selling drugs. Plus, a store brings up the prison's economy. We gotta buy all our shit from the commissary, so the better a store does, the more money being spent in this prison.

"The prison is the real winners son. They're making money all day and night. Niggas with stores are just the workers.

"Daf has a store in his cell upstairs too. You know a New York nigga gonna get paid wherever he's at.

"Shit, it beats having one of these slave-ass Unicor jobs in this bitch for twenty cents an hour, making furniture and military uniforms, or some shit. Fuck that son!"

"You ain't even lying bro. I don't want a job in here," I said.

"No worries homie. I'm gonna have Mr. Britt give you a job cleaning one of the TV rooms before they put you in the kitchen with all the other new people.

"And you won't even have to clean the TV room...just pay some amigo ten dollars a month to do your five dollar a month job—and you good! Your entire day is free to do what you want basically."

"Hell yea Zane, I got better things to do in here than be a fucking slave. Plus, I will be OK financially. Can't spend but $250 a month in here anyway. That's chump change!"

"I know, but you won't even have to spend that if you get a store or hustled. I don't even go to commissary. I just send the people who owe me.

"But for real Manzo, if you wanted to get down with this store just let me know, because my celly Flav from North Carolina is in the hole for some dumb shit, so I don't have a celly.

"But if Flav gonna be transferred I gotta find a new celly, and we could go half on everything! It's just something to think about, no worries, and no homo. I know how you Harlem cats have to say that shit after every damn sentence it seems."

"Ha-ha, no bullshit Zane. Shit is stupid for real. I'm gonna stop."

"I hear that son. But here's some shit to get you on your feet." He handed me the sack of sustenance.

"And after y'all game Manzo, we gonna tear up that fried rice I just made, oh yea—banana pudding too. Daf got some fried chicken upstairs from the kitchen, so we're good money son."

"Yooo, Zane man—you didn't have to give me all this shit! This bag is heavy bro!"

*Banana pudding, fried rice...**and** fried chicken!*

I can't wait until after the game!

"Man stop fronting son! You a big nigga! I know you like to eat, ha-ha!

"And there's ten books of stamps, some picture tickets, so you can send some flicks home, some headphones and a Walkman in there.

"Son you wolfing like a motherfucker, so if you want a haircut I will get Country Mike to holla at you.

Hurry up and go to your cell and get dressed—the move is in like five minutes. You miss that, and you're hit son."

"Aight, cool Zane—"

"Oh yea, before I forget, there's a brand-new lock in your bag, so make sure you lock all your valuable shit all up. I love these D.C. niggas because they go hard, but some of these cats are grimier than you could ever imagine.

"But I need to go make a call real quick, and then I will meet you out front." Zane cautioned and then opened the door.

"Damn, that's love homie. Thank you, Zane," I said. "I will repay you bro."

"No worries son. Just repay me on that court, by you and brother Daf beating Big John...*and* Big Clops' ass."

Chapter Thirty-Two

ASS BET

Walking through the metal detectors of Cumberland's recreational center, I followed Zane, Daf, and a stampede of inmates past an unoccupied humid indoor gymnasium, exiting the back through double-doors leading to the outside area, universally known in any American prison as—*the yard*.

The second I entered Cumberland's main attraction, the hair-raising energy converged all around me, and I didn't know where to look first, so I stopped and viewed it all.

After almost ten months of being trapped in fresh-airless accommodations, my senses were happily confused, and I was ready to attack and experience every activity surrounding me. I finally felt alive.

A few yards from the entryway, lively men of all races partook in card games —making best of the hands they were dealt.

The inmates ate junk food and drank sodas on six lawn-green round tables that extended the width of a cemented area, which mimicked a Las Vegas gambling floor. After each card hand, tiny paper-wrapped square bundles that I assumed were books of stamps, exchanged from dealer to player or vice-versa.

Cigarettes and Black & Mild cigars burned everywhere freely, with a taste of marijuana and fermented fruit lingering in the air.

Shirtless inmates of all ages, but mainly men of color and with bodies of Egyptian gods, exercised on and near six stations of rusted-steel pull-up bars— positioned between the casino and a softball field, which set inside an expansive oval dirt track, surrounded by a towering fence.

Like gymnasts, the men, some wearing work gloves, gracefully yanked themselves up and over the bars with precision and strength, in a display of muscle defining acrobats that I had neither seen, nor experienced.

Focusing on explosiveness and power, I had always lifted heavy weights when I trained for football. But there were no weights at Cumberland, and when my lawyer revealed that I had chosen a prison without even a dumbbell, I was deeply disappointed.

For a week in RCJ, I contemplated changing my prison destination, but decided that I'd rather have been close to Brittney and Ruby.

I would be able to hold my babies routinely, so I could never request somewhere further from *home* based on Cumberland not fitting my training standards.

After looking at the men on the *bars*, I knew getting in top shape wouldn't be a problem, even without pumping steel.

The rawness of calisthenics had me intrigued, and I was eager to transform my bulky physique—by strictly using bodyweight movements.

* * *

"One more! Get that money yo! OK, that's my doug!" a slim, golden-poppy tanned inmate with a fresh Caesar haircut and thick beard willed his partner's chin over the bar.

'Doug'? Ha-ha, Keion Carpenter talks like that.

Baltimore dudes can't ever say 'dog' right.

Man, I need to find a barber...I'm wolfing.

"Yooo Manzo!" someone called my name, and I immediately turned left.

Searching through a cluster of men, I spotted Zane on the second of two parallel full-length basketball courts that stretched perpendicular to the track's fence.

He waved for my attention as he stood with Daf by his side, under the right-side basket.

Relieved, I scrambled through the unacquainted faces on the first court until finally reaching my homeboys.

Before speaking, I was sidetracked by a group of nine Muslim men dressed in kufis and high-watered khakis, prostrated while making Salat.

They prayed in a corner patch of grass located between the fence and the second court's far-baseline, and I admired the restraint of the brothers to keep their faith a priority, even with the yard's distractions.

None of this bullshit matters to them.

I need that type of discipline in my life.

"OK Manzo, you ready son?" Zane asked while Daf handed me a dusty basketball.

"Hell yea, I'm ready homie," I answered.

"Go Ciscoooo!" a guy screamed, after a walloping hit on the softball field, and I rubbernecked to see the runner.

"Manzo!" Zane snapped.

"I'm here! I'm ready!" I returned my attention to Zane.

"Listen Manzo, you need to focus right now! This shit is not a game son! There's 300 books on the motherfucking line homie!"

"*300 books?*" I repeated.

"Yea, 300 *books*! That's fifteen hunnit dollars son!"

"*$1,500* Zane?"

"That's right, and that's just mine and Daf's bet alone. Ain't no telling what these other cats got on it. One book of stamps is five dollars in here.

"We're betting 300. And *when* we win, your cut is 100 books, and you don't have to put a up a dime. Just win son!" Zane placed his right hand on my shoulder.

"Don't even worry about the money part brother Manzo. Just play your game and this will be a piece of cake. You played for Riverside and Ernie Lorch, so I know you got game.

"We're not losing to these D.C. brothers. Not a chance," Daf professed his sureness, snatched the ball back from me, and bungled a two-foot-lay-up, missing the entire rim.

Holy shit!

Daf is a fucking bum!

Why the FUCK did I brag about balling?

"My hands are a little slippery," Daf rationalized and then shot a five-foot *jump shot*, hammering it off the backboard.

This nigga is a BUM! We can't win with him!

Oooh shit, they're here!

As the inmates began to gather around, Big John and another guy, who I assumed was Big Clops, stepped onto our court, under the opposite goal from my *squad*.

Big John had bulk and could've been the first draft pick in a movie about football. He also had size and could've been the only rapist, in a novel about prison.

African American and massive, Big John could've *played* most of the typical roles—but he still didn't match the enormity of his running mate.

Six feet, seven inches of oak, with mighty biceps like mutated pistachio shells—Big Clops had stovepipe arms that dragged, and touched his kneecaps even if he walked with perfect posture.

His traps slid from his ears to his shoulders with zero consideration for missing a neck.

Just as rude, the two split-boulders below his collarbone refigured his wife beater's support, and slightly caused his tank top to rise at the hem as he moved.

Seven cornrows stopped abruptly halfway down the back of his skull as if the grizzly hairs were on strike.

Clops' eyes jammed fairly into an undersized head, but his overbite, and the lengthiness of his cartoon bird's nose—nearly had given the illusion that he only had one eye.

His pencil-thin beard was coal black, but his outfit was *movie*-cocaine white —a tad brighter than the wad of paper in his fist.

Although he wore Nike high-tops and gym shorts, Big Clops clearly didn't come to play basketball. He came to take pictures.

Are those picture tickets in his hand?

This motherfucker doesn't even plan on getting dirty!

"OK let's get this shit on the road! I have shit to do!" Big Clops yelled to the spectators.

"Hell yea Cyclooooopss!" a voice cheered.

Cyclops...of course.

"Let's go Daf! We ready to take you and your home-*girl's* money!" Big John insisted while stretching in his sweat suit at the opposite free throw line.

What? Is this guy is playing in sweats? It's eighty-five degrees out here!

"Yeeeaaa! Get in their ass Big John!" support for the two monsters spewed from everywhere.

"Get me paid Big John!"

"Make that young boy your bitch big homie!"

"Kiiill-Moe! On my momma Joe—Big John about to kill these bamas!"

"New York niggas don't want it!"

"That bama too big to ball!"

"Y'all not playing football Daf!"

"Cyclops these dudes a fucking joke slim!"

"Fifty books on Big John and Cyclops! Who wants this bet?"

"Ain't nobody gonna take that bet Hootie! That's eaaasssy money!"

Is anybody here from goddamn New York?

"Manzo?" Zane tapped my arm.

"Yea...what's up Zane?

"It's showtime baby! Come on and get a couple of warm-up shots on this goal down here, where these fools are at...that's where y'all playing!" Zane advised, pointing to the enemy's territory.

"Cool," I agreed.

Fuck man!

Ah shit what am I doing?

"Your homie looking real scared Zane!" the hecklers continued.

"Big boy, you look real cute in them Jordan's slim!"

"Big John gonna take your sneakers, *and* ya ass!"

Why am I playing against these savages?

"Manzo, this game is gonna be up to you son. Daf isn't that great," Zane *revealed* as we walked.

"No shit Zane," I replied as Daf continued to warm-up, and erratically dribbled past our opponents and missed another lay-up.

"He can't score, but the brother will do the little things, like rebound and play defense. You know that shit nobody else wants to do, he will do Manzo."

"I know homie, but I'm gonna need some help against these fucking animals," I pleaded once crossing half-court.

"Manzo you got this! These niggas are big, but you're athletic and got skills, and you can think homie! Yooo Daf—let me see that ball!" Zane praised *blindly* before Daf chucked him the ball.

"Yooo, why do you believe in me so much? You never even saw me play before Zane! I could be a bum!"

"Just calm down son—let me explain," he said.

"Please do...because I'm confused as fuck!"

"Listen Manzo, there's an All-American AAU tournament in Jersey that my nephew played in years ago, called Little Lads, and my brother Jack was one of the coaches.

"Jack just told me on the phone that they had pictures of the past Mr. Little Lads, or rather the MVP's of the tournament...and the last three Mr. Little Lads at that time was Felipe Lopez, Stephon Marbury, and *motherfucking* Manzo!

"I truly believe that *none* of those dudes I mentioned is bums, plus, they don't give *bums* football scholarships to schools like Virginia Tech son!"

Of course this dude did his homework! He named 100 of my peoples back home!

"So tighten up son and go show Big John, Big Clops, or Big goddamn *whoever* in here that tries to treat you like a punk—that you ain't. Why?"

"Because you're from New York *fucking* City!" He handed me the ball, winked, and walked away to a bench.

Zane's words had doused fresh gasoline over my old courage. He was totally correct though—I have never been a punk!

I'm gonna kill these motherfuckers!

"Manzo we're about to start! Shoot the rock! Warm up!" Daf ordered, standing a foot from Cyclops and Big John at the free throw line.

"*Manzo?* Oooh shit, Daf got a Mexican to play with him slim!" Big John joked to the crowd.

"Ha-ha—Daf got an *amigo!*" Cyclops added to the insults. "We gonna blow him and this pointy-shoe-wearing motherfucker out Big John!"

Yea right!

"Bring it in, *New York City!*" a gruff-sounding individual instructed.

Who's that?

Facing the ensuing flow of felon fanatics, an elder gentleman with knotted braids under a black kufi full of lint, twirled a stringed whistle around his right index finger. He stood at the free throw line between Daf, and our adversaries—who had their wide backs to the goal.

The old timer had a compact Vietnam veteran's beard that covered half of his mug which shined like a slice of raw liver.

Fat from cheeks to gut, the man wore a soiled khaki uniform, and decrepit 585 New Balance sneakers that leaned over the soles better than a Baltimore dope fiend.

He only conversed with Cyclops and Big John, while Daf licked his own finger and stuck it in the air.

This dude is the ref? I bet my life he's from D.C.!

"OK Mangee, you know which way to call this shit homie! I got twenty-five books on this motherfucking game! Don't give them bamas a damn thing, akki!" one of the Muslim brothers hollered, as he folded his prayer rug.

Man, he won't call a fair game! Fuck!

The odds of Daf and I beating the two brutes had not been favorable even without them gaining any unfair advantages, but with Mangee refereeing, our chance at victory was inconceivable.

Surely, Mangee would show bias, and I didn't have to be a seasoned convict to know that anyone in his position would've taken a bribe, not just for the money—but for the sake of staying in the good graces with the homeboys who protected him.

I could've dealt with simply losing, but Daf and I being played for suckers was impossible for me to accept. Frustrated, I hoisted the ball from the three-point line.

"Told y'all the New York bama was a bum!" an inmate to my left declared after I barely missed the shot.

Hold up.

That rim is sweet!

"I don't know y'all! Kid's form is pretty as fuck!" someone rebutted.

Daf was on point!

The wind blowing a little to the left.

"Bring it in, *New York City!*" Mangee repeated, and I stood next to Daf.

I can kill that rim! I know I can with a good look!

"It's about to be on nigga! Don't get scared now!" Big John said, and we locked eyes.

Damn he's ugly.

I see somebody tried to slice his face off.

"Aight, save it for the game Big John!" Mangee advised.

He's too big to guard me. I just need a little space.

"Aight y'all, here's the rules: Game goes to ten points, by ones! You score, you keep the damn ball! I will call the fouls and shit! No crying like fucking babies! Just play basketball!

"Things get too physical, on some other type shit, then we will have to stop 'cuz them guards looking at us like hawks! And if we stop, *nobody* gonna get paid! Y'all understand da rules gentlemen?" Mangee explained.

You forgot the part about you cheating.

"Yes sir," I answered first.

"*Yes sir*?" Cyclops taunted. "Brother Daf, you got you a proper mama's boy, don't ya slim?"

"Yes sir brother Mangee," Daf replied.

Daf is focused as fuck!

"Yea-yea Mangee—let's just play!" Big John demanded as he swayed from side to side.

This Black motherfucker is hyped and ready!

"Yea Mangee—let's go! Hold up, one sec! " Cyclops yelled, and suddenly trotted toward the far sideline. "J-Lo baby...hold these for daddy!

'J-Lo'?

What grown-ass man has the name 'J-Lo'?

"That's right Cyclops! Let wifey hold you down while we kill these bamas Moe!" Big John shouted.

From behind the bench where Zane and three other men sat and literally faced adversity, a *man* emerged from within a batch of "brothers" and proceeded to prance his kids-sized all white Reebok classics onto the court.

The petite inmate's black hair fell sleekly down the chest pockets of his close-fitting khaki shirt that was tied in a knot just above his frail midriff.

He had refashioned his khaki pants into skintight capris that had an unbuckled pink-dyed belt, looped at the top of his authentic britches.

With a prominent chin, and an Adam's apple, ample enough to share with Eve, J-Lo was made-up in eyeliner, red lipstick, and possibly, also with blush—but he still couldn't mask the dark shadow of shaved hairs on his cheekbones.

J-Lo certainly *looked* like a "J-Lo," but I was sure that the inmate wasn't Jennifer Lopez. The *real* Jenny didn't pee standing up, on her block.

Although I didn't consider myself homophobic at all, I had been caught off guard and did feel strange witnessing homosexuality in prison.

That's Cyclops' wifey?

I don't care how much time I had; I couldn't mess with a man!

I will beat off until my hands fall off!

"Thanks boo," Cyclops said.

"Anything for you honey! Now go win mama some dinero!" J-Lo replied and then returned to the bench area.

"OK, I'm ready Mangee! Let's make this quick Big John!" Cyclops said and winked at Big John.

"OK fellas! Y'all can shoot for first ball!" Mangee said.

"Nah fuck that! They can have the ball first! Y'all chumps ain't getting the shit back!" Big John promised.

Yea, we want the ball first!

"OK, it's y'all ball Daf! Somebody throw me a good ball!" Mangee said before catching the basketball. "Thanks slim! Oh yea, one last thing—three pointers count as two points!"

What?

Two pointers?

"Don't mean shit to these jokers! Let's play!" Cyclops added.

I'm gonna show this whole pound who's the man now!

"Aaaah shiiiiid!" The crowd had begun to get rowdy.

"Yeeaaaa, that's y'all asses New York bamas!"

"Big New York look soft as fuck slim!"

"Hell yea Moe! He gonna be Big John's number one gump!"

"One last time! Fifty books on Cyclops and Big John! Who don't like 'em?"

"Ain't nobody gonna take that bet Hootie! They know better!"

"I'll take that bet! I don't like them!" a relatively familiar voice yelled, and everyone muted with staggering curiosity.

Oh shit!

Who's betting with us?

"Who said that? Who wanna lose fifty books?" a brown-skinned brother in his forties with an unexceptionably trimmed beard and freshly braided cornrows repeated the wager after pushing his way to the court's baseline.

Big John and Cyclops spun around to behold the commotion.

"Right here, next to you brother! I don't like them! Bet fifty jawns...or *more!*" the man called the bet, but I couldn't see him through Lil Junie and the six hulking brothers with heavy beards.

"Fifty books is good brother!" Hootie settled for the minimum.

"OK, bet!" the ironclad gambler yelled and squeezed past his security. "Let's go Manzo! Make these niggas a believer today!"

Oh shit, that's Boo!

"Aaaah man! The New York kid might be the truth!" an inmate ignited a shift of support.

"The Philly bama just bet fifty books on New York! This gonna be a goody!"

"Let's go New York!"

"Show them how we do from up top!"

There are other New Yorkers in this place! I'm gonna kill these niggas now!

Let's go!

"Here's the ball Daf! Let's get it fellas!" Mangee handed Daf the basketball at the top of the key. I shuffled to my left, beyond the three-point line, to give Daf some space.

They gonna know my name after this!

"You get Daf, Cyclops! I got this big *bitch!*" Big John stepped closer to me.

"Hey New York, if you win...I ain't paying y'all bamas shit. But I will...fuck you in that tight lil' cornhole...*real* hard."

What the fuck this nigga just say? Is he serious?

I should just walk away!

"And I'm *dead* ass, as you New York bamas say!" Big John reassured as his *good* eye twitched.

This shit ain't worth it!

He said he was gonna fuck me! This ain't that serious!

Don't play!

The enthusiasm I had about displaying my basketball skills in front of the compound was short-lived.

I changed my mind and didn't want to participate in any physical activity against a guy like Big John, who had just threatened to rape me after a basketball *game.*

I didn't know if he were serious or just trying to intimidate me, but was playing the game worth the risk?

There were no guarantees Big John and Cyclops' emotions wouldn't flare *when* they lost.

I wasn't just another dude trying to pass time on the court, I was a true baller —*especially* when I played for money!

Even having lost a step, I could compete in any sport at a high level.

* * *

Twice a week I hooped while at RCJ, and every game I embarrassed a guy who wasn't too happy about the outcome.

I didn't take anybody's feelings into consideration, and I trash talked from the moment I dribbled, until the moment I hit the usual game winning shot like I did at Woodberry before switching to play football.

The badgering elevated my game and demoralized my opponents, but just like the Virginia Prep League, the inmates at RCJ had never gotten personal.

After rec-time had ended, we would all go back to the pod and recap the ass whipping, wait for our separate turns to shower, we would eat lunch, and then not mention another word about basketball—unless there were a popular game on TV.

No one held grudges in jail, but in the feds, there were too many unknown variables to deliberate, like if a man was ever going home or if he craved to taste blood again.

Not to mention, in RCJ, there were only nineteen probable enemies, but on Cumberland's yard alone—there were at least 500 inmates.

Big John and Cyclops weren't the only psychopaths betting, and a lot of pride and money were at stake. I was the new kid. I couldn't imagine every murderer betting *with* me.

Athletics were tests of manhood and pride, and some people behind bars couldn't handle losing.

Many fights in prison, I was sure, had derived from *friendly* competition.

So, adding another "L" to an inmate's record was risky and could be psycho-logically damaging for the loser.

Unlike chess, sports examined carnal-will, experience, *and* mental strategies; hence, a defeat went way beyond the final score.

Add the gambling aspect, losing could go deep into an inmate's pockets.

The All-American athlete had been still alive inside me, and I always played to win and never backed down from a challenge.

My will to succeed was precisely my reasoning for wanting to excuse myself from the basketball game and ask Daf to find another partner, but I couldn't.

I was smart and not scared, but my self-removal would send a resounding message saying the latter. Quitting would make my time at Cumberland incurable from the stigma of being a punk.

Like my Woodberry ninth grade history teacher, Mr. Dick Glover, used to say —I had *crossed the Rubicon*, and there was no turning back!

If I didn't want to face men like Big John and Cyclops, then I shouldn't have ever sold drugs. I had to play the game.

* * *

"Let's get this money Daf!"

"OK Manzo, I hear you! Let's get this motherfucking money!" Zane cheered.

"Play baaalll!" Mangee shouted, and I ran to the top of the key. Daf handed me the ball.

"Just get out of my way," I whispered to Daf, who trotted to the right wing of the court.

Holding the ball with both hands, I prepared to attack the rim, but Big John held his ground in a crouched defensive stance at the free throw line—five feet in front of me.

Cyclops flanked to the wing to cover Daf, leaving Big John and me, one on one.

He's giving me too much room.

If I drive Cyclops will come help.

Can I trust Daf to make the lay-up if I pass it to him? Fuck No!

Shoot the three!

After analyzing the options, I suddenly jumped—releasing the ball off my fingertips at the top of my elevation, as Mangee's Blue Nile fragrance reeked heavily in the air.

Watching the ball rotate toward the rim, Daf crashed the basket in hopes for an offensive rebound—but there wouldn't be one.

SWISH!

"Oooooooh!" The crowd went berserk!

"Bone, that nigga jumper is wet yo!"

"Yoooo, kill these niggas New York!"

"Big John you better get up on him yo, before he doug you!"

That rim is sweet!

"Shaka he's welling! That shit was luck!" Big John hollered back at the inmate.

Luck?

Nigga I'm nice!

"That's a two-pointer! The score is 2-0! Daf and Big New York!" Mangee fetched the ball and threw it to Daf, who stood next to me at the top of the key. "Play ball!"

"I got this homie," I told Daf after he passed me the ball and hopped to the right-wing area again.

Big John is too far!

He's scared I will blow by him. He's giving me the shot again.

SWOOSH!

"Aaaaahhhh! Oooooohhhh!" The inmates watched the ball go through the net again.

"Good Lord that nigga got a jumper!"

"Y'all letting this big bama fuck up the church's money!"

"That's that Rucker Park shit homie! Let them know!"

"Them shits ain't even hitting the goddamn rim slim!"

"Big John—you some shit Joe!"

"Big New York ain't scared of you fucking clowns!"

"That's another two-pointer! The score is 4-0! Daf and Big New York! Mangee announced. "Here's the rock Daf! Play ball fellas!"

"Big John, you want me to get him slim?" Cyclops offered.

Won't make a bit of difference.

"Man I got him!" Big John irately responded.

"OK, well tighten up! Let's go slim!" Cyclops insisted.

Big John is mad. He's going to play tight now.

He doesn't know I can dribble. Top of the key is still the shot.

There's still a light breeze blowing.

Back up Manzo.

Once Daf tossed me the basketball, Big John rushed out to me with his hands up, not giving me an inch of space to maneuver.

I held the ball at my side as Big John's sweat poured onto my flesh, and the stench of canned mackerel steamed the back of my neck.

Big John was worked up, and his feelings were too involved. I had studied him as he warmed up before the game, and he didn't have the footwork or coordination to guard me.

He shouldn't have been so close, and I planned on using his aggression against him, just as I did to kids for years when I played for Riverside Church.

Thank you, Coach Dermon Player.

* * *

'When an angry, bigger player is on you Manzo and you have him pinned on your left hip, quickly jab step to the right, and he's going to fly that way because he's so hellbent on stopping you—but he won't be able to stop his momentum.

'So just give a quick jab step, and either dribble-drive to your left, or take one dribble with your left hand, as you step backward.

'Square up, nail your jumper...and watch the life drain out your opponent's face!'

* * *

SWISH!

"Ooooooooooh!" The inmates were in a state of pandemonium after I hit my third shot, a couple of feet beyond the three-point line.

"Is it the shoes?"

"Big New York whipping these niggas ass slim!"

"This new bama is balling like-shit!"

"Yoooo, I knew I shudda bet with this dude!"

"Ain't no grass in New York! All them bamas do is hoop!"

"He too big to be shooting like that!"

"Mangee, you can't cheat today for your homies! You gonna eat cold Ramen noodles tonight nigga!"

"*Another* two-pointer—shit! The score is 6-0! Big New York and Daf! Play ball!" Mangee announced with evident disappointment and tossed the ball to me, instead of Daf.

"Man—fuck that, I'm guarding him! You get Daf, Big John! I will show you how to guard this fool!" Cyclops snarled at his teammate.

"That's right, you get'em zaddy!" J-Lo hollered.

"Fuck! That shit is luck slim! OK, I got Daf!" Big John said.

This is skill asshole.

Same shit gonna happen to Cyclops too. He's too slow.

"Here Daf!" I threw the ball to Daf and grabbed it out of his hand immediately as I spoke the plan in his ear. "After two dribbles set a *solid* pick."

Cyclops was just as slow as his *other* partner, but his arms were considerably longer than Big John's. Because of Cyclops' length, I wouldn't be able to shoot with a clean look at the rim!

Considering that overpowering my new defender was impossible, I suddenly noticed Cyclops' *eyes*—he squinted whenever he focused on anything.

Eyesight was crucial in the game of basketball, and I didn't believe that Cyclops had the peripheral vision to avoid being attacked *laterally*, making him the perfect victim for a screen, or *pick* play.

All I needed was Daf to give me an extra second to shoot, by interfering with Cyclops' ability to block my shot, and then Big John would be *my* bitch again.

"I'm on you! What you gonna do now pussy?" Cyclops asked with his hands in my face.

Damn, I can't even see the basket! Jab step right.

Fuck, he didn't even move!

Swing your right foot in front of him. Give yourself some room.

Let him know you going left. Lean your shoulder into a little. Damn he's strong as shit!

"Yea, you ain't going nowhere now motherfucker!" Cyclops guaranteed, and the crowd applauded his tenacity.

"Hell yea Cyclops!"

"Lock that nigga down!"

"You can't do shit with Big Clops on dat ass!"

"They gonna come back and whip that ass Moe!"

Find Daf!

Make eye contact with Daf now!

OK he saw me. Make your move!

With two hard dribbles to my left, I planted my left foot, and hop-dribbled the ball behind my back to my right hand, reversing my direction of attack.

Cyclops did a good job of recovering, and he moved with me but never saw Daf, who was positioned stiffly like an Academy Award.

Cyclops crashed into Daf, and I dribbled to *my* spot with an unobstructed view at the basket as Big John shuffled his feet to defend me—but he was way too late.

Release...

Follow through...

Money.

SWAP!

"Oooooohhhhhh...aaaaahhhh!" the men witnessing the onslaught howled, and some even ran on the court.

"He's on fi-yaahh!"

"That big nigga can shoot kid!"

"Yooooo, he should be overseas! Kiiill Moe...that bama nice!"

"Magoo, we got us a bona-fide hooper in B-1!"

"No bullshit Tuffy! He's abusing these big niggas!"

"That's my homeboy!"

"Stop letting him get to the top of the key motherfuckers!"

"That's the easiest two-pointer on the goddamn court, you ass-holes!"

"Nice pick Daf!"

"Eaaassyy money!"

Just one more bucket!

We got this!

"WHHEEEEEP! WHHEEEEEP!" Mangee blew his whistle to maintain order. "Get off the motherfucking court! It ain't over! This shit ain't over!"

This shit is over! One more bucket!

I'm gonna embarrass them now! Y'all wanna call me a pussy?

I ain't no punk!

Fuck them!

I'm not scared of anyone! Fuck these dudes!

"WHHEEEEEP! That was a two pointer! The score is 8-0! Big New York and Daf! Play ball!"

"Let me get this fool!" Big John insisted.

"Motherfucker—you didn't call out the pick!" Cyclops argued but still switched to guard Daf.

"Daf give me the rock and move out the way, *my brother*! I'm gonna bake this fucking clown!" I ordered.

The onlookers had heard my voice for the first time, and no one dared to talk.

I was a man possessed and there had been no denying my intentions through my actions and play. I wanted everyone, particularly my enemies and the doubters, to *hear* my need to abuse the men who had so much to say *before* the game.

Prison was new to me, but being a man wasn't.

Big John and Cyclops had disrespected me with rhetoric that in many places, like prison, would have been sanctioned by death.

So, I didn't want to just beat them—I yearned to humiliate them. They were zeros, and I was determined to leave their asses on *my* court with a zero.

Big John said he would fuck me if I won, but I refused to let his threats change the outcome of the basketball game.

An inmate's ass and life hung in the balance every day in prison, and whether I won or lost wouldn't necessarily prevent anyone from attempting to violate me in some way.

I surely would make it known that I wasn't easily rattled and would fight until the death.

"We meet again big fella!" I greeted Big John as he played defense, steadily looking over his left shoulder.

"Nah B, ain't no picks!" I promised while dribbling between my legs at the top of the key. Big John was already putting too much weight on his heels.

I'm gonna break this nigga's ankles!

"You better get close BJ. They say I can shoot a lil' bit." I head-faked like I was shooting, while still maintaining my dribble. Big John jumped.

"Ha-ha, stop jumping! I'm right here, *Blow-job!*" I taunted, and Big John grew livid.

"Should I cross your big-ass like my homie Shamgod or hit another jumper like my homie Poodah?" I asked.

Just get it over with. You made your point.

This ain't Dyckman or the 'Together We Chill' tournament.

This is prison, not fucking Barry Farm.

Don't drop to their level.

Too dangerous!

"OK, let me stop messing with you Big John!" I said and swiftly shot a jumper before he had the opportunity to get one of his toes off the ground.

As the ball headed toward the basket I looked in Big's eyes and said, "Take that L...

SWISH!

"And *please*, don't be a..."

Chapter Thirty-Three

SORE LOSER

"Blood on my knife or shit on my dick?"

It was a tough question to have to answer on my first night in federal prison. As a matter of fact, it's probably the toughest question in the universe.

An hour after my game winning shot, Big John opened my cell door and asked his question. He didn't yell. He didn't grunt. He simply asked.

He asked this life-changing question with zero emotion. When a six-foot four-inch, 250-pound Black ass-bandit spoke while gripping a four-inch dagger, people listened.

Murderers listened. Rapists listened, and even Mafioso types listened. Well, now add an ex-football jock/drug dealer to the audience.

All this shit over a damn basketball game?

"Hey *baller!* I said blood on my knife or shit on my dick?" Big John repeated, but with the intensity of someone who had looked like he snorted an eight ball of coke for dinner and smoked crack for dessert. I had fried rice and banana pudding.

Big John's eyes bulged, and his nostrils pumped as sweat seeped through his wife-beater tank top.

Please God, tell me this motherfucker isn't serious!

I had seconds to decide whether I wanted to be stabbed or rammed in the ass. With a name like *Big John*, I wasn't certain which option would hurt less.

Think motherfucker! What the fuck can I do?

I scanned my cell for a weapon. Nothing.

Run!

My prison cell was the standard four feet by nine feet, with only one way in and one way out. Big John represented both.

Scream for help!

Die a coward.

Go for the shank!

Die with courage.

Maybe the best way out of this is to get into it.

Bingo!

If I don't answer he's going to carve me up for sure!

Shit!

Too late!

Big John lifted his right size-sixteen Air Force Ones as if he were going to charge, I put both my hands up and submitted, "OK! Shit on your cock! I mean shit on your dick Big John!"

Fuck, I should've let him win the basketball game! Sore fucking loser!

Big John stopped! Drool raced from both sides of his mouth as if the floor were the finish line.

Shaking with excitement, Big John started rubbing on his cock with his left hand and never let go of the shank with his right. He wanted my buns badly, and he could not contain it. I bet he sucked at poker.

I'm smarter than this dude!

Come on! Think!

Big John was a career criminal, but suddenly, I had realized that even the smartest of criminals weren't always the smartest of people.

To survive, I had to concede that Big John was the superior criminal; a superior criminal with a fucking shank.

I could not attempt to think like a hardened convict because I wasn't. Today was only my first day in federal prison! Shit, I still had McDonald's on my breath.

I had not gone through the battles, shed blood, shed tears, or lost comrades. I had never been to the hole, trained in the art of *prison* manipulation, or tested in the art of war.

I had no stripes, no medals, no accolades and not even a certificate for my mother to put on the wall in the living room. I was just a petty officer in the ranks of five-star-general killers and psychopaths.

In any hierarchy there is the fundamental belief that anyone, for the most part, can rise in the ranks by earning his way.

I was determined to be reclassified after this experience but not because I wanted more respect—I was determined, because I wanted to survive.

The odds were against me because I was a fresh *fish* without direction or a weapon.

I quickly realized survival was my direction, and I did have a weapon far more exceptional and deadlier than anything Big John could assemble or sharpen–I had my brain.

Big John wiped his mouth with the back of his cemented fist which held the knife.

Clenching his teeth, Big John whispered, "Don't be playing no fucking games with me New York City."

Visibly trembling, I muttered, "Big John I would never fuck with you. Just please don't hurt me. I will give you *whatever* you want. Please Big John, please don't hurt me dude. I'm sorry. It was just a basketball game! I beg you sir!"

He was from Washington, D.C., but I assumed I should treat Big John like he was from Missouri—*the Show Me State*.

I didn't wait for a reply, and I quickly turned around. I dropped my dank basketball shorts to the ground and exposed my bare ass.

With both hands, I grabbed the cold steel top-bunk as I slipped one leg out of my shorts.

Moving so fast, I got the boot on my right foot caught in my shorts and almost fell. My death grip on the bunk, as well as the fear of being found butchered in my cell with cut-off sweatpants around my ankles—helped me maintain my balance.

"See Big John, I wouldn't play with you," I said a little bit too softly for a guy, six feet and 250 pounds.

"Nigga don't play with—"

"I'm not!" I screamed, rotating my head around.

His eyes were soulless.

Oh my God, he ain't convinced! Fuuuuccckkkk!

The shuddering increased, and I turned my back around in submission. A half of a second passed, and I took a deep breath.

The moonlight broke through my tiny cell window, and I began to think about aliens and outer space before wondering about heaven and the afterlife.

I didn't know what was out there waiting for me when I died, but I knew that I wasn't ready to find out.

Where do our souls go when—

"Are you fucking listening faggot?" Big John barked, snapping me out of the astrological trance.

I had not heard a word he had said, but before I could answer he whispered, "Bend the fuck over, and I am not going to say the shit again nigga."

I heard you loud and clear Big John!

Mommy give me strength!

As tears ran down my cheeks, I stuck my tongue out my mouth to lick my upper lip. I felt the prickly sensation of my mustache and sampled the salty mix of sweat and mucous. My sense of touch and taste were still there.

This shit here ain't a dream Manzo!

Think motherfucker!

All that could be heard in my cell were Big John's heavy breathing, and my punk-ass sniffling.

Suddenly someone hollered, "Yooooo, Big John Stud in there laying that pipe to the *new,* New York bama!"

When I heard some asshole conjecturing that I was getting *piped,* and referring to me as the "*new,* New York bama" a volcano erupted in my soul. I wanted hot lava to burn the prison to ashes.

Did all New Yorkers get fucked in the feds?

Shaking almost uncontrollably, I released my grip of the top bunk.

Left hand.

Right hand.

I closed my eyes and began to bend over, tilting my pelvis. My knees buckled a bit as I reached out my palms to place them on the bottom bunk.

Left palm.

Right palm.

Oddly enough, the texture of the wool blanket rubbing against my wet skin was a welcomed distraction. I tried not to think about how I looked at this moment.

I was bent over, my ass hang-gliding in the air, sporting a pair of damn steel-toe boots, not even Timberlands. I was live on stage, in the flesh, and Big John had a front row seat.

Showtime.

"Mmmm..." moaned Big John, as he touched himself—aroused by tonight's entertainment.

"*New York, New York*—you better not fucking move. Just take this gristle like a good boy, so your moms won't have to buy a new black dress...*sweetie pie.*"

Sweetie pie?

"Don't tear his asshole up too much Big John! Save me some of that tight cooter!" an inmate screamed outside of my cell. "Ha, ha, ha!"

Oh no!

Please God, save me!

During the muffled laughter, I opened my eyes, ducked my head, and peeped between my legs.

I heard the *clank* from the shank being placed on the edge of the porcelain sink, and my spirit shook.

From what I could tell, Big John remained four feet behind me. I could only see his quads stuffed in his sweatpants, and never have a pair of limbs been scarier.

"Come do it already," I said almost inaudibly, lips almost dry-walled together.

I awaited Big John's instructions, but no words came out of his mouth—only his breathing. His panting. His grunting.

I couldn't see his face, and didn't know what he was doing, but then I heard that unmistakably familiar sound. I heard his belt buckle.

The CLICK-CLACK noise that a belt made had always signified two things in my life—either I was getting an ass whipping from my parents, or I was getting some pussy. I wasn't quite ready to add anything new to the list.

"I'm gonna pop this pussy real proper!" Big John had sworn, almost talking to himself.

Fucking psychopath! He unzipped his zipper! This ain't happening!

I remained positioned with my hands clenching the blanket, my butt raised, and my head looking through my legs.

Perspiration stung my eyeballs, but I could still see through the jungle. The predator eyed his prey and prepared for the kill.

Three feet.

Hell No!

Two feet.

Someone help me please!

One foot.

This is gonna be so fucking painful!

In a swift motion, I picked my right leg off the floor, almost trying to touch my chin with my knee.

Tightening my core, I kicked backward powerfully as if my first name was Jack and my last name was Ass, simultaneously letting out a monstrous roar.

"Raaaahhhhh!"

Simba had some competition.

CRUNCH!

The sound was reminiscent of when I was a child, when I poured a quart of milk into a pot of Rice Krispies, but this time, there was no break in the melody —just one big *SNAPCRACKLEPOP*!

My size-thirteen jackhammer sunk deep into the serial rapist's flesh, and I was confident my foot hit the end zone.

"Aaahhh!" Big John howled in agony as he flew back four feet, crashed into the cell door, and slid to the floor.

Touchdown motherfucker!

"Aaahhh! Aaahhh! Aaahhh! Aaahh!" Big John *Stud* screamed. "Oh-my-God! Oh-my-God! Oh-my-God!"

Don't cry now bitch!

Oh shit! The shank!

Realizing that the shank was still on the sink, I quickly let go of the bunk. I spun around without a care or the realization that I looked like a big toddler who was wearing only a t-shirt and some booties—I needed *my* rattle!

I spotted the shank and grabbed it. Caressing the duct tape with my thumb, I ignored Big John's shrieks and cries. I held the weapon up to the light and stared.

"Just kill me faggot!" Big John whimpered as he laid on the ground in the fetal position.

He was smothering his crotch with both hands, while blood escaped his fingers and leaked onto the floor.

Big John was now the one who was trembling. He was now the one that was crying with a blood pancake forming between his legs on *my* cell floor, and I had no sympathy for the bastard. The more he cried, the more my rage and disregard grew.

"Stop crying—you pathetic little bitch!" I shouted as I stood over him choking the knife. "Ain't no fun when the motherfucking rabbit has the gun, huh?"

I was like a proud hunter who had to access the damage of his kill shot.

With my left hand, I put the knife to his throat.

With my right hand, I slowly removed his red mitts from his disfigured bat and balls.

Like a used ketchup packet, the sore loser's cock was smashed, and red paste oozed out of the top.

His testicles resembled overcooked falafel dipped in beet soup. I never wanted to eat Halal again.

I looked at the shank and saw a slither of my reflection. I no longer recognized even a piece of me.

The junior high school Drama major was gone.

The straight "A" student vanished.

The Virginia Tech football player was dead.

A real man was born.

I bent down and put my lips next to Big John's ear and whispered, *"Blood on my knife, or shit on my dick?"*

"Ha, ha, ha," I chuckled.

"Picture that...I'm from New York *fucking* City!"

Chapter Thirty-Four

KEY INFO

After my fight with Big John, I had spent the last thirty days in the Special Housing Unit (SHU), also referred to as *the hole*, isolated in a one-man-cell with a few books and plenty of thoughts.

Once a day for an hour I had the privilege to leave my cell and enter a cramped, outside space, consisting of one large cage divided into five individual cages.

Because my potential infraction was of a violent nature, I was restricted to time alone in my pen. No other animals could share the same kennel.

Each day, I would exercise underneath the sun while broiling and communing with the four other troubled inmates in their respective enclosures.

Surprisingly, all the men I shared recreational time with had heard about my incident with Big John even before I got to the hole.

Everyone treated me with a newfound respect that I clearly didn't have when I had first arrived on the compound.

There were no taunts, threats, or name calling. The men spoke to me like I was a man, an equal, and we appreciated each other's company.

We shared funny stories about sexual conquests, debated about sports, and exchanged intellects about life, space travel, drugs, and history.

We never discussed the crimes, which led to our incarceration—although, Michael Moretti, an old Italian fellow with huge bifocals, and a wooden cane that he used to beat his celly while he slept—divulged that he had been locked up for so long that Rudy Giuliani was the federal prosecutor on his case.

Regardless of the subject discussed, I regularly returned to my cell grateful that I had other voices to listen to beside the ones in my head, and I waited anxiously for the next twenty-three hours to pass to free myself from mental limbo.

I was only allowed to make one phone call per week that I used to check on Brittney and the baby.

Each call was limited to fifteen minutes, of which, Brittney would use 870 seconds of the allotted time mourning to me about her solemn loneliness and my not being home.

I would normally feel worse about myself than I did before hearing her voice, but two nights ago, at the end of our *conversation*—Brittney said that she'd been bringing the baby to Annapolis to visit Reese Malone and his two sisters, Evelyn and Charlene, who were the only family I had in the area.

Just before the phone automatically ended, Brittney also relayed that my parents were coming to visit me on Saturday.

For the first time, I had smiled and didn't punch the wall after hanging up the phone.

* * *

After limited sleep and reading *The Count of Monte Cristo* from cover to cover, Saturday had finally come, and I restlessly sat in FCI-Cumberland's visitation room in the SHU section—anticipating my parents to parade through the visitor's entrance, twenty-feet to my left.

Facing a wall and a chair that was an arm's length away, I had been seated at the second of four small tables.

Several yards behind me, two coextending rows of five identical olive-brown tables passed along the length of the room, ending a few feet from the far wall where a slender prison-photographer with a black scarf that swaddled fat gold-enrod dreadlocks was standing.

The inmate's head ensemble resembled an albino python partially stashed under a flipped basket. Meanwhile, an airbrushed backdrop of Tupac and Biggie with bad nose jobs and throwing up the peace sign displayed behind the *imposta-farian.*

All decked-out in fresh khaki uniforms, spotless boots, sneakers, and Rockports, inmates lounged at their personal tables with their families, friends, and significant others.

Everyone sat in purple, enameled plastic-chairs while engaging in a collection of playful, romantic, and crucial conversations.

Some people chugged beverages and devoured food from the vending machines and microwave that were positioned to the right of the entrance, against a wall, and directly across from the officer's desk—which sat twenty-feet away at the center of the room.

The essence of radiated meat-like substances, and homemade perfumes coalesced and filled the room with a mixed sense of nostalgia. Part of me missed shopping at Barneys, the other part missed eating at Wendy's.

Strategically placed to keep a special eye on the *special inmates*, a correctional officer with closely cropped whey-washed hair and sideburns—rested twenty-feet behind me at an imitation beech-wood desk that faced the SHU section.

He was pretending to read a *Guns & Ammo* magazine while he ogled at the female visitors in his vicinity.

Burly with a Nestle's Strawberry Quik *suntan*, the officer wheezed when he breathed, and bit his nails nervously after each turn of the page.

The lone guard appeared to be scared and guilty as if he were the one under surveillance, although, right outside of the visitation room, more officers kept tabs of everyone through the security cameras—even the babies and children were being watched closely.

Because most of the SHU inmates had been sanctioned already, and the loss of visitation was part of the punishment, my desolate area of the room had a completely different vibe than the Disney World to my rear.

Emulating my current living arrangements, the SHU section had been word-less with a hovering dead energy that had even pacified the cute Asian boy with spiked hair and a teensy LA Dodger's uniform.

The kid was situated quietly at the table to my right, with his back against the wall—and across from his parents.

Five feet away, the family were the only other people in the designated area, and I kept peeping at the child's mamacita—who sat closest to me and to the left of Chino.

With wet, jet-black, curly hair falling to her bare shoulders and flat chest, she was dressed in a flowing white strapless dress with a collection of life-sized carnations, sans the stems, budding throughout the light fabric that hid her paunch—but failed to produce past the midway point of her meaty thighs.

Her thin kissers were heavily covered in hot-pink lipstick that added to her sex appeal but did little to distract from the hot-pink bumps on her hooked nose.

The young Hispanic lady with the alluring Pacifica Cocoa perfume was not my type, but she was *very* fuckable. The date was July 18th, but my cock was ready for Cinco de Mayo.

Of course, since my incarceration, my standards had dropped to a "just have a vagina" level, and I unashamedly sexually fantasized about every woman.

Although uncommon, I did feel guilty each instance my eyes met with the eyes of the MILF (Mexican I'd Liked To Fuck), because the inmate attached to her right hip with his hand underneath her dress was not just her husband.

He was an inmate I conferred with every day, who went by the name, *Chino.*

* * *

Chino, a Sureños gang member from East Los Angeles, was from Thailand but embraced the Mexican street-culture more than drunk tourists watching a Tijuana donkey show.

Squatty and hairless with heavy eyelids and a snub nose, Chino was inked from his neck to his calves.

An exemplary piece of penitentiary art and Chino's favorite tattoo, a portrait of a female Sphinx cat, face-painted in clown make-up, and cutting her wrist with a razor blade—fully covered his left forearm.

Chino had been in the hole for two weeks after a guard found a homemade tattoo gun and some alleged heroin in his locker during a prison shakedown.

During our rec-time two weeks ago, Chino admitted to owning the makeshift device but said the dope couldn't have come from his locker for one fool-proof reason: He already snorted all of his shit!

He also confided in me that he had been very concerned about his visitation privileges most likely being stripped before his wife and son could finally visit him for the first time during his prison bid.

Chino's wife had already bought non-refundable plane tickets to come in August, but he didn't have the loot to change the flights—his scheduled sanction date was July 20, 2001.

After learning that Chino had been crowned the best tattoo artist on the compound, *and* just happened to live in my unit, I offered to send his wife $500 from my prison account in exchange for full arm-sleeves and a back-piece.

Chino happily accepted the offer.

Any type of dealings with another criminal that involved currency was risky, especially a druggy inmate in a gang, but I was too arrogant and had too much money on my books to care.

Chino knew I wasn't broke and could fight, so I figured he would honor our agreement, either because he respected me, or because he desired more of my business.

In any case, after witnessing the gratifying expression on his wife's face, I was happy that I could be of some help. Chino was super cool, and I already considered him a friend.

* * *

Strutting behind a plumpish White woman with a Silky terrier inspired haircut, my father nodded and grinned at me while holding the entrance's door, inevitably for my mother.

A hood aristocrat with a graying Caesar and divinely shaped-up five o'clock shadow, Daddy looked dapper in form-fitting blue jeans, and a gray Dsquared2 crew neck that cropped slightly above a brown leather Louis Vuitton belt with the classic gold *LV* buckle.

His bare feet tucked into a pair of Louis Vuitton loafers that matched the style and precision of the belt, complementing his gold Patek Philippe watch, and two-carat-diamond-stud earrings.

Having lost some weight, my father had an unusual slenderness to his cheeks with a youthful radiance like he had been sleeping regularly and washing his face in holy water.

Daddy looked very fresh and very clean, but neither he nor anyone else in the room could transcend the exquisiteness of the celestial creature who entered and floated by my father.

Mommy!

My mother swayed gingerly from side to side, but the metallic double-chain of her leather sapphire Chanel handbag remained fixed to her right shoulder.

Her white, tailored Balenciaga swing collar button-down accented a midriff, too thin for a woman who had one kid—Mommy had five.

The denim of her Moussy skinny jeans stretched with each stride, and her Chanel heels, unvaried in the style and color of her bag, click-clacked toward me with understanding and boldness—like she already knew my location. A satellite had nothing on a mother's intuition.

An almost six-foot-doll with three-carat-diamond-studs in each ear, she didn't wear any make-up, and she didn't need any.

Her skin had smoothness like a brand-new tub of margarine, and I couldn't believe she had no wrinkles.

"Damn, New York girl's bad," I heard someone say.

They think she's my girl.

Creeps!

"Hey Mommy!"

I just know she gonna say something about my hair and my tooth.

"Oh my God, my son! How are you?" she asked as we tightly embraced.

"Hanging in there Mommy. You know me."

Still the most beautiful woman I've ever known.

"What's up, my big son?" My father greeted me with a hug and a kiss on the forehead.

"What's up Daddy?"

"Damn look at you—all hairy. Let me see that missing tooth boy." Mommy pulled down my bottom lip with her finger.

"Which one of these bastards put their hands on my baby?" she asked while scanning the room.

"Mommy it's OK. Y'all sit down please, before I get in some more trouble," I urged.

"Daddy sit in this chair, so you can see the room and not break your neck *people*-watching. Mommy sit right here next to me."

"It's OK, it's just a tooth. Manzo can handle himself...right son?" my father spoke and pulled the chair from the table for my mother.

You have no idea Daddy.

"That's right Daddy, no need to worry about me. I'm good."

"OK, I'm just saying—got my baby looking like a bootleg Michael Strahan up in here," she remarked.

"Ha, ha, ha...*Michael Strahan* though Mommy?"

"Karen, you're still crazy." Daddy laughed and sat across from my mother and me.

Fuck, I wished they were still together.

"Shut up Carlos. I mean that brother Strahan still fine though. What team does he plays for again?" she inquired.

"The Giants. Your *husband's* team Karen." My father glanced at her wedding ring.

Daddy still misses her.

"Shit, Eugene already knows—me and Jason are *out* if I get my hands on that young fella. But anyway, *seriously*, how are you Manzo?" My mother touched my hand.

"I'm fine really Mommy, no worries. You look amazing as always. You really don't age. These dudes think you're my girl, or maybe my sister, ha-ha. They def don't think you're my moms."

"Black don't crack son," Mommy said.

"It *sure* don't," Daddy mumbled.

"Anyway, how much longer do you have to be in the hole? It's been like a month already," she asked.

"For real Mommy, I don't know, but it can't be that much longer, because the dude I fought already got shipped away a few days ago."

"So they gonna ship you too?" my father asked.

"From what the jailhouse lawyers in the hole are saying, I won't be shipped off. I should go back on the compound soon."

"But do these people know that you didn't do anything wrong son?"

"Well, kind of Mommy."

"What do you mean, *kind of*?" Mommy pried.

No sense in lying now.

"Well, I didn't make a statement and neither did the other guy. Sooo, *technically*...nobody is at fault," I said.

"*What*?" Mommy questioned.

"What the hell are you talking about son? So, you're telling me some motherfucker tried to go spearing for doo-doo sharks up your ass and *nobody* is at fault?" Daddy grilled.

"Why didn't you give a statement then?" Mommy asked.

"Because I'm in prison, and you just don't do that type of stuff in here Mommy."

"Why the hell not?" Mommy pressed.

"Because if I wrote a statement, it's the same as ratting, no matter who the victim was and that stuff follows you *everywhere*, and I'm not walking around here or anywhere else labeled as a rat. So now I can leave out the hole and have the respect that I earned."

This is my world now!

"OK, but what if they would've let both of you out on the compound son?"

"Then I would've whipped his motherfucking ass again Daddy!"

The chattering in the visitation room stopped in a harsh silence, and although I never looked behind me, I could feel everyone focusing their attention on our area.

My outburst startled my mother, and Chino's son flinched while he scattered Uno cards on a Monopoly board placed atop their table, but neither Chino nor his wife, who inconspicuously gyrated her hips under a Washington Times newspaper—was fazed.

The couple continued with their agenda, and I knew Chino wouldn't wash his left hand for a week.

Watching Mommy's eyes enlarge in panic as she peered over my shoulder, I knew the guard was coming to conceivably terminate my visit, and a sharp sadness clung to the insides of my chest—but the pain wasn't for me. I didn't want my parents to leave, because I wanted my parents to get all *their* time.

The oncoming squeaky steps of timeworn boots, and tinkling keys were like ticks from the second hand of a clock for a man on death row, and for my parents.

I was surprisingly calm and had already accepted going back into the comfort of solitude.

Gradually transforming into inmate 09485-084, I enjoyed the detachment from all outside contact, and comforted in not worrying about phone calls, commissary, or keeping up with current events.

Every meal was delivered to my *house*, the guards supplied me with plenty of toiletries, and all I did was read, write letters, do push-ups, sleep, and masturbate undisturbed.

Without concern or care, I had begun to accept the culture and all possible contingencies of prison life. I was becoming institutionalized.

"Manzo is everything OK over here?" the guard investigated.

'Death in the family' always works.

"Yes sir, everything is OK. I truly apologize about the noise sir. Just got some bad news from my parents about a death of a friend. No worries sir, I will keep it down. Won't happen again," I promised.

"OK no worries Manzo, but no more outburst please or I will be forced to end your visit. So just keep it down big fella," the guard warned casually.

"Yes sir," I said as the guard glanced at Chino's wife and strolled back to his desk.

Damn that was easier than I thought.

"I, for sure, thought he was going to kick our Black asses out," Mommy admitted. "Manzo, what's up with your temper these days?"

We can start with I'm in fucking prison.

"Karen here's some money, please take this and go get us some food from the machines. Get us anything please. Everything is OK—let me talk to Manzo for a minute." My father handed Mommy a meager roll of dollar bills.

Daddy must've left his bread in the car.

"But Manzo, he can't—"

"It's OK Karen, I got it. Just get us some food please. Take your time...and don't forget—"

"I know, I know—*don't forget to get mustard for the burger*," Mommy impersonated my father and snatched the money.

All the inmates *and* Daddy followed her every stride to the vending machines.

"Hello...Daddy?"

"Yea, yea, I'm just making sure your mother knows where to go son."

"Yea, I bet," I teased. "You two are staying the night in town?"

"No, Gregory is outside. He's driving us back to the city *right* after we leave here."

"Just checking," I said.

"Hey Daddy, I'm sorry for my tone—"

"Son just be quiet for a moment and let me talk, OK?"

Damn, he's not playing around.

"Yes sir. Of course," I replied.

"Manzo, I could only imagine what you are going through in this place, but you can't let this situation break you or make you become something that you aren't. I'm worried about you, and you see that your mother is worried about you too.

"It's understandable that you adjust to your environment for your own good and survival, but you're not like most of these people in here.

"You're different. You have always been and will always be different. Use this time to better yourself in every way and don't conform to the bullshit.

"The few years you have left will fly by, and it's important that you keep sight that this place *isn't* your home.

"It's just a temporary stop for you. You'll make it through this ordeal a better person, only if you choose to.

"I know I've never been to prison, but I do know that just like on the outside, you can involve yourself in a lot of bullshit in here that can get you in more trouble...*like* playing a damn basketball game on your first fucking day, without processing the people in here or the situation you're putting yourself in.

"You don't have to prove to anyone how tough you are, or prove that you ain't a punk, because you're smarter than that. Do *your* time. Do your time and use your head.

"Unfortunately, there are guys in here who will be in this place for a very long time, if not forever, but they aren't *you* son.

"You have about four years left, which I'm sure a lot of these dudes would kill just to have your time. You made some mistakes, but you will grow from them and come out on top.

"I must live with the fact that even though I tried teaching you to do right, I *showed* you otherwise, and I'm truly sorry for letting you down as a parent.

"I only tried to put food on the table for my family, and if I could do things all over again, I would've done things differently.

"Don't be like I *was* Manzo. Be better than me. I'm not perfect. I made mistakes like the next man, but don't use my choices as *your* choices.

"I know I should've had this talk with you a long time ago, and some days I hate myself for not sitting you down when I noticed the changes in you and your behavior.

"I'm your father, so I don't need to see what you're doing to know what you're doing. It's called experience.

"I guess I felt too ashamed to confront you about what I sensed was going on when you were out doing your thing, and again...I'm sorry.

"But you're still alive and have so much more to live for. This place *is* and never will be a place you should be at. Don't succumb to the bullshit.

"Elevate yourself past it, and be that special boy, rather *man*, who I knew you would be from the moment you were born.

"Son, I ain't gonna lie, I was beyond hurt and upset when I found out that your momma didn't give you the Peña last name—*your* family's last name, but throughout the years I started to understand.

"You are special, and you need to understand this. You're unlike any of us.

"Your Uncle Henry and Aunt Joyce always said that you were a bona fide genius and can accomplish whatever you put that big head to—and I agree whole heartedly.

"But you don't even know it yet, because you've been following the moves of a *fool* and not your own,"

Daddy had spoken compassionately, and I put my head down, placing both of my hands on my forehead to conceal my wet eyes.

"It's OK son. Let it out," my father said.

"It's not your fault Daddy...I was just stupid."

"No son, this is totally my fault."

"I can't blame this on you. I did what I wanted to do and now I'm paying for it—I knew better," I admitted.

"Well when you come home, you will have a better example to follow, because I'm living my life right these days, and I'm not going back to that lifestyle. *You* have showed me it's not worth it," he claimed.

"Wait a minute—are you serious Daddy?"

"Hell yea, time to get on some new shit son."

No wonder he only has singles.

"What are you going to do for bread?" I asked as I patted my eyes with my sleeve.

"Well, after blowing a shit load of money on that damn club, the limousine company and the grocery store, I still have a couple of dollars saved up.

"Sooo, I will manage...but...I saw this place for sale on 105th and Second that would make a nice spot for a restaurant, but it cost way more than I—"

"Get it." I said.

"Damn son, you didn't even let me finish."

Can't talk about this here!

"*Whatever* it takes Daddy—just get it," I said while staring into his eyes.

I don't trust this visitation room!

Convo might be monitored and recorded!

Spend however much of my bread you need!

"It will be a good look for you to make an honest paycheck when you get out —Lord knows son, you will need the money after spending it *all* on those expensive lawyers—"

"Some lady and her twenty-five kids ate up all the damn burgers in the machine. I got waters and some peanut M&M's," Mommy interrupted my father's acting job, setting the candy and drink on the table.

"Thank you, Mommy."

"Thanks Karen."

"Maaan, there's some fine-ass brothers up in *here*—but why they all with fat White girls?" My mother inquired.

"And look Carlos, all them girls rocking that funny short hair style like they poodles or some shit. They all are wearing boot-cut jeans and white Reeboks like *they're* the ones in prison, ha-ha. What's up with that Manzo?"

Yooo, Mommy is still mad funny!

"Ha, ha, ha—I don't know Mommy. You would have to ask them."

"I did notice that coming in here Karen. I guess the sisters are tired of their shit. You know how *y'all* do."

"Yup...I can't blame the sisters either," Mommy agreed and opened a bottle of water. "Speaking of fat White girls...how's Brittney?"

"*Karen*—you know you wrong for that."

"That's messed up Mommy."

Mommy never bites her tongue.

"I'm just saying son, she *finally* sent some pics of her and Ruby, and Brittney doesn't look like she's missing any meals, is all I'm saying," my mother elaborated.

"Mommy, she just had a baby," I said.

"Karen you're crazy."

"Carlos don't play dumb, because you said the same thing in the car. *Just* had a baby, my ass. Child-please, that was six months ago. That girl gonna be big. Watch what I tell you son."

"Everybody can't bounce back as fast as you Mommy. You're a freak of nature. Glad you're still rocking the earrings I got you."

"Of course, I still have to keep my shit together, but stop trying to change the subject son.

"I still mean what I said about your baby-momma. How's Ruby, and when are you going to finally get to hold your daughter?"

"Ruby's fine Mommy, from what Brittney tells me, and the pictures she sends. I will see them soon, just not with me looking like *this*."

"I hear that. Y'all talk on the phone? Are you guys still together? I mean, what's the deal?" Mommy cross-examined.

"Since I've been in the hole, we only talk once a week. But we're still together...I love her. I plan on being with her and Ruby when I get out. I'm going to marry her in here."

"*Married*?" Mommy asked. "*This* nigga done bumped his goddamn head Carlos."

"Yes...*married* Mommy."

"You still have like four years left. I think you should wait and see how things go before thinking about marriage," my mother strongly advised. "You really think she's going to wait around and not get a piece of ding-ga-ling while you're in here?"

"Nah Mommy, Brittney's a good woman. She would never cheat on me. I trust her with all my heart. She will stay faithful. You don't know *our* relationship."

"Son, I don't need to know *your* relationship, I know *women*, and that one you got is as sneaky as she is bitter right now.

"*Trust me*, she'll be getting the Black pipe long before the next four years are up. I hate to be the one to pull your coat son, but you're going to see," she warned.

"Carlos stop making me look like the bad guy all the time—school your son, please."

Brittney would never do that! She loves me!

Mommy just saying that because she's White!

"Okaaay Karen...let's change the subject. You don't want your son hanging himself over no pussy."

"Shut up Daddy. Ha, ha, ha. I'm cool. Mommy's entitled to her opinion."

Brittney would never cheat on me! Never!

"Damn—Carlos don't even play like that."

"Nah, it's cool Mommy. I'm good."

"Son, I love you and didn't mean to upset you, and I already know what you're thinking, but my feelings have nothing to do with the color of her skin.

"Let's just nip that shit in the bud—because if race mattered to me, I would've never allowed you to go Woodberry with all them White kids, so don't use her being White as a copout.

"A crab comes in many complexions and many *shapes* son, but let's talk about your brothers who are starting to act like fools in these streets."

She's not a crab! She's my heart! Brittney would never! Never!

"It's cool Mommy, I'm not upset. What's up with my brothers and Sandy?"

She won't mess around on me!

"Well, Sandy, Donté, and Jason are fine. You have to ask your father about Chink. Javier and Alejandro are up to no good, and I can feel it in my bones."

"Why you say that?" I asked.

Why does she think Brittney will cheat? Brittney is faithful to me!

"They said they were going to Miami for a few days to promote Alejandro and his music.

"He's rapping now, and I thought that the trip was a good idea, but when they came back, I saw QB's girlfriend in Miguelina's when I was getting my hair done.

"She was bragging and showing her friend pictures from their trip. And *your* brothers had rented all kinds of Lamborghini's and shit.

"Alejandro had a neck full of diamonds, and both your brothers had on Breitlings, and I knew that your father didn't give them *that* type of money.

"So now I'm wondering where the hell they got that type of money from?"

"Hold up Mommy, when did Alejandro start rapping?" I asked.

"For a while now. Chink got him started, and Alejandro, I mean, *Al-Money* is hot with that rapping stuff.

"Although things didn't work out with Reb and their Diamonds in Da Rough group, Chink still set up a meeting with his Rock-A-Fella peoples...not Jay-Z. What's the other guys' names Carlos?"

"Your mother is talking about Damon Dash and Biggs. *Hip-Hop*, I think is the guy Chink is talking to though."

Hold up!

Today's the eighteenth!

"Uuh...yea...y'all act like I've been dead or something. I know who you're talking about—Hip-Hop is Kyambo, Biggs little brother.

"I used to play basketball with Kyambo at Milbank. He's a great guy. That's amazing. Better than *Al-Money* working in that cell phone store. I hope he keeps it up," I said.

Today's Chinks birthday!

"Well he's not gonna keep up shit if he's in these streets flossing. I swear I saw his little-bony-ass speed by me and Eugene in a convertible Corvette when we were on the Deegan. I'm not 100% sure. But you can bet your ass I will find out," she cautioned.

Corvette?

That couldn't have been Alejandro.

"Seriously Mommy, are you sure?"

Where are they getting all this money from?

What I have Daddy give them can't buy all that!

"Son I know your mama is getting old, but I know what I heard, and I know what I *saw*," my mother said.

"And did you ask them?" I questioned.

I swear something else happened today.

Glad I don't smoke anymore—can't remember shit!

"Yes, but you know they looked me in the eyes and lied. They were talking about one of their friends rented all the stuff. I know you're having someone send me those money orders every month."

"I'm not stupid son. So I'm going to ask you, and don't lie in my face...did *you* give your brothers that money?"

"No, no, no, Mom—I didn't give them any money. I'm in prison and I'm broke!"

"You a damn liar...*just* like your daddy," my mother expressed after a few seconds of scrutinizing my face with her squinty eyes. "I tell you; the truth just ain't in you Peña men."

"Stop acting like a cop Karen. The boy is telling you the truth," Daddy lied.

"*Really* Carlos? Just save the bullshit for your *new* bitches. I'm not your wife anymore. You don't have to lie to me."

That's it!

July fucking eighteenth!

Today was their anniversary!

"I'm a changed man Karen—"

"Mmmm-hmmm, like I said Carlos...save the petty larceny for your new bitches—"

"Come on Mommy, please chill. I didn't give them any money. *If* I had that type of money laying around, I would never let my brothers just blow it. Come on, please give me a little credit."

Where did they get that type of bread from?

"Weeell, someone did, and the shit has me worried, so please talk to them— because I'm getting too old to be visiting three different sons in prison.

"Plus, they don't need that type of attention with the way these guys killing over a nickel in these streets."

"You're right," my father agreed.

"Yes, you're right Mommy. I will talk to them. I promise."

"Well you better, because if they are involved in some bullshit, and you knew about it, then I'm holding *your ass* responsible," my mother vowed and drank some more water.

"Manzo, DO NOT play with me."

"Mommy, I would *never* play with you. I will find out what's going on. I promise. I'm on it. No worries."

"OK good, because I know they're up to something, but since they moved out your father's place and got their *own* apartments, we can't keep track of what they are doing anymore.

"Every time I go to see Javier, him and his girl ain't there. It's always that pretty little Dominican babysitter, that Aimee O-*something* girl, who is watching your nephews." she conveyed.

"Well, it's showing they're growing up and being responsible," I said.

"*Responsible* my ass. Listen to me one more time...DON'T PLAY WITH ME."

"Okaaay, I'm on it Mommy."

"But enough about them...let me ask you something. What are you going to do when you get out? Have you thought about *your* future? Are you going to take that one class somewhere to get your degree?" she asked.

"Yea son, what do you want to do?" Daddy asked.

"I'm not thinking about college right now. I really don't know. I just want to educate myself in here in any and every way possible that I can while I'm locked up.

"I figure that somewhere along the way I will come up with something that God has already planned for me."

"*OK*, but you really need to get that degree. At least to make your ole momma proud, if anything. You've come too far to stop."

"I know Mommy...I will."

"But look at you, talking about God and plans—I like that. Since when you have become so religious?" my mother wondered.

"I'm not real religious Mommy. I just know God has a plan for me. I can feel it."

"You know we're Catholic, so are you going to attend church if they have it in there? I'm sure they do," my father asked.

"Nah Daddy, I won't be going to church, but I've been reading the Quran in the hole to pass time."

"What? The *Quran*?" he questioned.

"Well, I be damned Karen. You mean to tell me that my son is going to give up bacon *and* White women?

"Get the fuck outta here. No wonder why he didn't touch the M&M's, Karen."

"Why? What's wrong with the M&M's?" Mommy went for the bait as usual.

"You know them shits are made with *pork*!" Daddy delivered his punch line. *Classic Daddy shit.*

I see where I get it from.

"You're right Carlos, ha-ha! Got me wasting your damn money."

"Ha, ha, ha—Mommy I told you don't feed into him. You know how he does."

"Well that's good son. No bullshit. As long as you're reading something," he said.

"But on the serious-side though...all joking aside. At least he will be able to work on any street in Harlem when he comes home," he said.

"What do you mean, 'he will be able to work on any street in Harlem'?" Mommy mulled over Daddy's comment. "Doing what Carlos?"

"Selling *bean pies* and newspapers on the motherfucking corner!" my father roasted.

"Carlos, you are a *fooool*...ha, ha, ha! Leave your son alone!"

"You play too damn much Daddy. I'm not in the Nation of Islam...or a Muslim."

"I hope they have bowties to fit around that big-ass head of yours!" my father wisecracked.

"Bowties go around your neck silly!" Mommy corrected.

"Ha, ha, ha...well you know what I mean Karen."

"Daddy this is the last time I'm telling you shit—I swear"

"Karen, Manzo is gonna be like that guy on that movie, *Don't Be A Menace* something-something. I always forget the full damn name."

"What guy?" she asked.

"You know the one...the one in that Wayans brothers' movie—the Muslim guy. The one who tapped the Black girl at the party and said, 'Excuse me sister... but can you tap that White girl right there!'"

"Oh yeeeaaaa—ha, ha, ha! I remember we saw that in the movies at White Stone!"

"You always say the same jokes! I won't front though—shit is still mad funny!" I laughed

"That was too funny. I needed a good laugh," Mommy said, dabbing her eyes with her fingers.

"Son, I'm just messing with you...because I miss you."

"I know Daddy. I miss you too...*both* of you."

"Well Moose, it's 3:30 and we have to unfortunately hit the road. Your mama still has to work tomorrow," Mommy said.

I will always be Moose to her.

Fuck, I don't want them to go!

"Yes son, I have to get working on my new project first thing in the morning. I will keep you posted." Daddy winked.

"What project?" Mommy pried.

"Mind your business, woman. This is men's talk," he playfully ordered.

"Mmmmm-hmmm—better be *legal* men's talk, is all I know," she said.

"Always Mommy. It's a new day. Have a little faith."

Daddy's finally getting his shit together. So proud of him!

"I will believe it when I see it," Mommy said.

"Oooh yea...oh man—we almost forgot. Your father has a letter for you from Matthew."

Really? Oooh shit! Dirt!

Yes!

"When did you see him Daddy?"

"I didn't see him at all. The letter was under my windshield when I came out the house last week. Thought I had got a damn parking ticket."

"You have the letter on you now?" I asked, attempting to mask my excitement.

"Yea hold up," my father said and dug into his back pocket.

"Here you go son. We didn't open it either, ha-ha. We don't want to know *anything* y'all two slick motherfuckers are plotting."

"Thank you, Daddy. Please just give me a minute to read this," I requested, after receiving the folded white envelope.

Fuck yea!

My nigga Dirt!

About time!

"Sure, go ahead. Just don't tell me shit," Mommy joked.

"Shiid, me either Karen," Daddy agreed.

"OK thanks. One moment please," I said and ripped the envelope, extracted the slice of loose-leaf paper, and began to read the red ink.

'My nigga what up? Just letting you know that I'm OK don't worry about me. Kills me that these rat motherfuckers got you in there but hold your head you will be home soon.

I'm still making it do what it do out here but I fell back and let these lil niggas hit the trenches while I'm all the way out the way.

Streets ain't playing fair these days but that's just how the game goes I guess. All I know is that I ain't ever going back to VA again!

'But you ain't never gonna believe what I'm about to tell you my nigga. Our plan was that I supposed to come to the spot the day after you got bagged to square things up, but I was already in town a day early fucking with that redbone bowlegged bitch from the mall I had met.

Bitch pussy was mean my nigga but anyway the bitch was mad annoying, so I left her crib with the quickness to come and check you before you bounced and when I'm a couple blocks away I see you pulling off with the fat white bitch.

'But before I had a chance to honk or try and catch you the fucking feds were already behind you on the low in a black Tahoe, so I stopped and turned off my lights and didn't move.

I called you but you didn't answer, and I was shook so I just parlayed in the cut but I didn't see any police around the crib yet at all besides the rednecks that followed you.

'So I'm mad paranoid and I don't really know if I should jet or be easy for a few longer and then I see your homie coming out the crib with the bag and I never seen your homie before but I know our fucking bag my nigga.

I didn't know if he was a fed but the way he was looking that nigga was paranoid too so I said fuck it and grabbed the hammer and ran up on him and took the two birds and the bread and his ID and told that nigga if he said a word I was going to tie his grandmother up.

Funny thing is that I didn't even know the nigga really lived with his grandmother, but the message got across crystal clear and your homie didn't put up a fight.

'I drove back to that annoying redbone bitch crib and told her I would give her my whip and a month salary to drive me to the city, and God bless that big booty girl heart because she got me up outta there by the skin of my fucking teeth my nigga.

After I took my slice of the bread I had your loot in the stash since then but I didn't know what to do with it so I had one of my lil niggas take the money to your pop's crib to give to him but your pops wasn't home so the dumb lil nigga left it with your lil brothers!

And you already know it's prolly a wrap for that bread because I'm sure they gonna do exactly what we would've done if a nigga gave us that bag at their age. BALL!!!

'Anyway my nigga if you need ANYTHING then just hit Keisha, Tye-Tye,

Stacks, or Flow Money up and they know how to find me! It's sad but you know how the game goes Manzo. Unfortunately I can't visit you and I sure as hell don't want my voice on the fed jacks yall got in there so I can't take any calls!

But when you get out a nigga gonna have a gang of big booty BLACK GIRLS and a bag of cash waiting for you on the other side of that fence for what you didn't do because I owe you like a motherfucker. Love you Manzo!

P.S. Oh yea your Jesus chain looks better on me! Ha ha! Don't even ask for details on how I got it back my nigga. You know how I gets down. See you on the other side rock star!!!'

"Love you too Dirt. You don't owe me anything," I whispered.

"Is everything OK son?" my father investigated.

"Yes Daddy...everything is cool," I answered and smiled, handing him the letter. "Please don't read and burn this letter *as soon* as you get outside. It would mean *a lot*."

"OK, no problem. You have my word son," Daddy promised, and he and Mommy stood up. I followed.

"Thank you, Daddy."

"No, thank you son," he said and hugged me firmly, and I felt like I was five years old again. "Everything will be OK. I love you so much."

"I love you so much too Daddy," I said, and we unclasped after a few seconds.

"Come here Mommy," I told my mother, who nibbled on her bottom lip, conspicuously on the verge of a breakdown.

"Take care of yourself Moose," my mother wailed madly in my ear after wrapping her arms around my neck.

I was in her stomach twenty-five years ago today when they were getting married.

Bet she never thought this would be my future.

Ah man—she's going to make me cry!

"I will Mommy—I'm good. I'm alive and will be out this place before you know it."

How could I hurt her like this?

"I'm sorry I failed you Moose. I tried to raise you right, but I failed. I'm so sorry for putting you in here. My heart hurts every fucking day son, and I don't know what to do. I need you.

"You're *my* oldest child. This family needs you. What am I going to do without you for four more years? Oooh God, I wish I could trade places with you. I'm sorry. Please forgive me. You shouldn't be here!"

"You *never* have failed me Mommy, you did the best you could. I failed you. I was hardheaded and I'm paying for it.

"You were the best mother...the absolute best...and it's you that's going to keep me safe in this place and get me through this hell that I put myself in.

"What you have instilled in me will help me make better decisions as a man. I love you. I love you so much Mommy...and I will make you proud one day—I will. I'm never coming back here. Please forgive me. I love you. I will never hurt you again Mommy. You have my word."

Chapter Thirty-Five

HOT POTATO

Although my transition into prison life did not start on ideal terms, after seven months at FCI-Cumberland I felt as if I had finally adjusted to my new world with a clearer mind, and with the mentality that I would use each day to improve the faulty thinking that had led to my incarceration.

My parents' visit while I was in the hole was the key factor in my character transformation, especially considering that I was furiously disappointed with my loss of two-months-good-time for my fight with Big John, who was shipped to United States Penitentiary-Terra Haute, a maximum-security prison in Indiana.

Because I didn't cooperate and tell the truth about the attempted sexual assault, I was found guilty of fighting, and sanctioned to a punishment that I did not deserve but had no choice to accept.

Following the testimony of several anonymous inmates, the Special Investigative Services (SIS) determined that I had not been the aggressor, but without a detailed statement from Big John or myself that covered the accounts of the fight, I was equally held responsible.

My first day back in B-1, I had been moved to a top-tier-cell with Marvin Hill after I was denied my request to live with Zane.

Counselor Britt thought I needed to *slow down* and be around someone who was new to Cumberland like I was. The counselor was right.

Zane had been involved in a lot of different hustles that I would've joined in willingly, because I loved action and making money.

But chasing a stamp and a dream was only beneficial to my growing as a successful inmate—not a successful man.

Zane and I remained close and we hung out, ate together, and talked in the unit every day, but it was with Hill that I had grown.

* * *

Hill, a compact country boy around my age with a chin-strap beard, and corn-rows the girth of a braided jump rope, had broiled lemon colored skin with red clay undertones, and prided himself on being from Knoxville, Tennessee just as much as I did to be from New York City.

A drug offender outside *and* inside of prison, he had been transferred from FCI-Manchester in Kentucky to Cumberland for attempting to bring an ounce of compressed marijuana into the institution after a visit from his son's mother.

He had been stripped of visitation from anyone, couldn't buy commissary, and lost his phone privileges—all for six months.

He kept to himself, and apart from working out, Hill spent most his time in the cell reading and didn't get caught up in the homeboy politics of prison, and I subsequently adapted to his style of *bidding*.

We both read a book day, worked out, smoked Black & Mild cigars, and played a game of chess before lights out. I virtually never won.

The entire fall had gone by where I had spent two hours a day on the yard in the morning, either exercising or playing a *friendly* game of basketball in the gym before being trapped in my cell and reading while Hill did the same.

I only watched TV when the New York Giants' games were broadcasted, but I didn't participate in gambling on my team or any other team like countless of the men did to pass the time.

Winning a bet was just a side effect of not having to think about real life for hours at a time.

My football passion had been replaced with the eagerness to learn, and to inwardly escape to new lands as anyone other than myself.

Regardless of how much I read and spent time away from the compound, and the unit's common areas, I still had the reputation as a scrapper and one of the best at hoops in the prison.

Whether standing online for chow on fried chicken day or for mail call, guys would attempt to befriend me with hopes of my joining their gangs or religious groups.

No one would ever just come flat out and ask, but the routine was consistent and often. Always with the yard being the meeting place, men offered me spiritual guidance, weed, or White Lightening (moonshine).

I respectfully listened but never committed to anyone, and I never accepted any examples of their *generosity* in public because inmates would immediately associate me with that particular sect.

Understanding the outcome of Big John's attempted savagery, the men repeatedly stated that by no means did they intend any disrespect or want any *funny business*. I appreciated the disclaimer, but I was still cautious of my surroundings.

I trusted no one.

I politely declined in every instance, and eventually the disguised initiation invites stopped, but efforts to get me to lace up for FCI-Cumberland's winter league basketball tournament didn't.

After some convincing from some of the guy's in my unit, I had joined B-1's A-Division team for the opening of the January 2002 season.

The holidays were the most depressing time in prison, so I welcomed being involved in a team sport to take my mind off of home, even if only for a moment.

After seven games our unit had a 5-2 record, but whether we won or lost, when the final whistle had blown, I couldn't shake thoughts of Brittney and wondering what she was doing, and if another man was around my daughter.

I tried terribly to not focus on things that I had no control over, but picturing another man playing *Daddy* with my family was a disease that needed more than basketball and some books to cure.

* * *

During Brittney's visit last August when I held my daughter for the first time, I cradled Ruby on my chest and I could feel her tiny heartbeat, but my untold love for the precious soul in my arms was overshadowed with panic and guilt.

My dormant insecurities had awakened. For the next four years, I wasn't going to be a part of Ruby's life and I hated myself for leaving her and her mother alone.

I feared that the same way that I looked into my baby's eyes and kissed her chubby cheeks, some replacement father would too as if the child was of his own flesh and blood.

When I closed my eyes at night, Brittney was all that I saw, and often I had nightmares about her being in different sexual positions, screaming in ecstasy as a variety of Black men without faces ravaged her every hole.

The pants and moans played in my ears with clarity, and I would jump out of my bed and into my desk chair to illustrate my love for her through twenty pages of heartfelt letters that I hurriedly mailed right when my cell door unlocked in the morning.

As soon as the phones turned on, I would call Brittney just to hear her voice, and she promised me that everything was fine.

She told me I was acting *crazy*, because she didn't want anyone else and never would let another man besides me touch her.

She said that she wouldn't have driven two hours to see me virtually every week if she did not love me or intended to have a future with me, and I believed her—until the next bad dream.

The cycle of worry and re-assurance continued for months, and I saw no end from the insanity, until Valentine's Day when Brittney came for a surprise visit without the baby.

Brittney stated that we needed some alone time, so she paid the normal babysitter double her rate to work on the most romantic night of the year.

When she visited, I was intoxicated with happiness and disbelief for the duration of our time spent together, and I knew then that Brittney really loved me. I had been in fear of her infidelity without merit.

We discussed marriage and having more kids while she fondled my cock for hours and kissed my neck.

Surprisingly, she even scooped her fingers in her vagina and shoved her stickiness into my mouth and ordered, "Taste *your* pussy."

Elated, I left the visitation room with a brand-new confidence and a brand-new set of blue balls.

I trusted my future wife more than I ever did. Brittney was my *ride or die* chick, and I would never doubt her commitment to me again, the loyalty she had was rare.

I couldn't let my crazy thoughts ruin the solid foundation of love I shared with the woman that I honestly would had jumped in front of a bullet for.

When I had returned to B-1 from Brittney's visit, I wanted to give her a little time to get situated for her trip home before I called her, so I decided to call my friend from Woodberry Forest, Michael Starke.

Other than Freddy *Spaghetti* Hollins, Mike was the only guy who had written me, and I appreciated that I was in his thoughts.

Mike had recently gone to Jamaica and sent me pictures of him on the beach with beautiful young women, drinking fruity drinks and enjoying life.

Each time I talked to Mike, I lived vicariously through him to the point that I burned his memory in my mind like I had doubtlessly experienced the adventure, and I couldn't wait to involve myself in his newest conquests.

* * *

Unseen in a corner of my unit, twenty yards to the left of B-1's entrance, four conjoined door-less phone booths with stools set alongside double doors that led to the counselor's office.

Big Ed, and Hill occupied the first and second booths, respectively, while the third and fourth booths remained empty.

After selecting to sit at the last booth, to give the other men some privacy, I wiped the scent of sweat and Sandalwood musk from the receiver with my t-shirt, placing the phone to my ear and dialed Mike's number.

I had really hoped he could talk, because I was thrilled to tell someone other than my parents about my plans to marry Brittney.

9-2-0-2-5-5-5-5-6-8-2.

OK, it's ringing.

RING...

Shit sounds too low. Hit the volume button.

TAP.

RING!

Better.

"Hello?" Mike answered.

The computerized operator spoke, "*You have a prepaid phone call from—*"

BEEP!

"Hello?" he repeated, after pressing *five* to accept the call.

"Yooo...what's up Mike?"

"My nigga Manzo! What's up slim?"

"Damn, you didn't even wait for the robot lady to tell you who the call was from," I said.

"Shit, no need Manzo, you the only dude I know in prison, and you know I will always accept."

"That's why I fucks with you lil' bro, but I hope I'm not interrupting anything...it *is* Valentine's Day."

"Never, plus—you already know I have too many girls around this piece to dedicate an entire holiday to just one of them."

"Ha-ha, I figured that. That's why I didn't feel bad calling. You never gonna change, huh?"

"One day... just not *to*-day. But what's good with you? You sound like you in great spirits—talk to me big bro!" Mike replied.

"Man, no complaints over here. Just doing my time. Staying out these people way."

"I hear that slim. Damn, you always on the phone though. You Dee-Boing the phone time?"

"Ha-ha...Mike it's not like that here.

"We each get 300 minutes a month, and we have to wait fifteen fucking minutes in between calls, you know, so nobody can Dee-Bo these shits, as you say," I explained.

"Damn, just 300 minutes a month?" he asked.

"Yup, just 300 minutes. Shit is lame!"

"Maaaan, so if you have mad bitches, you have to choose between talking to them and your family?" he asked.

"Always thinking about the bitches...but yup, you are correct my friend."

Unless you paid a couple of dudes for their phone codes like I do.

"Oooh, OK slim. I won't even ask my next question then."

"Ha-ha, please don't," I warned.

Mike knows me like a motherfucker.

"My nigga Manzo...but anyway...you still hoopin' in that joint slim?"

"Hell yea Mike, and I'm killing your homies! I average like twenty-six or something, but they have some good dudes here. Just can't guard me to save their motherfucking lives."

"I already know, but no more *fights* though, right?" he asked.

"Nah bro, I don't beef with anyone. Just play my game and keep it moving," I assured.

"Good shit slim, because it's not worth it. I heard they stab people every day there!"

"Nah, not every day...but between your crazy-ass D.C. homeboys and these Mexican gangs, shit gets crazy here," I said.

"Damn, I forgot they have gangs there."

"*Gangs?* Maaaan, Mike, this place has GD's, Bloods, Crips, Vice Lords, Nazi's...man you name it, Cumberland has it."

"That shit sounds scary bro," he spoke with concern.

"Shit...some days it is, but I'm here. Can't run from anything, just have to make sure I'm not doing anything that comes with confrontation—so I just workout and read, and write mad letters, as you can assume," I explained and sat on the stool.

"Ha-ha, I know! I write you two pages like I'm doing something, and you reply with a goddamn book," Mike stated.

"That's what everyone says about us prison dudes. No worries though. I'm just happy you write a nigga. I would appreciate just a sentence, no bullshit."

"Of course big bro...but slim...you're looking real cut in the pics you sent—*no homo.* Gotta watch what I say. Don't know if you got niggas doing the Tootsie-Roll in your cell in thongs and shit—ha, ha, ha, ha!"

"Ha, ha, ha, ha—fuck you Mike! You know I would have to kill you if you said that shit to me in here, don't you?"

"Go 'head with that shit! These is just *jokes!* But seriously though slim—you got mad tattoos now! I didn't even recognize you at first!"

"Yea I'm working out something serious, and I changed my diet. I'm in prison, it kinda comes with the territory. But the *tats?* I had these shits before I got locked up. We can talk about that another time," I conveyed, attempting to switch topics.

Please don't say another word about tattoos. Phones are monitored Mike.

"Oooh...oh yea...OK. Did you get my Jamaica pics?" he asked.

Thank God he caught on!

"Yessir! Thanks bro! That's why I was originally calling you...good looking out lil bro!"

And to tell you I'm getting married.

"No problem. Yea, it was a fun trip slim. You would've killed it there! Mad girls!"

"I bet bro! The girls looked mad good, but let me ask you this though Mike?"

"What?" he asked.

"Tell me why your boy Gene in every flick with you and a girl?" I harassed.

"Ha, ha, ha—go 'head with that bullshit Manzo!"

"Y'all dudes were swinging out there in Jamaica, or there was a shortage of bitches?"

"I knew your dumb-ass would say something slim! Gene jumped in every pic—"

"I know! I saw...fifteen times!" I teased.

"Only you bro!" Mike cackled into the phone.

"Gene has to be a good dude if that's your ace, but just do me a favor and crop him out next time please.

"Man, because I got your envelope and opened the shit right during mail call, and I pulled out the big-ass *posters* you sent.

"And I'm looking at them...and these gumps in my unit were looking over my shoulder, as I'm pulling out *page* after fucking *page* of two shirtless light skin niggas with arched eyebrows—on a beach standing next to *one* different girl in each flick!"

"Yoooo...you're a fucking fool bro! Nigga our eyebrows ain't arched!"

"No bullshit Mike...when I turned around, they were whispering at each other looking at me! I was scared! I hauled ass!"

"You just not right in the head Manzo! If I didn't know you, I would believe this bullshit!"

"Ha-ha—for real though Mike! Your pics gonna get me stabbed in this bitch...fuck basketball! But I *appreciate* you though bro!" I joked.

"Ha-ha...ah man...you still the same, slim."

"Still me Mike...just on a little vacation is all. Gotta laugh to keep from crying sometimes. How's the fam though?"

"Zack is out here beasting in football. Lil' bro said he's going to the NFL. Moms and pops are good. They always ask about you."

"Ah man, I'll be looking out for Zack *Starke* on TV one day. Send everyone my love." I said.

"No doubt. But his last name is Williams though asshole."

"Ha-ha, you know I'm just fucking with you Mike. The Starke kids play flag football."

"Ha, ha, ha—shut up fool! How's your fam though?" he asked.

"Family is good. My moms enrolled in Monroe College to get her bachelors, and my pops is about to open a club/restaurant. So, if they good...I'm good," I replied.

"Man...OK pops! That's what's up—but your moms not playing around I see!"

"Nah, she's on a mission! She's where I get my fight from. My moms never gives up—so I'll never give up."

"I know slim, this just a bump in the road for you. If people are counting you out, then they're just some fucking fools Manzo."

"Thanks lil' bro. Glad you believe in me."

"Maaan, cut it out—always! How's Ruby doing though?" he asked.

"She's good, just turned two."

"Oh shit slim. She was just born like yesterday!"

"I know Mike! Shit is crazy!"

"Ruby still being distant with you?" Mike asked.

"Yea, it's gotten a little better though, but shit is annoying. She acts like I'm a stranger."

"Just give it time big bro—she knows who her father is," he said.

Tell him about the wedding.

"I know, but the shit is hard to take sometimes. I can only imagine how she will behave at our wedding."

"Nigga—the *what*?" Mike asked.

"The *wedding*...when Brittney and I get married probably next month in here."

"Oooh OK...but slim, you still have some time though before you come home. *A lot* can change by then!"

"I know, but I feel I'm doing the right thing...Brittney's my soul mate."

"*Soul mate*? Do you hear yourself Manzo?"

Why does he think this shit is so funny? I love her.

"Yes, I do—and I'm serious!" I said.

"OK, OK, calm down—I get it Manzo, but five years is a long time! That's a long time for a woman to *wait* for anyone! Just saying big bro!"

I'm done talking about this!

"Brittney is different! Relax! She's not like these other girls! Now can we spend the few minutes we have left talking about something else...please?"

Nobody is happy for me!

"Of course! Listen, I'm happy for *whatever* you do in life big bro. Just don't forget about a nigga when the world knows your name."

As long as you accept my wife.

"I would never forget any of my *real* homies. Speaking of that, how's Reese? I called him last week, but he didn't accept my call—must've been bad a connection," I wondered.

"*Reese?*" he asked after a few seconds of silence.

"Yes, *Reese Malone*. How's Reese?" I repeated.

Mike is acting funny again.

"Oh yea...Reese is cool. I just talked to him the other day," Mike finally answered.

Something's not right.

"Is there something wrong with Reese? Did something happen?" I grilled, beginning to panic.

Please God say he's OK!

"Nooo, it's nothing like *that*—" Mike said.

"OK, so what is it like Mike? I know when you aren't telling me something... it's my gift! Now tell me what's wrong with Reese!"

"All right, all right! Listen slim...Reese said that...he said that you're mad at him—that's why you don't talk to him."

"What the fuck are you talking about Mike?"

"Yea, he said you aren't talking to him...because you probably hate him."

"*Hate Reese*? For what? Is this a joke Mike?" I probed, shifting in my stool.

Why would I hate Reese?

Makes no sense!

"Maaan, you *really* need to talk to Reese, Manzo. My word he didn't tell me why."

But from the sound of your voice you already figured it out, didn't you Mike?
What possible reason would I be upset with Reese?
He doesn't owe me any money.
What could he have done to me while I'm in—wait!
Oh no!
Nooo!
Not possible! He would never! Not Reese!
"Uuuh, Mike—I gotta go! I gotta go! I will call you back! Love you, lil bro!"
"Manzo wait—"
SLAM!

* * *

After I hung up, my body felt weightless as my chest tightened to console my battered heart. I trembled while I watched the numbers on the phone and contemplated making the call that I was sure would impact the rest of my life.

Paranoid thoughts pumped perspiration from my forehead and palms, and my stomach rejected reality. I wanted to vomit!

Ignoring the nausea, I shut my eyes hoping life's circumstances had changed when I opened them. I'd rather have been anywhere besides in a phone booth suspecting that my best friend, and my future *wife* were intimate while I served my debt to society.

When I opened my eyes, the same phone hung in front of me, and I was in the same booth—life still sucked!

Reese said that I *hated* him, but I had no reason to have any ill feelings toward the man that I loved like a brother.

He didn't snitch on me, and he did not owe me any money, but I knew that he and Brittney had recently been spending time together. Unbothered, I had never worried about their friendship, until now.

Prior to Mike's conversation I would have bet my life that I could trust Reese. If our roles were reversed, he could trust me around his girlfriend, wife, baby-momma, sidepiece, or whomever—but the more my brain marinated with logic, a mere hunch had transformed into fact.

* * *

Call her! Ask her!
No don't ask her! Tell her you already know!
But how? Trick her!

How?

Tell her Reese told you! That won't work!

Yes it will!

Reese didn't do it! Yes he did!

No...

He FUCKED Brittney!

Call her!

It's hasn't been fifteen minutes though!

Use Benny's phone code! What the fuck is it again? Oh yea!

9-6-9-0-6-5-6.

Volume.

TAP! TAP! TAP!

"Please enter the number you would like to call."

9-7-5-7-5-5-5-2-2-4-5.

"Thank you. One moment please."

RING!

Bitch better answer! Fuuucck, this is crazy!

"Hello?" Brittney answered.

"You have a prepaid phone call from—"

BEEP!

"Hello?" I spoke after Brittany accepted the call.

Please tell me I'm buggin'!

"Manzo, ha-ha, why you talking so low baby? Are you OK?"

No, I'm not.

"Yes, I'm fine," I lied.

"Well you don't sound fine," she stated.

Ask her.

Tell her Reese told you already!

"I'm...good," I said.

"Oooo-kaay, if you say so. I'm on the highway and was just thinking about getting married. I can't wait to be *your* wife!"

See, she loves me!

It's probably nothing! Let her know you know!

"Yeeeaaa, I can't wait either," I said.

"Manzo what is wrong? Tell me, or I'm going to hang up—because I know you too damn well! *What's* wrong?"

Stop being a pussy! Tell her you know!

"I...I...I *know* Brittney," I stammered.

"You *know* what Manzo?"

"I...I know...about...I know about you...and...you and Reese."

"*Whaaaat?*" she asked.

Fuck, I know I'm wrong!

"About you and Reese...I know," I continued the deception.

I'm so stupid for this! Brittney would never cheat!

"Manzo, how can you say such crazy things to me? Are you trying to sabotage us? Our *marriage?* Why would you say such a thing? Who would tell you such nonsense?"

She would never cheat! Too late!

Keep going!

"Reese told me everything Brittney—he confessed to me."

She's going to know I'm lying now!

"*What?* Wait Manzo! Reese told you...*everything?*"

Keep it going! Make up something!

"Yes, he told me everything...and I told him I would call him back after I called you. And he didn't mind me telling you that I talked to him. He even said if we all needed to be at a visit together, he would say the same things in our faces.

"But he said it wouldn't come down to a visit, because you would tell the truth also." I concocted a fitting scenario.

This is ridiculous!

Why am I doing this to her?

"Oh...is that what *he* said?" she questioned.

Shit!

She knows I'm making this shit up!

"Yes, now *what* is he talking about, you and him... fucking?" I continued.

Just deny it so I can quit this bullshit!

Can't believe I'm doing this?

"*Brittney,* are you still there?"

"Yes I'm still here," she sobbed.

She's crying!

Oh no!

Come on!

"Brittney, why are you crying baby?" I asked while fighting back my own tears.

Why is she crying?

"Uumm, I dunno."

"You *dunno?* Brittney you better talk to me!" I yelled.

You better say he's fucking lying! Please say he's lying!

OK, calm down! Stop yelling!

"Come on Brittney—you know you can tell me anything. I'm in here. I can understand anything, if you're honest. Ha-ha—I'm in here, not you babe.

"I will never get mad at you, if you keep it real with me, because that's the type of love we have...that real shit. *Unconditional shit.* Either way—you're my future wife."

Bitch, I will crack your motherfucking forehead if you're fucking my best friend!

"You really mean that?" she asked tenderly.

"Of course, my vanilla-pudding-doll-face. People make mistakes. We live, and we learn from them my love. Life is too short to leave your soulmate for a blunder.

"We are all human. Lord knows, I made my mistakes, and our love is stronger than ever. *We are built to last.*"

I'm gonna kill this nigga when I see him if she says some crazy shit! Just tell me he's lying!

Please God, make her tell me she's lying!

"Reese...Reese is... Reese is telling the truth—but Manzo, I'm so sorry!" Brittney confessed.

* * *

Many nights I sat in my cell and listened to the cries of the tormented inmates on the phone who had just been told that their significant others were cheating on them.

I dared not to laugh or judge, because if the day ever came that I learned of an infidelity over a prison phone, I knew that I would not be strong enough to hold in the pain. I was right.

I wanted to run home to my mother.

I wanted to escape and grieve around loved ones.

I wanted to call Brittney, not the monster on the phone, and have her help me heal.

I wanted to call Reese like I had done since I was fifteen years old and ask him for his guidance.

I wanted to get on a Greyhound to Annapolis, the same way that I did when Tanisha shred my life to pieces, and the Malone family provided me with shelter and an outlet to get my bearings together.

I just wanted to feel the comfort and love from the people who I could always depend on, before I would lose my mind and self-destruct on a prison phone, trapped in the mountains of Maryland—but I couldn't.

Simultaneously, both of my safe havens crumbled, leaving me to deal with my agony alone, because I would never call my mother and give her the satisfaction of saying she was right—mothers were *always* right!

A stubborn child, I was stuffed in a shrinking phone booth with literally nowhere to turn except inward—into a mind of a maniac with warmth removed from his heart, and pornographic images filled in his head.

Remaining deathly silent, I locked my jaw and welcomed the blaze of unrestricted thoughts, before I exploded.

* * *

"How could you fuck my best friend—you fucking slut?" I screamed.

"I'm sorry!" she bawled.

"You're *sorry*?"

"Manzo you said you wouldn't get mad! Why are you yelling?"

"Bitch shut up! This ain't the fucking movies!" I spat.

'Beat this pussy up Reese!'

'Stick that big Black thang deep inside me!'

"It was just one time—I swear!"

"Stop lying, bitch!"

"It was! I promise Manzo! I love you baby! It was only one time! I wasn't in my right mind—"

"It was that fucking night you stayed over there, wasn't it?" I asked.

"Yes—I was wasted! I'm sorry! I love you! Please forgive me! I was confused! Ooooh God—why is this happening? It was a bad period for me! I wasn't myself!" she pleaded.

"Bitch—you had my motherfucking daughter in the same room when you were sucking my best friend's dick?"

"Uh...uh, I was wasted—"

"You're the worst type of woman Brittney! You're the fucking worst, and Ruby is going to grow up to be a whore just like you as long as I'm not around! You're a fucking slut! I hate you for doing this to me!"

"Nooo—" she cried.

"Did you enjoy it? Did he fuck you good?"

"Stop Manzo! I love *you*!"

"Did he fuck you better than me? Is his dick bigger than mine?"

"Stop Manzo! Stop! Ooooh God! I'm sorry! I'm sorry!"

"FUCK YOU! It's over! You can have him!" I cried.

"Noooo! Noooo! Don't say that! Don't *ever* say that! We can work through this —I promise! We can be a family!" she wept insanely.

"A *what*? A *family*? Y'all ain't shit to me! Are you fucking kidding? Reese is the worst type of slime ball! And you're just my whore-ass-baby-momma now! That's what I will always see you as—"

"Don't say that! Manzo please don't say that! But what about Ruby? What about the baby?"

"Don't mention my daughter! You killed our future when you couldn't keep your fucking legs closed! Fuuuccckk!

"You and that motherfucker are selfish and only care about yourselves—y'all don't love me!

"I hope you catch a fucking disease and your nasty pussy falls off—you fucking cunt!" I roared, and saliva savagely dripped from my mouth.

"Noooo! We can still be together as a family! And yes, I do love you! It was a mistake! I love you! Reese still loves you!"

"Shut the fuck up! No you don't! No, he fucking doesn't either! Reese was my *brother*! His mom and dad were like my mom and dad!

"His family was my family! My family was his family, and you two selfish motherfuckers have just stripped me of *my* family!

"Y'all just took away people that I loved like we had the same blood, and things will *never* be the same again!

"I can never look the Malones in their eyes again—all because some stupid White slut couldn't control herself around some Black dick!"

"This isn't all my fault!" she disputed.

"You're right! You *are* right! Reese is to blame as much as you, and this is exactly why this hurts so fucking bad!

"I loved you two just as much as anybody walking this earth...and now I've lost my best fucking friend...and I lost the girl I wanted to marry!

"Fuck you and Valentine's Day! Go home and put a fucking bow on his dick and suck it—you whooore!"

"Don't say that! Please don't fucking say that! I love you soooo much—pleeeeeaaaasssee...don't saaaay that!" she pleaded.

"Shut the fuck up! You don't have a right to tell me shit anymore! Why? Why? Why?

"I know I wasn't always perfect, and this is what I probably deserve, but let me tell you something bitch—I don't have *life* in prison Brittney! I have *mother-fucking* a release date!

"I will be home before you know it, and I fucking guarantee that you and that fucker Reese will regret this shit!

"I will get out! I will do big things! I will be successful and people around the fucking world will know my goddamn name!

"And I will act like you two don't even exist! Just watch! And it will eat at you two cheating, lowdown, backstabbing motherfuckers before it eats at me... because I'm done!"

"Nooo Manzo, please don't say such things!"

"As a matter of fact, have a nice life Brittney!"

"I have to go, so I can call Reese and hear some other things he wanted to tell me before our phone call ended!" I bluffed and peeped out of the booth to find Hill had left, but Big Ed was on the phone—staring directly at me like a disappointed father.

Unashamed, I ignored his presence and pushed on with the madness.

Fuck Big Ed!

Fuck everybody!

"WAIT!" she squealed.

"What do you want bitch?"

"He said...he had some other *stuff* to tell you?" she asked delicately.

She's worried!

Fuck!

There's more!

"Yes, he said he had some other *stuff*, so please let me go—it's over! You're a fucking liar! At least Reese found it in his heart to tell me *stuff* I should be hearing from you bitch!"

God this hurt so bad!

I don't know what to do! I still love her so much!

Why Brittney?

Why Reese?

"You know what? You're right Manzo. You should be hearing everything from me. I fucked up, and I love you too much to lie to you anymore...so let me just tell you," Brittney sobbed.

I can't take any more! I'm broken!

Get off the phone Manzo! Hang up!

"Bitch, if you have something you need to say you better hurry—because I'm hanging up!" I cautioned.

Don't listen!

Just hang up!

This won't be good!

"OK, OK—Manzo! I don't want you hearing this from anyone else...but... but...I...I also...well...I just want us to have a clean slate...if we could...so...I—"

"Stop fucking stalling and spit it out!" I screamed.

She's pregnant!

She has an STD?

What?

"Okaaaay...I did have sex with Reese *once*...but...oh man...I—"

"WHAT did you do Brittney?"

Ruby isn't mine? What is it?

Hang up!

Don't listen!

"OK! OK! I *did* have sex with Reese...but there's something else you should know...I didn't want you finding out like this...but...but...please forgive me but...I had sex with Reese's little brother Kamari too...and we kinda dated."

Chapter Thirty-Six

DEAD END

After Brittney confessed her sexual trysts with a third of the Malone siblings, I slumped into an abysmal state of depression that maintained its power for several months.

During this time, I had no correspondence with Brittney other than letters and cards of her begging for my forgiveness.

I missed her and Ruby dearly, but I absolutely didn't want to hear Brittney's voice, so I never called and even denied their visits the couple of times Brittney drove down with my daughter.

Cold, I felt nothing about sending my *family* away and asked the guard to relay one message to Brittney, "Go fuck yourself!"

At times, I wished I were dead. I sailed around the prison like a lost ship with no sight of land or support, without ever disclosing to anyone the root of my wretchedness, but I knew my relationship status was no secret.

Every toxic syllable that I had snarled at Brittney bounced off my unit's walls and into an inmate's gossip column.

Big Ed and Hill, the only eyewitnesses to my tirade, would often give me looks of concern but had never mentioned to me what they heard.

They refrained from prying into my personal life, and I appreciated how they minded their own businesses.

At night, Hill and I no longer played chess, instead I sat at the desk intermittently staring at a picture of Brittney while I wrote her a ten-page letter, split evenly with five pages of soul-crushing hatred and five pages of heart-warming love.

Hill would just read his book until the pen's final stroke, followed by me ripping up the evidence of my confusion, and turning off the light.

The undeviating ritual did little to ease my mind, and I wanted to confide in my "celly" about my feelings and thoughts that concerned my *relationship* as I had done with many other topics, but I chose to internalize the distress.

I feared of Hill one day using my truths against me, although we had a solid friendship.

He already had known more than I'd liked, and I didn't feel comfortable escorting him any further into my weaknesses, but the pressure of concealing my sentiment was becoming too much.

My spirit was broken, and I no longer recognized whom I had transformed into—I wasn't Manzo.

Playing basketball and working out were outlets that provided an interim distraction from my sorrow, but when the cell door's locked and trapped me with my demons, I needed help and protection from myself.

Unwilling to vent the pain, I would bang my head against the wall just to fall asleep once I heard Hill snoring on the top bunk.

I was afraid that the longer that I stayed conscious, the higher the chance was of me physically harming myself.

Sleep brought peace, unlike being awake in the darkness where I could see Brittney and Reese fucking like Puerto Rican rabbits.

Each blink they switched positions, and with each position—I switched murder plots.

One morning I had awakened with a terrible migraine and noticed blood on my pillow before feeling the lump on my forehead.

Frightened, I realized that I'd better humble myself and open-up to someone immediately, so I jumped out of my bunk, got dressed, and ran to the phone.

In desperate need of unconditional wisdom, I called my mother.

* * *

My mother listened diligently and after the initial shock subsided, she cursed the day that Brittney was born.

After she simply stated that Reese was not my friend and never was, I was too ashamed to tell Mommy about Kamari, so I hid the crucial information that would have made me look like more of a sucker than I already was.

Mommy was very protective of us, so I also couldn't risk her knocking on Brittney's door with my aunts to *talk*.

Even though Ruby's mom was a slut in my book—Brittney was still, in fact, Ruby's mom.

Nonetheless, my mother's sympathy didn't last long, and she made it clear that I truly deserved my karma because of the way that I had treated Brittney and other girls in the past.

Mommy knew that I had cheated on Brittney numerous times and even knew a few of the girls with whom I dipped out of my relationship.

I didn't know who exactly the tattletale was, but apparently, someone with the Peña last name had a big fucking mouth!

Mommy loved her children but would never let any one of us, especially her eldest, separate her from her morals and values as a woman, and I respected her convictions.

Considering that I witnessed my father's strain on my mother, she told me that she'd always been disappointed at my lack of loyalty for any girlfriend I ever had.

My mother believed as long as I continued *my* whoring around—God had no choice but to deny my happiness.

Mommy's perspective helped me understand that I wasn't the victim, because I put myself in prison, and no one behind bars was exempt from his significant other seeking comfort in another man's arms. Treachery at home was a part of doing time.

She advised me to "man the fuck up," take a deep look at the person I was and the person I desired to be, and make the required changes that would better my position to succeed when it was my turn to walk out of those prison gates.

She said Brittney wasn't the one for me, Brittney never was the one for me, and that God showed me the *truth* early in my prison sentence, so I could heal with plenty of time to transcend into the man that my mother raised—and the father that Ruby needed.

I was not religious at all, but I could feel God speaking through Mommy to free me from my tribulation.

When the phone call finally ended—my spirit had been cleansed like I had drunk holy water from the River Jordan.

I smiled and returned to my cell with the demons uplifted from my soul!

I still had no plans on ever going to church or preaching the gospel, but I had decided to not let anyone have power over me.

What Brittney chose to put in her vagina would never determine my fate.

Mommy's blueprint to worthiness was an ultra-precise creed that laid out the steps for self-elevation.

Beginning with changing my daily regime, I listened to my mother and had taken the vital steps to reprogram my thinking.

My body was in chains, but my mind was not.

* * *

No longer isolating myself in my cell, I frequented the yard more with Zane and my other New York homies, because being around guys who I had something in common gave me mental comfort.

Amongst laughing and joking, we discussed whatever popped into our heads.

But it was the conversations about our law-breaking and trifling ways that had given me better insight as to how awful of a person that I really was.

Granted that not everyone involved in our powwow had spoken out of remorse, I saw the life and excitement in a few guys' eyes as they illustrated details of high-level drug deals, robberies, schemes, assaults, and sexual adventures.

I used my homies' glorification of mayhem to help me identify that the core of whom I really was, and how I was raised, did not correlate with that of a typical convict—even though my past actions said otherwise.

I didn't think that I was better than any of the guys from New York, but none of them had my education or my upbringing—yet, we still ended up at the same place.

I completely felt that I was the fool of the bunch.

I had been provided with the people and tools to prosper toward greatness that the others didn't have as youth.

But I neglected to stay the course and take advantage of the unimaginable opportunities presented to a boy from the projects.

The more the city boys talked on the yard, the more I kept asking myself, "What am I doing here?"

Unlike the rec-time group-thinks when I was in the hole, I wasn't entertained by the stories my homies bragged about and didn't enable the men by replicating their demeanor when I revealed street tales of my own.

I used the guys to clear my head, so I could admit out loud some regrettable events that I had never communicated to another individual—who was not directly involved in the incident.

I never divulged into any incriminating subject matter that could have led to any further troubles with the law.

All my stories dealt with lack of scruples rather than criminality issues, because I still didn't trust anyone.

As additional months passed, my jailhouse psychiatric sessions, along with an increase in recreational activities, aided in propelling my sanity to steady levels.

Now, the only times I spent in my cell were for count-time and nightly lockdown.

Of course, I still missed Brittney and thought about her and Reese, but I wasn't emotionally drowned in the situation anymore.

The mania was gone, and in December 2003, I finally asked Brittney to bring Ruby for a visit. After twenty-two months—I could no longer take not seeing my daughter.

Brittney never stopped sending pictures of Ruby, and the guilt of my being absent while I was absent had gotten to me.

I wanted to hold my little girl.

* * *

During the visit, Ruby wined and cried persistently each instance I attempted to touch her, as if I were a stranger.

Although I had a boner like a free Yankee's bat on Kid's Day, I was emotionally numb to Brittney's presence, and I borderline detested her.

The only part of me that yearned for her was beneath my zipper, but the urge to fuck Brittney was expected, because the only action I had gotten in over three years was from my close friend, *Depalma Myhand*.

Karma did bite me, but I couldn't compartmentalize my doing wrong from having wrong done to me, and I still had not forgiven Brittney.

She had taken a job in Oxon Hill at Potomac High School as a home economics teacher, and the bulk of our conversations revolved around her students and was as bland as her cooking.

The spice and spark between us that once had zest and flash were transparently absent. Annoyed, I just needed to get the fuck away from Brittney.

I preferred to have spent another month in the SHU than to smell another dehydrated petal of her sunflower perfume—while I faked interest in baking blueberry muffins.

Brittney and Ruby stayed only an hour before I fabricated a story about me not feeling well.

Kissing both of them on the cheek, I signaled for the guard that I was *done*, and I left frustrated—but only about the non-existing interaction between Ruby and me.

I didn't give a fuck about Brittney *or* the Maryland Board of Education. The spell had been officially broken.

With Brittney, virtually off my mind, my confidence returned, and I felt good—maybe too good.

* * *

New Year's Eve rolled around, and Hill and I decided that while on lockdown in our cell for the night, we would celebrate another year closer to freedom by drinking a Sprite bottle full of White Lightning and smoking weed.

I had scored the party supplies from an amigo that I used to watch "Caliente" and "Niña Amada Mía" with in B-1's Spanish TV room.

Arrogantly, I believed that I could handle one night of indulgence, because I deserved to *chill* in the manner that most of the inmates did leading up to the stroke of midnight.

Besides, I had been sober for 1,242 days, and in my mind, I conquered my substance-abuse struggles. A little marijuana and fermented fruit had never hurt anyone.

After inhaling the spec of weed rolled in a micro-square of toilet paper wrapping, I grabbed the moonshine from my desk and took a swig before glancing at my watch to commence counting down to a new beginning of the same bid.

However, Hill and I had been talking about our respective children and failed to keep track of the time, so there would be no count down.

My watch read 12:01 AM—the official time of my relapse.

Reacquainted with my sins, I was high off the one pull of smoke that I sucked into my born-again lungs as the dead apples doused my brain with feelings and hallucinations extracted from the depths of my subconscious.

1999 permeated my stomach, and I had started tripping! My eyes saw a storm of $100 bills and white powder swirl around in a felonious dreamland.

Jane, naked and positioned with her elbows and knees planted on my bottom bunk, snorted lines of cocaine off a Juvenile CD case while her ass wiggled in the air.

Jane's shimmy was her normal sign to let me know the front door was locked, but the backdoor was wide open.

I had lost contact with Jane after RCJ, and I really missed her, but proportionate with my priorities and urges from the most titillating year of my life—I was more turned on by the coke rather than the cokehead.

As I sat at the desk staring at my empty bunk, I could taste the blow's bitterness without an interrupting memory from the sweet and sourness of Jane's vagina.

Cocaine had seeped through Cumberland's walls and found me, and I would have taken the White girl back without question if she really were in my arms again.

Hill, witnessing my mind drift, tapped my shoulder from his own chair while he burned the tips of his right fingers as he smoked every postage stamp worth of weed out of the tiny joint.

Snapping out of the love affair, I enjoyed the poisons traveling through my body and told myself that it was perfectly fine to have a moment of stupidity and carelessness.

Relapse was a part of recovery.

Hill and I finished our party supplies while we laughed and listened to the Disney Radio through both of our Coby headphones hanging from a bedpost.

The station seemed to play nothing but the Cheetah Girls, Miley Cyrus, and Hilary Duff.

I was drunk and before I passed out, I butchered every word to every teeny-bopper song, until I promised myself to renounce abusing any more substances for the extent of my incarceration—but I had lied.

Hungover with the monsters reenergized and still alive in my soul, I woke up the next day craving to be high and free from distress, so I bought some more weed and smoked a joint alone in my cell while Hill went to breakfast.

The flight from reality was awesome, and I didn't think about home, Brittney, Ruby, or my imprisonment. Time and family were neither a worry nor a factor.

My head cleared from the strain, I didn't want the phenomenon to end!

After a day of eating junk food, watching funny movies, and masturbating to five Butt-Man magazines while holding a ten-day-old, empty tuna can to my nose—I topped off my *best day* in prison with another round of White Lightening, more weed, and an evening of unruffled sleep.

* * *

Mommy's words dissolved with each pull of marijuana, and for the better part of 2004—I chased green clouds of comfort and courage, rather than conditioning my mind to change my undisciplined thinking.

I stopped reading books and became lost in prison pleasures that in no way would prepare me for real-world obstacles.

I rejoiced in gambling, and I partook in poker on the yard when I wasn't betting on professional and college sports.

I loved to watch rap videos celebrating the lifestyle that had been a catalyst to my adverse circumstances.

Repeating the lyrics, I never considered that my favorite jams illustrated the *wrong* moves of most men in prison.

Seventy-three percent of the Cumberland's inmates had been convicted on drug-related charges.

Just another convict content with the movement of the clock rather than the movement of his character, I had no intellectual growth—and I didn't give a fuck either.

Athletics. Food. Women. With my mental development stagnated, I stuck with the subject matter that I found worthy of my energy.

I played basketball, coached my unit's flag football team, created culinary masterpieces in the microwave, and corresponded with as many females as possible.

In both sports, my squads had lost disappointingly in the league's championship.

But when it came to receiving letters, dirty pictures, phone sex, and visits from girlfriends—I won the Heisman, the Cy Young, and the Conn Smythe trophies.

Some of the women were old acquaintances that I had reconnected with through mutual friends, but most were neglected souls that I had met on a *dating* website, prisonpenpal.com.

* * *

One evening in early August of 2004, I called Kieta—my childhood friend from Harlem. He had just come home from doing a ten-year-bid in Albany, so I was excited to hear from him.

Mid-conversation, he talked about the amount of mail he used to get from a lovely Latina who lived in London. She had found him looking for love on prisonpenpal.com.

After disclosing the pond he'd used to find such a catch, Kieta admitted that the girl wasn't *real*—his whole fish was really half cat. Still hooked, I remained on the line.

As long as it were indeed a female writing back, a pen pal pretending to be a hot girl was unimportant. She could lie about *her* persona—because I planned to definitely lie about mine.

I just wanted to correspond with someone who didn't have a peter and a nut sack.

A week after Kieta's conversation, I received a brochure from the site and went back to my cell.

Immediately, I picked through a few dozen shirtless pictures, before choosing a flick of me on the yard wearing Timberlands and gray sweats. And of course, my muscles were coated in baby oil.

Filling out the brochure, I had written my name, my referral, and the necessary billing information.

While circling "straight man seeking women only," and arriving at the bio section—I couldn't stop laughing!

I never thought that I would be *seeking* attention and companionship from random women on the Internet, but I was no longer at home with unlimited female options.

I was in prison where only freedom trumped vagina as the highest commodity. Desperation *was* the standard.

As I gazed at the empty box on the brochure, the humor of the situation ended, but I couldn't formulate the lies and tender prose to describe myself and what I wanted from the *prison pen-pal experience*—I was too high.

Reaching deep into my lexicon of love, I decided to not bullshit the precious creatures who just wanted to be wanted.

Instead, I straightforwardly asked a question that would convey my true feelings and reflect the type of partner I desired, so I wrote, "WHO WANTS THIS BIG BLACK DICK?"

I just couldn't take any part of having my image plastered on the World Wide Web for meat-hungry women to select like a steak from the butcher seriously.

Unbothered, I just figured that the $109 I sent to the site was squandered away with my optimism of romantic prosperity.

I took the pen pal fiasco as a sign that I should just do *my* time and stop looking for lust in all the the wrong places.

For two consecutive weeks, I went to mail call with no expectations for letters from any *new friends*.

But on that thirteenth day, when I decided to stay in the sports TV room with my homie, Tuffy—I thought I heard the guard shout out my name for mail, twenty-seven times!

Confused, I concluded that my ears had been mistaken.

So, I continued waiting for the game's final score between the Oakland A's and Los Angeles Dodgers.

I needed the Dodgers to cover the two-point-spread for me to win ninety-two books of stamps.

Moments later, Zane walked in with a stack of envelopes in his hands. Dropping most of the mound on my lap, he grinned as ESPN's Stewart Scott announced that I was $460 richer. *Boo-yaaah!*

In complete denial of my good fortunes, I searched every letter with anticipation of my name not being on any of them.

On each envelope though, *Manzo* had been spelled correctly on them all, and in a variety of handwritings and ink colors. Barbie-Pink was my favorite.

Fleeing like O.J. Simpson in a Hertz commercial, I firmly toted my parcel up to my cell, settled at my desk, and commenced to indulge in my newest obsession. I already forgot about my latest positive-stamp-flow.

Out of the twenty-seven letters, nineteen were from women and eight were from men.

I left the men's letters unopened and discarded them into the trash—because there was absolutely nothing a man had to say that I wanted to hear.

The remaining envelopes were perfumed with a medley of flowery scents that I recurrently held under my nose.

Besides inspirational cards and an array of stationary, the women sent pictures of their families, their houses, their trailers, their cars, and of themselves.

Some women were clothed, and some women were completely naked, and I yearned to fuck them all—and they all yearned to fuck me.

I shouldn't have been surprised by the raw intentions of these ladies, considering the brazenness of my introductory question, but I was shocked—yet quite flattered.

For hours, I savored the abundance of lust, infatuation, and adoration the strangers had for me, without ever questioning their motives or thinking.

Women of various ages and races spoke like they had known me for a lifetime as they explained that I was a perfect fit in their worlds.

Some revealed their relationship fears and hoped that I wouldn't hurt them like their previous or even current partners.

Most of the women started their letters with a generic "Dear Sexy," and they offered me money, visits, and "the best pussy you ever had."

Isabella from Orlando, Florida said she couldn't wait for me to come home to her, so she could suck me off in the Disney World parking lot until I was "cock-less like a chocolate Donald Duck."

Lilly, a musician from Stockholm, Sweden, stated that she wanted me to "anally defile" her while she played Frederic Chopin's "March Funebre" on her deceased racist grandfather's grand piano, and even though I didn't know the song—I liked the tune.

Many of my suitors clearly had psychological issues, but so did I. Nothing suggested was taboo to me.

I read every line of different penmanship with an erection and had to take breaks in between letters to please myself. My testicles would have exploded and nuked the prison if I hadn't.

I wasn't attracted to many of the women, but they were all beautiful to me.

If given five minutes alone in a bedroom with any of them, I would have screwed each different woman with the exact beast-like effort and passion.

Willing to try *almost* anything with a woman, I couldn't deny that I was a hyper-sexual animal when I was home, but prison sank its savagery into my blood and remodeled the structure of my inhibitions.

Not having any sex made me yearn for *forbidden* sex, and the pen pals helped identify my limitless appetite for a woman's flesh.

Every mail-call since the inception of my perverse curiosities, I would acquire a consistent twenty or so letters, but I would wait until the unit had been locked down for the night to read them.

Although I could no longer masturbate with Hill present, at night, I could zone out and attentively respond to my old and new darlings without interruption, in a cell of literary enthusiasts. Hill read gangster novels. I authored romantic short stories.

One by one, I tirelessly read and answered each letter at my desk into the morning hours while Hill slept.

Never generic with *my* rhetoric, I treated the women as separate entities, and I felt as if I were in a monogamous relationship with whomever's name was penned on the return envelope.

Effortlessly, I had convinced myself that my words were sincere and special, because part of me really believed that they were.

I was one person, but I wasn't the same *my love* to everybody. There was no proof that I had been only giving just a part of me, because in my mind—I wasn't.

Like the same character in a different play, I displayed devotion, loyalty, and even love on an individual basis, The language I spoke was only coherent to the reader.

I always remembered minute details, such as birthdays, zodiac signs, and children's names. Everyone was important. Everyone was special.

I encouraged the women to eat properly, pray often, and love themselves.

I complimented them regularly, and routinely asked them how their days were, how was work, and if they were getting enough sleep at night?

I told them that they were jewels, and that it would be an honor for any man to call them his *wife*.

I expressed compassion and interest in who they were and their wellbeing, because I knew them better than they had known themselves.

Most importantly, I knew what was absent in their lives—someone like me.

Many had boyfriends and spouses, but the women lacked men who raised their confidences, put their feelings first, challenged their thoughts, and made their pussies tingle with the power of words—rather than the power of touch.

The pen was mightier than the penis, and my voice was my advantage—because the bulk of males in society were naturally selfish and needy, focusing on the physical and ignoring the mental.

It had been easy for me to detect the deficiency within my gender. When I was home, I was also a selfish male who just wanted to get laid and not be hassled.

I could have cared less about the oral communication between most women and myself.

While locked up, I couldn't have sex or hold my pen pals tight at night, but I could listen and give insightful, constructive, yet positive feedback.

I righteously paid attention to *their* needs and desires as if I were a student of their anxiousness.

I made their minds *come* with each delivery from their local postmen, and the effect I had on the women was more profound than sex.

No matter where the ladies traveled, I was in their heads, sustaining a longer impact than if my head were inside of them.

Their consciences were interchangeable with my prison cell, because I lived in both places.

The women had the same probability of escaping the thought of me as I did of escaping FCI-Cumberland.

The connections developed into something far more intense when a few of my pen pals transitioned into *phone* pals.

They could now hear the intense conviction of my feelings with an immediate chance to respond. I was no longer having to wait days to articulate answers and reactions.

Within two conversations of fun and serious dialogue, the lingo switched to an erotic wordplay of wishes and fantasies. Subsequently—every pair of sweats I owned now had a hole in the right pocket.

Missing meals, I had phone sex for breakfast, lunch, dinner—and even dessert.

Vibrators buzzed in my ear so often, a few times on the yard, I swatted the air around my head—because I thought I was being chased by bees!

Phone-sex relaxed me, and I thoroughly appreciated the daily releases, but the women had become more insecure and possessive with each orgasm.

I had been the only form of intimacy for many of them, and the thought that I was being unfaithful caused them to question me about my interactions with other women.

Momentarily easing their suspicions, I professed my love, honor, and respect for them. I swore that I was a good boy and would rather die than take advantage of their trust.

I promised all eight of my girlfriends that I wanted a future and children with them, although I hadn't known any of the women for more than a few weeks.

Without any remorse, I thought nothing of telling the women whatever they needed to hear because our dealings were a game to me.

I had been incarcerated for over four years, and with eleven months left on my sentence, I was using them to help my time go a faster.

Considering my girlfriends' feelings was not an option that I had given much thought. The women really were expecting me to walk out Cumberland's gates and into their arms—but that was not my plan.

They needed soulmates, but I wanted playmates. My girlfriends and I had very different objectives.

The women were my puppets and I loved them for being part of the cast, but on my release day, the strings would be cut, the curtain would fall, and I would have stage-left their lives forever. I didn't care if they could stand on their own.

I had many chances to emancipate their souls from my deceitfulness, but I didn't because I was addicted to the attention as much as they were addicted to me.

Therefore, I offered the women an advancement in our relationship and correspondence to show them that my love was real—I invited all my girlfriends to come see me.

Excited, they all agreed! After I added them on my visitation list, the women and I set up respected dates for our first physical encounters.

Their dreams had come true.

* * *

From East Stroudsburg, Pennsylvania—Joanne, a red-headed thirty-seven-year-old with an ass as wide as the cattle she raised, was a porcelain divorcee with two kids and two clit rings.

She lived the closest to Cumberland, so I made plans to see her first in September of 2004. Joanne had an insatiable marijuana habit, so I persuaded her to compress an ounce of weed and sneak it into the visiting room to give to me.

I've never attempted to bring any form of contraband into the prison, but I knew Officer Crocker, the only Black guard, and a Virginia Tech fanatic—would be on duty.

The last three times I left visitation, he and I chatted about football before I exited without him searching me at all. I prayed he still loved those mother-fucking Hokies.

* * *

The day had arrived for my biggest girlfriend to come bless me with her present, and I was *excited* to finally meet her.

In her sexy polka dot dress and Aldo flats, Joanne seductively swayed all 282 pounds of her between the visitation room doors.

Instantly, my cock thickened as if Tyra Banks just had bent over naked and picked up a brand new penny.

Although there was something beautiful about every woman, I was never attracted to larger women while out on the streets.

But prison wasn't the streets, and Joanne had three major things going for her: a vagina, some weed, and the fact that I was a sick fuck!

She was the hottest piece of tail in the room in *my* eyes, and when she approached me, I stood up and greeted her just as any other inmate greeted his *bae*—with a big kiss.

Our mouths touched and split as my tongue found hers, and we lunged for one another's throats.

Oblivious to the stunned onlookers, I unrelentingly lapped her saliva—tasting the spinach fondue and cheddar biscuits Joanne had for lunch.

I dug my fingers into the sides of her cushiony belly and listened to her mild moans while I inhaled her spice, the essence of cinnamon buns.

The sweat on her forehead rolled onto my cheek, and I felt Joanne's fingers slide into my opened pants zipper.

After steadily withdrawing my lips from hers, I looked into her emerald eyes, and told her I loved her. She said that she loved me too.

As I pulled out a chair for Joanne, I could feel everyone's eyes.

Scanning the room, I found several inmates and their guests watching us with disgust—especially the stunning, barefaced, young woman with the melanin rich complexion of a swallowtail butterfly, standing at the visitor's entrance.

The height of a volleyball player, she had remarkable ever-changing light eyes set in a taut velvety even-toned face.

Her nose was bulbous tipped and hovered beautifully above plump centre lips that I would've spent another year in the hole just to kiss.

Extravagant dark fine glossy hair swooped past a heart shaped chin and twin tear-drop breast, ending gracefully at her ribcage with perfection.

The Black beauty's ass and thighs were thick and dense like semi-dried cement. She appeared to have done walking lunges from her home to the prison, before switching outfits in the visitation room.

Fierce and fashioned in all black, the woman wore jeans and a long-sleeved shirt that complied sweetly with the sleekness of her build as if she had on a bodysuit.

The gold H of her Hermes belt, and the knee-high Bottega Veneta leather boots with four-inch-heels—gave the super woman the appearance of a comic book character. I suddenly yearned to be saved.

She held an Hermes Kelly clutch in her right hand, and acid in both eyes. And while everyone in the room stared at her, the demigoddess stared at me.

The gorgeous woman's face was familiar to the point where I even thought I knew her name, which rested where I wanted her butt to be, on the tip of my tongue.

Although when I saw the tears well up in her eyes and she shook her head, my memory recharged.

I abruptly filled with confusion and embarrassment, because I totally figured out whom the woman was—and what unlucky bastard she had come to see.

My first time ever seeing the young lady without a face full of makeup, I almost didn't recognize her.

The tortured dime-piece's name was Celeste, and she must've come to FCI-Cumberland to meet her "amazing new boyfriend."

I proved quickly that I was far from amazing, but we were in a *committed* relationship.

Celeste was also one of my girlfriends.

* * *

Creole and twenty-two years old, Celeste Baptiste lived in Atlanta and owned a real estate firm, Baptiste Realtors.

A recent graduate of the University of Alabama, she was the only woman that I had met from pen pal site that was not an actual member of the site.

She came across my profile when her fifty-six-year-old assistant showed Celeste my bio just for a giggle.

After they both laughed, her assistant went to the bathroom—and Celeste covertly wrote down my information from the woman's computer screen.

Celeste deliberated contacting me but had decided to *follow her heart,* so she sent me a letter and a picture of herself in a black single-breasted Givenchy business suit.

In her letter there were no words except a question, written at the top in Barbie-Pink ink, "WHO WANTS THIS PUSSY?"

I hysterically laughed when I read her question because I had instantly gotten her humor and recognized that she was mocking me.

I liked how different her approach was from all of the other women, and I also found her to be one of the most attractive.

* * *

Since our introduction, we had written one another every day, and I thoroughly delighted in our banter and engaging dialogue, especially when we started talking on the phone.

A fast-witted foxy woman who challenged my thoughts, Celeste accepted who I was with no expectations from our relationship, only that I always had to be real with her.

She said there wasn't anything that I couldn't tell her, and I believed her, but I refused to speak the truth to any woman in my life. Honesty wasn't a part of the game, but manipulation was.

Celeste was my favorite, and I thought about her all the time, but not enough to stop thinking about the other women.

I had no idea what Celeste was doing out in the world, and there was no way that I would ever commit to a young lady that I felt like I could love but didn't really know—*especially* while I was in chains.

Celeste was wife material, but I wasn't willing to risk the shredding of my life again with a woman that I knew everybody wanted. Besides being the only dark skinned Creole girl I had ever met, Celeste was different.

Super attractive, she made me change my core beliefs about *long distance* relationships, because Celeste possessed an intense desirability that could easily charm any man who entered her zone.

Even a potential wife had sexual needs that I didn't think could be fulfilled by mutual masturbation sessions over a prison phone.

I had rather remained a confident hypocrite and believe that no man's physical presence could ever break the mental bond we shared—but at the same time still fear that my fleshly absence wasn't adequate to sustain a functional relationship for the remainder of my bid.

Celeste gave off no impressions that she wanted any involvement with another man, but her bold move of reaching out to me had always puzzled me.

Insecure, I wondered why such a stunning young woman with a great career, her *own* assets, and a prestigious southern family background, would want anything to do with a convict?

So, I asked her about my concerns, during our last discussion—a day prior to her twenty-third birthday, and ironically, the day before Joanne had come to visit me.

Celeste disclosed that she was highly attracted to me and saw an *adorable* hurt in my eyes that begged for a love that my mouth would never concede.

She further stated that her last three boyfriends, who all cheated, were too serious and lacked the entertaining frankness that she perceived were my strong points, judging from the ridiculousness of my online bio.

Lastly, with the purity of a child, she confessed that the two biggest blessings ever in her life were attending the University of Alabama—and finding me.

Falling fast, Celeste wanted me to descend into the fairytale at the same rate, and I did.

Years had passed since someone besides my parents endorsed my character and saw me for something other than my mistakes.

Celeste's affectionate praise and openness during our conversation pulled me closer to our union, and all my doubts about the woman's loyalty had vanished.

I was relieved that God had mercy on me, and brought the perfect mate into my life, even though I wasn't worthy of His blessings.

My sanctity induced tears, and I had begun to cry.

The final twenty-one ticks of the call, I told her that I loved her, I needed her, and in under eleven months her future husband was coming home to her and no one else.

And I meant every word spoken, for fifteen minutes, until I was able to call Rosie from Virginia—the next girlfriend in the rotation.

* * *

Watching Celeste blast out of the visiting room after witnessing me slurping on my extra-large juice, I panicked and ran to the inmate's entrance and knocked, leaving Joanne devoid of a bidding farewell.

Permitting me into the search room that was comparable to the square footage of two prison cells, Officer Crocker shut the metal door behind me.

He then double-stepped to an adjacent exit that led to the compound, and erratically right-hand-waved for me to leave as he spoke into his walkie-talkie, notifying the guards posted in Times Square of my release.

Officer Crocker's demeanor and compliance to escort me out so expeditiously, revealed that he had seen my Jerry Springer Show's tryout on the security monitor that rested at the center of the room on a plastic yellow chair.

Skipping the normal small talk about *our* football team, or even a pat down, I left the search room in a gratified haste.

Speed-walking to my unit, I sprinted directly to the phones upon entering my unit.

* * *

Wishing she would accept my call, I repeatedly dialed Celeste's cell phone number with the will of a single mom on welfare who called a radio station to win groceries. And just as I zipped my pants, secured the tube of cellophane-wrapped-weed Joanne wedged below my wiener—Celeste pressed five and answered.

Barely able to breathe, Celeste wept and yelled, spewing profanity and insults every other word—while describing me as a "ghetto Shallow Hal" and a "sick chubby-chaser."

She said that I was "Satan," and she had been a fool for driving ten hours to surprise a "narcissistic sociopath with *mommy* issues," but also stated that she couldn't resist seeing and holding the most important person in her life on *her* birthday.

Proceeding to disclose her evaluation of my self-worth, Celeste ended the verbal assassination by shouting that I would never change and "good luck raising your piglets!"

There should have been something in Celeste's torment that affected me enough to reflect upon her perception, but I thought that nothing she said had applied to me. She evidently didn't know who I was at all.

I especially couldn't have been a narcissist, because narcissists felt they could do no wrong.

Throughout her rant, I had been busy formulating a rebuttal, and only her name-calling had gotten my full attention, because her metaphors used to describe my *preference* in women were hilarious.

Presumptuous, I had supreme faith that Celeste still loved me, and I could get her to trust me again, but I knew that I had to allow her to speak freely and not interrupt the mourning process.

Our *misunderstanding* was merely an embarrassing moment for me that could be corrected with time and communication, so I gave her most of the call to clear her mind.

After we hung up, I called her every ten minutes for hours, but all my attempts went straight to her voicemail, and I could not think about anything else beside Celeste.

I *had* to speak to my girlfriend!

Smelling deathly from deep sweat and a lack of a shower, I aimlessly paced throughout the unit, unable to sit for even a minute.

When the prison locked down for the night, and Hill finished counting his last sheep, I sat at my desk like I spiked my Mountain Dews with lithium.

A pile of unopened pen pal letters accompanied my madness as I conjured images of Celeste and I getting married and having kids—until the guards reopened the cell doors at 5:30 AM.

After forcing myself to go to breakfast just to kill time, I returned to the unit and waited by the phones until they turned back on at 7:00 AM.

I continued to obsess. I would've killed to hear Celeste's voice.

Sick, I genuinely didn't want anything to do with her, but her ignoring me made me feel that I would have died without her.

At no time did I ever think about what was best for Celeste, or even her well-being for that matter, because I didn't care.

I wasn't hurt. My *ego* was hurt, and I had to get the woman who *portrayed* that she didn't want any dealings with me—to consent that she did.

My infatuation to win had been masked by a craving to be loved, but I didn't love Celeste.

I only loved myself, but the "crazy cat" that waited by the phone couldn't comprehend the meaning behind his compulsiveness.

I had felt like I could have called Celeste for the rest of my bid until she had spoken to me, but to my good fortune, I didn't have to wait that long.

At 7:25 AM *she* picked up and accepted the call.

* * *

There was just a distant hissing after I said hello, and I anxiously awaited Celeste's southern twang.

Exhausted, I spoke again, but oddly, a gentleman with a Creole accent responded, and I had thought that I dialed the wrong number somehow, or that Celeste spitefully had another man pick up her phone to infuriate me.

Before I questioned the guy, he identified himself as "Celeste's father," and I readied myself for "the talk" about his demands that I leave his daughter the hell alone and to never call her again. I was *almost* right.

The father-in-law that I would never have, conveyed that he knew of my relationship with Celeste and wanted me to be aware that she was in a car accident on her birthday—while returning home from visiting me.

He reported that his daughter crashed her Range Rover into a truck on I-85 South near Petersburg, Virginia, and was immediately rushed to Southside Regional Medical Center in critical condition.

She had suffered intense head trauma, as well as, rupturing several vital organs.

Mr. Baptiste paused his speech, and gasped before he persevered with the update.

My chest tightened, and I gripped the edge of the phone booth to support my legs that suddenly had gone numb.

Mr. Baptiste said that the doctors did everything that they could, and there was no need to bother her again, because his "little girl" was gone...forever.

On September 24, 2004, at 8:06 PM—Celeste Aliza Baptiste was pronounced dead.

Chapter Thirty-Seven

LIFE COACH

"Let's go Boo! Get this money kid! Get ten! Come on, get ten—you got it! Pull-motherfucker-pull! Good shit!" I encouraged Mark "Boo" Elliot to complete his repetitions of pull-ups.

Fuck, it's cold out here. I have to take a piss.

No time.

Training is everything!

"Manzo, you been trying to kill us in this jawn lately. You can't fool me homie. You're going through something or some shit," Boo said, lowering himself from the rusted steel platform.

A seven-foot-post, welded between the platform and the center of a horizontal five-foot-pole that curved downwards at both ends, served as the spine of the pull-up bars that I nicknamed, the Bank.

Nope, I'm not going through shit! I'm perfectly fine!

"Just turning you into a savage homeboy! Now step away from that motherfucker and let Hill get some of this money! Let's go Hill! Your turn! You up, country boy!" I commanded.

"Maaan, dis will make twenty-four sets!" Hill complained.

"No shit! I didn't know you could count that well! I salute the state of Tennessee's public-school system! Now let's go Hill!"

"Nigga you sed we were just doin' twenty-five sets dis mornin!" Hill reminded.

"I know I did, but shit has changed! Twenty-five sets for bitches, not us! We gonna keep going until the ten-minute move!"

"What the fuck Manzo?" Boo interjected. "That jawn ain't until thirty-seven minutes from now!"

I don't give a fuck! We gotta get this money!

"You niggas should've been math-ah-*fucking*-maticians instead dope dealers! Stop whining and let's go! It didn't take you that long to get in the damn police car!" I shouted.

"Fuck you nigga!" Hill laughed, leaping to the bar.

"Ha-ha—yooo, you stupid Manzo!" Boo hollered.

"We gotta make our baby-mommas throw up a little in their mouths when they see us shining on the streets!" I said.

"Aaaah!" Hill howled, now pulling like a machine.

"That's' right Hill! Pull! Get that money! I need seven more! Pull motherfucker! Pull! Yessir, three more! This ain't shit for you Hill! You got this! Bingo!" I yelled.

This is all that matters. Train hard.

Gotta keep training hard. Keep this body tight.

Train like a savage.

"Goddamn Manzo—you think we goin' to the Olympics or some shit?" Hill asked.

"I know Hill! This nigga is crazy! Manzo, we ain't you!" Boo added, and the vapor from his mouth masked his face.

My turn! Let's get this money!

"Get out my fucking way lil' buddy! I need to make a withdrawal!" I warned, soaring to my *mental* therapy as Hill hopped off the platform.

"Manzo is possessed!" Boo yelled.

Although I didn't realize it, Boo had been totally correct, I was *possessed*.

* * *

In the weeks since Celeste's passing, I exercised three times a day with three different sets of inmates who followed my every routine.

For a minimum of two hours each training session, I led my *car* in advanced routines that challenged the men's strength and endurance.

The combination of calisthenics, and conditioning drills I learned from Coach Gentry were something the guys in prison had never seen.

I invented workouts that pushed the men in the icy mountain air, while most of the compound was sleeping.

With no regard for the below freezing temperatures, we attacked the record-cold-October elements—clothed in charcoal skull caps, double-layered sweat suits over long johns, and orange work gloves that we bought for ten stamps apiece from the UNICOR workers.

We didn't have any hoodies or scarves, so we wrapped towels around our necks and tucked the towels under our sweatshirts like we were preparing to shoot a Saturday Night Live skit with Hans and Franz.

Numb to weather and tragedy, I was in the best shape of my life—*physically*. I maintained a dense physique and could not pinch an inch of fat anywhere on my body.

I had action figure abs, and a plastic soul that had been suffused with unrefined narcissism. No matter how toned and shredded my muscles had become, I wasn't satisfied.

I appreciated my physique, but I was always upset that I didn't look better.

Scrutinizing my body every chance I could, I paid attention to my aesthetics and nothing else.

Vain, I spent every night in my cell doing crunches, dips, and push-ups, and I would *forget* to call my family as promised, because I was staring in the mirror for an hour—looking at a god.

Brittney, Mommy, or anyone else hadn't heard from me, but the Bank did.

The yard was my sanctuary and way of coping with the untimely death of one of the most precious human beings I had ever met. I felt guilty, like I was solely to blame.

Whenever I thought about Celeste, I elevated the intensity of the workout, and sweat the images out of my brain.

In denial, I had disclosed to no one the supplement responsible for my physical prowess.

I just continued to suppress the sadness, and increase the reps.

* * *

Get this money! Four more Manzo! Don't stop!

"Eighteen...nineteen...twenty—good shit NEW YORK CITY!" Hill cheered.

"Daaaamn Manzo—your big-ass couldn't do a single pull-up when we first got here!" Boo said.

"Shiiiid, I remdist when Zane had'ta hold ya damn feet!" Hill joked. "Now that was some funny-ass shit!"

"You ain't lying either Tennessee!" Boo added.

"Ha, ha, ha! Fuck y'all!" I responded from the ground, feeling the frigidness of the concrete through my gloves as I did push-ups.

Rising to my feet, I looked up at the gray clouds that lingered over the convict country club before spotting Big Ed standing with his scuffed black boots dangling from the platform of *his* pull-up bar, ten feet to the right of my area—facing the basketball courts.

Big Ed's odd facial expression puzzled me.

Bundled in the identical insulation as Boo, Hill and me—Big Ed appeared to study me like a father did when his glossy-eyed-son came home after curfew, but I didn't know what he had wanted.

What the fuck is Big Ed looking at? I thought we were mad cool.

Only the inmates with an overwhelming dedication to their appearance, health, or both, exercised outside in the penetrating coldness at 6:00 AM every morning *before* breakfast.

Besides Big Ed and my car, only a handful of old timers jogged or walked the track, attempting to cheat death.

Big Ed had always trained alone with his headphones on, and no one ever bothered him or his *almost* pull-ups, but what he lacked in range of motion, he made up with respect.

Content in his own world, he listened to the classic R&B station on the gym's satellite radio as he crooned songs from the O'Jays, Earth, Wind & Fire, and the rest of the bands that aided in my parents' baby making.

But for the first time, Big Ed wasn't singing, and even though he and I had gotten closer over the span of three consecutive holiday seasons, mainly because of our affinity for sports—I really feared I had upset the aged warrior in some way.

"Now this motherfucker thinks he's Tarzan on the bar and shit," Boo said.

Shit, I have to use the bathroom.

"Y'all some fools, I swear. I'm going inside to the bathroom really quick. Hill watch Boo—you know how he likes to *miscount* his money!"

"Man, cut that bullshit out!" Boo said, and I made my way to the restroom in the gym.

"Hur-ruh up too!" Hill hollered to my back.

Trotting past Big Ed in the middle of willing himself through a set of dips, I avoided his eye contact, but my back singed from the heat of his gaze.

I wasn't scared of Big Ed or any man at Cumberland, and there was no chance that I would let another inmate who bled like I did, make me feel uncomfortable—so I decided to approach Big Ed when I returned from relieving myself.

I didn't owe the man any stamps, and it was impossible that I had sex any of his women, so I reckoned that my being assertive was the best option.

There's never been any miscommunication between us, and I knew the risk of invading on any man's time with himself, his workout, and his music. But I felt more comfortable addressing Big Ed in an open space than the bounds of our unit.

With my mind momentarily off of Big Ed and back on my bladder, I walked through the side entrance of the gym.

* * *

The warmth from the gymnasium massaged my skin, and the stench of timeless sweat circulated through the air while a lithesome Asian inmate with huge calves, a bowl haircut, and glasses taught a nine-man yoga class that tranquilly conducted at the far end of the basketball court.

Stretched from goal to goal, the wooden stands consisted of five rows that sloped from a white wall which served as a backrest to a pink-lipped teen with a gamboge glow, maze-like braids, and dressed in a khaki uniform and Timberlands.

The adolescent was seated in the center of the top level with his legs snuggled around a seasoned gentleman's back as the gangster grandpa, also in khaki uniform, relaxed and got his gray hairs greased and braided. The old inmate rested his wrinkled neck in the kid hairdresser's crotch.

This place is crazy. I've done seen everything in this motherfucker.

If only people knew what really goes down in this place.

Immediately as I turned right to head for the little convict's room, three amigos, all wearing government-issued basil-green overcoats, black skullcaps, gray sweatpants, and black boots, crossed my path and advanced toward the door that I had just entered.

I didn't catch a solid look at them, and from behind, the diminutive figures could've been triplets, so I didn't wreck my brain to attempt to distinguish who they were. Besides Chino's fellow Sureños in my unit, I didn't know any of the amigos by their names, just by their faces.

Most South American Latinos were gang members who dealt strictly with their respected crews, such as the aforementioned Sureños, the Norteños, the Mexican Mafia, Los Zetas, and MS-13—to name a few.

On most federal prison compounds, the amigos were the smallest group of people in number and stature, but they arguably were the craziest—they simply didn't give a fuck about anything!

I didn't have a problem with any of the amigos, but I waited until I saw them step outside before I proceeded to the restroom, simply because I've never seen those guys at recreation that early. Their ethnicity, affiliation, or reputation made no difference to me.

There were mass murderers of all shades and heights at FCI-Cumberland, and in the three-plus-years, I had always remained alert and on point.

With the amigos departing the gym, I peeped my surroundings, and after I deemed it *safe* to finally relieve my full bladder, I pushed through the restroom doors—but I wished that I had not.

OK, they're gone—

What the fuck?

"Uuuuhh...uuuuuhhh...yea papi...fuck this pussy! Gimme that Black pipe nigga!"

A feminine voice with a Spanish accent hollered from inside the last of three stalls as ten massive tan fingers gripped the top edges of the stall's door.

"That's right! Take it ma-ma! Take all this meat!" a man ordered as the stall thunderously shook, and I rushed out the bathroom's door.

This place is fucking siiiiccck! What the FUCK?

I can't take this shit anymore!

Frustrated, I hotfooted back to the side entrance, composed myself, and strolled out of the gym.

I vigorously shook my head and tried to erase the sounds of the two inmates' butt-love, but I knew who they were, so the added visuals had me terribly disturbed.

The only early morning regulars at rec that I had not seen were Cyclops and J-Lo, who usually played ping-pong together in one of the activities rooms before Cyclops hit the pull-up bars to workout.

And although circumstantial, I had all the evidence needed to convict the inseparable couple—dubbed, *J-Clo*.

* * *

My head briefly in a daze, I walked several strides up the pathway, only to halt my travels at the benches, along the first basketball court's sideline, and halfway the distance to the pull-up bars.

To my surprise, Big Ed was standing at the benches with his headphones around his neck and appearing unsettled, seemingly waiting for me.

Shit...now this!

"Wha...what's up Big Ed?" I asked.

Man, I will kick this nigga in his old-ass knees he tries some bullshit.

"What's going on New York? Can I holla at you for a moment youngin'?" he asked.

What the fuck could he want?

"Of course Big Ed...I always got time for you OG—what's good?"

Don't try nothing crazy Big Ed...please!

"First off, relax Manzo. You look like you saw a damn ghost or something. I come in peace," Big Ed said as he smiled, and I was relieved for the moment.

Shit, I wish it were a ghost I saw.

"Ha-ha—I'm relaxed Big Ed. No ghost, just a little tired from working out, I guess."

"Shit I hear that, I'm kinda tired my damn self. I just wanted to kick it with you a sec because I know you're short, and you're going home soon."

"Yea I'm real short, I got less than ten months," I confirmed and glanced over at Boo and Hill chatting away.

What are they gonna do without me?

"Yea, I see you working out like a madman all day...getting right for the streets, huh?" Big Ed asked.

"Yes sir, those girls are not gonna be ready for me when I get back to the crib."

"*Neeew Yooork*...the ladies' man. I hear that—hey, what happened to your mail? I don't hear your name called anymore," he asked.

Damn this nigga nosey as hell.

"Yea man, I had to let those women go. I just thought it was time, you know?"

"Oooh OK...best thing to do since you're going home. No need to string them along for no reason. You had your fun," he said.

Is he talking to me because he wants my bitches?

"Yeeaa...plus...you know...I need to focus on me a little—read more."

Damn, I don't know when the last time I read a book.

"OK, well listen youngsta—I'm not gonna bullshit with you right now New York. It's hard to read anything when you drunk and high every day, and gambling on everything from sports, to whether the next TV commercial will have grass or a Black person in the commercial.

"I see you. I *know* what you've been doing with your time lately. And I *know* about what happened to the girl who came to see you too, so let's start this convo over without the bullshit, if you don't mind?"

How the hell he knows? I never told anyone!

"Uuuh, what are you talking about Big Ed?"

"Listen, you know don't shit go down in this place that I don't know about, *especially* with someone in *my* unit."

This motherfucker is a psychic!

"I kind of figured that," I said.

"So with that said...talk to me. Tell me where your heads at New York, because it's not where it's supposed to be. We both know that."

Tell him everything's OK.

Tell him to mind his fucking business.

"I'm good for real—"

"New York I'm try'na help ya, but if you want to look me in my motherfuckin' face after all these years and lie to me, then that's your choice," he spoke sternly and slipped his headphones over his ears.

"Wait!" I yelled. Big Ed stopped and removed his headphones.

I can't keep on like this! Talk to him!

He's trying to help me! I need help!

Talk to him!

Throughout my bid, I had followed the unwritten law of not speaking too much to any man about my problems, thoughts, concerns, and fears. But when I looked into Big Ed's eyes, I could see his empathy. I could feel his virtue.

The compartment in my soul that obtained all the pain that I never shared was full, and I now had the opportunity to empty some of the hurt that has weighted my life with melancholy, contempt, and regret.

After four-plus years, I was almost a free man but still a shell of myself. I understood that it was in my best interest to reveal some of the things that I only confronted at night when my body slept and then my subconscious had suddenly awakened.

Breaking the rules for the better, I yearned healing and direction, so sanely, I switched strategies with an expectance for different results.

Opening my baggage of sorrow and frustration, I allowed Big Ed to take a look.

"All right, all right...I will talk to you," I agreed.

"OK Manzo...just say whatever is on your mind young brother. I'm listening."

Just let it out. It's time!

"Man, where do I even begin Big Ed?"

"Just start with something different youngsta. Start with the truth."

I can't keep all this shit bottled inside anymore!

Just let it out! It's time!

"Man Big Ed...it's like...it's like—like, I'm in this place, and I know I should be doing things to better myself.

"I feel like I should do things to make me a better person, but I only do shit that's going to make my time go faster.

"Ever since I found out my baby-momma fucked my best friend *and* his little brother, my spirits have been crushed, and I don't trust anyone.

"I don't give a fuck about anyone but myself, and I don't care about who I hurt.

"I'm not even trying to be a real part of my daughter's life either. I get so damn frustrated that she doesn't love me like a daughter loves her father, and instead of trying harder I just accept the bullshit and give up.

"I mean, you have seen the way my daughter won't let me touch her in visitation. That shit hurts Big Ed!

"I know that my baby-momma is out there sucking mad niggas' dicks around my daughter, and I don't know what to do from in here to make my little girl see that I'm her father, not them other dudes.

"She's only going on four, but she's smart as hell, and she's very perceptive. Kids know more than we want to admit as parents, and I think my daughter really believes that I'm a piece of shit.

"I feel like I abandoned her and my baby-momma, and God is punishing me in every way. And I know I should be praying and fighting, but instead I'm getting high every day, drinking every day.

"I'm doing whatever I can to numb the pain and not take responsibility for my responsibilities.

"And I blame my daughter's racist-ass grandparents for putting shit in her head about me, but I'm not doing things to make her see me in a different light either. I was too busy with all these pen pal chicks.

"I started messing with all these girls and they made me feel like I was the man again...made me feel like I was a *king*.

"I manipulated these women. I lied to these women. I sold dreams to these women, because it's like a game to me, and their feelings don't even matter man.

"My mother didn't raise me to treat women like this. She would be devastated to find out the shit I've been doing in this motherfucker.

" I've used women like real live toys...until better toys came along.

"And the shit with these pen pal girls was all fun and games until Celeste died.

"She died because she came to see her *boyfriend*, but I wasn't her man! I'm nobody's fucking man!

"If I would've let her know that shit Big Ed, and not sold her a dream, she would've never got in that goddamn car! She would still be alive today!

"She would still be with her family, but I'm a selfish motherfucker who had to have it all!

"She was a good girl! She was too good for me, and her blood is on my hands forever!

"And the crazy shit Big Ed, is that I really liked the girl! She was a beautiful woman who had her shit together, who was all about me, but I played her for a fool and got caught messing with another damaged soul—just because I wanted some fucking weed!

"That ain't right! I'm not *right*! How dumb could I be Big Ed?

"So I work out like a fucking savage, because the yard and the bars are like my medicine! I look good, but I *feel* like shit!

"On the outside, I'm a diamond, but on the *inside*...I'm a pebble—a soulless fucking pebble!

"I'm short—but I'm in here living like I have twenty, thirty more years on my bid!

"I have like ten measly-ass-months left, and I feel almost like the same motherfucker that walked in this hellhole!

"It scares the shit out of me too, because I don't ever want to hurt anyone, *especially* women, the way that I have!

"I also don't want to give these...these...*mother-fucking* people any more time!

"I'm sick of this place! I am *sick* of this *god-damn* place...and...I want to go home Big Ed. I *need* to go home...but not like this Big Ed...not like this."

When I finished speaking my hands trembled, but I wasn't emotional—I was liberated.

I had finally spoken my truth aloud, and to hear the profound honesty leave my mouth had given me energy, unlike how the lies fatigued my spirit.

Nothing I had admitted I was proud of, but everything was from the heart and without filter, and I knew I could grow and build from my words, converting my rhetoric into action.

I had no concerns what Big Ed would do with my secrets, albeit, I did worry that I had bored him with my rambling, but he appeared to have taken a keen ear as he rubbed his beard, maintained eye contact, and nodded calmly.

"How do you feel right now Manzo?" he asked.

"I still feel like shit, but I do feel better that I don't have this shit still all bottled up. It was eating me alive."

"That's good young brother, and I know that took a lot, and I thank you for..."

Stopping mid-sentence, Big Ed tilted his head slightly, and squinted over my shoulder, so I swiftly turned around to see the distraction.

The three amigos I had previously encountered in the gym were huddled in a corner to the right of the side entrance while they laughed, and smoked roll-ups. I didn't know if they had been there the entire time or had just arrived.

The amigos were doing nothing out of the ordinary, but neither was Big Ed, who was always aware of his surroundings.

I was the unfocused one who committed a grave sin: *thou shall never have his back to any door.*

I reverse pivoted, so I could face the entrance and still engage in our conversation.

With no one on the basketball courts behind us, I felt more secure, but I still sensed Big Ed's internal alarm had not stopped ringing.

He had spent the last eighteen years in prison, and I had no authority to ever question Big Ed's paranoia, so when he continued to school me, I was reassured that the amigos were not the menaces of the moment.

Big Ed would had never dedicated any of his attention to me if he considered anyone in the vicinity a threat to his safety.

They're just chilling.

No big deal but watch those motherfuckers!

"Like I was saying...I appreciate your honesty New York, because I knew that you weren't right in the head, and because you're smarter than the way that you've been acting.

"You're smoking and drinking that shit with the rest of them fools, but you're better than that. Shit, you're hella-smart—ya fooled me!

"Slim, I thought you was a Redskins fan for damn near two years!"

Oh shit he knew?

"But all bullshitting aside, one thing that I don't want you *ever* to forget is that none of these women out here belong to you.

"You're in prison young brother. Once these people lock our Black asses up, all that pussy you *think* is yours is ups for grabs.

"There are no exceptions to the rules. Shit, prison breaks up families, and you can't trust ya own daddy around ya baby-momma.

"If the stars align right, you best believe ya daddy would burn that fat-White-ass up like he didn't know you from a can of paint. That's just how the game is played.

"Now, it's messed up, without a doubt, and you shouldn't be with her, because if you do then you are a damn fool—but a hoe is gonna be a hoe, but you still have to be a father Manzo.

"Ya little girl will always be ya little girl, and if you have to fight for her love until the day you die, then that is what you have to do.

"You made the choice to sell dope, not ya daughter. She's suffering every day without you.

"She needs you, and she does love you, so don't blame anyone but ya'self for the way she feels about you, because if you were home, she wouldn't feel the way she does.

"I have five kids that have spent more time visiting me in prison than on the streets...but I still do whatever I can from in here to be a part of their lives.

"You have an opportunity to do great things and be a great dad. Don't fuck it up because ya baby-momma had an itch that she needed to be scratched.

"She will always be in ya life as the mother of ya child. Concentrate on building a relationship with *her* as such.

"Call her when you get back to the unit and ask her to bring ya daughter for Christmas. Show some initiative.

"If she says no, then you keep asking until she comes. Call ya daughter everyday like you do those smuts from that Internet thang.

"Put ya energy in ya family, fuck these women who don't give a shit about ya for real. Call ya mama. Tell *her* ya love her—she matters more than anybody else.

"And as far as the young lady who passed away...it's natural you feel guilty but understand that God takes who He wants and when it's ya time to go, it's ya time to go.

"You described a special young lady who is watching over you from heaven. She's OK New York.

"I know it's hard to let go and believe that, but if you are really sorry, then change your life young brother.

"*You* are here for a reason, and there's nothing you can do about the past but learn from it.

"I see the way you train the fellas on the yard, and I tell everyone that you have a gift.

"I've seen some dudes that you trained. You have no idea, but some of them bamas killed their *entire* motherfucking families!

"Those guys listen to everything you ask them to do—I saw it with my own two eyes. Those savages would run through a brick wall if you asked them to.

"I even seen your homeboy...Riddick Bowe...boxing champion of the motherfucking *world*, come to you for guidance with his workouts—because you were doing some shit, he or me, or any brother on this pound have *never* saw.

"So take your talent and do something with it! Train those rich White folks when ya get out of prison!

"Show them White gals how to get asses like our Black sisters and you will get *paid* my brother! Whatever it is, just give ya all to it and stay out of here!

"And Manzo...I *strongly* suggest you get the hell away from Cumberland before you hit the streets."

What?

"How the hell I do that?" I asked.

"There's this nine-month drug program called RDAP in FCI-Butner that inmates are eligible for when they are thirty-six months short," he said.

"Yea, I heard of the program—but I have less than ten months left. I don't have time Big Ed!"

"Yes you do! I will talk to Mr. Britt today to put ya in for it, and you will make it to Butner in time to start. They have new enrollment every two months, I believe, so you can get there by the next one. The counselor will do it for me—he owes me a favor," he explained.

Shit I heard Butner was sweet! Big Ed got some pull in this bitch!

"No bullshit?" I asked.

"No bullshit New York. You need to get away from here and get ya mind right before you hit them streets...make plans for the future.

"You're too damn comfortable here, and *comfortable* is dangerous young brother."

What's the catch though? Be careful!

There's always a catch!

"Big Ed all this sounds good, and I'm appreciative, but I have to ask, and I mean no disrespect...but *why* are you giving me all this advice? Why do you want to help me? I'm not even from D.C.—we ain't even homies."

"Listen New York...*Manzo*—I don't give a shit where ya from to begin with, but that's a fair question and the answer is simple.

"When I was your age, I was just like you, but no one talked to me like I'm talking to you, and if someone did, maybe I wouldn't be stuck in this place like the way I am.

"And maybe God will give me blessings when I finally meet him, so I'm helping both me *and* you out."

"Damn Big Ed, you're talking like you're dying or something. You've been down a long time; your day will come one day to get out this place too," I said.

"Yes...yes young brother...my day *will* come when I get out of here. That day will come. That day will come all right...when I'm in a casket.

"Manzo...I'm never going home. I was sentenced to life—"

"OK-OK fellas! My turn to get this money!" Cyclops announced as the gym's side door flew open.

"Oh shit—let's go son—COME ON!" Big Ed suddenly commanded.

"Huh?" I turned to Big Ed, but he was already *running* toward the pull-up bars!

What's happening?

"AAAAAAHHH! AAAAAHHHH!" Cyclops howled.

What the—Oh nooo!

"STOP! STOP! AAAAAAHHHHH!" Cyclops' agonizing screams echoed through the compound.

"Manzo let's goooo!" Hill yelled as he, Big Ed, and Boo raced past the tables and into the gym's main entrance, but I couldn't move.

A couple of feet from where I stood in petrified fright, the three amigos systematically poked and sliced Cyclops from his scalp to his thighs as if he were choice-cut meat, and the grill was hot and ready.

Each amigo held four-inch-shanks, with white tape wrapped around their enclosed right fists.

With their weapons secured from dropping, the trio plunged the sharpened steel through flesh and bones.

Smoke blew from the amigos' mouths as blood spewed and sprinkled on their tattooed faces, but the butchers didn't blink a spec of vengeance from their eyes.

The locos' motive was to slaughter and eat, and the carving of the one-eyed-lamb did not stop.

Cyclops fell to his knees and raised his left hand in a hopeless plea, until one of the little demons stabbed him in the throat several times.

Toppling to the ground, Cyclops crept his right hand up to the fatal wounds, but even the immensity of his hand couldn't plug his neck-punctures, as he rested on his back, and looked up at his assailants.

All the amigos spat on him before fleeing back into the gym without saying a word in English *or* Spanish, and in no instance—did they ever acknowledge my presence. I felt invisible.

"Get on the fucking ground!" a guard ordered from a distance.

"Get on the fucking ground—NOW!" a deeper voice yelled.

My senses had shut down, and I momentarily couldn't process the sounds or the situation. I had gone into a semi-shock. I just stared at Cyclops gasping for air while his sprawled legs swayed, and his spirit decided whether to leave or re-enter one of the seventeen holes in Cyclops' torso alone.

Look at all that blood.

That sure is a lot of blood.

That's a pretty color.

A viscous red wetness, leaking life from lacerated organs, saturated his sweat suit with certain death—breaking the promise he made on the back of his driver's license.

Cyclops' head steadily titled until his right cheek settled in gobs of crimson neck fluid which steamed from a puddle on the ground—evaporating his soul.

"Convict get on the goddamn ground!" a third guard ordered.

Manzo!

Snap out of it motherfucker! They will kill you!

Get down—

"NOW ASSHOLE!" he repeated.

Regaining my bearings, I took heed of the guards' instructions and promptly situated my body on the floor with both arms outstretched to my side, as my right fingers warmed in the carnage.

Erroneously, I planted the left side of my head toward Cyclops and stared at his dilated, hazel eye that stared right back at me.

Four gashes striped his face diagonally, and comparable to a sedated tiger, Cyclops laid motionless with the tip of his tongue overhanging in the right corner of his mouth.

A red river gushed from his throat and marched toward my left cheek. I observed the parade of gore seep under my skin before I felt the blood and smelled it.

I lifted my face slightly away from the aroma of Mommy's copper scouring pad, and suddenly there was a hand pressed against my temple—mashing my opened lips into the blood.

I watched Cyclops gasp and take his final breath while his vital fluid swirled on my tongue. I didn't fancy the taste of death, or my current predicament.

The four big-game hunters violently bent my arms and squeezed handcuffs on me, before they grabbed my feet and hoisted me in the air like *Moose* was my species and not just the nickname my mother called me as a child.

As I bounced away, looking at the heavens—I made a promise to myself.

I ain't never coming back!

Chapter Thirty-Eight

FINAL TEST

Following Cyclops' death, I was once again placed in the hole and under investigation for suspicion that I may have been an accomplice to the murder, even though the entire massacre was caught on the yard's security cameras. And again, I declined to cooperate or give a statement.

After SIS concluded that the amigos killed Cyclops because of *J-Lo's* outstanding gambling debt, I was found innocent of any involvement after spending a sleepless week in the SHU reliving every high definition prod and shred of Cyclops' intestines.

But instead of being allowed back on the compound, a week later I was shipped away from FCI-Cumberland and headed to North Carolina, because I had been accepted into FCI-Butner's Residential Drug Abuse Program (RDAP).

Big Ed kept his word and I wish I could've thanked him personally before I left.

I didn't get a chance to say goodbye to any of my friends, and I would miss them all, but I was so thankful and happy to be leaving, because I needed a change of scenery to help me change.

The transportation accommodations to FCI-Butner were the same, and I had to fly Con Air from Harrisburg, Pennsylvania to USP-Atlanta. After a week in solitary confinement, I was bused to North Carolina.

Unlike my first transfer, I hadn't stressed about anything, and thought mainly about my sobriety and making the best of the opportunity to address my drug addiction.

Ahead of making a single plan, I would have to confront the root of my hardships and take the crucial steps to maintain a new life of sobriety when I was released.

My ambitions were strong, but my substance abuse issues proved to be stronger, and I refused to let my disease contribute to the destruction of my life again.

Hungry for self-improvement, I was grateful for RDAP, and I was willing to learn *and* apply anything the program had to offer even before officially enrolling.

* * *

When I walked into FCI-Butner from the Receiving and Discharge building, I immediately noticed the undeniable similarities to FCI-Cumberland.

Other than being built on a treeless flat plane, and having buildings with Chapel-Hill blue trim, the prison virtually looked the same—just smaller. The outer surroundings and the energy made Butner *feel* different from the gladiator school in the mountains.

My new prison had an unobstructed view of the horizon from every direction, and the sky traveled forever to a freedom that seemed assessable. I felt as if I were permitted to leave whenever I wanted.

Consistent with all medium security institutions, Butner had controlled moves, but none of the predominantly muscular inmates with a healthy glow migrated throughout the compound in a rush or panic.

Since the distances between the units and other buildings were half as widespread as Cumberland, inmates could commute from point A to point B, and back to point A again with minutes to spare before lockdown.

The men strolled the compound with smiles on their faces and no apparent signs of stress, which amplified the aura that each man chose to be at the prison as much as the students at Virginia Tech had elected to go to class, rather than drive back to their respected hometowns.

Butner was considered, arguably, the "sweetest joint" in the federal system— and there were many reasons: Minimum violence, inmate programs, Black correctional officers and staff, canopied weight room, many female employees, band room, karaoke machine, tennis courts, track, indoor gym, delectable cuisine, and an extensive commissary list.

Even the men who had only experienced the prison through animated tales and reenactments, spoke of the place like it was a convict utopia on a hidden tropical island with a marijuana field and a translucent blue beach.

I almost thought that Leonardo DiCaprio was the warden.

I wholeheartedly agreed that Butner was well deserving of its high praise and reputation, and any inmate privileged enough to spend even a day of his bid there was considered blessed.

I appreciated being in an environment where I could read undisturbed, focus on future goals, and dissect my character-flaws.

My perception of what made Butner special was different from most of the 741 inmates, because my situation was special. I was a participant in the Residential Drug Awareness Program.

Housed in the Drug unit or "(NC)-State" (All the units were named after universities from the Atlantic Coast Conference), I had been sheltered and *forced* to adhere to certain rules and regulations that didn't apply to the inmates who weren't in the program.

Fighting and any involvement with illegal drugs or alcohol, whether using, drinking, selling, or simply possessing, were grounds for immediate dismissal.

Any man that failed the routine breathalyzers or drug screens were sent to the hole, and subsequently transferred back to the prison from which he came.

I loved to get high, but the thought of having to go back to Cumberland was enough incentive to remain sober without hindrance for the duration of my sentence.

I had made some terrible decisions in my life, but with the consequences so dire, the urge to relapse disappeared like I had a rabbit under my top hat.

I had just come from a prison where raunchiness and shady endeavors were conventional, and no one cared about foul language, a friendly wager between gentlemen—or watching a movie that showed a line of coke being snorted and licked off some dime-sized nipples.

Rejoicing in the societal wrongs of life were a common element of the bid, and there was a universal acceptance—regardless of a man's religious ties, age, or occupation. At Cumberland, Inmates were not judged negatively for holding on to a few *non-threatening* vices.

No one cared if even the prison's pastor lost his stamps on the Washington Redskins at 3:30 PM, and at 8:00 PM screamed at the TV during a Ford Taurus commercial about wanting to "bang grandma in the backseat," who drove her grandkids to school in the featured automobile.

Vulgarity and shenanigans were expected, but not at RDAP.

In the program, cursing and gambling were prohibited, along with watching movies, TV shows, or music videos that showed nudity, guns, drugs, or any unlawful activities.

Basically, all the visual forms of entertainment I took pleasure in were not allowed and were considered *glorifying* our criminal lifestyles. I wasn't a *My Name is Earl* type of fellow, so I stayed in my cell and read.

RDAP made it easy for me to concentrate on bettering myself, because I couldn't partake in any of the distractions that I had been accustomed to.

I read many educational booklets that I had received in the classes that helped me identify the flaws in my priorities and core beliefs, and although the material was useful, dealing with my sexual addiction was still a battle.

* * *

During the orientation phase of the program, each inmate was assigned to a counselor for *personal development* meetings with a counselor, and I just happened to get hitched with RDAP's only female employee—Ms. Morgan.

With jet-black hair down to her shoulders, she had pale skin and ex-big-girl cheeks that moved gently against her curls when she talked.

Her face was pumpkin-pie-round with seventeen nutmeg freckles dotted on the bridge of her deviated nose, and her chin fluffed to the base of her neck whenever she gestured in agreement.

Under her Chico's outfits, Ms. Morgan had a doughy, yet slender figure, and a low-hanging butt that barely applauded with each step, as if she hadn't known if the word *squats* were an exercise or a city in Alaska.

Her *unintentionally* enticing scent of roses that were marinated in honey, trailed profoundly throughout the unit and caused me to think about her with every breath I'd taken, but ironically, the more time that I spent with Ms. Morgan, the more I yearned for her help—not her flesh.

A week into the program, I had gotten a job in the educational department as a class tutor for inmates aspiring to receive their GED.

After the interview with Mr. Ragsdale, the class' teacher, I had my first meeting with Ms. Morgan in her office, where I truthfully disclosed my behavioral struggles.

She urgently attacked my apathy for women as real people, and how I viewed women as objects and means for sexual conquest.

As I sat at Ms. Morgan's desk fantasizing about her, she said that there wasn't anything wrong with having strong sexual urges for women that I felt a physical connection with—*especially* in a prison setting.

She compared men trying to fight their lust for the opposite sex while incarcerated, to starving animals around food.

She further explained that the root of the problem was with how I *treated* women, not so much as how much I wanted them physically.

Continuing, she looked me in the eye and stated that I was *immature, selfish, greedy, a coward,* and *pathetic*—and if I didn't start to respect women, my daughter would end up with a man just like her father!

I wasn't prepared for such an honest and bold evaluation, and I left Ms. Morgan's office livid, but my anger was not directed at her. I loathed the thought of Ruby mixed up with a man that shared any kind of likeness to myself.

I was all of Ms. Morgan's few *choice words*, plus many more, that my counselor did not use to describe me.

Instead of denying who I had become, I mentally committed myself to RDAP, because I didn't know how many chances that I would have in life to get the professional guidance I needed to become a better man and a better father.

The rest of my meetings with Ms. Morgan, I rejected the lust but kept the faith.

I considered each day that I had not taken the program seriously, a day closer to having *myself* as a son-in-law, which would never have worked—because I didn't get along with douche bags.

Months into the program, I had been consistently applying the information that I acquired to my life, rather than complying and faking behavioral changes, purely to appease the staff and fellow peers.

I totally refrained from using profanity, and I quit saying *nigga, bitch, retard, midget, fat,* and any hurtful words used to describe a person's race or anyone in the lesbian, gay, bisexual, and transgender community.

I thought about others' feelings before I spoke or reacted, and I also used my phone minutes for conversations with my family and friends—never for manipulating women!

Embracing most of the RDAP philosophies, I thought I was being an exemplary pupil, but Ms. Morgan pointed out that I had not been connecting with my peers outside of classes and group meetings—and my isolation would be a factor in whether I advanced to the next stages of the program.

Complete participation was a requirement, but I still didn't trust anyone. I didn't want inmates in my personal life, because I didn't want them to rat me out to the counselors for a potential mishap.

I wasn't ever going to rat on them for *anything*, so I thought it would be best that I stay to myself but staying to myself wasn't part of the treatment—accountability was.

* * *

The keystone to RDAP's success had been the ability to have the participants *police* themselves. Since the staff went home to their *regular* lives at 5:30 PM and had weekends off, accurately keeping track of an inmate's conduct was impossible.

The RDAP inmates were responsible for themselves and one another. We had to raise our hands during the group meetings to admit if we personally had broken any program rules, or if we had *witnessed* any of our peers that did.

The counselors and the RDAP handbook described telling on an inmate as *accountability*, or *holding someone accountable* for his actions and decisions.

Although, I described the providing of information of an unknown illegal act to a government employee exactly for what it was—snitching!

I thought it was comical to expect convicts to stand up in a meeting and point to another inmate that he knew committed a program offense, or even a prison offense, but all the humor ended quickly.

Every meeting, several different peers gave eyewitness accounts of anything —from napping during the day, to bringing food into the unit from the kitchen.

The inmate in question would have to stand and receive *feedback* about his negative behaviors, and then repeat the feedback to ensure he was listening.

With no shame, men spied on one another to catch an inmate slipping, because holding a peer accountable was the highest form of showing the counselors that we were changing.

Letting go of the prison code of silence was paramount in securing an RDAP diploma.

Many men were eligible for a sentence reduction for completing the program and would have held Jesus accountable for having his hair longer than his collar, if it meant they could leave prison up to eighteen months early.

Personally, even if I had entered the program two years ago, I was never eligible for a time-cut because of my concurrent state conviction, so my motive to transfer to Butner was only to get help and get far away from Cumberland.

I couldn't go anywhere a day before August 2, 2005, but my release date played zero part in my decision to never hold anyone accountable other than myself.

I believed in the program, but I didn't believe in being a law enforcement agent, so I gained participation points by confessing to some of the mistakes that I had made.

* * *

Every week I held *myself* accountable for something that I had really done, like sneaking into the TV room during quiet time to watch the highlights of my bum-ass-Knicks lose another game, or when I bet a bag of chips with Black, my Harlem homeboy from Clemson Unit—that I could bench 425 pounds eight times.

I thought all my transgressions had little to do with my criminality, and I considered my *charges* petty, but the feedback I had gotten from my bloodthirsty peers wasn't.

Each surrender, the men eagerly *helped* by spitting verbal bullets at me, and the recurring caliber of slug was their labeling me as a "Master Manipulator with entitlement issues," and having the qualities of a "Dominican Ted Bundy."

I didn't know whether my peers were being malicious or if their diagnoses of my behaviors were genuine, but either way, I was open and receptive to their feedback—even the Dominican part.

Examining their words with scrutiny, I concluded that intent had little to do with the truth, and there was nothing that had been said that I could contest.

My time in prison was coming to an end, and if a group of strangers could easily identify the person who I hid, then the deception was over.

Exposed, I realized that opening up would have been in my best interest to get the treatment that I traveled across the country in shackles to get.

And in the third and final phase of the program, I treated State Unit as if it were a Catholic church. I bared my soul every chance that I got.

Unsolicited, I disclosed my current mental conflicts without holding back any details.

I cried many times whenever I discussed how I had let down my coaches, friends, family, and *especially* my mother with some of the self-destructive decisions that I had made that resulted in a sixty-month-stint in federal prison.

Many instances I stood amongst my peers thinking of my Woodberry Forest School days, and how an African American kid from Harlem not only co-existed but loved and bonded with Caucasian kids from all over the world, who loved him back.

The color of anyone's skin didn't matter!

Those kids looked to me as their leader on and off the football field and basketball court, and they thought that I was special enough to follow and respect.

* * *

Donnie Bergin's family, who graciously housed some of the Woodberry boys during a basketball tournament in Charlotte, was even comfortable enough to let their only daughter spend the night in the same room as I did, because they trusted me.

I went to sleep forgetting that the captain of her high school cheerleading squad had been a mere ten feet away.

An affluent White family, the Bergins—didn't see me as a thug, a peddler of death, an addict, or a threat to their children and society, because I wasn't.

I was a good boy, but the drugs were better.

* * *

I revealed to my peers that there was a time where the older folks pointed to me and told their children, "I want you to be *just* like him."

I walked around my neighborhood with pride, in contrast to when I quit playing football, and I purposely bypassed anyone who I knew would ask me about college.

I even crossed the street one time when I saw Jay Black's older brother, Snookum, but I couldn't shake him because he hollered my name so loud that my not responding would have been a blatant sign of avoidance and disrespect.

* * *

Larry "Snookum" Black, a career oil truck driver, had already heard the news that I had turned my back on being a student-athlete, and when he approached me, I could see the deep disappointment in his face.

I didn't even get in a *hello* before he said that I had let everyone down, and that my smoking weed would be the beginning of all my failures in life.

Snookum gave me a hug, told me he loved me, and left me in front of Palma's corner store on 123rd Street and Second Avenue with eyes full of THC, and a brown paper bag full of blunts.

I was embarrassed and felt horrible, but for only a minute or two, because I was too high to grasp the impact at which Snookum rooted for me to succeed. I never considered that he had been one of my guardians since I was a child.

My only experience ever playing any type of football as a kid was the Sunday morning games of *two-hand-touch* in the concrete baseball field in front of my building.

Snookum was the quarterback, and although I was a fat nine-year-old boy, he and Jay always picked me to be on their team.

I was as athletic as any boy my size and age could have been, but I was no match for the men, mostly hustlers and murderers, lined up across from me.

Snookum and Jay kept me close so they could watch me, and I could learn from them, rather than the *usual* project guys with the unusual occupations.

The Black brothers knew that I handicapped the team, but Snookum and Jay didn't care about the outcome of the game. They cared about the outcome of my life, and so did the RDAP community.

* * *

In the nine months that I had been in the program, my peers had given me invaluable feedback that was essential for me to grow as a man—regaining confidence in myself, and in my potential.

At my RDAP graduation on August 1, 2005, where I had been selected as the class speaker by my peers and the counselors, I thanked everyone for being a primary element to my continuing recovery.

I spoke about how the eighteen-year-old-boy whom Frank Beamer had once felt *honored* to have the opportunity to coach, had now been awakened.

I spoke on how I would let the values, respect, and discipline that had laid dormant for ten years—lead me through the rest of my adulthood.

I advised my peers to keep striving for greatness and always stay positive, because God was giving us another chance at living purposefully. In time—He would show us that purpose. We just had to stay out of trouble during the process!

Completing RDAP was such a gratifying accomplishment and an ideal way to finish my prison bid, but on the morning of my release from FCI-Butner, I felt as if I had an obligation that I had not fulfilled.

* * *

Technically, I was not a GED tutor anymore, so I wasn't required to go to my 9:00 AM class, but August 2nd was the day that my students would receive their math scores back from North Carolina's educational board—and I wanted to be the one who showed the men how well they did.

The only three remaining students, Rock, Sun, and Big Dave had already passed the social studies, science, reading, and writing portions of the exam, and were waiting to find out if they had the same success with the commonly most difficult section, mathematics.

For months my students and I worked restlessly to get them to comprehend the basics of algebra and geometry, but fully learning the subjects before the upcoming test would take more than just the scheduled class times.

So, every Sunday at 11:00 AM for six consecutive weeks in the prison library, I had an unofficial class for the men who needed the extra help.

After all the hard work and hours my students had put forth to obtaining their diplomas, there was no way that I would not be there to share in their special moment.

My parents weren't scheduled to pick me up until 10:00 AM sharp, so with the permission of Mr. Ragsdale, at 9:37 AM I peeked into the classroom's door window with a mesh bag full of my property in my left hand, and a manila envelope containing the students' scores in my right—prepared to enter one final time.

* * *

I normally closed the blinds to lessen the distractions while I taught, but without me around, I wasn't surprised to see that the blinds were completely opened, so the class was extraordinarily bright, magnifying its vacancy.

Most of the desks and chairs were disorganized and empty, but the three spacious round tables were in their normal spots against the back wall that faced the door.

With their backs almost touching the window—Big Dave and Rock were seated together at the middle table.

Sun, positioned the same as Big Dave and Rock, slumped in his chair several feet away at the table on the right, near the teacher's oak desk which rested in front of a wall-length white marker-board with the word "abuse" written in red at the center.

The letter A had been partially erased.

Ahead of twisting the doorknob and surprising the last of my students, I couldn't help but look at each of them for a moment, because whether they passed or failed, I was proud of the guys.

Attaining a GED for these men wasn't mandatory, but they chose school over socializing with their homeboys at the yard, watching frivolous television shows, getting high, or participating in any of the *traditional* norms of a doing a bid.

Their decision to educate themselves and think about their lives beyond prison was commendable, and after nine months I had a bond with the three students that was deeper than a tutor-student relationship.

Big Dave, Sun, and Rock represented how much I matured as a man. They were the foundation of my redemption.

They think I helped them, but they really saved me.
Big Dave is mad cool but needs to chill with that Nu-Nile.

Big Dave's hair rippled under the sunlight, and his forehead was coated with a secondhand-wave-grease shine, which explained the acne scars scattered from his hairline to his eyebrows.

The ginormous youngster possessed undefined mega-muscles that puffed the third button off his khaki shirt, and his face swelled with a cinnamon-honey tinge, giving him the likeness of a Teddy Graham on steroids.

Big Dave, a North Carolina native, always squeaked his words through a clenched jaw as if he hid twenty of his little bear cousins in his mouth.

He had an affinity for New York hip-hop music, and we made a deal that after every surprise quiz, in which he passed, I would tell him a fun story about some of the rappers that I grew up with in Harlem.

("Killa" Cam'ron and Jim Jones, along with Juelz Santana and Freekey Zekey–formed the infamous rap group "the Diplomats," while Mase was a multi-platinum selling artist with P Diddy and Bad Boy Records.)

Sun is brilliant. I just hope he realizes it before he gets out.

Sun was an animated New Yorker who took pride in being from Harlem despite residing in North Carolina for ten of his twenty-three years on earth, and whatever room he was in—he was the loudest and the funniest.

His dreads, the staple of his character, were a little longer than the wind in his lungs. Butner's favorite rapper, and the only non-Jamaican on the *all-Jamaican* prison soccer team, loved to talk.

Sun *acted* like a giant with a black soul, but he was five-inches under six-feet, he had straw-hay-shaded skin, and his jokes were just as colorful as his *real* personality.

Multifaceted and smart, Sun was harmless, and everyone knew it —even him.

Sun's false bravado gave him the confidence to deal with his fifteen-year prison sentence, and only at a place like FCI-Butner could Sun's attitude be looked at as entertainment and not a threat.

I was going to really miss the kid. Sun was truly a good person and a great friend.

Man, I'm glad I don't have to hoop against Rock anymore. That's a hacking dude!
Happy he's going home soon too. Those kids need their daddy!

Rock, also a North Carolina native and the oldest of the three students, had a milk-caramel complexion, and a granite physique that made him well deserving of the moniker given to him by his high school football teammates.

He donned the signature prison fade, but unlike many inmates who compulsively brushed their hair to the front, Rock brushed his midnight waves to the side.

Rock's *classic man* façade filled its task of making the six-foot seven-inch, 285-pound father of six more approachable.

His prickly eyebrows, resembling the bristles of an old vacuum cleaner, linked with the impenetrability of his goatee.

Rock's bullnose matched his bull-strength, and we hated each other on the basketball court, but in the classroom our bond was like Jordan and Pippen. He was one of my favorite students.

* * *

"Whaaaat's up my brothers?" I said as I pushed the door open, setting my mesh bag on top on a stack of newspapers on the desk.

"Ooooh shiiid...what you doing here Manzo?" Big Dave asked.

"Damn, we said our goodbyes and shit yesterday! I thought you'd be in some pussy by now homie!" Sun hollered.

"Maaaan, you don't want to go home do you, I see," Rock said.

"Y'all know I wasn't going to leave without *personally* giving you guys your scores!" I announced and walked to each of them, giving them dap.

"Aaah man Manzo, they don't make 'em like you no more! That's solid!" Rock said.

"You a better man than me Manzo...'cuz my Black-ass wudda been like *peeeaaaacccceee!*" Sun stated.

"Shut up Sun!" I laughed and hustled to the desk.

"Sun stop fronting all the damn time!" Rock spoke.

What time is it?

What the heck is that nasty ass smell though? One of these dudes didn't shower or something?

"Yea Sun, relax! Manzo just did some real shit!" Big Dave added.

"Damn fellas—ease up! I was just fucking with the nigga!" Sun said.

"And stop cussing and saying *nigga* all the time! You know Manzo don't like that motherfucking shit!" Big Dave scolded Sun.

"Thanks Big Dave, but it's cool. What time is it Rock?" I asked.

"9:46 bro," Sun answered.

"I guess we got two Rocks up in this bitch," Dave wisecracked.

"Y'all niggas...my bad...y'all *Black* gentlemen, who are kings of the universe and the leaders of the community—"

"Thanks Sun, but I have to go!" I cut Sun's sarcasm short.

"Y'all still silly as ever. I have to make this quick, but for real fellas, which one of you didn't shower though?"

"Come on Manzo—don't even try us like that. You know those sex offender dudes have class before us. I don't know why they be scared to shower; them chomos all live together," Sun ranted.

* * *

FCI-Butner was indeed like no other federal prison in the country, besides RDAP, the Sex Offender Treatment Program (SOTP) was offered at the safe haven and had been a major element to prison's uniqueness.

Only at Butner could pedophiles and child molesters (*chomos*) have a comfort and a sense of safety to cohabit in an institution full of killers, without any concern for targeted acts of violence.

An isolated group within the prison, SOTP participants were not involved with anything other than their program and personal agendas. Activities such as recreation league tournaments were prohibited for their own safety.

At Butner, sex offenders were protected and literally couldn't be touched, because a fight with a chomo was the fastest way for an inmate, outside of SOTP, to get bounced from the compound—and *nobody* wanted to transfer from Butner.

* * *

When I first arrived at Butner, and the guys in my unit briefed me about the Sex Offender Treatment Program, I really didn't dwell on the fact that I would be living amongst sexual predators.

I was only focused on fixing myself, and anything not pertinent to RDAP was irrelevant.

But as I roamed the compound daily and would see the chomos, I had become furious.

I could not stop thinking about the demonic deeds that *may* have led to their incarceration.

Sex offenders came in all colors and flavors of shit, but I could only imagine each stereotypical ghastly pale, balding, and stout, middle-aged White man that I encountered on the compound—as someone who mentally and physically terrorized children.

On sight, I visualized the chomo, with his two-inch-bifocals, his belt barely strapped around his belly button, his beady eyes, and his clammy, fat hands—violating children.

I depicted a bottomless pit of affliction, and the highly graphic nature of my imaginations drove me mad!

I had a young child and envisioned Ruby being a potential victim of the same scum who shared a breakfast table with me, who sat across from me in the library, and who jogged along the track with me.

The twisted pictures in my mind had me on the brink of vengeance for all the children who couldn't fight back.

I had a profound compulsion to lash out at the evil men, but regardless of how compelling the valiant exploit had appeared, nothing would have ever materialized out of my vindictiveness.

I was too smart to let my yearning for vengeance stop me from coming home to my *own* child.

I loved Ruby too much for further stupidity. Someone else would have to play hero.

* * *

"I kinda blocked those guys out of my mind Sun, *but*...you're right. I should've known that funk wasn't from any of you. My bad brother," I apologized.

I'm so glad my peers talked some sense into me!

"Shiiid, you ain't say nothing wrong Manzo. Sun thinks he's a fucking Jamaican, so who the hell knows what he might come in here smellin' like," Big Dave teased.

"Man shut up—you greasy Care Bear!" Sun counterattacked.

"Ha-ha—I'm gonna miss you crazy dudes! No more clowning for a minute please though! I have to hurry! Who wants to get their score first?" I asked.

God please let these dudes get up out this class.

"Shit...I mean...I'll go, but I'm as nervous as a big White girl on the Maury Show," Rock confessed, ascending from his chair.

What?

Maury Show?

"What does that even mean Rock?" I asked.

They all laughed and looked at each other before replying in unison, "The bitch don't know *which* nigga's the daddy!"

"Ha, ha, ha, ha, ha!" I died laughing.

"OK-OK, no more bad language! But booooy, you shudda seen your damn face Manzo! That was classic, I tell ya!" Big Dave said.

"Ha-ha! Yea y'all got me! OK, let's go Rock!" I said as Rock dropped back into his chair with an uncustomary facial expression.

Damn, is he that scared?

"Rock, what's wrong big fella? Let me show you your score brother," I said.

"It's cool Rock. I'm sure you did OK homie," Big Dave encouraged.

"Yea Rock, no pressure," Sun added.

"Man, I'm not scared to see my grades y'all," Rock finally had spoken.

"I'm cool fellas. I just don't need to see my score in no secret. I'm going to tell y'all eh-neh-way, so just call mine out, 'cuz this my third time taking the math part.

"So if I didn't pass then the whole compound gonna know...'cuz my Black-ass will be in class tomorrow. And if I leave prison without my GED, my proba-tion officer won't trip 'cuz that's what's expected of us.

"And my baby-mommas will just have some more shit to talk about me to my lil' ones...'cuz daddy is still dumb as hell."

The room fell hush, and I let Rock's words filter before I responded.

For the first time, I had consciously become aware that the men in front of me were reconstructing their lives for reasons other than to create a higher personal value in the workforce.

Like me, they were brawling against the doubters to validate that they could change, and in the process our kids and loved ones surveyed every transforma-tional step.

People have often said, "I don't have to prove anything to anyone but myself," but convicts and ex-convicts didn't have the luxury of being so blasé—virtually our every move required substantiation.

Whether it were seeking employment or a wife, we would forever have to prove that we weren't the same people our criminal records said we were, before we were given the opportunity to *show* our worth.

We put ourselves in this hole and we will get ourselves out of this hole. No crying.

Without uttering a sound, I bent the two-pronged, golden clasp and removed the scoresheet from the manila envelope.

After carefully scanning the paper for Rock's government name, Roderick Eubanks, I slid my eyes to the corresponding number in bold black print on the right.

He needed a minimum score of 145 to have obtained his General Education Diploma—recognized nationwide as the equivalent of graduating from high school.

My heart beats per minute were probably one and the same as the number I was about to reveal to the daddy—who *wasn't* dumb as hell.

Math...

GED scores...

Ellison, David...

Tinsley, Lashawn...

Eubanks, Roderick...175.

Yes!

"Mr. Eubanks...tell your baby-mommas stop talking *crap*! You got a 175!" I shouted. "Rock, you did it!"

"Hell yea Rock!" Big Dave cheered and grabbed Rock's shoulders, playfully shaking them. "Fuck yea Rock! You out this motherfucker!"

"Rock, you'sa a goddamn Einstein bro!" Sun hollered. "Good shit!"

"Thank God! Finally! I'm sick of this place!" Rock yelled and stood up.

"You did it bro!" I said and strolled to his table to shake his hand.

"Congratulations Rock! You earned it, and no one can ever take this away from you!"

"Maaaan...thank you, Manzo! I couldn't have done it without you bro!" Rock said.

"Man stop it brother! This is all you! I didn't take the test...you did," I said.

"Seriously Manzo, thank you. And good luck out there. Stay sucker free. You're not like these dudes. 'Use your gifts for good' as you always tell us," Rock advised.

"Oh man, happy to see you were paying attention Rock," I said.

"Of course I paid attention. We *all* paid attention...even though these jokers won't admit it."

"Stop it Rock. Manzo you be spitting those jewels. Just hope you practice what you preach homie, and don't go sniffin' coke off those big booty White girls' asses the first chance you get!" Sun said.

"Nah Sun...God willing...those days are long gone. But I am trying to find that fine-ass *Rihanna* girl though." I said.

Gotta be strong...one day at a time.

"Sun stop that shit! You're talking about Manzo's triggers in a glorifying manner!" Big Dave mocked.

"Ooooh...OK Big Dave—you're ready for RDAP!" I said.

"I don't mean to break up this real live after school special, but Manzo it's 9:55!" Sun informed. "Just tell us our scores and get the hell outta here homie!"

Is this really happening? I'm going home!

Just breathe. Relax.

"Oh man you're right! They gonna call for me in a minute!" I stated, steadily getting super nervous. "OK...Big Daaave...you gooot aaahh..."

Math...

GED scores...

Ellison, David...190.

Not surprised at all.

"Mr. Ellison, congratulations! *Super* Dave...you got a 190!" I hollered and shook Big Dave's hand.

"Hell yea Dave!" Rock shouted.

"Daaaamn, 190 though? That's what's up Big Dave!" Sun yelled.

Oh man, it's almost time!

"Thank you, Manzo, because I was about to say fuck a GED if I failed!" Big Dave said.

"Good job big fella! Never doubted you brother. You worked hard. Now keep moving forward!" I said.

I'm about to be a free man! I can't believe this!

"OK Sun, are you *ready* lil' homie?" I asked.

"Yessir, but damn, I don't want to be in here with a new group though. I wish I had studied more," Sun admitted.

"You got this Sun...chill," Rock encouraged, and then everyone seemed to stop breathing.

"Sun, whatever happens, I know you did your best, and that's the important thing," I said.

"Suuun...your score iiisss..."

Tinsley, Lashawn...

KNOCK-KNOCK.

CLICK.

"Maaanzooo! Time to go home my brother! Let's go!" Mr. Ragsdale opened the classroom door, poking his head inside.

Oh shit!

"OK...OK...let me just read Sun his score please! One sec!" I said and continued.

"OK...Okaaay...Suuun...you got... aaahh..."

Tinsley, Lashawn...145.

Fuck yea!

I mean, heck yea!

Damn, not cursing is hard.

"Mr. Tinsley...my Harlem homie...you got a 145!" I delivered the amazing news and hugged Sun.

Phew!

Ha-ha, he just made it!

"Hallelujah!" Sun screamed. "Yes...*God!*"

"You did it Sun! You ain't that stupid after all!" Big Dave joked.

"I'm proud of you kid!" Rock added.

"Hold up! Hold up! Hold up!" Mr. Ragsdale hollered as he walked to desk.

Why is he angry? Sun passed!

Who cares it's only a 145?

"What...what's the problem Rags?" I asked.

What is his problem?

"Soooo...I guess none of you told Manzo?" Mr. Ragsdale questioned as he smirked.

"Told me what Rags?" I pressed as all three of my passing students stared at the floor. "What the hell is going on fellas?"

I don't have time for this stuff!

"Sun...go 'head and tell your homie. Don't want him keeping his family waiting," Mr. Ragsdale spoke.

What's this about?

Are Big Dave and Rock trying not to laugh?

They think I'm a joke or something?

"It's like this Homie. Manzo...umm...yea... buuut—"

"But *what* Sun?" I grilled.

What's so funny?

"Relax...but...uuuumm...yea...we all...we all kinda...knew our scores... before...man, we knew our scores before you even got here!" Sun confessed, and everyone convulsed in laughter.

"Are y'all fucking kidding me?" I asked.

"Ha, ha, ha, ha, language Manzo—language! That's not the RDAP way—ha, ha, ha!" Big Dave howled.

"You assholes!" I yelled and all the guys stood up. "Y'all got me good! Y'all deserve the prison Oscars!"

"Yea we gotcha good Manzo!" Rock said.

"You not even lying Rock! Tyler Perry needs to put your ass in a Madea movie with that emotional performance you pulled!" I said.

"Yeeeaa, they're some real joke'stas Manzo. I thought you would've figured it out by now. Hold up! Now I'm wondering...how many lies y'all pulled on me?" Mr. Ragsdale asked.

Can't believe they fooled me.

"Maaan Rags...if we lie to you, then who are we gonna tell the truth to? We some honest-Abes in this bitch!

"But in all seriousness Manzo. I know you gotta bounce, but real talk, I got something I want to say," Sun spoke, and everyone stopped laughing.

"Rags had to tell us our grades before you got here, because today is the deadline to sign up for the Vance-Granville College courses, and we couldn't sign up unless we passed the GED, and *nobody* knew you were coming to tell us our scores.

"But when Rags said you wanted to come, we wanted you to still come homie —because we appreciate all you have done for us. We would never have passed without you. Plus, I know I'm gonna miss you.

"You made this bullshit fun, and I for damn sure wouldn't be thinking about College *anything* if weren't for you. You even got my ass wanting to write a book one day!

"Now go home to your folks and do special shit out there like we know you gonna do. One love, Manzo."

"Aaah man Sun, you're trying to make me cry. One love, my brothers...one love." I gave everyone dap and a hug.

I'm really going to miss these dudes.

My job here is done.

"One love, Manzo," Big Dave said.

"One love, Manzo," Rock repeated.

"OK Manzo grab your bag 'cuz your folks are here!" Rags ordered, and repetitively nodded—his way of thanking me.

I'm gonna miss you too Rags.

* * *

After my first week at Butner, I was forced to work in the kitchen like the rest of the new inmates who entered the compound.

On my first day, while slicing potatoes for the prison's lunch, I looked to my right at the inmate with the two thick braids hanging down the front of his apron working just inches away from me.

Although we never introduced ourselves to one another—I felt like I knew him.

Finally recognizing the inmate, I suddenly panicked and was overcome with a warm disgust.

The guy was light skinned and resembled the Native American sidekick in every Western movie, but his disguise didn't fool me!

I waited for the ten-minute-move, twirled the kitchen knife in my hand before placing it on the cutting board, and walked out of the kitchen for good.

I had no *personal* beef with the fake Indian chief and was the biggest Tupac fan, but I still loved all the great New York rappers.

So, there was no way that I could work or even be near David Mack, the former LA police officer and prime suspect in the murder of Brooklyn legend—the Notorious B.I.G.

Knowing my limitations, I reminded myself that I was going home in nine months as I headed straight to the Education Department to seek a tutoring job.

* * *

Upon entering, I walked around the building until I found the first instructor who was actually working.

In a classroom of twenty-one students, I explained to Mr. Ragsdale who I was, my academic level, and my love for helping others achieve their goals, whether physical or intellectual.

Simply handing me a test and a pen, he said, "You have forty-five minutes, *rock star.*"

With the voice of Mr. Szydlowski, my Algebra III teacher at Woodberry, scrambling in my head—I had taken the entire mock GED math section in seven minutes amongst the inmates' lively *conversations.*

Mr. Ragsdale checked my answers, but I already knew the results. I had gotten a perfect score, and then I was paired with the perfect teacher—he hired me immediately.

Since my first day as Mr. Ragsdale's tutor, the man with the devil's-food-cake hue, and sable stole-like mustache, always wore oversized suits and square-front shoes like he was the fourth king of comedy. Rags was funny, but not that damn funny.

The big-eyed teacher saw the way the students responded to me, so he gave me the liberty to run the class how I wanted, and he often remained in his office. The arrangement was ideal.

The inmates kept passing their exams, Mr. Ragsdale kept getting the credit, and I kept from having to look over my shoulder—everybody won.

* * *

"Ok, I'm out fellas—"

Oooh shit!

What the hell?

As I announced my final departure, I reached to snatch my bag off the stack of old newspapers, but I froze in place after noticing the ghost on the front page of an old Daily News—at very top of the pile.

I hadn't seen the man's face in nearly twenty-five years, but there he was looking up at me with those same thickset pair of black-framed glasses, and the identical condescending grin—as if I had just missed an uncontested lay-up against Gary "G-Dogs" Saunders and the Gauchos to win the game.

From the angle of the photo, the man seemed to have aged gracefully, but there was no mistake that the headshot taken in front of a Bronx courthouse, of a soulless old White man with the raw-chicken-thigh-cheeks, white dress shirt, and purple tie that squeezed the stuffing out of his turkey neck—was my former Riverside Church Hawks basketball coach, Mr. Ernie Lorch.

The headlines read, "HOOPS COACH IN KID SEX PROBE."

'April 30, 2002. DA eyes molestation charges, $2m payments.'

In utter disgust, I quickly read the rest of the cover of my hometown news-paper and suddenly remembered the wise advice that *current* NBA superstar, Stephon Marbury, had given me the last time I had ever stepped a sneaker in Riverside Church. He may never know, but his words were a great assist.

'Manzo...don't ever let anybody make you do something you don't want to do.'

Thank you, Steph—

"Damn sex offender teachers always leaving that mess in here," Rags complained as I headed toward the door.

"You knew that man Manzo?"

A couple of feet shy of exiting the first door to freedom, I momentarily stopped moving, and before I slid past Rags with my belongings slung over my right shoulder—I turned and replied as I pointed to Mr. Lorch's picture.

"No sir Mr. Ragsdale. I never knew...*that* man."

Chapter Thirty-Nine

BABY STEPS

Standing at the main entrance of Butner's Receiving and Discharge building, I waited calmly for my release from the wild and into the wilder.

I was beyond anxious, and my mind sped with an onslaught of questions and erratic thoughts as my nose slightly burned from the smell.

The synthetic sting of bleach fumed the air as an aging African American inmate artistically weaved a wet mop across the tiled floors, swaying backward down the hallway.

Officer Jackson, a beefy, ash-brown, southern throwback of a gentleman with a Shar-Pei-wrinkled scalp, stripped upper lip, and chin hairs that formed an inverted pyramid—stood by my side, remaining speechless as always.

Still having an inmate's mentality, I wouldn't initiate a conversation with a guard, but subconsciously, I had wished officer Jackson said something. I was a nervous wreck.

Wearing slim-fit Prps blue jeans, a black Affliction t-shirt with a skull on the front, and an olive green, orange, and black pair of Air Jordan IV Undefeated sneakers, an outfit that my brother, Javier, had sent to the prison for my home-coming—I felt awkward in the non-convict duds.

But my uneasiness hadn't been solely from the unfamiliarity of the fresh fabrics on my skin. The clothes were too tight!

The pop-fashion evidently had evolved to less-baggy styles, but I already missed my oversized Iceberg jeans and white tees.

Before I got locked up, if I would've worn the nut-huggers that I currently had on, then I might as well had started rollerblading and *only* dating Asian women. I looked like I was one "Best of Madonna" CD away from crossing the borderline.

Javier had always been hip and up to date on the latest trends, so for the moment I ignored the dinosaur stylist in my brain and centralized my reflection on more significant issues—my family, my future, and my past.

* * *

The ideal way for many inmates to exit prison was in a limousine full of bottom of the barrel hookers and top shelf liquors, but I appropriately had chosen for my parents to escort me into a new life.

Sobriety was the key for me to prevail over my demons, and a detour into a hole of fornication and drunkenness had not been in my itinerary for change.

The savage in me would have loved to celebrate and party like the common men I had just left who made plans to fail even before the shackles had been unlocked, but I had to stay focused. My mission wasn't the same, and I wasn't the same. I was different.

I knew my limitations just as much as I had known that my drug addiction was by no means cured and having my parent's support on my first day out of the joint was pivotal for traveling the road to redemption.

Relapse was a part of recovery, and if by some chance that I used drugs again once I was free, I'm sure that I would get the necessary treatment that I needed from probation-mandated outpatient programs, but I refused to set myself up for any downfalls.

I needed to have an agenda—and my parents were the pillars to my agenda.

Instead of getting my own apartment right away, my mother *suggested* that I live with Eugene, Jason, and her in their two-bedroom apartment in River Park Towers in the Bronx.

I would have to humble myself and sleep on an air mattress in their living room, but I had no qualms with the probable arrangement at all, because I needed to slowly reconnect with society.

If I lived alone, I would have nine kids—nine months after signing the lease.

Sleeping on a prison bunk for five years had a way of making a man grateful for simply having a place that he could call home other than a cell, and I more than appreciated Mommy and Eugene's hospitality.

Having left my mother when I was just fifteen years old, I figured that living with her would strengthen our strained relationship.

And as much as she wanted me around in order to take care of me during my transition, I wanted to take care of her.

Mommy looked like she was thirty-years old, but her youthful appearance didn't erase the fact that she was fifty.

My active participation around the house would help my mother relax and have more time to enjoy life.

As a middle-aged woman, she already had enough pressure—such as doing the daily chores, paying bills, raising Jason, and doing her homework. Yes, *her* homework.

Besides being a full-time mom and working as a medical assistant at St. Luke's hospital for the last ten years, Mommy was a junior at Monroe College in her pursuit to attain her bachelor's degree in Child Psychology. I profoundly believed that she would succeed.

After raising five bad-ass kids *and* Jason, my mother could've taught the dang course. I was so freaking proud of her!

A supreme inspiration, my mother was my motivation and proof that as long as I had air in my lungs, any goal I had was obtainable—age, past mishaps, or limitations *others* put on me were trivial.

Mommy showed me a lineage of commitment, faith, determination, and dedication that I had forgotten existed in my blood.

My mother's continued perseverance and refusal to settle for mediocrity was infectious, and if I could feel her strength while I was trapped inside a dungeon, hundreds of miles away—I figured that being in her presence would propel my penchant for prominence to a higher position.

So, I had decided that I would take Mommy up on her generous offer, but I had known better than to have taken my father up on his.

With the accumulating good fortune of *Peña's*, my father had permanently stepped away from any illegal activity.

He concentrated on his East Harlem bar, vowing to never re-enter the cruel game that had taken his son away from him for five years.

He had played with the devil long enough, and although he had escaped from cocaine's gauntlet of evil relatively unscathed, the avid churchgoer still carried with him the burden of his son's collapse.

My incarceration represented my father's resurrection into a world of legitimacy, voting, and paying taxes.

My father didn't want to suffer the same fate that I did or persist to have been the gold standard of irresponsibility, ignorance, and illegality to my younger, more impressionable siblings. Daddy's every move was still being watched very closely.

Peña's had become a family business, and my brothers, Chink, Alejandro, and Javier worked with my father full-time, while my sister Sandy bartended after school and on the weekends.

* * *

My cousin, Chris (the younger brother of Harlem street legend, Hen-Dog—who was murdered during my freshman year at Woodberry) was the deacon of his church and also worked at the bar in between taking classes at Baruch College.

A victim of New York's harsh Rockefeller Drug Laws, Chris, who was a University of Pennsylvania finance major before his arrest—had recently come home from Green Haven Correctional Facility after serving a fifteen-year prison sentence.

My junior year at Virginia Tech was the last time I had seen Chris' face, during an A&E *special* episode about his case.

His lawyers, Ron Kuby and Bill Kunstler, couldn't keep Chris out of prison—but I prayed that my father's bar would.

* * *

The thought of the Peña posse thriving as a unit, with my father at the helm of hard work, was as unimaginable as it was heartening—I was eager to witness the kindred dynamic.

Naturally, Daddy asked me to come run the bar with him upon my release and to allow the same establishment that had saved him from the cruel Harlem streets to save me, but unfortunately, I could *never* work at a place like Peña's.

I was a drug addict. I would forever be a drug addict.

I had a disease that could only have been suppressed and contained, yet never annihilated, because there was no cure, but there were many stimulators —and alcohol was the biggest of them all.

With just one sip of alcohol, I could activate the coke-blowing-beast who slept with one nostril open and waited to be awakened by a splash of booze over its wicked face.

I would've been insane to ever have thought that I could work somewhere that served my damnation to the brim to individuals just as, or even sicker than I was.

All it would have taken was a drink and a pretty girl with pretty-bad habits, and I would already have had one boot back in federal prison.

Factor in that many old neighborhood friends with their same neighborhood jobs would frequent Peña's once word had spread that I was home, and my *grand* collapse was imminent.

I had been proud of my father's accomplishments with the bar, and his remarkable integration of his children within the business. Although the prospect of being around family was enticing, staying out of prison or a casket seemed like the better deal.

Daddy and I would just have to build on our relationship *outside* of a bar, or any other setting that wasn't conducive to my sobriety.

I wished I had the strength of my father and could have a cocktail without thoughts of getting high swirling in my head like the ice in the glass, but I didn't —so I disclosed to him over the phone that I wanted to be a personal trainer and *never* wanted to work at Peña's.

With evident disapproval in his voice, Daddy told me that I was not going to be a personal trainer, and my nerves unhinged before my father chuckled and said, "Son, you are going to be the *perfect* personal trainer."

My father's support of my potential profession reassured me that listening to Big Ed's advice had been wise, because I couldn't deny my love for exercising and helping others reach their fitness goals.

My mother had already purchased the books that I needed from the National Academy of Sports Medicine (NASM) to take the exam for my personal training certification, so that when I got home, I could avoid procrastination and begin studying.

Maintaining employment was a must while I was on five years of probation, but I didn't want to just have *any* job for the sole purpose of fulfilling my requirements, therefore it was imperative that I pursued my desired career immediately.

Plus, I needed some positive income as quickly as possible—I was flat broke.

Along with the women, fake friends, expensive cars, jewelry, and clothes, all *my* money was gone!

After paying legal fees, court fines, and helping my family when I could, I was only left with my smile and my brain—and I didn't care.

Wanting to set a good example for which my daughter could mold her own morals, I preferred to come home and have to work hard for everything that I had.

A hustler's blood still ran strong in my veins, and if I put my mind and my grind toward getting money *legally* with the same ferociousness that I did when I sold drugs, then there was no doubt that having money would never be an issue.

But obtaining fortune wasn't a priority to me at all—what I desired didn't have any monetary value.

I yearned for what money could *not* buy, like the taste of Mommy's fried chicken and the smell of the New York streets just after it rained.

I ached for being a better father to Ruby and building my relationship with her—showing her that her daddy was worthy of her affection.

I wanted to be rich with the love of my daughter and my family, and experience some of the simple pleasures of life that I missed because of my greed and selfishness—such as walking in the park with my daughter while I held her hand.

I couldn't wait to take my daughter to school and watch her enter her classroom with her tiny backpack, running to her little clique.

I dreamt of enjoying a movie with Ruby as we simultaneously reached into a large box of buttered popcorn, and I could feel her little fingers brush against mine—reminding me that my baby girl was near and to never abandon her again.

I craved many things, and money or materialistic items weren't on my list, but *forgiveness* was at the very top.

* * *

My final couple of years in prison, I prayed quite often, even though I was not religious.

Many times, I asked God for forgiveness, but in my heart, I felt that God, my daughter, or anyone else would never absolve me of my infringements if I didn't show forgiveness myself.

I knew that I had to let go of any grudges I had with any individuals that I believed had done me an injustice.

To move on with my life and receive all the blessings that would be bestowed upon me, I had to not harbor any feelings toward Brittney, and instead love her as the mother of my child.

No matter what she may have done while I was in prison, I left her all alone to raise *our* daughter without a father.

I wasn't the victim, Brittney and Ruby were.

For five years, Brittney had to act as both parents without a choice and fend for herself because of the choices that I made.

She had done an amazing job with Ruby and deserved my praise rather than my contempt.

I appreciated Brittney tremendously, and the time had come for me to show her how much I did, by coming home and doing all that I could as a co-parent to make her life easier, with my presence and not my presents.

No longer a hypocrite, I realized that the anguish I put that courageously strong woman through since we met had far outweighed her few indiscretions, and I should seek *her* forgiveness.

I couldn't take back the affair between Brittney and the Malone brothers. To progressively advance in the direction of change, I had to set aside my resentment for all three—including my eternal hatred for the woman I had exclusively held accountable for my five years of imprisonment, Katherine "Biscuit" Jones.

* * *

Many a night in my prison cell, I had vivid dreams of murdering Biscuit, and I would wake up enraged—instantly closing my eyes to relive the handsome horror again.

At one point, the dreams occurred so systematically that I could predict which vengeful dish would be served on any given night of the week:

Monday
Battered Biscuit with a bat
Tuesday
Sliced Biscuit neck
Wednesday
Charred Biscuit with gasoline marinade
Thursday
Biscuit throat with acid drizzle
Friday
Biscuit with shotgun pellets
Saturday
Chopped head Biscuit
Sunday
Filleted Biscuit

The dreams started to scare me, and with my high blood pressure, Biscuit had to get removed from the menu.

I considered getting therapy, but had decided to go another route first, thus had begun my ritual of praying before bed.

I prayed every night. I prayed for my family, my loved ones, and even for Biscuit's safety.

I asked God to end the nightmares, and the terrors subsided, and so did my abomination for Biscuit.

Steadily, I stopped accusing her for my incarceration and proceeded to recognize the real person accountable for the crimes that I had committed. His name was Manzo.

I was in prison because *Manzo* sold drugs.

I was in prison because *Manzo* broke the law.

I was not in prison because of anyone's doing but myself, and at last, I had finally taken responsibility for my actions and decisions—lifting the blame for my love of sin from Biscuit *and* my father.

I picked my own path in life while I was fully aware of the critical consequences.

Daddy, regardless if I agreed with his parenting or lifestyle, led me to one of the best boarding schools in the United States, and an elite university on a football scholarship—I led myself to federal prison.

The energy I had spent on finger pointing could have been used to mentally prepare for my return into society.

With the guidance of RDAP during my final months in chains, I concentrated on my future success, rather than dwelling on past failures.

Excited to face new challenges, I knew my life was far from over—it was just the beginning.

With an adjustment of attitude, I would have plenty of opportunities to conquer being a slave to my passions and desires, but I had to slow down and to remain focused.

Change was a process!

There were so many monumental lessons from prison that I would take with me, yet *the Five P's of life* was one of the main philosophies that I would never forget and thought about as I stood with Officer Jackson—anticipating my admittance into the free world.

* * *

"Goddamn Manzo, ya looking like ya could still play for the Hokies again. You swole as a motherfucker son!" Officer Jackson broke the silence.

Proper...Planning...Prevents...Poor...Performance—

"Manzo?"

"Uh...yea—what's up Jackson?" I said.

"Ha-ha! Damn brother, you spaced the hell out over there."

"My bad Jackson, just a lot on my mind...as you can imagine."

"Shit, I bet. Ya probably thinking 'bout all that damn coochie you bout'ta get."

"Man, not even. Just trying to stay focused brother."

"I hear that, but like I was saying—you looking like you ready to play for the Hokies again. You a *swole* motherfucker Manzo!"

"Ha-ha, Jackson—you are crazy brother. I may *look* like I can play, but I don't want to mess with any those young boys."

How did he know I was a Hokie?

Word travels fast around here I see.

"Shiiid, I bet'cha could at least play for them sorry-ass Redskins," he said.

"Thanks, but I wouldn't stand a damn chance. Not happening. Even them dudes would rearrange my bones. They hit too hard in the league."

How Javier got me in these 'come and pump me' shits though?

These pants feel too tight!

"Ya ain't lyin' either Manzo. Them jokers got mouths to feed, ha-ha. But sorry to keep ya standing here. The ten-minute-move is on, and you know the policy. Nothin' in, nothin' out—until the shit is over."

"No problem sir, patience is a strong point of mine at this point. I've waited five years, so another few minutes won't kill me," I expressed.

"I know that's right Manzo. Speaking of *Manzo*...all the officers here—*especially* the fee-males, was always wondering why don't ya have a last name? You a damn rock star or something?"

Oh, I have good story ready—no stop this nonsense!

Be truthful for once!

"Ha-ha—I knew you would ask me that for some reason," I said.

"Am I a rock star? Well Jackson, that all depends on who you ask...but I got my name, because my mother didn't want me having the same last name as my father when she found out that my pops had a son two months before I was born."

Finally, the truth!

"Wooow, that's some heavy shit—huh Manzo?"

"Sure is Jackson, but we all grow from our mistakes," I said.

"Ya daddy must've been slangin' that dick something serious! Shit, ain't no difference from my poppa—except I have *four* half siblings. Sooo...I feel'ya rock star."

What's a male camel toe?

"My pops is a changed man though—but I need your honest opinion on something Jackson, if you don't mind brother?" I asked, switching topics.

"Shoot," he said.

Oh yea, I have a moose knuckle. You can see my print!

"Are these jeans too tight? I mean, they feel too tight. Is this really what *men* are wearing these days?"

"I saw ya kept checking ya'self out, and I knew ya were thinking that."

"No for real Jackson, let me know! I can't leave prison looking like I was walking around the yard holding some big dude's back pocket my entire bid!"

"Ha, ha, ha! Manzo, you too damn funny!" Jackson laughed, and turned up the volume on his walkie-talkie.

"Every damn time a guy leaves here, he asks me 'bout the way he's dressed. It's like ya fellas have been in a time capsule or some shit! That baggie clothes nonsense is over with young man. It's about *form-fitting* clothes these days.

"You good though brotha. Better get with the times, ha, ha, ha—don't you watch rap videos? As a matter of fact, don't answer that Manzo—you was in RDAP! You mothafuckahs ain't even allowed to watch women's tennis, 'cuz the girls' nipples be too hard!"

"You have no clue how on point you are!" I laughed and my eyes watered.

"I love working State Unit though. Ain't noooo trouble in *that* boring-ass unit!

"No bullshit though Manzo, one time a fella told me that hard nipples was a *trigger* for him...*could I turn the TV?*

"I looked that fool in the eyes...and said, *heeeell naaah!* Hard nipples a trigger for me too...a *trig-gaah* for a *nig-gaah* to get some pussy when I get up out dis mothafuckah!"

"Yooo...stop...please! You sounded just like Richard Pryor right there! Man, you're killing me! I never knew you were this funny Jackson!"

"Shiiid, I told that Chinese fella, I think his name was Hung. First off, how the hell is a Chinese nigga named *Hung* in the first place? Manzo, you know Hung?"

"Yes, I know who you're talking about. Hung graduated and went home a week after I got here."

"So I tells this Hung motherfuckah...the next time you ever in your *life* try and change this-here TV when my baby Serena is on...I'm going to *Hung* my foot in your ass!"

"Seriously? What did Hung say after that?" I asked.

"He ain't say shit Manzo—but what the lil' shrimp-dick-mothafuckah did do was, was go to the counselor. Uuum, what's the Black counselor name that wears the suits? Lookin like he sells bean pies and shit?"

"You're talking about Mr. Devereux?" I asked.

Oooh, sooo Hung was the reason why Jackson was always quiet and mean mugging.

"Yea him—Mr. Devereux! So this lil' rice-cake-eating-mothafuckah goes and tell Mr. Devereux that I'm a racist...and I need to hold myself *accountable*.

"He act like I was in the damn program! But Manzo can you believe that shit? He called *me*, out of all people...a goddamn *racist*."

"Naaah, he must have you confused with another officer. Definitely not you Jackson," I lied.

Totally a racist.

"Exactly! That's what I told the captain! I said that Hung was a damn liar and must think all Black people look alike because—"

"*TEN MINUTE MOVE OVER! SECURE THE COMPOUND!*" a boyish voice blared from Jackson's walkie-talkie, causing my nerves to jitter.

Oh man, this is it!

"*PERMISSION TO RELEASE MR. MANZO!*" the officer officially granted me a new lease on life.

That's me!

He said, 'Mister'! Not 'inmate'!

"Well you heard 'em, *Mis-tah* Manzo," Jackson said while placing his left hand on the door handle.

"*Rock star*—You are freeee to go."

Free? He just said 'free'!

"Ah man...*pheeew*. I never thought this day would come Jackson," I admitted.

It's over!

This can't be happening! I made it!

Breathe. Calm down.

"It's here my brotha...it is here! Ya folks 'round back filling out paperwork and will be out front in a couple of minutes," he confirmed and raised the walkie-talkie midway to his mouth but stopped, turned around, and looked at me.

"OK...now ya *sure* ya wanna go without hearing the rest of my story? Shit was about to get good as mothafuckah Manzo!"

"I'm sure Jackson, but thank you for easing my mind brother. I forgot where I was for a moment."

I can't leave yet!

The world is too different! I'm not ready!

"Of course brotha. I can only imagine how ya feel. Glad to see I still got it though. Now please...go do something special," Jackson said, and then spoke into the walkie-talkie.

"Copy control...unlock main entry. Jackson, releasing Mr. Manzo!"

Oooh my God!

Officer Jackson pulled the door open, and freedom's brilliance spread over my existence.

* * *

Squinting from the dazzle of daylight, I welcomed the sun, and relished in the fiery rays of hope while an organic breeze cooled my fright of flight, whisking away the smog from my wings.

The air on this side of the cage was fresh and seductive. My pores opened with a rabid thirst to overfill on the purity of an uncontaminated life.

Jackson shut the portal of darkness behind me, and the infinite lanes to redemption had emerged from my soul.

In spotless footwear, I trod on my stained reputation, toward the sterilizing heat, cleansing my priorities and polishing my sight.

Seven paces into my revival, I stopped moving at the center of FCI-Butner's desolate visitor's parking lot and tried on my new eyes. I could see again!

The delicious colors conjointly saturated my vision and palate. If I had licked the sky, it would have tasted like a blue raspberry Slurpee.

A healthy growth of pistachio-green leaves extended from a nearby tree, while a northern cardinal landed on the highest branch.

The cherry on top rocked to the rhythm of the American Flag which hung from a white pole directly in front of the prison and flapped freely in the open air.

The tri-colored symbol of my achievement had reiterated that I was free and no longer an inmate.

Even though I would be on probation, I wouldn't have a curfew, and I now made my own decisions about my bedtime, visits, phone usage, food options, TV programming, sex life, and occupation.

It was solely up to me if I would smoke a joint with the guys from my old neighborhood while we rolled dice on Second Avenue.

Unrestraint, I could drink a pint of Hennessy and drive 105 miles per hour up the FDR Drive, with my little princess unbuckled in the backseat—just like my cousin, Fernando, did before fatally crashing into a cement post. He and his baby girl were killed instantly.

A former inmate at FCI-Fort Dix, *Nando* had just been released after serving a six-year prison sentence. Like my departed cousin, I would have to live or die with my decisions.

If I wanted to snort 105 lines and screw 105 times, without 105 condoms, I could—because I was now responsible for myself, and nobody could snatch the rolled $100 bill out of my hand or take the straw out of my nostril.

The feds weren't my babysitters anymore, and I should've been thrilled by the prospect of self-government, but I wasn't.

Paranoid, I freaked out and panicked!

Oh no!

I'm not ready!

I am a fuck up!

I can't say no!

As my eyes tingled from sweat, I could see my heart violently pumping from under my t-shirt, and I hyperventilated with insuppressible fear.

Super anxious, my breathing was heavy and swift.

I panted like a miniature schnauzer humping a teddy bear.

The air failed to reach my brain, and a nauseating lightheadedness temporarily made me lose balance.

The world launched into rapid rotation, and my skin burned.

My blood scratched my muscles and boiled the saliva in my mouth.

Dropping my bag, I coughed, and my tonsils tumbled against the back of my throat and scraped my esophagus.

Gagging, I almost toppled to one knee, but the sudden crunching of gravel behind me prompted my limbs to stiffen.

Instantaneously, I whipped myself around to inspect the sounds and prepare for any sneak attack.

Droplets of delirium flung from my brow and sailed into a sea of oxygen, docking at a pair of pearly white Prada boat shoes as I noticed the set of toned, muscular calves—smaller versions of mine.

Staying the course, my attention traveled past white Balmain shorts and anchored to the weeping grin of the ex-stud who stood—a hug's distance away from his terrified son.

My dad's tears splashed onto the buttons of his white Armani shirt, with the untucked tails and the sleeves freshly folded at his forearms.

His battleship-grays glistered on his cheeks from the rainstorm of emotions that I witnessed just once in my lifetime, twenty-five years ago—at my grand-mother's funeral.

Following the flow from my father's quarter-centennial surge of sentiment, flushed the foreboding from my frontal lobe, and I suddenly had forgotten to fear anything.

As my backbone stiffened, I spotted his platinum necklace with both of my eyes, but I could only see a fraction of *who* I used to be.

Fringed by silvery ringlets of chest hairs, a modest medallion, the left piece of a perfectly broken heart, suspended from the matching metal and rested on my father's chest.

Set inside the pendant, was a bisected black and white headshot of a young man at his junior high school graduation.

Although just half of my pimply face and my cap appeared in the photo—I totally remembered *how* I used to be.

My confident smile, filled with aspirations and limitless potential, had a bulletproof brightness that the jewelry's jagged edge couldn't pierce.

* * *

The fifteen-year-old in the photo viewed society's unattainable dreams as practical options for his future, and failure was just a word in the dictionary between *failsafe* and *fain*.

Special, he prided himself on being different, and lived mainly by his mantra —*if anybody can have it, then I don't want it*.

Marijuana was as accessible as cigarettes, and a cocaine-tree grew in his home, but the All-American kid wasn't interested in the self-destructive tendencies that the *average* guys his age coveted.

The boy never fancied the flood of fermented fruit funneled from liquor stores that failed to card adults, teenagers, rotten-mouthed kids, or even babies —having a pulse was the only prerequisite for purchasing the poison.

The boy on the pendant was the annoying goofball on New Year's Eve who drank sparkling apple cider and pretended to be drunk, just to mock the adult-juveniles and old-delinquents.

He just couldn't fathom depending on alcohol or any other substances to enhance the enjoyment of any engagement.

In his young mind, he was the Salvador Dali of East Harlem.

Manzo didn't need drugs; he was drugs.

People got addicted to him, and he was only addicted to making his mom proud with his budding success.

* * *

The image of the Drama major with higher standards spiked my courage, and Daddy's presence gave me strength, alleviating most of my physical and psychological woes.

Just like the photo, I had been incomplete—my *power* was still missing; however, I could smell the source of my energy.

The familiar flavor of the woman's scent invigorated my joints like God had washed His hands in adrenaline and smacked my soul.

Awakened and standing taller than the emasculated individual I was seconds before, I leaned my head slightly to the left and peeked around Daddy's shoulder, coincidentally as my mother, always the slower walker—stepped from behind my father and stopped timidly right by his side.

With her hair slicked back into a bun, revealing the widow's peak that only her and I shared out of all her kids, Mommy was flawlessly clad in a white sleeveless Brunello Cucinelli jumpsuit.

The cotton-silk fabric harmoniously molded to her torso and spread gently at the hips, before elegantly reshaping at her upper thighs—maintaining its slenderness down to a white pair of Jimmy Choo, Attila leather-trimmed flats.

My mother didn't wear any makeup, and the naturally bronzed warmth of her skin sparkled as she sobbed in a controlled hush, cupping her mouth with her right hand.

Lobster-claw-clasped around my mother's neck, a twenty-four-carat gold replica of my father's chain held the right-half of my headshot that showed the yellow tassel hanging from my cap and kept my mother's piece of the broken heart from falling.

The pendant safely rested on my mother's bosom like a newborn, and the sight of my picture in her possession made me realize how truly blessed I was.

With all my worries vanishing, I believed that I had the courage to keep pushing toward success, because after fourteen years of having gone astray, I still had the foundation to my prosperity standing right in front of me.

Through all the turmoil that I had put Mommy through, she had remained my guardian.

She had kept the faith that one day I would rise from the fires of my misjudgments and become *her* son again.

I understood that struggle would be a part of the journey, but the path to greatness would be a less difficult one by accepting Mommy's love and direction —the woman had never given me bad advice.

As a man, I knew that I had to make split decisions on my own though, especially regarding alluring temptations.

Despite my mother's availability to give me assistance, I still couldn't forget that the choices I made in life didn't just affect me.

I would never leave my mother or Ruby alone again, so it was critical that I paid strict attention to the *people, places, and things* in my zone.

With little margin for error, I had to move intelligently and with complete understanding for what was at risk if I slipped.

I didn't have any more bids left in me, and I preferred death over another imprisonment, so now I had to *just do things right.*

* * *

Looking at my mother stare at me as if I were a mirage, I was confused because I didn't know what to do, and my body froze with an overwhelming cheerfulness.

Rushed with the need to hold her, I couldn't move and momentarily settled for hugging my mother tightly—in my mind.

Since my incarceration, I had wondered what it would be like to finally step out of prison as a free man and embrace the woman who birthed me.

Fighting back tears, sixty months in the making, I impulsively dropped my bag when I noticed the vintage piece on her left wrist.

Instead of her Cartier watch, Mommy accented her outfit with a stringed elbow-macaroni bracelet.

Immediately, I recalled who the designer of the edible jewelry was, even though I hadn't seen the accessory since the Christmas of 1982—when I had given the Kindergarten assignment to my mother...as a birthday gift.

My heart, heavy with emotions, was defenseless against the twenty-one pieces of pasta, but I still had not shed a tear—until Mommy finally removed her hand from her mouth, smiled and said, "Hey Moose."

THANK YOU

I would like to thank my amazing wife Bamz, our best friend Mira, Charli,
Pablo, Richard T. Schmeglin,
and of course—Adderall.

ABOUT THE AUTHOR

MANZO is a writer, entrepreneur, and celebrity personal trainer. He lives in NYC with his wife Bamz, their bully rescues, Charli and Pablo, and their beloved bearded dragon—
Richard T. Schmeglin.

For more updates and upcoming books:
www.goodboymanzo.com
@goodboybetterdrugs

f facebook.com/goodboymanzo
🐦 twitter.com/goodboymanzo
📷 instagram.com/goodboymanzo

COMING SOON

GOOD BOY,
BETTER TOYS

MANZO

Free from federal prison, Manzo falls in love with Olivia Newcastle, niece of deceased iconic artist, Anderson Newcastle, and enters New York City's high society while struggling with his sobriety and independence. On a quest for power, fortune, and acceptance from his new family, Manzo becomes a celebrity personal trainer and a fixture in the art world. Moving fast toward success, Manzo trips on the savage within, but this time...he might not get up.

CPSIA information can be obtained
at www.ICGtesting.com
Printed in the USA
LVHW010343110720
660357LV00001B/2

9 781734 135428